SUPERMAN

ARCHIVES ▾ VOLUME 1

JERRY SIEGEL & JOE SHUSTER

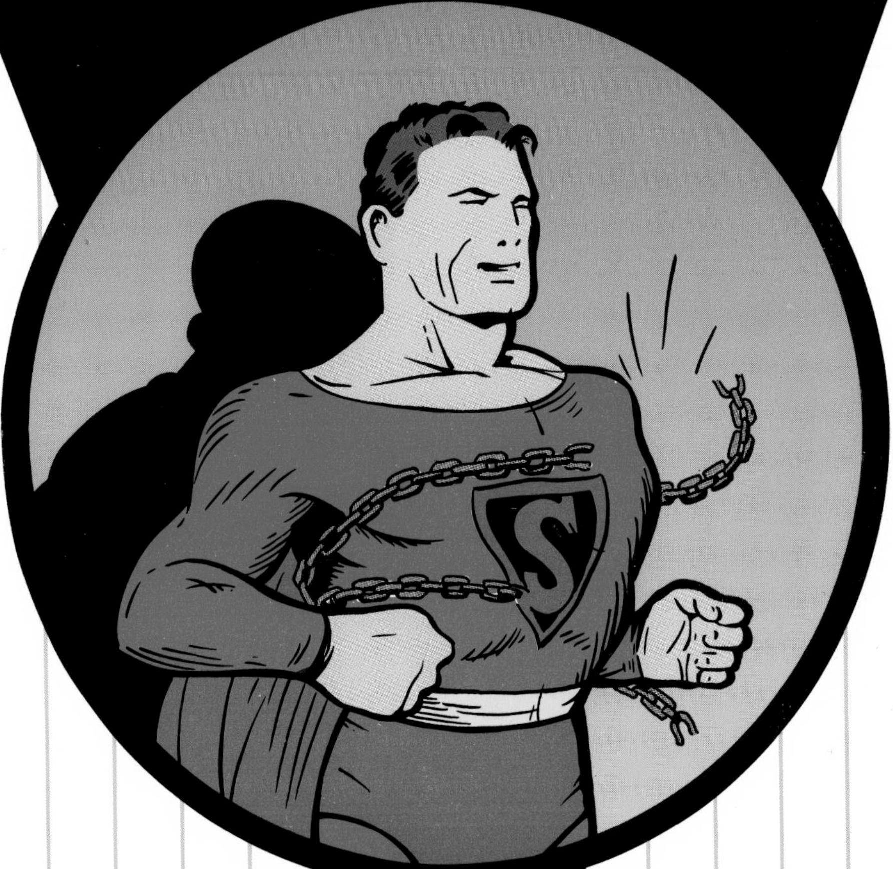

ARCHIVE DC® EDITIONS™

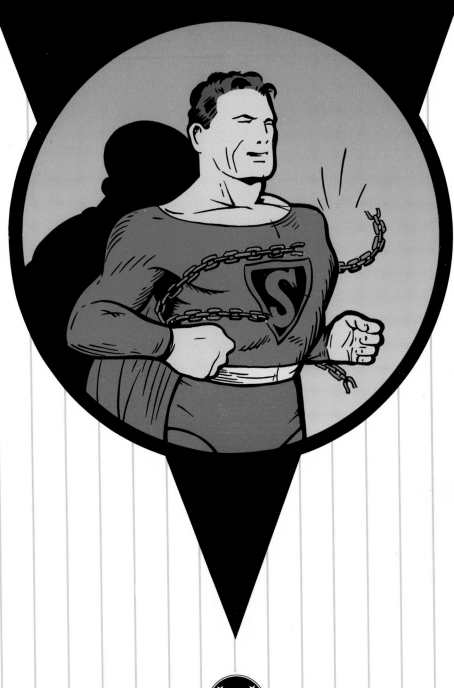

DC COMICS

DAN DIDIO
VP-EDITORIAL

MARK WAID
RICHARD BRUNING
EDITORS-COLLECTED EDITION

ROBBIN BROSTERMAN
SENIOR ART DIRECTOR

PAUL LEVITZ
PRESIDENT & PUBLISHER

GEORG BREWER
VP-DESIGN & RETAIL PRODUCT
DEVELOPMENT

RICHARD BRUNING
SENIOR VP-CREATIVE DIRECTOR

PATRICK CALDON
SENIOR VP-FINANCE & OPERATIONS

CHRIS CARAMALIS
VP-FINANCE

TERRI CUNNINGHAM
VP-MANAGING EDITOR

ALISON GILL
VP-MANUFACTURING

RICH JOHNSON
VP-BOOK TRADE SALES

HANK KANALZ
VP-GENERAL MANAGER, WILDSTORM

LILLIAN LASERSON
SENIOR VP & GENERAL COUNSEL

JIM LEE
EDITORIAL DIRECTOR-WILDSTORM

DAVID MCKILLIPS
VP-ADVERTISING &
CUSTOM PUBLISHING

JOHN NEE
VP-BUSINESS DEVELOPMENT

GREGORY NOVECK
SENIOR VP-CREATIVE AFFAIRS

CHERYL RUBIN
SENIOR VP-
BRAND MANAGEMENT

BOB WAYNE
VP-SALES & MARKETING

SUPERMAN CREATED BY JERRY SIEGEL AND JOE SHUSTER

SUPERMAN ARCHIVES
VOLUME ONE

ISBN: 1-4012-0630-1

PUBLISHED BY DC COMICS
COVER, FOREWORD, AFTERWORD AND
COMPILATION COPYRIGHT © 1989 DC COMICS

ORIGINALLY PUBLISHED IN SINGLE MAGAZINE
FORM IN SUPERMAN 1-4. COPYRIGHT 1939-
1940 DC COMICS. ALL RIGHTS RESERVED.

SUPERMAN AND ALL RELATED CHARACTERS,
THE DISTINCTIVE LIKENESSES THEREOF AND
RELATED ELEMENTS ARE TRADEMARKS OF
DC COMICS. THE STORIES, CHARACTERS AND
INCIDENTS FEATURED IN THIS PUBLICATION
ARE ENTIRELY FICTIONAL. DC COMICS DOES
NOT READ OR ACCEPT UNSOLICITED SUBMIS-
SIONS OF IDEAS, STORIES OR ARTWORK.

DC COMICS
1700 BROADWAY
NEW YORK, NY 10019

A WARNER BROS. ENTERTAINMENT COMPANY
PRINTED IN HONG KONG.
FIFTH PRINTING.

SELECTED STORIES
BLEACHED AND RECONSTRUCTED
BY PURE IMAGINATION;
GREG THEAKSTON, SUPERVISOR.
STEVE SCANLON, SCOTT MITCHELL,
SEAN LEONG, STAFF.

COLOR RECONSTRUCTION BY
BOB LE ROSE AND DANIEL VOZZO.

JACKET AND TEXT DESIGN BY
ALEX JAY/STUDIO J.

FOREWORD

BETWEEN THE TIME THAT HEMINGWAY created Nick Adams and Tolkien conjured Bilbo Baggins, he came to life.

He was born in the company of Mr. Chips, Joseph K, Lady Chatterley, Conan, Studs Lonigan, Anthony Adverse, Tom Joad, Perry Mason, Horatio Hornblower, Jeeter Lester, Cthulhu, and Walter Mitty—and became more famous than all of them.

Even more remarkable is that as the hero of heroes, he was the brainchild of two 19-year-olds whose greatest ambition was to fill the pages of their small mimeozine, **Science Fiction**. As childhood friends living twelve blocks apart in Cleveland, Ohio, Jerry Siegel and Joe Shuster shared and combined their interests—words and pictures—in the amateur literary endeavor.

Although in 1930 the SF genre was still in its formative stages, the teenagers found their imaginations ignited by the form. Only three pulp magazines—**Amazing Stories, Astounding Stories,** and **Air Wonder Stories**—were devoted exclusively to fantastic fiction. Their families still suffering from the Depression, the two fans scraped pennies together to afford their newsstand habit. Siegel submitted stories to the pulps under the pseudonym Bernard J. Kenton; together the boys collaborated on illustrated fiction and newspaper-strip samples.

Superman was one of them.

Conceived in 1933, he dominated their efforts throughout the next five years, even after they

sold a half-dozen projects to the comics company that would eventually herald the DC banner. Believing in their creation, they doggedly sent numerous versions to newspaper syndicates, all of which rejected the strips as crude and immature.

Superman was filed under "failure" by the youthful team, who, after a Niagara of submissions, ran out of potential markets. Their Man of Steel was too offbeat for editors schooled in traditional comic-strip sensibilities to accept. Fantasy and SF had shaken hands with the four-color form decades earlier: Lyonel Feininger's **The Kin-der-Kids** and Winsor McCay's **Little Nemo in Slumberland** date back almost to the turn of the century, while **Buck Rogers, Flash Gordon, Brick Bradford, Alley Oop,** and **Mandrake** paced the '30s Industrial Era, preparing the way for the Atomic Age. Super beings, however, were another matter. Perhaps the period's most outstanding was pulp hero Doc Savage, whose advertisements headlined him as a "superman" as early as 1934.

The word *ubermensch* was coined by German philosopher Friedrich Nietzsche before the turn of the century. The term, translated into English, was popularized through such references as George Bernard Shaw's play **Man and Superman** and such pulp tales as *The Superman* (August, 1931) and *The Supermen* (October, 1933) in **Amazing Stories**.

Until June 1938, comic books were only an echo of the funny papers. Some of the most successful merely reprinted the popular newspaper strips—**Blondie, Popeye, Li'l Abner, Terry and the Pirates, Buck Rogers, Dick Tracy, Flash Gordon, Tarzan,** and **Mickey Mouse.** Publishers who could not afford major-league characters simply nurtured a multitude of imitations.

Comic books needed a superman of their own—a bold new champion who could leap off the page in an unexpected direction that would herald the Golden Age of Comics—and they got him! According to legend, the event was solely the result of chance. McClure Syndicate agent M. C. Gaines, an early comics pioneer, just happened to have the Siegel and Shuster submission on his desk when president Harry Donenfeld phoned, inquiring about original material to fill a new magazine he was assembling. Coincidentally, the artist/writer team was already supplying several strips to his line, including **Dr. Occult, Federal Men, Henri Duval, Radio Squad, Spy,** and **Slam Bradley.**

Donenfeld recognized the material's appeal and ordered the newspaper strip repasted into comic-page format, with the first week eliminated to accommodate available space in the magazine, which was christened **Action Comics.** On the cover, Superman hoisted an automobile as if it were a toy wagon.

(The opening tale was reprinted in its entirety in **Superman** 1, as it is here. That story and those that immediately followed are collected within these pages exactly as they appeared then. Retouching is minimal, and only to restore artistic detail. Coloring, including airbrushing and color-holds, duplicates that of the original books.)

Initially, the Man of Steel was "a genius in intellect, a Hercules in strength, a nemesis to wrong-doers," dressing in street clothes, not very different from the source that inspired him: Philip Wylie's 1930 novel **Gladiator.** In the book, the hero evidences super-strength as a baby, discovers he can leap 40 feet in the air at ten years old, and, as a young man in the war, finds that machine-gun bullets and exploding shells cannot penetrate his skin. The tale was one of Siegel's favorites, reviewed with praise in his fanzine.

As the concept developed, he put a spin on the idea by grafting it to the Biblical story of Moses' concealment from the Pharaoh, with outer space substituting for the Nile. The concept of aliens visiting Earth dates back as far as Voltaire's 1752 fantasy **Micromegas,** which countless SF authors, including H. G. Wells in **The War of the Worlds,** have used as a dramatic device.

The explanation of Superman's strength relating to the gravity factor (detailed on the filler page between the second and third stories in this volume, but contradicted by a newspaper-strip synopsis) was first suggested in John W. Campbell's Aarn Munro tales about a descendant of Earthmen raised on the planet Jupiter who is a physical and mental superman on our world. The analogy between the strength of insects and man was also derived from Wylie's novel.

Although the Superman premise was incomplete, the existing elements fit together with perfect logic. To reinforce the concept, Siegel added the dual-identity bit (standard fare for dozens of characters from Zorro to The Shadow, traceable to 1905's **The Scarlet Pimpernel**), while Shuster provided the crowning touch: the super-hero costume. Previously, few fictional men of adventure had been associated with their clothes. Superman changed all that by becoming comic books' first—and most important—icon.

The pulps had no correlative SF character, but newspapers did, in **Flash Gordon.** Beginning in January 1934, the blond spacehawk and his retinue were four-color fashion plates difficult for an impressionable young artist to ignore. In his first fantastic sequence, Flash was garbed in a form-fitting shirt with a yellow chevron on his chest, trunks over blue tights (like a circus acrobat's) girded by a belt, and stretch boots. All that was missing was a red cape—which he acquired a few weeks later. Flash Gordon's influence was pervasive. By coincidence or design, the costume Superman ultimately wore made him the most recognizable hero in the comics universe and beyond.

By today's standards, Joe Shuster's art is primitive, but what it lacks in sophistication and pretention, it makes up for in raw, energetic imagery. His approach is the essence of correspondence-school simplicity. Although the artist learned to draw after winning a scholarship to the Cleveland School of Art, and while attending the John Huntington Polytechnical Institute (where he paid for lessons a dime at a time), he was more influenced by the humor and adventure strips of the period. Roy Crane's superb **Wash Tubbs** provided Shuster with an ideal model for style and storytelling. Superman, especially as seen in these tales, bears an interesting resemblance to Captain Easy.

Solid and straightforward, the art was a perfect match for its subject matter—and so successful it became the DC-hero house style for decades to follow. Suddenly, the young draftsman had more work than he could handle. On January 16, 1939, the Superman strip debuted in four newspapers, with a Sunday page starting on November 5. By 1941, more than 300 papers carried the Man of Steel's adventures for a combined circulation of 20 million. The **Superman** comic book began as a quarterly in summer 1939 and was followed in spring 1941 by **World's Finest** (originally **New York World's Fair**).

As the demand escalated, Siegel and Shuster rented an office that qualified as the smallest in Cleveland, set up four drawing tables, and hired a staff of assistants (including Joe's brother). Paul Cassidy, Dennis Neville, and Leo Nowack were among Superman's early ghosts, but the best— and the most enduring—was Wayne Boring, a Chicago Art Institute student who pencilled, inked, and even lettered the strip, ultimately defining the quintessential Superman.

Siegel continued to scribe the Kryptonian's saga, but Shuster was forced to relinquish drawing duties as the character's popularity exceeded their wildest expectations. Failing eyesight and a Sisyphean workload forced him to function primarily as the strip's art director, concentrating his artistic efforts on layouts that were finished by the shop crew with varying degrees of competence. The stories reproduced in this volume, however, have a maximum input from Shuster; most were originally created or published as newspaper strips.

The earliest tales reveal a wealth of surprises about the Man of Steel's past, details that, over the last half-century, have been refined, modified, adapted, and ultimately changed beyond recognition—an evolution authentic legends must often endure.

It is little remembered that baby Kal-I (Kal-El in later versions) was "turned over to an orphan asylum" after being found by the elderly Kents. (Siegel appropriately manages to advance the story, characterize the awesome infant, and squeeze a laugh into the two-panel sequence; remarkably, the parents appear to get younger as their adopted son ages in the following panel.) Superman sticklers will also note that young Clark begins his career at **The Daily Star** in the first story, moves to **The Evening News** (coincidentally based near his creators, in Cleveland) in the second, and switches back to the **Star** by his fourth adventure. Almost an entire year passes before he finally settles down in Metropolis (named after Fritz Lang's dystopian film masterpiece). Whether he follows Lois during his job-hopping or she follows him is still disputed.

Changes in costume abound throughout the early period. Years will pass before Superman's boots are standardized. (Although we've accepted the fact that he wears his outfit under street clothes, has no one ever wondered how he wears boots under his shoes?) The boot tops are sometimes pointed below the knee, sometimes curved, and often simply straight across. Occasionally, they aren't drawn at all! The belt holding up his trunks also appears and disappears with alarming regularity (luckily they have no zipper), as do the chevrons on his chest and cape, the latter of which is also missing sporadically during every adventure. The seeming incongruities may perhaps be explained by the comforting notion that not even Superman is perfect.

The most significant changes, however, concern the hero's powers. As he was originally created, "nothing less than a bursting shell" could penetrate his skin. He had the limited ability to "leap" an eighth of a mile and had no extras (super-ventriloquism, indeed!). There is no evidence to support his X-ray vision; to the contrary, in the first story, Clark requests a look at a newspaper headline from a man not three feet away! The Man of Tomorrow is obviously no longer the Man of Yesterday. One-upmanship has taken him a long way in the past 50 years. He now withstands nuclear explosions, can fly to the ends of the universe, and has more super bits of business than Freddy Krueger has lives. Those born in the fast-lane era must remember that Superman came to Earth in an age of innocence, a time amply reflected in the following stories. Simpler times called for simpler measures; major problems could easily be resolved by the threat of violence, though the Man of Steel displays little restraint in resorting to violent action whenever the spirit moves him. In his most basic form, Superman is the embodiment of the ultimate Adlerian adolescent fantasy: the most powerful man in the world. A hero created for kids by kids.

It is impossible to overestimate Superman's pre-eminence in the comics universe, and this collection represents the dawn of an era that can only be categorized as an American phenomenon. In February 1940, the Man of Steel made his radio debut. The following year, the first of 17 magnificently rotoscoped cartoons was released to breathless worldwide audiences. A decade later, two film serials and a TV series would fur-

ther propagate the Superman legend. As a comic-book character, he is the foremost of three—the others being Batman and Wonder Woman—whose adventures have been in continuous publication since their inception. Like Hamlet and Mickey Mouse, he is a figure of fictional immortality, a giant we have come to know best as a friend.   — STERANKO

JIM STERANKO is a writer/designer/historian of contemporary popular culture. As a comics writer and artist whose most noted works include **Nick Fury—Agent of S.H.I.E.L.D.**, **Captain America**, and **Superman**, as well as the **Outland** film adaptation and the graphic novel **Chandler**, he has exhibited his work around the world, including in the Louvre. A prolific illustrator in the fantasy and adventure genres, he has painted a profusion of movie posters, record albums, and book covers (including 30 Shadow paperbacks), in addition to working with Steven Spielberg as production artist on **Raiders of the Lost Ark**. His two volumes of **The History of Comics** have sold over 100,000 copies. He is currently the editor and publisher of **PREVUE Magazine**.

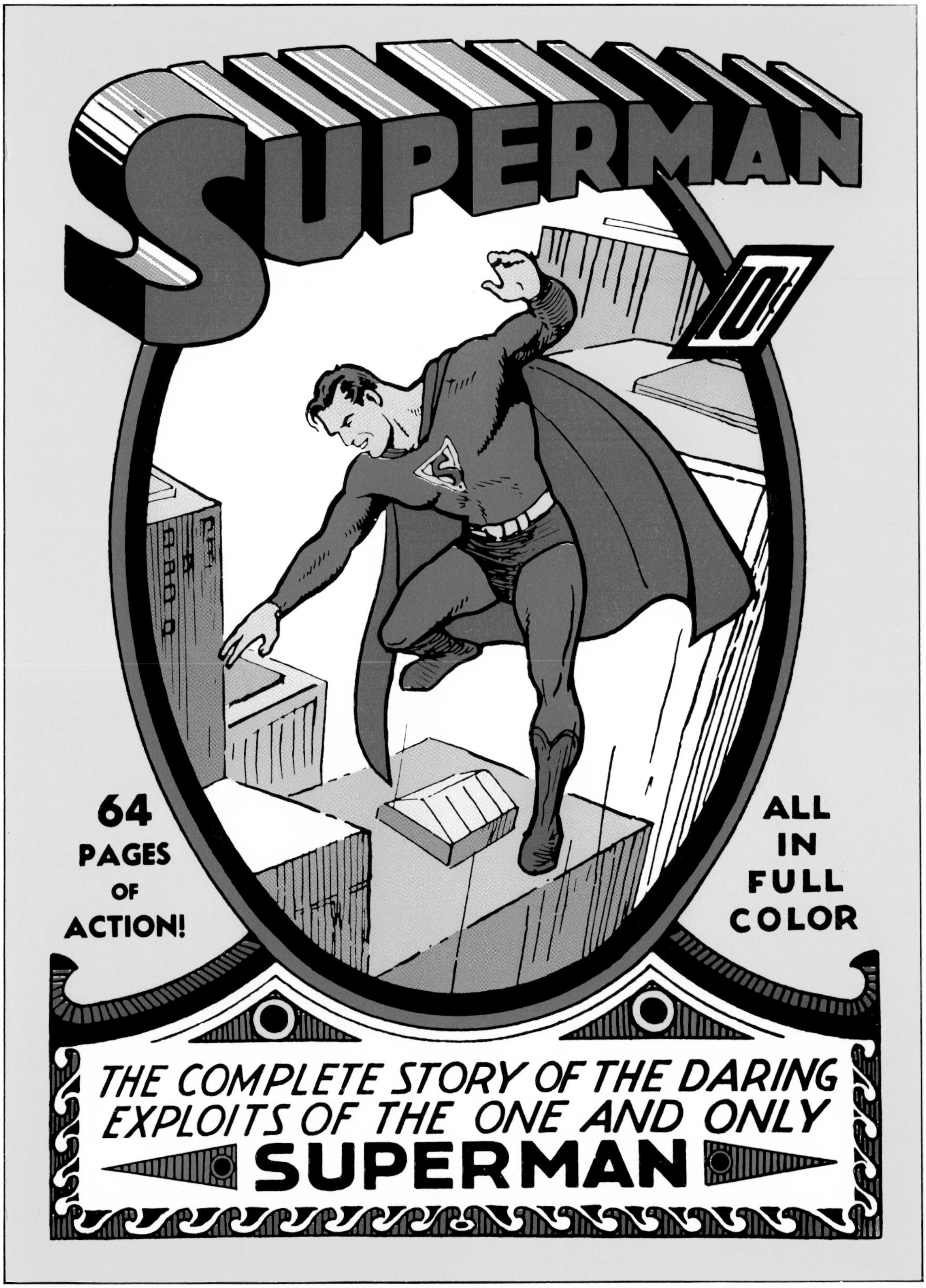
SUPERMAN
10¢
64 PAGES OF ACTION!
ALL IN FULL COLOR
THE COMPLETE STORY OF THE DARING EXPLOITS OF THE ONE AND ONLY
SUPERMAN

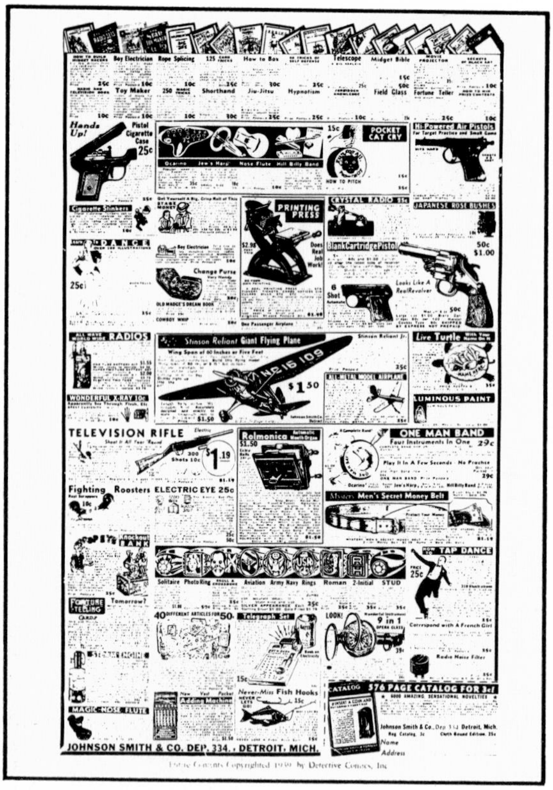
Hands Up!
Pistol Cigarette Case 25c
Hi-Powered Air Pistols
POCKET CAT CRY
Ocarina
Jew's Harp
Nose Flute
Hill Billy Band
CRYSTAL RADIO
JAPANESE ROSE BUSHES
Cigarette Stinkers
DANCE
PRINTING PRESS
Blank Cartridge Pistol
Looks Like A Real Revolver
50c
$1.00
Change Purse
OLD MADGE'S DREAM BOOK
COWBOY WHIP
One Passenger Airplane
RADIOS
Stinson Reliant Giant Flying Plane
Wing Span of 60 Inches or Five Feet
NC16109
$1.50
Live Turtle
ALL METAL MODEL AIRPLANE
WONDERFUL X-RAY 10c
LUMINOUS PAINT
TELEVISION RIFLE
Shoots 10c
$1.19
Rolmonica
ONE MAN BAND
Four Instruments In One 29c
Play It In A Few Seconds
No Practice
Fighting Roosters
ELECTRIC EYE 25c
Mystery Men's Secret Money Belt
Knockout BANK
TAP DANCE
Solitaire
Photo Ring
Aviation
Army Navy Rings
Roman
2-Initial
STUD
FORTUNE TELLING
40 DIFFERENT ARTICLES FOR 50c
Telegraph Set
9 in 1
Correspond with A French Girl
Radio Noise Filter
Adding Machine
Never-Miss Fish Hooks
MAGIC NOSE FLUTE
576 PAGE CATALOG FOR 3c!
Johnson Smith & Co., Dep. 334 Detroit, Mich.
JOHNSON SMITH & CO. DEP. 334, DETROIT, MICH.
Entire Contents Copyrighted 1939 by Detective Comics, Inc

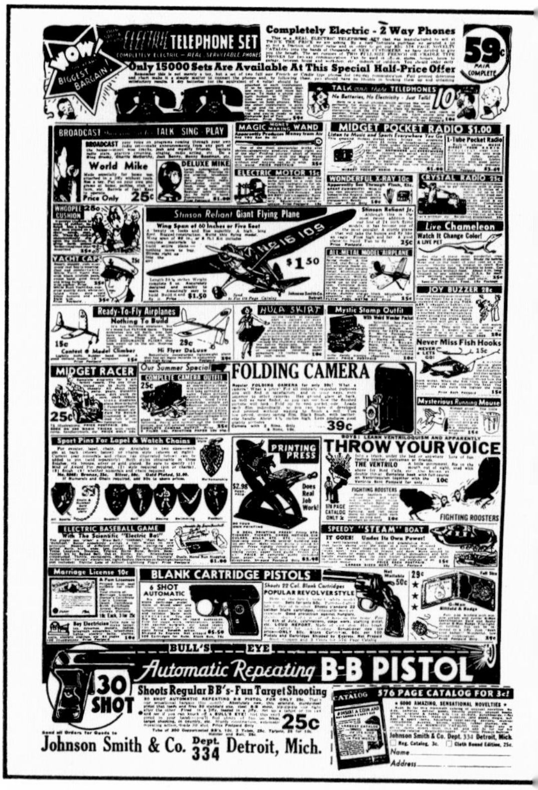
WOW! BIGGEST BARGAIN
ELECTRIC TELEPHONE SET
Completely Electric - 2 Way Phones
59c PAIR COMPLETE
Only 15000 Sets Are Available At This Special Half-Price Offer
TALK thru these TELEPHONES 10c
BROADCAST TALK SING PLAY
World Mike
DELUXE MIKE
Price Only 25c
MAGIC WAND
MIDGET POCKET RADIO $1.00
ELECTRIC MOTOR
WONDERFUL X-RAY 10c
CRYSTAL RADIO
WHOOPEE CUSHION
Stinson Reliant Giant Flying Plane
Wing Span of 60 Inches or Five Feet
NC16109
$1.50
Live Chameleon
Watch It Change Color!
YACHT CAP
ALL-METAL MODEL AIRPLANE
JOY BUZZER
Ready-To-Fly Airplanes
Nothing To Build
HULA SKIRT
Mystic Stamp Outfit
Never Miss Fish Hooks
MIDGET RACER
Our Summer Special
FOLDING CAMERA
39c
Mysterious Running Mouse
Sport Pins For Lapel & Watch Chains
PRINTING PRESS
THROW YOUR VOICE
FIGHTING ROOSTERS
ELECTRIC BASEBALL GAME
SPEEDY "STEAM" BOAT
Marriage License 10c
BLANK CARTRIDGE PISTOLS
6 SHOT AUTOMATIC
POPULAR REVOLVER STYLE
50c
BULL'S EYE
Automatic Repeating B-B PISTOL
30 SHOT
Shoots Regular B B's-Fun Target Shooting
25c
576 PAGE CATALOG FOR 3c!
Johnson Smith & Co. Dept. 334 Detroit, Mich.

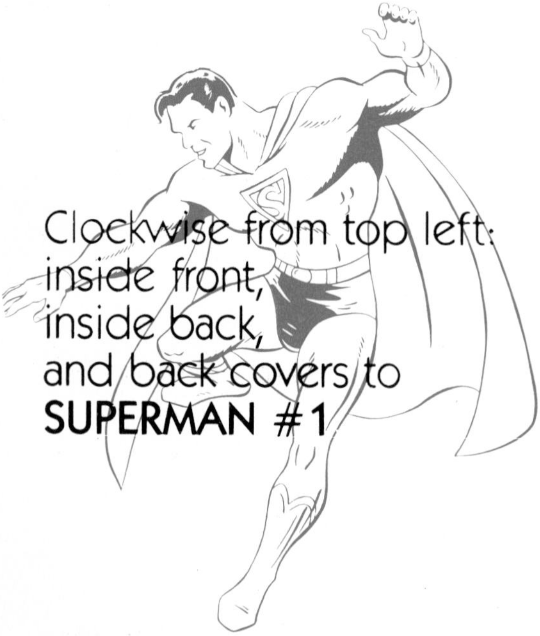

Clockwise from top left:
inside front,
inside back,
and back covers to
SUPERMAN #1

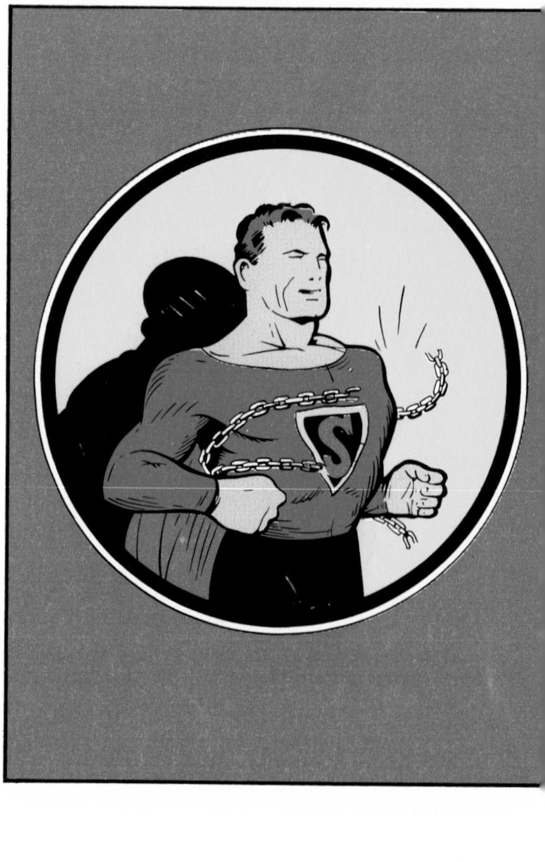

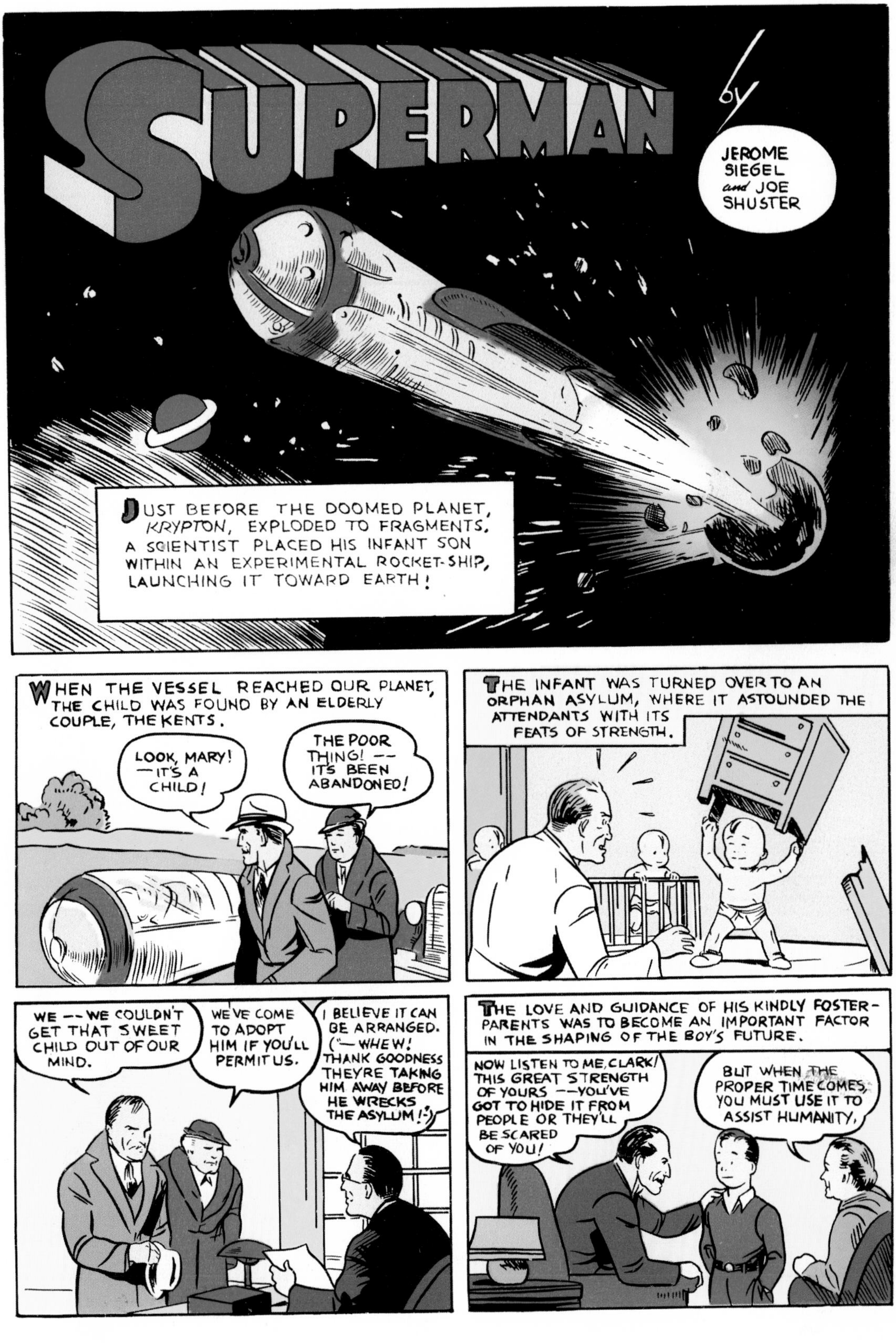
SUPERMAN
by
JEROME SIEGEL and JOE SHUSTER
JUST BEFORE THE DOOMED PLANET, KRYPTON, EXPLODED TO FRAGMENTS, A SCIENTIST PLACED HIS INFANT SON WITHIN AN EXPERIMENTAL ROCKET-SHIP, LAUNCHING IT TOWARD EARTH!
WHEN THE VESSEL REACHED OUR PLANET, THE CHILD WAS FOUND BY AN ELDERLY COUPLE, THE KENTS.
LOOK, MARY! —IT'S A CHILD!
THE POOR THING! — ITS BEEN ABANDONED!
THE INFANT WAS TURNED OVER TO AN ORPHAN ASYLUM, WHERE IT ASTOUNDED THE ATTENDANTS WITH ITS FEATS OF STRENGTH.
WE — WE COULDN'T GET THAT SWEET CHILD OUT OF OUR MIND.
WE'VE COME TO ADOPT HIM IF YOU'LL PERMIT US.
I BELIEVE IT CAN BE ARRANGED. ("—WHEW! THANK GOODNESS THEY'RE TAKING HIM AWAY BEFORE HE WRECKS THE ASYLUM!")
THE LOVE AND GUIDANCE OF HIS KINDLY FOSTER-PARENTS WAS TO BECOME AN IMPORTANT FACTOR IN THE SHAPING OF THE BOY'S FUTURE.
NOW LISTEN TO ME, CLARK! THIS GREAT STRENGTH OF YOURS —YOU'VE GOT TO HIDE IT FROM PEOPLE OR THEY'LL BE SCARED OF YOU!
BUT WHEN THE PROPER TIME COMES, YOU MUST USE IT TO ASSIST HUMANITY.

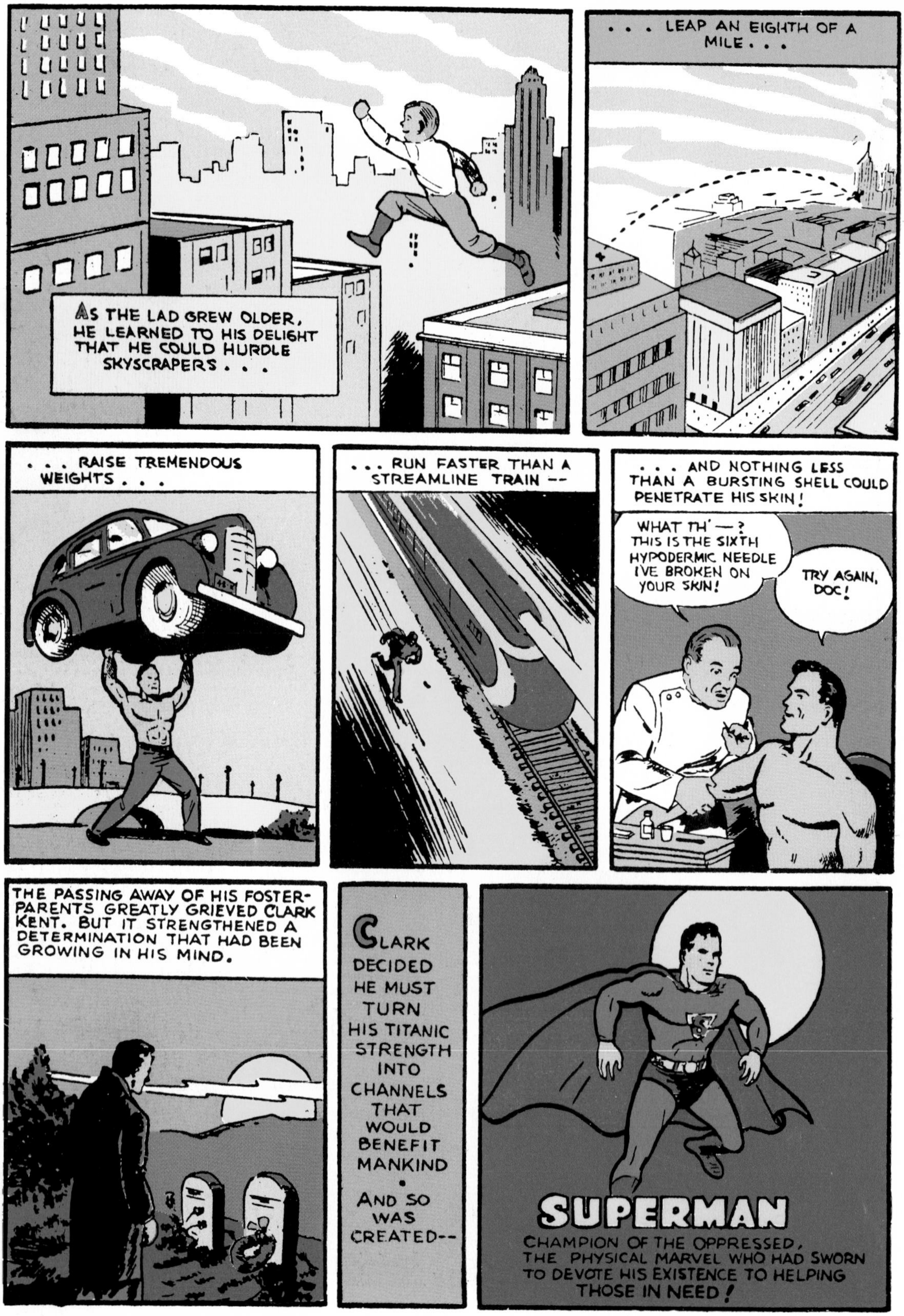
AS THE LAD GREW OLDER, HE LEARNED TO HIS DELIGHT THAT HE COULD HURDLE SKYSCRAPERS . . .
. . . LEAP AN EIGHTH OF A MILE . . .
. . . RAISE TREMENDOUS WEIGHTS . . .
. . . RUN FASTER THAN A STREAMLINE TRAIN --
. . . AND NOTHING LESS THAN A BURSTING SHELL COULD PENETRATE HIS SKIN!
WHAT TH' — ? THIS IS THE SIXTH HYPODERMIC NEEDLE I'VE BROKEN ON YOUR SKIN!
TRY AGAIN, DOC!
THE PASSING AWAY OF HIS FOSTER-PARENTS GREATLY GRIEVED CLARK KENT. BUT IT STRENGTHENED A DETERMINATION THAT HAD BEEN GROWING IN HIS MIND.
CLARK DECIDED HE MUST TURN HIS TITANIC STRENGTH INTO CHANNELS THAT WOULD BENEFIT MANKIND
AND SO WAS CREATED--
SUPERMAN
CHAMPION OF THE OPPRESSED, THE PHYSICAL MARVEL WHO HAD SWORN TO DEVOTE HIS EXISTENCE TO HELPING THOSE IN NEED!

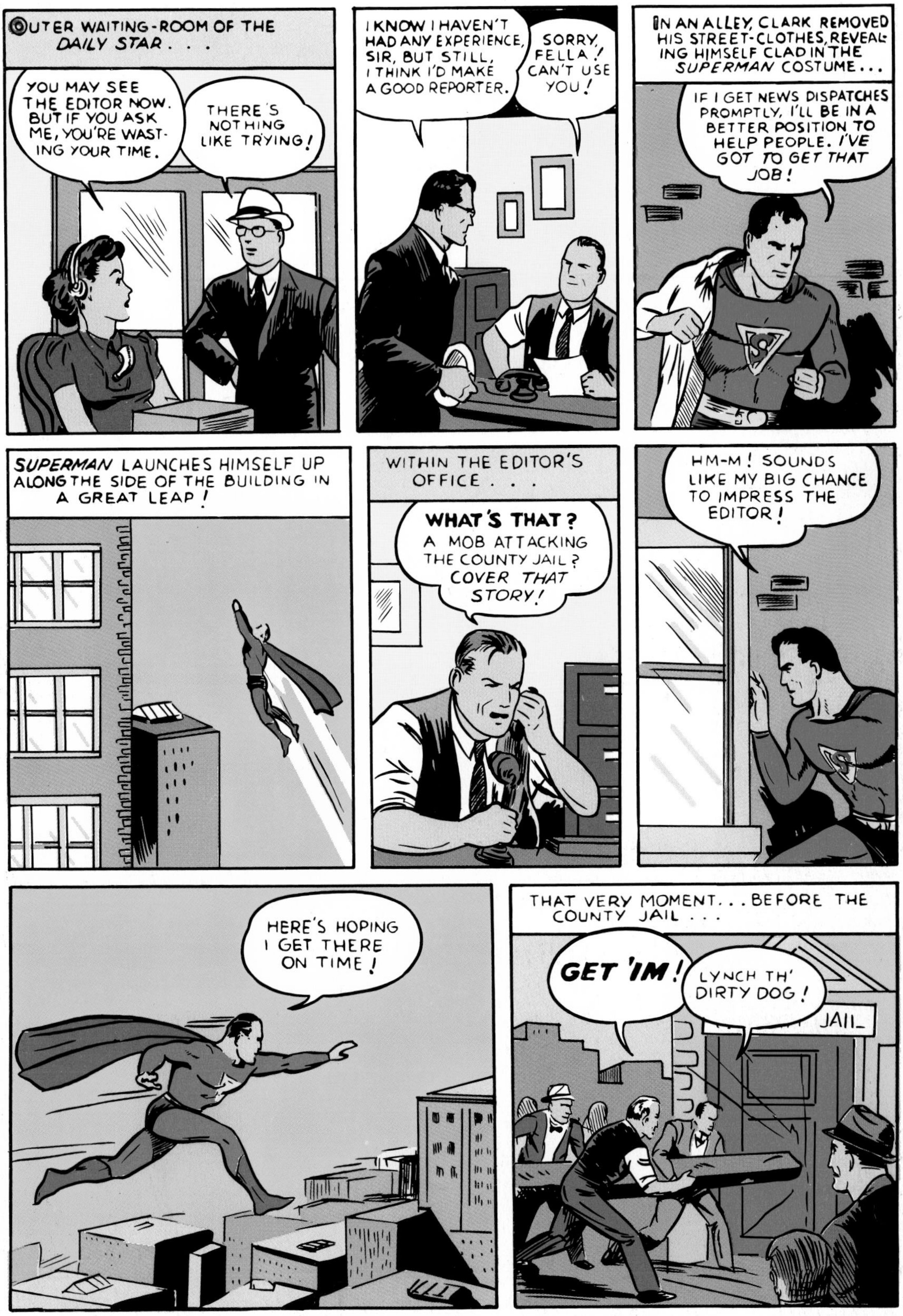
OUTER WAITING-ROOM OF THE DAILY STAR . . .
YOU MAY SEE THE EDITOR NOW. BUT IF YOU ASK ME, YOU'RE WASTING YOUR TIME.
THERE'S NOTHING LIKE TRYING!
I KNOW I HAVEN'T HAD ANY EXPERIENCE, SIR, BUT STILL, I THINK I'D MAKE A GOOD REPORTER.
SORRY, FELLA! CAN'T USE YOU!
IN AN ALLEY, CLARK REMOVED HIS STREET-CLOTHES, REVEALING HIMSELF CLAD IN THE SUPERMAN COSTUME . . .
IF I GET NEWS DISPATCHES PROMPTLY, I'LL BE IN A BETTER POSITION TO HELP PEOPLE. I'VE GOT TO GET THAT JOB!
SUPERMAN LAUNCHES HIMSELF UP ALONG THE SIDE OF THE BUILDING IN A GREAT LEAP!
WITHIN THE EDITOR'S OFFICE . . .
WHAT'S THAT? A MOB ATTACKING THE COUNTY JAIL? COVER THAT STORY!
HM-M! SOUNDS LIKE MY BIG CHANCE TO IMPRESS THE EDITOR!
HERE'S HOPING I GET THERE ON TIME!
THAT VERY MOMENT . . . BEFORE THE COUNTY JAIL . . .
GET 'IM!
LYNCH TH' DIRTY DOG!
JAIL

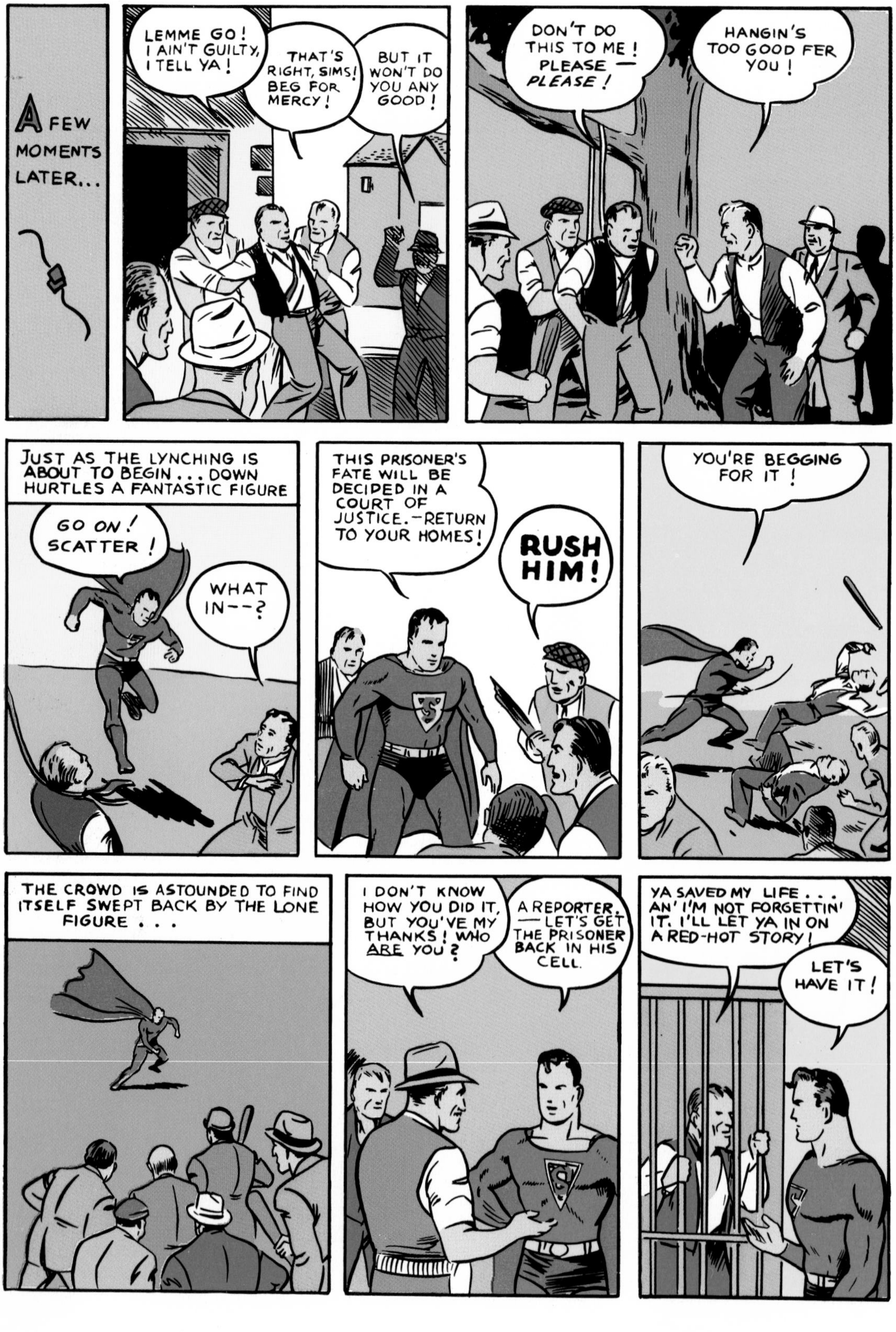
A FEW MOMENTS LATER...
LEMME GO! I AIN'T GUILTY, I TELL YA!
THAT'S RIGHT, SIMS! BEG FOR MERCY!
BUT IT WON'T DO YOU ANY GOOD!
DON'T DO THIS TO ME! PLEASE — PLEASE!
HANGIN'S TOO GOOD FER YOU!
JUST AS THE LYNCHING IS ABOUT TO BEGIN... DOWN HURTLES A FANTASTIC FIGURE
GO ON! SCATTER!
WHAT IN--?
THIS PRISONER'S FATE WILL BE DECIDED IN A COURT OF JUSTICE.—RETURN TO YOUR HOMES!
RUSH HIM!
YOU'RE BEGGING FOR IT!
THE CROWD IS ASTOUNDED TO FIND ITSELF SWEPT BACK BY THE LONE FIGURE...
I DON'T KNOW HOW YOU DID IT, BUT THANKS! YOU'VE MY THANKS! WHO ARE YOU?
A REPORTER. — LET'S GET THE PRISONER BACK IN HIS CELL.
YA SAVED MY LIFE... AN' I'M NOT FORGETTIN' IT. I'LL LET YA IN ON A RED-HOT STORY!
LET'S HAVE IT!

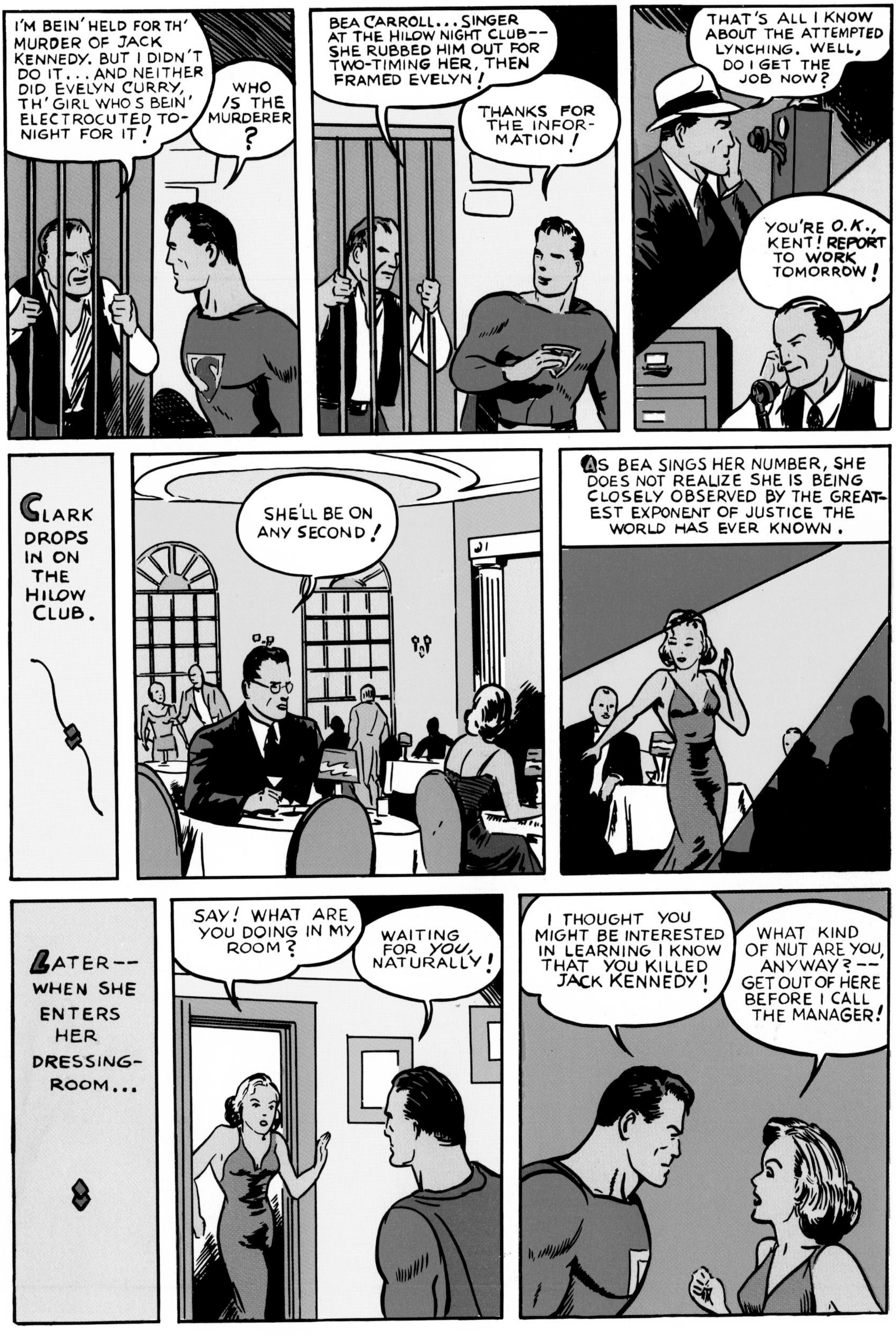
I'M BEIN' HELD FOR TH' MURDER OF JACK KENNEDY. BUT I DIDN'T DO IT... AND NEITHER DID EVELYN CURRY, TH' GIRL WHO'S BEIN' ELECTROCUTED TO-NIGHT FOR IT!
WHO IS THE MURDERER?
BEA CARROLL... SINGER AT THE HILOW NIGHT CLUB-- SHE RUBBED HIM OUT FOR TWO-TIMING HER, THEN FRAMED EVELYN!
THANKS FOR THE INFOR-MATION!
THAT'S ALL I KNOW ABOUT THE ATTEMPTED LYNCHING. WELL, DO I GET THE JOB NOW?
YOU'RE O.K., KENT! REPORT TO WORK TOMORROW!
CLARK DROPS IN ON THE HILOW CLUB.
SHE'LL BE ON ANY SECOND!
AS BEA SINGS HER NUMBER, SHE DOES NOT REALIZE SHE IS BEING CLOSELY OBSERVED BY THE GREAT-EST EXPONENT OF JUSTICE THE WORLD HAS EVER KNOWN.
LATER-- WHEN SHE ENTERS HER DRESSING-ROOM...
SAY! WHAT ARE YOU DOING IN MY ROOM?
WAITING FOR YOU, NATURALLY!
I THOUGHT YOU MIGHT BE INTERESTED IN LEARNING I KNOW THAT YOU KILLED JACK KENNEDY!
WHAT KIND OF NUT ARE YOU, ANYWAY? -- GET OUT OF HERE BEFORE I CALL THE MANAGER!

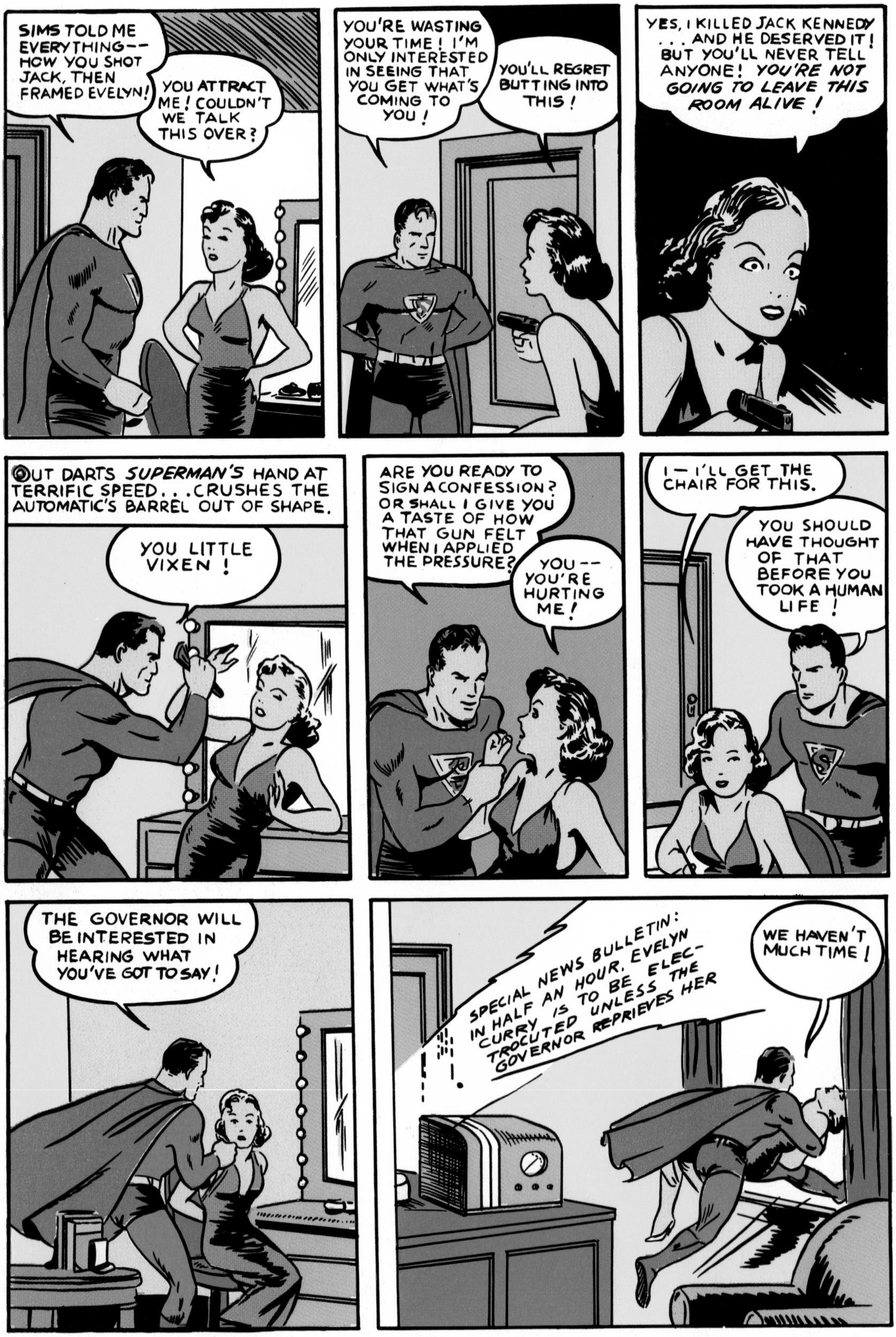
SIMS TOLD ME EVERYTHING-- HOW YOU SHOT JACK, THEN FRAMED EVELYN!
YOU ATTRACT ME! COULDN'T WE TALK THIS OVER?
YOU'RE WASTING YOUR TIME! I'M ONLY INTERESTED IN SEEING THAT YOU GET WHAT'S COMING TO YOU!
YOU'LL REGRET BUTTING INTO THIS!
YES, I KILLED JACK KENNEDY . . . AND HE DESERVED IT! BUT YOU'LL NEVER TELL ANYONE! *YOU'RE NOT GOING TO LEAVE THIS ROOM ALIVE!*
OUT DARTS *SUPERMAN'S* HAND AT TERRIFIC SPEED. . .CRUSHES THE AUTOMATIC'S BARREL OUT OF SHAPE.
YOU LITTLE VIXEN!
ARE YOU READY TO SIGN A CONFESSION? OR SHALL I GIVE YOU A TASTE OF HOW THAT GUN FELT WHEN I APPLIED THE PRESSURE?
YOU-- YOU'RE HURTING ME!
I-I'LL GET THE CHAIR FOR THIS.
YOU SHOULD HAVE THOUGHT OF THAT BEFORE YOU TOOK A HUMAN LIFE!
THE GOVERNOR WILL BE INTERESTED IN HEARING WHAT YOU'VE GOT TO SAY!
SPECIAL NEWS BULLETIN: IN HALF AN HOUR, EVELYN CURRY IS TO BE ELEC-TROCUTED UNLESS THE GOVERNOR REPRIEVES HER
WE HAVEN'T MUCH TIME!

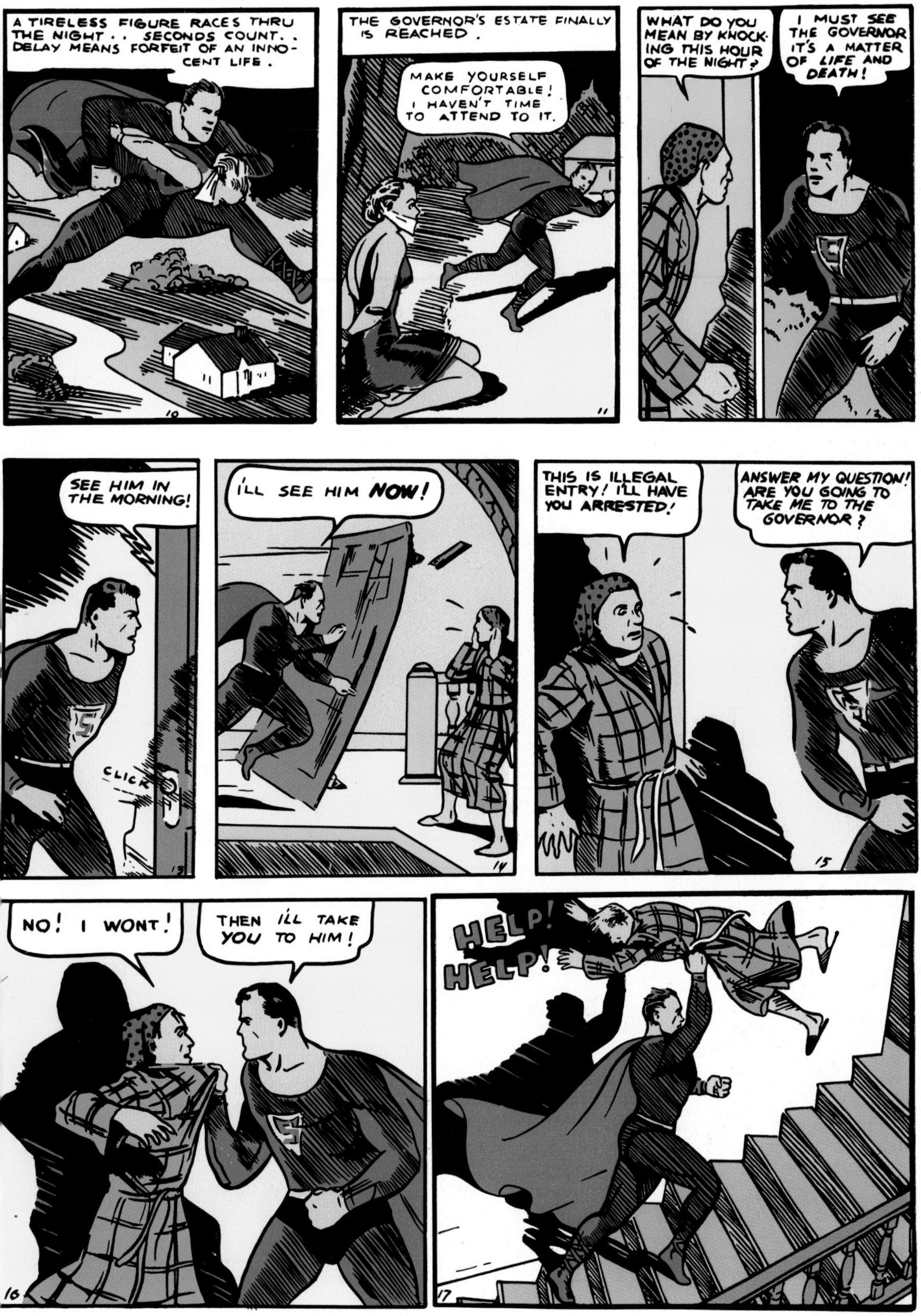
A TIRELESS FIGURE RACES THRU THE NIGHT . . SECONDS COUNT. . DELAY MEANS FORFEIT OF AN INNOCENT LIFE .
THE GOVERNOR'S ESTATE FINALLY IS REACHED .
MAKE YOURSELF COMFORTABLE! I HAVEN'T TIME TO ATTEND TO IT.
WHAT DO YOU MEAN BY KNOCKING THIS HOUR OF THE NIGHT?
I MUST SEE THE GOVERNOR IT'S A MATTER OF LIFE AND DEATH!
SEE HIM IN THE MORNING!
CLICK
I'LL SEE HIM NOW!
THIS IS ILLEGAL ENTRY! I'LL HAVE YOU ARRESTED!
ANSWER MY QUESTION! ARE YOU GOING TO TAKE ME TO THE GOVERNOR ?
NO! I WONT!
THEN I'LL TAKE YOU TO HIM!
HELP! HELP!

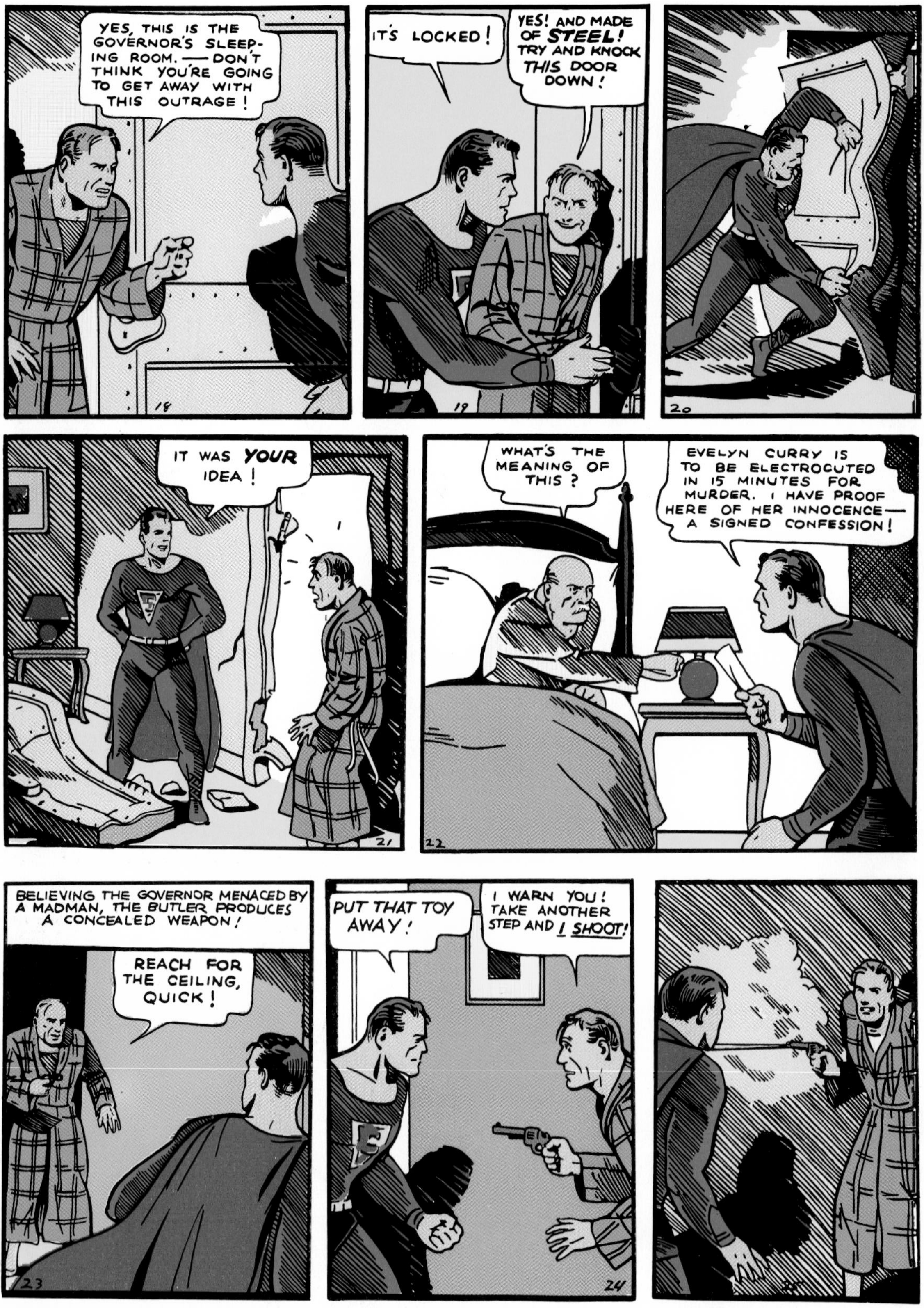
YES, THIS IS THE GOVERNOR'S SLEEPING ROOM. — DON'T THINK YOU'RE GOING TO GET AWAY WITH THIS OUTRAGE!
18
IT'S LOCKED!
YES! AND MADE OF STEEL! TRY AND KNOCK THIS DOOR DOWN!
19
20
IT WAS YOUR IDEA!
21
WHAT'S THE MEANING OF THIS?
EVELYN CURRY IS TO BE ELECTROCUTED IN 15 MINUTES FOR MURDER. I HAVE PROOF HERE OF HER INNOCENCE— A SIGNED CONFESSION!
22
BELIEVING THE GOVERNOR MENACED BY A MADMAN, THE BUTLER PRODUCES A CONCEALED WEAPON!
REACH FOR THE CEILING, QUICK!
23
PUT THAT TOY AWAY!
I WARN YOU! TAKE ANOTHER STEP AND I SHOOT!
24
25

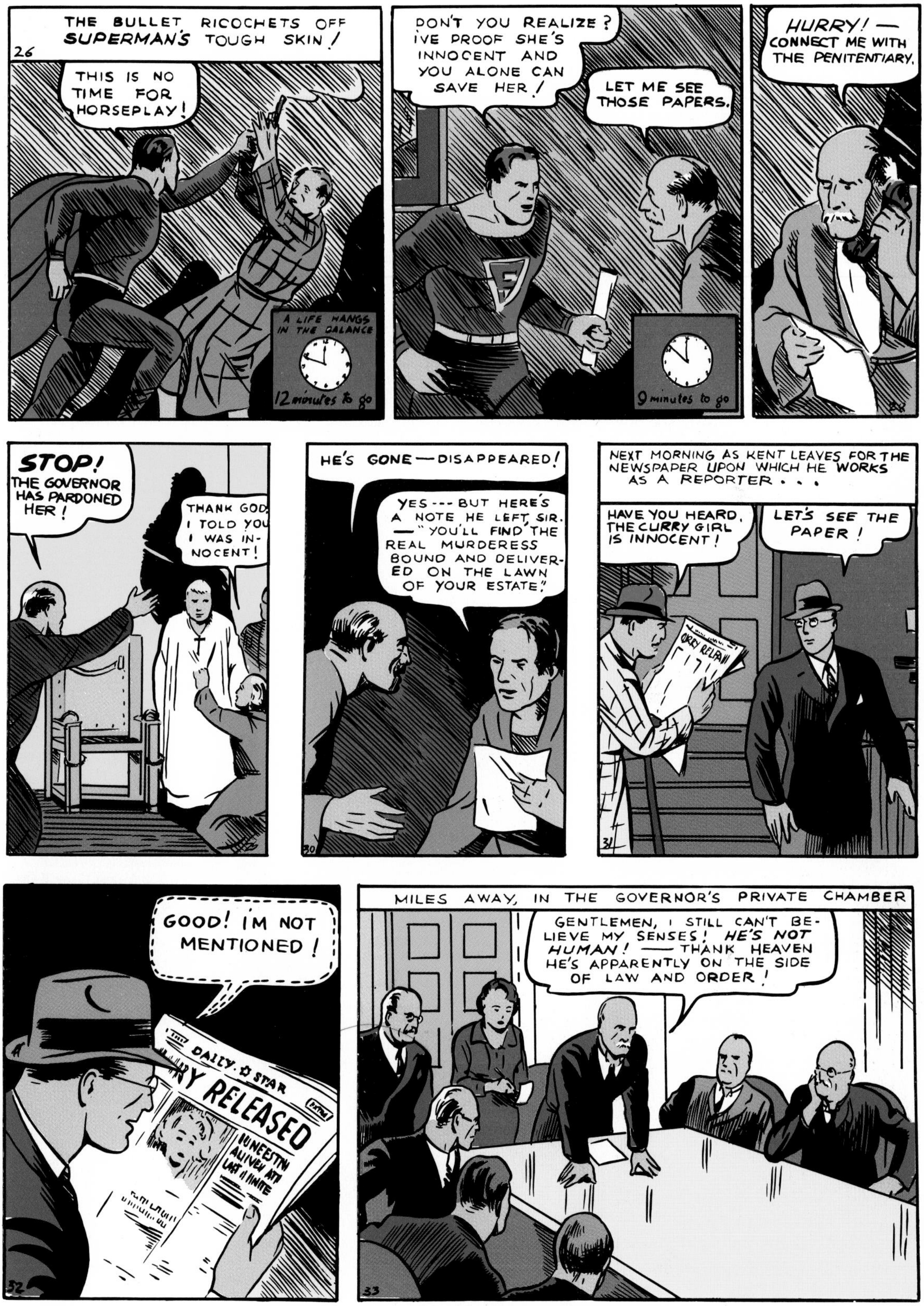
THE BULLET RICOCHETS OFF SUPERMAN'S TOUGH SKIN!
THIS IS NO TIME FOR HORSEPLAY!
A LIFE HANGS IN THE BALANCE
12 minutes to go
DON'T YOU REALIZE? I'VE PROOF SHE'S INNOCENT AND YOU ALONE CAN SAVE HER!
LET ME SEE THOSE PAPERS.
9 minutes to go
HURRY! — CONNECT ME WITH THE PENITENTIARY.
STOP! THE GOVERNOR HAS PARDONED HER!
THANK GOD! I TOLD YOU I WAS INNOCENT!
HE'S GONE — DISAPPEARED!
YES --- BUT HERE'S A NOTE HE LEFT, SIR. — "YOU'LL FIND THE REAL MURDERESS BOUND AND DELIVERED ON THE LAWN OF YOUR ESTATE."
NEXT MORNING AS KENT LEAVES FOR THE NEWSPAPER UPON WHICH HE WORKS AS A REPORTER . . .
HAVE YOU HEARD, THE CURRY GIRL IS INNOCENT!
LET'S SEE THE PAPER!
GOOD! I'M NOT MENTIONED!
DAILY STAR
RELEASED
MILES AWAY, IN THE GOVERNOR'S PRIVATE CHAMBER
GENTLEMEN, I STILL CAN'T BELIEVE MY SENSES! HE'S NOT HUMAN! — THANK HEAVEN HE'S APPARENTLY ON THE SIDE OF LAW AND ORDER!

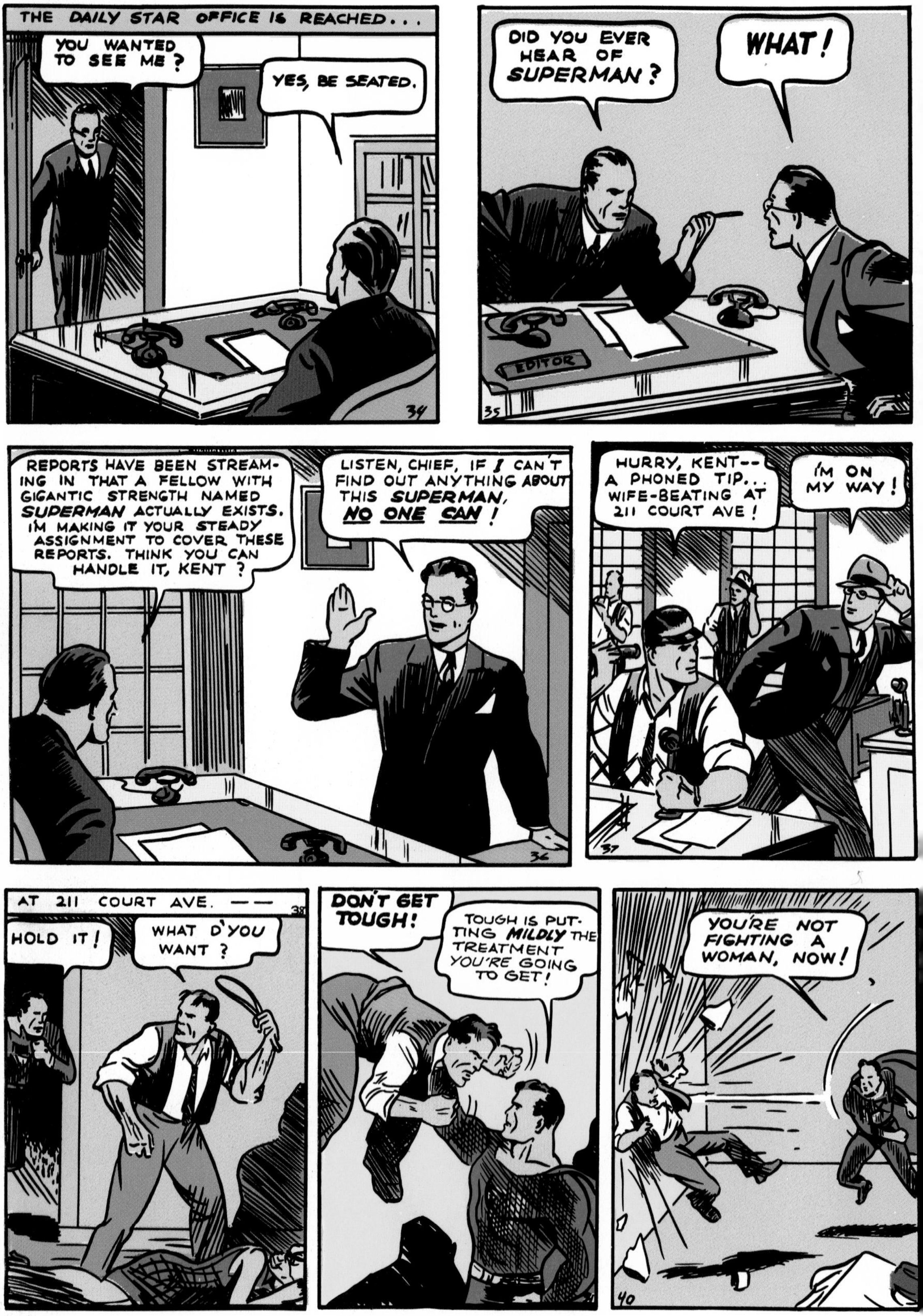
THE DAILY STAR OFFICE IS REACHED...
YOU WANTED TO SEE ME?
YES, BE SEATED.
DID YOU EVER HEAR OF SUPERMAN?
WHAT!
EDITOR
REPORTS HAVE BEEN STREAMING IN THAT A FELLOW WITH GIGANTIC STRENGTH NAMED SUPERMAN ACTUALLY EXISTS. I'M MAKING IT YOUR STEADY ASSIGNMENT TO COVER THESE REPORTS. THINK YOU CAN HANDLE IT, KENT?
LISTEN, CHIEF, IF I CAN'T FIND OUT ANYTHING ABOUT THIS SUPERMAN, NO ONE CAN!
HURRY, KENT-- A PHONED TIP... WIFE-BEATING AT 211 COURT AVE!
I'M ON MY WAY!
AT 211 COURT AVE. ——
HOLD IT!
WHAT D'YOU WANT?
DON'T GET TOUGH!
TOUGH IS PUTTING MILDLY THE TREATMENT YOU'RE GOING TO GET!
YOU'RE NOT FIGHTING A WOMAN, NOW!

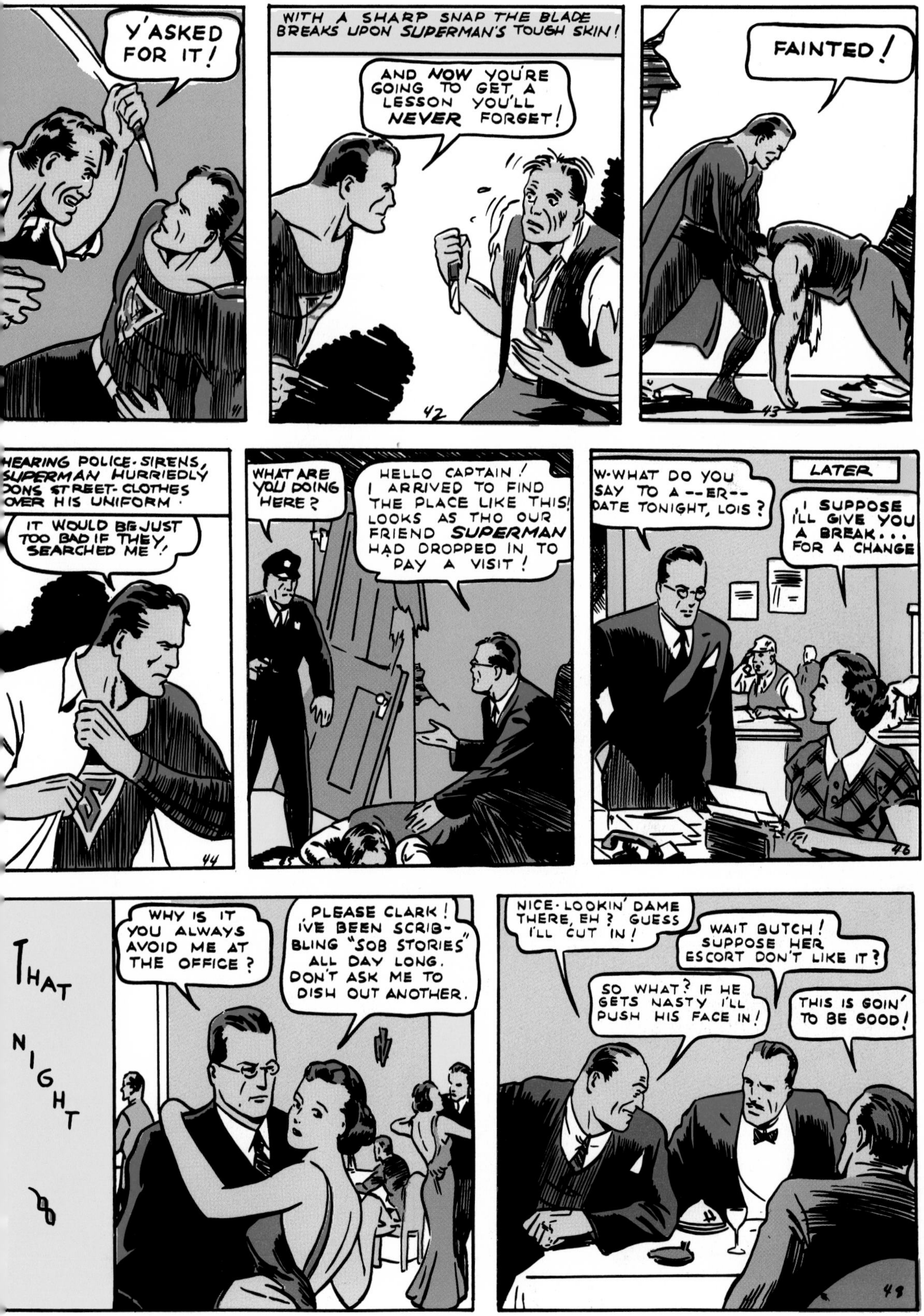
Y'ASKED FOR IT!
WITH A SHARP SNAP THE BLADE BREAKS UPON SUPERMAN'S TOUGH SKIN!
AND NOW YOU'RE GOING TO GET A LESSON YOU'LL NEVER FORGET!
FAINTED!
HEARING POLICE-SIRENS, SUPERMAN HURRIEDLY DONS STREET-CLOTHES OVER HIS UNIFORM.
IT WOULD BE JUST TOO BAD IF THEY SEARCHED ME!
WHAT ARE YOU DOING HERE?
HELLO CAPTAIN! I ARRIVED TO FIND THE PLACE LIKE THIS! LOOKS AS THO OUR FRIEND SUPERMAN HAD DROPPED IN TO PAY A VISIT!
W-WHAT DO YOU SAY TO A--ER--DATE TONIGHT, LOIS?
LATER
I SUPPOSE I'LL GIVE YOU A BREAK... FOR A CHANGE
THAT NIGHT
WHY IS IT YOU ALWAYS AVOID ME AT THE OFFICE?
PLEASE CLARK! I'VE BEEN SCRIBBLING "SOB STORIES" ALL DAY LONG. DON'T ASK ME TO DISH OUT ANOTHER.
NICE-LOOKIN' DAME THERE, EH? GUESS I'LL CUT IN!
WAIT BUTCH! SUPPOSE HER ESCORT DON'T LIKE IT?
SO WHAT? IF HE GETS NASTY I'LL PUSH HIS FACE IN!
THIS IS GOIN' TO BE GOOD!

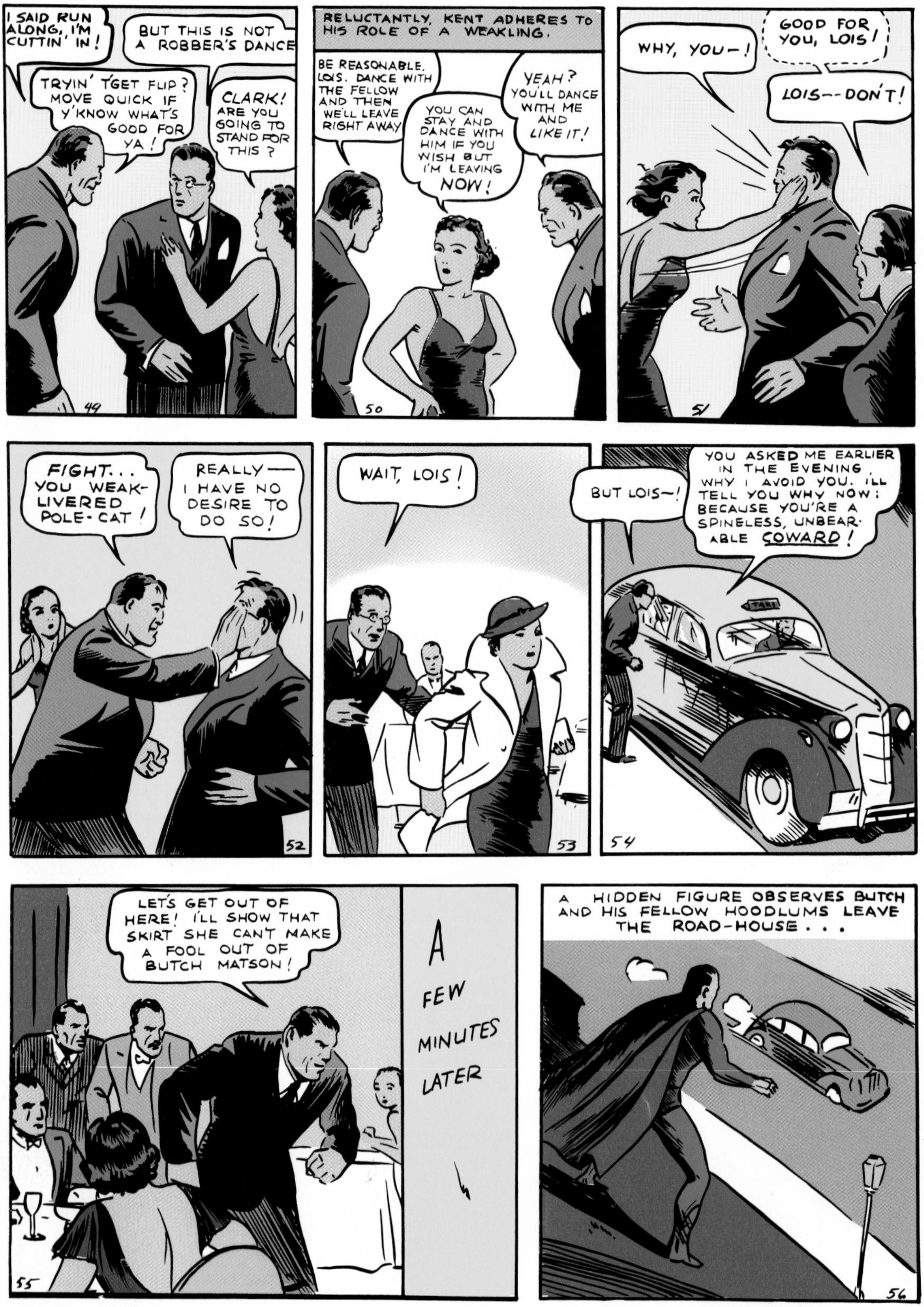
I SAID RUN ALONG, I'M CUTTIN' IN!
BUT THIS IS NOT A ROBBER'S DANCE
TRYIN' T'GET FLIP? MOVE QUICK IF Y'KNOW WHAT'S GOOD FOR YA!
CLARK! ARE YOU GOING TO STAND FOR THIS?
RELUCTANTLY, KENT ADHERES TO HIS ROLE OF A WEAKLING.
BE REASONABLE, LOIS. DANCE WITH THE FELLOW AND THEN WE'LL LEAVE RIGHT AWAY
YOU CAN STAY AND DANCE WITH HIM IF YOU WISH BUT I'M LEAVING NOW!
YEAH? YOU'LL DANCE WITH ME AND LIKE IT!
WHY, YOU--!
GOOD FOR YOU, LOIS!
LOIS--DON'T!
FIGHT... YOU WEAK-LIVERED POLE-CAT!
REALLY-- I HAVE NO DESIRE TO DO SO!
WAIT, LOIS!
BUT LOIS--!
YOU ASKED ME EARLIER IN THE EVENING WHY I AVOID YOU. I'LL TELL YOU WHY NOW: BECAUSE YOU'RE A SPINELESS, UNBEARABLE COWARD!
TAXI
LET'S GET OUT OF HERE! I'LL SHOW THAT SKIRT SHE CAN'T MAKE A FOOL OUT OF BUTCH MATSON!
A FEW MINUTES LATER
A HIDDEN FIGURE OBSERVES BUTCH AND HIS FELLOW HOODLUMS LEAVE THE ROAD-HOUSE...

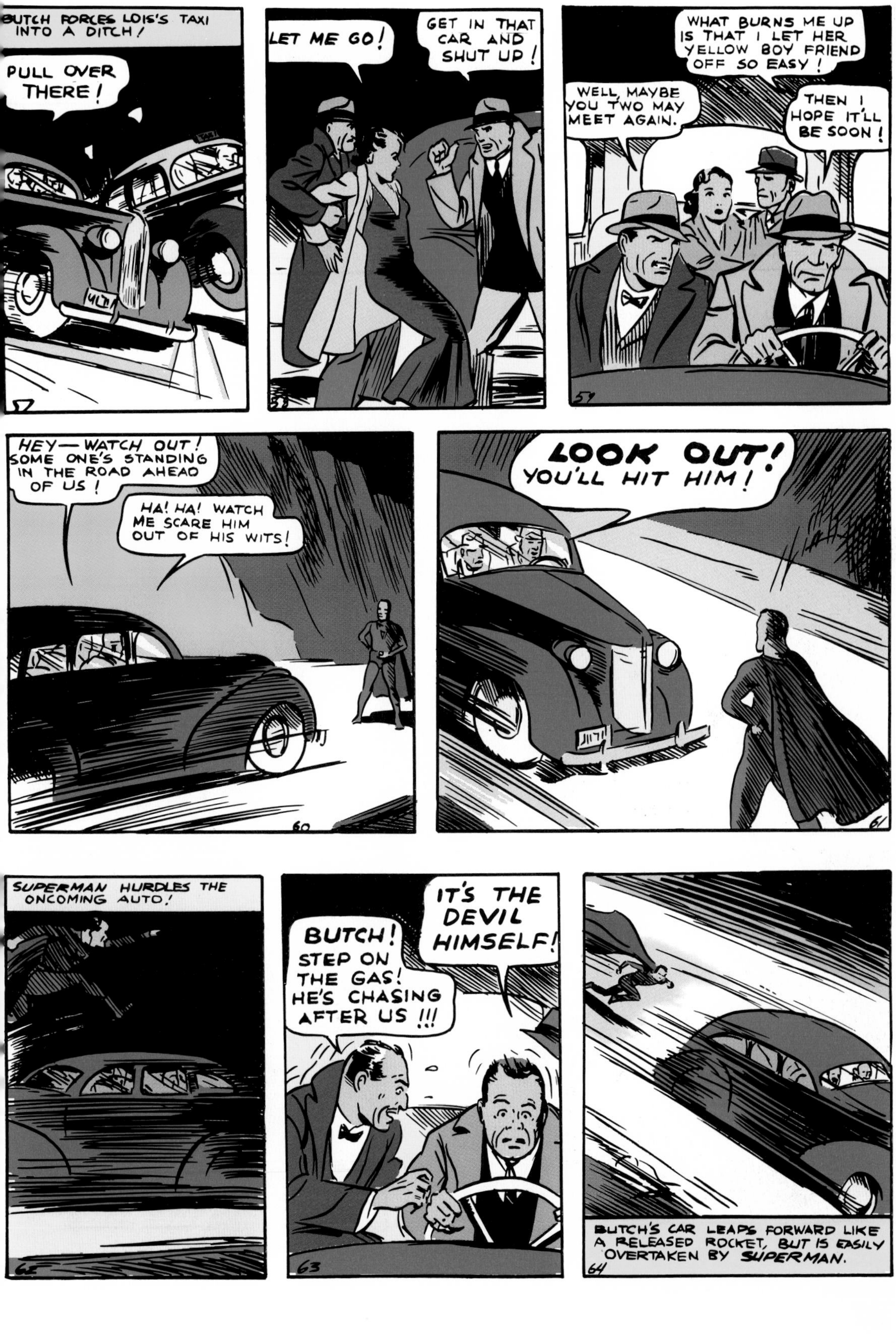
BUTCH FORCES LOIS'S TAXI INTO A DITCH!
PULL OVER THERE!
LET ME GO!
GET IN THAT CAR AND SHUT UP!
WHAT BURNS ME UP IS THAT I LET HER YELLOW BOY FRIEND OFF SO EASY!
WELL, MAYBE YOU TWO MAY MEET AGAIN.
THEN I HOPE IT'LL BE SOON!
HEY—WATCH OUT! SOME ONE'S STANDING IN THE ROAD AHEAD OF US!
HA! HA! WATCH ME SCARE HIM OUT OF HIS WITS!
LOOK OUT! YOU'LL HIT HIM!
SUPERMAN HURDLES THE ONCOMING AUTO!
BUTCH! STEP ON THE GAS! HE'S CHASING AFTER US!!!
IT'S THE DEVIL HIMSELF!
BUTCH'S CAR LEAPS FORWARD LIKE A RELEASED ROCKET, BUT IS EASILY OVERTAKEN BY SUPERMAN.

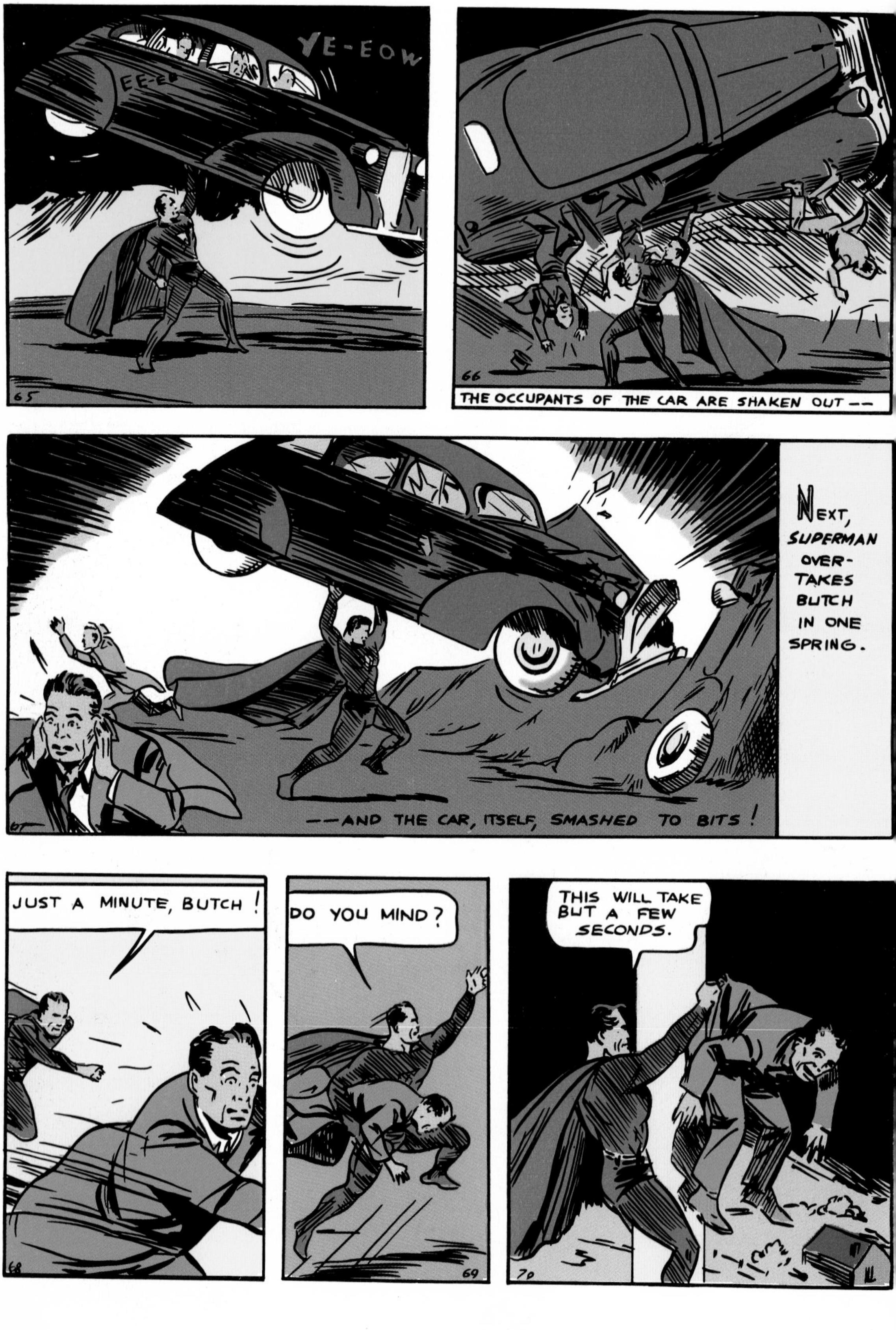
YE-EOW
EE-EE
65
66
THE OCCUPANTS OF THE CAR ARE SHAKEN OUT --
NEXT, SUPERMAN OVER-TAKES BUTCH IN ONE SPRING.
67
--AND THE CAR, ITSELF, SMASHED TO BITS!
JUST A MINUTE, BUTCH!
68
DO YOU MIND?
69
THIS WILL TAKE BUT A FEW SECONDS.
70

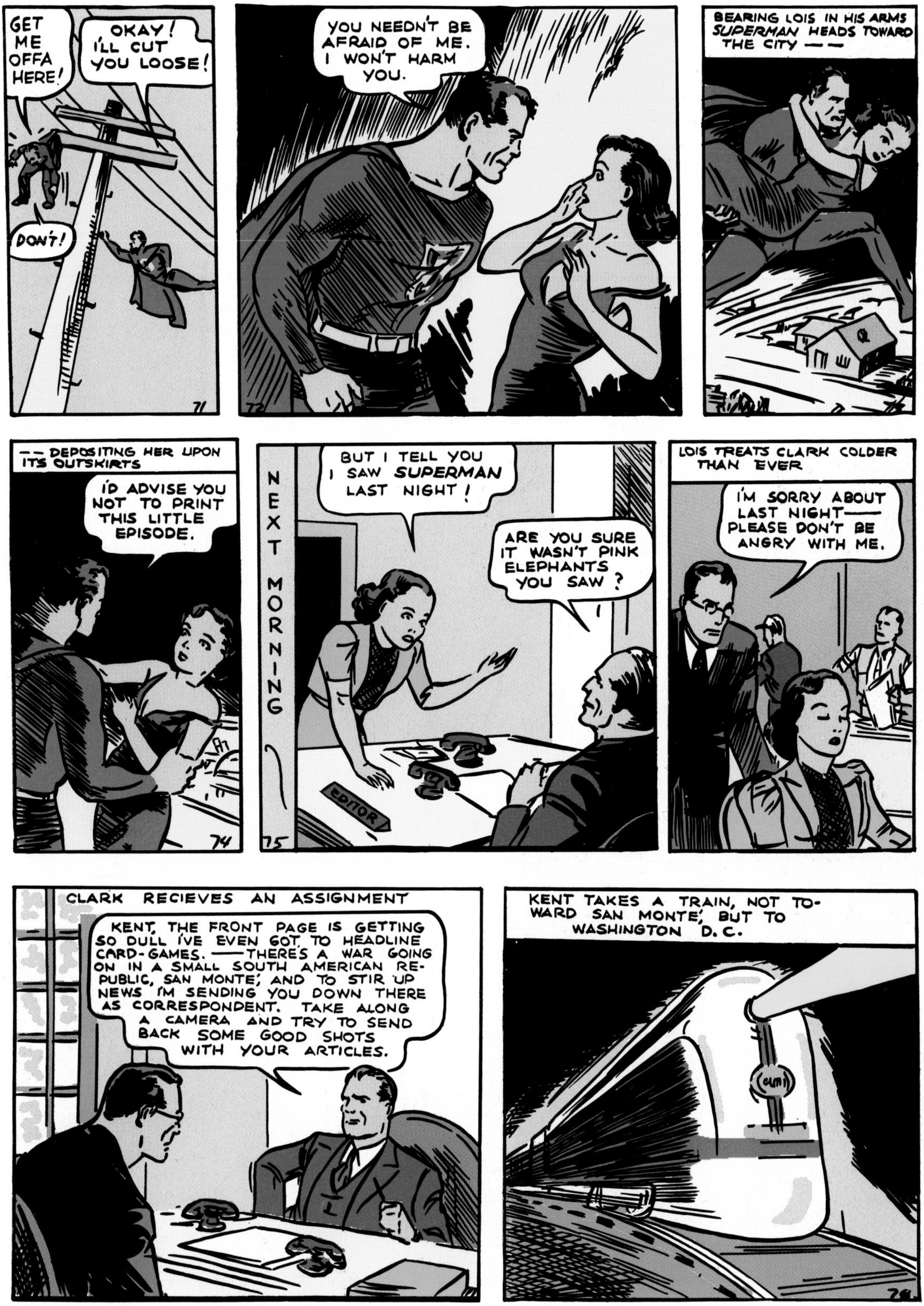
GET ME OFFA HERE!
OKAY! I'LL CUT YOU LOOSE!
DON'T!
YOU NEEDN'T BE AFRAID OF ME. I WON'T HARM YOU.
BEARING LOIS IN HIS ARMS SUPERMAN HEADS TOWARD THE CITY — —
— — DEPOSITING HER UPON ITS OUTSKIRTS
I'D ADVISE YOU NOT TO PRINT THIS LITTLE EPISODE.
NEXT MORNING
BUT I TELL YOU I SAW SUPERMAN LAST NIGHT!
ARE YOU SURE IT WASN'T PINK ELEPHANTS YOU SAW?
EDITOR
LOIS TREATS CLARK COLDER THAN EVER
I'M SORRY ABOUT LAST NIGHT—— PLEASE DON'T BE ANGRY WITH ME.
CLARK RECIEVES AN ASSIGNMENT
KENT, THE FRONT PAGE IS GETTING SO DULL I'VE EVEN GOT TO HEADLINE CARD-GAMES.——THERE'S A WAR GOING ON IN A SMALL SOUTH AMERICAN REPUBLIC, SAN MONTE; AND TO STIR UP NEWS I'M SENDING YOU DOWN THERE AS CORRESPONDENT. TAKE ALONG A CAMERA AND TRY TO SEND BACK SOME GOOD SHOTS WITH YOUR ARTICLES.
KENT TAKES A TRAIN, NOT TOWARD SAN MONTE, BUT TO WASHINGTON D.C.

IN THE CAPITAL CITY, HE ATTENDS A SESSION OF CONGRESS, SITTING IN THE GALLERY

IS THAT SENATOR BARROWS SPEAKING?

YES.

UPON LEAVING THE SENATE *CHAMBERS*, CLARK SNAPS A PICTURE OF A FURTIVE MAN SPEAKING SWIFTLY TO SENATOR BARROWS

WHEN CAN I SEE YOU?

I TOLD YOU NEVER TO SPEAK TO ME IN PUBLIC!...UH.. MY HOME..TONIGHT AT 8:30.

AT THE "MORGUE" OF A LOCAL 'NEWSPAPER....

WHO'S THE CHAP SPEAKING TO SENATOR BARROWS.?

WHY, THAT'S ALEX GREER, THE SLICKEST LOBBYIST IN WASHINGTON. NO ONE KNOWS WHAT INTERESTS BACK HIM.

EIGHT-THIRTY P.M.! OUTSIDE SENATOR BARROWS' RESIDENCE...
AN EAVESDROPPER LISTENS IN ON AN INTERESTING CONVERSATION!

I'VE TOLD YOU TO AVOID ME IN PUBLIC. WHAT WOULD PEOPLE THINK IF THEY KNEW I HAD ANYTHING TO DO WITH YOU?

QUIT SPUTTERING! I HAD TO SEE YOU. TELL ME: DO YOU THINK YOU'LL SUCCEED IN PUSHING THE BILL THRU?

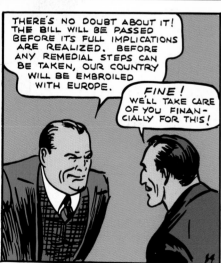

THERE'S NO DOUBT ABOUT IT! THE BILL WILL BE PASSED BEFORE ITS FULL IMPLICATIONS ARE REALIZED. BEFORE ANY REMEDIAL STEPS CAN BE TAKEN, OUR COUNTRY WILL BE EMBROILED WITH EUROPE.

FINE! WE'LL TAKE CARE OF YOU FINAN-CIALLY FOR THIS!

I SUPPOSE YOU'RE GOING TO BE WELL TAKEN CARE OF YOURSELF?

YOU BET HE WILL!

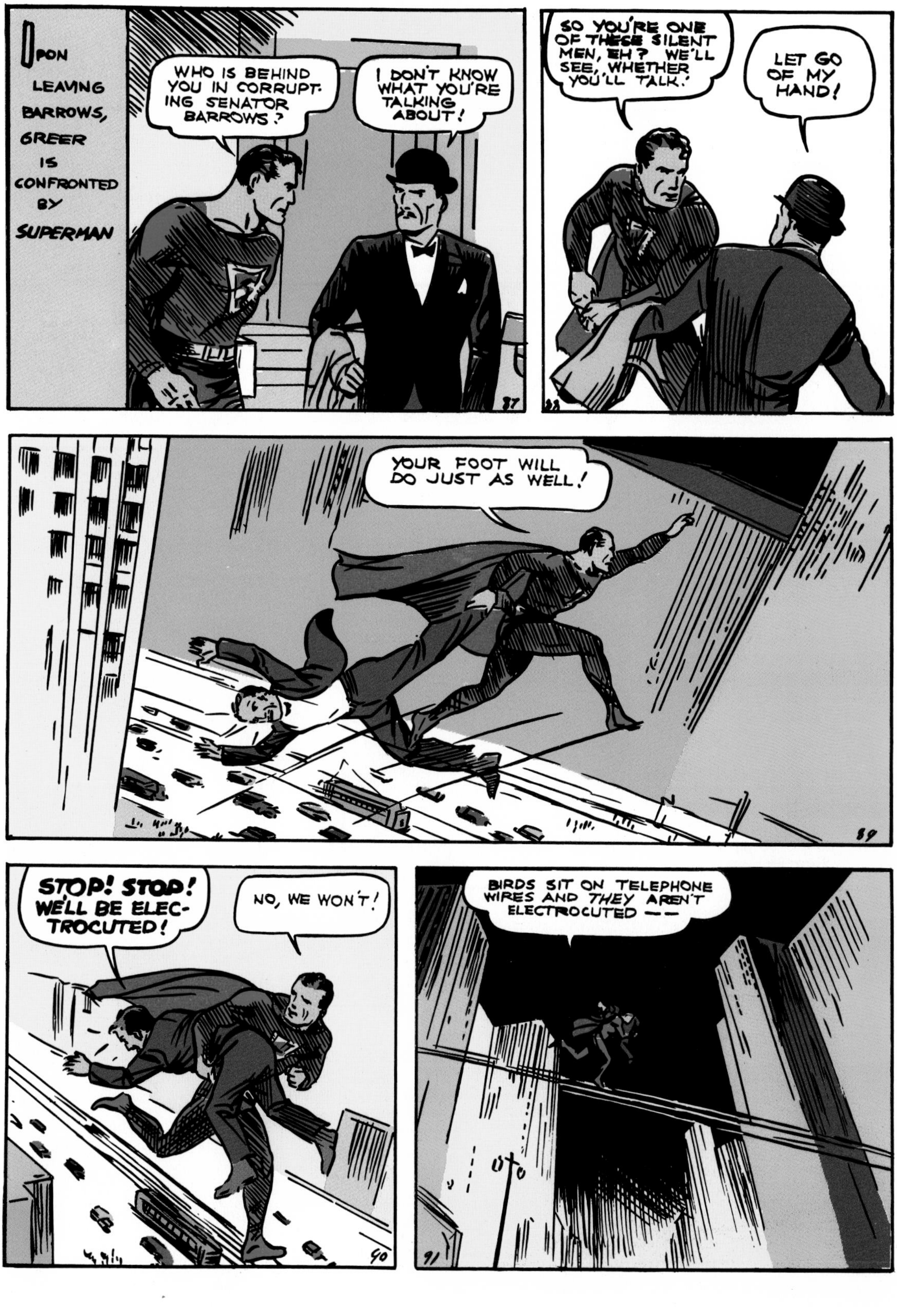
UPON LEAVING BARROWS, GREER IS CONFRONTED BY SUPERMAN
WHO IS BEHIND YOU IN CORRUPTING SENATOR BARROWS?
I DON'T KNOW WHAT YOU'RE TALKING ABOUT!
SO YOU'RE ONE OF THESE SILENT MEN, EH? WE'LL SEE, WHETHER YOU'LL TALK!
LET GO OF MY HAND!
YOUR FOOT WILL DO JUST AS WELL!
STOP! STOP! WE'LL BE ELECTROCUTED!
NO, WE WON'T!
BIRDS SIT ON TELEPHONE WIRES AND *THEY* AREN'T ELECTROCUTED --

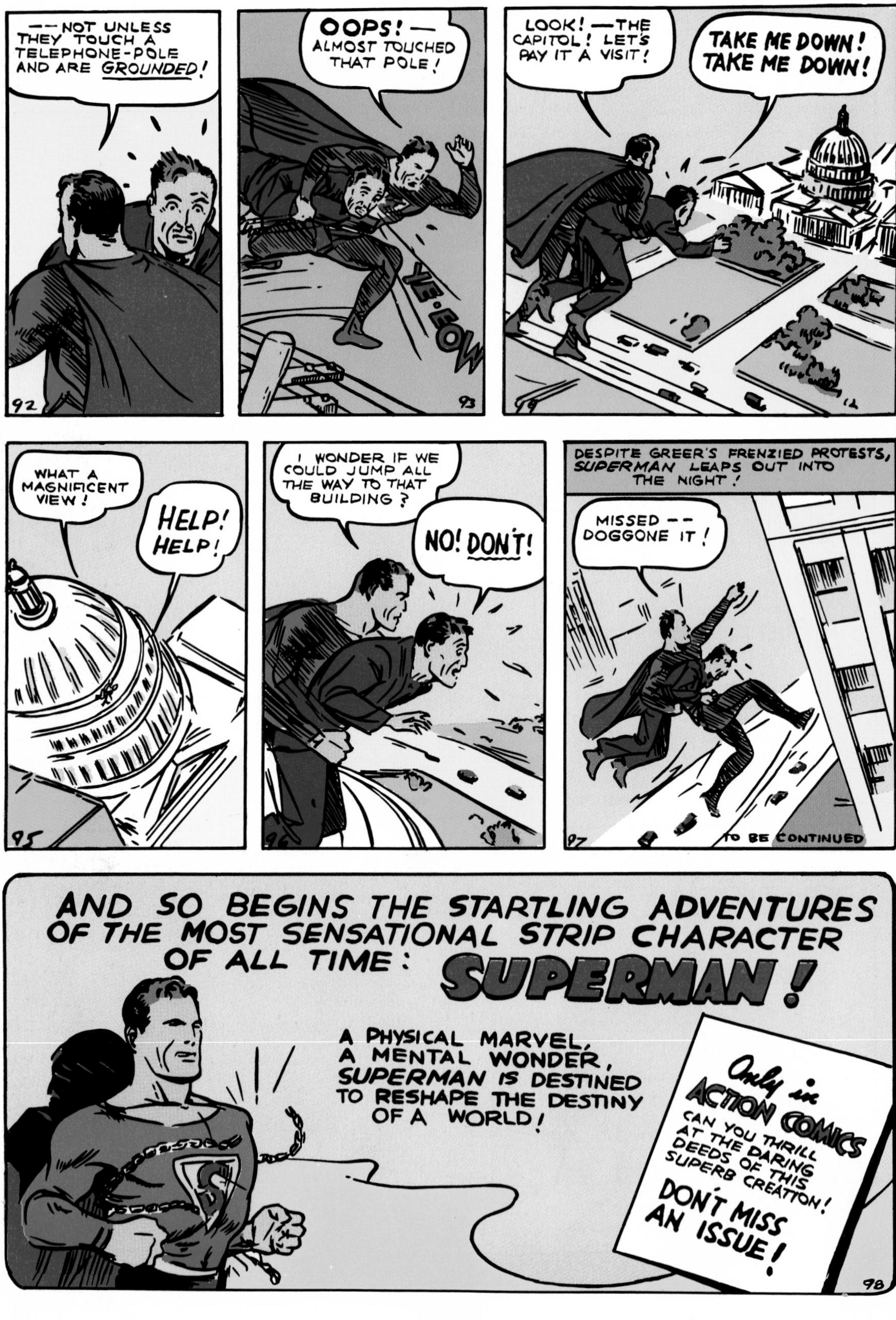
--NOT UNLESS THEY TOUCH A TELEPHONE-POLE AND ARE GROUNDED!
OOPS!— ALMOST TOUCHED THAT POLE!
YE-EOW
LOOK!—THE CAPITOL! LET'S PAY IT A VISIT!
TAKE ME DOWN! TAKE ME DOWN!
WHAT A MAGNIFICENT VIEW!
HELP! HELP!
I WONDER IF WE COULD JUMP ALL THE WAY TO THAT BUILDING?
NO! DON'T!
DESPITE GREER'S FRENZIED PROTESTS, SUPERMAN LEAPS OUT INTO THE NIGHT!
MISSED -- DOGGONE IT!
TO BE CONTINUED
AND SO BEGINS THE STARTLING ADVENTURES OF THE MOST SENSATIONAL STRIP CHARACTER OF ALL TIME: SUPERMAN!
A PHYSICAL MARVEL, A MENTAL WONDER, SUPERMAN IS DESTINED TO RESHAPE THE DESTINY OF A WORLD!
Only in ACTION COMICS CAN YOU THRILL AT THE DARING DEEDS OF THIS SUPERB CREATION!
DON'T MISS AN ISSUE!

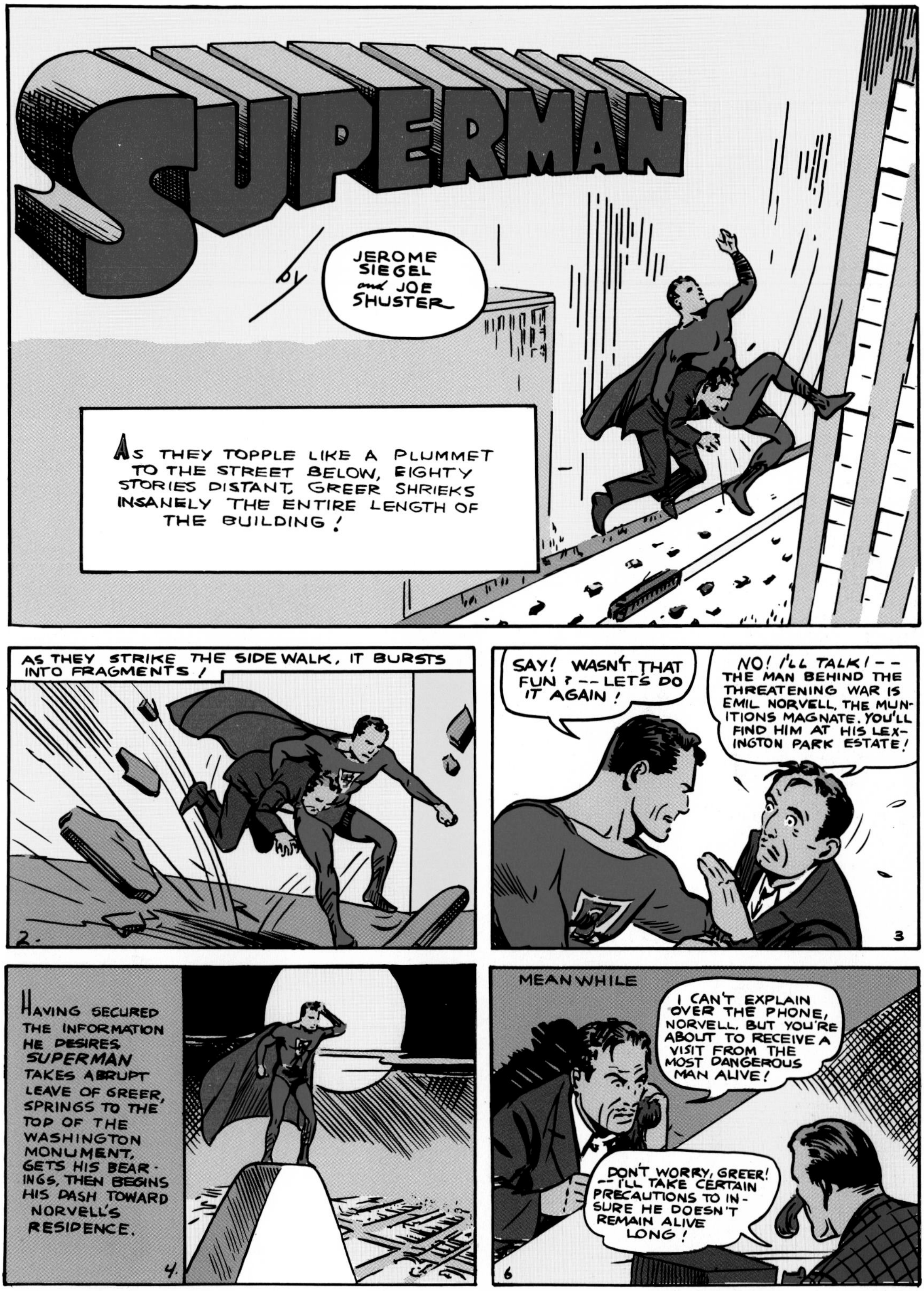
SUPERMAN
by
JEROME SIEGEL and JOE SHUSTER
AS THEY TOPPLE LIKE A PLUMMET TO THE STREET BELOW, EIGHTY STORIES DISTANT, GREER SHRIEKS INSANELY THE ENTIRE LENGTH OF THE BUILDING!
AS THEY STRIKE THE SIDEWALK, IT BURSTS INTO FRAGMENTS!
2.
SAY! WASN'T THAT FUN? -- LET'S DO IT AGAIN!
NO! I'LL TALK! -- THE MAN BEHIND THE THREATENING WAR IS EMIL NORVELL, THE MUNITIONS MAGNATE. YOU'LL FIND HIM AT HIS LEXINGTON PARK ESTATE!
3
HAVING SECURED THE INFORMATION HE DESIRES SUPERMAN TAKES ABRUPT LEAVE OF GREER, SPRINGS TO THE TOP OF THE WASHINGTON MONUMENT, GETS HIS BEARINGS, THEN BEGINS HIS DASH TOWARD NORVELL'S RESIDENCE.
4.
MEANWHILE
I CAN'T EXPLAIN OVER THE PHONE, NORVELL, BUT YOU'RE ABOUT TO RECEIVE A VISIT FROM THE MOST DANGEROUS MAN ALIVE!
DON'T WORRY, GREER! -- I'LL TAKE CERTAIN PRECAUTIONS TO INSURE HE DOESN'T REMAIN ALIVE LONG!
6

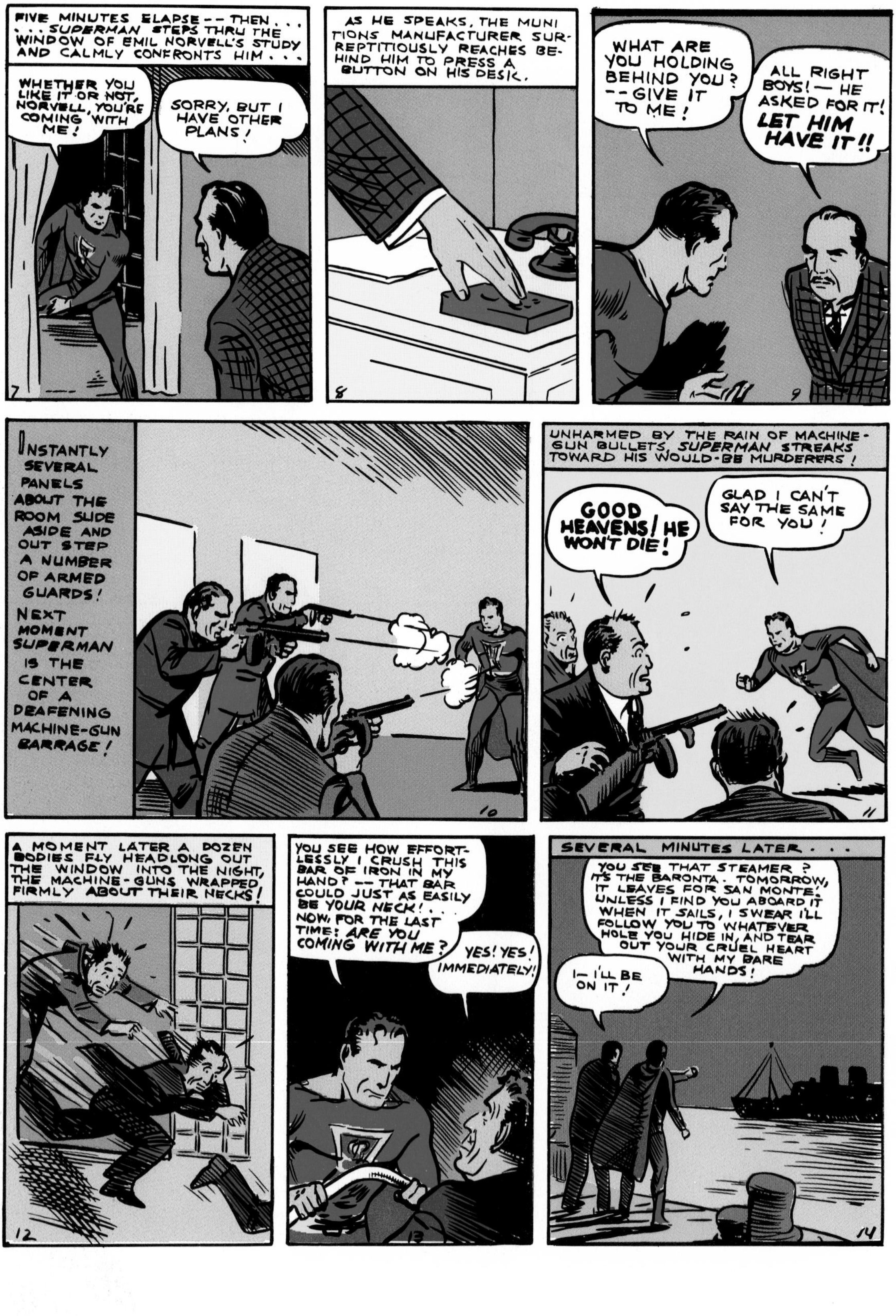
FIVE MINUTES ELAPSE -- THEN . . . . . . SUPERMAN STEPS THRU THE WINDOW OF EMIL NORVELL'S STUDY AND CALMLY CONFRONTS HIM . . .
WHETHER YOU LIKE IT OR NOT, NORVELL, YOU'RE COMING WITH ME!
SORRY, BUT I HAVE OTHER PLANS!
7
AS HE SPEAKS, THE MUNITIONS MANUFACTURER SURREPTITIOUSLY REACHES BEHIND HIM TO PRESS A BUTTON ON HIS DESK.
8
WHAT ARE YOU HOLDING BEHIND YOU? -- GIVE IT TO ME!
ALL RIGHT BOYS! — HE ASKED FOR IT! LET HIM HAVE IT!!
9
INSTANTLY SEVERAL PANELS ABOUT THE ROOM SLIDE ASIDE AND OUT STEP A NUMBER OF ARMED GUARDS! NEXT MOMENT SUPERMAN IS THE CENTER OF A DEAFENING MACHINE-GUN BARRAGE!
10
UNHARMED BY THE RAIN OF MACHINE-GUN BULLETS, SUPERMAN STREAKS TOWARD HIS WOULD-BE MURDERERS!
GOOD HEAVENS! HE WON'T DIE!
GLAD I CAN'T SAY THE SAME FOR YOU!
11
A MOMENT LATER A DOZEN BODIES FLY HEADLONG OUT THE WINDOW INTO THE NIGHT, THE MACHINE-GUNS WRAPPED FIRMLY ABOUT THEIR NECKS!
12
YOU SEE HOW EFFORTLESSLY I CRUSH THIS BAR OF IRON IN MY HAND? -- THAT BAR COULD JUST AS EASILY BE YOUR NECK! . . NOW, FOR THE LAST TIME: ARE YOU COMING WITH ME?
YES! YES! IMMEDIATELY!
13
SEVERAL MINUTES LATER . . .
YOU SEE THAT STEAMER? IT'S THE BARONTA. TOMORROW, IT LEAVES FOR SAN MONTE. UNLESS I FIND YOU ABOARD IT WHEN IT SAILS, I SWEAR I'LL FOLLOW YOU TO WHATEVER HOLE YOU HIDE IN, AND TEAR OUT YOUR CRUEL HEART WITH MY BARE HANDS!
I— I'LL BE ON IT!
14

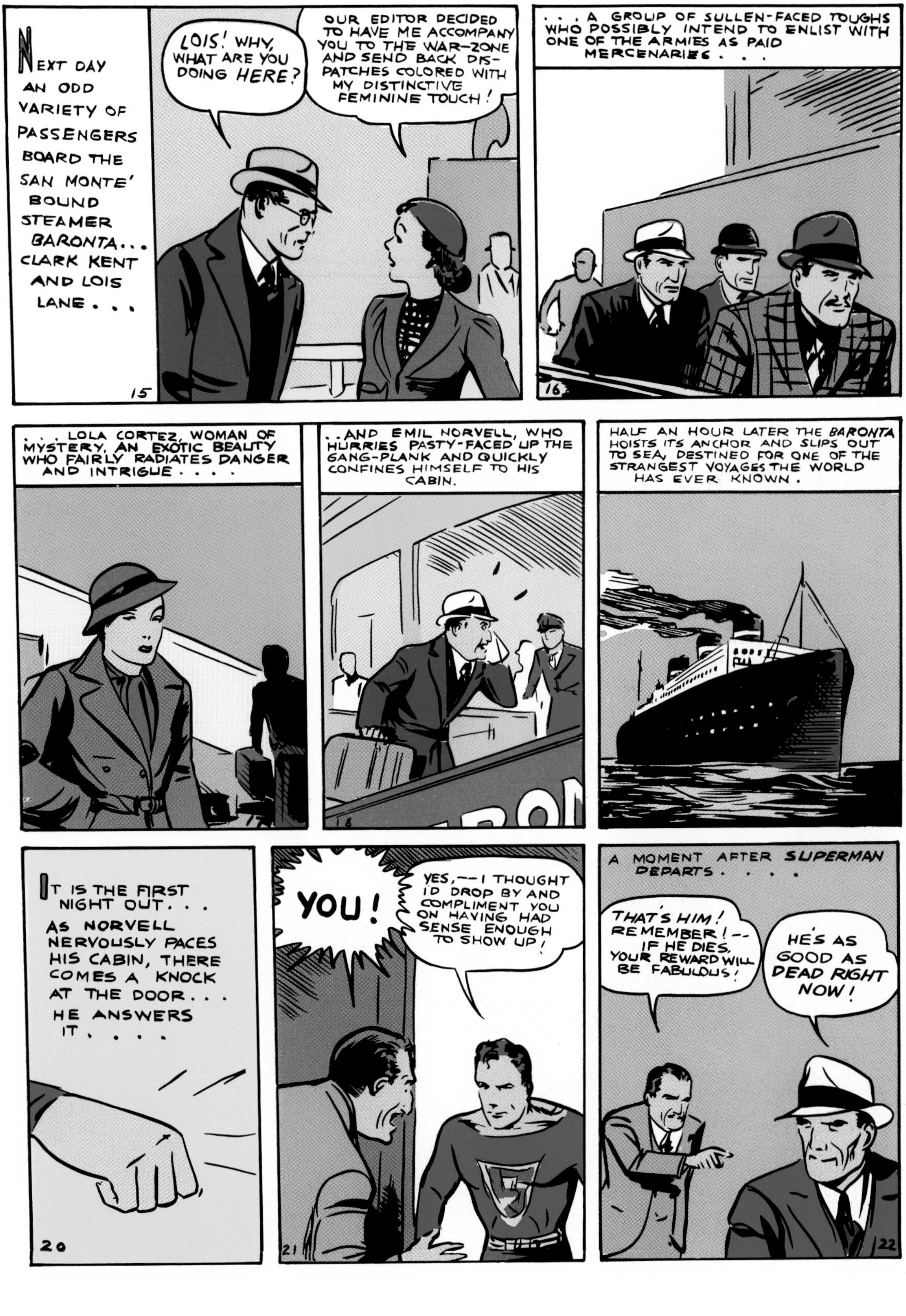
NEXT DAY AN ODD VARIETY OF PASSENGERS BOARD THE SAN MONTE' BOUND STEAMER BARONTA... CLARK KENT AND LOIS LANE . . .
LOIS! WHY, WHAT ARE YOU DOING HERE?
OUR EDITOR DECIDED TO HAVE ME ACCOMPANY YOU TO THE WAR-ZONE AND SEND BACK DIS-PATCHES COLORED WITH MY DISTINCTIVE FEMININE TOUCH!
. . . A GROUP OF SULLEN-FACED TOUGHS WHO POSSIBLY INTEND TO ENLIST WITH ONE OF THE ARMIES AS PAID MERCENARIES . . .
. . . LOLA CORTEZ, WOMAN OF MYSTERY, AN EXOTIC BEAUTY WHO FAIRLY RADIATES DANGER AND INTRIGUE . . .
. . AND EMIL NORVELL, WHO HURRIES PASTY-FACED UP THE GANG-PLANK AND QUICKLY CONFINES HIMSELF TO HIS CABIN.
HALF AN HOUR LATER THE BARONTA HOISTS ITS ANCHOR AND SLIPS OUT TO SEA, DESTINED FOR ONE OF THE STRANGEST VOYAGES THE WORLD HAS EVER KNOWN.
IT IS THE FIRST NIGHT OUT. . . AS NORVELL NERVOUSLY PACES HIS CABIN, THERE COMES A KNOCK AT THE DOOR . . . HE ANSWERS IT . . .
YOU!
YES,--I THOUGHT I'D DROP BY AND COMPLIMENT YOU ON HAVING HAD SENSE ENOUGH TO SHOW UP!
A MOMENT AFTER SUPERMAN DEPARTS . . .
THAT'S HIM! REMEMBER!-- IF HE DIES, YOUR REWARD WILL BE FABULOUS!
HE'S AS GOOD AS DEAD RIGHT NOW!

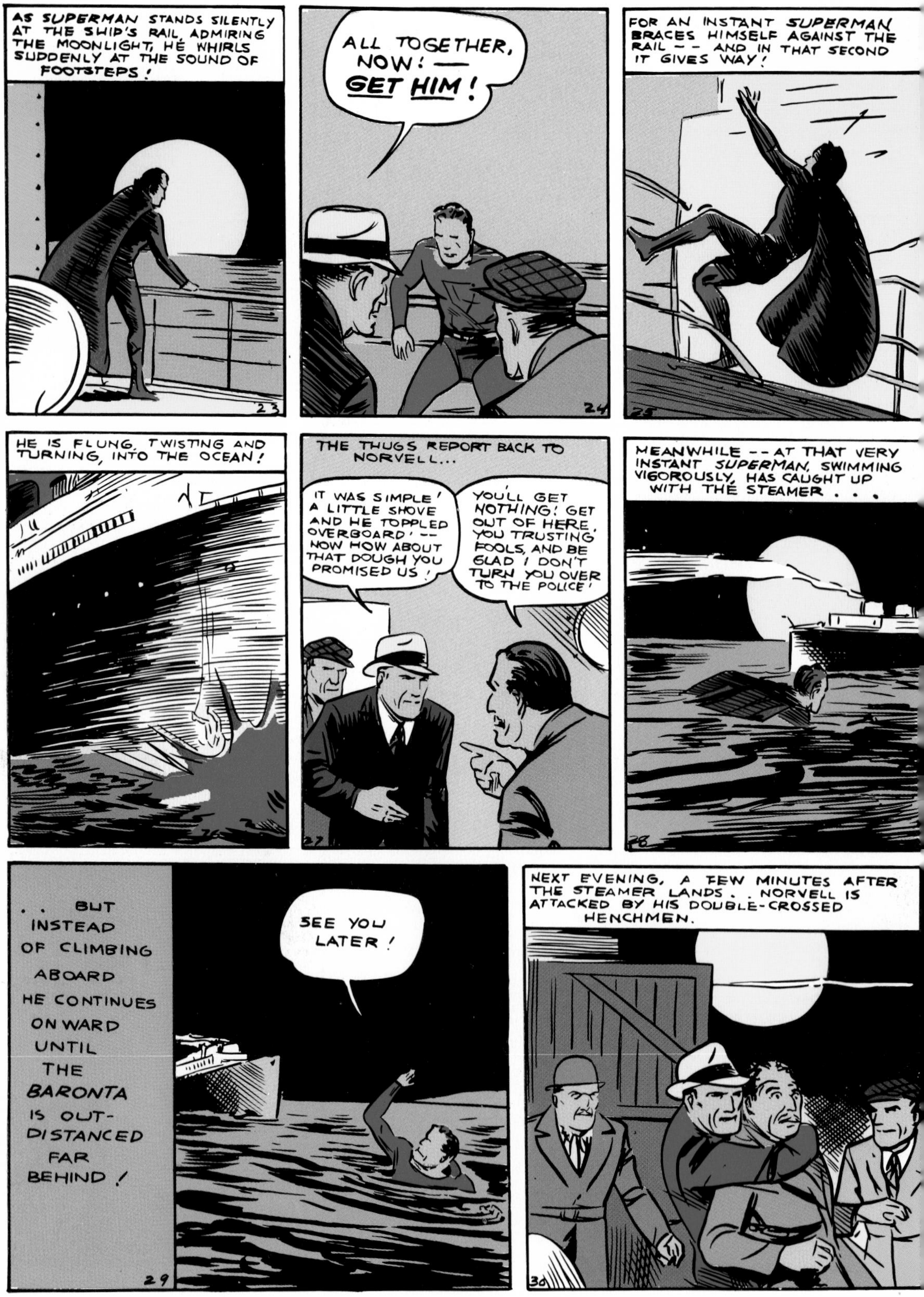
AS SUPERMAN STANDS SILENTLY AT THE SHIP'S RAIL, ADMIRING THE MOONLIGHT, HE WHIRLS SUDDENLY AT THE SOUND OF FOOTSTEPS!
ALL TOGETHER, NOW! — GET HIM!
FOR AN INSTANT SUPERMAN BRACES HIMSELF AGAINST THE RAIL -- AND IN THAT SECOND IT GIVES WAY!
HE IS FLUNG, TWISTING AND TURNING, INTO THE OCEAN!
THE THUGS REPORT BACK TO NORVELL...
IT WAS SIMPLE! A LITTLE SHOVE AND HE TOPPLED OVERBOARD! -- NOW HOW ABOUT THAT DOUGH YOU PROMISED US!
YOU'LL GET NOTHING! GET OUT OF HERE, YOU TRUSTING FOOLS, AND BE GLAD I DON'T TURN YOU OVER TO THE POLICE!
MEANWHILE -- AT THAT VERY INSTANT SUPERMAN, SWIMMING VIGOROUSLY, HAS CAUGHT UP WITH THE STEAMER . . .
. . BUT INSTEAD OF CLIMBING ABOARD HE CONTINUES ONWARD UNTIL THE BARONTA IS OUT-DISTANCED FAR BEHIND!
SEE YOU LATER!
NEXT EVENING, A FEW MINUTES AFTER THE STEAMER LANDS . . NORVELL IS ATTACKED BY HIS DOUBLE-CROSSED HENCHMEN.

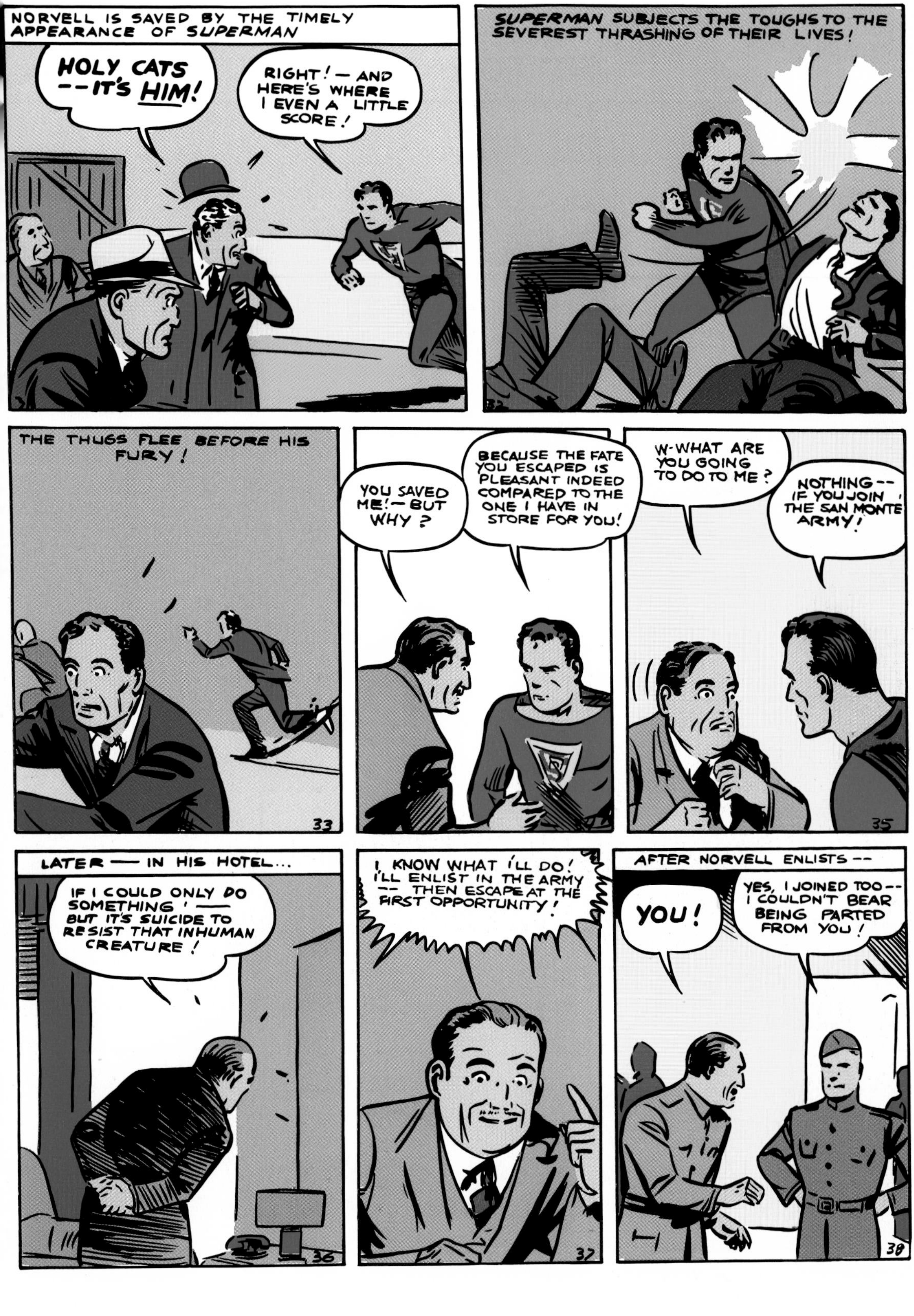
NORVELL IS SAVED BY THE TIMELY APPEARANCE OF SUPERMAN
HOLY CATS --IT'S HIM!
RIGHT! — AND HERE'S WHERE I EVEN A LITTLE SCORE!
SUPERMAN SUBJECTS THE TOUGHS TO THE SEVEREST THRASHING OF THEIR LIVES!
32
THE THUGS FLEE BEFORE HIS FURY!
33
YOU SAVED ME!— BUT WHY?
BECAUSE THE FATE YOU ESCAPED IS PLEASANT INDEED COMPARED TO THE ONE I HAVE IN STORE FOR YOU!
W-WHAT ARE YOU GOING TO DO TO ME?
NOTHING -- IF YOU JOIN THE SAN MONTE ARMY!
35
LATER — IN HIS HOTEL...
IF I COULD ONLY DO SOMETHING! — BUT IT'S SUICIDE TO RESIST THAT INHUMAN CREATURE!
36
I KNOW WHAT I'LL DO! I'LL ENLIST IN THE ARMY -- THEN ESCAPE AT THE FIRST OPPORTUNITY!
37
AFTER NORVELL ENLISTS --
YOU!
YES, I JOINED TOO -- I COULDN'T BEAR BEING PARTED FROM YOU!
38

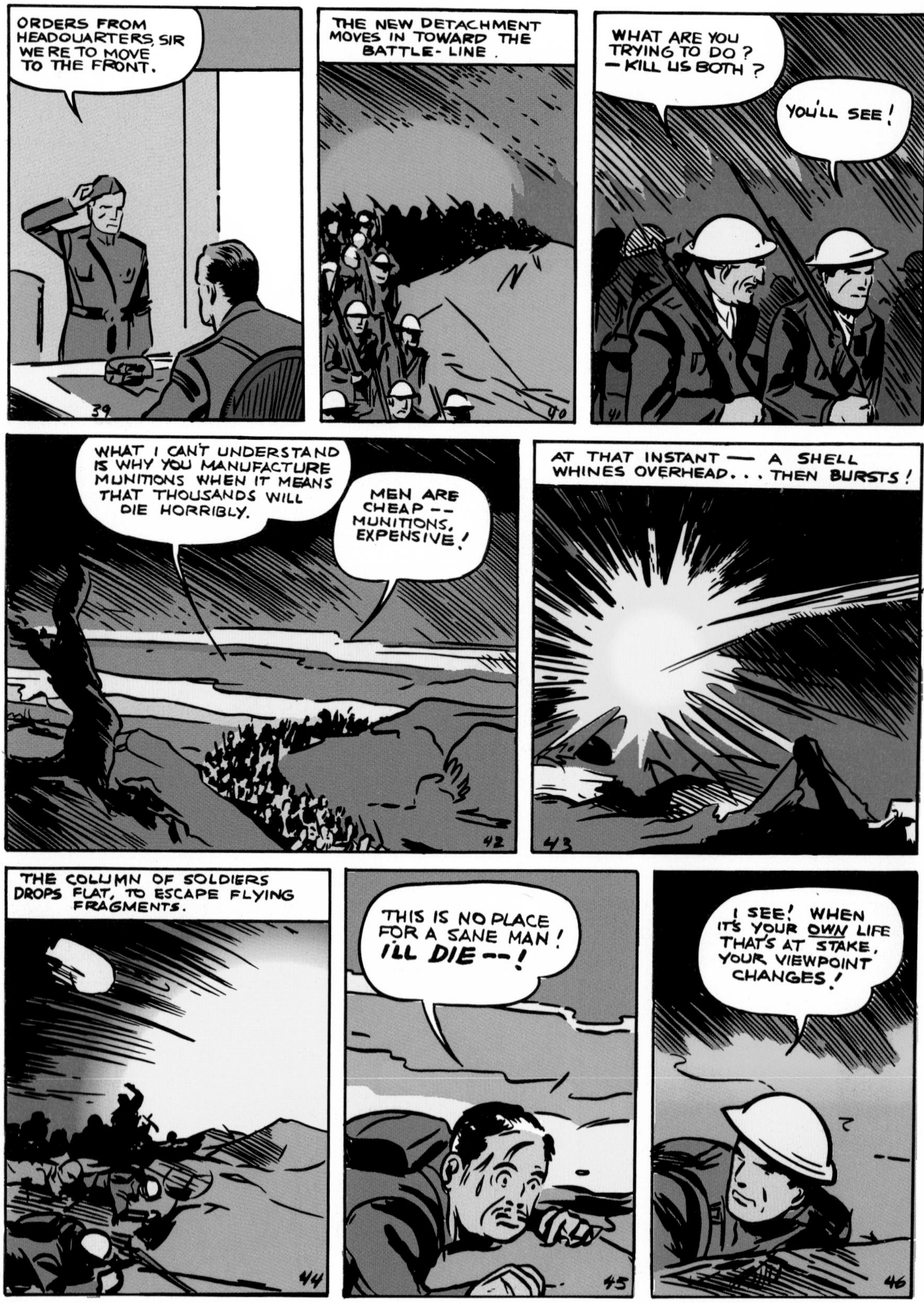
ORDERS FROM HEADQUARTERS, SIR WE'RE TO MOVE TO THE FRONT.
THE NEW DETACHMENT MOVES IN TOWARD THE BATTLE-LINE.
WHAT ARE YOU TRYING TO DO? —KILL US BOTH?
YOU'LL SEE!
WHAT I CAN'T UNDERSTAND IS WHY YOU MANUFACTURE MUNITIONS WHEN IT MEANS THAT THOUSANDS WILL DIE HORRIBLY.
MEN ARE CHEAP -- MUNITIONS, EXPENSIVE!
AT THAT INSTANT — A SHELL WHINES OVERHEAD. . . THEN BURSTS!
THE COLUMN OF SOLDIERS DROPS FLAT, TO ESCAPE FLYING FRAGMENTS.
THIS IS NO PLACE FOR A SANE MAN! I'LL DIE --!
I SEE! WHEN IT'S YOUR OWN LIFE THAT'S AT STAKE, YOUR VIEWPOINT CHANGES!

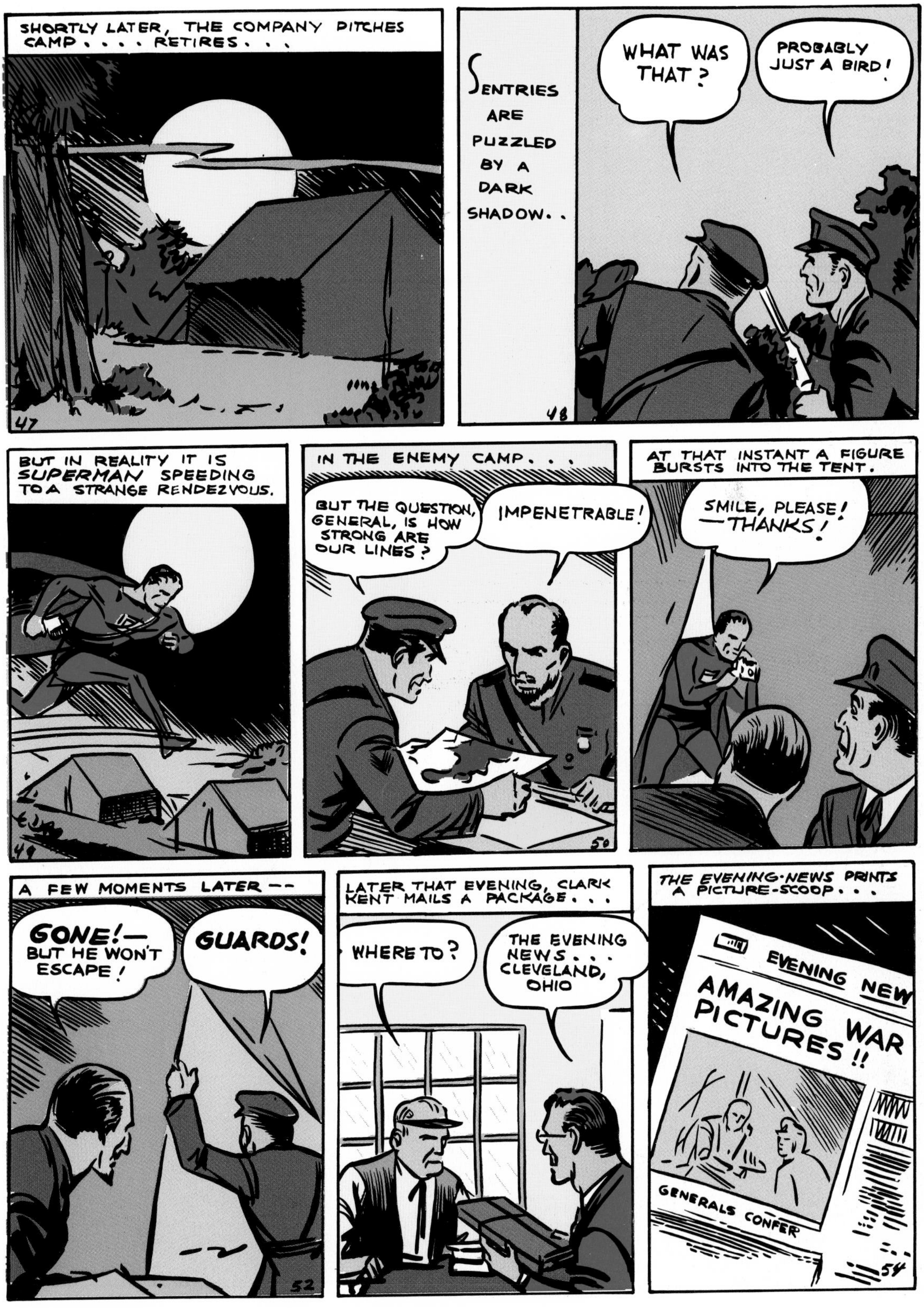
SHORTLY LATER, THE COMPANY PITCHES CAMP . . . . RETIRES . . .
SENTRIES ARE PUZZLED BY A DARK SHADOW. .
WHAT WAS THAT?
PROBABLY JUST A BIRD!
BUT IN REALITY IT IS SUPERMAN SPEEDING TO A STRANGE RENDEZVOUS.
IN THE ENEMY CAMP . . .
BUT THE QUESTION, GENERAL, IS HOW STRONG ARE OUR LINES?
IMPENETRABLE!
AT THAT INSTANT A FIGURE BURSTS INTO THE TENT.
SMILE, PLEASE! —THANKS!
A FEW MOMENTS LATER --
GONE!— BUT HE WON'T ESCAPE!
GUARDS!
LATER THAT EVENING, CLARK KENT MAILS A PACKAGE . . .
WHERE TO?
THE EVENING NEWS . . . CLEVELAND, OHIO
THE EVENING-NEWS PRINTS A PICTURE-SCOOP . .
EVENING NEW
AMAZING WAR PICTURES!!
GENERALS CONFER

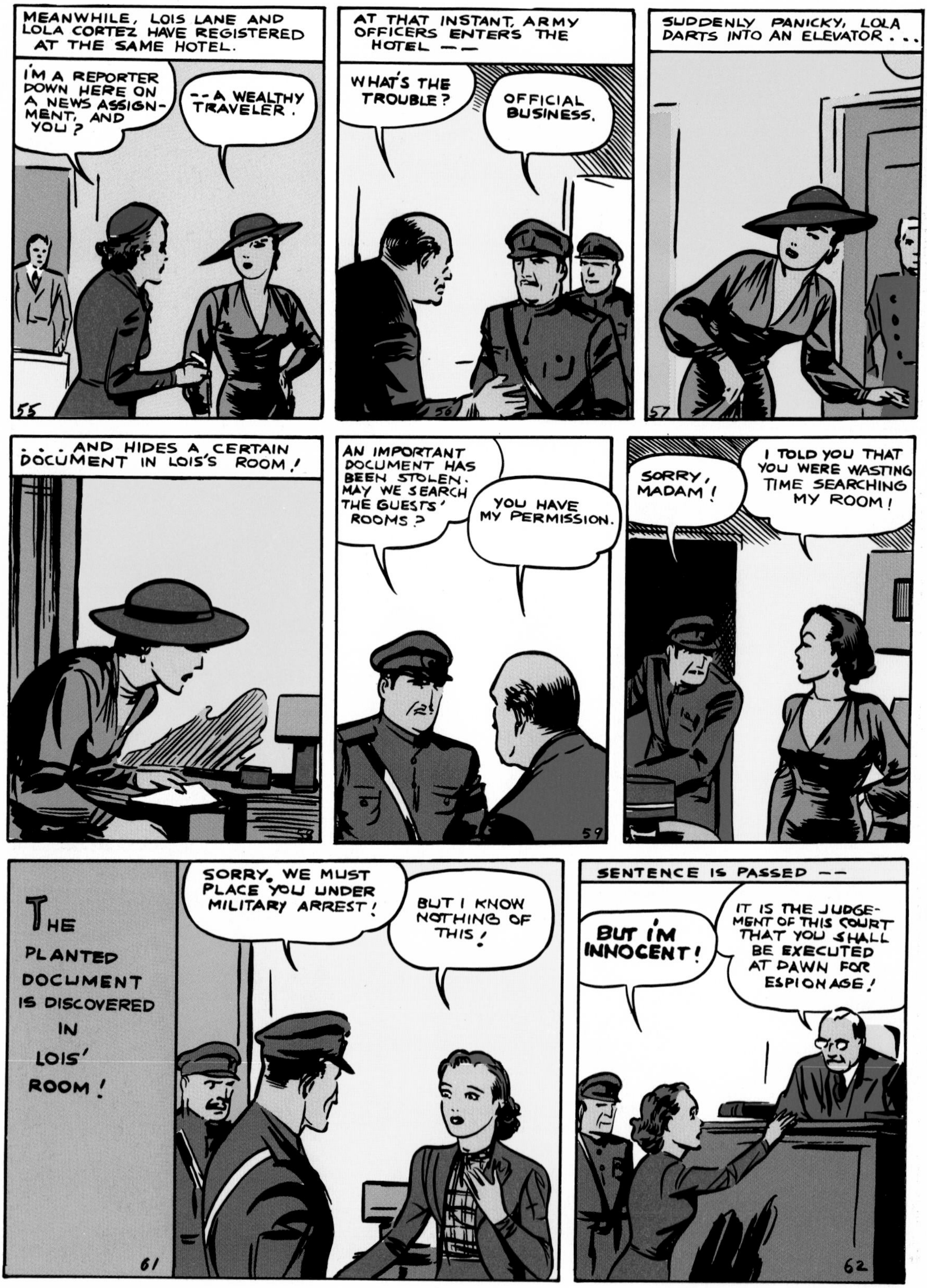
MEANWHILE, LOIS LANE AND LOLA CORTEZ HAVE REGISTERED AT THE SAME HOTEL.
I'M A REPORTER DOWN HERE ON A NEWS ASSIGNMENT, AND YOU?
--A WEALTHY TRAVELER.
55
AT THAT INSTANT, ARMY OFFICERS ENTERS THE HOTEL --
WHAT'S THE TROUBLE?
OFFICIAL BUSINESS.
56
SUDDENLY PANICKY, LOLA DARTS INTO AN ELEVATOR . . .
57
. . . AND HIDES A CERTAIN DOCUMENT IN LOIS'S ROOM!
58
AN IMPORTANT DOCUMENT HAS BEEN STOLEN. MAY WE SEARCH THE GUESTS' ROOMS?
YOU HAVE MY PERMISSION.
59
SORRY, MADAM!
I TOLD YOU THAT YOU WERE WASTING TIME SEARCHING MY ROOM!
THE PLANTED DOCUMENT IS DISCOVERED IN LOIS' ROOM!
SORRY, WE MUST PLACE YOU UNDER MILITARY ARREST!
BUT I KNOW NOTHING OF THIS!
61
SENTENCE IS PASSED --
BUT I'M INNOCENT!
IT IS THE JUDGEMENT OF THIS COURT THAT YOU SHALL BE EXECUTED AT DAWN FOR ESPIONAGE!
62

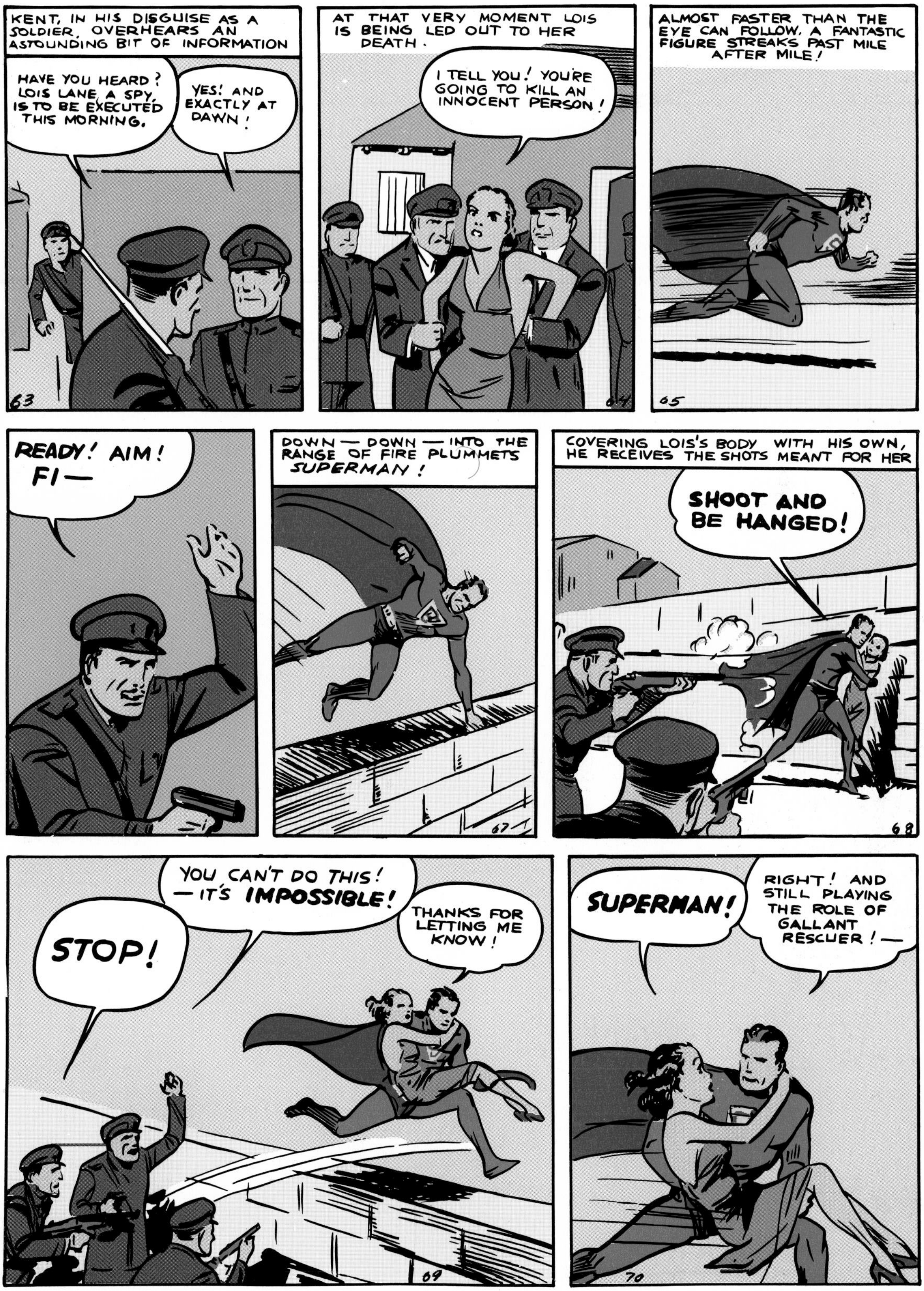
KENT, IN HIS DISGUISE AS A SOLDIER, OVERHEARS AN ASTOUNDING BIT OF INFORMATION
HAVE YOU HEARD? LOIS LANE, A SPY, IS TO BE EXECUTED THIS MORNING.
YES! AND EXACTLY AT DAWN!
AT THAT VERY MOMENT LOIS IS BEING LED OUT TO HER DEATH.
I TELL YOU! YOU'RE GOING TO KILL AN INNOCENT PERSON!
ALMOST FASTER THAN THE EYE CAN FOLLOW, A FANTASTIC FIGURE STREAKS PAST MILE AFTER MILE!
READY! AIM! FI—
DOWN — DOWN — INTO THE RANGE OF FIRE PLUMMETS SUPERMAN!
COVERING LOIS'S BODY WITH HIS OWN, HE RECEIVES THE SHOTS MEANT FOR HER
SHOOT AND BE HANGED!
STOP!
YOU CAN'T DO THIS! — IT'S IMPOSSIBLE!
THANKS FOR LETTING ME KNOW!
SUPERMAN!
RIGHT! AND STILL PLAYING THE ROLE OF GALLANT RESCUER! —

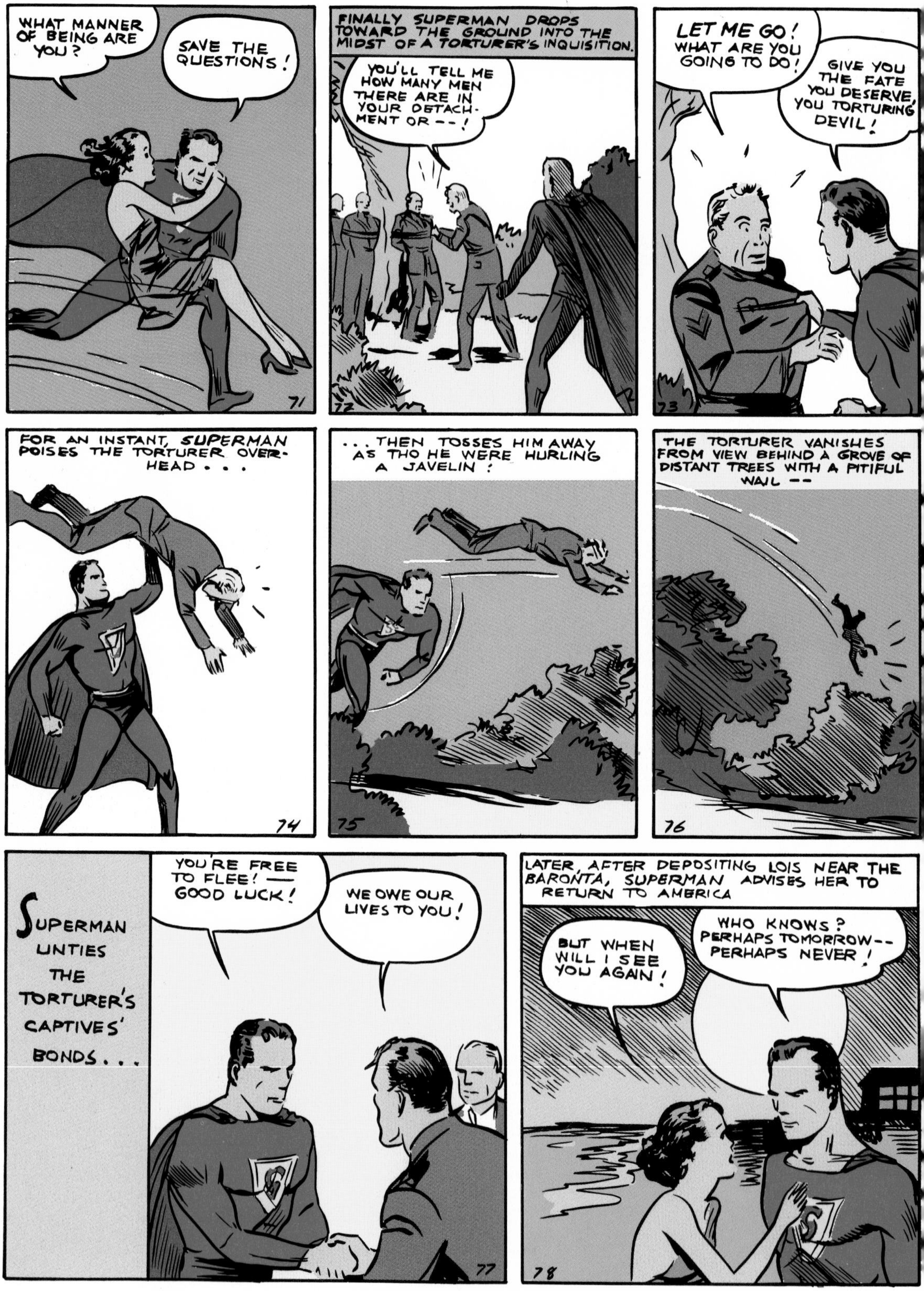
WHAT MANNER OF BEING ARE YOU?
SAVE THE QUESTIONS!
FINALLY SUPERMAN DROPS TOWARD THE GROUND INTO THE MIDST OF A TORTURER'S INQUISITION.
YOU'LL TELL ME HOW MANY MEN THERE ARE IN YOUR DETACH-MENT OR --!
LET ME GO! WHAT ARE YOU GOING TO DO!
GIVE YOU THE FATE YOU DESERVE, YOU TORTURING DEVIL!
FOR AN INSTANT, SUPERMAN POISES THE TORTURER OVER-HEAD . . .
. . . THEN TOSSES HIM AWAY AS THO HE WERE HURLING A JAVELIN!
THE TORTURER VANISHES FROM VIEW BEHIND A GROVE OF DISTANT TREES WITH A PITIFUL WAIL --
SUPERMAN UNTIES THE TORTURER'S CAPTIVES' BONDS . . .
YOU'RE FREE TO FLEE! — GOOD LUCK!
WE OWE OUR LIVES TO YOU!
LATER, AFTER DEPOSITING LOIS NEAR THE BARONTA, SUPERMAN ADVISES HER TO RETURN TO AMERICA
BUT WHEN WILL I SEE YOU AGAIN!
WHO KNOWS? PERHAPS TOMORROW-- PERHAPS NEVER!

AND NOW TO ATTEND TO NORVELL!

79

BUT WHEN *SUPERMAN* RETURNS TO HIS DETACHMENT, HE FINDS ANTI-AIRCRAFT GUNS BOOMING.

80

THE CAMP IS BEING MERCI-LESSLY RIDDLED BY A BLOOD-THIRSTY AVIATOR!

DIE! -- LIKE CRAWLING ANTS!

81

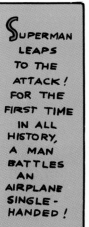

*S*UPERMAN LEAPS TO THE ATTACK! FOR THE FIRST TIME IN ALL HISTORY, A MAN BATTLES AN AIRPLANE SINGLE-HANDED!

82

THE PLANE ZOOMS TOWARD *SUPER-MAN'S* FIGURE, GUNS BLAZING!

83

-- INTO A HEAD-ON CRASH!

84

ITS PROPELLER SHATTERED UPON *SUPERMAN'S* SKIN, THE AIRPLANE FALLS TO ITS DOOM!

85

NORVELL HAD WITNESSED THE CRASH.

GOOD! --THAT FINISHES MY NEMESIS!

86

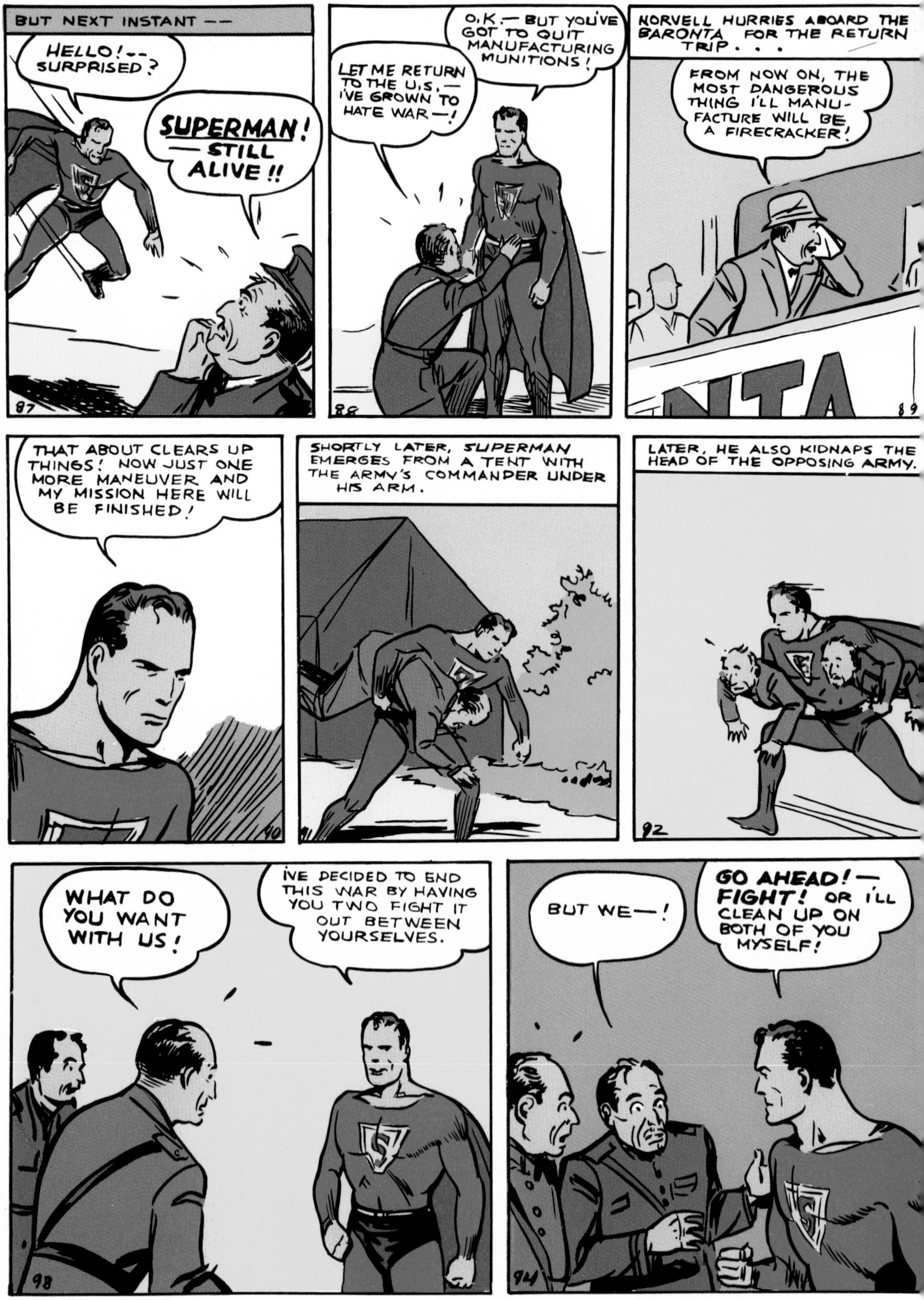
BUT NEXT INSTANT --
HELLO!-- SURPRISED?
SUPERMAN! — STILL ALIVE!!
87
LET ME RETURN TO THE U.S.— I'VE GROWN TO HATE WAR—!
O.K.— BUT YOU'VE GOT TO QUIT MANUFACTURING MUNITIONS!
88
NORVELL HURRIES ABOARD THE BARONTA FOR THE RETURN TRIP . . .
FROM NOW ON, THE MOST DANGEROUS THING I'LL MANUFACTURE WILL BE A FIRECRACKER!
NTA
89
THAT ABOUT CLEARS UP THINGS! NOW JUST ONE MORE MANEUVER AND MY MISSION HERE WILL BE FINISHED!
90
SHORTLY LATER, SUPERMAN EMERGES FROM A TENT WITH THE ARMY'S COMMANDER UNDER HIS ARM.
91
LATER, HE ALSO KIDNAPS THE HEAD OF THE OPPOSING ARMY.
92
WHAT DO YOU WANT WITH US!
I'VE DECIDED TO END THIS WAR BY HAVING YOU TWO FIGHT IT OUT BETWEEN YOURSELVES.
93
BUT WE—!
GO AHEAD!— FIGHT! OR I'LL CLEAN UP ON BOTH OF YOU MYSELF!
94

BUT WHY SHOULD WE FIGHT ?
WE'RE NOT ANGRY AT EACH OTHER!
95
THEN WHY ARE YOUR ARMIES BATTLING ?
96
I DON'T KNOW! CAN YOU TELL ME ?
NO. CAN YOU ?
97
GENTLEMEN, IT'S OBVIOUS YOU'VE BEEN FIGHTING ONLY TO PROMOTE THE SALE OF MUNITIONS! — WHY NOT SHAKE HANDS AND MAKE UP ?
98
AND SO, DUE TO THE CONCILIATORY EFFORTS OF *SUPERMAN*, THE WAR IS HALTED.
99
WHEN KENT REPORTS BACK TO HIS EDITOR . .
SINCE YOU'VE BEEN GONE, THERE'S BEEN NO *SUPERMAN* NEWS. MAYBE HE'S RETIRED FOR GOOD!
SOMEHOW, CHIEF, I'VE A HUNCH HE'LL MAKE HIS APPEARANCE AGAIN--SOON!
THE END
100

FOLLOW THE ADVENTURES OF THE ONE AND

THE OPPORTUNITY OF A LIFE TIME!

SUPERMAN & ACTION COMICS INVITE YOU TO BECOME A CHARTER MEMBER OF THE

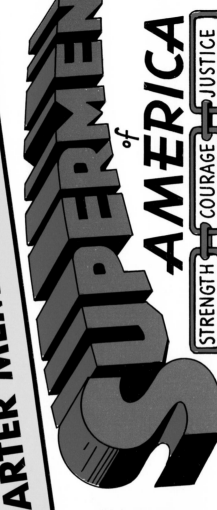

SUPERMEN of AMERICA

STRENGTH COURAGE JUSTICE

CALLING ALL RED-BLOODED YOUNG AMERICANS!

How would you like to become a Charter Member of the only club devoted to strength, courage and justice — SUPERMEN of AMERICA?

CHARTER MEMBERSHIP IS LIMITED! DON'T WAIT!

You *must* hurry if you want to become a Charter Member of SUPERMEN of AMERICA and get your membership card, badge and secret code! All you have to do is sign

Superman's Secret Code that you must know in order to read the *hidden* message from SUPERMAN that will appear in every issue of *Action Comics* from now on! Remember, you won't be able to read SUPERMAN'S message unless you know the code and you can't get the code unless you're a member of SUPERMEN of AMERICA.

The best part about becoming a Charter Member is that it costs *nothing!* No dues and no initiation fee! Just 10c to cover the cost of mailing your membership Certificate, Button and Secret Code.

And that's not the half of it! All members will receive special instructions from SUPERMAN on how to develop strength, courage, and agility, and how to protect yourself in times of danger. Later on we will tell club members how they can earn many valuable prizes!

Wait until you see the beautiful SUPERMAN Button! You'll be proud to wear it and every one in your neighborhood will envy you and ask you where you got it. That's why you should be the *first* to get your button and know the absolutely secret SUPERMAN code!

You must promise *not* to tell *anyone* the code and you must promise to strive for strength, courage and justice — just like SUPERMAN does.

Now, do you think you'd like to be a Charter Member? You do? That's great! Fill out the application blank and mail it *immediately,* before you forget. This is the chance of a lifetime to become a charter member of this newest and finest organization of its kind — SUPERMEN of AMERICA!

LY SUPERMAN IN EVERY ISSUE OF ACTION COMICS AMERICA'S LEADING COMIC MAGAZINE!

HERE'S WHAT YOU GET WHEN YOU BECOME A MEMBER OF THIS GREAT NEW ORGANIZATION

1. A beautifully colored Certificate of Membership, suitable for framing!
2. A large Membership Button in full color, with a patented clasp!
3. Superman's Secret Code which you must have to read Superman's Secret Message in every issue of ACTION COMICS!

BE SURE TO FILL IN AND MAIL THIS APPLICATION BLANK AT ONCE!

S U P E R M A N,
c/o ACTION COMICS
480 LEXINGTON AVE., N. Y. C.

Dear Superman:

Please enroll me as a Charter Member of the SUPERMEN of AMERICA. I enclose 10c to cover cost of mailing. It is understood that I am to receive my Membership Certificate, Button and Superman Code.

NAME..AGE..................

STREET ADDRESS..

CITY AND STATE..

DON'T FORGET TO ENCLOSE TEN CENTS (10c) IN COINS OR STAMPS FOR MAILING COST!

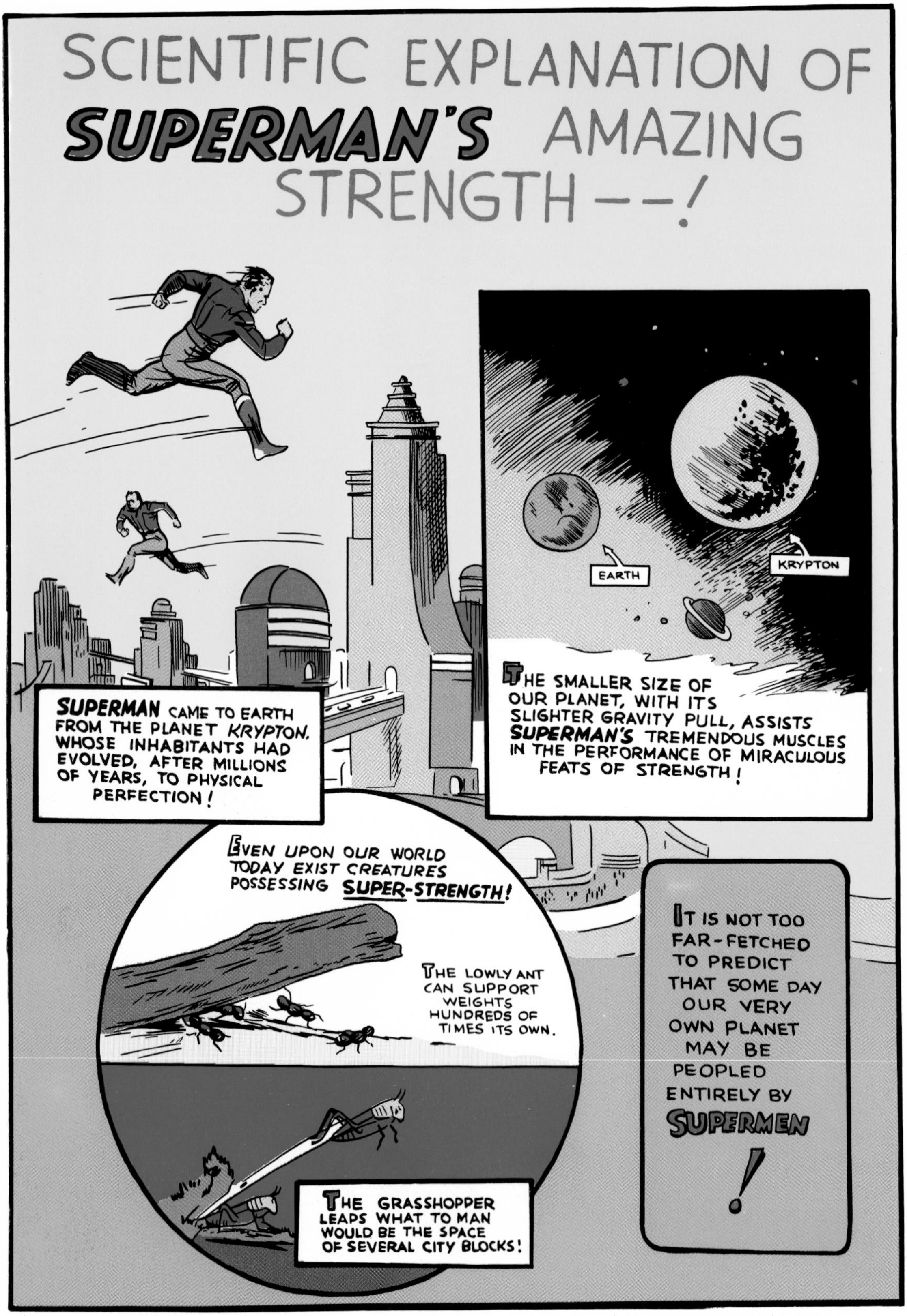
SCIENTIFIC EXPLANATION OF SUPERMAN'S AMAZING STRENGTH--!
SUPERMAN CAME TO EARTH FROM THE PLANET KRYPTON, WHOSE INHABITANTS HAD EVOLVED, AFTER MILLIONS OF YEARS, TO PHYSICAL PERFECTION!
EARTH
KRYPTON
THE SMALLER SIZE OF OUR PLANET, WITH ITS SLIGHTER GRAVITY PULL, ASSISTS SUPERMAN'S TREMENDOUS MUSCLES IN THE PERFORMANCE OF MIRACULOUS FEATS OF STRENGTH!
EVEN UPON OUR WORLD TODAY EXIST CREATURES POSSESSING SUPER-STRENGTH!
THE LOWLY ANT CAN SUPPORT WEIGHTS HUNDREDS OF TIMES ITS OWN.
THE GRASSHOPPER LEAPS WHAT TO MAN WOULD BE THE SPACE OF SEVERAL CITY BLOCKS!
IT IS NOT TOO FAR-FETCHED TO PREDICT THAT SOME DAY OUR VERY OWN PLANET MAY BE PEOPLED ENTIRELY BY SUPERMEN!

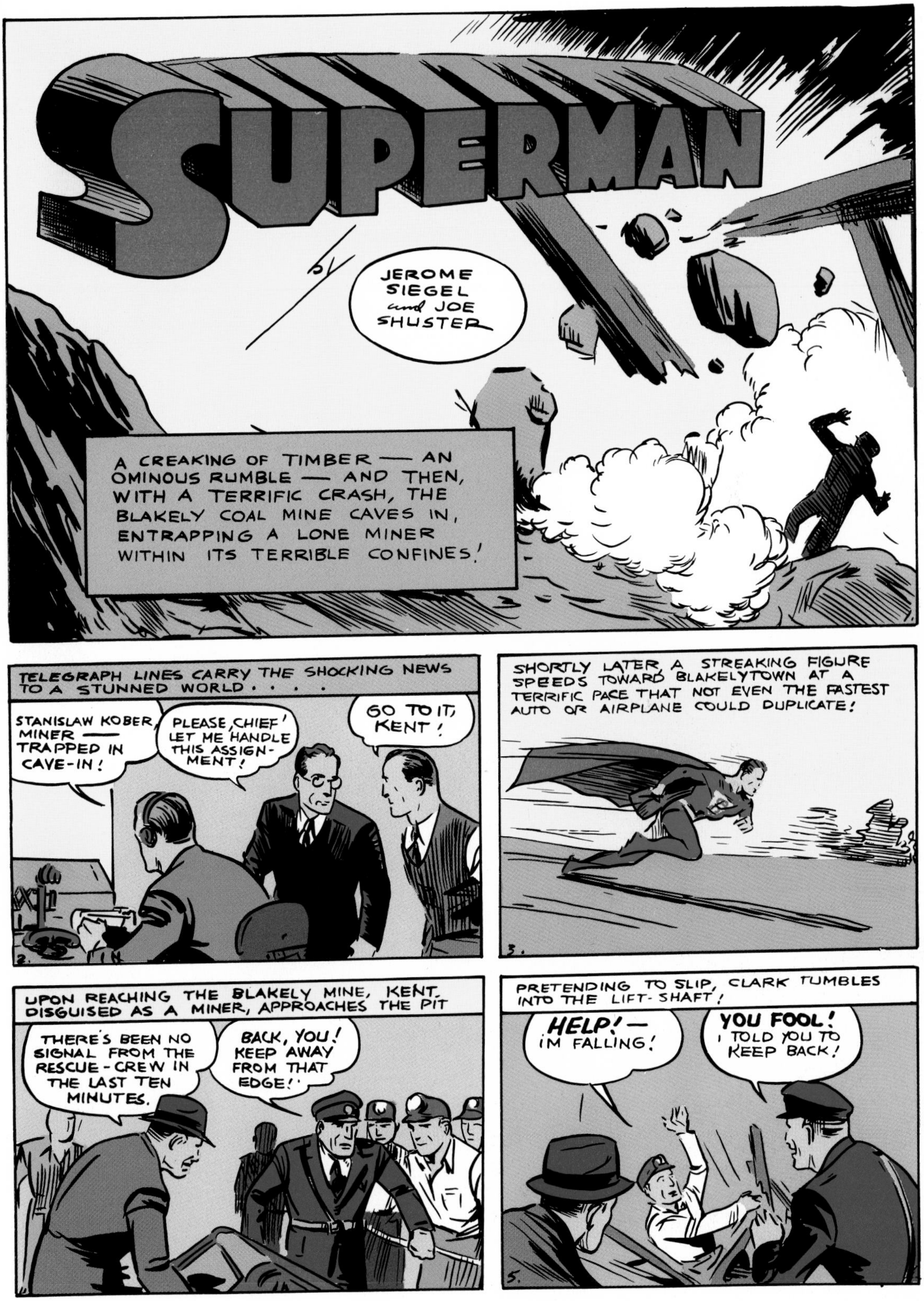
SUPERMAN
by
JEROME SIEGEL and JOE SHUSTER
A CREAKING OF TIMBER — AN OMINOUS RUMBLE — AND THEN, WITH A TERRIFIC CRASH, THE BLAKELY COAL MINE CAVES IN, ENTRAPPING A LONE MINER WITHIN ITS TERRIBLE CONFINES!
TELEGRAPH LINES CARRY THE SHOCKING NEWS TO A STUNNED WORLD . . . .
STANISLAW KOBER, MINER — TRAPPED IN CAVE-IN!
PLEASE, CHIEF! LET ME HANDLE THIS ASSIGNMENT!
GO TO IT, KENT!
SHORTLY LATER, A STREAKING FIGURE SPEEDS TOWARD BLAKELYTOWN AT A TERRIFIC PACE THAT NOT EVEN THE FASTEST AUTO OR AIRPLANE COULD DUPLICATE!
UPON REACHING THE BLAKELY MINE, KENT, DISGUISED AS A MINER, APPROACHES THE PIT
THERE'S BEEN NO SIGNAL FROM THE RESCUE-CREW IN THE LAST TEN MINUTES.
BACK, YOU! KEEP AWAY FROM THAT EDGE!
PRETENDING TO SLIP, CLARK TUMBLES INTO THE LIFT-SHAFT!
HELP! — I'M FALLING!
YOU FOOL! I TOLD YOU TO KEEP BACK!

DOWN PLUNGES *SUPERMAN* IN A FALL WHICH WOULD HAVE MEANT DEATH FOR AN ORDINARY MAN!

AS *SUPERMAN* STRIKES THE BOTTOM OF THE SHAFT, HE DETECTS --

GAS! — POISON GAS!

HIS PHYSICAL STRUCTURE UNAFFECTED BY THE GAS, *SUPERMAN* CONTINUES ALONG THE MINE'S BOTTOM --

-- UNTIL HE STUMBLES UPON A DOZEN UNCONSCIOUS FIGURES.

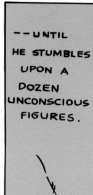

THE RESCUE-PARTY! I'D BETTER GET THEM OUT OF HERE *BEFORE* THE GAS FINISHES ITS DEADLY WORK!

A TRIFLE UNCEREMONIOUS -- BUT THE OCCASION DEMANDS IT!

PLACING THE MEN ON THE LIFT, *SUPERMAN* JERKS THE SIGNAL CORD, AND THE ELEVATOR BEGINS ITS UPWARD JOURNEY.

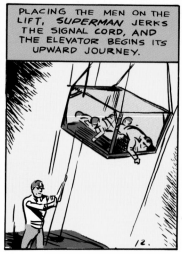

THAT'S THAT! — AND NOW TO *REALLY* GET TO WORK!

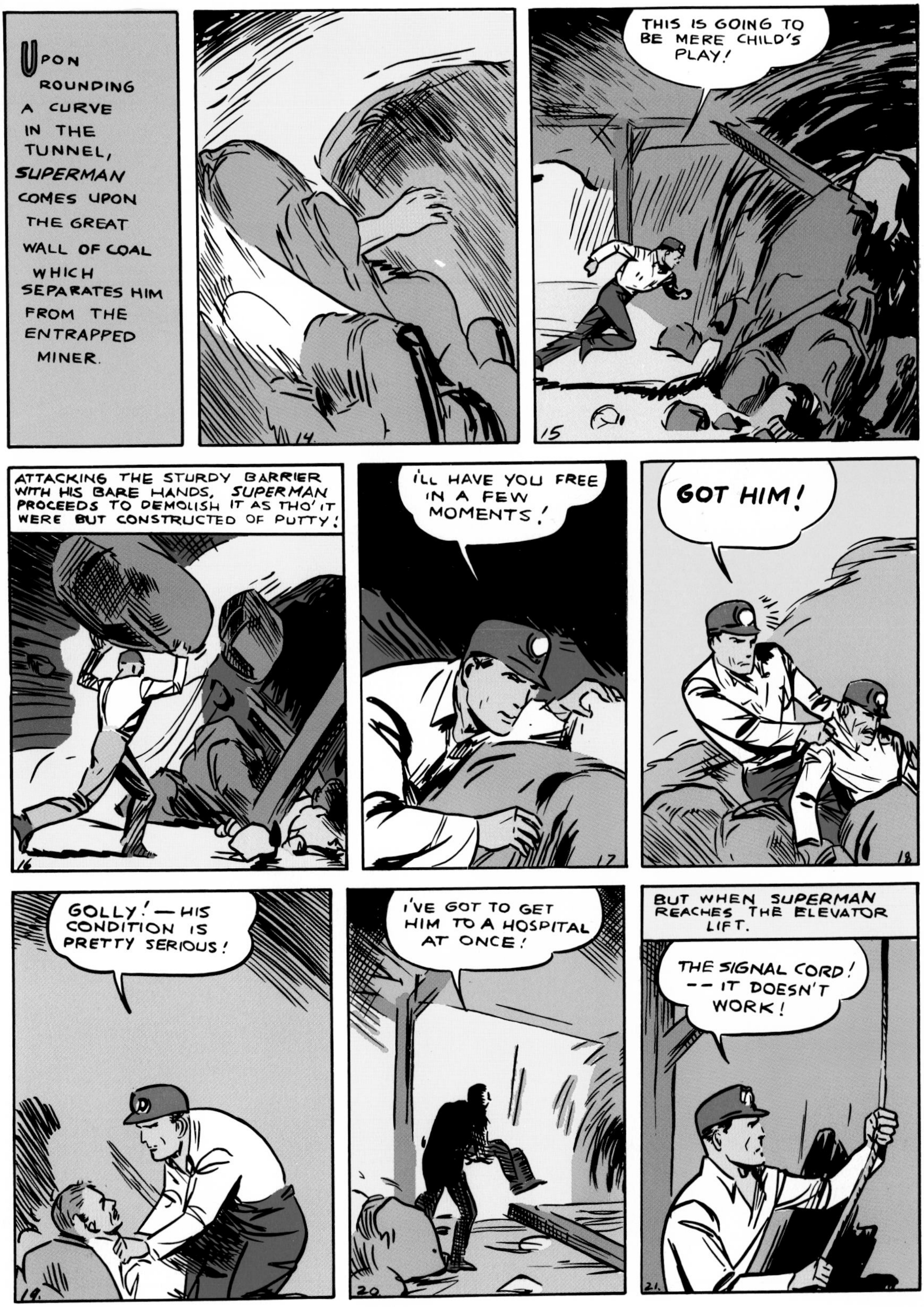
UPON ROUNDING A CURVE IN THE TUNNEL, SUPERMAN COMES UPON THE GREAT WALL OF COAL WHICH SEPARATES HIM FROM THE ENTRAPPED MINER.
THIS IS GOING TO BE MERE CHILD'S PLAY!
ATTACKING THE STURDY BARRIER WITH HIS BARE HANDS, SUPERMAN PROCEEDS TO DEMOLISH IT AS THO' IT WERE BUT CONSTRUCTED OF PUTTY!
I'LL HAVE YOU FREE IN A FEW MOMENTS!
GOT HIM!
GOLLY!—HIS CONDITION IS PRETTY SERIOUS!
I'VE GOT TO GET HIM TO A HOSPITAL AT ONCE!
BUT WHEN SUPERMAN REACHES THE ELEVATOR LIFT.
THE SIGNAL CORD! -- IT DOESN'T WORK!

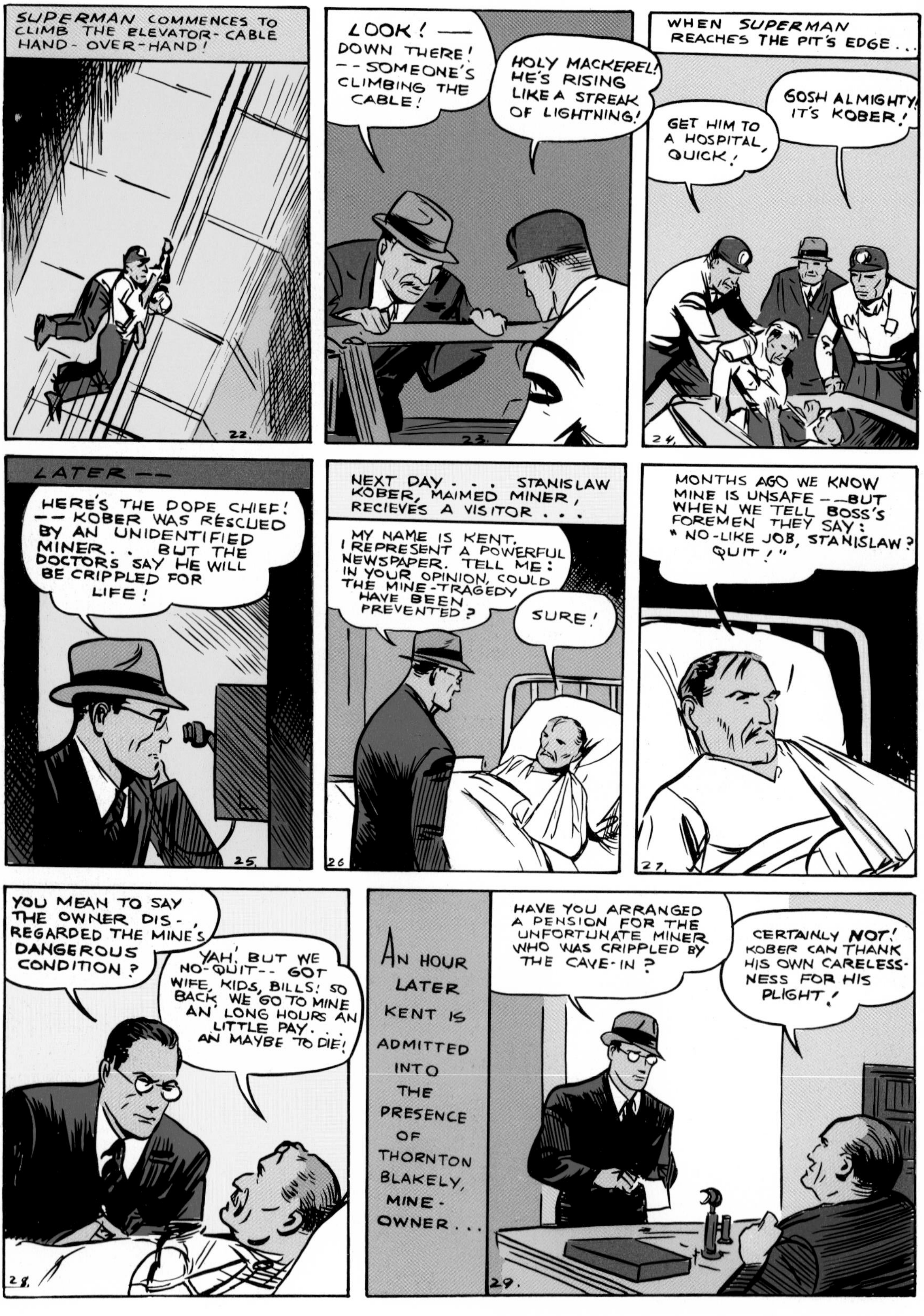
SUPERMAN COMMENCES TO CLIMB THE ELEVATOR-CABLE HAND-OVER-HAND!
22.
LOOK! — DOWN THERE! --SOMEONE'S CLIMBING THE CABLE!
HOLY MACKEREL! HE'S RISING LIKE A STREAK OF LIGHTNING!
23.
WHEN SUPERMAN REACHES THE PIT'S EDGE...
GET HIM TO A HOSPITAL, QUICK!
GOSH ALMIGHTY! IT'S KOBER!
24.
LATER --
HERE'S THE DOPE CHIEF! -- KOBER WAS RESCUED BY AN UNIDENTIFIED MINER. BUT THE DOCTORS SAY HE WILL BE CRIPPLED FOR LIFE!
25.
NEXT DAY... STANISLAW KOBER, MAIMED MINER, RECIEVES A VISITOR...
MY NAME IS KENT. I REPRESENT A POWERFUL NEWSPAPER. TELL ME: IN YOUR OPINION, COULD THE MINE-TRAGEDY HAVE BEEN PREVENTED?
SURE!
26
MONTHS AGO WE KNOW MINE IS UNSAFE --BUT WHEN WE TELL BOSS'S FOREMEN THEY SAY: "NO-LIKE JOB, STANISLAW? QUIT!"
27.
YOU MEAN TO SAY THE OWNER DIS-REGARDED THE MINE'S DANGEROUS CONDITION?
YAH! BUT WE NO-QUIT-- GOT WIFE, KIDS, BILLS! SO BACK WE GO TO MINE AN' LONG HOURS AN LITTLE PAY... AN MAYBE TO DIE!
28.
AN HOUR LATER KENT IS ADMITTED INTO THE PRESENCE OF THORNTON BLAKELY, MINE-OWNER...
HAVE YOU ARRANGED A PENSION FOR THE UNFORTUNATE MINER WHO WAS CRIPPLED BY THE CAVE-IN?
CERTAINLY NOT! KOBER CAN THANK HIS OWN CARELESS-NESS FOR HIS PLIGHT!
29.

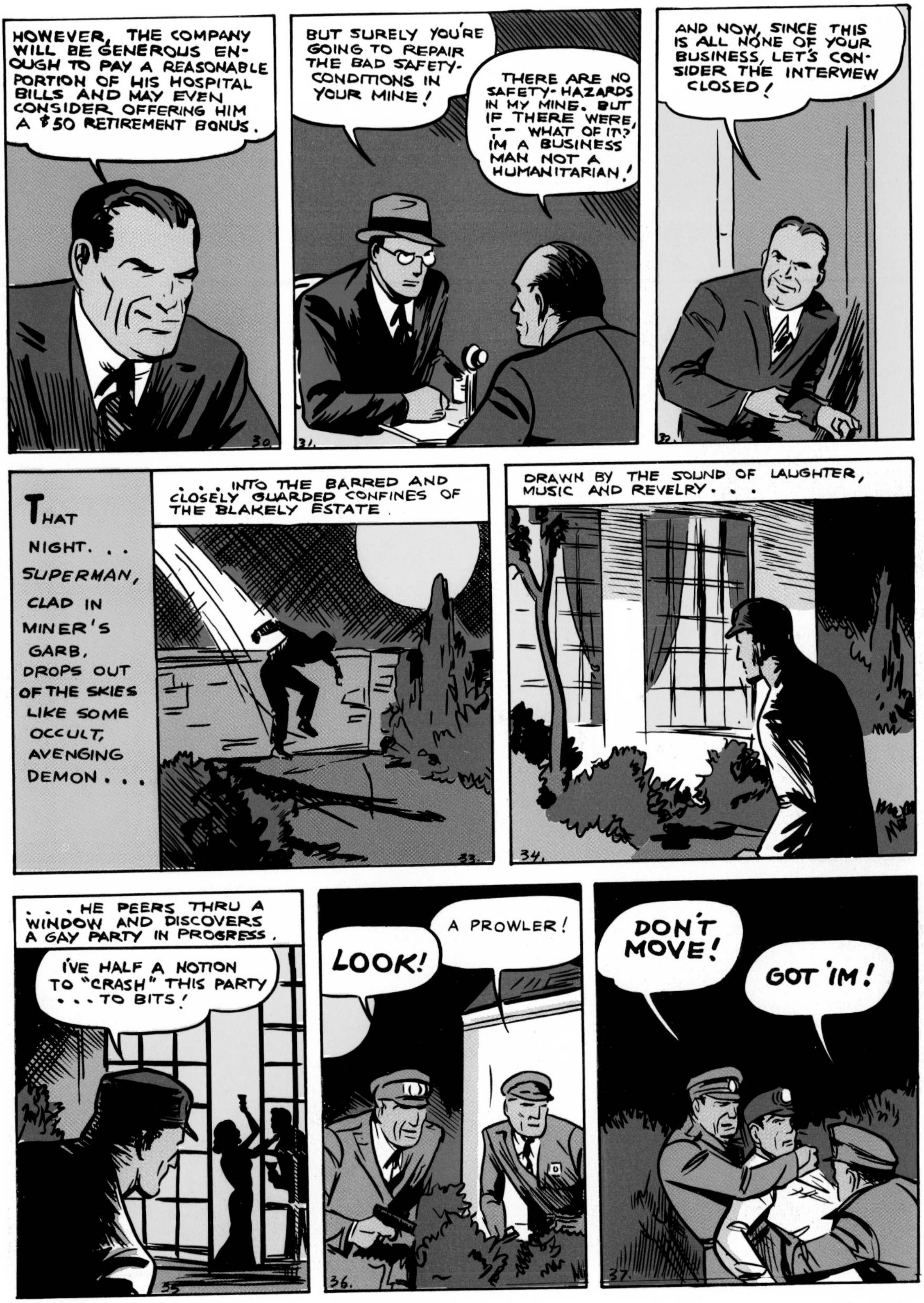
HOWEVER, THE COMPANY WILL BE GENEROUS ENOUGH TO PAY A REASONABLE PORTION OF HIS HOSPITAL BILLS AND MAY EVEN CONSIDER OFFERING HIM A $50 RETIREMENT BONUS.
30.
BUT SURELY YOU'RE GOING TO REPAIR THE BAD SAFETY-CONDITIONS IN YOUR MINE!
THERE ARE NO SAFETY-HAZARDS IN MY MINE. BUT IF THERE WERE, -- WHAT OF IT? I'M A BUSINESS MAN NOT A HUMANITARIAN!
31.
AND NOW, SINCE THIS IS ALL NONE OF YOUR BUSINESS, LET'S CONSIDER THE INTERVIEW CLOSED!
32.
THAT NIGHT... SUPERMAN, CLAD IN MINER'S GARB, DROPS OUT OF THE SKIES LIKE SOME OCCULT, AVENGING DEMON...
...INTO THE BARRED AND CLOSELY GUARDED CONFINES OF THE BLAKELY ESTATE.
33.
DRAWN BY THE SOUND OF LAUGHTER, MUSIC AND REVELRY...
34.
...HE PEERS THRU A WINDOW AND DISCOVERS A GAY PARTY IN PROGRESS.
I'VE HALF A NOTION TO "CRASH" THIS PARTY ...TO BITS!
35
LOOK!
A PROWLER!
36.
DON'T MOVE!
GOT 'IM!
37.

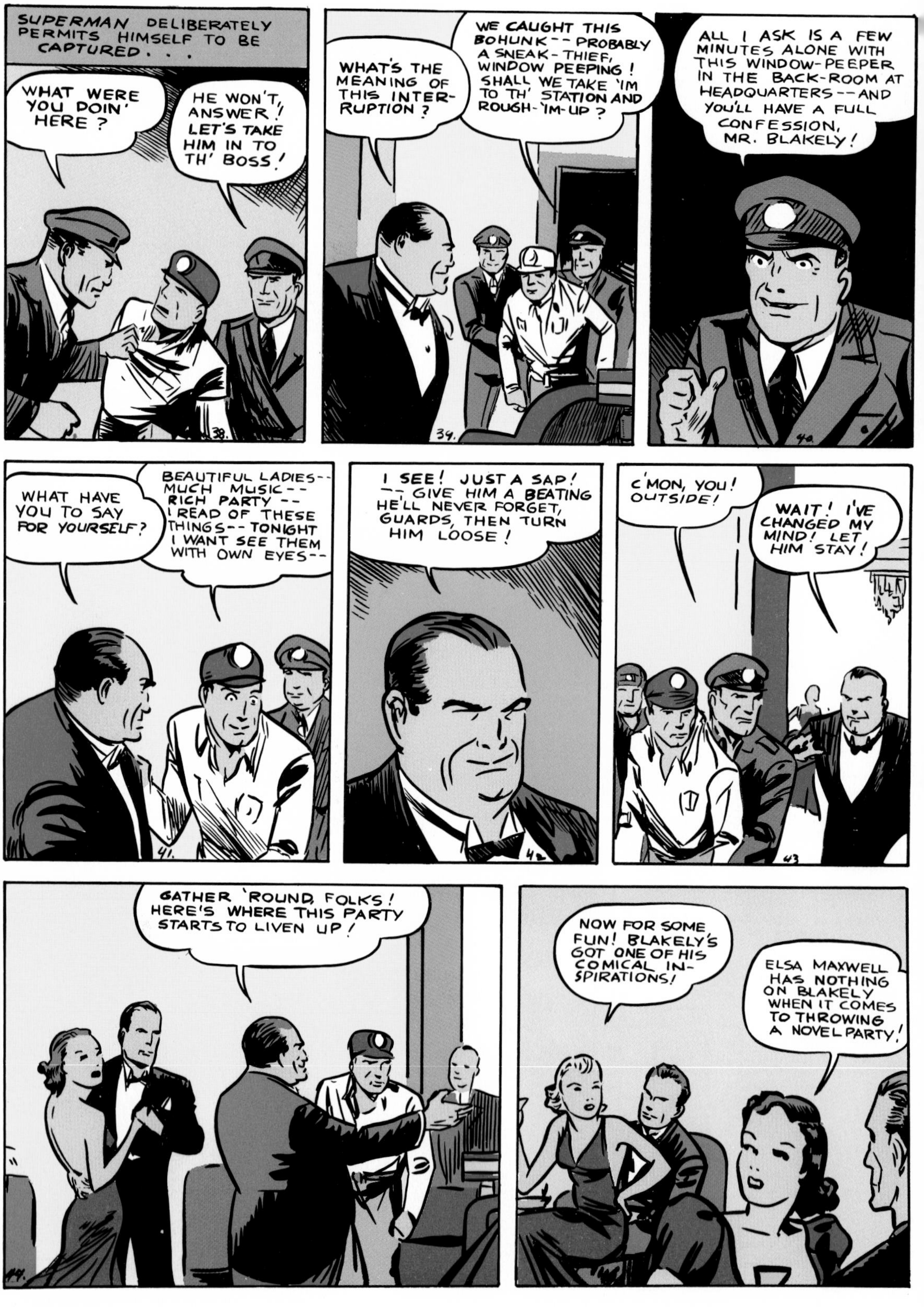
SUPERMAN DELIBERATELY PERMITS HIMSELF TO BE CAPTURED . . .
WHAT WERE YOU DOIN' HERE ?
HE WON'T ANSWER ! LET'S TAKE HIM IN TO TH' BOSS !
WHAT'S THE MEANING OF THIS INTER-RUPTION ?
WE CAUGHT THIS BOHUNK -- PROBABLY A SNEAK-THIEF, WINDOW PEEPING ! SHALL WE TAKE 'IM TO TH' STATION AND ROUGH-'IM-UP ?
ALL I ASK IS A FEW MINUTES ALONE WITH THIS WINDOW-PEEPER IN THE BACK-ROOM AT HEADQUARTERS -- AND YOU'LL HAVE A FULL CONFESSION, MR. BLAKELY !
WHAT HAVE YOU TO SAY FOR YOURSELF ?
BEAUTIFUL LADIES-- MUCH MUSIC-- RICH PARTY -- I READ OF THESE THINGS-- TONIGHT I WANT SEE THEM WITH OWN EYES--
I SEE ! JUST A SAP ! -- GIVE HIM A BEATING HE'LL NEVER FORGET, GUARDS, THEN TURN HIM LOOSE !
C'MON, YOU ! OUTSIDE !
WAIT ! I'VE CHANGED MY MIND ! LET HIM STAY !
GATHER 'ROUND, FOLKS ! HERE'S WHERE THIS PARTY STARTS TO LIVEN UP !
NOW FOR SOME FUN ! BLAKELY'S GOT ONE OF HIS COMICAL IN-SPIRATIONS !
ELSA MAXWELL HAS NOTHING ON BLAKELY WHEN IT COMES TO THROWING A NOVEL PARTY !

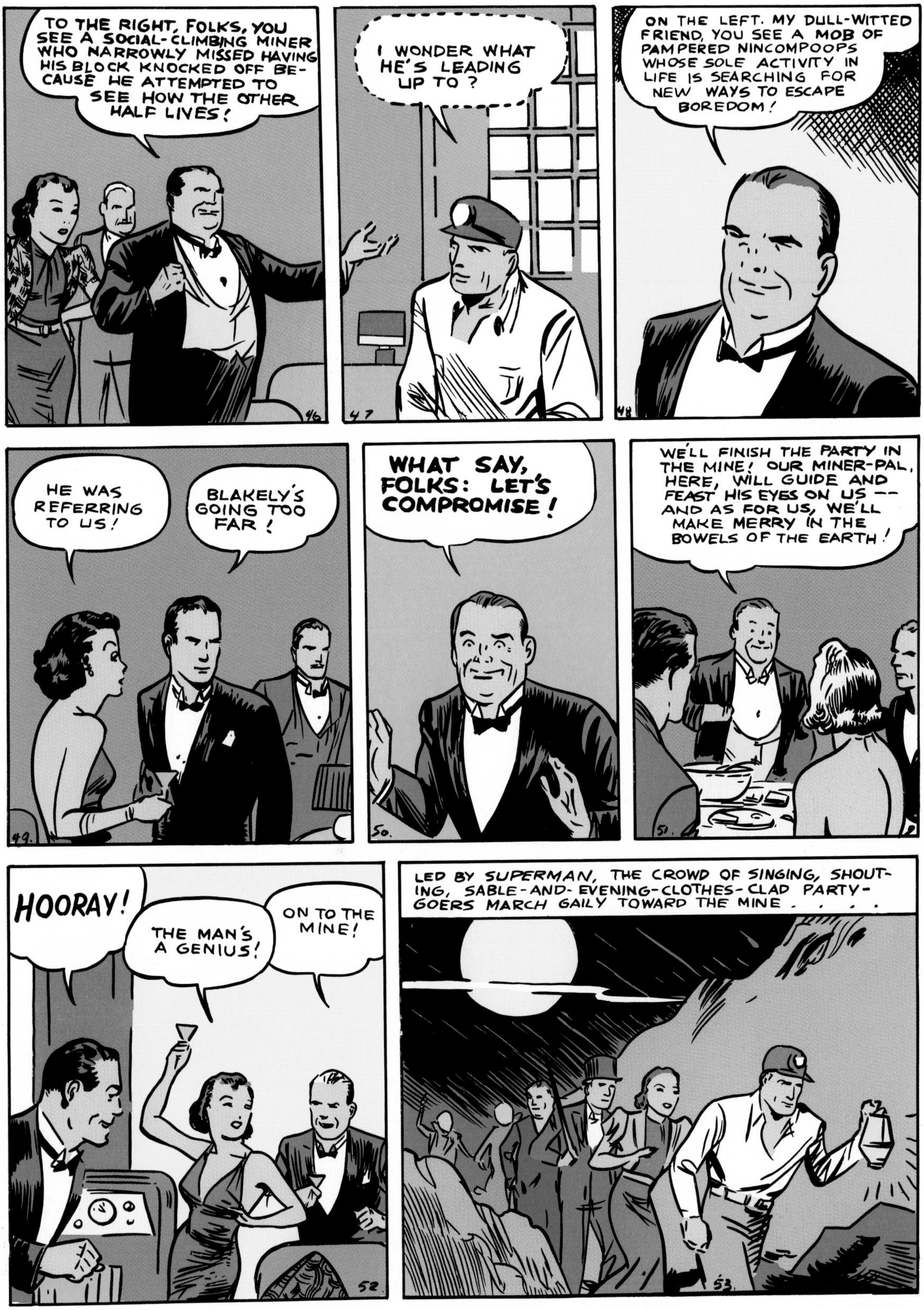
TO THE RIGHT, FOLKS, YOU SEE A SOCIAL-CLIMBING MINER WHO NARROWLY MISSED HAVING HIS BLOCK KNOCKED OFF BE-CAUSE HE ATTEMPTED TO SEE HOW THE OTHER HALF LIVES!
I WONDER WHAT HE'S LEADING UP TO?
ON THE LEFT. MY DULL-WITTED FRIEND, YOU SEE A MOB OF PAMPERED NINCOMPOOPS WHOSE SOLE ACTIVITY IN LIFE IS SEARCHING FOR NEW WAYS TO ESCAPE BOREDOM!
HE WAS REFERRING TO US!
BLAKELY'S GOING TOO FAR!
WHAT SAY, FOLKS: LET'S COMPROMISE!
WE'LL FINISH THE PARTY IN THE MINE! OUR MINER-PAL, HERE, WILL GUIDE AND FEAST HIS EYES ON US -- AND AS FOR US, WE'LL MAKE MERRY IN THE BOWELS OF THE EARTH!
HOORAY!
THE MAN'S A GENIUS!
ON TO THE MINE!
LED BY SUPERMAN, THE CROWD OF SINGING, SHOUT-ING, SABLE-AND-EVENING-CLOTHES-CLAD PARTY-GOERS MARCH GAILY TOWARD THE MINE . . . .

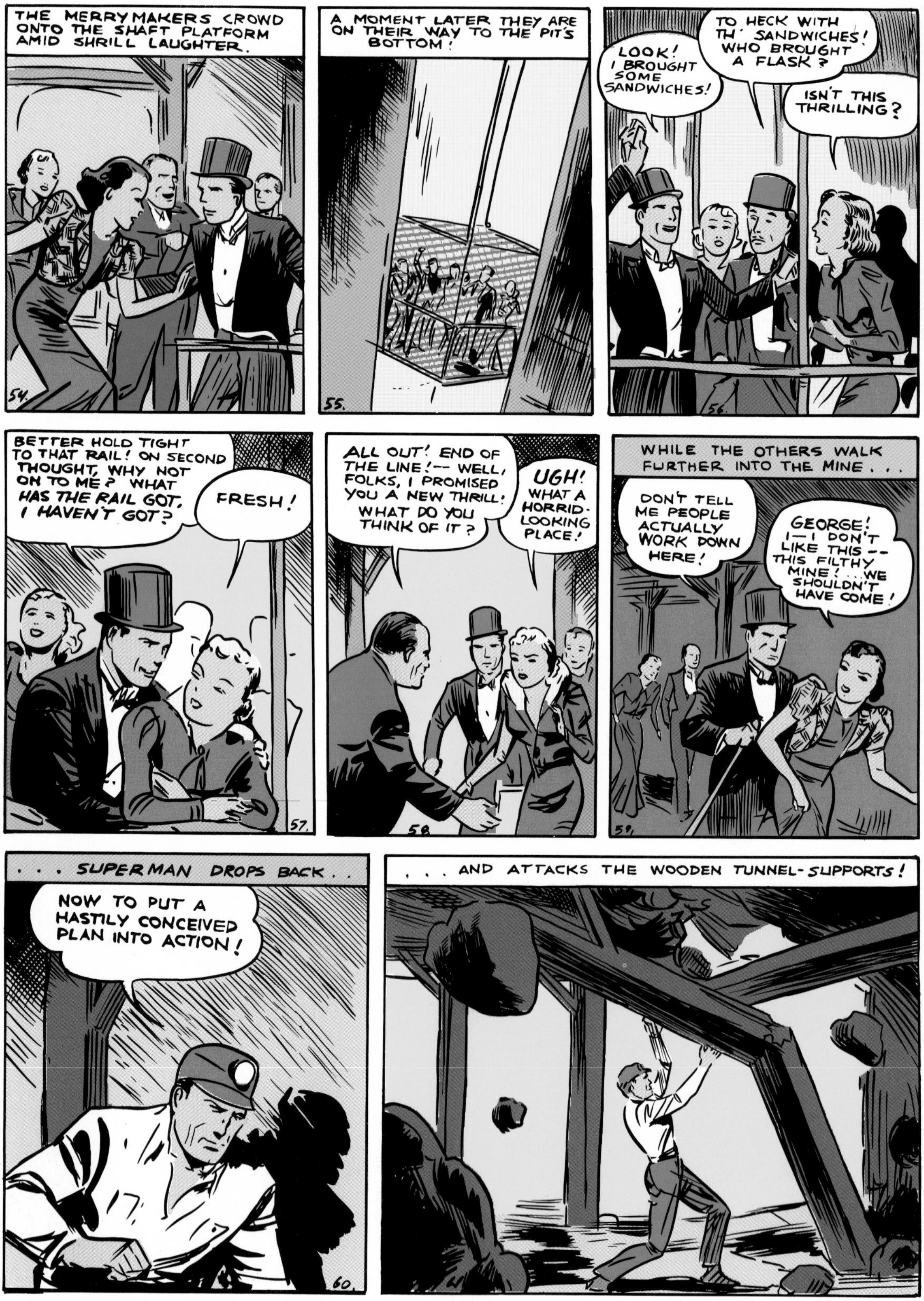
THE MERRYMAKERS CROWD ONTO THE SHAFT PLATFORM AMID SHRILL LAUGHTER.
54.
A MOMENT LATER THEY ARE ON THEIR WAY TO THE PIT'S BOTTOM!
55.
LOOK! I BROUGHT SOME SANDWICHES!
TO HECK WITH TH' SANDWICHES! WHO BROUGHT A FLASK?
ISN'T THIS THRILLING?
56.
BETTER HOLD TIGHT TO THAT RAIL! ON SECOND THOUGHT, WHY NOT ON TO ME? WHAT HAS THE RAIL GOT, I HAVEN'T GOT?
FRESH!
57.
ALL OUT! END OF THE LINE!-- WELL, FOLKS, I PROMISED YOU A NEW THRILL! WHAT DO YOU THINK OF IT?
UGH! WHAT A HORRID-LOOKING PLACE!
58.
WHILE THE OTHERS WALK FURTHER INTO THE MINE...
DON'T TELL ME PEOPLE ACTUALLY WORK DOWN HERE!
GEORGE! I--I DON'T LIKE THIS-- THIS FILTHY MINE! ...WE SHOULDN'T HAVE COME!
59.
...SUPERMAN DROPS BACK..
NOW TO PUT A HASTILY CONCEIVED PLAN INTO ACTION!
60.
...AND ATTACKS THE WOODEN TUNNEL-SUPPORTS!

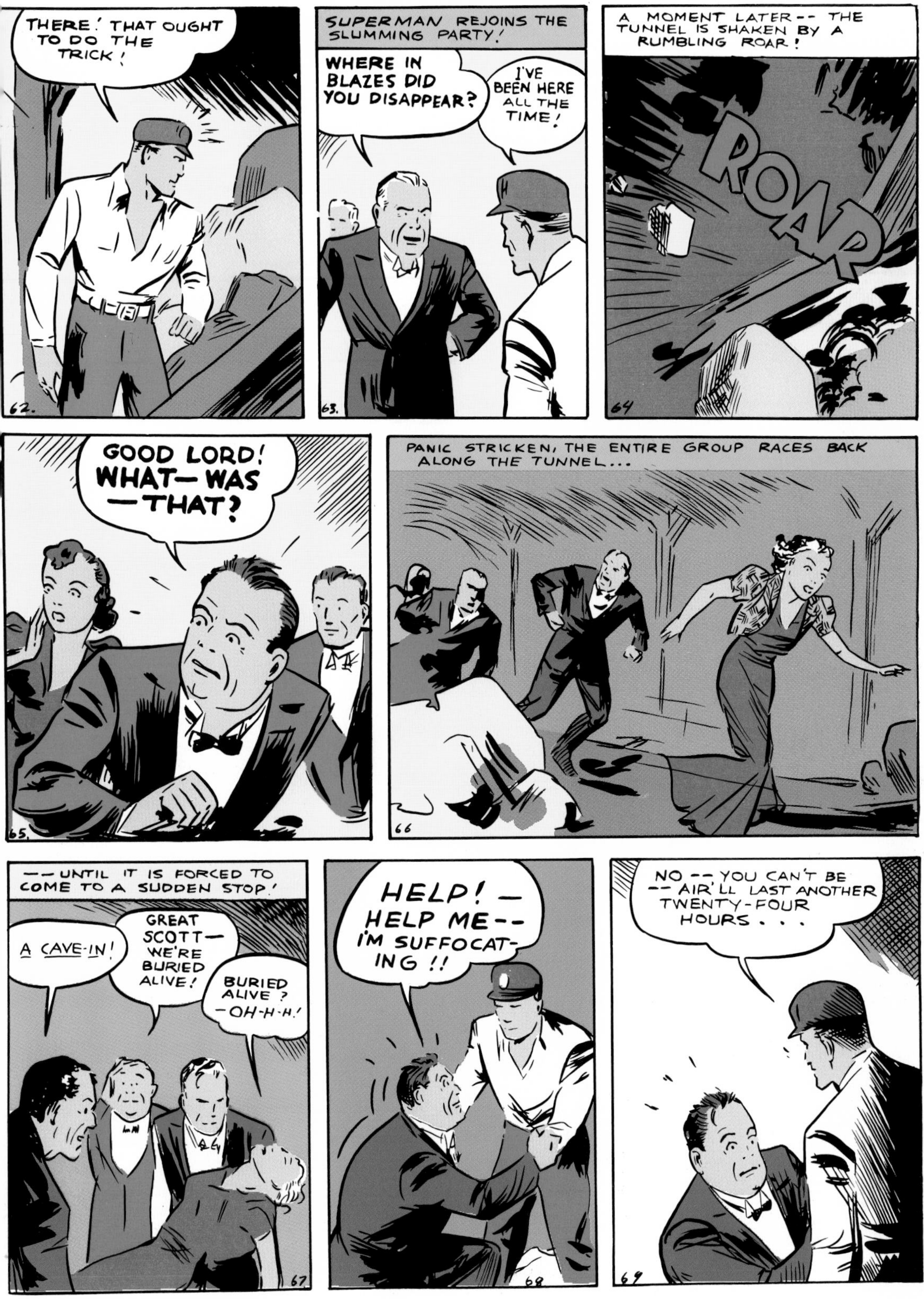
THERE! THAT OUGHT TO DO THE TRICK!
SUPERMAN REJOINS THE SLUMMING PARTY!
WHERE IN BLAZES DID YOU DISAPPEAR?
I'VE BEEN HERE ALL THE TIME!
A MOMENT LATER -- THE TUNNEL IS SHAKEN BY A RUMBLING ROAR!
ROAR
GOOD LORD! WHAT—WAS —THAT?
PANIC STRICKEN, THE ENTIRE GROUP RACES BACK ALONG THE TUNNEL...
-- UNTIL IT IS FORCED TO COME TO A SUDDEN STOP!
A CAVE-IN!
GREAT SCOTT— WE'RE BURIED ALIVE!
BURIED ALIVE? -OH-H-H!
HELP! — HELP ME-- I'M SUFFOCATING!!
NO -- YOU CAN'T BE -- AIR'LL LAST ANOTHER TWENTY-FOUR HOURS . . .

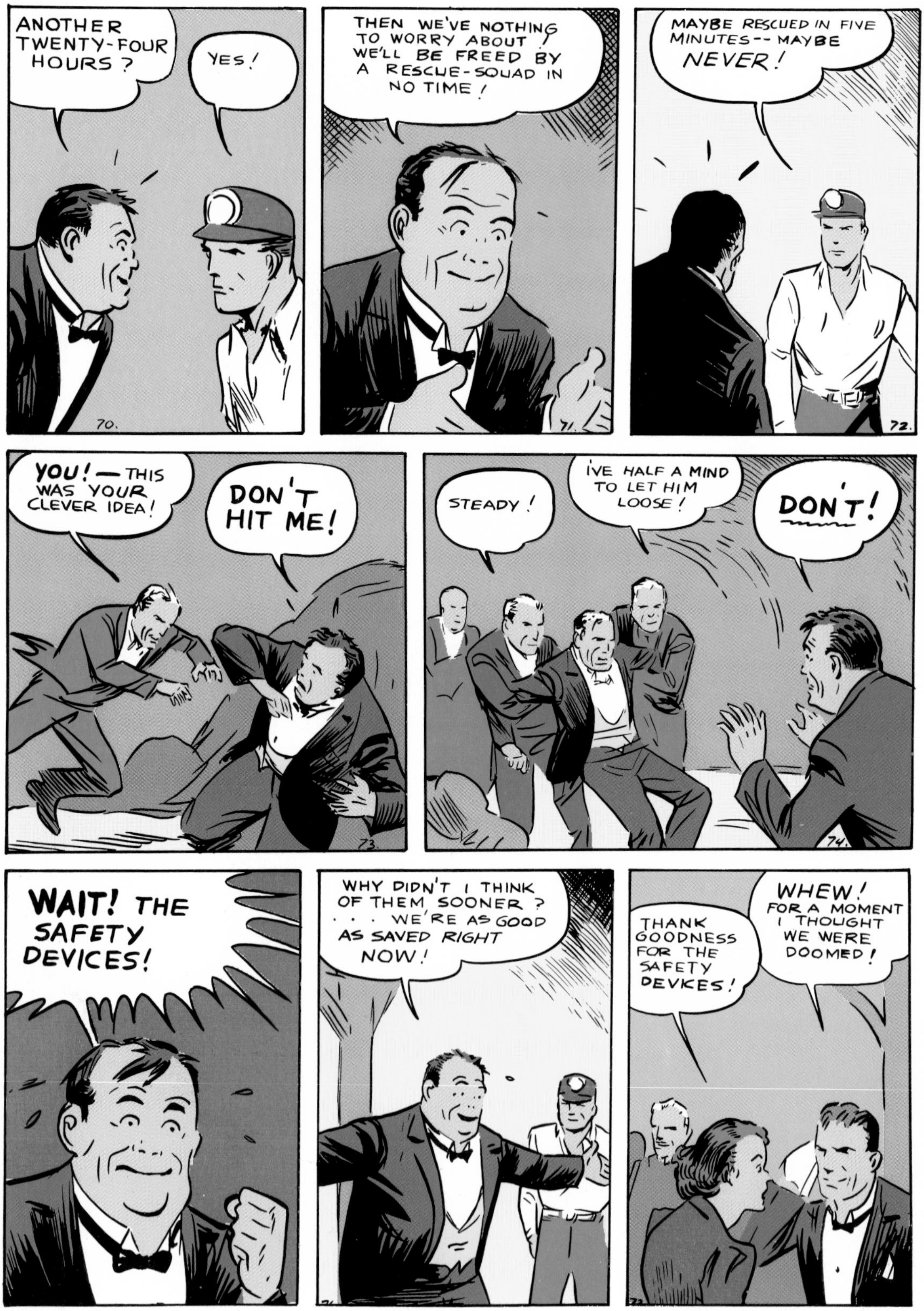
ANOTHER TWENTY-FOUR HOURS ?
YES!
THEN WE'VE NOTHING TO WORRY ABOUT! WE'LL BE FREED BY A RESCUE-SQUAD IN NO TIME!
MAYBE RESCUED IN FIVE MINUTES -- MAYBE NEVER!
YOU! — THIS WAS YOUR CLEVER IDEA!
DON'T HIT ME!
STEADY!
I'VE HALF A MIND TO LET HIM LOOSE!
DON'T!
WAIT! THE SAFETY DEVICES!
WHY DIDN'T I THINK OF THEM SOONER ? . . . WE'RE AS GOOD AS SAVED RIGHT NOW!
THANK GOODNESS FOR THE SAFETY DEVICES!
WHEW! FOR A MOMENT I THOUGHT WE WERE DOOMED!

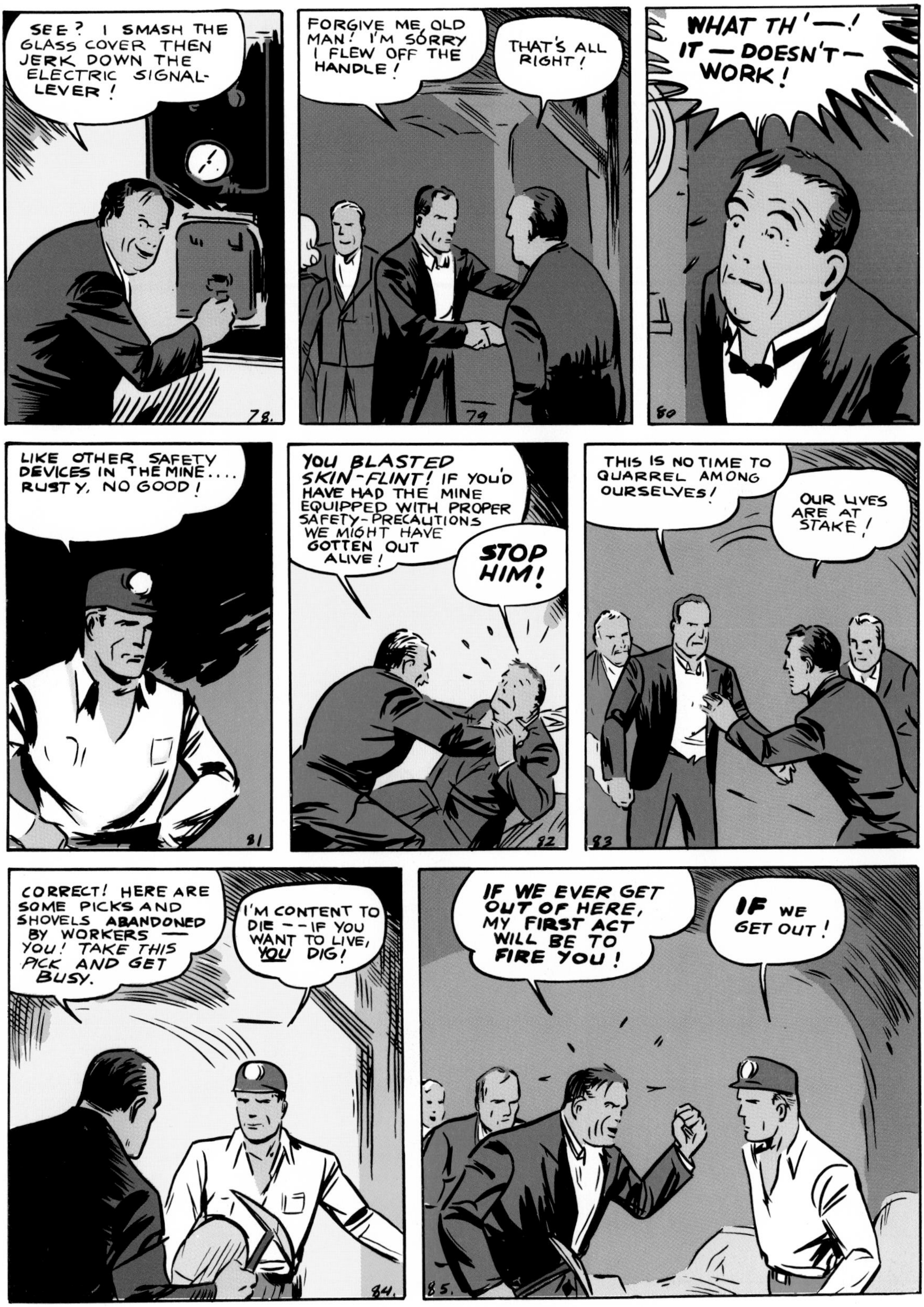
SEE? I SMASH THE GLASS COVER THEN JERK DOWN THE ELECTRIC SIGNAL-LEVER!
78.
FORGIVE ME, OLD MAN! I'M SORRY I FLEW OFF THE HANDLE!
THAT'S ALL RIGHT!
79
WHAT TH'—! IT—DOESN'T—WORK!
80
LIKE OTHER SAFETY DEVICES IN THE MINE.... RUSTY, NO GOOD!
81
YOU BLASTED SKIN-FLINT! IF YOU'D HAVE HAD THE MINE EQUIPPED WITH PROPER SAFETY-PRECAUTIONS WE MIGHT HAVE GOTTEN OUT ALIVE!
STOP HIM!
82
THIS IS NO TIME TO QUARREL AMONG OURSELVES!
OUR LIVES ARE AT STAKE!
83
CORRECT! HERE ARE SOME PICKS AND SHOVELS ABANDONED BY WORKERS — YOU! TAKE THIS PICK AND GET BUSY.
I'M CONTENT TO DIE — — IF YOU WANT TO LIVE, YOU DIG!
84.
IF WE EVER GET OUT OF HERE, MY FIRST ACT WILL BE TO FIRE YOU!
IF WE GET OUT!
85.

Knee-deep in stagnant water, struggling with unwieldy tools, slipping, frequently falling, the entrapped pleasure-seekers seek desperately, but vainly, to batter down the huge barrier of coal!

HURRY! WHILE THE AIR SUPPLY LASTS!

WE'VE GOT TO GET OUT-- WE'VE GOT TO!

I'M WINDED! I--I CAN'T KEEP THIS UP!

THINK OF THE MINERS! THEY HAVE TO DO THIS 14 LONG HOURS EACH DAY!

MEANWHILE -- A RESCUE-PARTY WORKS FRANTICALLY ON THE OTHER SIDE OF THE BARRIER!

IT'S NO USE! WE'LL NEVER GET OUT OF HERE! WE'LL ALL DIE!

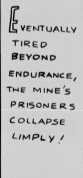

OH, IF I ONLY HAD THIS ALL TO DO OVER AGAIN! --I NEVER KNEW-- REALLY KNEW-- WHAT THE MEN DOWN HERE HAVE TO FACE!

THAT'S ALL I'VE BEEN WAITING TO HEAR!

Eventually tired beyond endurance, the mine's prisoners collapse limply!

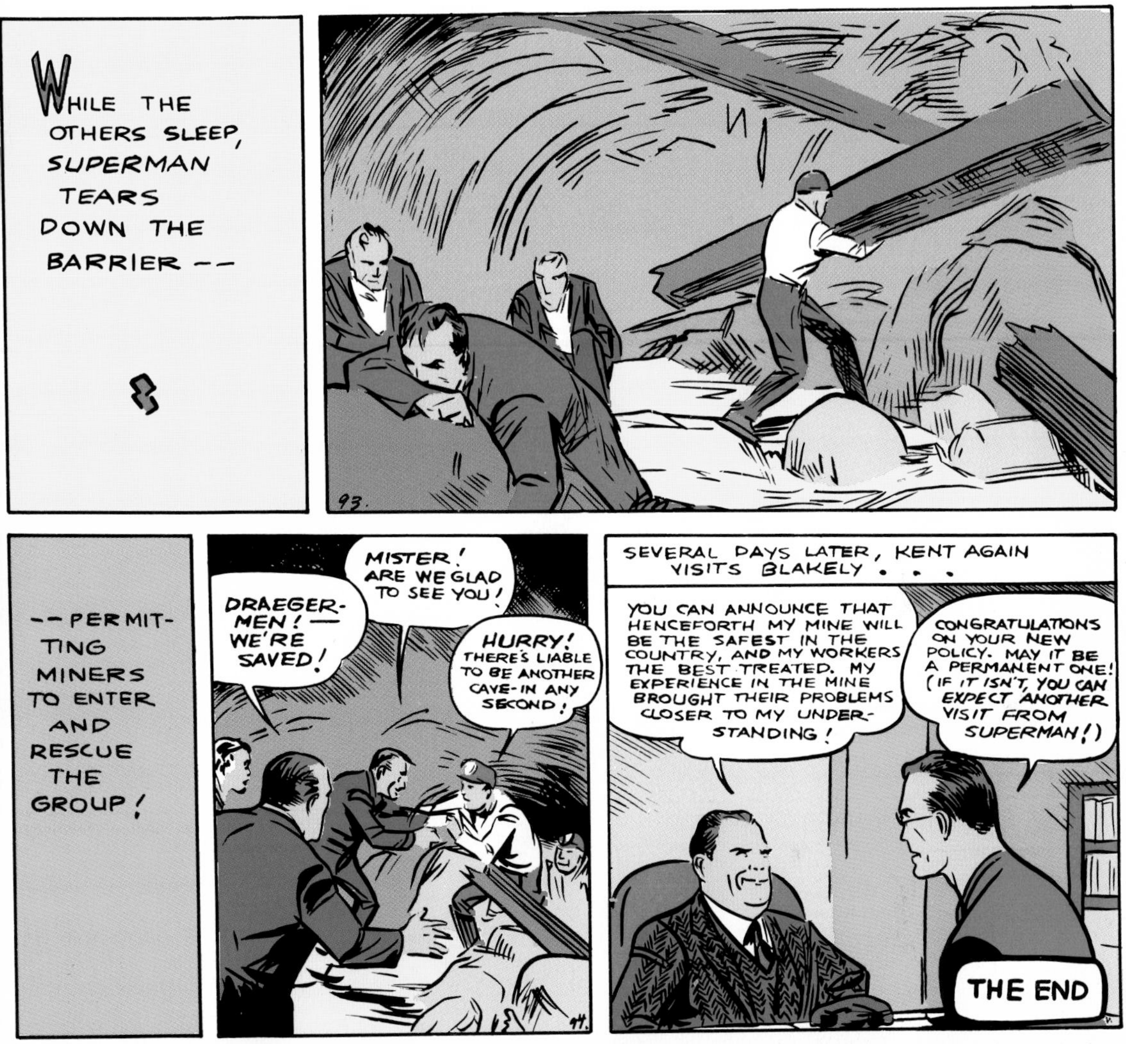
WHILE THE OTHERS SLEEP, SUPERMAN TEARS DOWN THE BARRIER --
--PERMITTING MINERS TO ENTER AND RESCUE THE GROUP!
DRAEGER-MEN! — WE'RE SAVED!
MISTER! ARE WE GLAD TO SEE YOU!
HURRY! THERE'S LIABLE TO BE ANOTHER CAVE-IN ANY SECOND!
SEVERAL DAYS LATER, KENT AGAIN VISITS BLAKELY . . .
YOU CAN ANNOUNCE THAT HENCEFORTH MY MINE WILL BE THE SAFEST IN THE COUNTRY, AND MY WORKERS THE BEST TREATED. MY EXPERIENCE IN THE MINE BROUGHT THEIR PROBLEMS CLOSER TO MY UNDERSTANDING!
CONGRATULATIONS ON YOUR NEW POLICY. MAY IT BE A PERMANENT ONE! (IF IT ISN'T, YOU CAN EXPECT ANOTHER VISIT FROM SUPERMAN!)
THE END

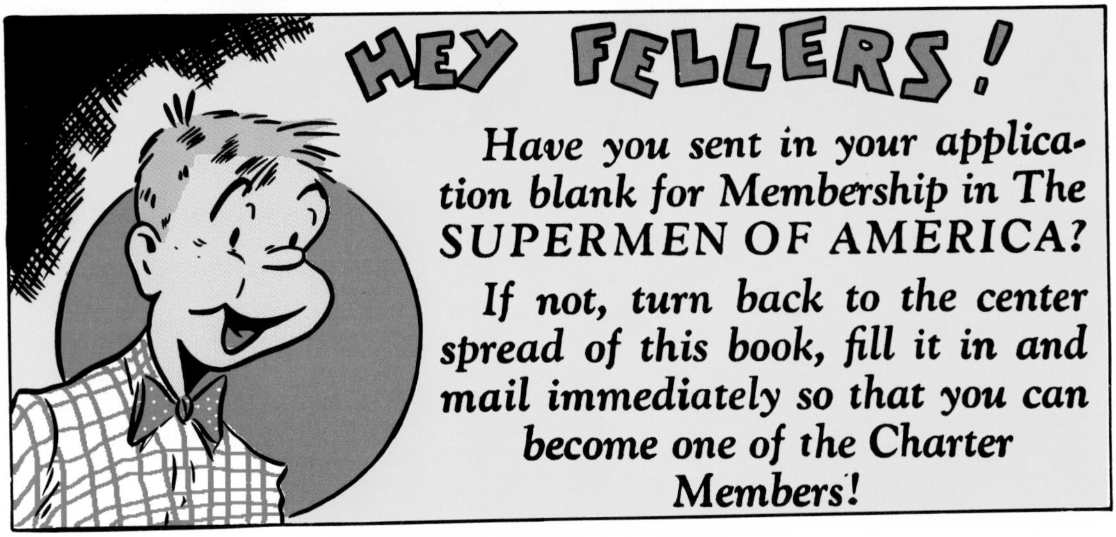
HEY FELLERS!
Have you sent in your application blank for Membership in The SUPERMEN OF AMERICA?
If not, turn back to the center spread of this book, fill it in and mail immediately so that you can become one of the Charter Members!

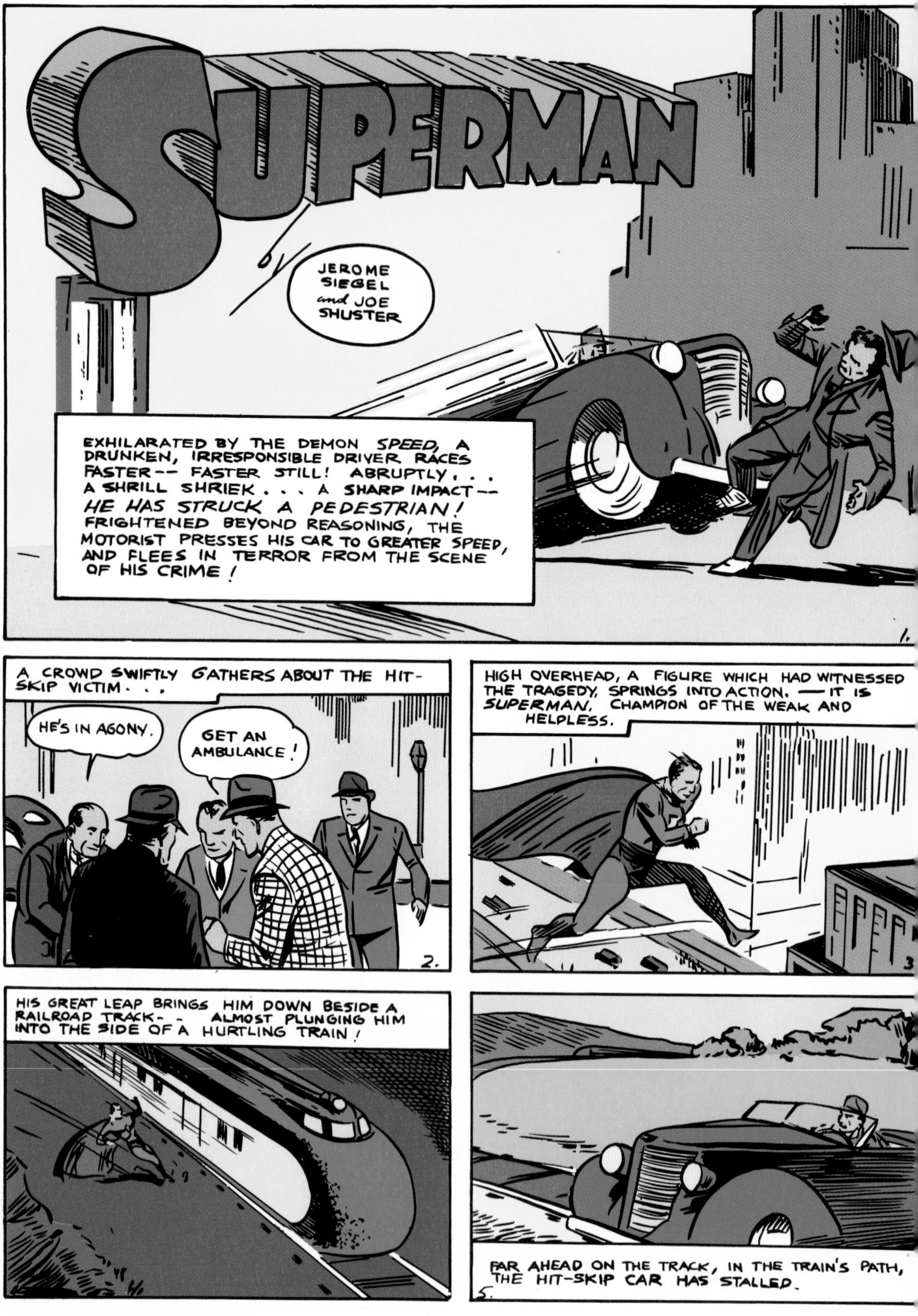
SUPERMAN
by
JEROME SIEGEL and JOE SHUSTER
EXHILARATED BY THE DEMON SPEED, A DRUNKEN, IRRESPONSIBLE DRIVER RACES FASTER-- FASTER STILL! ABRUPTLY. . . A SHRILL SHRIEK . . . A SHARP IMPACT-- HE HAS STRUCK A PEDESTRIAN! FRIGHTENED BEYOND REASONING, THE MOTORIST PRESSES HIS CAR TO GREATER SPEED, AND FLEES IN TERROR FROM THE SCENE OF HIS CRIME!
A CROWD SWIFTLY GATHERS ABOUT THE HIT-SKIP VICTIM. . .
HE'S IN AGONY.
GET AN AMBULANCE!
HIGH OVERHEAD, A FIGURE WHICH HAD WITNESSED THE TRAGEDY, SPRINGS INTO ACTION. — IT IS SUPERMAN, CHAMPION OF THE WEAK AND HELPLESS.
HIS GREAT LEAP BRINGS HIM DOWN BESIDE A RAILROAD TRACK-- ALMOST PLUNGING HIM INTO THE SIDE OF A HURTLING TRAIN!
FAR AHEAD ON THE TRACK, IN THE TRAIN'S PATH, THE HIT-SKIP CAR HAS STALLED.

...THIN THE ENGINE-CAR...

NOW'S ME CHANCE TO SNEAK A LI'L NIP WHILE HIS BACK IS TURNED.

GLANCING OUTWARD, THE ENGINEER DOUBTS HIS SENSES, AS HE SEES A FIGURE NOT ONLY RACING THE TRAIN...

W·WHAT--?

...BUT PASSING IT!

MIKE! — A MAN RACING US — RUNNING FASTER THAN TH' TRAIN-- I SAW IT WITH MY OWN EYES!

DRINKIN' AGAIN, EH?

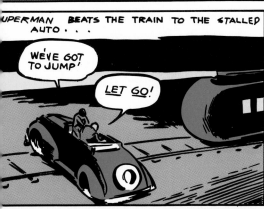

UPERMAN BEATS THE TRAIN TO THE STALLED AUTO...

WE'VE GOT TO JUMP!

LET GO!

YOU FOOL! YOU'LL KILL US BOTH!

WHEW! — JUST MADE IT! BUT THIS FELLOW HAS DIED OF A HEART ATTACK!

SEIZING THE EDGE OF A WINDOW, SUPERMAN SWINGS DOWNWARD . . .

. . . INTO A PRIVATE ROOM IN THE PULLMAN CAR.

OH-OH — SOMEONE'S ENTERING

WE CAN TALK HERE WITHOUT BEING OVERHEARD.

WHY HAS THE TRAIN BEEN STOPPED ?

IT HIT AN AUTO.

IF I DON'T WIN THIS GAME AGAINST CORDELL UNIVERSITY, IT MEANS I LOSE MY POSITION AS COACH AT DALE — I'M DETERMINED TO WIN AT ANY COST !

IN THAT CASE, WE'RE THE MEN FOR YOU, COACH RANDALL !

YOU'LL FIND OUR SERVICES EXPENSIVE , BUT EFFECTIVE ! ARE WE HIRED TO PLAY ON THE DALE FOOTBALL TEAM ?

YOU'RE IN ! — BUT REMEMBER I WANT YOU TO "GET" STEVENS, BURNS AND LEWISTON, OUR FOE'S BEST PLAYERS, RIGHT AT THE GAME'S BEGINNING !

LEAVE IT TO US !

ROUGH STUFF IS OUR SPECIALTY, COACH !

AFTER THE THREE DEPART.

HM-M ! A CROOKED COACH HIRING PROFESSIONAL THUGS TO PLAY FOOTBALL ! — SOUNDS LIKE JUST THE SORT OF SET-UP I LIKE TO TEAR DOWN !

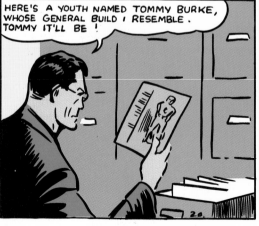

NEXT DAY — CLARK KENT, NEWSPAPER REPORTER, EXAMINES PHOTO-CLIPPINGS OF CORDELL'S FOOTBALL MATERIAL.

HERE'S A YOUTH NAMED TOMMY BURKE, WHOSE GENERAL BUILD I RESEMBLE. TOMMY IT'LL BE !

WITHIN THE PRIVACY OF HIS APARTMENT, CLARK DONS SOME MAKE-UP GREASE-PAINT.

SPLENDID ! NOW HIS OWN MOTHER WOULDN'T KNOW US APART !

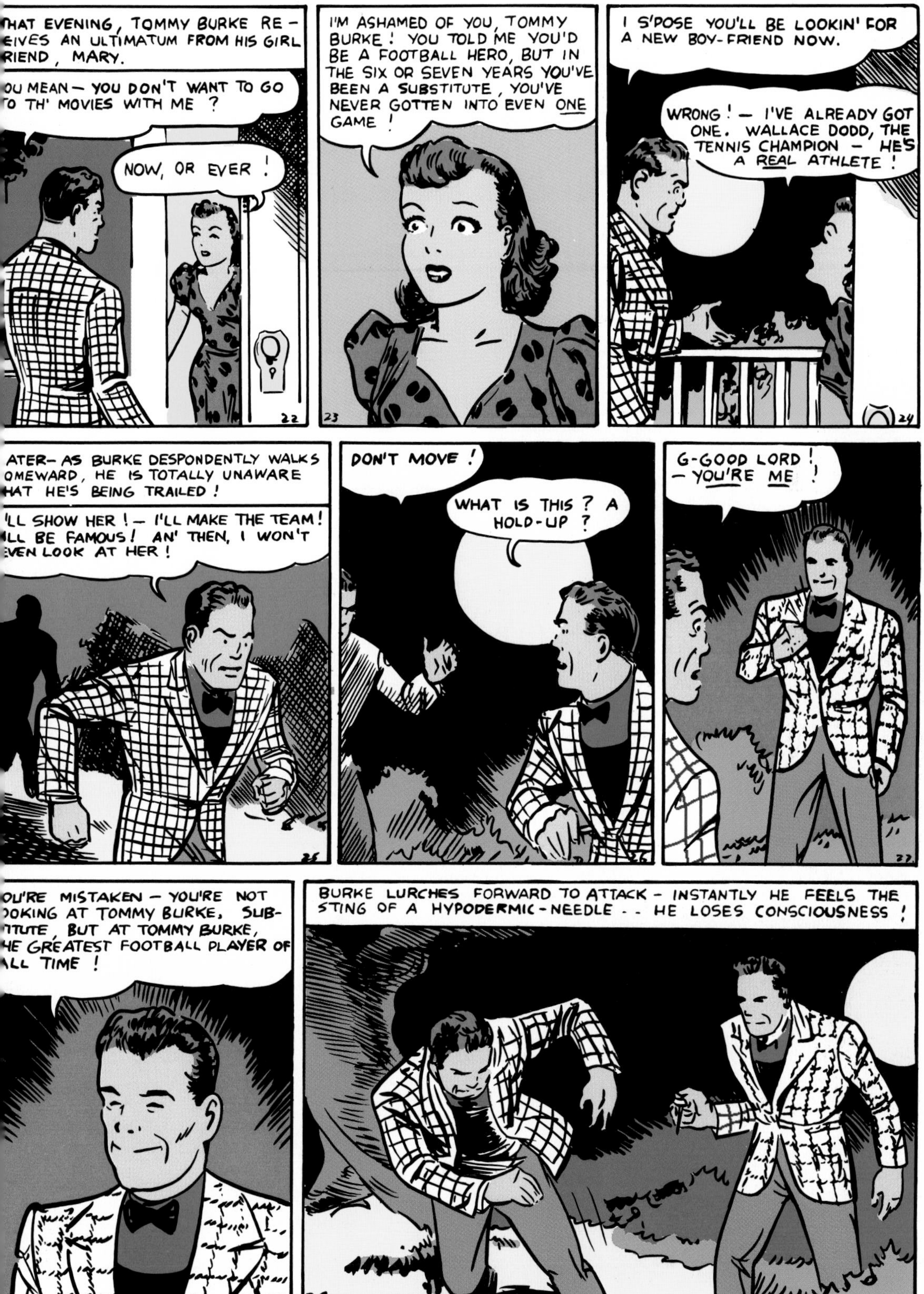
HAT EVENING, TOMMY BURKE RE-
EIVES AN ULTIMATUM FROM HIS GIRL
RIEND, MARY.
OU MEAN— YOU DON'T WANT TO GO
O TH' MOVIES WITH ME ?
NOW, OR EVER !
I'M ASHAMED OF YOU, TOMMY BURKE ! YOU TOLD ME YOU'D BE A FOOTBALL HERO, BUT IN THE SIX OR SEVEN YEARS YOU'VE BEEN A SUBSTITUTE, YOU'VE NEVER GOTTEN INTO EVEN ONE GAME !
I S'POSE YOU'LL BE LOOKIN' FOR A NEW BOY-FRIEND NOW.
WRONG ! — I'VE ALREADY GOT ONE. WALLACE DODD, THE TENNIS CHAMPION — HE'S A REAL ATHLETE !
ATER— AS BURKE DESPONDENTLY WALKS
OMEWARD, HE IS TOTALLY UNAWARE
HAT HE'S BEING TRAILED !
'LL SHOW HER ! — I'LL MAKE THE TEAM !
LL BE FAMOUS ! AN' THEN, I WON'T
EVEN LOOK AT HER !
DON'T MOVE !
WHAT IS THIS ? A HOLD-UP ?
G-GOOD LORD ! — YOU'RE ME !
OU'RE MISTAKEN — YOU'RE NOT
OOKING AT TOMMY BURKE, SUB-
TITUTE, BUT AT TOMMY BURKE,
HE GREATEST FOOTBALL PLAYER OF
LL TIME !
BURKE LURCHES FORWARD TO ATTACK - INSTANTLY HE FEELS THE STING OF A HYPODERMIC-NEEDLE - - HE LOSES CONSCIOUSNESS !

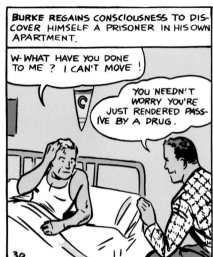

BURKE REGAINS CONSCIOUSNESS TO DISCOVER HIMSELF A PRISONER IN HIS OWN APARTMENT.

W- WHAT HAVE YOU DONE TO ME ? I CAN'T MOVE !

YOU NEEDN'T WORRY YOU'RE JUST RENDERED PASSIVE BY A DRUG.

30

BUT WHAT'S TH' BIG IDEA ?

MERELY THIS: I'M GOING TO TAKE YOUR PLACE IN LIFE FOR A FEW DAYS — SO LONG, FOR NOW !

31

DISGUISED AS BURKE, SUPERMAN REPORTS TO THE LOCKER-ROOM OF CORDELL UNIVERSITY, PREPARATORY TO FOOTBALL PRACTICE.

WELL, HERE GOES ! — WONDER IF I'LL GET AWAY WITH IT ?

LOCKER ROOM

32

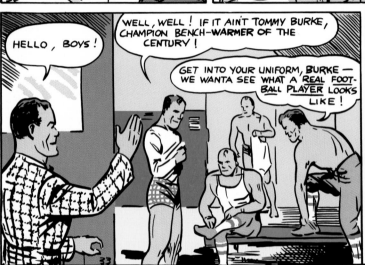

HELLO, BOYS !

WELL, WELL ! IF IT AIN'T TOMMY BURKE, CHAMPION BENCH-WARMER OF THE CENTURY !

GET INTO YOUR UNIFORM, BURKE — WE WANTA SEE WHAT A REAL FOOTBALL PLAYER LOOKS LIKE !

33

I DON'T KNOW IN WHICH LOCKER BURKE KEEPS HIS STUFF — I'LL JUST CHOOSE ONE AT RANDOM ... THIS ONE WILL DO.

34

SAY ! — WHAT TH' BLAZES YOU DOIN' IN MY LOCKER ?

SORRY -- MY MISTAKE.

35

I'LL GIVE YOU SOMETHING TO BE REALLY SORRY ABOUT !

36

DON'T STAND THERE GRINNING ! PUT UP YOUR HANDS AND FIGHT !

BUT IT'S MORE FUN TO SIMPLY WATCH !

37

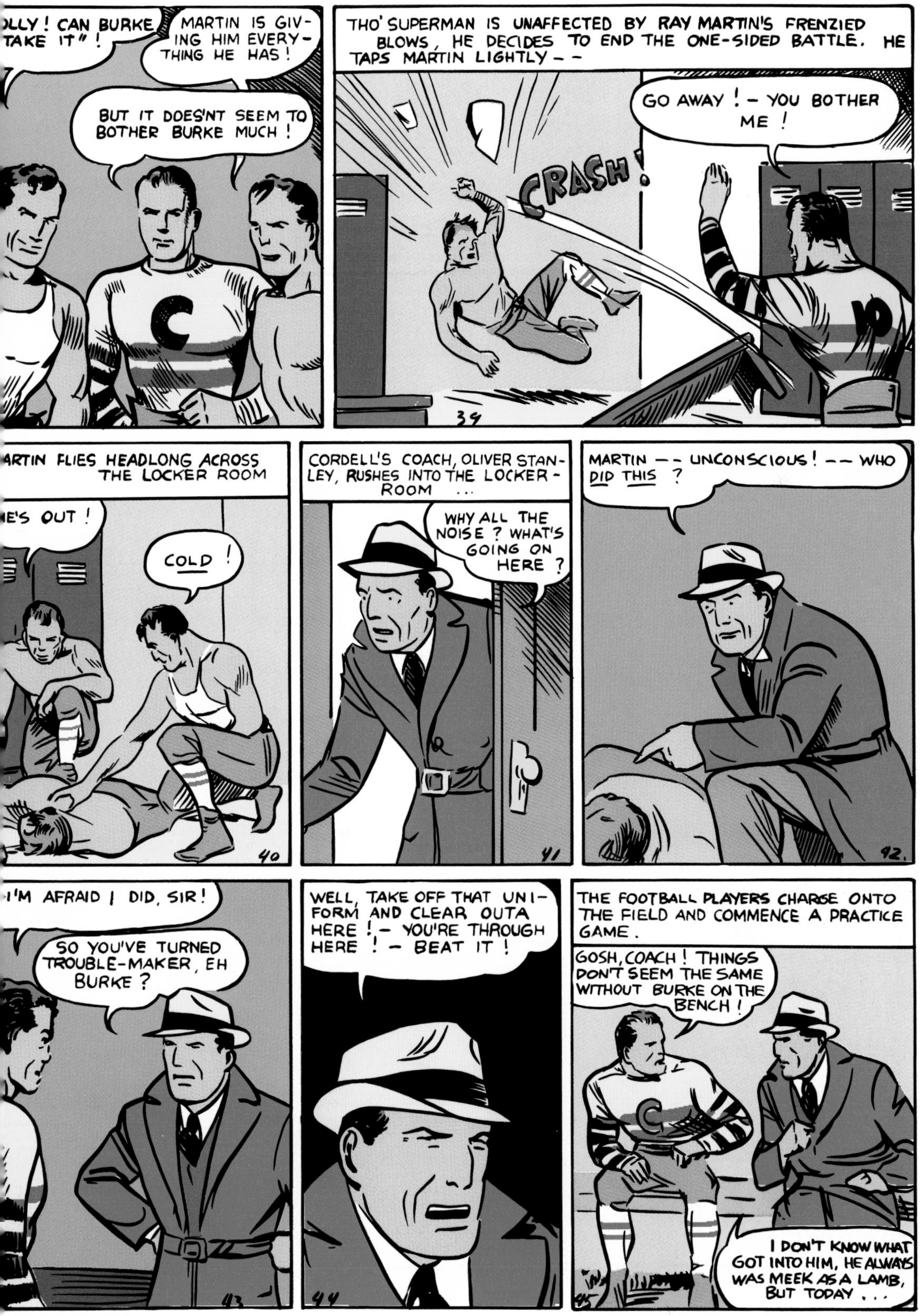
LLY! CAN BURKE TAKE IT"!
MARTIN IS GIVING HIM EVERYTHING HE HAS!
BUT IT DOES'NT SEEM TO BOTHER BURKE MUCH!
THO' SUPERMAN IS UNAFFECTED BY RAY MARTIN'S FRENZIED BLOWS, HE DECIDES TO END THE ONE-SIDED BATTLE. HE TAPS MARTIN LIGHTLY--
GO AWAY! - YOU BOTHER ME!
CRASH!
ARTIN FLIES HEADLONG ACROSS THE LOCKER ROOM
E'S OUT!
COLD!
CORDELL'S COACH, OLIVER STANLEY, RUSHES INTO THE LOCKER-ROOM...
WHY ALL THE NOISE? WHAT'S GOING ON HERE?
MARTIN -- UNCONSCIOUS! -- WHO DID THIS?
I'M AFRAID I DID, SIR!
SO YOU'VE TURNED TROUBLE-MAKER, EH BURKE?
WELL, TAKE OFF THAT UNIFORM AND CLEAR OUTA HERE! - YOU'RE THROUGH HERE! - BEAT IT!
THE FOOTBALL PLAYERS CHARGE ONTO THE FIELD AND COMMENCE A PRACTICE GAME.
GOSH, COACH! THINGS DON'T SEEM THE SAME WITHOUT BURKE ON THE BENCH!
I DON'T KNOW WHAT GOT INTO HIM, HE ALWAYS WAS MEEK AS A LAMB, BUT TODAY...

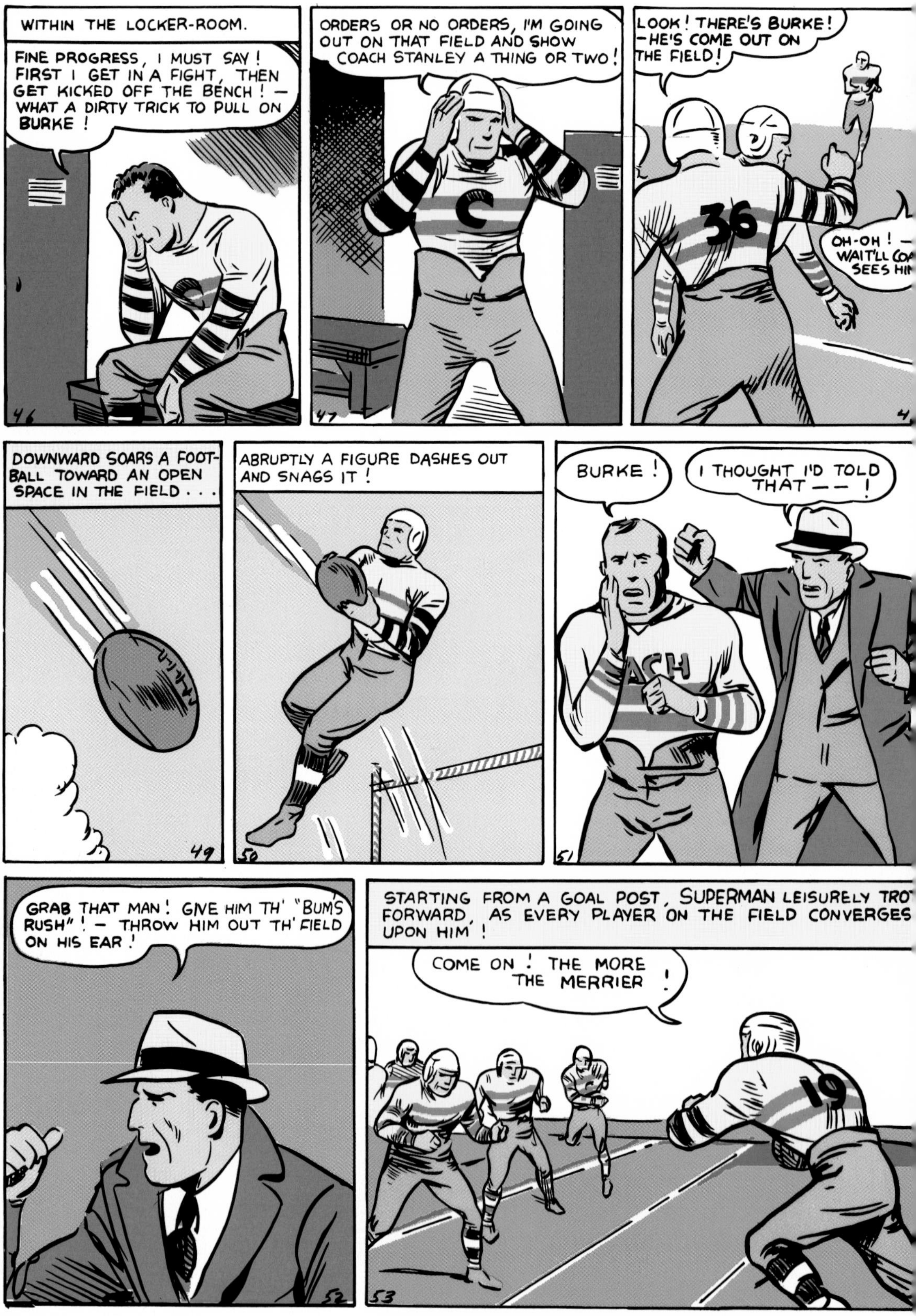
WITHIN THE LOCKER-ROOM.
FINE PROGRESS, I MUST SAY! FIRST I GET IN A FIGHT, THEN GET KICKED OFF THE BENCH! — WHAT A DIRTY TRICK TO PULL ON BURKE!
46
ORDERS OR NO ORDERS, I'M GOING OUT ON THAT FIELD AND SHOW COACH STANLEY A THING OR TWO!
47
LOOK! THERE'S BURKE! —HE'S COME OUT ON THE FIELD!
36
OH-OH! — WAIT'LL CO
SEES HI
DOWNWARD SOARS A FOOT-BALL TOWARD AN OPEN SPACE IN THE FIELD . . .
49
ABRUPTLY A FIGURE DASHES OUT AND SNAGS IT!
50
BURKE!
I THOUGHT I'D TOLD THAT — — !
51
GRAB THAT MAN! GIVE HIM TH' "BUM'S RUSH"! — THROW HIM OUT TH' FIELD ON HIS EAR!
52
STARTING FROM A GOAL POST, SUPERMAN LEISURELY TRO
FORWARD, AS EVERY PLAYER ON THE FIELD CONVERGES UPON HIM!
COME ON! THE MORE THE MERRIER!
19
53

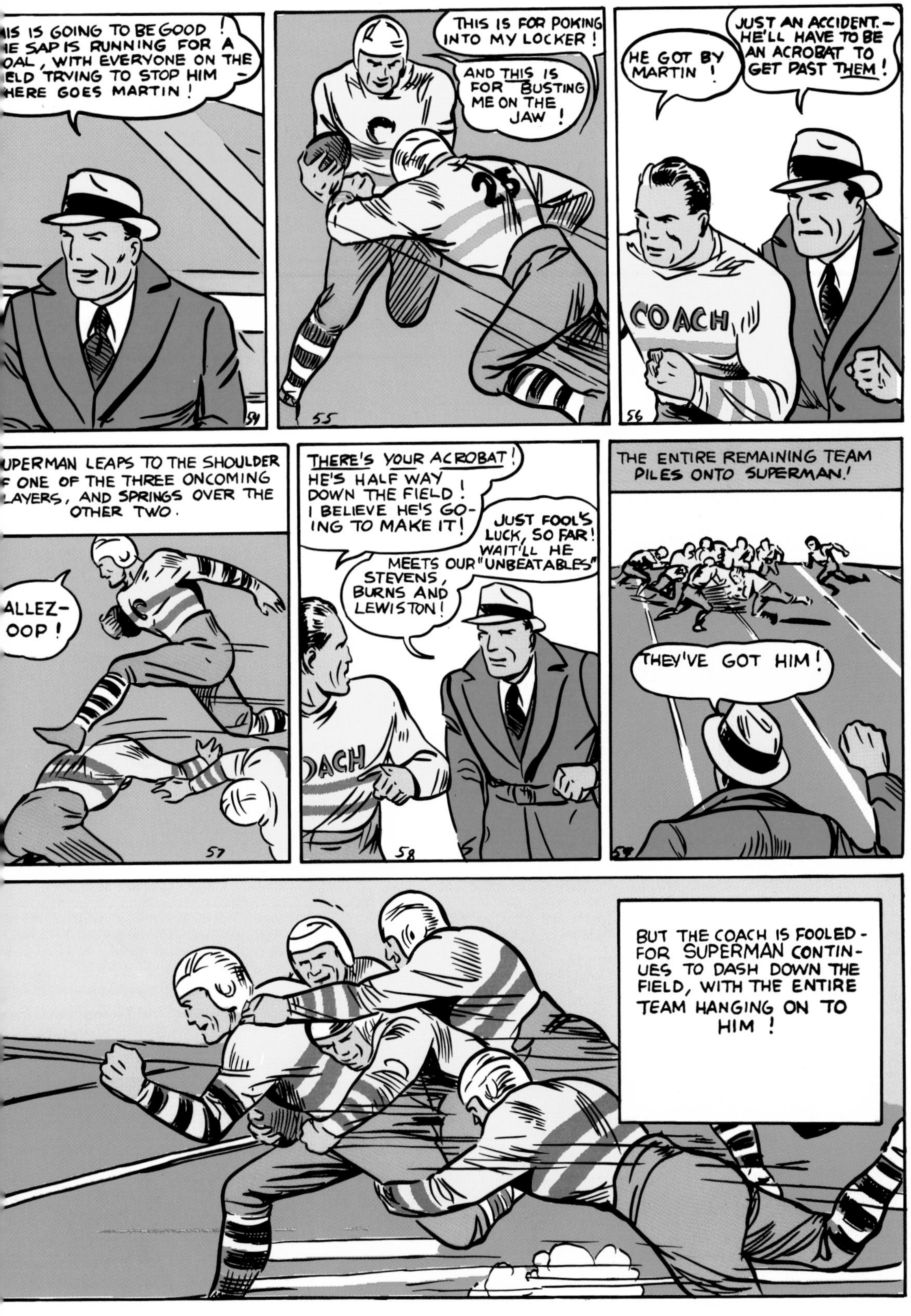
IS IS GOING TO BE GOOD! E SAP IS RUNNING FOR A OAL, WITH EVERYONE ON THE ELD TRYING TO STOP HIM — HERE GOES MARTIN!
THIS IS FOR POKING INTO MY LOCKER!
AND THIS IS FOR BUSTING ME ON THE JAW!
HE GOT BY MARTIN!
JUST AN ACCIDENT.— HE'LL HAVE TO BE AN ACROBAT TO GET PAST THEM!
UPERMAN LEAPS TO THE SHOULDER F ONE OF THE THREE ONCOMING LAYERS, AND SPRINGS OVER THE OTHER TWO.
ALLEZ-OOP!
THERE'S YOUR ACROBAT! HE'S HALF WAY DOWN THE FIELD! I BELIEVE HE'S GO-ING TO MAKE IT!
JUST FOOL'S LUCK, SO FAR! WAIT'LL HE MEETS OUR "UNBEATABLES" STEVENS, BURNS AND LEWISTON!
THE ENTIRE REMAINING TEAM PILES ONTO SUPERMAN!
THEY'VE GOT HIM!
BUT THE COACH IS FOOLED - FOR SUPERMAN CONTIN-UES TO DASH DOWN THE FIELD, WITH THE ENTIRE TEAM HANGING ON TO HIM!

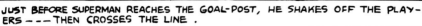

JUST BEFORE SUPERMAN REACHES THE GOAL-POST, HE SHAKES OFF THE PLAY-ERS --- THEN CROSSES THE LINE.

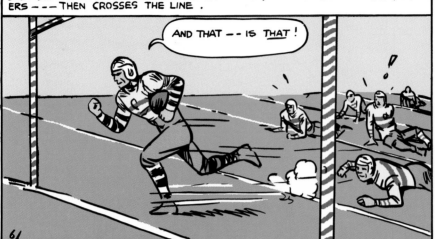

AND THAT -- IS _THAT_ !

TOUCHDOWN !

BURKE, HAVE YOU BEEN HOLDING OUT ON ME ?

WHAT'S COME OVER BURKE? BOY! WHATTA RUN !

AND TO THINK I LET THIS GUY SIT ON THE BENCH FOR SIX ENTIRE SEASONS !

BUT HE CAN BE IN OUR LAST GAME -- THE ONE AGAINST DALE, WHICH WILL DECIDE THE CHAMPIONSHIP !

THIS THE SPORTS EDITOR OF THE "NEWS"?-- LISTEN ! I'VE A PLA[Y]ER NAMED TOMMY BURKE WHO[']S A MARVEL, A SENSATION ! WHA[T] DO YOU THINK OF _THAT_ !

BURKE ?--DON'T MAKE ME LAUGH ! --IT'S NO SECRET HE'S THE JOKE OF THE CORDELL TEAM --WHAT IS THIS ? A GAG ?

IN BURKE'S APARTMENT --

WHAT'S SO FUNNY ?

THIS ARTICLE ABOUT YOU -- SATIRICAL BUT STILL, GOOD PUBLICITY!

AT DALE UNIVERSITY --

THIS ARTICLE PLAYS UP BURKE AS A CLOWN. BUT JUST THE SAME, I THINK [IT] WOULD BE A GOOD IDEA IF CORDELL[']S STAR PLAYER DISAPPEARED.

UNTIL THE GAME WAS OVE[R] EH, BOSS ?

WE GET YOU !

DURING THE FOLLOWING DAYS, THE CORDELL TEAM PRACTICES STEADILY FOR THE BIG GAME.

STILL DON'T GET IT! HOW IN THE WORLD CAN A PLAYER BECOME SO GOOD OVERNIGHT?

IF YOU KNEW, YOU'D BE THE GREATEST COACH IN THE WORLD!

TOMORROW'S THE GAME WITH DALE! NOW REMEMBER -- EARLY TO BED, NO SMOKING, NO DRINKING! - PLEASANT DREAMS!

THAT EVENING --

BURKE IS ASLEEP IN THAT A- PARTMENT, - YOU KNOW WHAT TO DO.

LATER-

HE'S COMPLETELY TIED!

STRANGE HE DIDN'T STRUGGLE AT ALL!

THE TWO THUGS ARE UNAWARE BURKE IS UNDER THE INFLUENCE OF A SLEEP-INDUCING DRUG OR THAT SUPERMAN IS OB- SERVING THEM FROM THE MOLD- ING OVERHEAD!

WHEN THE KIDNAPPERS DRIVE OFF, SUPERMAN RACES IN PURSUIT, EASILY KEEPING THEIR AUTO IN SIGHT!

BURKE IS BROUGHT INTO A DESERTED HOUSE!

W-WHERE AM I?

WHERE YOU WON'T BE ABLE TO GET INTO TOMORROW'S GAME.

BUT YOU DON'T WANT ME - I'M JUST A' SUB- STITUTE AND BESIDES-

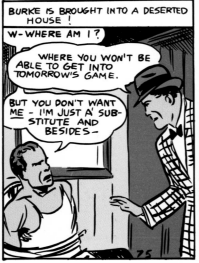

ARE YOU TOMMY BURKE?

YES, BUT IT ISN'T ME WHO--

THAT'S ALL WE WANTA KNOW - THIS GAG'LL QUIET YOU DOWN.

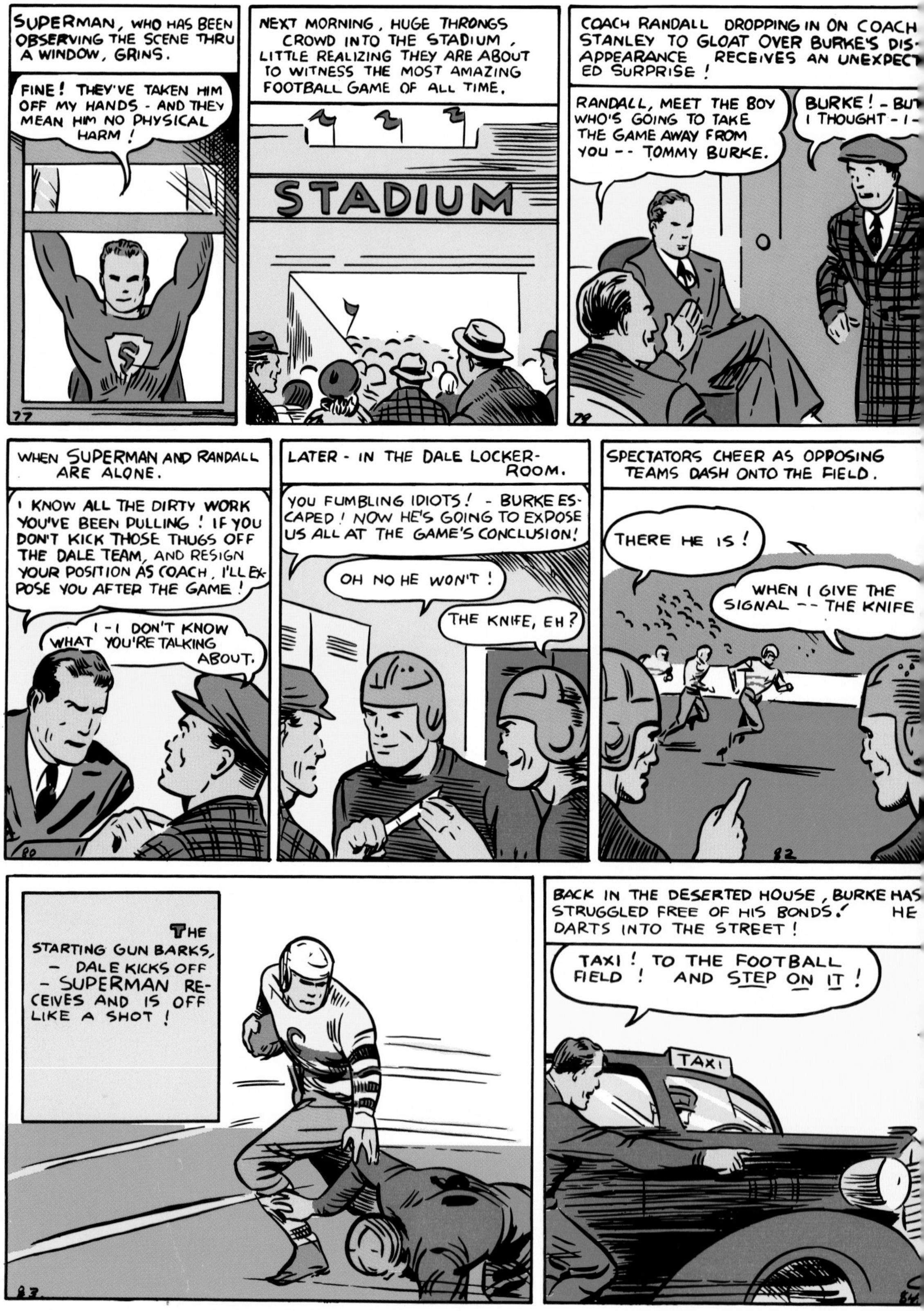
SUPERMAN, WHO HAS BEEN OBSERVING THE SCENE THRU A WINDOW, GRINS.
FINE! THEY'VE TAKEN HIM OFF MY HANDS - AND THEY MEAN HIM NO PHYSICAL HARM!
NEXT MORNING, HUGE THRONGS CROWD INTO THE STADIUM, LITTLE REALIZING THEY ARE ABOUT TO WITNESS THE MOST AMAZING FOOTBALL GAME OF ALL TIME.
STADIUM
COACH RANDALL DROPPING IN ON COACH STANLEY TO GLOAT OVER BURKE'S DISAPPEARANCE RECEIVES AN UNEXPECTED SURPRISE!
RANDALL, MEET THE BOY WHO'S GOING TO TAKE THE GAME AWAY FROM YOU -- TOMMY BURKE.
BURKE! - BUT I THOUGHT - I -
WHEN SUPERMAN AND RANDALL ARE ALONE.
I KNOW ALL THE DIRTY WORK YOU'VE BEEN PULLING! IF YOU DON'T KICK THOSE THUGS OFF THE DALE TEAM, AND RESIGN YOUR POSITION AS COACH, I'LL EXPOSE YOU AFTER THE GAME!
I-I DON'T KNOW WHAT YOU'RE TALKING ABOUT.
LATER - IN THE DALE LOCKER-ROOM.
YOU FUMBLING IDIOTS! - BURKE ESCAPED! NOW HE'S GOING TO EXPOSE US ALL AT THE GAME'S CONCLUSION!
OH NO HE WON'T!
THE KNIFE, EH?
SPECTATORS CHEER AS OPPOSING TEAMS DASH ONTO THE FIELD.
THERE HE IS!
WHEN I GIVE THE SIGNAL -- THE KNIFE
THE STARTING GUN BARKS, - DALE KICKS OFF - SUPERMAN RECEIVES AND IS OFF LIKE A SHOT!
BACK IN THE DESERTED HOUSE, BURKE HAS STRUGGLED FREE OF HIS BONDS! HE DARTS INTO THE STREET!
TAXI! TO THE FOOTBALL FIELD! AND STEP ON IT!
TAXI

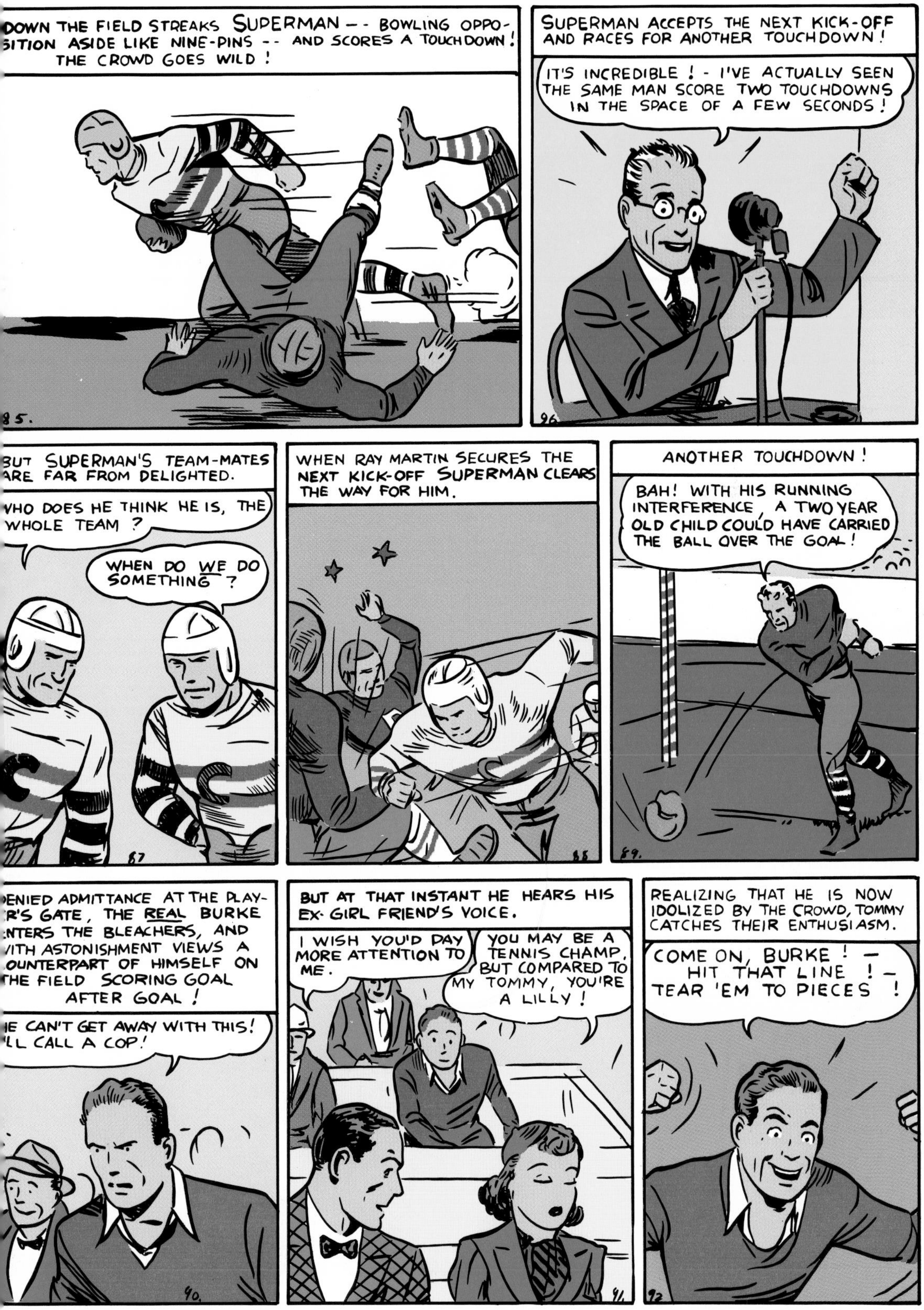
DOWN THE FIELD STREAKS SUPERMAN -- BOWLING OPPO-SITION ASIDE LIKE NINE-PINS -- AND SCORES A TOUCHDOWN! THE CROWD GOES WILD!
85.
SUPERMAN ACCEPTS THE NEXT KICK-OFF AND RACES FOR ANOTHER TOUCHDOWN!
IT'S INCREDIBLE! - I'VE ACTUALLY SEEN THE SAME MAN SCORE TWO TOUCHDOWNS IN THE SPACE OF A FEW SECONDS!
86
BUT SUPERMAN'S TEAM-MATES ARE FAR FROM DELIGHTED.
WHO DOES HE THINK HE IS, THE WHOLE TEAM?
WHEN DO WE DO SOMETHING?
87
WHEN RAY MARTIN SECURES THE NEXT KICK-OFF SUPERMAN CLEARS THE WAY FOR HIM.
88
ANOTHER TOUCHDOWN!
BAH! WITH HIS RUNNING INTERFERENCE, A TWO YEAR OLD CHILD COULD HAVE CARRIED THE BALL OVER THE GOAL!
89.
DENIED ADMITTANCE AT THE PLAYER'S GATE, THE REAL BURKE ENTERS THE BLEACHERS, AND WITH ASTONISHMENT VIEWS A COUNTERPART OF HIMSELF ON THE FIELD SCORING GOAL AFTER GOAL!
HE CAN'T GET AWAY WITH THIS! I'LL CALL A COP!
90.
BUT AT THAT INSTANT HE HEARS HIS EX-GIRL FRIEND'S VOICE.
I WISH YOU'D PAY MORE ATTENTION TO ME.
YOU MAY BE A TENNIS CHAMP, BUT COMPARED TO MY TOMMY, YOU'RE A LILLY!
91.
REALIZING THAT HE IS NOW IDOLIZED BY THE CROWD, TOMMY CATCHES THEIR ENTHUSIASM.
COME ON, BURKE! — HIT THAT LINE! — TEAR 'EM TO PIECES!
92

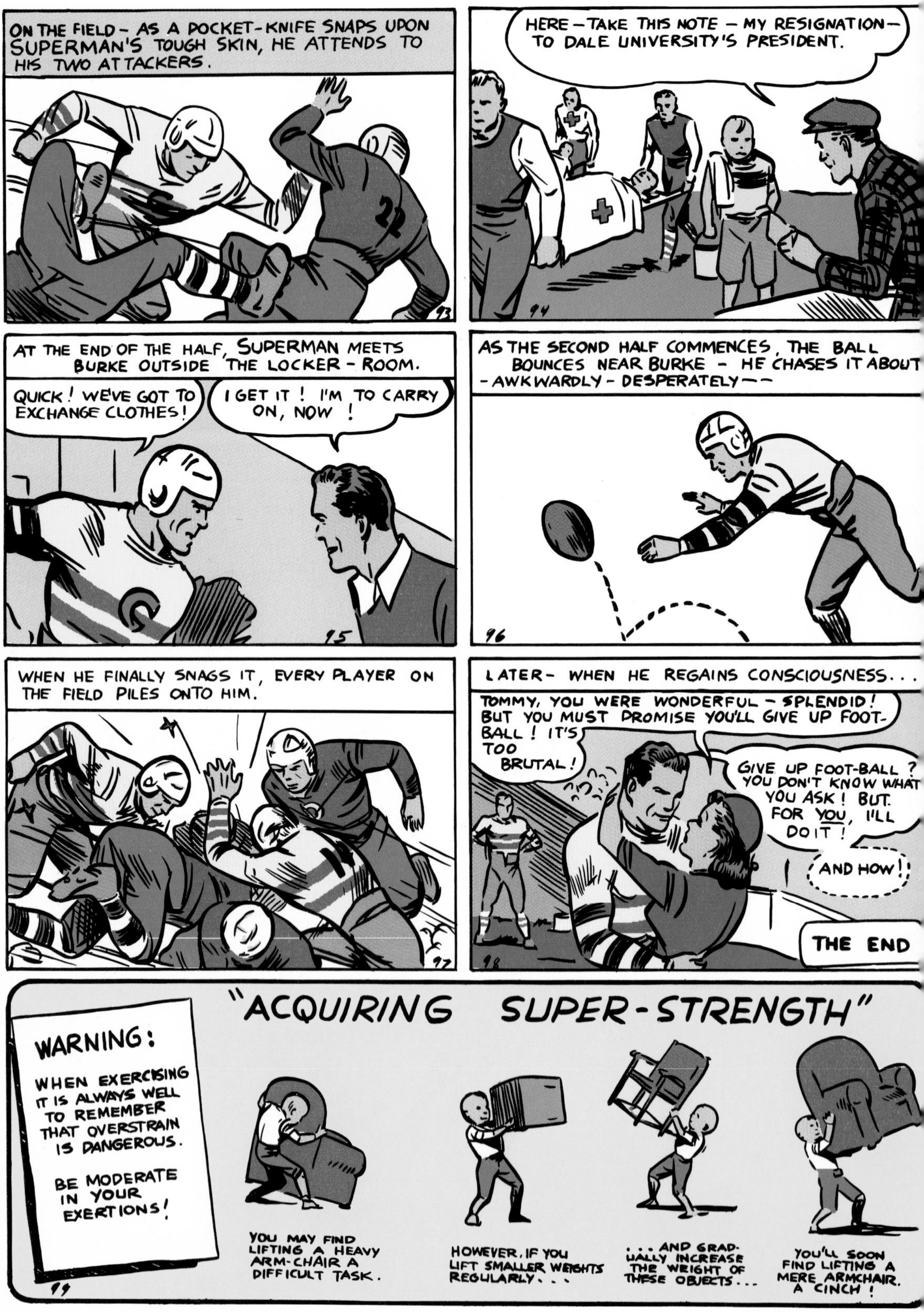
ON THE FIELD – AS A POCKET-KNIFE SNAPS UPON SUPERMAN'S TOUGH SKIN, HE ATTENDS TO HIS TWO ATTACKERS.
HERE – TAKE THIS NOTE – MY RESIGNATION – TO DALE UNIVERSITY'S PRESIDENT.
AT THE END OF THE HALF, SUPERMAN MEETS BURKE OUTSIDE THE LOCKER - ROOM.
QUICK! WE'VE GOT TO EXCHANGE CLOTHES!
I GET IT! I'M TO CARRY ON, NOW!
AS THE SECOND HALF COMMENCES, THE BALL BOUNCES NEAR BURKE – HE CHASES IT ABOUT – AWKWARDLY – DESPERATELY – –
WHEN HE FINALLY SNAGS IT, EVERY PLAYER ON THE FIELD PILES ONTO HIM.
LATER – WHEN HE REGAINS CONSCIOUSNESS . . .
TOMMY, YOU WERE WONDERFUL – SPLENDID! BUT YOU MUST PROMISE YOU'LL GIVE UP FOOT-BALL! IT'S TOO BRUTAL!
GIVE UP FOOT-BALL? YOU DON'T KNOW WHAT YOU ASK! BUT FOR YOU, I'LL DO IT!
AND HOW!
THE END
"ACQUIRING SUPER-STRENGTH"
WARNING:
WHEN EXERCISING IT IS ALWAYS WELL TO REMEMBER THAT OVERSTRAIN IS DANGEROUS.
BE MODERATE IN YOUR EXERTIONS!
YOU MAY FIND LIFTING A HEAVY ARM-CHAIR A DIFFICULT TASK.
HOWEVER, IF YOU LIFT SMALLER WEIGHTS REGULARLY . . .
. . . AND GRADUALLY INCREASE THE WEIGHT OF THESE OBJECTS . . .
YOU'LL SOON FIND LIFTING A MERE ARMCHAIR A CINCH!

Boys and Girls: *Meet the creators of the one and only* **SUPERMAN**—*America's Greatest Adventure Strip!*

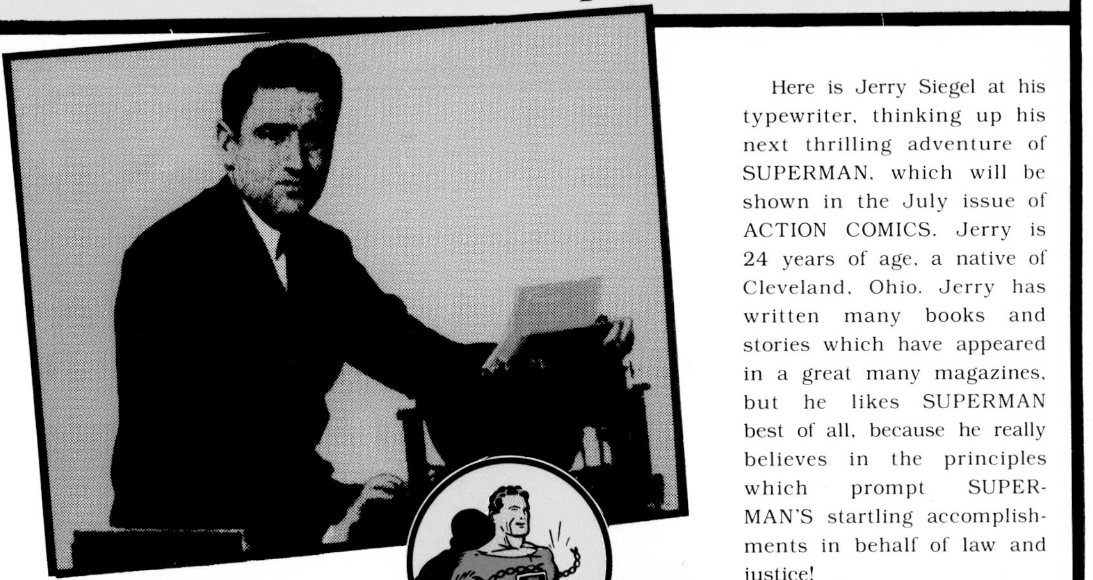

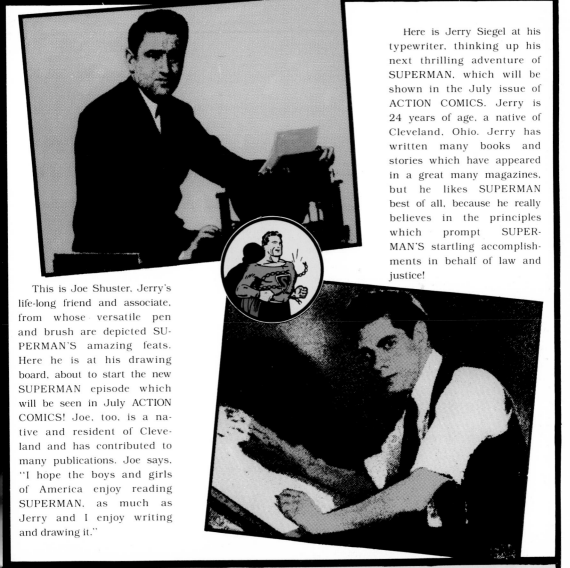

Here is Jerry Siegel at his typewriter, thinking up his next thrilling adventure of SUPERMAN, which will be shown in the July issue of ACTION COMICS. Jerry is 24 years of age, a native of Cleveland, Ohio. Jerry has written many books and stories which have appeared in a great many magazines, but he likes SUPERMAN best of all, because he really believes in the principles which prompt SUPERMAN'S startling accomplishments in behalf of law and justice!

This is Joe Shuster, Jerry's life-long friend and associate, from whose versatile pen and brush are depicted SUPERMAN'S amazing feats. Here he is at his drawing board, about to start the new SUPERMAN episode which will be seen in July ACTION COMICS! Joe, too, is a native and resident of Cleveland and has contributed to many publications. Joe says, "I hope the boys and girls of America enjoy reading SUPERMAN, as much as Jerry and I enjoy writing and drawing it."

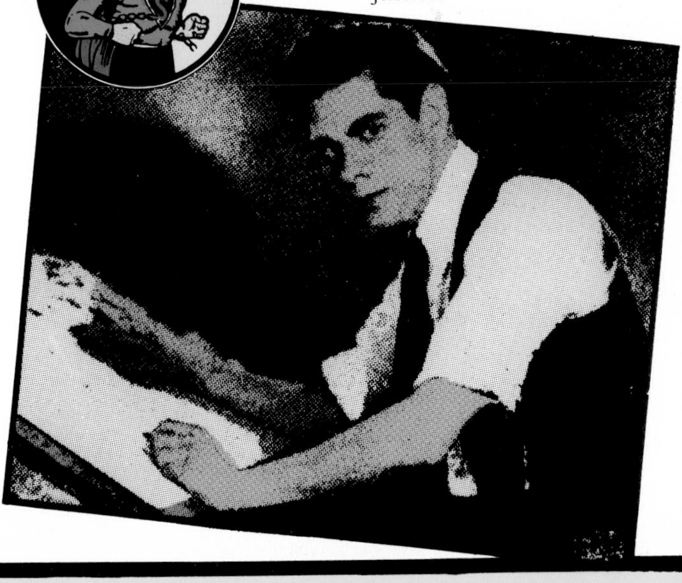

***JERRY SIEGEL and JOE SHUSTER are also the creators of "Slam Bradley" and "Spy" which appear in* DETECTIVE COMICS; *"Radio Squad" which appears in* MORE FUN COMICS; *and "Federal Men" which appears monthly in* ADVENTURE COMICS.**

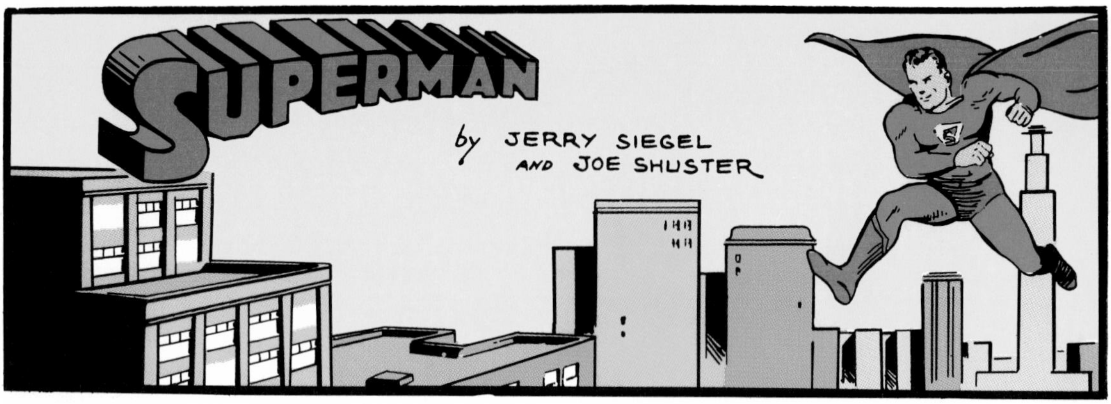
SUPERMAN
by JERRY SIEGEL
AND JOE SHUSTER

SMASHED desks, overturned filing cabinets, strewn plaster, gaping holes in the walls, shining steel fixtures drooping in sad caricature of their former modernistic splendor, greeted the startled Detective Sergeant's eyes, as he swung open the office door to the firm *Harvey Brown, Patent Attorney*

A quivering wreck of a man arose from the floor, stridently shrieked, "He can't do this to me! Get him! Arrest him!"

Sergeant Blake surveyed the fellow's torn clothing, mussed hair, and blackened eyes, then once again speechlessly regarded the carnage in the room. "What in blazes has happened here?" he roared, finding his voice at last, "A cyclone?"

"Cyclone, nothing!" exclaimed the trembling man. "Worse! I've just had a visit from SUPERMAN!"

"SUPERMAN!" The word burst from Blake's lips with the force of an explosion.

"Yes! He claimed I've stolen my clients' inventions. After he wrecked the place, he warned me that if I didn't go out of business, he'd come back and finish the job! I demand . . . " Brown halted his tirade. The Detective Sergeant was no longer in the room.

The remaining members of the riot squad were taken aback to see their superior officer come hurtling out into the hall at full tilt.

"Quick!" shouted Blake. "Seen anyone since I charged into the room?"

"No one," volunteered a puzzled officer. "That is, no one except a guy wearing a strange costume who asked what the trouble was, then stepped into the elevator."

A howl of baffled rage left the Sergeant as he sprang to the wall and desperately jabbed the elevator button. "Fools!" he roared. "That was SUPERMAN!"

Concerted cries left the policemen. "SUPERMAN! . . . and he's in that elevator! . . . What'll we do?"

Blake seized the hand of one of his men, and shoved it against the button. "Keep that pressed down for a full three minutes, Mooney—or I'll have your badge.—You others, come with me!"

Toward the nearby stairway dashed Blake, followed by his men. As they clattered down at top speed, he explained, "Fortunately, the elevator is automatically operated by the push-buttons on the various floors. As long as Mooney presses the button, SUPERMAN is trapped. And when the three minutes are up, and the Man of Steel gets off at the bottom floor, we'll be ready for him!"

Two minutes later found the policemen ranged before the first floor entrance to the elevator, guns out, all eyes strained on the indicator which showed that the car was stalled somewhere between the second and the first floor. Triumph blazed in Sergeant Blake's eyes. Visions of a pat on the back from the Commissioner, a promotion in rank, and a boost in salary, dangled tantalizingly in his mind.

"Careful, men!" he warned the officers grouped about him. "We've prayed for this break for months, and now that it's come, we don't want to muff it. He was seen going into that elevator . . . and he's bound to come out of that door any moment!"

"And *that's* what bothers me," muttered someone, "What'll we do when he *does* emerge?"

Said another "Our guns are useless against him!"

"Nonsense!" retorted Sergeant Blake. "All we've got to do is keep cool, and we've got him!"

But his glib comeback didn't satisfy even the Detective Sergeant himself. There were some very wild tales being circulated about this fellow who called himself SUPERMAN. He was said to be a modern Robin Hood . . . a person who had dedicated his existence to assisting the weak and oppressed. It was whispered that he possessed super-strength, could lift tremendous weights, smash steel with his bare hands, jump over buildings, and that nothing could penetrate his amazingly super-tough skin. But, of course, pondered the Sergeant, these were mere rumors, fantastic fairy tales. Probably SUPERMAN was just an ordinary person whose better than average strength had been immensely exaggerated Without a doubt!

Nevertheless, the hardboiled cop couldn't prevent an apprehensive shiver from creeping up his spine!

Suddenly, the arrow on the indicator began to move. The three minutes were up! Mooney had released the button, and the elevator was descending!

With a clash of metal the door to the elevator swung open. Fingers tensed on gun-triggers . . . Then . . .

A hesitant, alarmed voice broke the electric silence: "My word! Put down those guns!"

Out of the elevator stepped a slim, nervous figure. Meek eyes blinked fearfully behind thick-rimmed glasses. No SUPERMAN, this! Rather, a very much frightened young man.

From somewhere behind him, the dumbfounded Detective Sergeant heard a smothered titter. His face reddened. "Where's SUPERMAN?" he shouted at the mouse-like young man who stood before him. "What in all that's holy are *you* doing in that elevator?"

"I was just—er—descending to the lobby, when something apparently went wrong with the mechanism. "I'll admit I was terrified for a few moments, but . . . "

"Answer me!" thundered Blake. "Did you see a man in a strange uniform in that elevator?"

"No one at all . . . that is, except myself. I'm afraid there must be some mistake, Sergeant. I'm Clark Kent, reporter on the *Daily Star.*"

"But SUPERMAN was seen to enter the elevator by one of my men How do you explain that?"

Clark shrugged. "It's beyond me," he said. "Possibly your man was high-strung, or had an overactive imagination "

A loud laugh went up at this. The Detective Sergeant whirled to face his men, his features registering keen disappointment. "I guess it was just a false alarm, at that! Let's head back for headquarters, to turn in a report."

"I say, that's odd!" interrupted Kent. "I was just about to go to Police Headquarters myself, in search of a story. Do you mind if I accompany you?"

Later, as they sped through the streets with the squad car, Clark learned that people adjoining Brown's office had telephoned for a police car, complaining of a terrific rumpus going on in the Patent Attorney's office . . . and how Blake had expected SUPERMAN to emerge from the elevator.

"Very amusing," chuckled Clark. "It'll make a good feature article for the *Daily Star*."

"Hold on!" bellowed Blake in protest. "You can't print that. It would make me look like a sap!—Don't print it! And maybe some day I'll return the favor!"

The reporter shrugged. "Well, if you feel that strongly about it, I'll forget the yarn . . . temporarily."

The conversation was cut short as they parked before the police station. As they emerged from the car, an officer rushed up and exclaimed to Blake. "Have you heard? 'Biff' Dugan has just been captured!"

A happy grin quickly chased the glum expression from the Detective Sergeant's face. "Biff" was a long-sought murderer who had been eluding the law for months. "I knew we'd catch up with that rat," Blake chuckled.

Swift strides hurried Blake and Kent into the station. A few moments later the prisoner, an ugly hulking brute who sullenly refused to talk, stood before them.

"Thought you could evade the law, did you?" demanded the Sergeant. "Well, maybe you know better now!"

Clark tugged at Blake's sleeve. "Remember, Sergeant? You offered to do me a favor. I'd like to take you up, now!"

Suspiciously, Blake inquired: "What?"

"Allow me to interview the prisoner in private."

"And what," asked Blake, "is wrong with interviewing him right here in front of me?"

"You can see he's in no mood to talk. Perhaps if I could speak to him alone . . . "

"Are you looney? It's against regulations. It's . . . "

Clark smiled tauntingly. "If I can't have this interview, I'll have to write up a certain other story One about a dumb Detective Sergeant who had his men surround an elevator in the hope . . . "

"Wait!" cried Blake. "You can have that interview!" He added ominously. "But if anything happens to the prisoner, you'll be held personally responsible."

Shortly later, within an adjoining room, Clark was occupied with the task of prying replies from a glum prisoner when there came a knocking at the room's door.

Bart turned from the prisoner. Opened the door slightly.

It was Blake. He demanded: "Is the prisoner still there?"

"Naturally," replied Clark, exasperated. "See for yours . . . " Abruptly Kent's words were choked off in a gasp of astonishment. Alarmed, the Sergeant burst into the room. In one glance he saw the reporter's hand pointing toward an open window . . . and no sight of Dugan anywhere.

"He's escaped!" exclaimed Clark.

Sergeant Blake roared with rage, seized the frail reporter, and shook him angrily. "You—!" he choked. "It's *your* fault! This makes you an accessory to the fact!"

The Detective Sergeant will never completely remember what happened just then. One moment he was shaking a fear-struck reporter, and the next instant he was whirling up into the air, as though caught in the grip of a hurricane. Next instant, he struck the wall, uttered a groan, and lapsed into unconsciousness.

Clark Kent looked at the Sergeant's recumbent figure, muttered, "Sorry, but I haven't time to use

kid gloves," then, with amazing rapidity he stripped off his glasses and outer garments, revealing himself clad in a weird close-fitting costume, and flaring cape. In this apparel, it was apparent that he really possessed a fine physique of breathtaking symmetry.

One lithe leap brought him to the window-sill. There he poised momentarily, while his keen telescopic vision surveyed the vicinity. And then, as he sighted the figure of "Biff" scrambling into a parked auto, he dived out into space.

Out—out—sped the fantastic figure . . . its mighty muscles launching it across an incredible distance. The auto was a full three hundred yards away, but SUPERMAN smashed down into the gravel before it, just as the car's gears clashed and it leapt ahead.

Within the car, Dugan snarled. This solitary figure which had hurtled down from nowhere . . . it alone stood between him and escape. He pressed the accelerator down to the limit, with the intention of smashing into the body, crushing it beneath his auto's wheels.

He struck the figure with a *crash!* But then, the impossible happened! Instead of being flung beneath the wheels, SUPERMAN held his ground . . . actually kept the roaring machine from moving!

Astounded by this miracle, "Biff" threw the clutch into reverse, but again he was treated to an exhibition of super-strength. Having seized the front bumper, the Man of Steel prevented the automobile from backing up!

A shriek of sheer horror tore from Dugan's throat. Frenziedly, he flung open the door of the automobile, sprang out . . . and looked up to find himself faced by SUPERMAN'S grim figure.

Half mad with fright he leapt at the Man of Tomorrow, seeking to fight his way past. But it was like bucking against a stone wall. His fists encountered flesh as hard as metal, fracturing his knuckles!

Suddenly "Biff" was possessed with but one desire. To flee . . . to get away from this indestructible demon of wrath! He whirled, raced off with all his might, screeching at the top of his lungs. Next instant, arms of steel encircled him from behind. There was a pressure at the back of his neck. Then . . . unconsciousness. . .

SERGEANT Blake revived to find Clark Kent kneeling beside him. He felt his forehead groggily, then suddenly remembering what had occurred, seized the reporter. "You're under arrest!" he shouted.

"What for?" inquired Kent.

"For aiding 'Biff' Dugan to escape, that's why! And . . . "

Clark pointed to a figure huddled on the floor nearby. "Before you say any more, look over there!"

Blake looked, blinked uncomprehendingly, then exclaimed: "Dugan!—But how . . . ?"

"All I know," replied Clark, "is that a man wearing a strange costume jumped to the window-sill, tossed 'Biff' in, then leapt away."

The Detective Sergeant sprang erect. "Do you realize who that must have been! SUPERMAN!"

Clark's eyes widened. "Gosh! I guess you're right!"

"You know," grudgingly admitted Sergeant Blake, "sometimes I think SUPERMAN isn't such a bad guy, at that. But," he hastily amended, "don't think that doesn't mean I won't arrest him the minute I get my hands on him!"

"Let's hope you get within reaching distance," said Clark Kent.

Detective Sergeant Blake cast a quick suspicious glance at the reporter. For a moment he'd fancied he had detected a trace of mockery in Kent's voice. But Clark's visage was completely solemn.

THE END

Follow the Adventures of the one and only SUPERMAN *in every issue of* ACTION COMICS!!

HERE IS A MINIATURE REPRODUCTION OF OUR JULY ISSUE

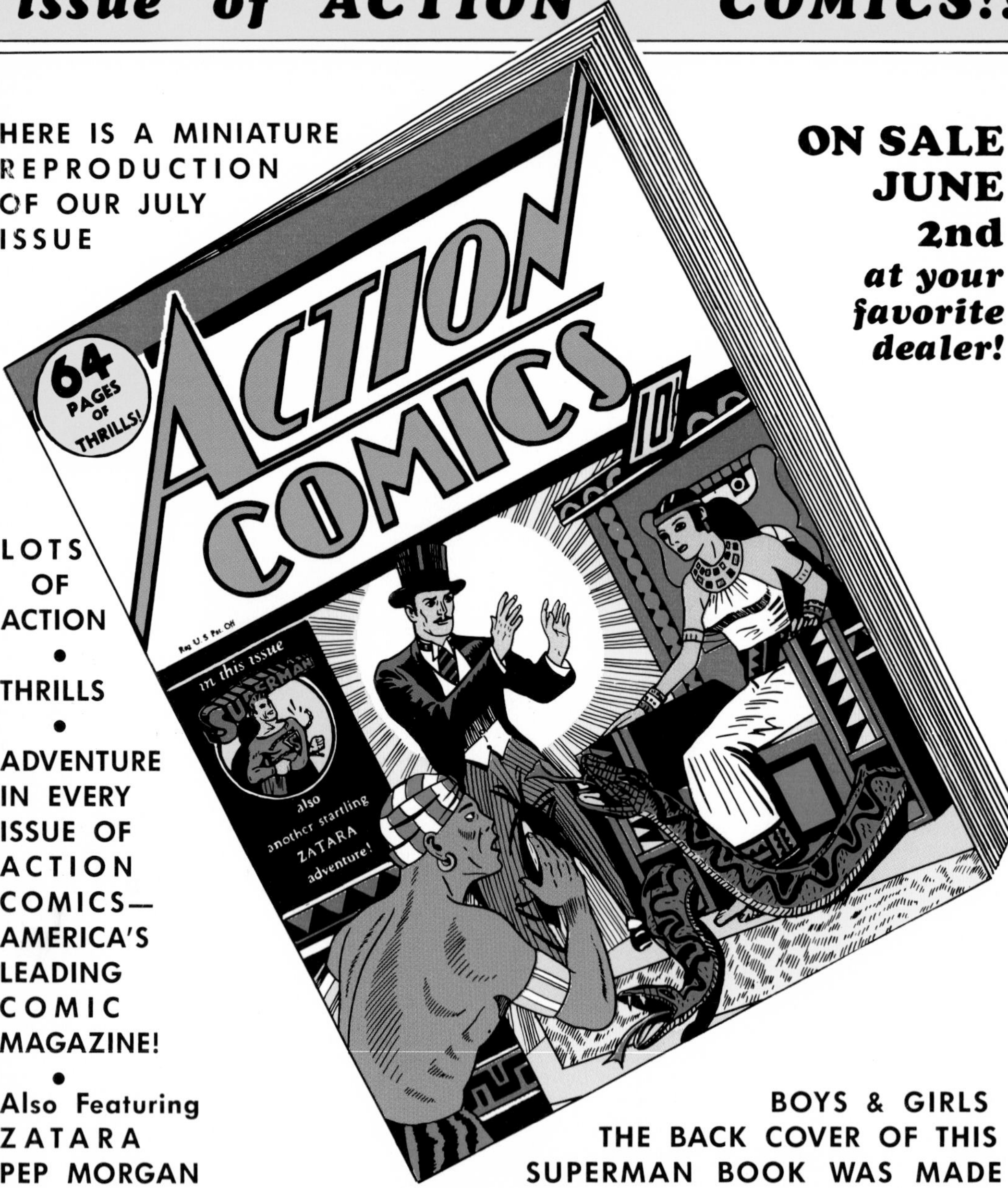
64 PAGES OF THRILLS!
ACTION COMICS 10¢
Reg. U.S. Pat. Off
in this issue SUPERMAN
also another startling ZATARA adventure!

ON SALE JUNE 2nd
at your favorite dealer!

LOTS OF ACTION
•
THRILLS
•
ADVENTURE IN EVERY ISSUE OF ACTION COMICS— AMERICA'S LEADING COMIC MAGAZINE!
•
Also Featuring
ZATARA
PEP MORGAN
TEX THOMSON
and many others!

BOYS & GIRLS THE BACK COVER OF THIS SUPERMAN BOOK WAS MADE ESPECIALLY FOR FRAMING! BE SURE TO CUT OFF ON THE DOTTED LINE!

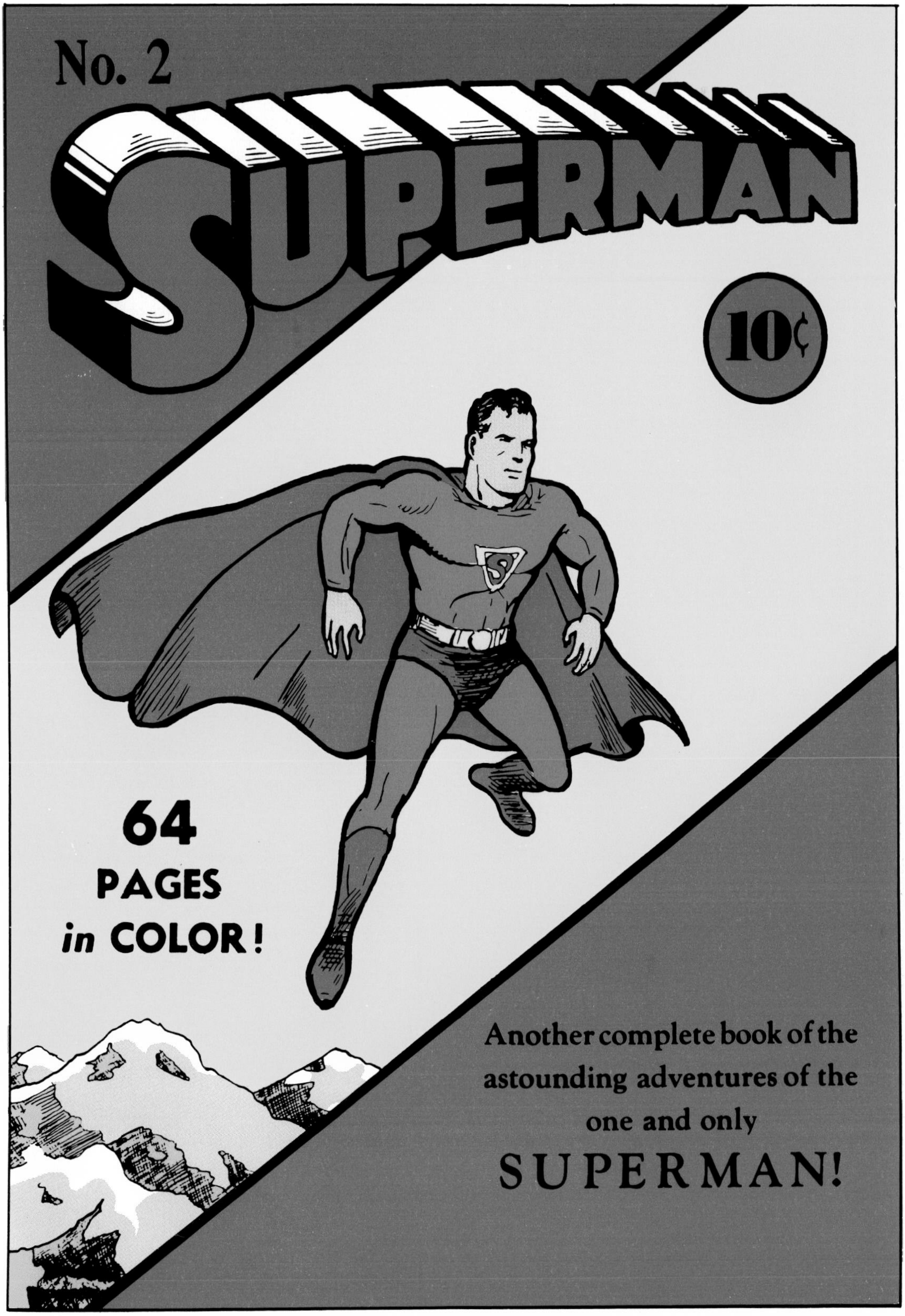
No. 2
SUPERMAN
10¢
64
PAGES
in COLOR!
Another complete book of the
astounding adventures of the
one and only
SUPERMAN!

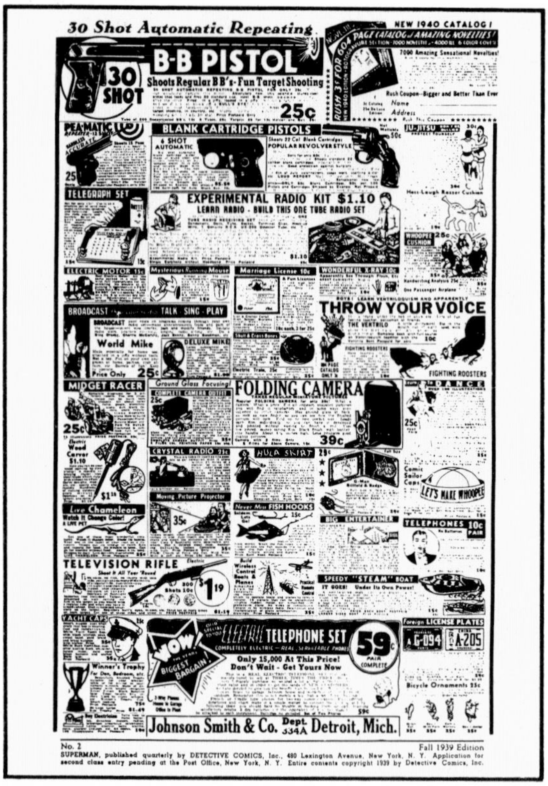
30 Shot Automatic Repeating
B-B PISTOL
30 SHOT
Shoots Regular BB's-Fun Target Shooting
25c
NEW 1940 CATALOG!
RUSH 3c FOR 604 PAGE CATALOG of AMAZING NOVELTIES
BLANK CARTRIDGE PISTOLS
JU-JITSU
TELEGRAPH SET
EXPERIMENTAL RADIO KIT $1.10
LEARN RADIO - BUILD THIS ONE TUBE RADIO SET
WHOOPEE CUSHION
ELECTRIC MOTOR
Marriage License 10c
WONDERFUL X-RAY 10c
BROADCAST
TALK · SING · PLAY
World Mike
THROW YOUR VOICE
MIDGET RACER
FOLDING CAMERA
DANCE
CRYSTAL RADIO
HULA SKIRT
LET'S MAKE WHOOPEE
Live Chameleon
Never Miss FISH HOOKS
BIG ENTERTAINER
TELEPHONES 10c
TELEVISION RIFLE
$1.19
SPEEDY "STEAM" BOAT
YACHT CAP
Foreign LICENSE PLATES
ELECTRIC TELEPHONE SET
WOW
59c
Only 15,000 At This Price!
Don't Wait - Get Yours Now
Bicycle Ornaments 25c
Johnson Smith & Co. Dept. 554A Detroit, Mich.
No. 2
Fall 1939 Edition
SUPERMAN, published quarterly by DETECTIVE COMICS, Inc., 480 Lexington Avenue, New York, N. Y. Application for second class entry pending at the Post Office, New York, N. Y. Entire contents copyright 1939 by Detective Comics, Inc.

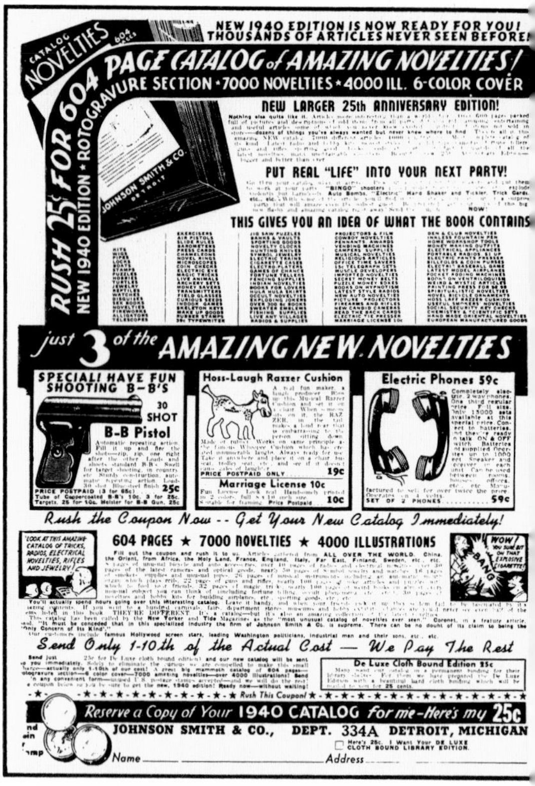
NEW 1940 EDITION IS NOW READY FOR YOU!
THOUSANDS OF ARTICLES NEVER SEEN BEFORE!
CATALOG NOVELTIES
RUSH 25c FOR 604
NEW 1940 EDITION · ROTOGRAVURE SECTION · 7000 NOVELTIES · 4000 ILL. 6-COLOR COVER
PAGE CATALOG of AMAZING NOVELTIES!
NEW LARGER 25th ANNIVERSARY EDITION!
PUT REAL "LIFE" INTO YOUR NEXT PARTY!
THIS GIVES YOU AN IDEA OF WHAT THE BOOK CONTAINS
JOHNSON SMITH & CO. DETROIT
just 3 of the AMAZING NEW NOVELTIES
SPECIAL! HAVE FUN SHOOTING B-B'S
30 SHOT
B-B Pistol
PRICE POSTPAID 25c
Hoss-Laugh Razzer Cushion
19c
Marriage License 10c
10c
Electric Phones 59c
59c
Rush the Coupon Now -- Get Your New Catalog Immediately!
604 PAGES ★ 7000 NOVELTIES ★ 4000 ILLUSTRATIONS
WOW!
Send Only 1-10th of the Actual Cost — We Pay The Rest
De Luxe Cloth Bound Edition 25c
Rush This Coupon!
Reserve a Copy of Your 1940 CATALOG for me-Here's my 25c
JOHNSON SMITH & CO., DEPT. 334A DETROIT, MICHIGAN
Name
Address

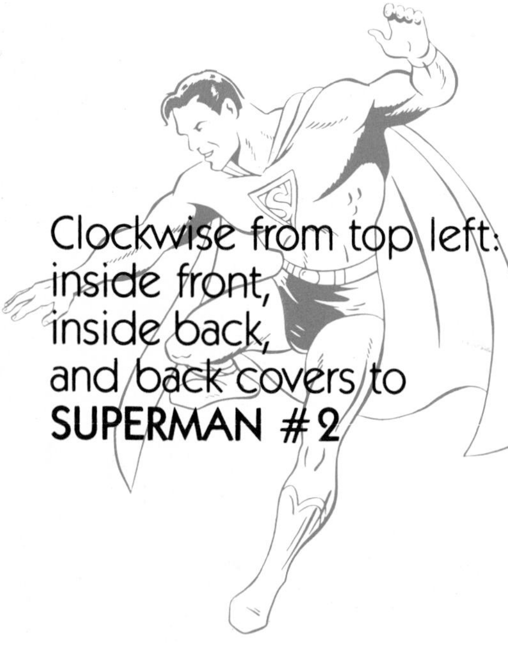

Clockwise from top left:
inside front,
inside back,
and back covers to
SUPERMAN #2

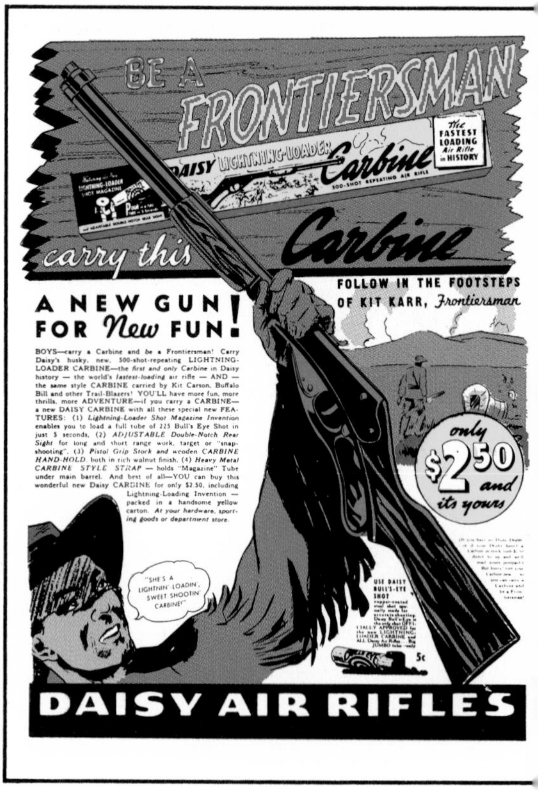
BE A
FRONTIERSMAN
DAISY LIGHTNING-LOADER Carbine
The FASTEST LOADING Air Rifle in HISTORY
carry this Carbine
FOLLOW IN THE FOOTSTEPS OF KIT KARR, Frontiersman
A NEW GUN FOR New FUN!
BOYS—carry a Carbine and be a Frontiersman! Carry Daisy's husky, new, 500-shot-repeating LIGHTNING-LOADER CARBINE—the first and only Carbine in Daisy history — the world's fastest-loading air rifle — AND — the same style CARBINE carried by Kit Carson, Buffalo Bill and other Trail-Blazers! YOU'LL have more fun, more thrills, more ADVENTURE—if you carry a CARBINE—a new DAISY CARBINE with all these special new FEATURES: (1) Lightning-Loader Shot Magazine Invention enables you to load a full tube of 225 Bull's Eye Shot in just 5 seconds, (2) ADJUSTABLE Double-Notch Rear Sight for long and short range work, target or "snap-shooting". (3) Pistol Grip Stock and wooden CARBINE HAND-HOLD, both in rich walnut finish, (4) Heavy Metal CARBINE STYLE STRAP — holds "Magazine" Tube under main barrel. And best of all—YOU can buy this wonderful new Daisy CARBINE for only $2.50, including Lightning-Loading Invention — packed in a handsome yellow carton. At your hardware, sporting goods or department store.
only $2.50 and its yours
"SHE'S A LIGHTNIN' LOADIN', SWEET-SHOOTIN' CARBINE!"
USE DAISY BULL'S-EYE SHOT
5c
DAISY AIR RIFLES

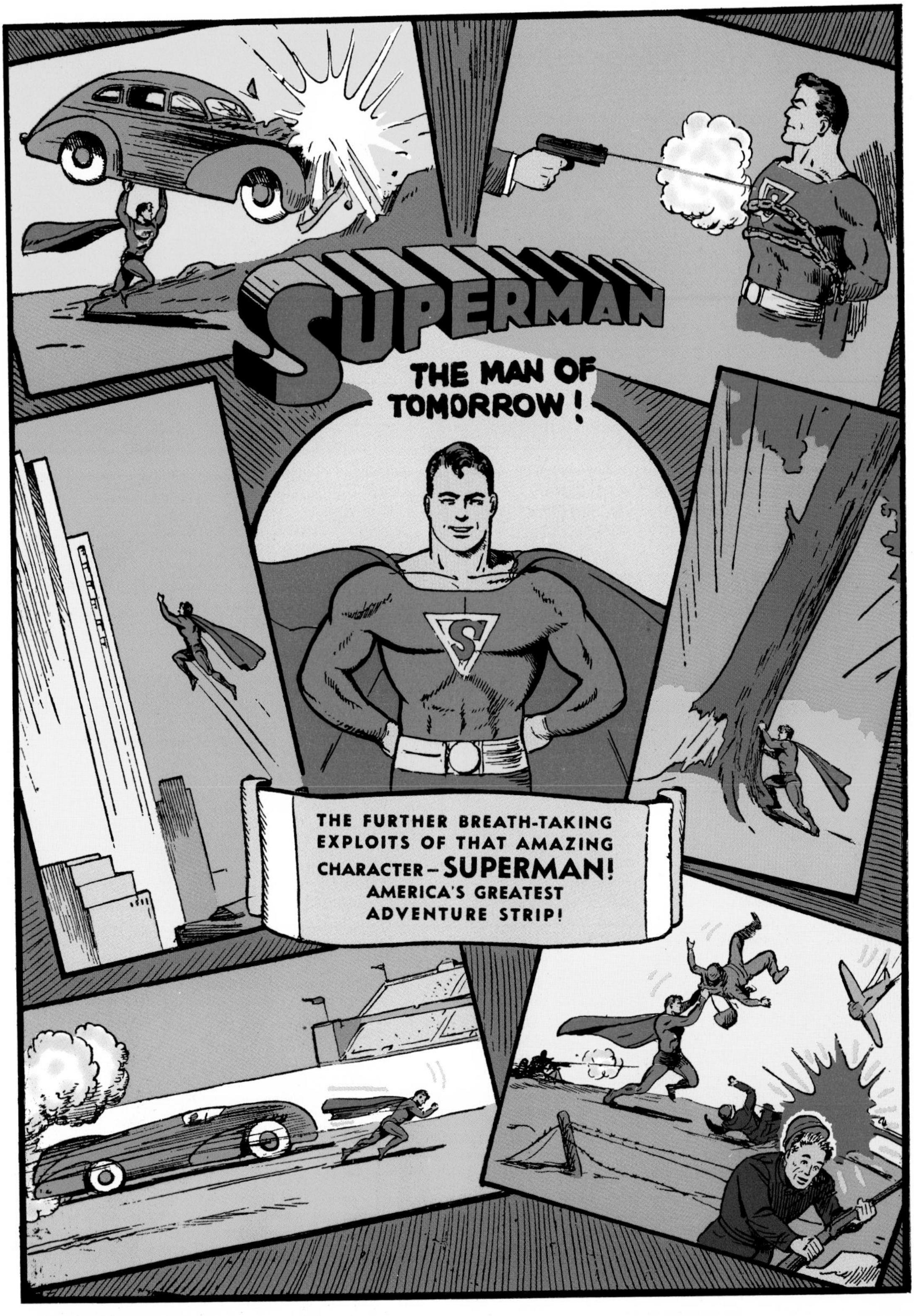
SUPERMAN
THE MAN OF TOMORROW!
THE FURTHER BREATH-TAKING EXPLOITS OF THAT AMAZING CHARACTER—SUPERMAN! AMERICA'S GREATEST ADVENTURE STRIP!

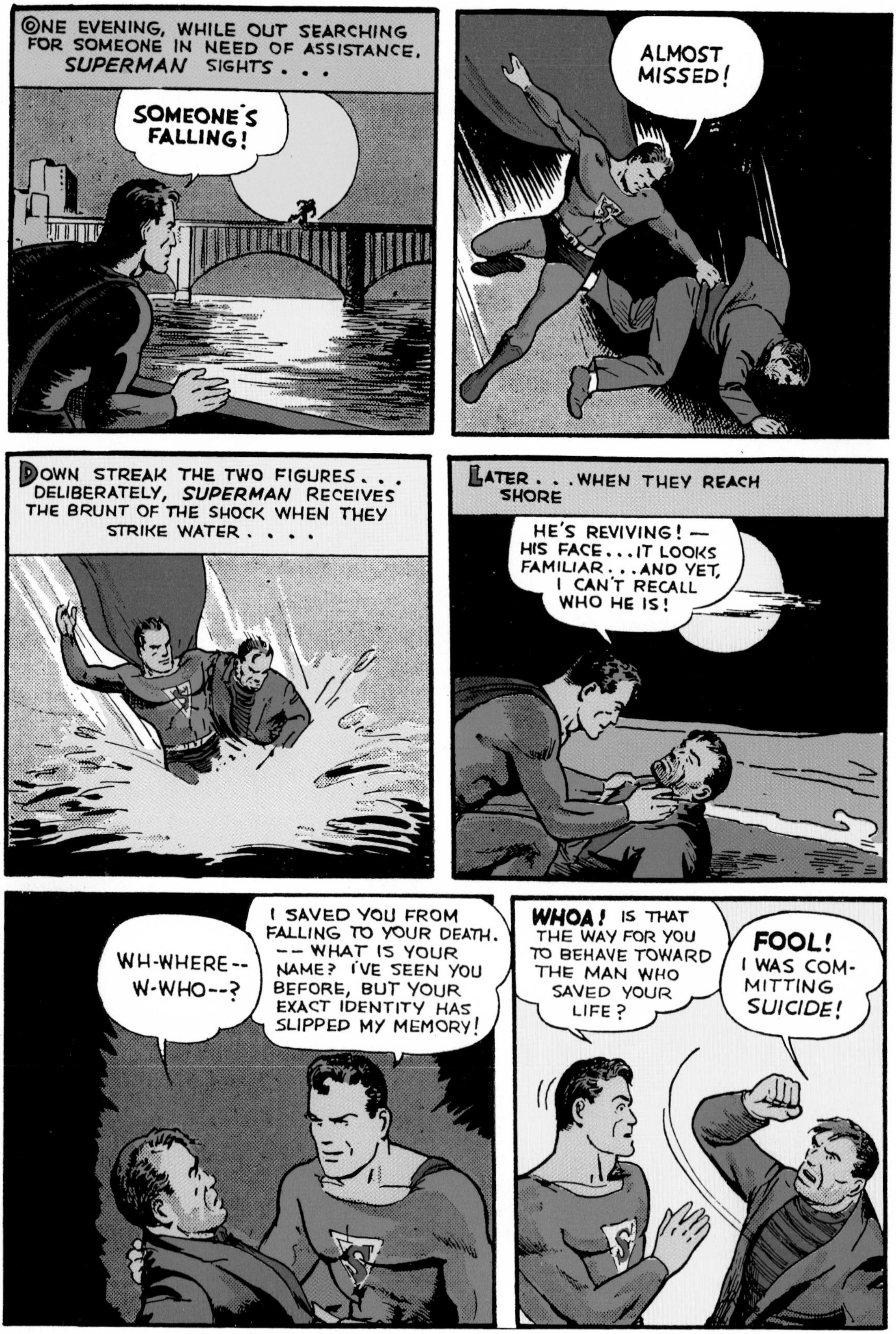
ONE EVENING, WHILE OUT SEARCHING FOR SOMEONE IN NEED OF ASSISTANCE, SUPERMAN SIGHTS . . .
SOMEONE'S FALLING!
ALMOST MISSED!
DOWN STREAK THE TWO FIGURES . . . DELIBERATELY, SUPERMAN RECEIVES THE BRUNT OF THE SHOCK WHEN THEY STRIKE WATER . . . .
LATER . . . WHEN THEY REACH SHORE
HE'S REVIVING! — HIS FACE . . . IT LOOKS FAMILIAR . . . AND YET, I CAN'T RECALL WHO HE IS!
WH-WHERE-- W-WHO--?
I SAVED YOU FROM FALLING TO YOUR DEATH. -- WHAT IS YOUR NAME? I'VE SEEN YOU BEFORE, BUT YOUR EXACT IDENTITY HAS SLIPPED MY MEMORY!
WHOA! IS THAT THE WAY FOR YOU TO BEHAVE TOWARD THE MAN WHO SAVED YOUR LIFE?
FOOL! I WAS COMMITTING SUICIDE!

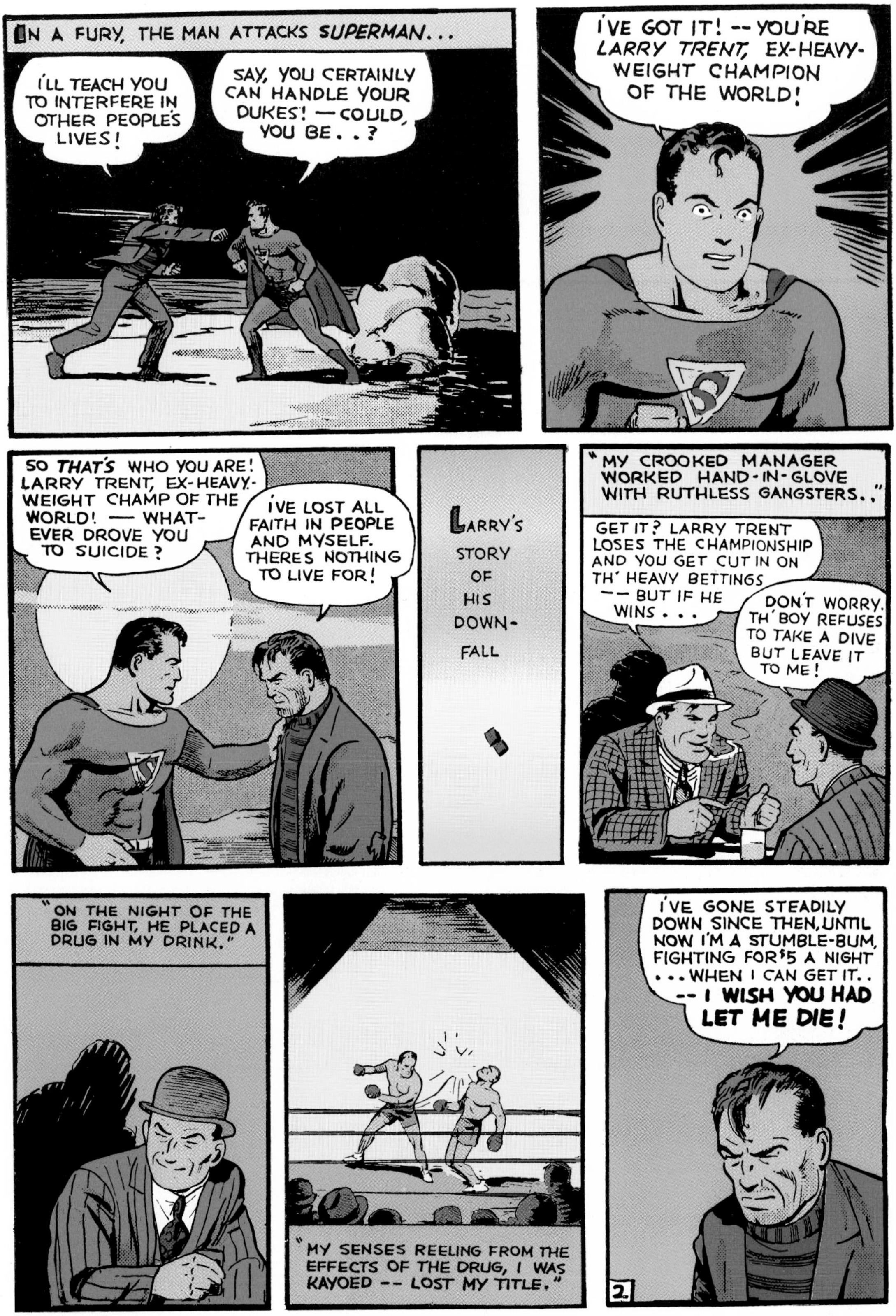
IN A FURY, THE MAN ATTACKS SUPERMAN...
I'LL TEACH YOU TO INTERFERE IN OTHER PEOPLE'S LIVES!
SAY, YOU CERTAINLY CAN HANDLE YOUR DUKES! —COULD, YOU BE..?
I'VE GOT IT! --YOU'RE LARRY TRENT, EX-HEAVY-WEIGHT CHAMPION OF THE WORLD!
SO THAT'S WHO YOU ARE! LARRY TRENT, EX-HEAVY-WEIGHT CHAMP OF THE WORLD! — WHATEVER DROVE YOU TO SUICIDE?
I'VE LOST ALL FAITH IN PEOPLE AND MYSELF. THERES NOTHING TO LIVE FOR!
LARRY'S STORY OF HIS DOWNFALL
"MY CROOKED MANAGER WORKED HAND-IN-GLOVE WITH RUTHLESS GANGSTERS.."
GET IT? LARRY TRENT LOSES THE CHAMPIONSHIP AND YOU GET CUT IN ON TH' HEAVY BETTINGS -- BUT IF HE WINS...
DON'T WORRY. TH' BOY REFUSES TO TAKE A DIVE BUT LEAVE IT TO ME!
"ON THE NIGHT OF THE BIG FIGHT, HE PLACED A DRUG IN MY DRINK."
"MY SENSES REELING FROM THE EFFECTS OF THE DRUG, I WAS KAYOED -- LOST MY TITLE."
I'VE GONE STEADILY DOWN SINCE THEN, UNTIL NOW I'M A STUMBLE-BUM, FIGHTING FOR $5 A NIGHT ...WHEN I CAN GET IT.. -- I WISH YOU HAD LET ME DIE!
2

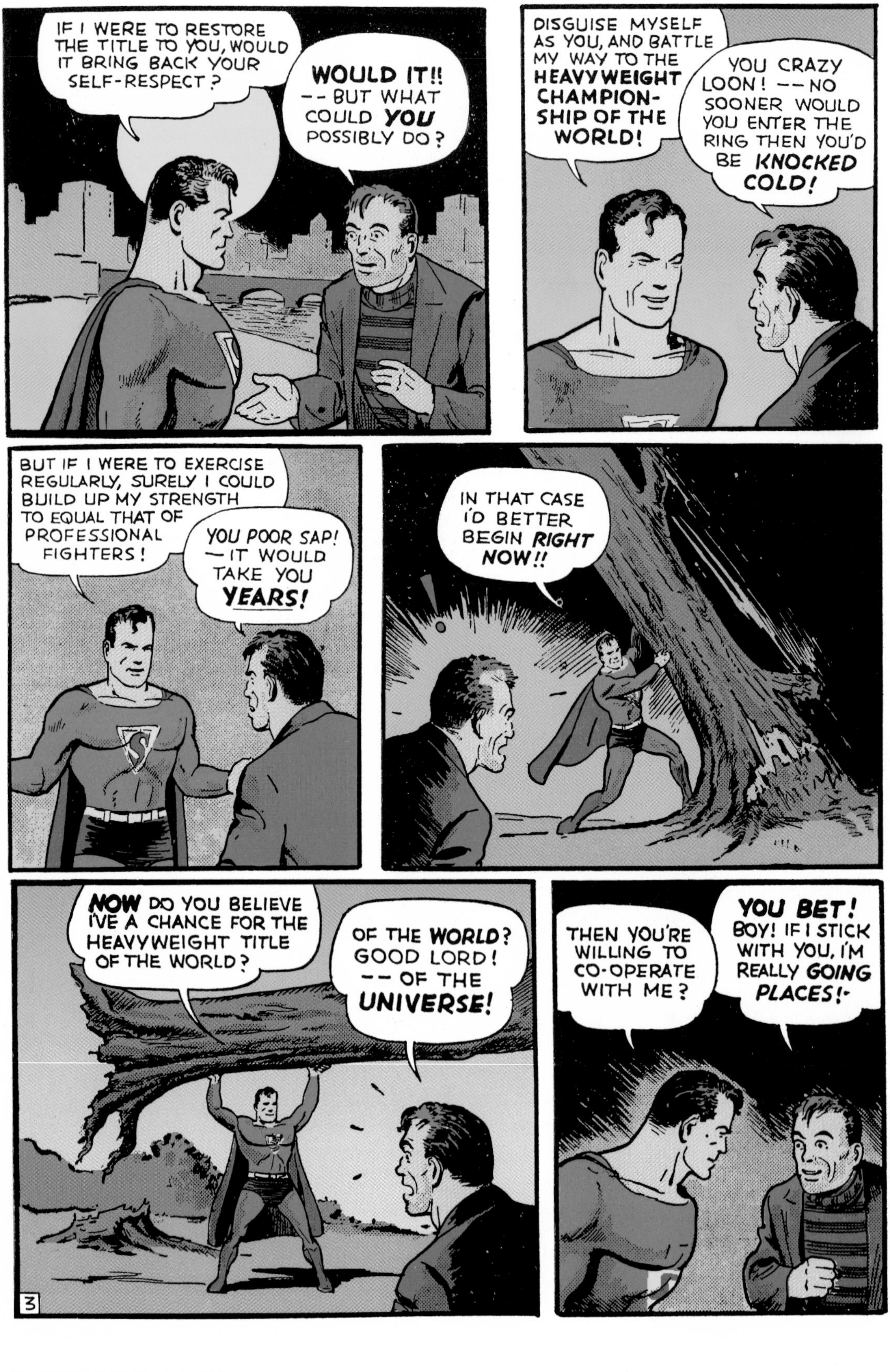
IF I WERE TO RESTORE THE TITLE TO YOU, WOULD IT BRING BACK YOUR SELF-RESPECT?
WOULD IT!! -- BUT WHAT COULD YOU POSSIBLY DO?
DISGUISE MYSELF AS YOU, AND BATTLE MY WAY TO THE HEAVYWEIGHT CHAMPIONSHIP OF THE WORLD!
YOU CRAZY LOON! -- NO SOONER WOULD YOU ENTER THE RING THEN YOU'D BE KNOCKED COLD!
BUT IF I WERE TO EXERCISE REGULARLY, SURELY I COULD BUILD UP MY STRENGTH TO EQUAL THAT OF PROFESSIONAL FIGHTERS!
YOU POOR SAP! —IT WOULD TAKE YOU YEARS!
IN THAT CASE I'D BETTER BEGIN RIGHT NOW!!
NOW DO YOU BELIEVE I'VE A CHANCE FOR THE HEAVYWEIGHT TITLE OF THE WORLD?
OF THE WORLD? GOOD LORD! -- OF THE UNIVERSE!
3
THEN YOU'RE WILLING TO CO-OPERATE WITH ME?
YOU BET! BOY! IF I STICK WITH YOU, I'M REALLY GOING PLACES!-

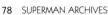

HEY! WHAT TH'—!

— DON'T BE ALARMED!

WE'RE GOING PLACES, ALL RIGHT, LARRY, BUT SHOOTING JUST A LITTLE HIGHER THAN YOU EXPECTED!

DOWN STREAKS **SUPERMAN** TOWARD THE WINDOW-SILL OF AN APARTMENT HE HAS RENTED FOR EMERGENCIES . . .

THIS IS WHERE YOU'LL STAY FOR THE NEXT SEVERAL MONTHS!

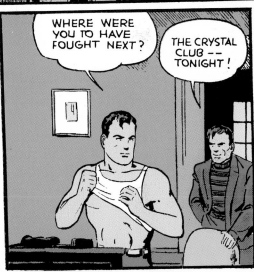

WHERE WERE YOU TO HAVE FOUGHT NEXT?

THE CRYSTAL CLUB —— TONIGHT!

GIVE ME SOME POINTERS ABOUT THE PEOPLE YOU KNOW!

APPLYING MAKE-UP, SUPERMAN EXPERTLY ALTERS THE APPEARANCE OF HIS FEATURES

SHORTLY AFTER

GOOD GOSH! — YOU'RE **ME**!

WRONG! YOU'RE NOT LOOKING AT LARRY TRENT, EX-CHAMP . . . BUT AT LARRY TRENT, THE COMING **CHAMPION OF THE WORLD!**

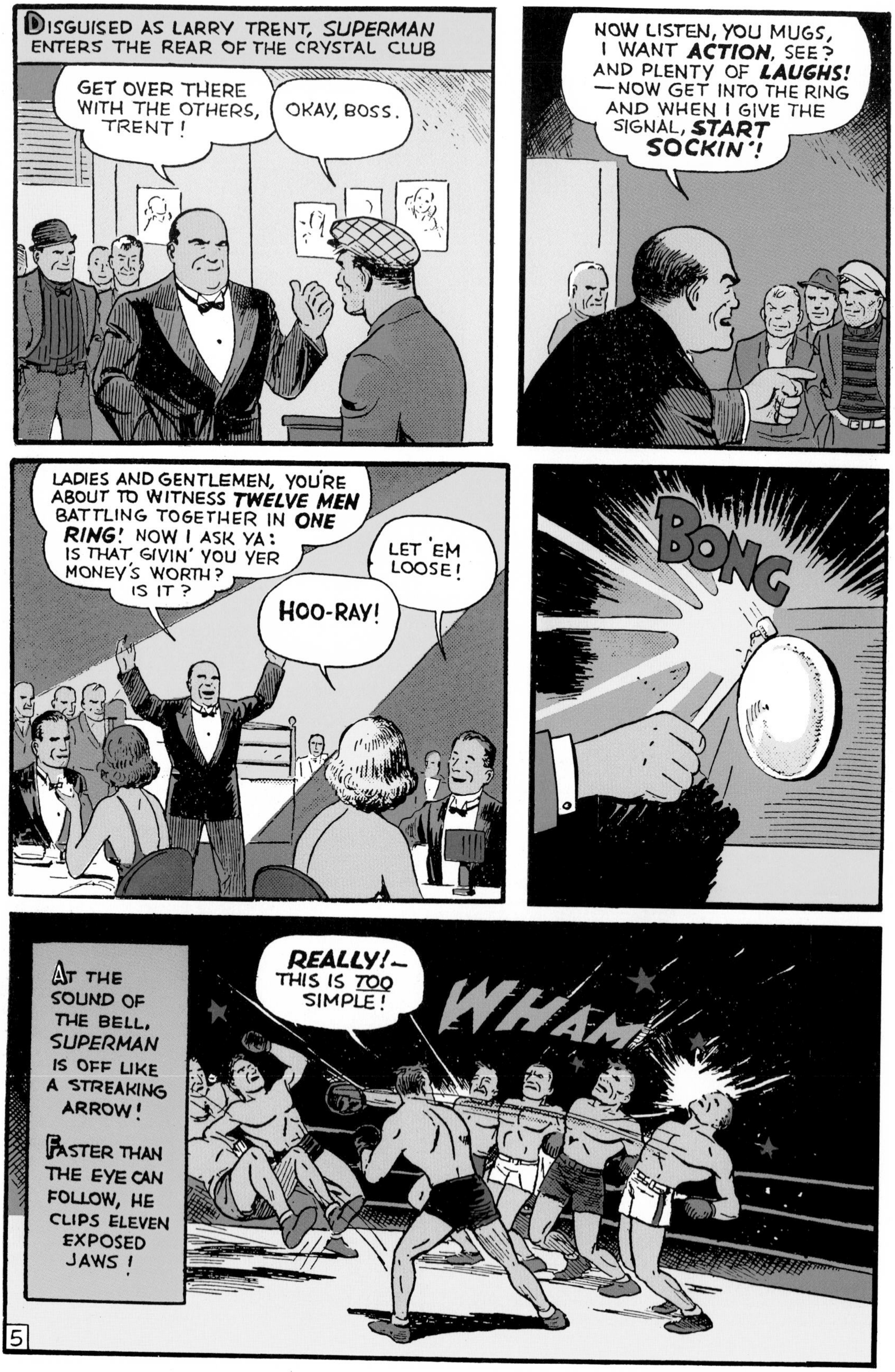
DISGUISED AS LARRY TRENT, SUPERMAN ENTERS THE REAR OF THE CRYSTAL CLUB
GET OVER THERE WITH THE OTHERS, TRENT!
OKAY, BOSS.
NOW LISTEN, YOU MUGS, I WANT ACTION, SEE? AND PLENTY OF LAUGHS! —NOW GET INTO THE RING AND WHEN I GIVE THE SIGNAL, START SOCKIN'!
LADIES AND GENTLEMEN, YOU'RE ABOUT TO WITNESS TWELVE MEN BATTLING TOGETHER IN ONE RING! NOW I ASK YA: IS THAT GIVIN' YOU YER MONEY'S WORTH? IS IT?
LET 'EM LOOSE!
HOO-RAY!
BONG
AT THE SOUND OF THE BELL, SUPERMAN IS OFF LIKE A STREAKING ARROW!
FASTER THAN THE EYE CAN FOLLOW, HE CLIPS ELEVEN EXPOSED JAWS!
REALLY!— THIS IS TOO SIMPLE!
WHAM
5

AND WITHIN THE SPACE OF **ONE SECOND** . . .

? !

. . . IS THE ONLY CONSCIOUS BATTLER LEFT IN THE RING!

GOT ANY MORE?

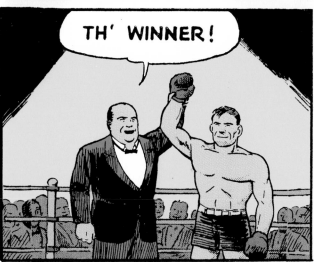

TH' WINNER!

JUMPIN' JITTERBUGS, LARRY, SEE JOCK KANE, TH' FAMOUS FIGHT PROMOTER AN' SAY I SENT YOU! -- KID, YOU'LL BE A **SENSATION** AGAIN!

THANKS.

LATER . . . THE MAN OF STEEL'S APARTMENT -- AS *SUPERMAN* SPARS WITH LARRY TRENT . . .

AND SO I WAS TOLD TO VISIT JOCK KANE.

KANE? -- EVER SINCE I LOST THE TITLE, I'VE BEEN THAT GUY'S PET HATE!

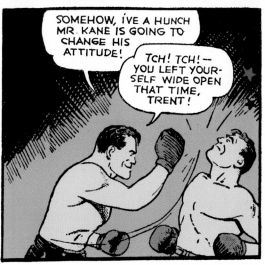

SOMEHOW, I'VE A HUNCH MR. KANE IS GOING TO CHANGE HIS ATTITUDE!

TCH! TCH! -- YOU LEFT YOURSELF WIDE OPEN THAT TIME, TRENT!

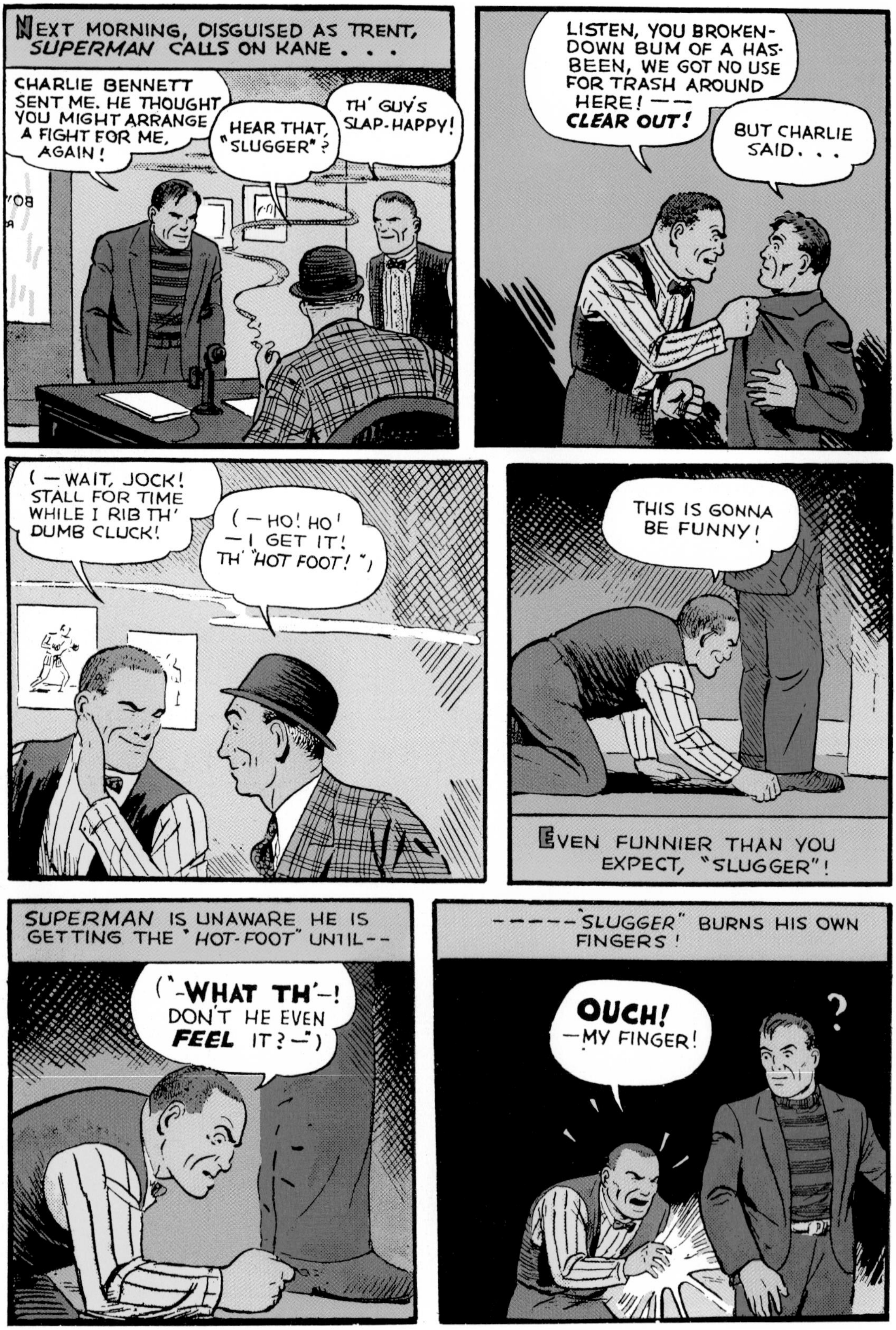
NEXT MORNING, DISGUISED AS TRENT, SUPERMAN CALLS ON KANE . . .
CHARLIE BENNETT SENT ME. HE THOUGHT YOU MIGHT ARRANGE A FIGHT FOR ME, AGAIN!
HEAR THAT, "SLUGGER"?
TH' GUY'S SLAP-HAPPY!
LISTEN, YOU BROKEN-DOWN BUM OF A HAS-BEEN, WE GOT NO USE FOR TRASH AROUND HERE! — — CLEAR OUT!
BUT CHARLIE SAID. . .
(— WAIT, JOCK! STALL FOR TIME WHILE I RIB TH' DUMB CLUCK!
(— HO! HO! — I GET IT! TH' "HOT FOOT!")
THIS IS GONNA BE FUNNY!
EVEN FUNNIER THAN YOU EXPECT, "SLUGGER"!
SUPERMAN IS UNAWARE HE IS GETTING THE "HOT-FOOT" UNTIL--
("-WHAT TH'-! DON'T HE EVEN FEEL IT?-")
-----"SLUGGER" BURNS HIS OWN FINGERS!
OUCH! —MY FINGER!
?

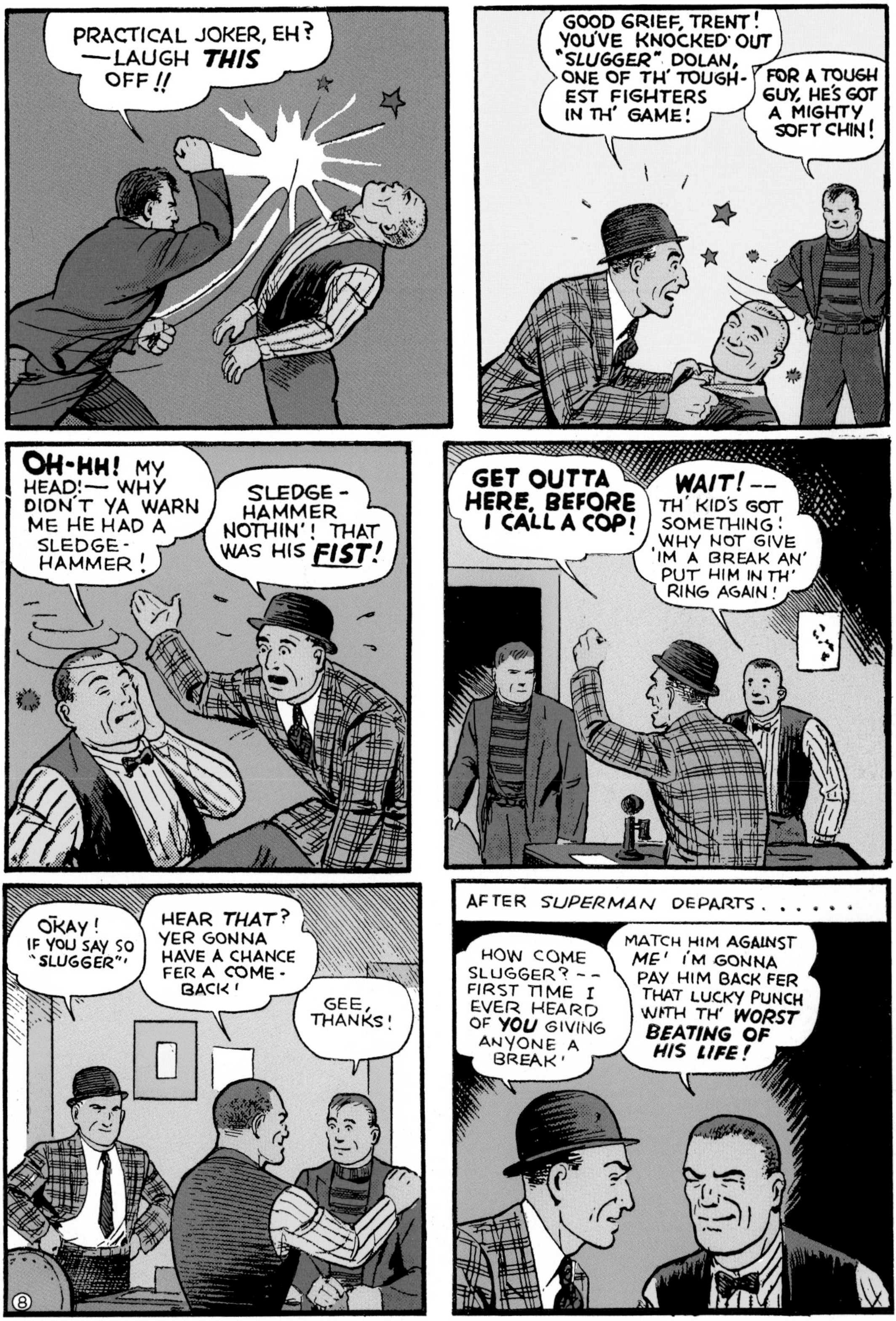
PRACTICAL JOKER, EH? —LAUGH THIS OFF!!
GOOD GRIEF, TRENT! YOU'VE KNOCKED OUT "SLUGGER" DOLAN, ONE OF TH' TOUGH-EST FIGHTERS IN TH' GAME!
FOR A TOUGH GUY, HE'S GOT A MIGHTY SOFT CHIN!
OH-HH! MY HEAD!— WHY DIDN'T YA WARN ME HE HAD A SLEDGE-HAMMER!
SLEDGE-HAMMER NOTHIN'! THAT WAS HIS FIST!
GET OUTTA HERE, BEFORE I CALL A COP!
WAIT!-- TH' KID'S GOT SOMETHING! WHY NOT GIVE 'IM A BREAK AN' PUT HIM IN TH' RING AGAIN!
OKAY! IF YOU SAY SO "SLUGGER"!
HEAR THAT? YER GONNA HAVE A CHANCE FER A COME-BACK!
GEE, THANKS!
8
AFTER SUPERMAN DEPARTS......
HOW COME SLUGGER? -- FIRST TIME I EVER HEARD OF YOU GIVING ANYONE A BREAK!
MATCH HIM AGAINST ME! I'M GONNA PAY HIM BACK FER THAT LUCKY PUNCH WITH TH' WORST BEATING OF HIS LIFE!

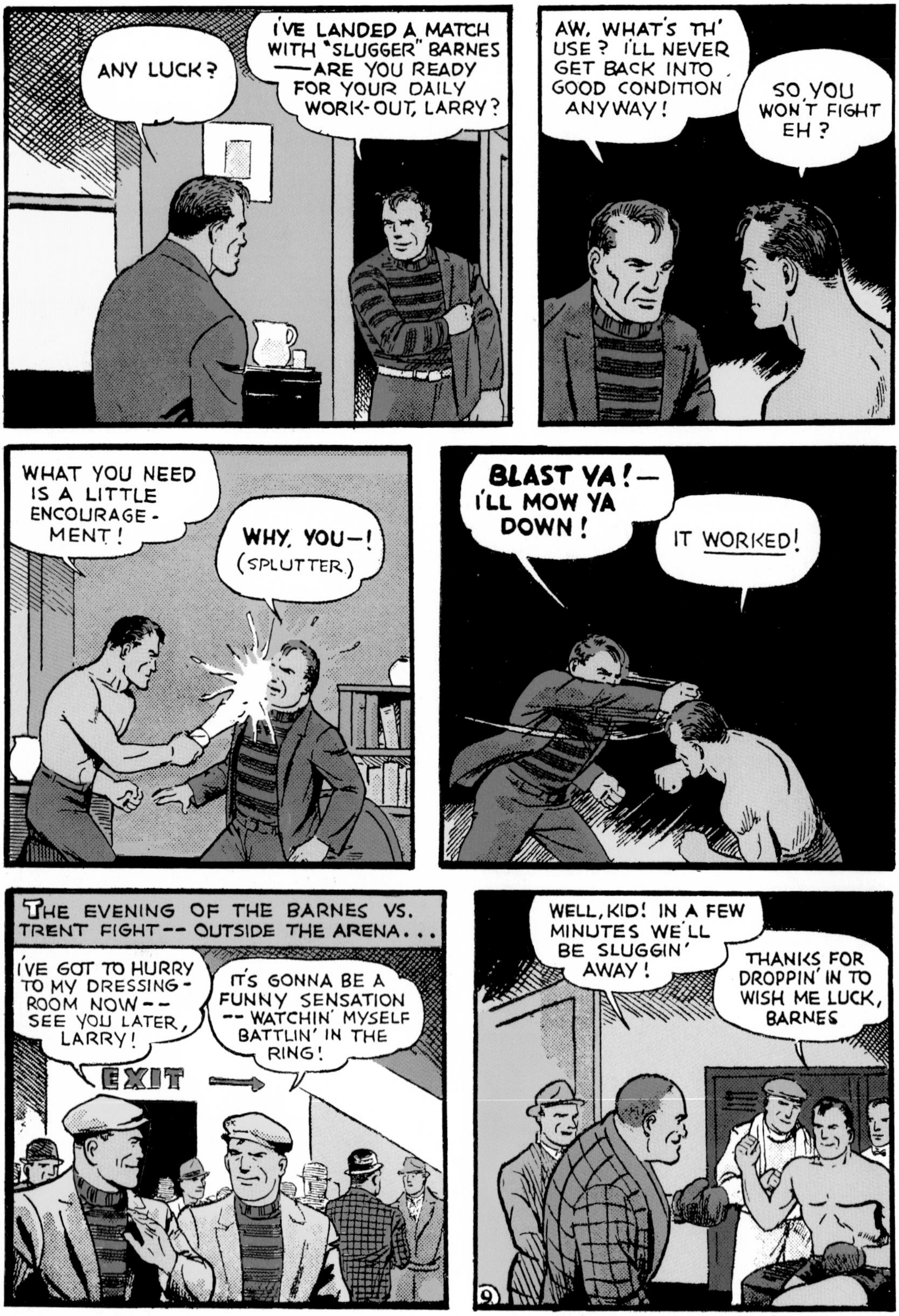
ANY LUCK?
I'VE LANDED A MATCH WITH "SLUGGER" BARNES — ARE YOU READY FOR YOUR DAILY WORK-OUT, LARRY?
AW, WHAT'S TH' USE? I'LL NEVER GET BACK INTO GOOD CONDITION ANYWAY!
SO, YOU WON'T FIGHT EH?
WHAT YOU NEED IS A LITTLE ENCOURAGE-MENT!
WHY, YOU—! (SPLUTTER)
BLAST YA!— I'LL MOW YA DOWN!
IT WORKED!
THE EVENING OF THE BARNES VS. TRENT FIGHT -- OUTSIDE THE ARENA...
I'VE GOT TO HURRY TO MY DRESSING-ROOM NOW -- SEE YOU LATER, LARRY!
IT'S GONNA BE A FUNNY SENSATION -- WATCHIN' MYSELF BATTLIN' IN THE RING!
EXIT
WELL, KID! IN A FEW MINUTES WE'LL BE SLUGGIN' AWAY!
THANKS FOR DROPPIN' IN TO WISH ME LUCK, BARNES
9

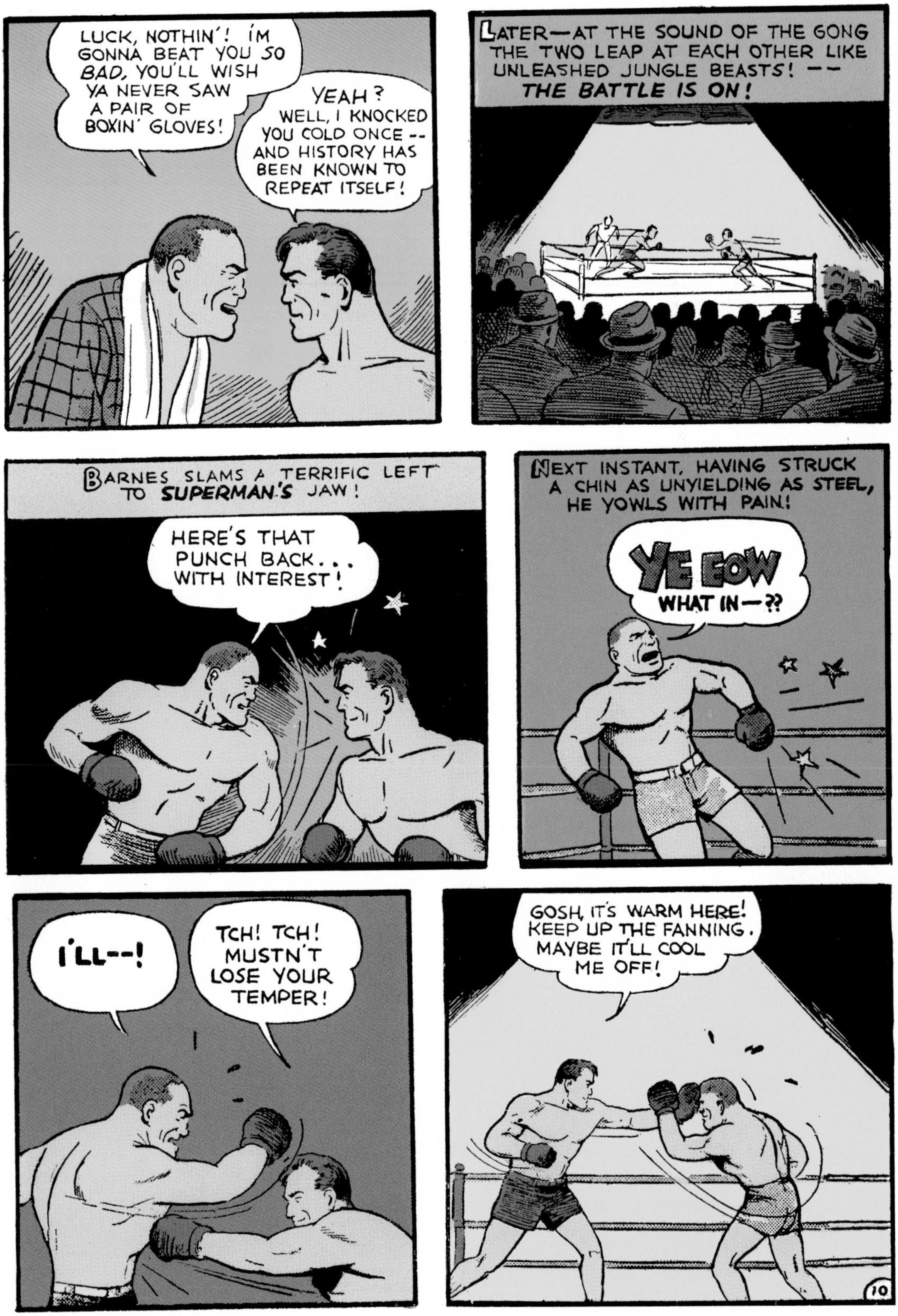
LUCK, NOTHIN'! I'M GONNA BEAT YOU SO BAD, YOU'LL WISH YA NEVER SAW A PAIR OF BOXIN' GLOVES!
YEAH? WELL, I KNOCKED YOU COLD ONCE -- AND HISTORY HAS BEEN KNOWN TO REPEAT ITSELF!
LATER—AT THE SOUND OF THE GONG THE TWO LEAP AT EACH OTHER LIKE UNLEASHED JUNGLE BEASTS! -- THE BATTLE IS ON!
BARNES SLAMS A TERRIFIC LEFT TO SUPERMAN'S JAW!
HERE'S THAT PUNCH BACK... WITH INTEREST!
NEXT INSTANT, HAVING STRUCK A CHIN AS UNYIELDING AS STEEL, HE YOWLS WITH PAIN!
YE EOW
WHAT IN—??
I'LL--!
TCH! TCH! MUSTN'T LOSE YOUR TEMPER!
GOSH, IT'S WARM HERE! KEEP UP THE FANNING. MAYBE IT'LL COOL ME OFF!
10

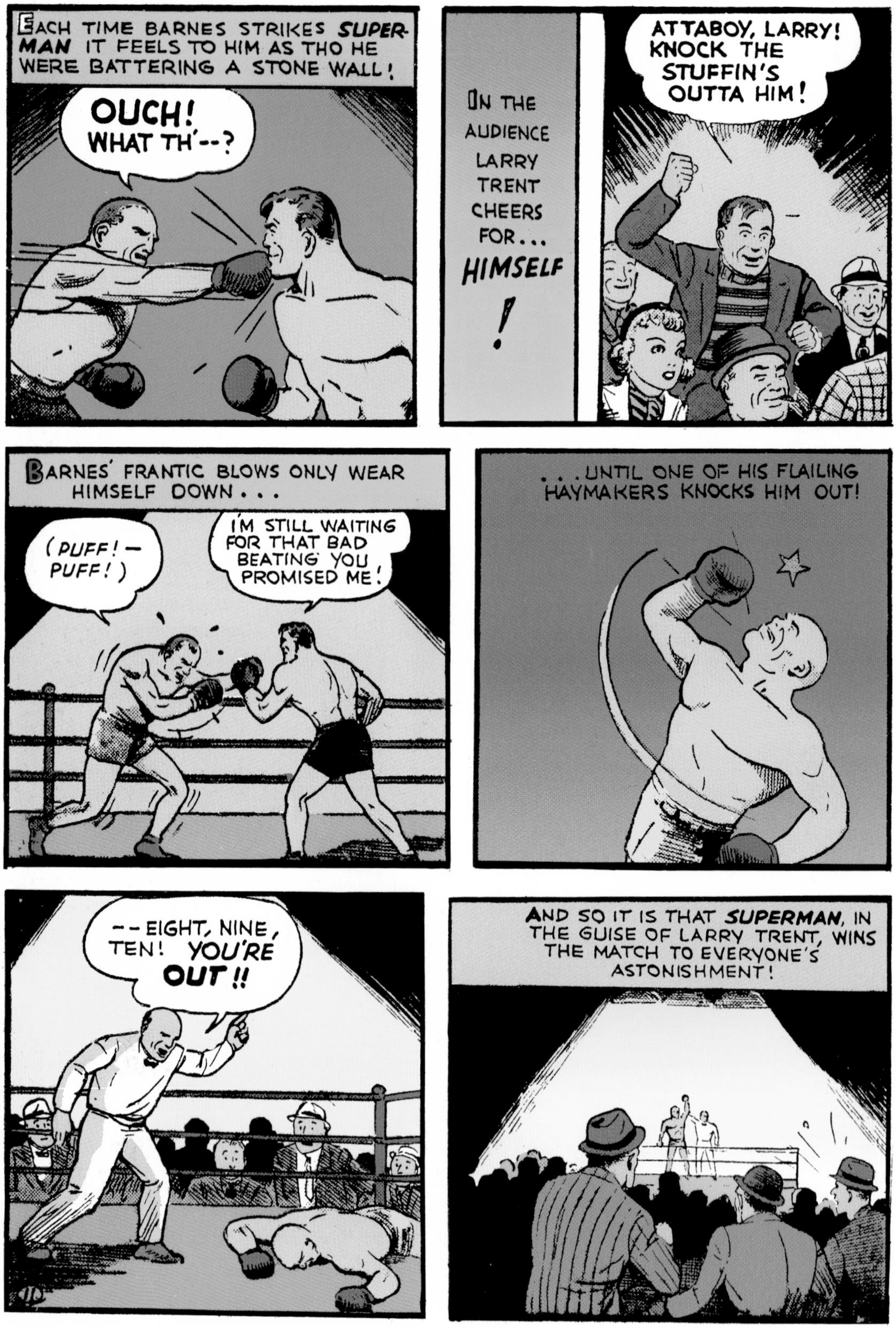
EACH TIME BARNES STRIKES SUPERMAN IT FEELS TO HIM AS THO HE WERE BATTERING A STONE WALL!
OUCH! WHAT TH'--?
IN THE AUDIENCE LARRY TRENT CHEERS FOR... HIMSELF!
ATTABOY, LARRY! KNOCK THE STUFFIN'S OUTTA HIM!
BARNES' FRANTIC BLOWS ONLY WEAR HIMSELF DOWN...
(PUFF! — PUFF!)
I'M STILL WAITING FOR THAT BAD BEATING YOU PROMISED ME!
...UNTIL ONE OF HIS FLAILING HAYMAKERS KNOCKS HIM OUT!
--EIGHT, NINE, TEN! YOU'RE OUT!!
AND SO IT IS THAT SUPERMAN, IN THE GUISE OF LARRY TRENT, WINS THE MATCH TO EVERYONE'S ASTONISHMENT!

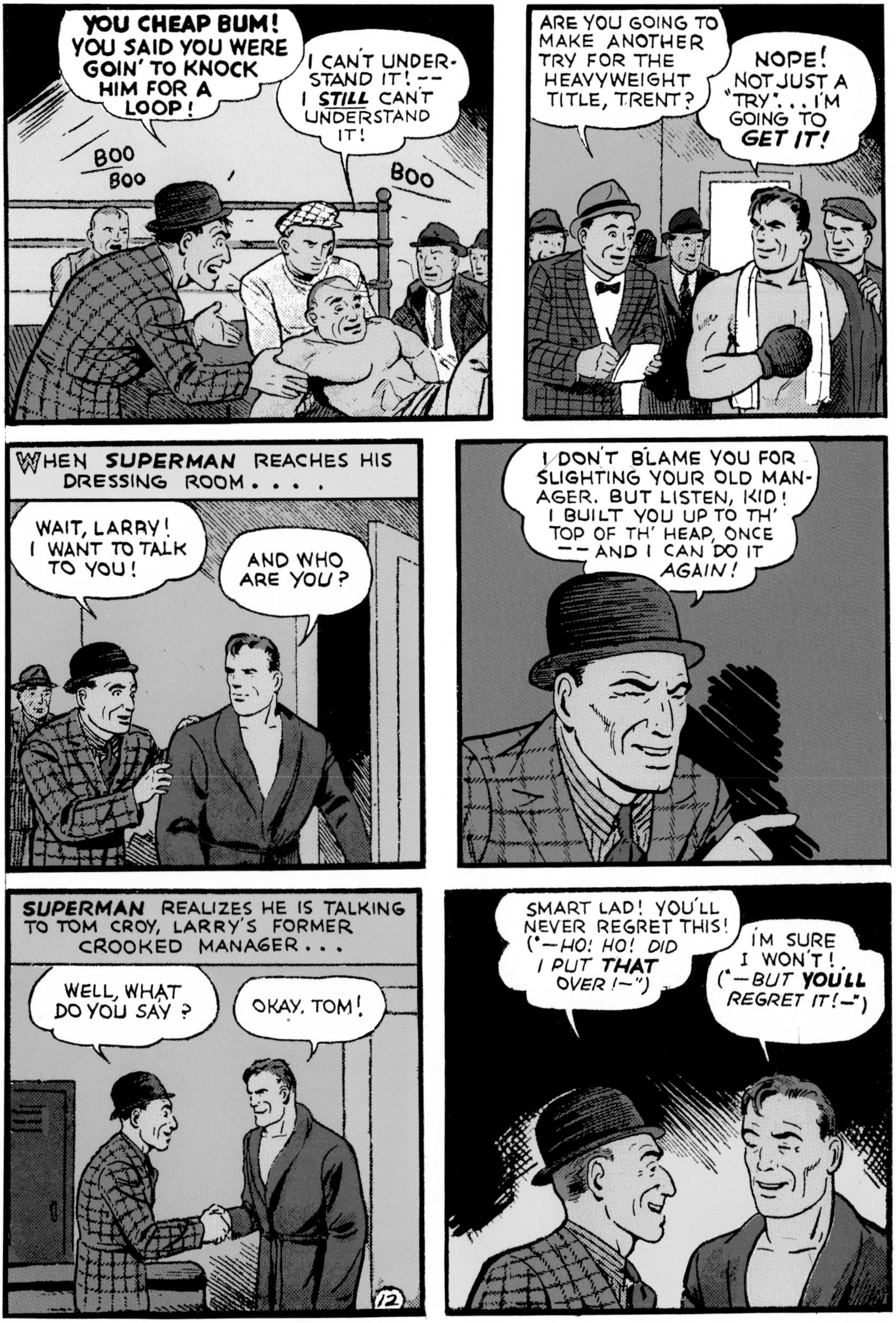
YOU CHEAP BUM! YOU SAID YOU WERE GOIN' TO KNOCK HIM FOR A LOOP!
I CAN'T UNDERSTAND IT! -- I STILL CAN'T UNDERSTAND IT!
BOO
BOO
BOO
ARE YOU GOING TO MAKE ANOTHER TRY FOR THE HEAVYWEIGHT TITLE, TRENT?
NOPE! NOT JUST A "TRY"... I'M GOING TO GET IT!
WHEN SUPERMAN REACHES HIS DRESSING ROOM....
WAIT, LARRY! I WANT TO TALK TO YOU!
AND WHO ARE YOU?
I DON'T BLAME YOU FOR SLIGHTING YOUR OLD MANAGER. BUT LISTEN, KID! I BUILT YOU UP TO TH' TOP OF TH' HEAP, ONCE -- AND I CAN DO IT AGAIN!
SUPERMAN REALIZES HE IS TALKING TO TOM CROY, LARRY'S FORMER CROOKED MANAGER...
WELL, WHAT DO YOU SAY?
OKAY, TOM!
12
SMART LAD! YOU'LL NEVER REGRET THIS! ("—HO! HO! DID I PUT THAT OVER!—")
I'M SURE I WON'T! ("—BUT YOU'LL REGRET IT!—")

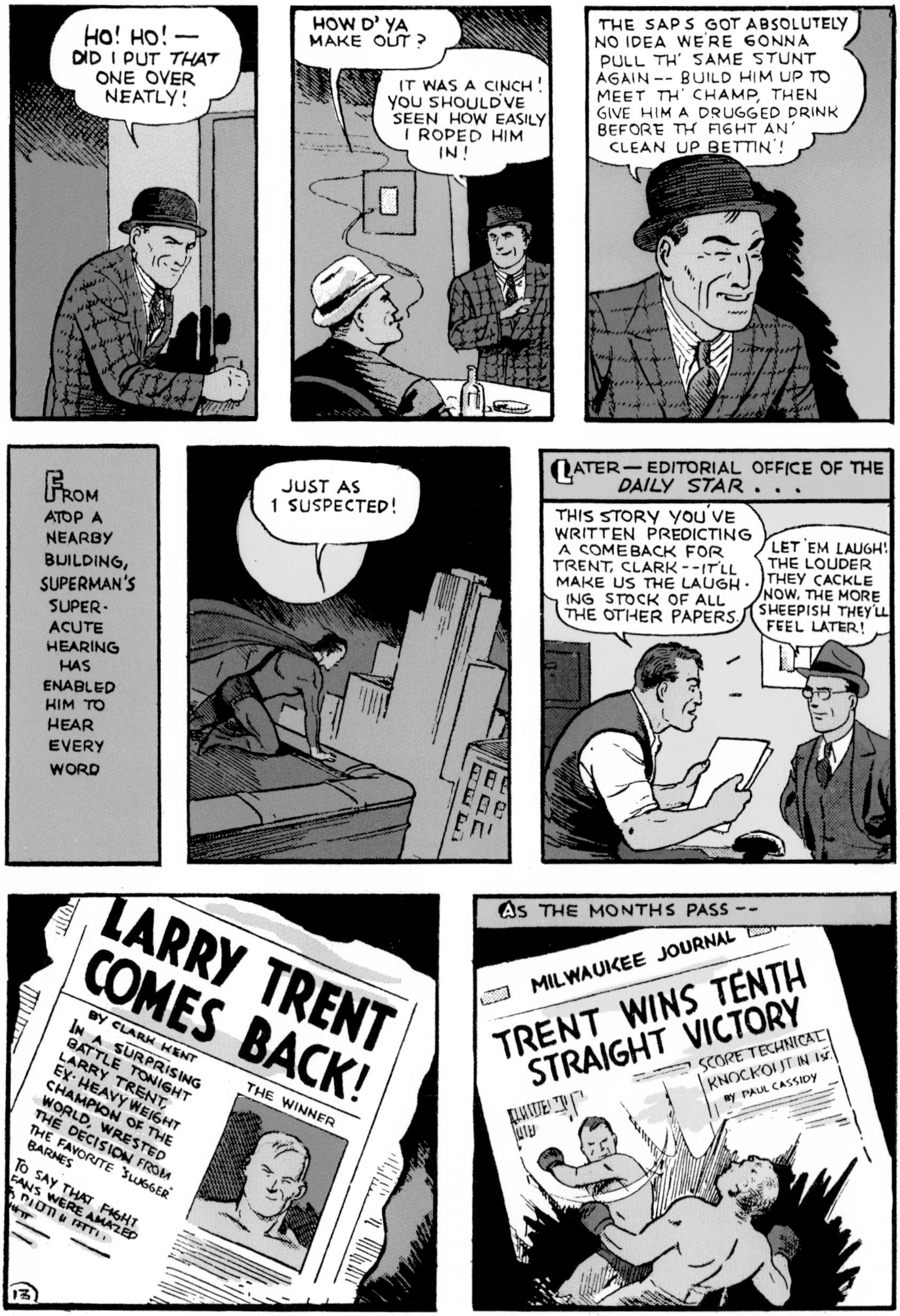
HO! HO! — DID I PUT *THAT* ONE OVER NEATLY!
HOW D' YA MAKE OUT?
IT WAS A CINCH! YOU SHOULD'VE SEEN HOW EASILY I ROPED HIM IN!
THE SAPS GOT ABSOLUTELY NO IDEA WE'RE GONNA PULL TH' SAME STUNT AGAIN -- BUILD HIM UP TO MEET TH' CHAMP, THEN GIVE HIM A DRUGGED DRINK BEFORE TH' FIGHT AN' CLEAN UP BETTIN'!
FROM ATOP A NEARBY BUILDING, SUPERMAN'S SUPER-ACUTE HEARING HAS ENABLED HIM TO HEAR EVERY WORD
JUST AS I SUSPECTED!
LATER — EDITORIAL OFFICE OF THE *DAILY STAR* . . .
THIS STORY YOU'VE WRITTEN PREDICTING A COMEBACK FOR TRENT, CLARK -- IT'LL MAKE US THE LAUGHING STOCK OF ALL THE OTHER PAPERS.
LET 'EM LAUGH! THE LOUDER THEY CACKLE NOW, THE MORE SHEEPISH THEY'LL FEEL LATER!
LARRY TRENT COMES BACK!
BY CLARK KENT
IN A SURPRISING BATTLE TONIGHT LARRY TRENT, EX-HEAVYWEIGHT CHAMPION OF THE WORLD, WRESTED THE DECISION FROM THE FAVORITE 'SLUGGER' BARNES
TO SAY THAT FIGHT FANS WERE AMAZED
THE WINNER
13
AS THE MONTHS PASS --
MILWAUKEE JOURNAL
TRENT WINS TENTH STRAIGHT VICTORY
SCORE TECHNICAL KNOCKOUT IN 1st.
BY PAUL CASSIDY

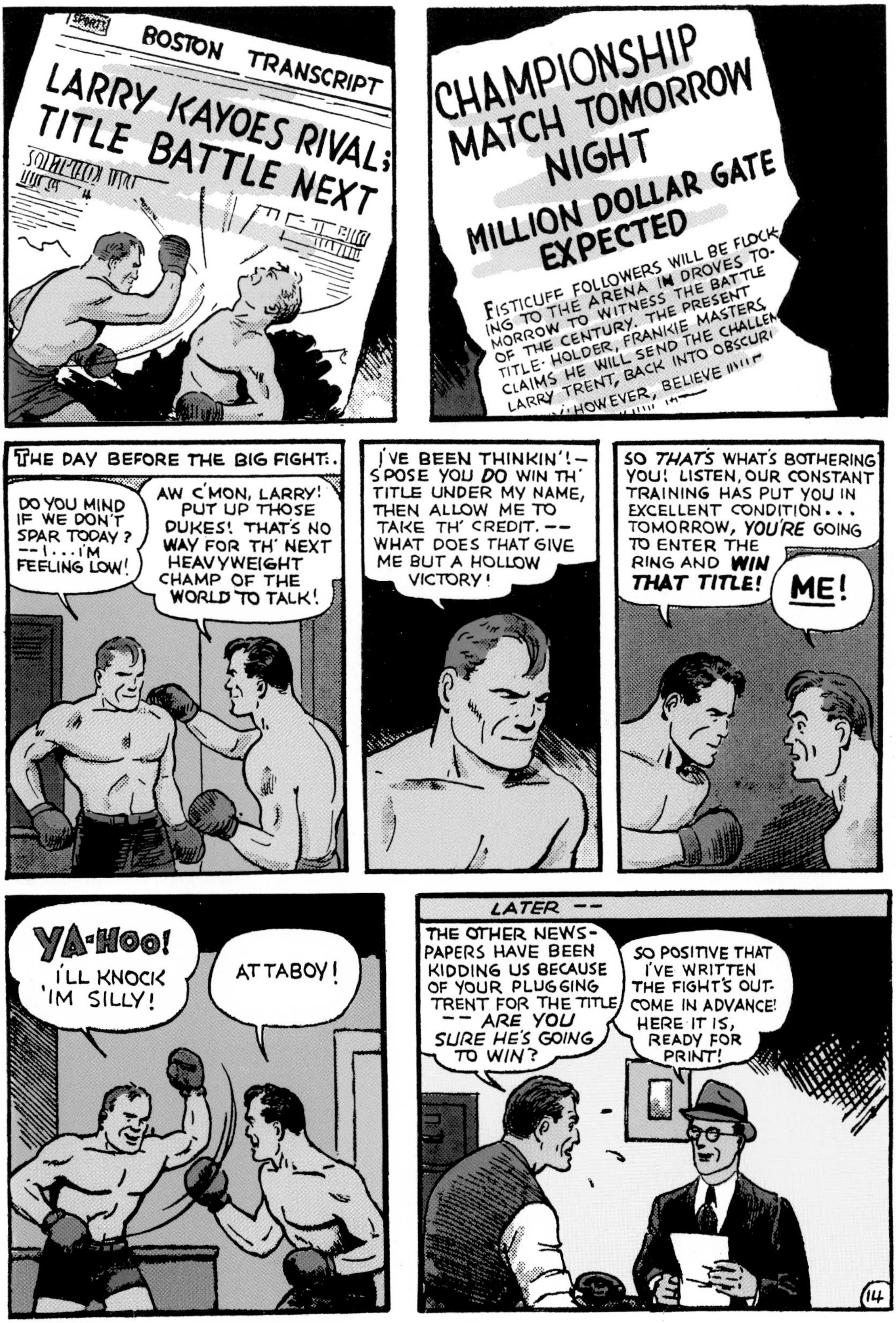
SPORTS
BOSTON TRANSCRIPT
LARRY KAYOES RIVAL; TITLE BATTLE NEXT
CHAMPIONSHIP MATCH TOMORROW NIGHT
MILLION DOLLAR GATE EXPECTED
FISTICUFF FOLLOWERS WILL BE FLOCK-ING TO THE ARENA IN DROVES TO-MORROW TO WITNESS THE BATTLE OF THE CENTURY. THE PRESENT TITLE HOLDER, FRANKIE MASTERS, CLAIMS HE WILL SEND THE CHALLEN LARRY TRENT, BACK INTO OBSCURI HOWEVER, BELIEVE
THE DAY BEFORE THE BIG FIGHT:.
DO YOU MIND IF WE DON'T SPAR TODAY? --I...I'M FEELING LOW!
AW C'MON, LARRY! PUT UP THOSE DUKES! THAT'S NO WAY FOR TH' NEXT HEAVYWEIGHT CHAMP OF THE WORLD TO TALK!
I'VE BEEN THINKIN'!-- S'POSE YOU DO WIN TH' TITLE UNDER MY NAME, THEN ALLOW ME TO TAKE TH' CREDIT.-- WHAT DOES THAT GIVE ME BUT A HOLLOW VICTORY!
SO THAT'S WHAT'S BOTHERING YOU! LISTEN, OUR CONSTANT TRAINING HAS PUT YOU IN EXCELLENT CONDITION... TOMORROW, YOU'RE GOING TO ENTER THE RING AND WIN THAT TITLE!
ME!
YA-HOO! I'LL KNOCK 'IM SILLY!
ATTABOY!
LATER --
THE OTHER NEWS-PAPERS HAVE BEEN KIDDING US BECAUSE OF YOUR PLUGGING TRENT FOR THE TITLE -- ARE YOU SURE HE'S GOING TO WIN?
SO POSITIVE THAT I'VE WRITTEN THE FIGHT'S OUT-COME IN ADVANCE! HERE IT IS, READY FOR PRINT!
14

THE EVENING OF THE CHAMPION-SHIP FIGHT . . .

REMEMBER! IF TH' DRUGGED DRINK DON'T WORK, *THIS* WILL!

DON'T WORRY! HE'LL SWALLOW ENOUGH DOPE TO KNOCK OUT A DOZEN MEN!

THE GONG CLANGS -- AND TRENT LEAPS FROM HIS CORNER, DETERMINED TO WIN BACK THE COVETED TITLE!

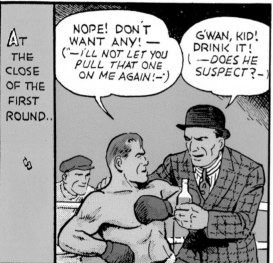

AT THE CLOSE OF THE FIRST ROUND..

NOPE! DON'T WANT ANY! — ("—I'LL NOT LET YOU *PULL* THAT ONE ON ME AGAIN!—")

G'WAN, KID! DRINK IT! (—DOES HE SUSPECT?—)

END OF ROUND SIX... WHEN LARRY IS TOO WEAK TO RESIST

I — DON'T — WANT — ANY!

GO AHEAD! *DRINK!*

AS CROY IS ABOUT TO FORCE LARRY TO SWALLOW THE DRUGGED DRINK, A GRIP OF STEEL ENCIRCLES THE REAR OF HIS NECK!

GO ON! DRINK IT YOURSELF!

GLUG! - GLUB!

HELP! I'M POISONED!

15.

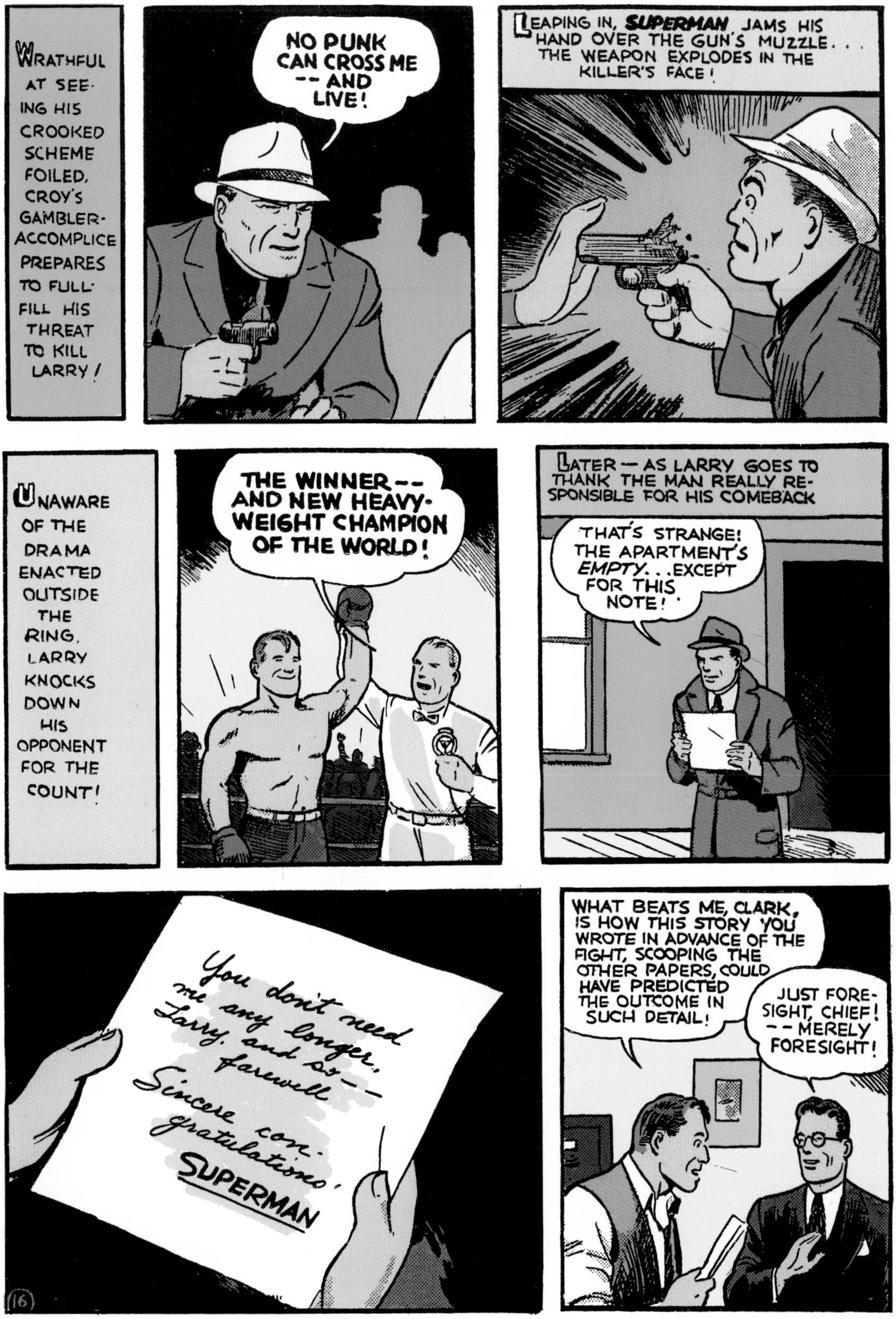
WRATHFUL AT SEEING HIS CROOKED SCHEME FOILED, CROY'S GAMBLER-ACCOMPLICE PREPARES TO FULL-FILL HIS THREAT TO KILL LARRY!
NO PUNK CAN CROSS ME -- AND LIVE!
LEAPING IN, SUPERMAN JAMS HIS HAND OVER THE GUN'S MUZZLE... THE WEAPON EXPLODES IN THE KILLER'S FACE!
UNAWARE OF THE DRAMA ENACTED OUTSIDE THE RING, LARRY KNOCKS DOWN HIS OPPONENT FOR THE COUNT!
THE WINNER-- AND NEW HEAVY-WEIGHT CHAMPION OF THE WORLD!
LATER — AS LARRY GOES TO THANK THE MAN REALLY RE-SPONSIBLE FOR HIS COMEBACK
THAT'S STRANGE! THE APARTMENT'S EMPTY...EXCEPT FOR THIS NOTE!
You don't need me any longer, Larry, and so-- farewell Sincere con-gratulations. SUPERMAN
(16)
WHAT BEATS ME, CLARK, IS HOW THIS STORY YOU WROTE IN ADVANCE OF THE FIGHT, SCOOPING THE OTHER PAPERS, COULD HAVE PREDICTED THE OUTCOME IN SUCH DETAIL!
JUST FORE-SIGHT, CHIEF! -- MERELY FORESIGHT!

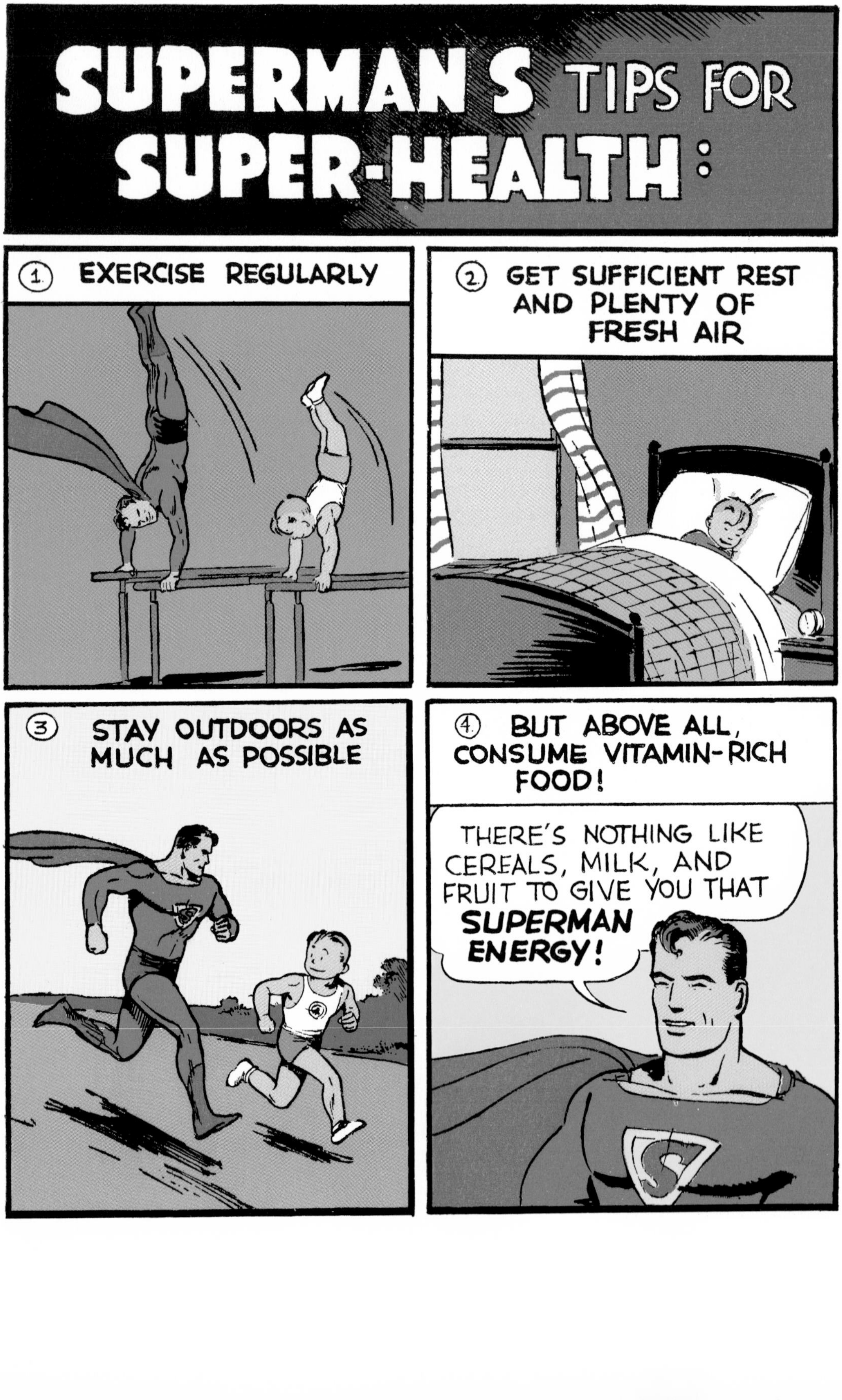
SUPERMAN S TIPS FOR SUPER-HEALTH:
1. EXERCISE REGULARLY
2. GET SUFFICIENT REST AND PLENTY OF FRESH AIR
3 STAY OUTDOORS AS MUCH AS POSSIBLE
4. BUT ABOVE ALL, CONSUME VITAMIN-RICH FOOD!
THERE'S NOTHING LIKE CEREALS, MILK, AND FRUIT TO GIVE YOU THAT SUPERMAN ENERGY!

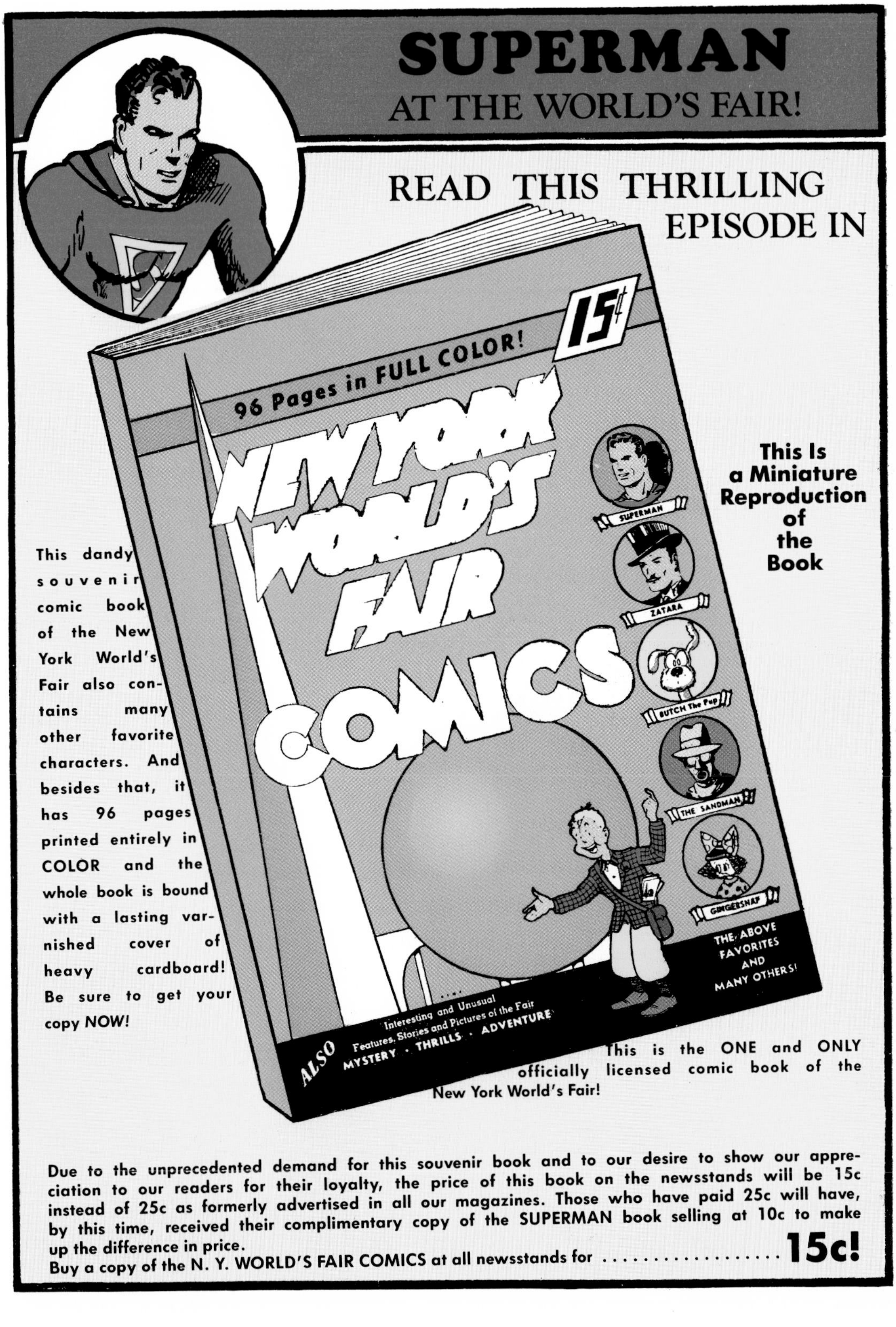
SUPERMAN
AT THE WORLD'S FAIR!
READ THIS THRILLING EPISODE IN
96 Pages in FULL COLOR!
15¢
NEW YORK WORLD'S FAIR COMICS
SUPERMAN
ZATARA
BUTCH The Pup
THE SANDMAN
GINGERSNAP
THE ABOVE FAVORITES AND MANY OTHERS!
ALSO Interesting and Unusual Features, Stories and Pictures of the Fair
MYSTERY · THRILLS · ADVENTURE
This Is a Miniature Reproduction of the Book
This dandy souvenir comic book of the New York World's Fair also contains many other favorite characters. And besides that, it has 96 pages printed entirely in COLOR and the whole book is bound with a lasting varnished cover of heavy cardboard! Be sure to get your copy NOW!
This is the ONE and ONLY officially licensed comic book of the New York World's Fair!
Due to the unprecedented demand for this souvenir book and to our desire to show our appreciation to our readers for their loyalty, the price of this book on the newsstands will be 15c instead of 25c as formerly advertised in all our magazines. Those who have paid 25c will have, by this time, received their complimentary copy of the SUPERMAN book selling at 10c to make up the difference in price.
Buy a copy of the N. Y. WORLD'S FAIR COMICS at all newsstands for .... 15c!

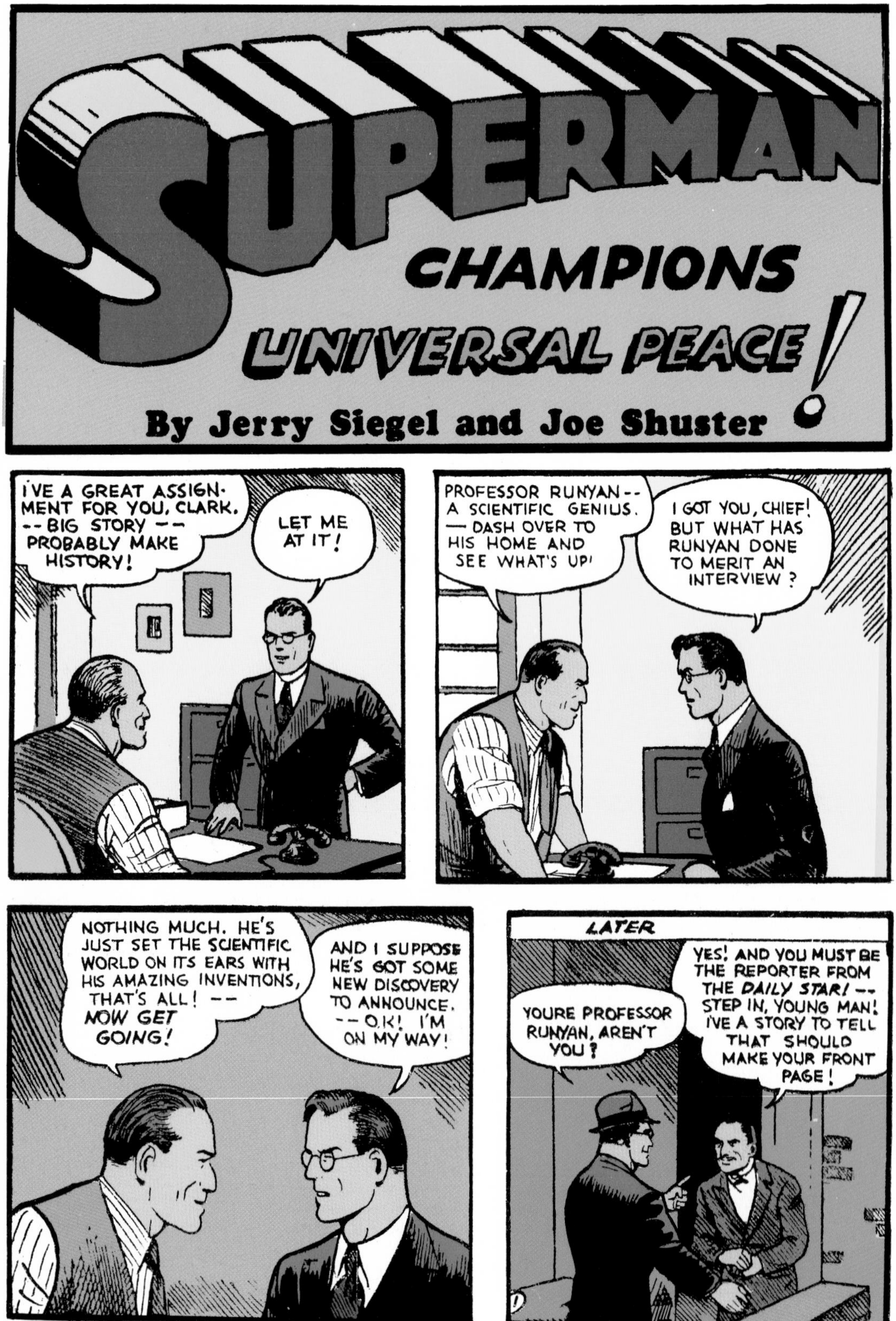
SUPERMAN
CHAMPIONS
UNIVERSAL PEACE!
By Jerry Siegel and Joe Shuster
I'VE A GREAT ASSIGNMENT FOR YOU, CLARK. -- BIG STORY -- PROBABLY MAKE HISTORY!
LET ME AT IT!
PROFESSOR RUNYAN -- A SCIENTIFIC GENIUS. — DASH OVER TO HIS HOME AND SEE WHAT'S UP!
I GOT YOU, CHIEF! BUT WHAT HAS RUNYAN DONE TO MERIT AN INTERVIEW?
NOTHING MUCH. HE'S JUST SET THE SCIENTIFIC WORLD ON ITS EARS WITH HIS AMAZING INVENTIONS, THAT'S ALL! -- NOW GET GOING!
AND I SUPPOSE HE'S GOT SOME NEW DISCOVERY TO ANNOUNCE. -- O.K! I'M ON MY WAY!
LATER
YOURE PROFESSOR RUNYAN, AREN'T YOU?
YES! AND YOU MUST BE THE REPORTER FROM THE DAILY STAR! -- STEP IN, YOUNG MAN! I'VE A STORY TO TELL THAT SHOULD MAKE YOUR FRONT PAGE!

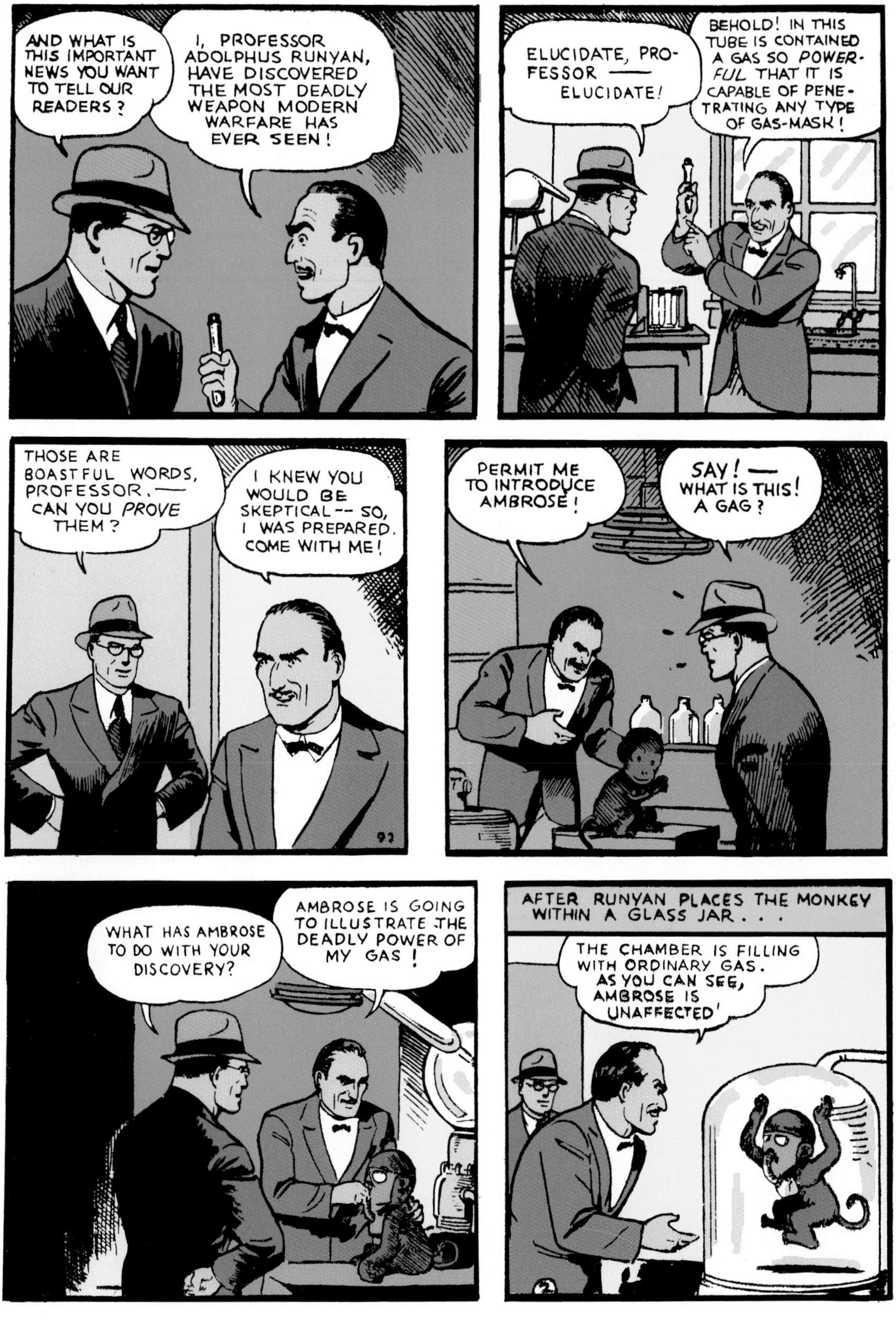
AND WHAT IS THIS IMPORTANT NEWS YOU WANT TO TELL OUR READERS?
I, PROFESSOR ADOLPHUS RUNYAN, HAVE DISCOVERED THE MOST DEADLY WEAPON MODERN WARFARE HAS EVER SEEN!
ELUCIDATE, PROFESSOR —— ELUCIDATE!
BEHOLD! IN THIS TUBE IS CONTAINED A GAS SO *POWERFUL* THAT IT IS CAPABLE OF PENETRATING ANY TYPE OF GAS-MASK!
THOSE ARE BOASTFUL WORDS, PROFESSOR. — CAN YOU *PROVE* THEM?
I KNEW YOU WOULD BE SKEPTICAL -- SO, I WAS PREPARED. COME WITH ME!
PERMIT ME TO INTRODUCE AMBROSE!
SAY! — WHAT IS THIS! A GAG?
WHAT HAS AMBROSE TO DO WITH YOUR DISCOVERY?
AMBROSE IS GOING TO ILLUSTRATE THE DEADLY POWER OF MY GAS!
AFTER RUNYAN PLACES THE MONKEY WITHIN A GLASS JAR . . .
THE CHAMBER IS FILLING WITH ORDINARY GAS. AS YOU CAN SEE, AMBROSE IS UNAFFECTED!

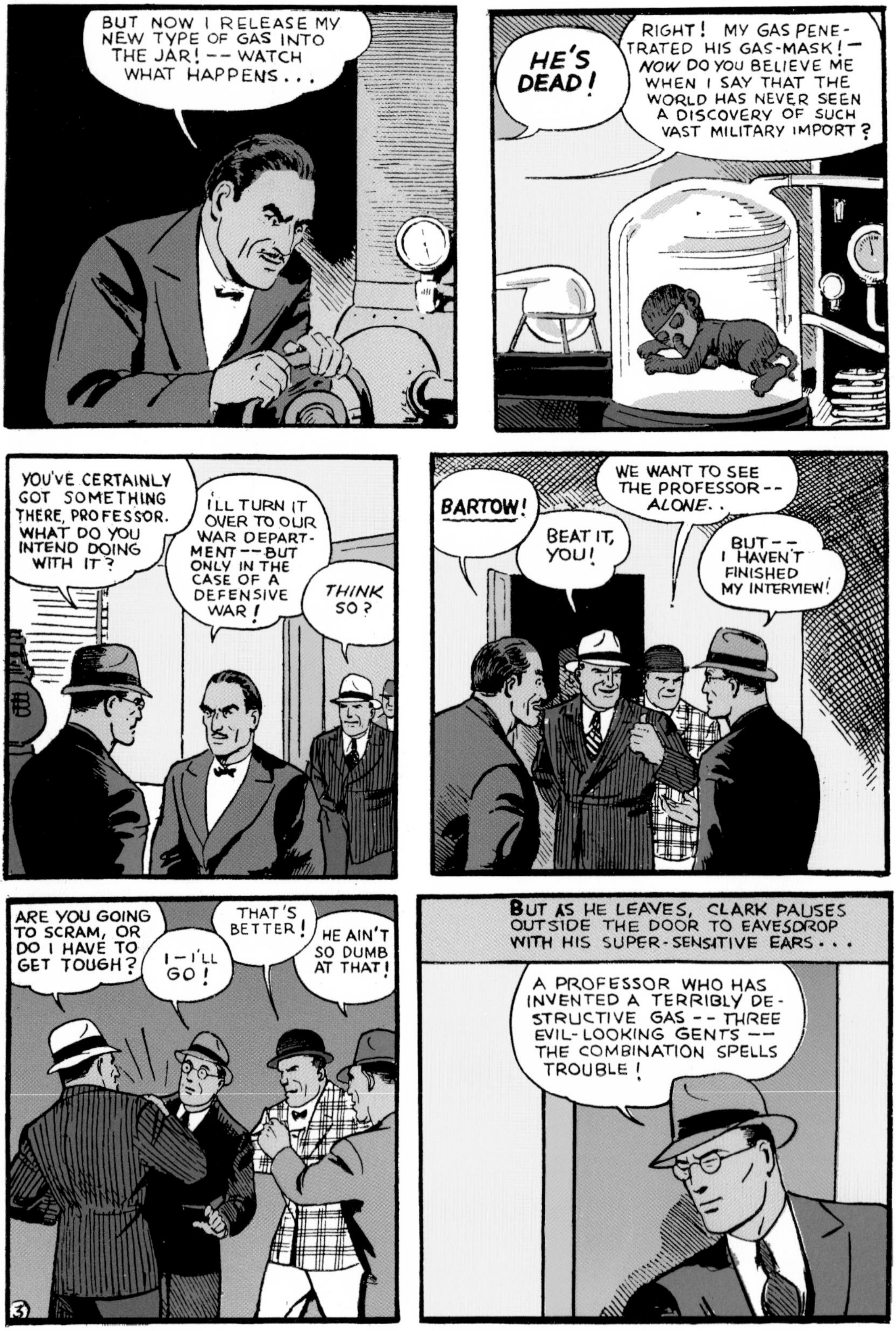
BUT NOW I RELEASE MY NEW TYPE OF GAS INTO THE JAR! -- WATCH WHAT HAPPENS...
HE'S DEAD!
RIGHT! MY GAS PENETRATED HIS GAS-MASK! — NOW DO YOU BELIEVE ME WHEN I SAY THAT THE WORLD HAS NEVER SEEN A DISCOVERY OF SUCH VAST MILITARY IMPORT?
YOU'VE CERTAINLY GOT SOMETHING THERE, PROFESSOR. WHAT DO YOU INTEND DOING WITH IT?
I'LL TURN IT OVER TO OUR WAR DEPARTMENT -- BUT ONLY IN THE CASE OF A DEFENSIVE WAR!
THINK SO?
BARTOW!
BEAT IT, YOU!
WE WANT TO SEE THE PROFESSOR -- ALONE..
BUT -- I HAVEN'T FINISHED MY INTERVIEW!
ARE YOU GOING TO SCRAM, OR DO I HAVE TO GET TOUGH?
I-I'LL GO!
THAT'S BETTER!
HE AIN'T SO DUMB AT THAT!
3
BUT AS HE LEAVES, CLARK PAUSES OUTSIDE THE DOOR TO EAVESDROP WITH HIS SUPER-SENSITIVE EARS...
A PROFESSOR WHO HAS INVENTED A TERRIBLY DESTRUCTIVE GAS -- THREE EVIL-LOOKING GENTS -- THE COMBINATION SPELLS TROUBLE!

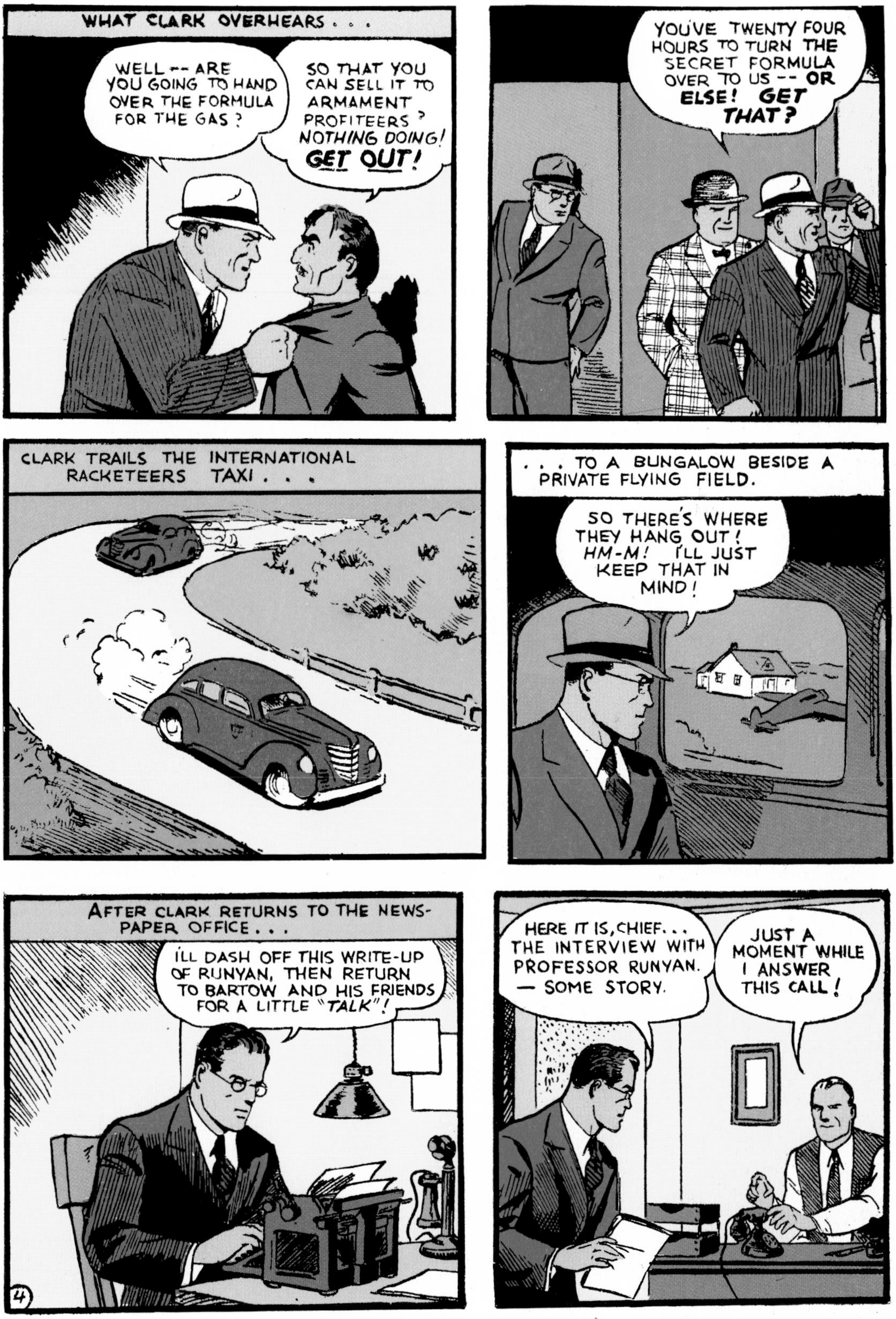
WHAT CLARK OVERHEARS . . .
WELL -- ARE YOU GOING TO HAND OVER THE FORMULA FOR THE GAS ?
SO THAT YOU CAN SELL IT TO ARMAMENT PROFITEERS ? NOTHING DOING! GET OUT!
YOU'VE TWENTY FOUR HOURS TO TURN THE SECRET FORMULA OVER TO US -- OR ELSE! GET THAT ?
CLARK TRAILS THE INTERNATIONAL RACKETEERS TAXI . . .
. . . TO A BUNGALOW BESIDE A PRIVATE FLYING FIELD.
SO THERE'S WHERE THEY HANG OUT! HM-M! I'LL JUST KEEP THAT IN MIND!
AFTER CLARK RETURNS TO THE NEWS-PAPER OFFICE . . .
I'LL DASH OFF THIS WRITE-UP OF RUNYAN, THEN RETURN TO BARTOW AND HIS FRIENDS FOR A LITTLE "TALK"!
4
HERE IT IS, CHIEF. . . THE INTERVIEW WITH PROFESSOR RUNYAN. — SOME STORY.
JUST A MOMENT WHILE I ANSWER THIS CALL!

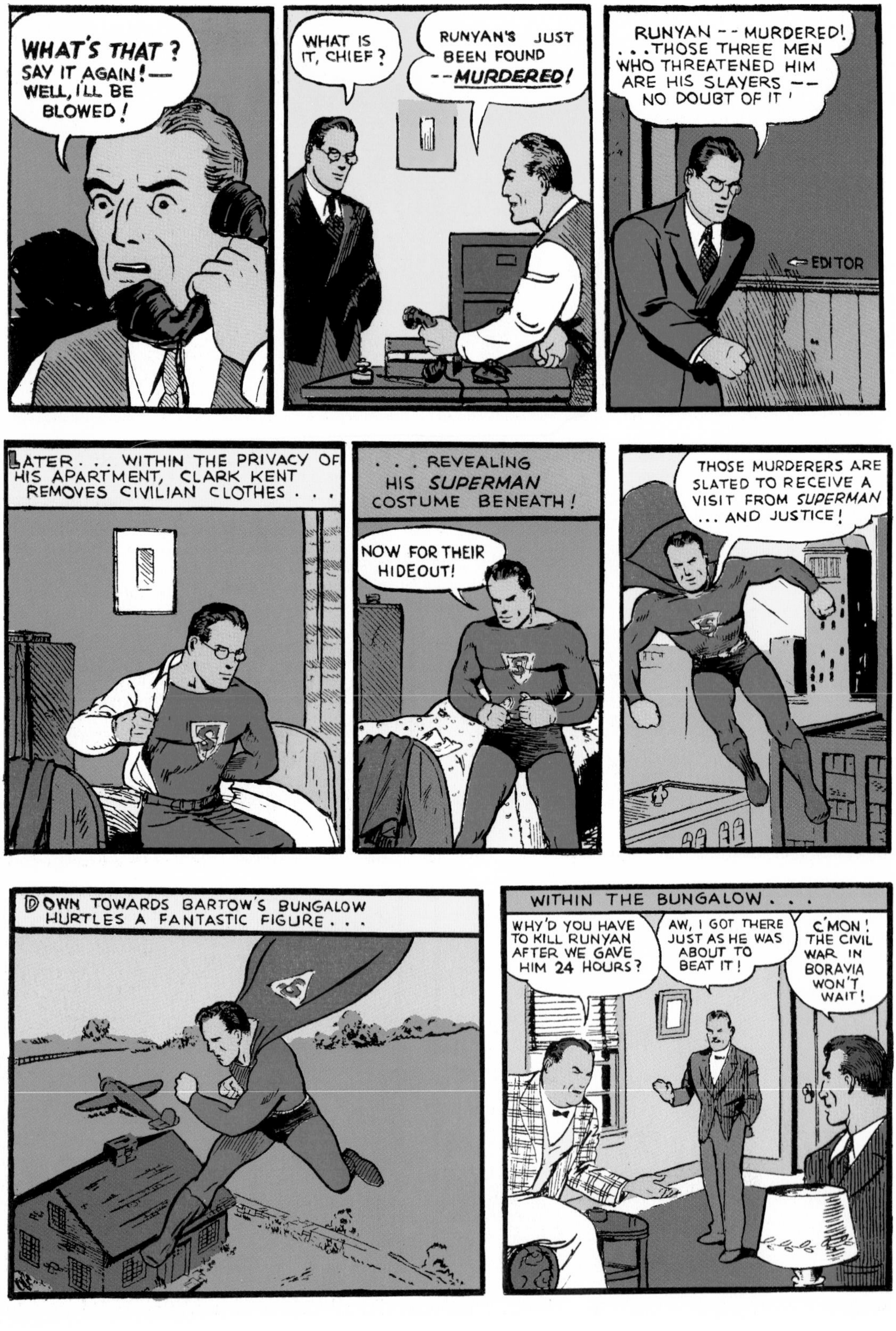
WHAT'S THAT? SAY IT AGAIN!—WELL, I'LL BE BLOWED!
WHAT IS IT, CHIEF?
RUNYAN'S JUST BEEN FOUND --MURDERED!
RUNYAN -- MURDERED! ...THOSE THREE MEN WHO THREATENED HIM ARE HIS SLAYERS -- NO DOUBT OF IT!
EDITOR
LATER... WITHIN THE PRIVACY OF HIS APARTMENT, CLARK KENT REMOVES CIVILIAN CLOTHES...
...REVEALING HIS SUPERMAN COSTUME BENEATH!
NOW FOR THEIR HIDEOUT!
THOSE MURDERERS ARE SLATED TO RECEIVE A VISIT FROM SUPERMAN ... AND JUSTICE!
DOWN TOWARDS BARTOW'S BUNGALOW HURTLES A FANTASTIC FIGURE...
WITHIN THE BUNGALOW...
WHY'D YOU HAVE TO KILL RUNYAN AFTER WE GAVE HIM 24 HOURS?
AW, I GOT THERE JUST AS HE WAS ABOUT TO BEAT IT!
C'MON! THE CIVIL WAR IN BORAVIA WON'T WAIT!

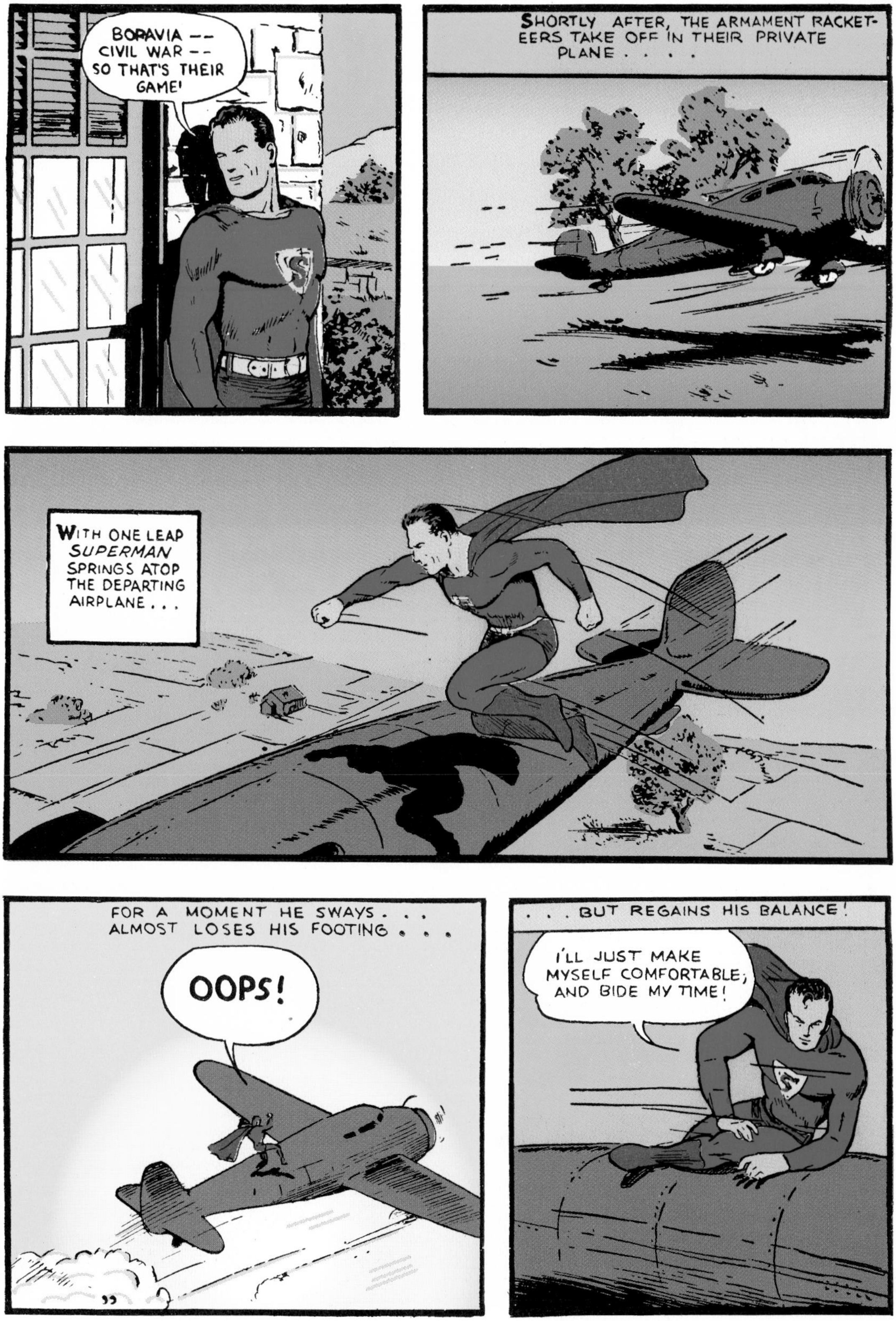
BORAVIA -- CIVIL WAR -- SO THAT'S THEIR GAME!
SHORTLY AFTER, THE ARMAMENT RACKETEERS TAKE OFF IN THEIR PRIVATE PLANE . . . .
WITH ONE LEAP SUPERMAN SPRINGS ATOP THE DEPARTING AIRPLANE . . .
FOR A MOMENT HE SWAYS . . . ALMOST LOSES HIS FOOTING . . .
OOPS!
. . . BUT REGAINS HIS BALANCE!
I'LL JUST MAKE MYSELF COMFORTABLE; AND BIDE MY TIME!

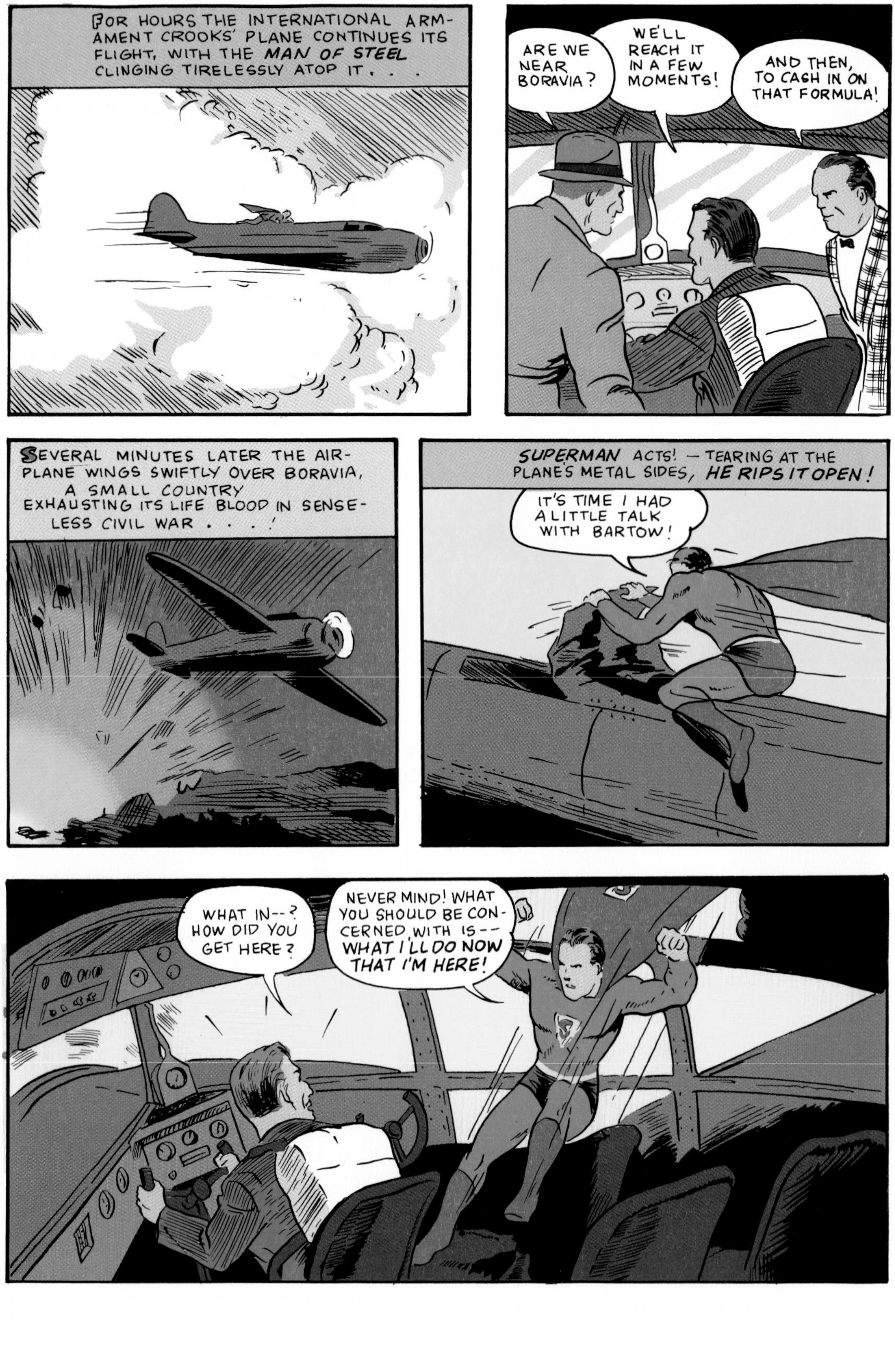
FOR HOURS THE INTERNATIONAL ARMAMENT CROOKS' PLANE CONTINUES ITS FLIGHT, WITH THE MAN OF STEEL CLINGING TIRELESSLY ATOP IT . . .
ARE WE NEAR BORAVIA?
WE'LL REACH IT IN A FEW MOMENTS!
AND THEN, TO CASH IN ON THAT FORMULA!
SEVERAL MINUTES LATER THE AIRPLANE WINGS SWIFTLY OVER BORAVIA, A SMALL COUNTRY EXHAUSTING ITS LIFE BLOOD IN SENSELESS CIVIL WAR . . . !
SUPERMAN ACTS! — TEARING AT THE PLANE'S METAL SIDES, HE RIPS IT OPEN!
IT'S TIME I HAD A LITTLE TALK WITH BARTOW!
WHAT IN--? HOW DID YOU GET HERE?
NEVER MIND! WHAT YOU SHOULD BE CONCERNED WITH IS -- WHAT I'LL DO NOW THAT I'M HERE!

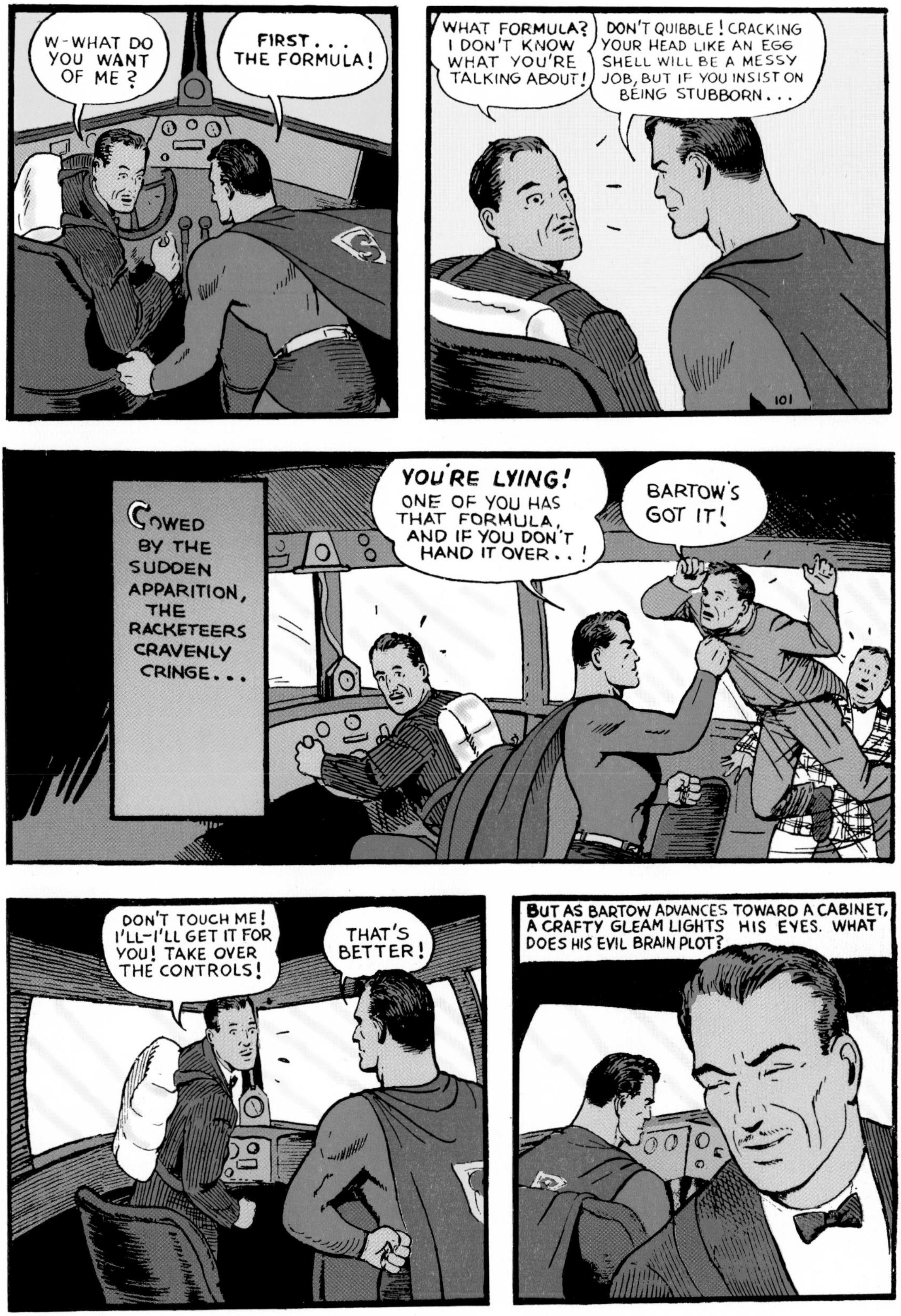
W-WHAT DO YOU WANT OF ME?
FIRST... THE FORMULA!
WHAT FORMULA? I DON'T KNOW WHAT YOU'RE TALKING ABOUT!
DON'T QUIBBLE! CRACKING YOUR HEAD LIKE AN EGG SHELL WILL BE A MESSY JOB, BUT IF YOU INSIST ON BEING STUBBORN...
COWED BY THE SUDDEN APPARITION, THE RACKETEERS CRAVENLY CRINGE...
YOU'RE LYING! ONE OF YOU HAS THAT FORMULA, AND IF YOU DON'T HAND IT OVER..!
BARTOW'S GOT IT!
DON'T TOUCH ME! I'LL-I'LL GET IT FOR YOU! TAKE OVER THE CONTROLS!
THAT'S BETTER!
BUT AS BARTOW ADVANCES TOWARD A CABINET, A CRAFTY GLEAM LIGHTS HIS EYES. WHAT DOES HIS EVIL BRAIN PLOT?

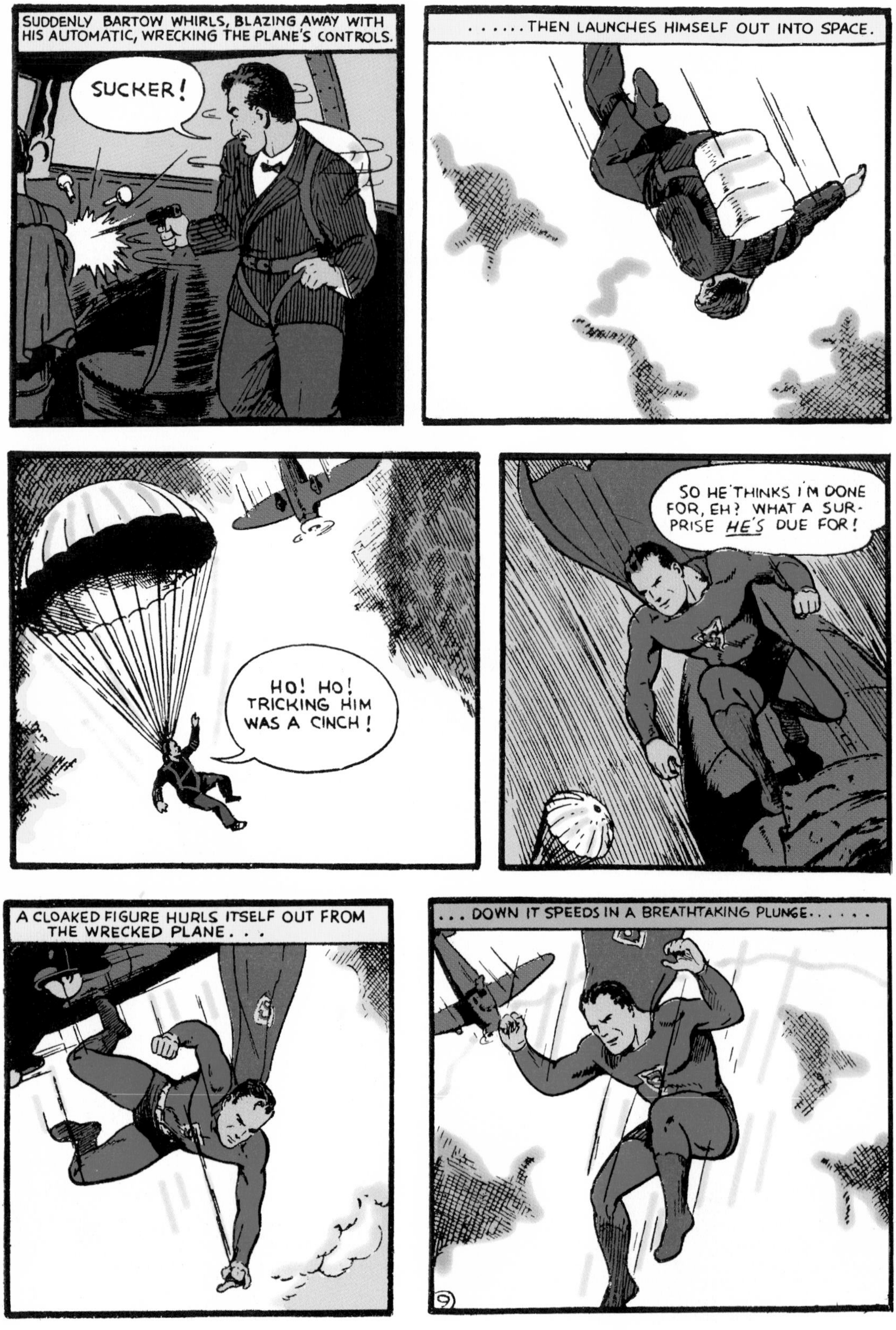
SUDDENLY BARTOW WHIRLS, BLAZING AWAY WITH HIS AUTOMATIC, WRECKING THE PLANE'S CONTROLS.
SUCKER!
. . . . . THEN LAUNCHES HIMSELF OUT INTO SPACE.
HO! HO! TRICKING HIM WAS A CINCH!
SO HE THINKS I'M DONE FOR, EH? WHAT A SUR-PRISE HE'S DUE FOR!
A CLOAKED FIGURE HURLS ITSELF OUT FROM THE WRECKED PLANE . . .
. . . DOWN IT SPEEDS IN A BREATHTAKING PLUNGE . . . . .
9

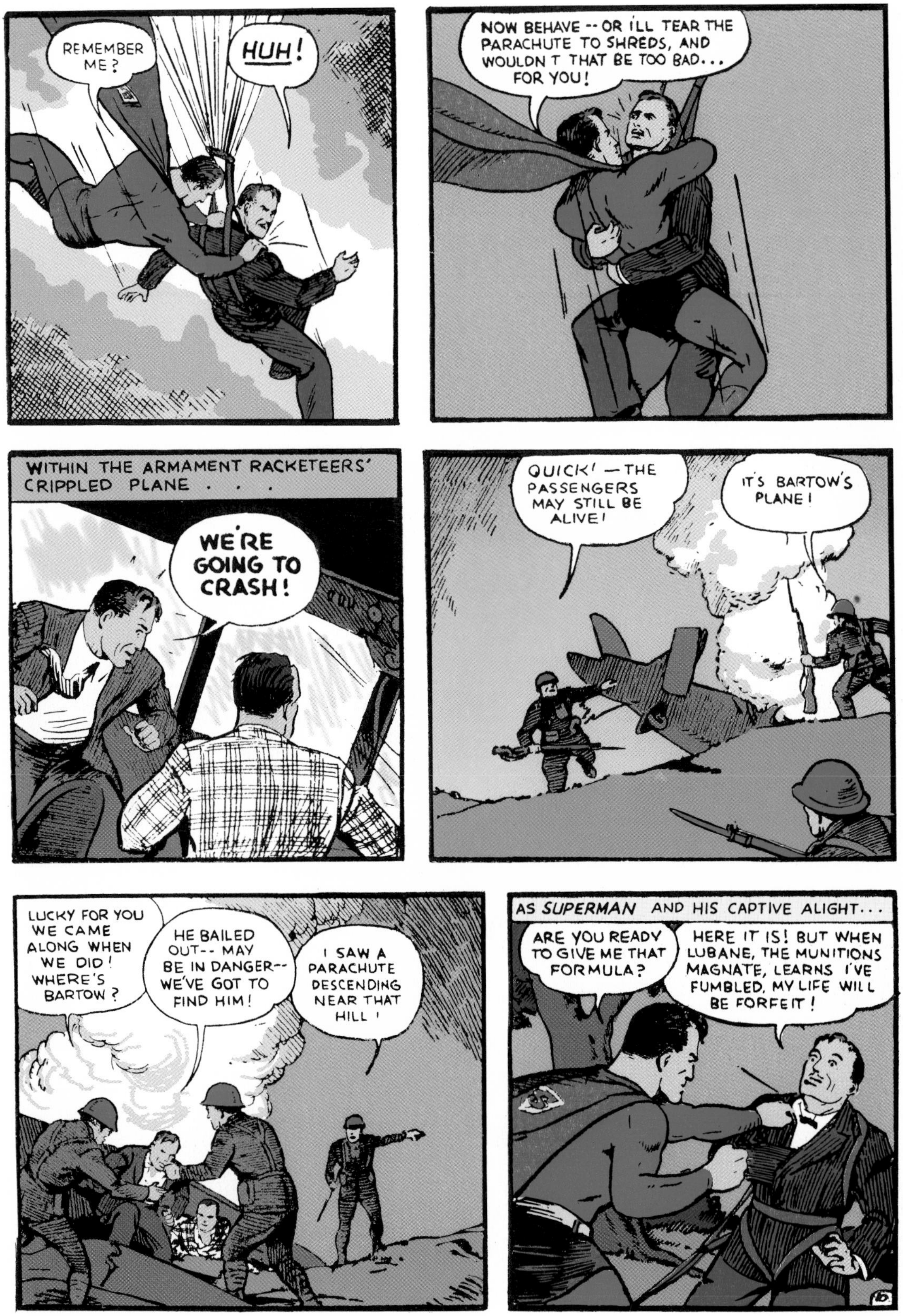
REMEMBER ME?
HUH!
NOW BEHAVE -- OR I'LL TEAR THE PARACHUTE TO SHREDS, AND WOULDN'T THAT BE TOO BAD... FOR YOU!
WITHIN THE ARMAMENT RACKETEERS' CRIPPLED PLANE . . .
WE'RE GOING TO CRASH!
QUICK! —THE PASSENGERS MAY STILL BE ALIVE!
IT'S BARTOW'S PLANE!
LUCKY FOR YOU WE CAME ALONG WHEN WE DID! WHERE'S BARTOW?
HE BAILED OUT-- MAY BE IN DANGER-- WE'VE GOT TO FIND HIM!
I SAW A PARACHUTE DESCENDING NEAR THAT HILL!
AS SUPERMAN AND HIS CAPTIVE ALIGHT...
ARE YOU READY TO GIVE ME THAT FORMULA?
HERE IT IS! BUT WHEN LUBANE, THE MUNITIONS MAGNATE, LEARNS I'VE FUMBLED, MY LIFE WILL BE FORFEIT!
6

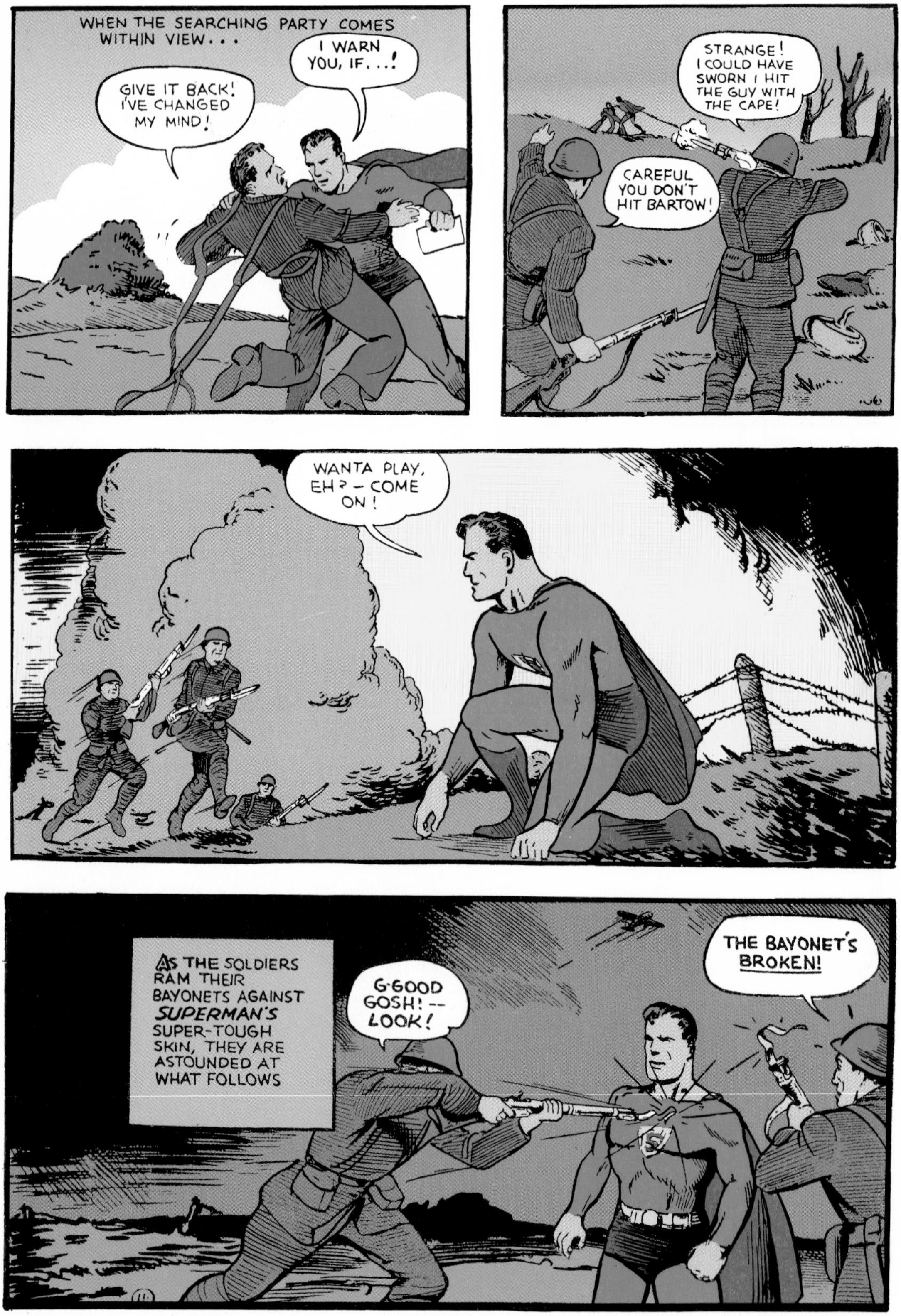
WHEN THE SEARCHING PARTY COMES WITHIN VIEW...
GIVE IT BACK! I'VE CHANGED MY MIND!
I WARN YOU, IF...!
STRANGE! I COULD HAVE SWORN I HIT THE GUY WITH THE CAPE!
CAREFUL YOU DON'T HIT BARTOW!
WANTA PLAY, EH? – COME ON!
AS THE SOLDIERS RAM THEIR BAYONETS AGAINST SUPERMAN'S SUPER-TOUGH SKIN, THEY ARE ASTOUNDED AT WHAT FOLLOWS
G-GOOD GOSH! -- LOOK!
THE BAYONET'S BROKEN!

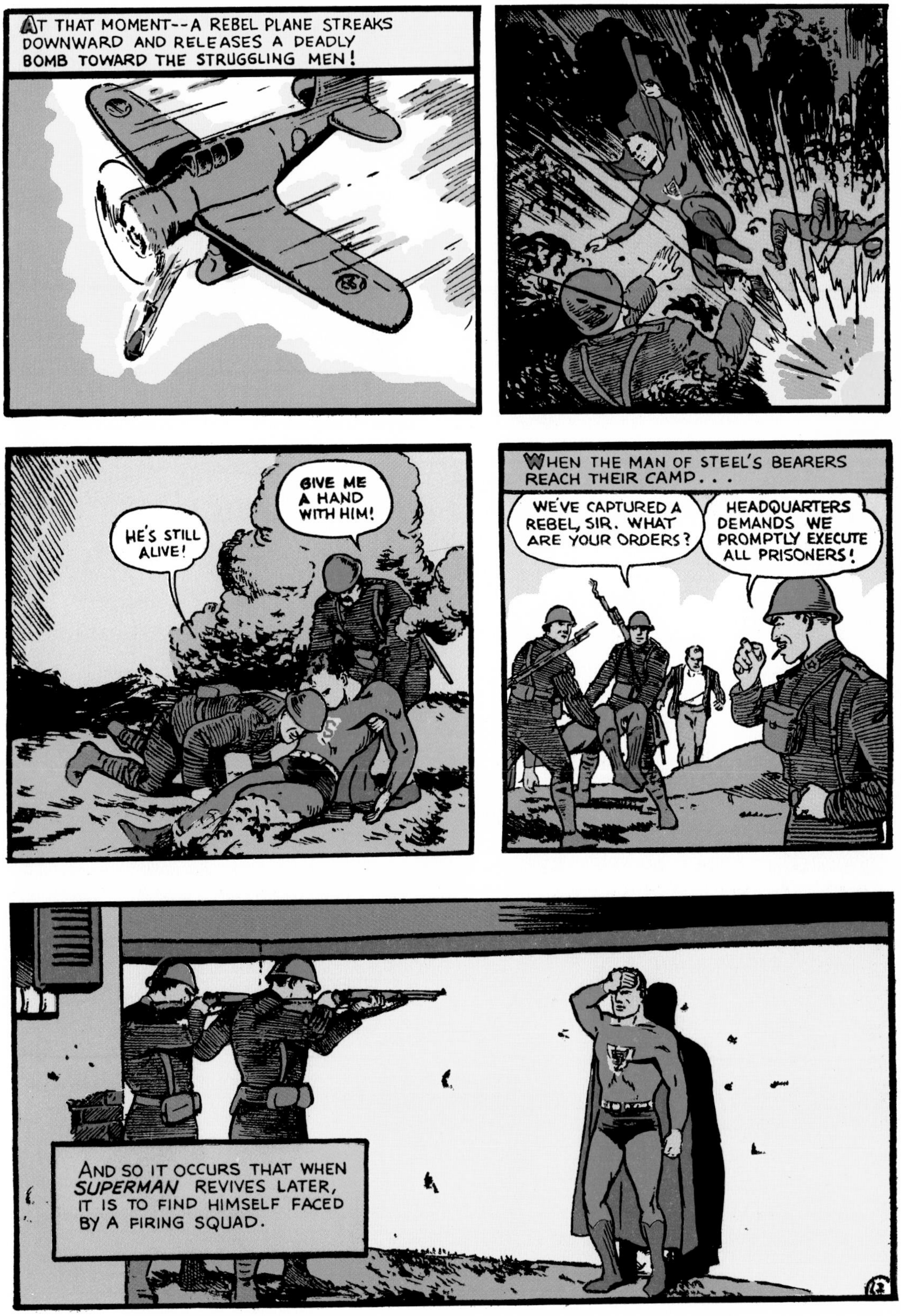
AT THAT MOMENT--A REBEL PLANE STREAKS DOWNWARD AND RELEASES A DEADLY BOMB TOWARD THE STRUGGLING MEN!
HE'S STILL ALIVE!
GIVE ME A HAND WITH HIM!
WHEN THE MAN OF STEEL'S BEARERS REACH THEIR CAMP . . .
WE'VE CAPTURED A REBEL, SIR. WHAT ARE YOUR ORDERS?
HEADQUARTERS DEMANDS WE PROMPTLY EXECUTE ALL PRISONERS!
AND SO IT OCCURS THAT WHEN SUPERMAN REVIVES LATER, IT IS TO FIND HIMSELF FACED BY A FIRING SQUAD.

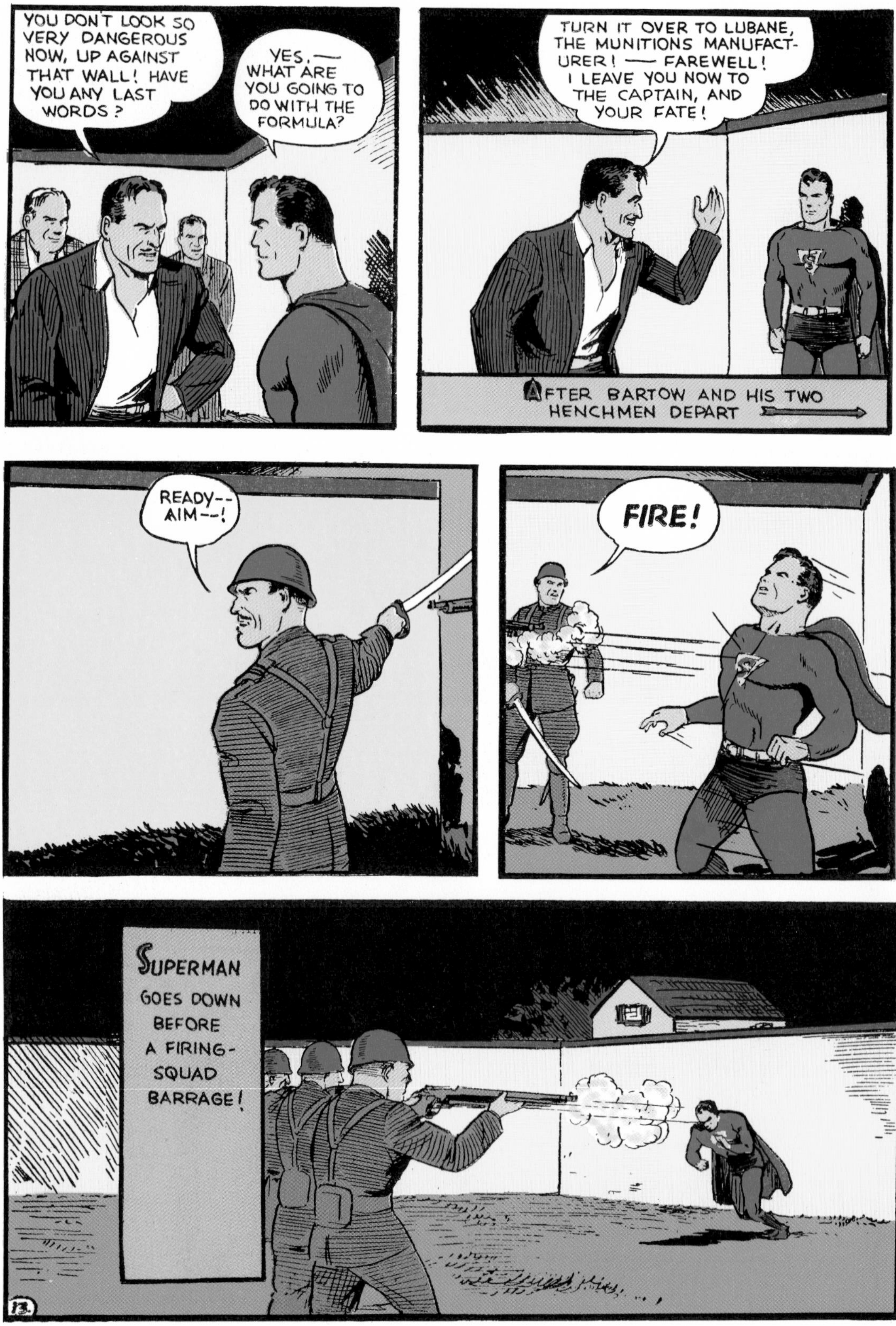
YOU DON'T LOOK SO VERY DANGEROUS NOW, UP AGAINST THAT WALL! HAVE YOU ANY LAST WORDS?
YES, — WHAT ARE YOU GOING TO DO WITH THE FORMULA?
TURN IT OVER TO LUBANE, THE MUNITIONS MANUFACT-URER! — FAREWELL! I LEAVE YOU NOW TO THE CAPTAIN, AND YOUR FATE!
AFTER BARTOW AND HIS TWO HENCHMEN DEPART
READY-- AIM--!
FIRE!
SUPERMAN GOES DOWN BEFORE A FIRING-SQUAD BARRAGE!
13.

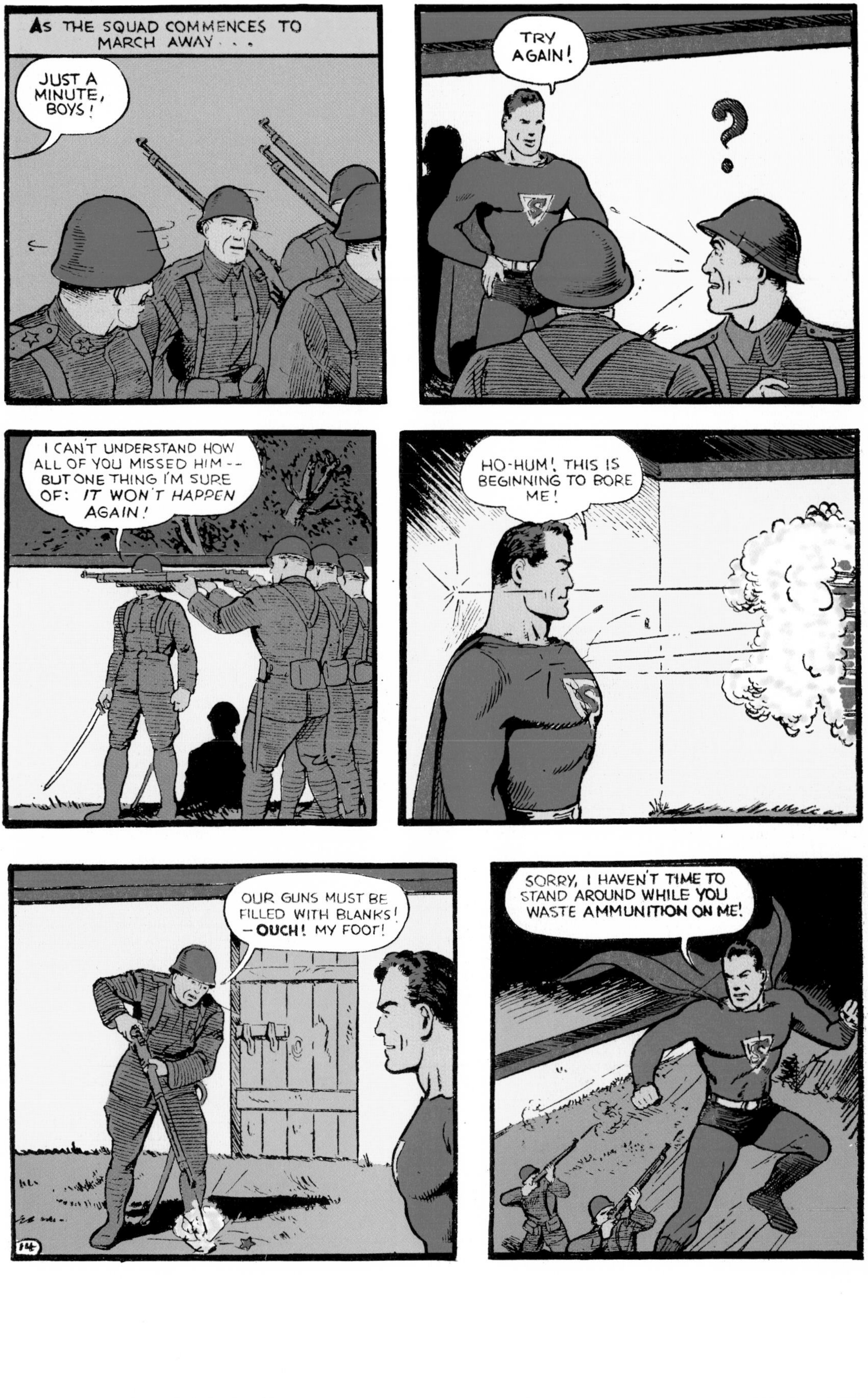
AS THE SQUAD COMMENCES TO MARCH AWAY . . .
JUST A MINUTE, BOYS!
TRY AGAIN!
I CAN'T UNDERSTAND HOW ALL OF YOU MISSED HIM -- BUT ONE THING I'M SURE OF: *IT WON'T HAPPEN AGAIN!*
HO-HUM! THIS IS BEGINNING TO BORE ME!
OUR GUNS MUST BE FILLED WITH BLANKS! —**OUCH!** MY FOOT!
SORRY, I HAVEN'T TIME TO STAND AROUND WHILE **YOU** WASTE **AMMUNITION** ON **ME**!

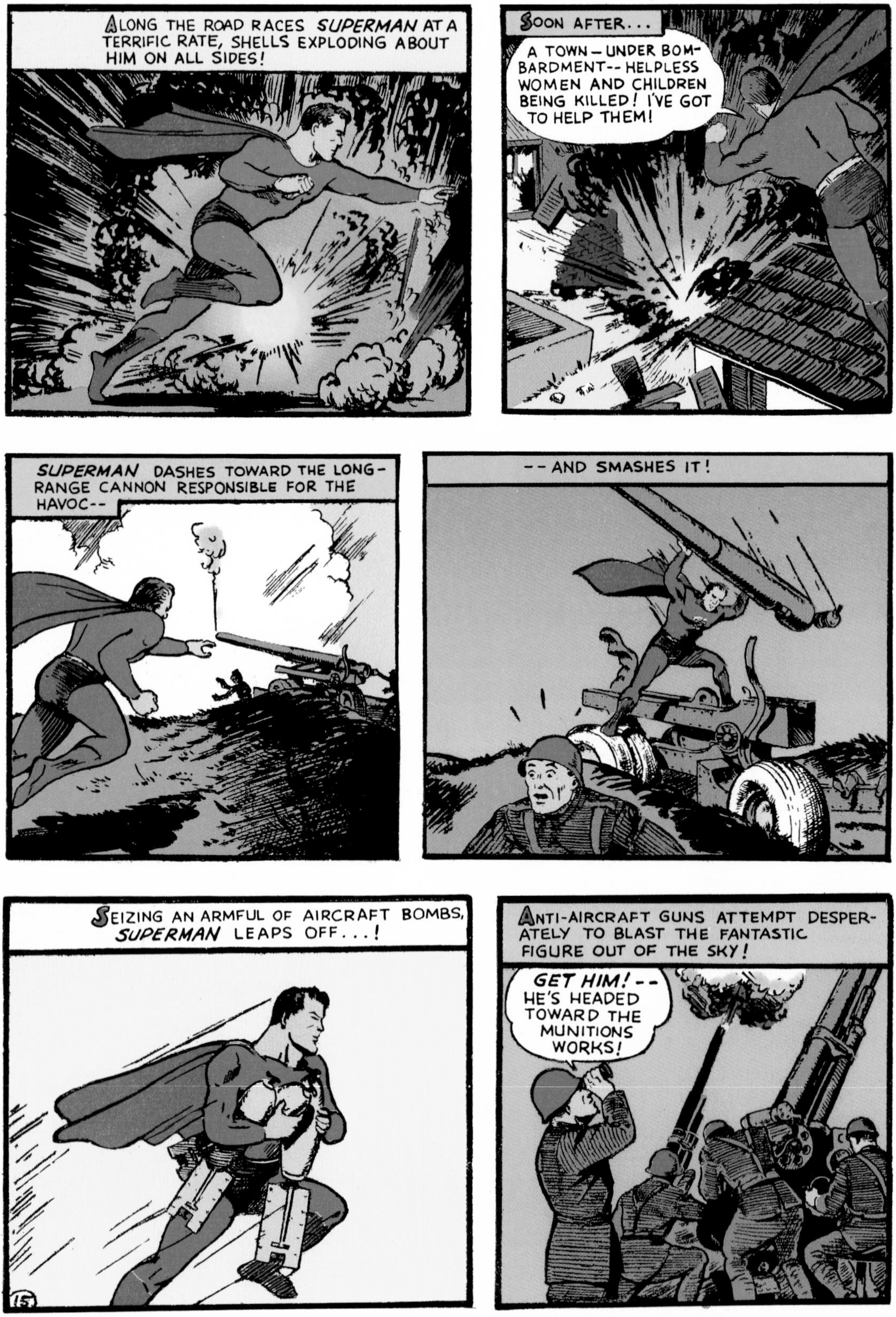
ALONG THE ROAD RACES SUPERMAN AT A TERRIFIC RATE, SHELLS EXPLODING ABOUT HIM ON ALL SIDES!
SOON AFTER...
A TOWN — UNDER BOMBARDMENT-- HELPLESS WOMEN AND CHILDREN BEING KILLED! I'VE GOT TO HELP THEM!
SUPERMAN DASHES TOWARD THE LONG-RANGE CANNON RESPONSIBLE FOR THE HAVOC--
--AND SMASHES IT!
SEIZING AN ARMFUL OF AIRCRAFT BOMBS, SUPERMAN LEAPS OFF...!
15
ANTI-AIRCRAFT GUNS ATTEMPT DESPERATELY TO BLAST THE FANTASTIC FIGURE OUT OF THE SKY!
GET HIM!-- HE'S HEADED TOWARD THE MUNITIONS WORKS!

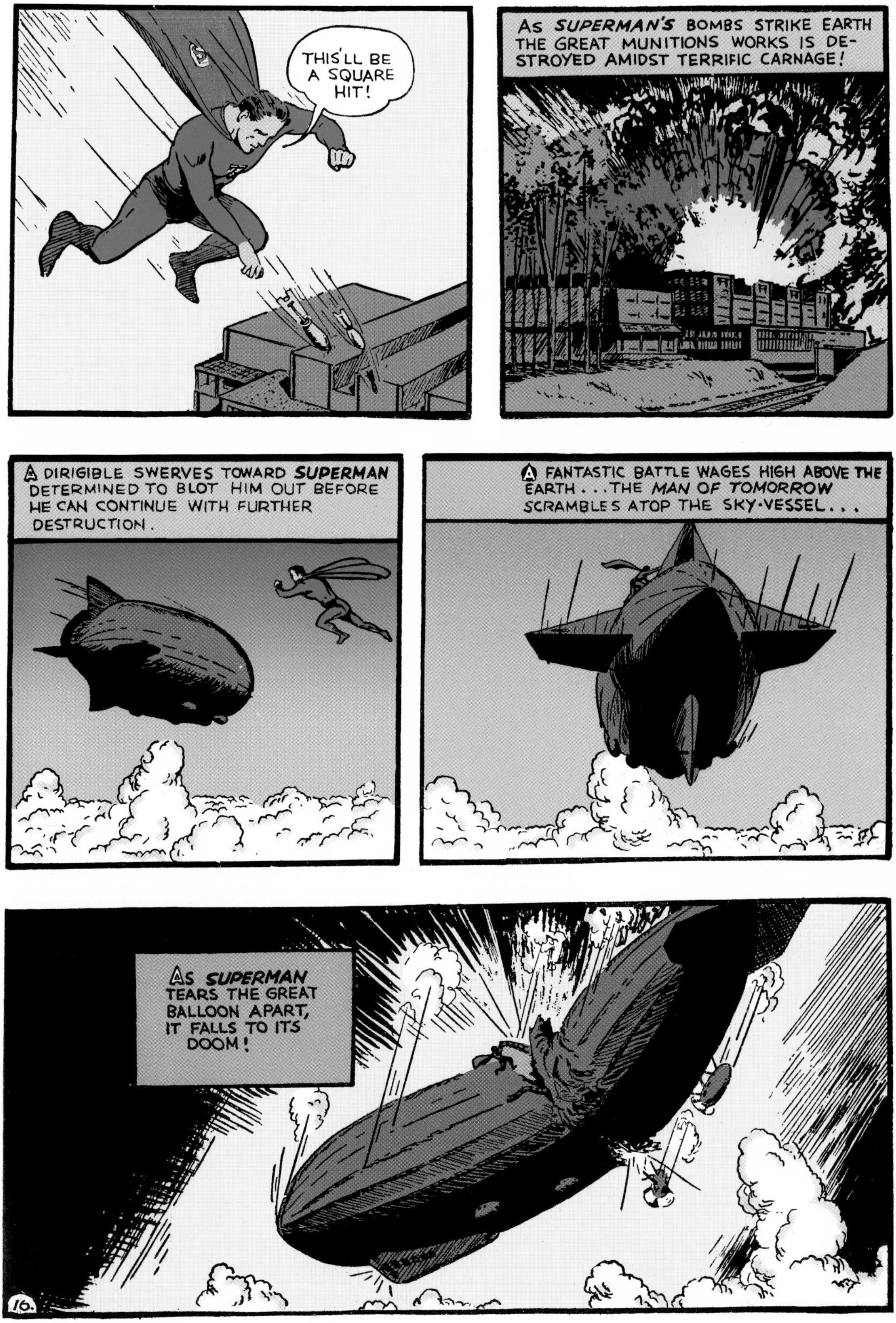
THIS'LL BE A SQUARE HIT!
AS SUPERMAN'S BOMBS STRIKE EARTH THE GREAT MUNITIONS WORKS IS DESTROYED AMIDST TERRIFIC CARNAGE!
A DIRIGIBLE SWERVES TOWARD SUPERMAN DETERMINED TO BLOT HIM OUT BEFORE HE CAN CONTINUE WITH FURTHER DESTRUCTION.
A FANTASTIC BATTLE WAGES HIGH ABOVE THE EARTH...THE MAN OF TOMORROW SCRAMBLES ATOP THE SKY-VESSEL...
AS SUPERMAN TEARS THE GREAT BALLOON APART, IT FALLS TO ITS DOOM!
16.

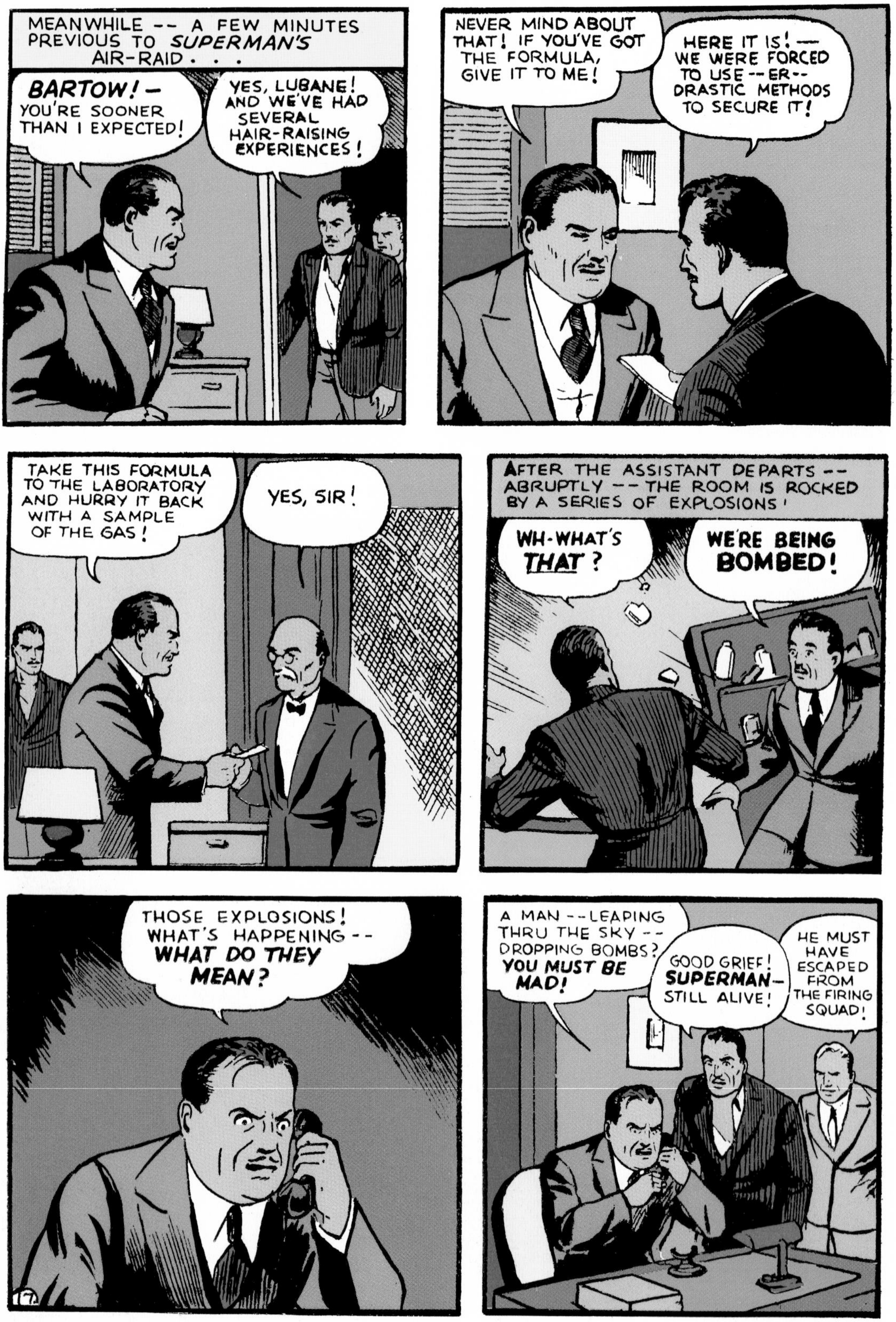
MEANWHILE -- A FEW MINUTES PREVIOUS TO SUPERMAN'S AIR-RAID . . .
BARTOW! — YOU'RE SOONER THAN I EXPECTED!
YES, LUBANE! AND WE'VE HAD SEVERAL HAIR-RAISING EXPERIENCES!
NEVER MIND ABOUT THAT! IF YOU'VE GOT THE FORMULA, GIVE IT TO ME!
HERE IT IS! — WE WERE FORCED TO USE -- ER -- DRASTIC METHODS TO SECURE IT!
TAKE THIS FORMULA TO THE LABORATORY AND HURRY IT BACK WITH A SAMPLE OF THE GAS!
YES, SIR!
AFTER THE ASSISTANT DEPARTS -- ABRUPTLY -- THE ROOM IS ROCKED BY A SERIES OF EXPLOSIONS!
WH-WHAT'S THAT?
WE'RE BEING BOMBED!
THOSE EXPLOSIONS! WHAT'S HAPPENING -- WHAT DO THEY MEAN?
A MAN -- LEAPING THRU THE SKY -- DROPPING BOMBS? YOU MUST BE MAD!
GOOD GRIEF! SUPERMAN — STILL ALIVE!
HE MUST HAVE ESCAPED FROM THE FIRING SQUAD!

SUPERMAN? WHO'S THAT?
OUR NEMESIS -- A MAN POSSESSING TERRIFIC STRENGTH. HE'S AFTER THE FORMULA!
HERE'S THE GAS AND FORMULA AS YOU REQUESTED.
SUPERMAN, EH? WELL, WHOEVER HE IS, HE CAN'T FRIGHTEN ME! AS LONG AS I HAVE THIS GAS, I NEED FEAR NO ONE!
LATER--AS HE DROPS DOWN ALONG THE SIDE OF THE MUNITIONS ADMINISTRATION BUILDING, SUPERMAN CATCHES HOLD OF A WINDOW. . .
WITHIN LUBANE'S OFFICE. . .
YOU'VE GOT THE FORMULA -- NOW GIVE US OUR DOUGH!
WE'RE CLEARING OUT!
TAKE IT AND GO.
WE'RE GRABBING THE FIRST PLANE OUT OF HERE THAT WE CAN GET! AND IF YOU'RE WISE, YOU'LL DO THE SAME.
STILL REFERRING TO A MYTHICAL SUPERMAN, EH? SUPERSTITIOUS FOOLS!
I THINK I'LL GIVE LUBANE A LITTLE TASTE OF SUPERSTITIOUS FEAR!

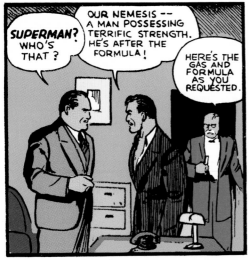

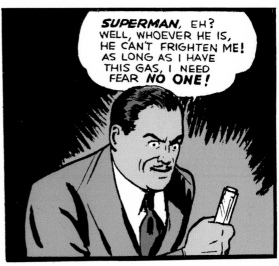

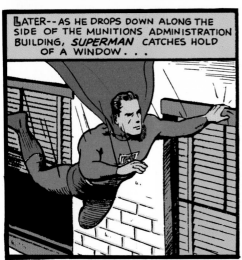

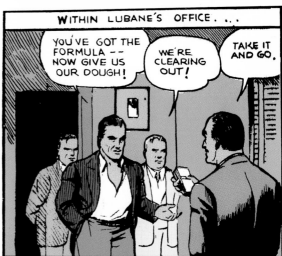

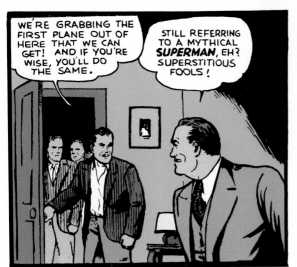

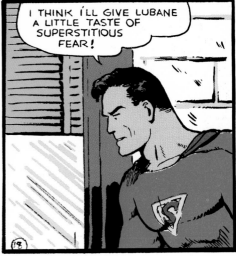

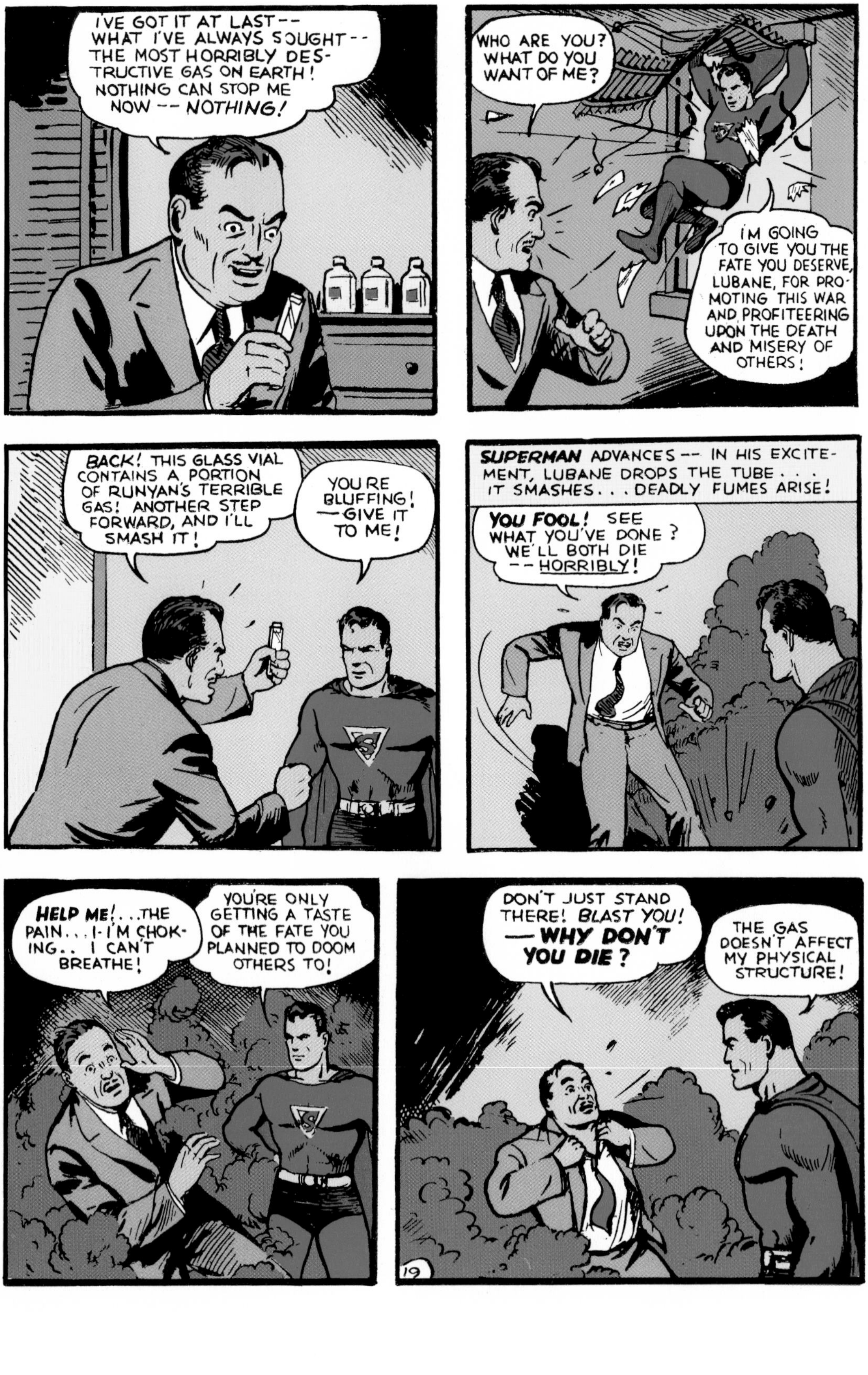
I'VE GOT IT AT LAST-- WHAT I'VE ALWAYS SOUGHT-- THE MOST HORRIBLY DESTRUCTIVE GAS ON EARTH! NOTHING CAN STOP ME NOW -- NOTHING!
WHO ARE YOU? WHAT DO YOU WANT OF ME?
I'M GOING TO GIVE YOU THE FATE YOU DESERVE, LUBANE, FOR PROMOTING THIS WAR AND PROFITEERING UPON THE DEATH AND MISERY OF OTHERS!
BACK! THIS GLASS VIAL CONTAINS A PORTION OF RUNYAN'S TERRIBLE GAS! ANOTHER STEP FORWARD, AND I'LL SMASH IT!
YOU'RE BLUFFING! —GIVE IT TO ME!
SUPERMAN ADVANCES -- IN HIS EXCITEMENT, LUBANE DROPS THE TUBE . . . IT SMASHES . . . DEADLY FUMES ARISE!
YOU FOOL! SEE WHAT YOU'VE DONE? WE'LL BOTH DIE --HORRIBLY!
HELP ME!...THE PAIN... I-I'M CHOKING.. I CAN'T BREATHE!
YOU'RE ONLY GETTING A TASTE OF THE FATE YOU PLANNED TO DOOM OTHERS TO!
DON'T JUST STAND THERE! BLAST YOU! —WHY DON'T YOU DIE?
THE GAS DOESN'T AFFECT MY PHYSICAL STRUCTURE!
19

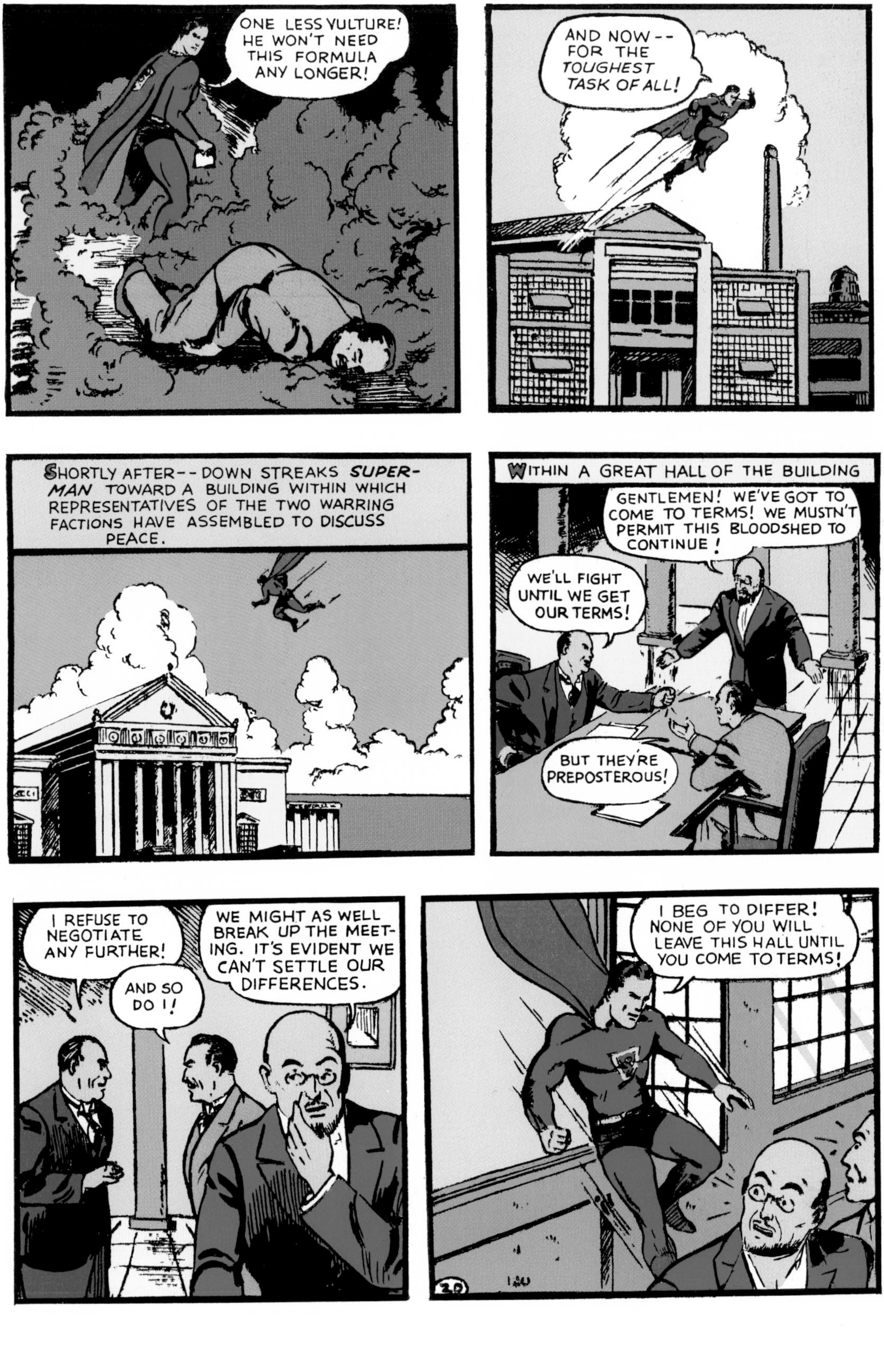
ONE LESS VULTURE! HE WON'T NEED THIS FORMULA ANY LONGER!
AND NOW -- FOR THE *TOUGHEST* TASK OF ALL!
SHORTLY AFTER -- DOWN STREAKS *SUPERMAN* TOWARD A BUILDING WITHIN WHICH REPRESENTATIVES OF THE TWO WARRING FACTIONS HAVE ASSEMBLED TO DISCUSS PEACE.
WITHIN A GREAT HALL OF THE BUILDING
GENTLEMEN! WE'VE GOT TO COME TO TERMS! WE MUSTN'T PERMIT THIS BLOODSHED TO CONTINUE!
WE'LL FIGHT UNTIL WE GET OUR TERMS!
BUT THEY'RE PREPOSTEROUS!
I REFUSE TO NEGOTIATE ANY FURTHER!
AND SO DO I!
WE MIGHT AS WELL BREAK UP THE MEETING. IT'S EVIDENT WE CAN'T SETTLE OUR DIFFERENCES.
I BEG TO DIFFER! NONE OF YOU WILL LEAVE THIS HALL UNTIL YOU COME TO TERMS!

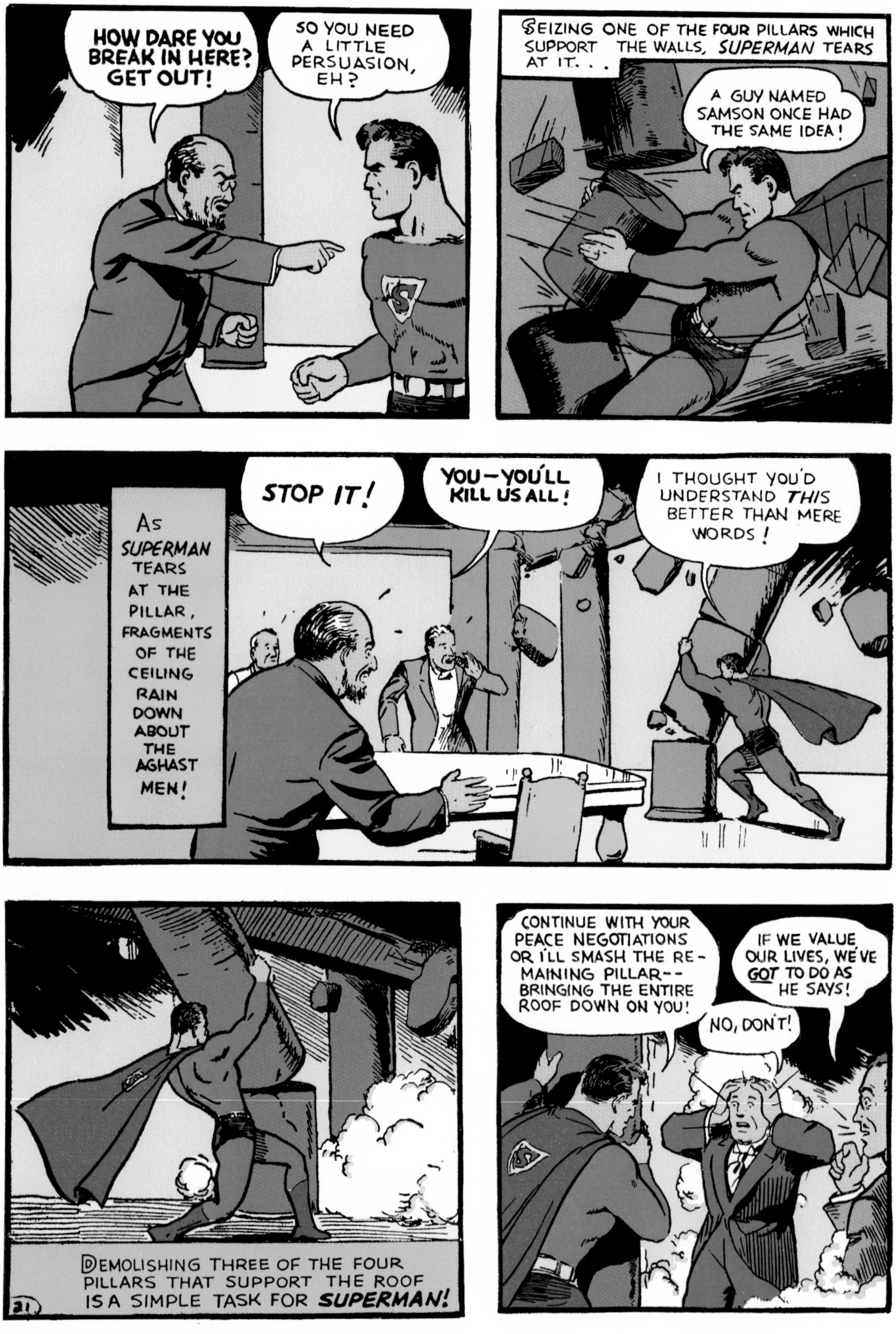
HOW DARE YOU BREAK IN HERE? GET OUT!
SO YOU NEED A LITTLE PERSUASION, EH?
SEIZING ONE OF THE FOUR PILLARS WHICH SUPPORT THE WALLS, SUPERMAN TEARS AT IT. . .
A GUY NAMED SAMSON ONCE HAD THE SAME IDEA!
AS SUPERMAN TEARS AT THE PILLAR, FRAGMENTS OF THE CEILING RAIN DOWN ABOUT THE AGHAST MEN!
STOP IT!
YOU—YOU'LL KILL US ALL!
I THOUGHT YOU'D UNDERSTAND THIS BETTER THAN MERE WORDS!
DEMOLISHING THREE OF THE FOUR PILLARS THAT SUPPORT THE ROOF IS A SIMPLE TASK FOR SUPERMAN!
21
CONTINUE WITH YOUR PEACE NEGOTIATIONS OR I'LL SMASH THE RE-MAINING PILLAR-- BRINGING THE ENTIRE ROOF DOWN ON YOU!
IF WE VALUE OUR LIVES, WE'VE GOT TO DO AS HE SAYS!
NO, DON'T!

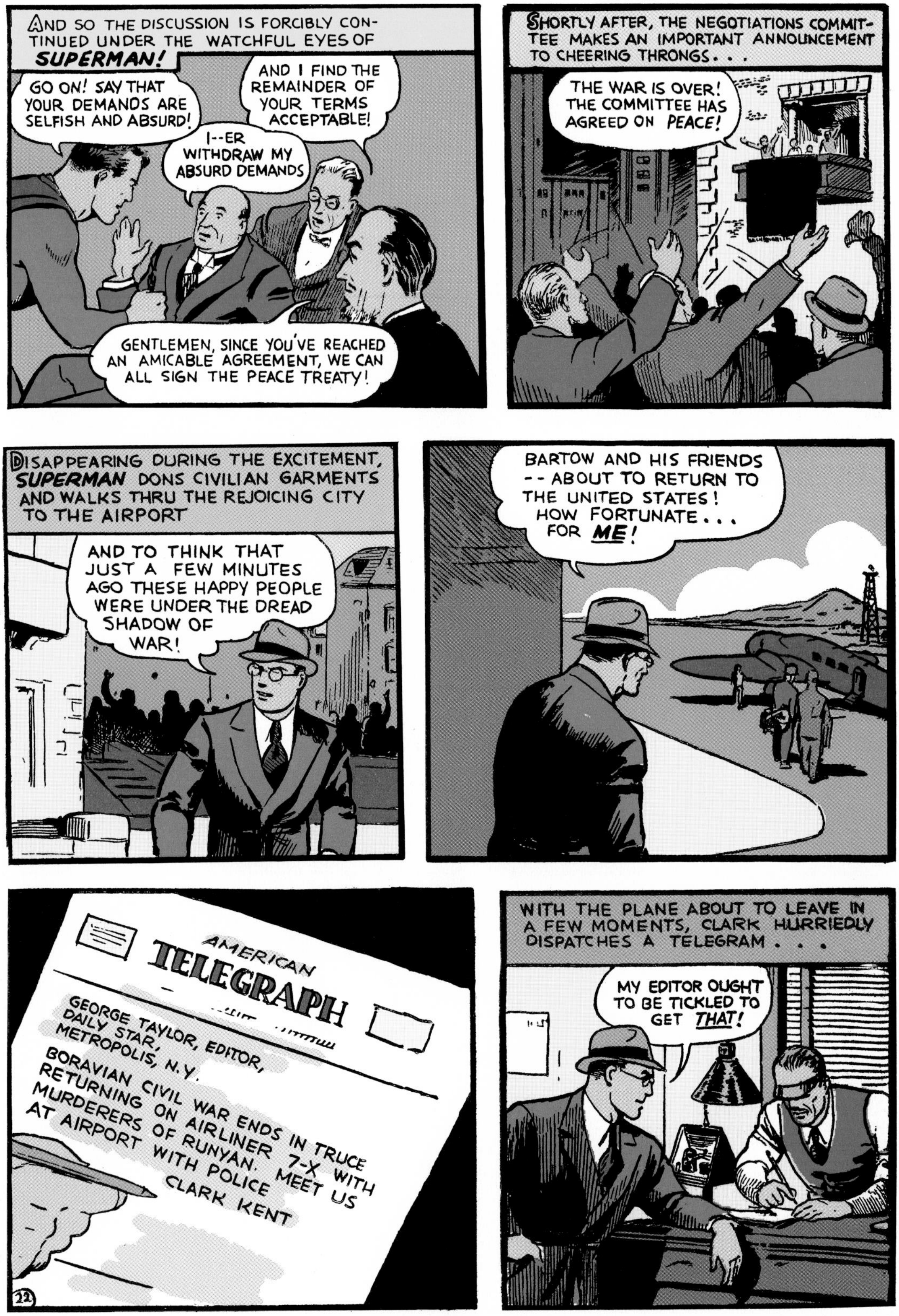
AND SO THE DISCUSSION IS FORCIBLY CONTINUED UNDER THE WATCHFUL EYES OF SUPERMAN!
GO ON! SAY THAT YOUR DEMANDS ARE SELFISH AND ABSURD!
I--ER WITHDRAW MY ABSURD DEMANDS
AND I FIND THE REMAINDER OF YOUR TERMS ACCEPTABLE!
GENTLEMEN, SINCE YOU'VE REACHED AN AMICABLE AGREEMENT, WE CAN ALL SIGN THE PEACE TREATY!
SHORTLY AFTER, THE NEGOTIATIONS COMMITTEE MAKES AN IMPORTANT ANNOUNCEMENT TO CHEERING THRONGS . . .
THE WAR IS OVER! THE COMMITTEE HAS AGREED ON PEACE!
DISAPPEARING DURING THE EXCITEMENT, SUPERMAN DONS CIVILIAN GARMENTS AND WALKS THRU THE REJOICING CITY TO THE AIRPORT
AND TO THINK THAT JUST A FEW MINUTES AGO THESE HAPPY PEOPLE WERE UNDER THE DREAD SHADOW OF WAR!
BARTOW AND HIS FRIENDS -- ABOUT TO RETURN TO THE UNITED STATES! HOW FORTUNATE . . . FOR ME!
AMERICAN TELEGRAPH
GEORGE TAYLOR, EDITOR, DAILY STAR, METROPOLIS, N.Y.
BORAVIAN CIVIL WAR ENDS IN TRUCE RETURNING ON AIRLINER 7-X WITH MURDERERS OF RUNYAN. MEET US AT AIRPORT WITH POLICE
CLARK KENT
22
WITH THE PLANE ABOUT TO LEAVE IN A FEW MOMENTS, CLARK HURRIEDLY DISPATCHES A TELEGRAM . . .
MY EDITOR OUGHT TO BE TICKLED TO GET THAT!

TOWARD THE U.S. WINGS THE GREAT BORAVIAN AIRLINER

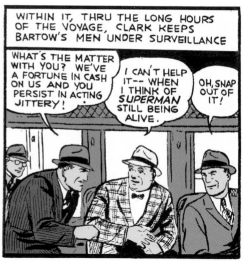

WITHIN IT, THRU THE LONG HOURS OF THE VOYAGE, CLARK KEEPS BARTOW'S MEN UNDER SURVEILLANCE

WHAT'S THE MATTER WITH YOU? WE'VE A FORTUNE IN CASH ON US AND YOU PERSIST IN ACTING JITTERY!

I CAN'T HELP IT-- WHEN I THINK OF SUPERMAN STILL BEING ALIVE.

OH, SNAP OUT OF IT!

AS METROPOLIS IS REACHED . . .

YOU'RE UNDER ARREST FOR THE MURDER OF ADOLPHUS RUNYAN!

BUT -- BUT THERE MUST BE SOME MISTAKE! WHO MAKES THIS RIDICULOUS CHARGE?

AIRLINES

I DO! -- AND YOU WON'T THINK IT SO RIDICULOUS WHEN A COURT OF LAW MAKES YOU PAY FOR YOUR CRIME!

NICE GOING, CLARK! NOW GET DOWN TO THE OFFICE AND TURN OUT THE STORY BEFORE ANOTHER PAPER SCOOPS US!

RIGHTO!

DAYS LATER -- KENT TAKES THE WITNESS STAND . . .

AND I DISTINCTLY OVERHEARD BARTOW THREATENING RUNYAN'S LIFE!

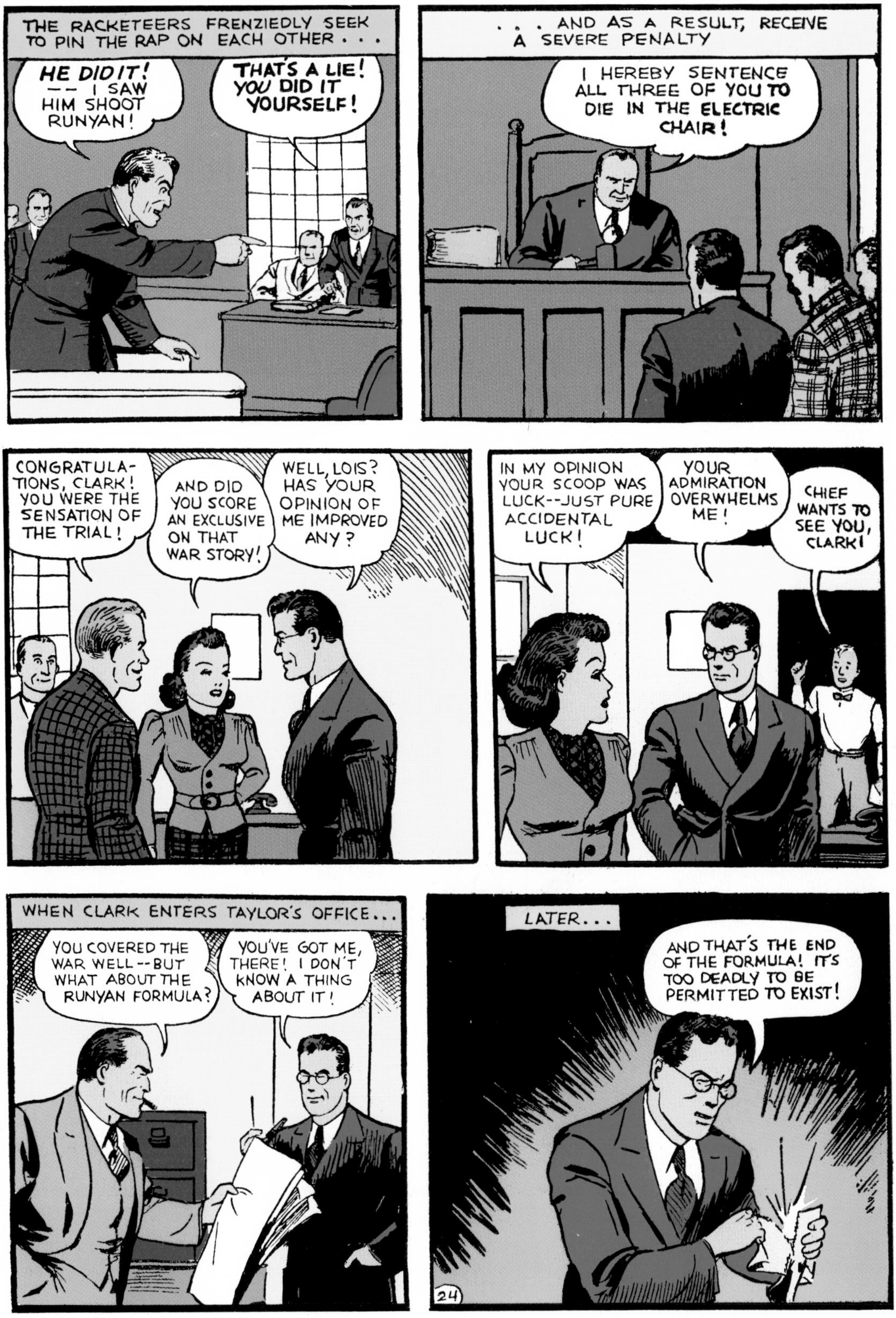
THE RACKETEERS FRENZIEDLY SEEK TO PIN THE RAP ON EACH OTHER . . .
HE DID IT! -- I SAW HIM SHOOT RUNYAN!
THAT'S A LIE! YOU DID IT YOURSELF!
. . . AND AS A RESULT, RECEIVE A SEVERE PENALTY
I HEREBY SENTENCE ALL THREE OF YOU TO DIE IN THE ELECTRIC CHAIR!
CONGRATULATIONS, CLARK! YOU WERE THE SENSATION OF THE TRIAL!
AND DID YOU SCORE AN EXCLUSIVE ON THAT WAR STORY!
WELL, LOIS? HAS YOUR OPINION OF ME IMPROVED ANY?
IN MY OPINION YOUR SCOOP WAS LUCK--JUST PURE ACCIDENTAL LUCK!
YOUR ADMIRATION OVERWHELMS ME!
CHIEF WANTS TO SEE YOU, CLARK!
WHEN CLARK ENTERS TAYLOR'S OFFICE...
YOU COVERED THE WAR WELL--BUT WHAT ABOUT THE RUNYAN FORMULA?
YOU'VE GOT ME, THERE! I DON'T KNOW A THING ABOUT IT!
LATER...
AND THAT'S THE END OF THE FORMULA! IT'S TOO DEADLY TO BE PERMITTED TO EXIST!
24

Thousands of Supermen of America members are already wearing this beautifully colored SUPERMAN EMBLEM!

Get yours! **It's free!**

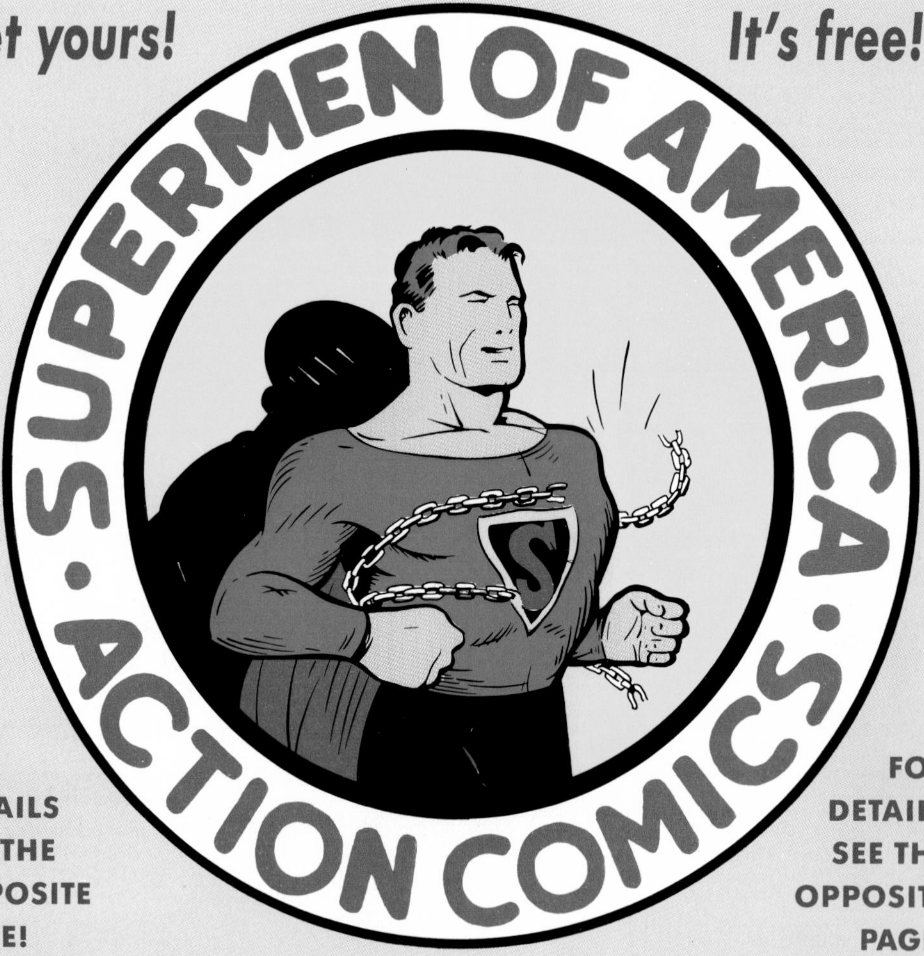
SUPERMEN OF AMERICA
• ACTION COMICS •

FOR DETAILS SEE THE OPPOSITE PAGE!

FOR DETAILS SEE THE OPPOSITE PAGE!

THIS IS THE ACTUAL SIZE OF THE EMBLEM!

This dandy felt SUPERMAN EMBLEM is made in four brilliant colors and can be sewed on your sweater, bathing suit, polo shirt or sweat-shirt.

Be sure to get yours *right away!* You'll be proud to wear it and everyone in your neighborhood will envy you.

HERE'S ALL YOU HAVE TO DO TO GET THIS BEAUTIFUL FREE SUPERMAN EMBLEM!

1. If you are already a member, get three (3) of your friends to join the SUPERMEN OF AMERICA. Get 10c from each of them to cover the cost of mailing.

2. Print the 3 names, addresses and ages on the large coupon below and send it in to Superman, c/o Action Comics, 480 Lexington Avenue, New York City, together with the 30c. Also, on this coupon print your own name and your Membership number. *This is important!*

3. Each of these new Members will receive a Membership Certificate, a Button and a Superman Code . . *and you'll receive this fine emblem FREE!!* So be sure to get at least three of your friends to join the SUPERMEN OF AMERICA.

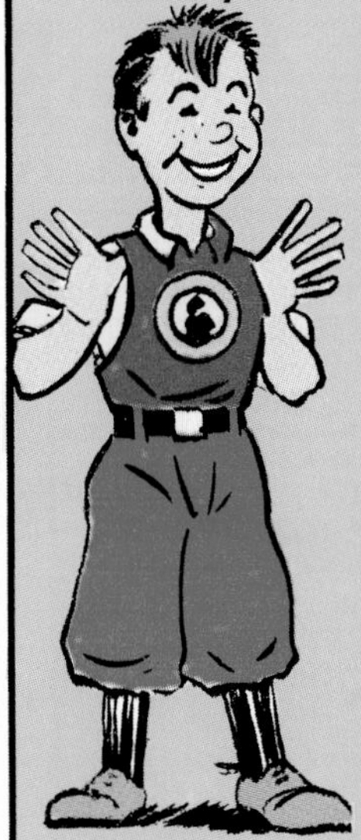

SUPERMAN, c/o ACTION COMICS
480 LEXINGTON AVENUE, N. Y. C. S/2

Below are the names and addresses of three of my friends who wish to join SUPERMEN OF AMERICA. I enclose 30c to cover cost of mailing. It is understood that I am to receive the Superman Emblem FREE of charge.

1.
NAME______________________ AGE______
ADDRESS______________________
CITY & STATE______________________

2.
NAME______________________ AGE______
ADDRESS______________________
CITY & STATE______________________

3.
NAME______________________ AGE______
ADDRESS______________________
CITY & STATE______________________

MY NAME IS______________________ No.______
ADDRESS______________________
CITY & STATE______________________

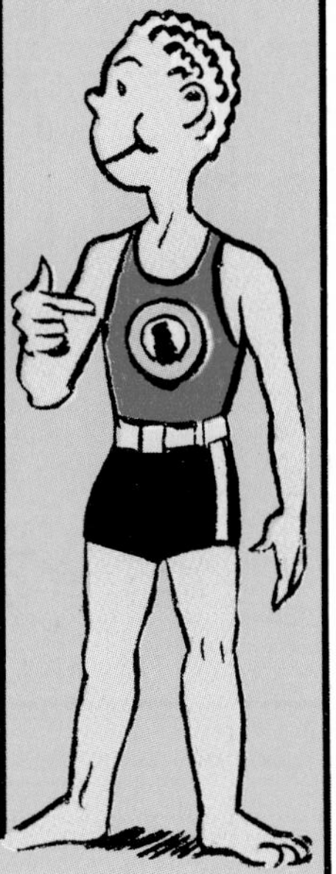

If you are *not yet* a Member of the SUPERMEN OF AMERICA, you can join by filling in the coupon on right and take advantage of this FREE emblem offer by getting three others to join with you! SEND in the coupon on the right and the coupon above properly filled in, together with 40c, and you'll receive a FREE emblem, too!

SUPERMAN, S/2
c/o ACTION COMICS,

Dear Superman:

Please enroll me as a Charter Member of the SUPERMEN OF AMERICA. I enclose 10c to cover cost of mailing. It is understood that I am to receive my Membership Certificate, Button and Superman Code.

NAME______________________ AGE______
STREET ADDRESS______________________
CITY AND STATE______________________

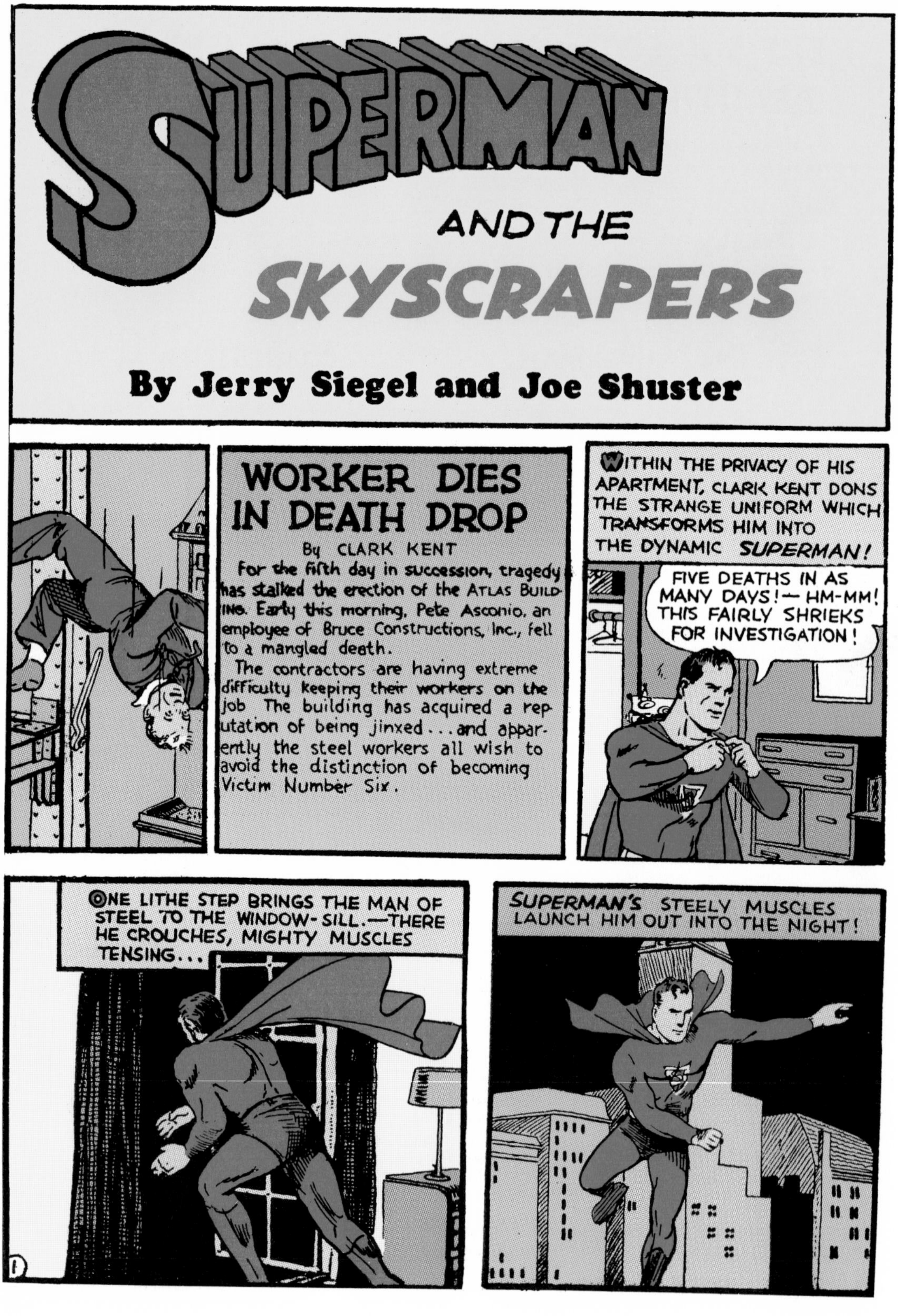
SUPERMAN
AND THE
SKYSCRAPERS
By Jerry Siegel and Joe Shuster
WORKER DIES IN DEATH DROP
By CLARK KENT
For the fifth day in succession, tragedy has stalked the erection of the ATLAS BUILDING. Early this morning, Pete Asconio, an employee of Bruce Constructions, Inc., fell to a mangled death.
The contractors are having extreme difficulty keeping their workers on the job The building has acquired a reputation of being jinxed . . . and apparently the steel workers all wish to avoid the distinction of becoming Victim Number Six.
WITHIN THE PRIVACY OF HIS APARTMENT, CLARK KENT DONS THE STRANGE UNIFORM WHICH TRANSFORMS HIM INTO THE DYNAMIC SUPERMAN!
FIVE DEATHS IN AS MANY DAYS!—HM-MM! THIS FAIRLY SHRIEKS FOR INVESTIGATION!
ONE LITHE STEP BRINGS THE MAN OF STEEL TO THE WINDOW-SILL.—THERE HE CROUCHES, MIGHTY MUSCLES TENSING...
SUPERMAN'S STEELY MUSCLES LAUNCH HIM OUT INTO THE NIGHT!

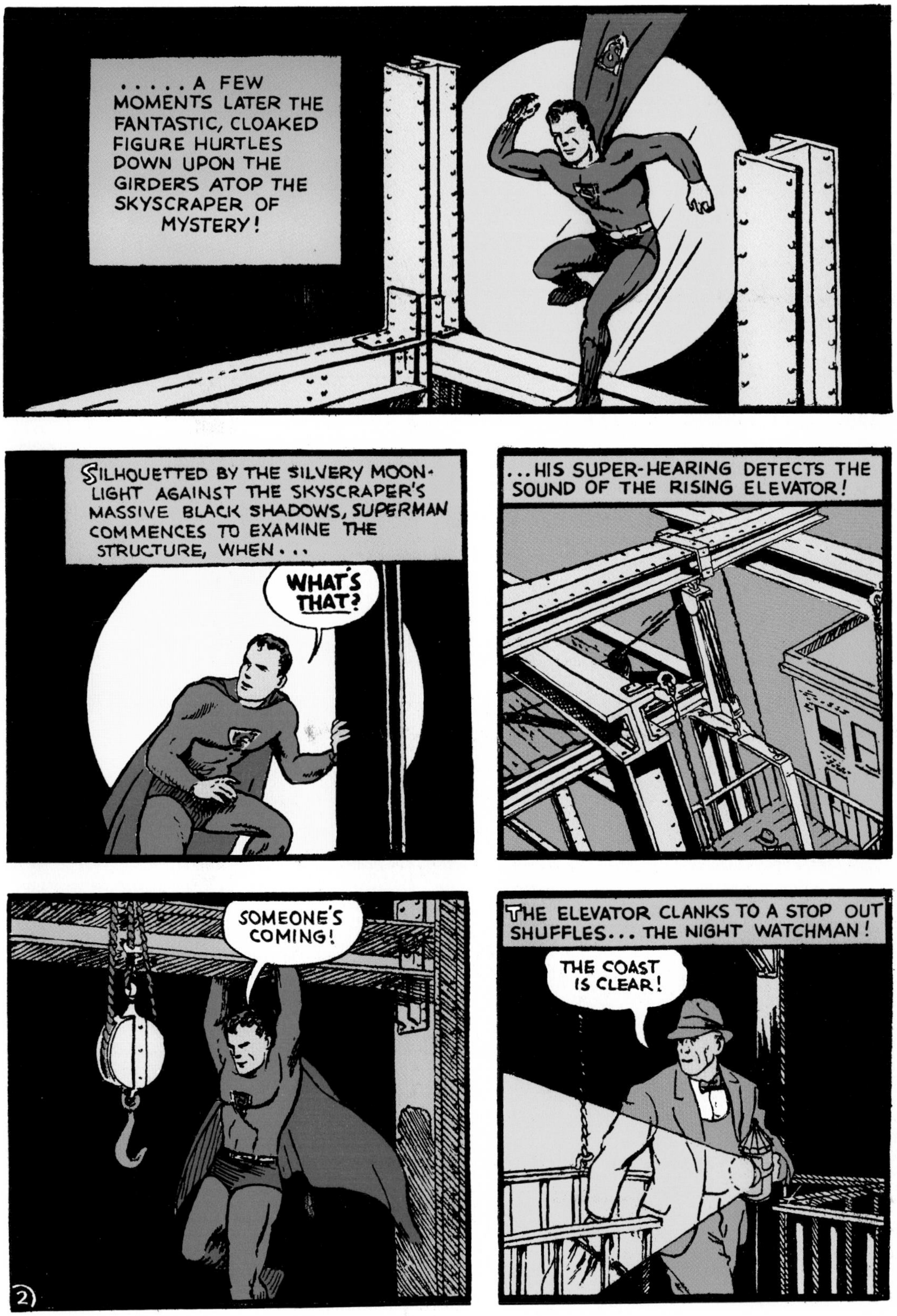
.....A FEW MOMENTS LATER THE FANTASTIC, CLOAKED FIGURE HURTLES DOWN UPON THE GIRDERS ATOP THE SKYSCRAPER OF MYSTERY!
SILHOUETTED BY THE SILVERY MOON-LIGHT AGAINST THE SKYSCRAPER'S MASSIVE BLACK SHADOWS, SUPERMAN COMMENCES TO EXAMINE THE STRUCTURE, WHEN...
WHAT'S THAT?
...HIS SUPER-HEARING DETECTS THE SOUND OF THE RISING ELEVATOR!
SOMEONE'S COMING!
THE ELEVATOR CLANKS TO A STOP OUT SHUFFLES... THE NIGHT WATCHMAN!
THE COAST IS CLEAR!

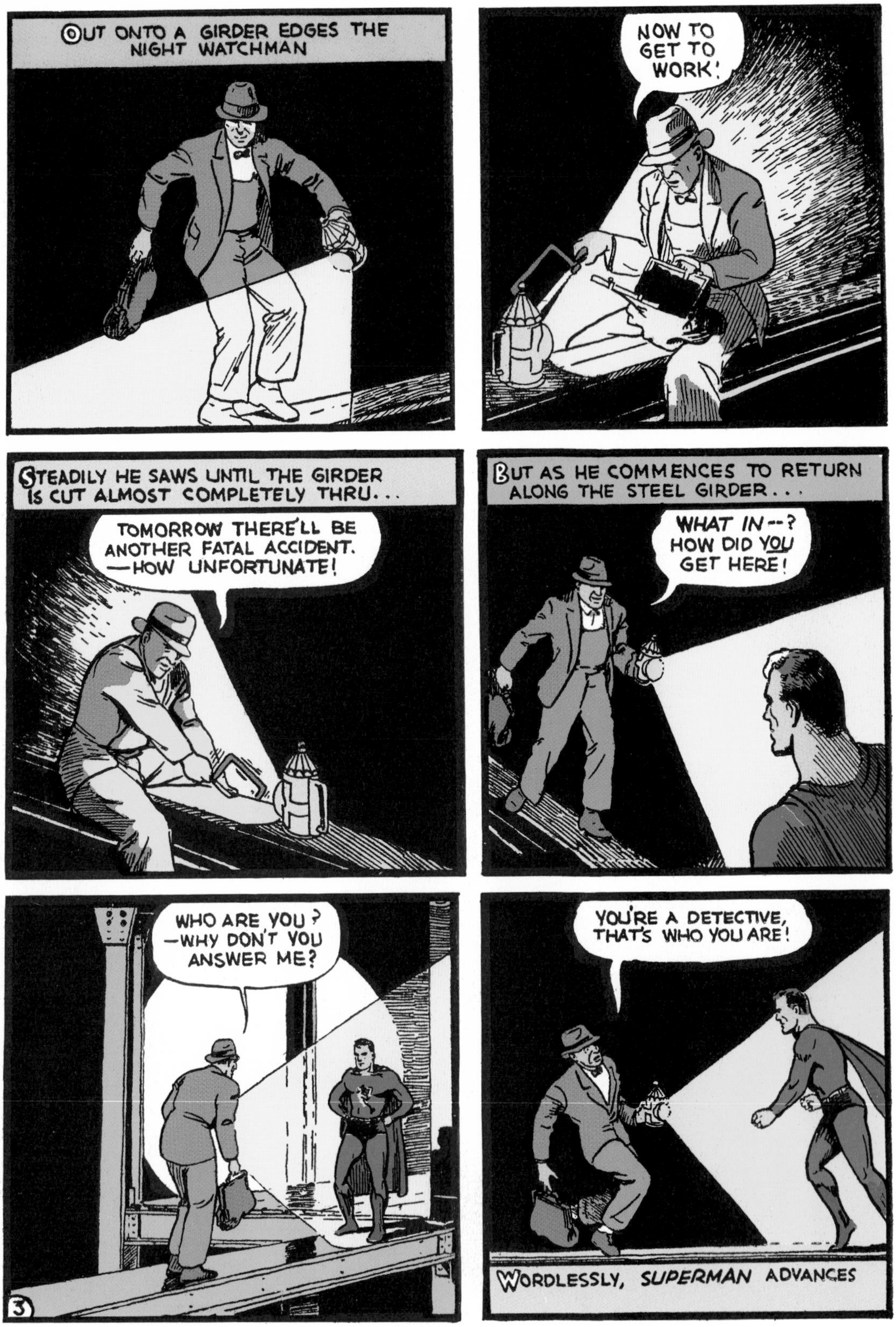
OUT ONTO A GIRDER EDGES THE NIGHT WATCHMAN
NOW TO GET TO WORK!
STEADILY HE SAWS UNTIL THE GIRDER IS CUT ALMOST COMPLETELY THRU...
TOMORROW THERE'LL BE ANOTHER FATAL ACCIDENT. —HOW UNFORTUNATE!
BUT AS HE COMMENCES TO RETURN ALONG THE STEEL GIRDER...
WHAT IN--? HOW DID YOU GET HERE!
WHO ARE YOU? —WHY DON'T YOU ANSWER ME?
3
YOU'RE A DETECTIVE, THAT'S WHO YOU ARE!
WORDLESSLY, SUPERMAN ADVANCES

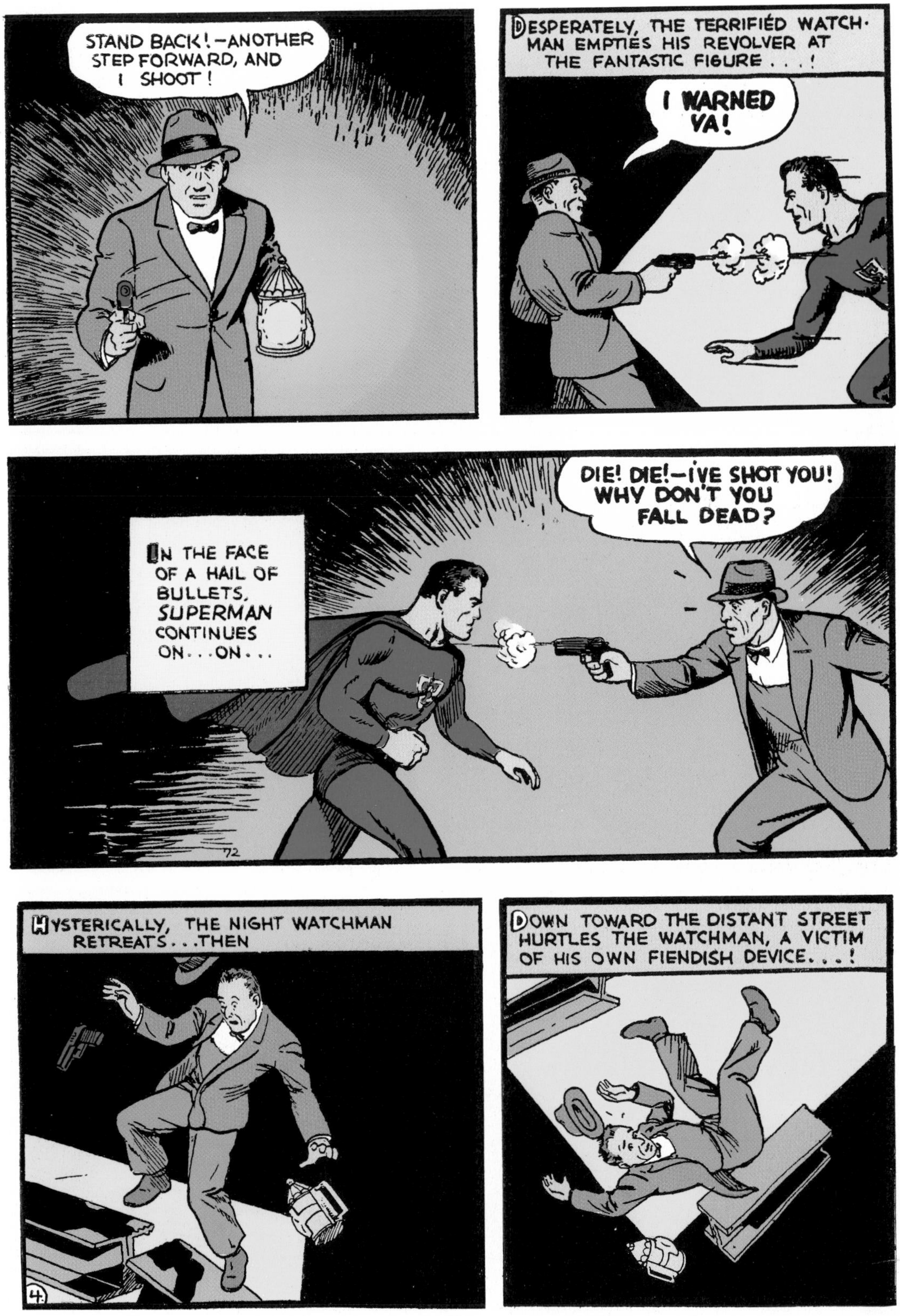
STAND BACK!-ANOTHER STEP FORWARD, AND I SHOOT!
DESPERATELY, THE TERRIFIED WATCH-MAN EMPTIES HIS REVOLVER AT THE FANTASTIC FIGURE...!
I WARNED YA!
IN THE FACE OF A HAIL OF BULLETS, SUPERMAN CONTINUES ON...ON...
DIE! DIE!-I'VE SHOT YOU! WHY DON'T YOU FALL DEAD?
HYSTERICALLY, THE NIGHT WATCHMAN RETREATS...THEN
DOWN TOWARD THE DISTANT STREET HURTLES THE WATCHMAN, A VICTIM OF HIS OWN FIENDISH DEVICE...!

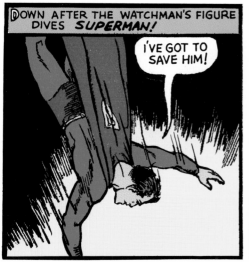

DOWN AFTER THE WATCHMAN'S FIGURE DIVES SUPERMAN!
I'VE GOT TO SAVE HIM!
CLOSER TOWARD THE EARTH HURTLE THE TWO BODIES, THE SPACE BETWEEN THEM GRADUALLY NARROWING...
HE'S HAD A HEAD-START! — CAN I REACH HIM?
GOT HIS HEEL!
BRUCE CONST. -INC-
WITH THE GROUND BUT INCHES AWAY HOW CAN SUPERMAN SAVE THE WATCHMAN FROM A MANGLED DOOM?
WITH ONLY INSTANTS TO ACT, SUPERMAN WHIRLS THE WATCHMAN UP INTO THE AIR ABOVE HIM...
UPSY-DAISY!
5
WHAM! — SUPERMAN STRIKES THE GROUND AMIDST FLYING EARTH.... TREMENDOUS MUSCLES CUSHION THE SHOCK...

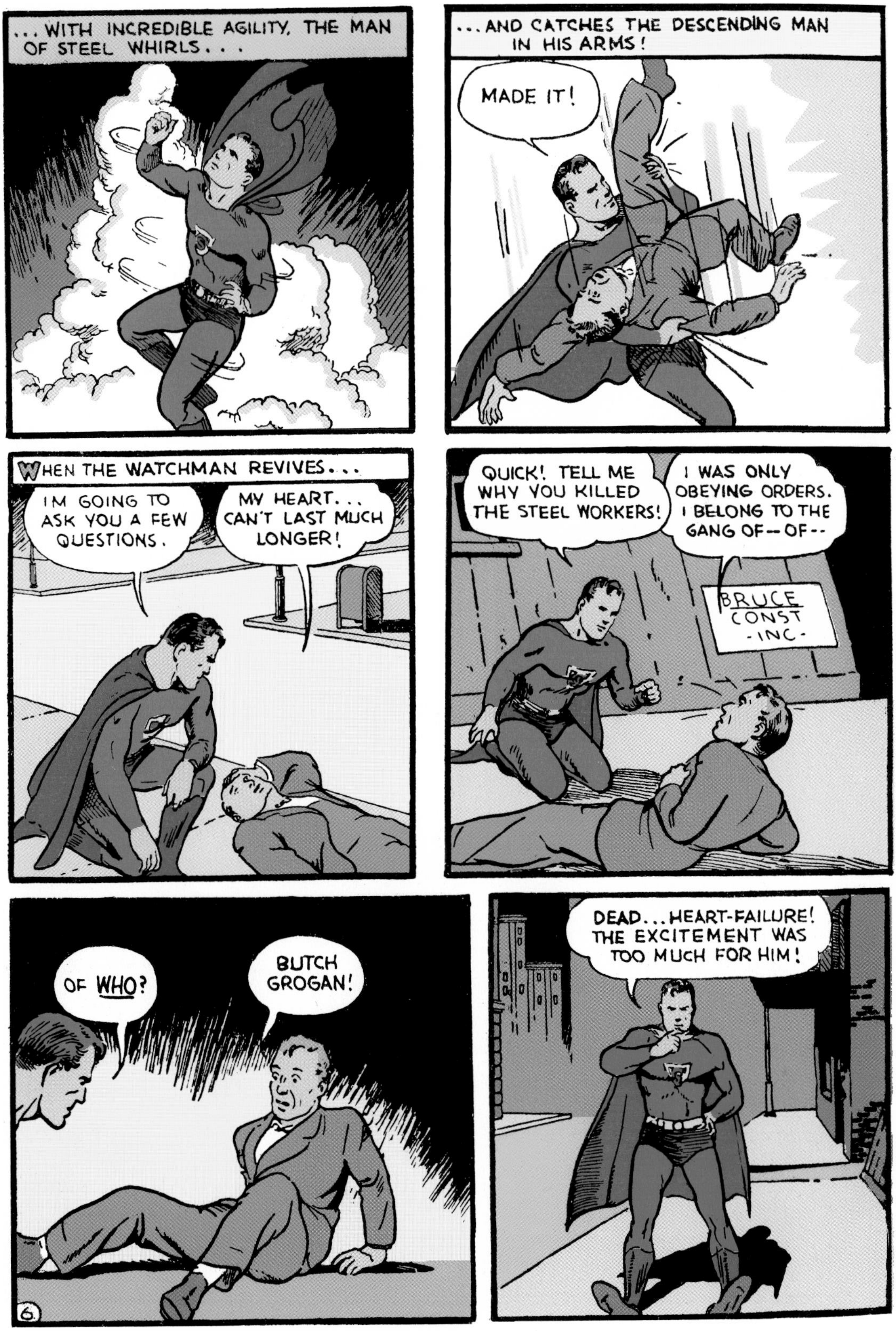
...WITH INCREDIBLE AGILITY, THE MAN OF STEEL WHIRLS...
...AND CATCHES THE DESCENDING MAN IN HIS ARMS!
MADE IT!
WHEN THE WATCHMAN REVIVES...
I'M GOING TO ASK YOU A FEW QUESTIONS.
MY HEART... CAN'T LAST MUCH LONGER!
QUICK! TELL ME WHY YOU KILLED THE STEEL WORKERS!
I WAS ONLY OBEYING ORDERS. I BELONG TO THE GANG OF--OF--
BRUCE CONST -INC-
OF WHO?
BUTCH GROGAN!
6
DEAD...HEART-FAILURE! THE EXCITEMENT WAS TOO MUCH FOR HIM!

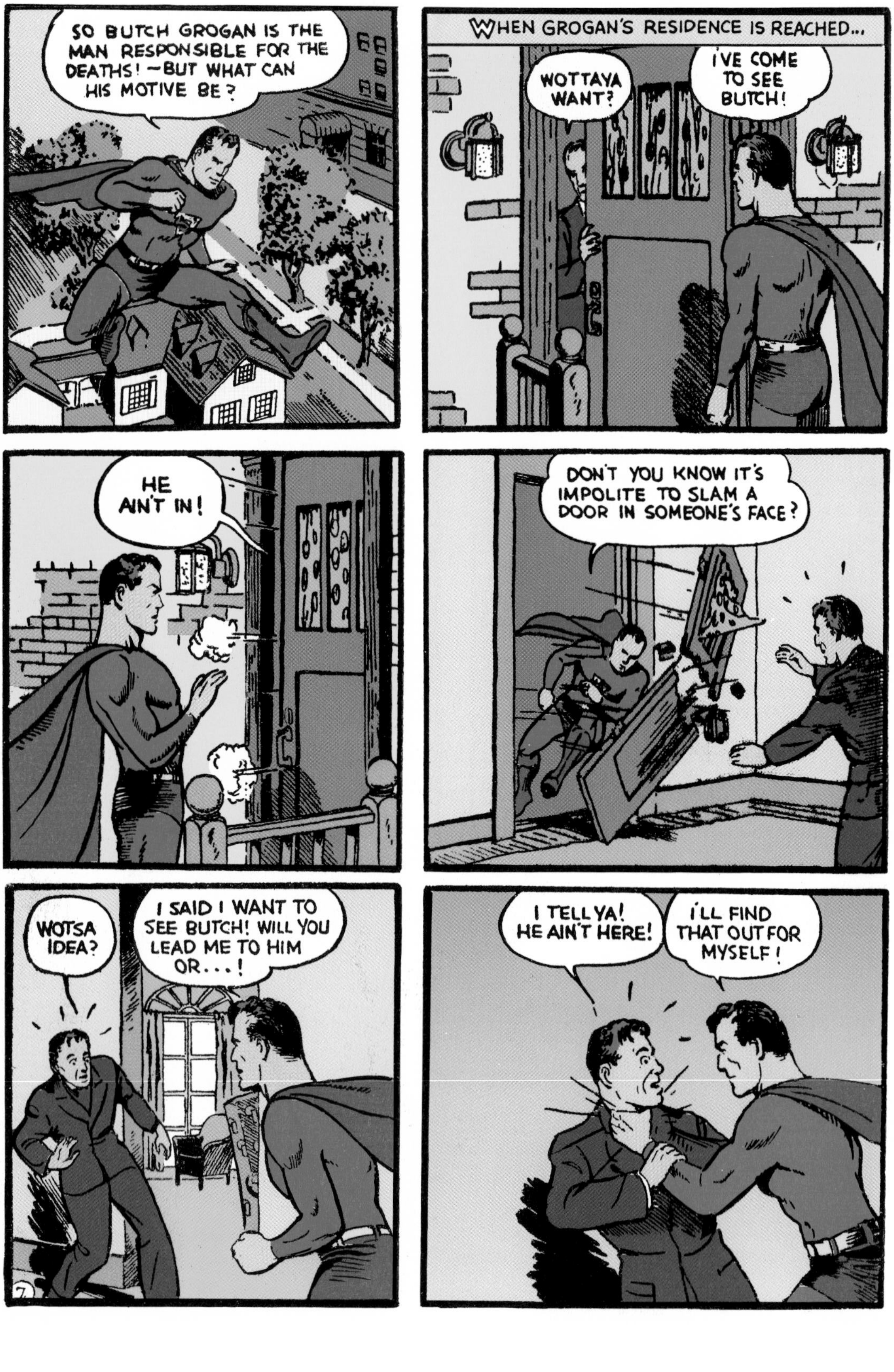
SO BUTCH GROGAN IS THE MAN RESPONSIBLE FOR THE DEATHS! —BUT WHAT CAN HIS MOTIVE BE?
WHEN GROGAN'S RESIDENCE IS REACHED...
WOTTAYA WANT?
I'VE COME TO SEE BUTCH!
HE AIN'T IN!
DON'T YOU KNOW IT'S IMPOLITE TO SLAM A DOOR IN SOMEONE'S FACE?
WOTSA IDEA?
I SAID I WANT TO SEE BUTCH! WILL YOU LEAD ME TO HIM OR...!
7
I TELL YA! HE AIN'T HERE!
I'LL FIND THAT OUT FOR MYSELF!

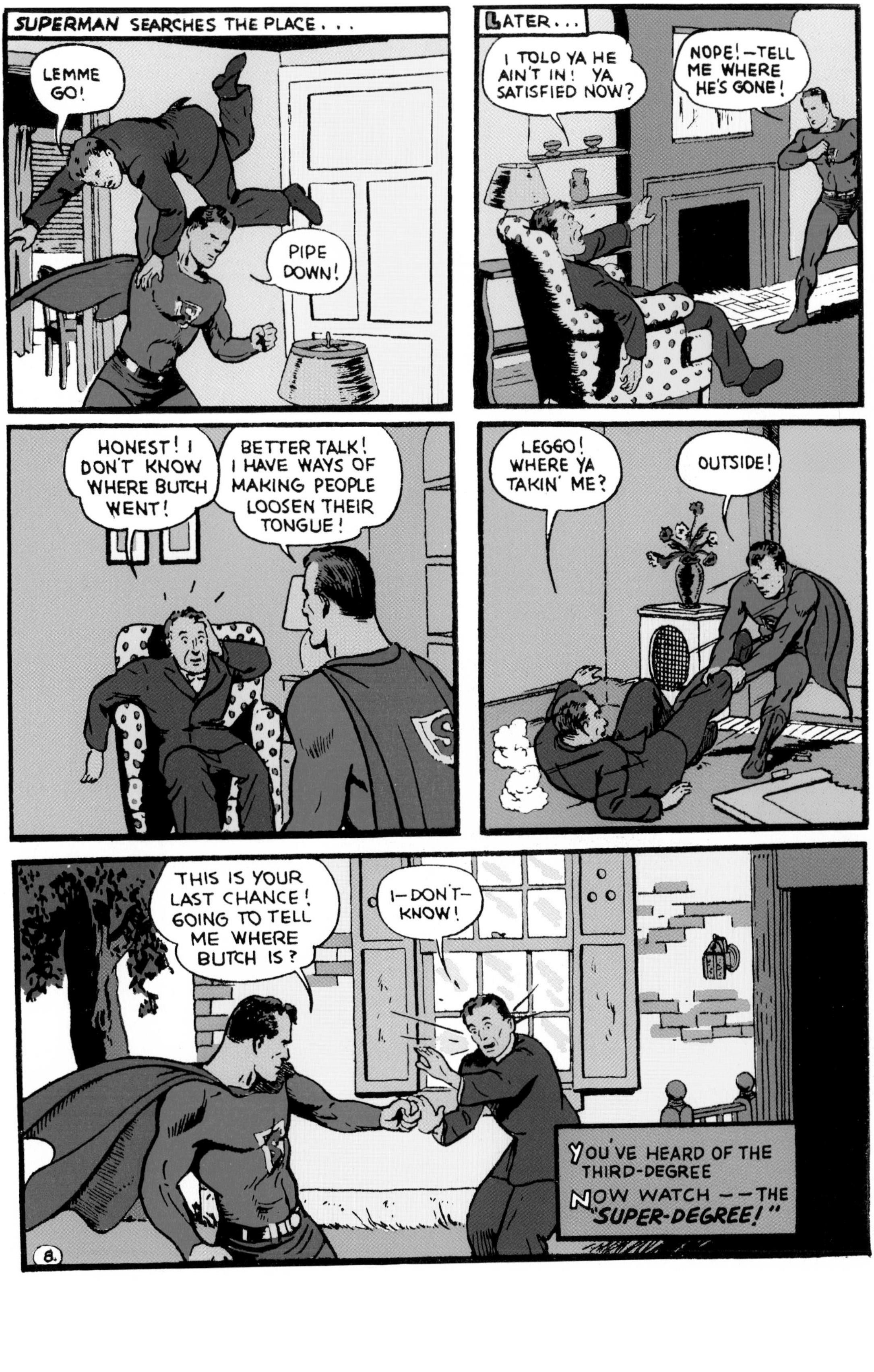
SUPERMAN SEARCHES THE PLACE . . .
LEMME GO!
PIPE DOWN!
LATER...
I TOLD YA HE AIN'T IN! YA SATISFIED NOW?
NOPE!—TELL ME WHERE HE'S GONE!
HONEST! I DON'T KNOW WHERE BUTCH WENT!
BETTER TALK! I HAVE WAYS OF MAKING PEOPLE LOOSEN THEIR TONGUE!
LEGGO! WHERE YA TAKIN' ME?
OUTSIDE!
THIS IS YOUR LAST CHANCE! GOING TO TELL ME WHERE BUTCH IS?
I—DON'T—KNOW!
YOU'VE HEARD OF THE THIRD-DEGREE
NOW WATCH — — THE "SUPER-DEGREE!"
8.

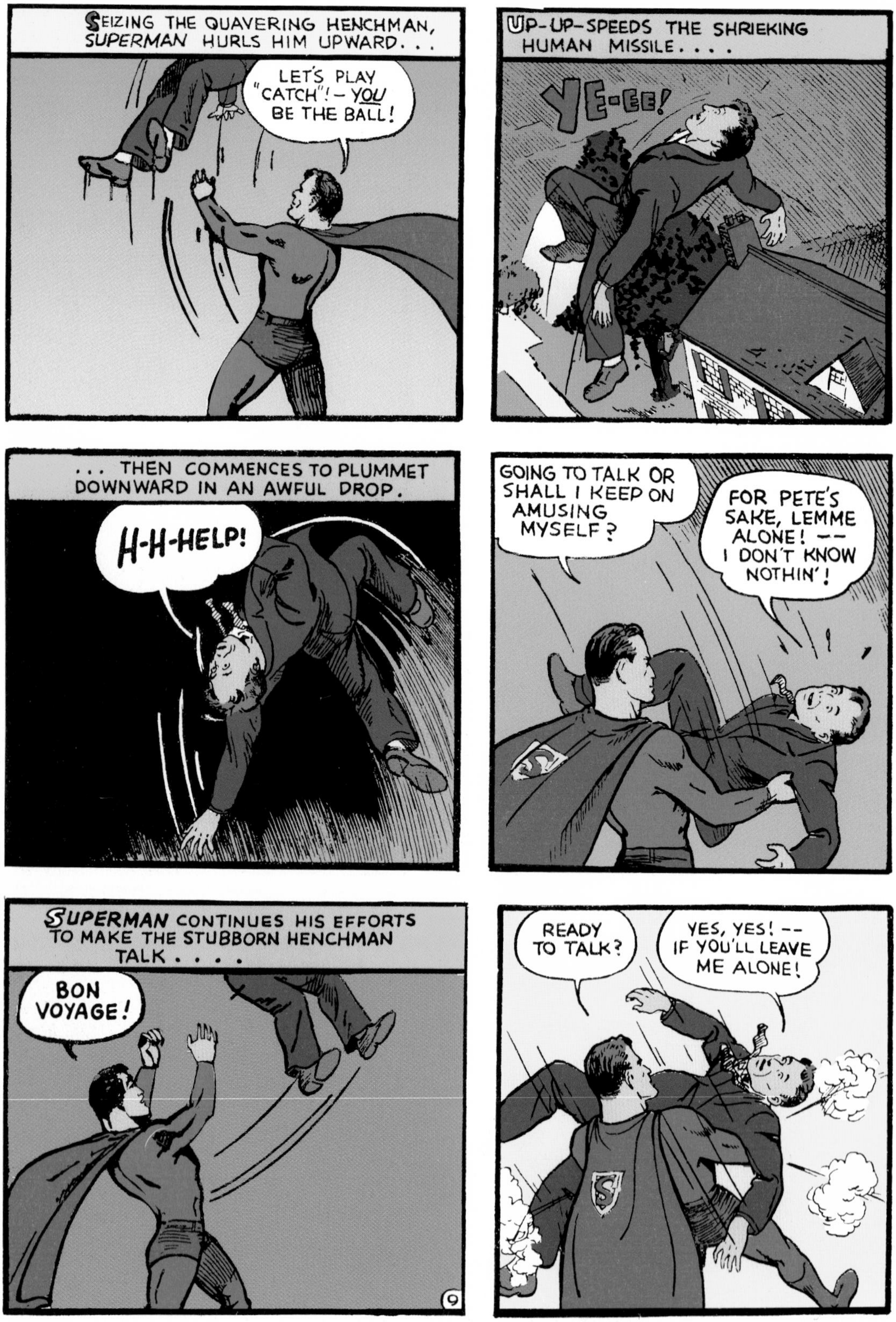
SEIZING THE QUAVERING HENCHMAN, SUPERMAN HURLS HIM UPWARD. . .
LET'S PLAY "CATCH"! – YOU BE THE BALL!
UP-UP–SPEEDS THE SHRIEKING HUMAN MISSILE. . . .
YE-EE!
. . . THEN COMMENCES TO PLUMMET DOWNWARD IN AN AWFUL DROP.
H-H-HELP!
GOING TO TALK OR SHALL I KEEP ON AMUSING MYSELF?
FOR PETE'S SAKE, LEMME ALONE! -- I DON'T KNOW NOTHIN'!
SUPERMAN CONTINUES HIS EFFORTS TO MAKE THE STUBBORN HENCHMAN TALK. . . .
BON VOYAGE!
9
READY TO TALK?
YES, YES! -- IF YOU'LL LEAVE ME ALONE!

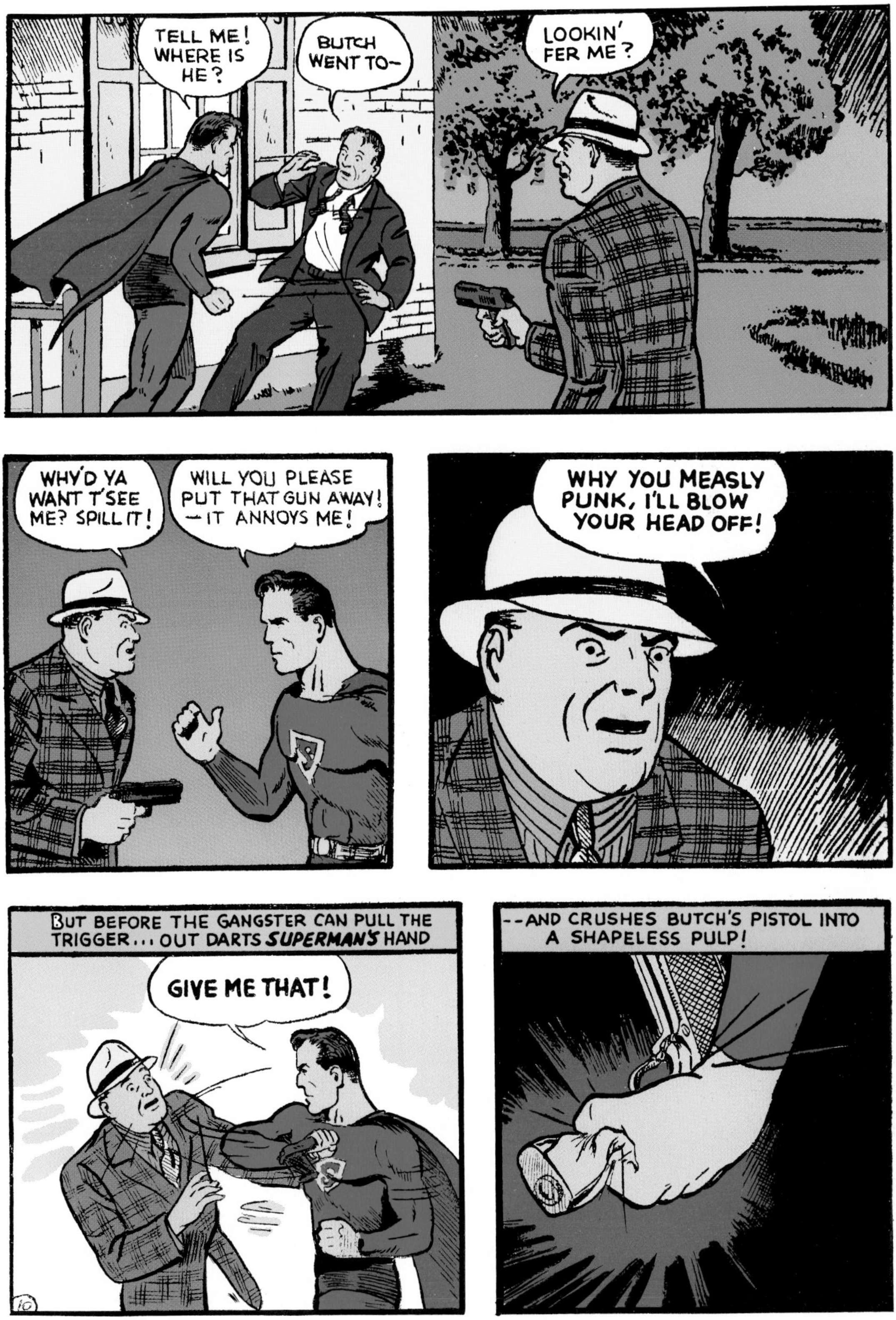
TELL ME! WHERE IS HE?
BUTCH WENT TO—
LOOKIN' FER ME?
WHY'D YA WANT T'SEE ME? SPILL IT!
WILL YOU PLEASE PUT THAT GUN AWAY! —IT ANNOYS ME!
WHY YOU MEASLY PUNK, I'LL BLOW YOUR HEAD OFF!
BUT BEFORE THE GANGSTER CAN PULL THE TRIGGER... OUT DARTS SUPERMAN'S HAND
GIVE ME THAT!
10
--AND CRUSHES BUTCH'S PISTOL INTO A SHAPELESS PULP!

TH' GAT! YA CRUSHED IT LIKE IT WAS MADE OUTA PUTTY!

RIGHT! AND IF YOU DON'T TELL ME WHAT I WANT TO KNOW, I'LL GET TO WORK ON YOU!

SEIZING A HEAVY CLUB, BUTCH'S HENCHMAN STEALS UP ON TIP-TOE TOWARD THE MAN OF TOMORROW'S BACK...

TAKE THAT!

SUPERMAN SCARCELY FEELS THE BLOW ...BUT THE CLUB BOUNCES BACK AND KNOCKS OUT ITS WIELDER!

CR-RACK

LET'S YOU AN' I GO FOR A RIDE, EH, BUTCH?

WHAT IN--??

WHEN THE ATLAS BUILDING IS REACHED...

BEFORE HE DIED THE WATCHMAN NAMED YOU AS THE MAN WHO HIRED HIM TO KILL THE MEN WORKING ON THIS BUILDING.

HE MUSTA BEEN CRAZY!

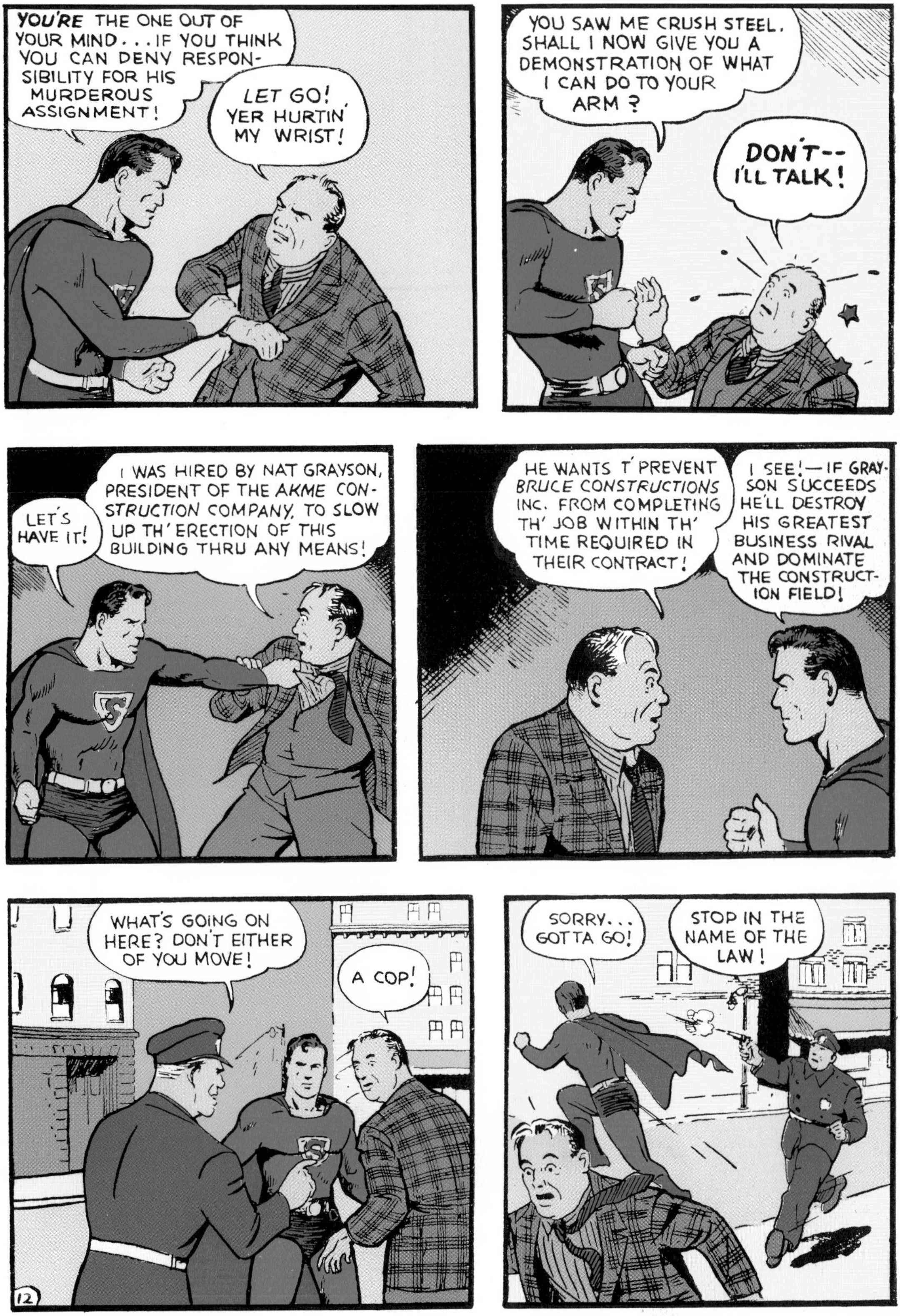
YOU'RE THE ONE OUT OF YOUR MIND. . . IF YOU THINK YOU CAN DENY RESPONSIBILITY FOR HIS MURDEROUS ASSIGNMENT!
LET GO! YER HURTIN' MY WRIST!
YOU SAW ME CRUSH STEEL. SHALL I NOW GIVE YOU A DEMONSTRATION OF WHAT I CAN DO TO YOUR ARM?
DON'T-- I'LL TALK!
LET'S HAVE IT!
I WAS HIRED BY NAT GRAYSON, PRESIDENT OF THE AKME CONSTRUCTION COMPANY, TO SLOW UP TH' ERECTION OF THIS BUILDING THRU ANY MEANS!
HE WANTS T' PREVENT BRUCE CONSTRUCTIONS INC. FROM COMPLETING TH' JOB WITHIN TH' TIME REQUIRED IN THEIR CONTRACT!
I SEE!—IF GRAYSON SUCCEEDS HE'LL DESTROY HIS GREATEST BUSINESS RIVAL AND DOMINATE THE CONSTRUCTION FIELD!
WHAT'S GOING ON HERE? DON'T EITHER OF YOU MOVE!
A COP!
12
SORRY. . . GOTTA GO!
STOP IN THE NAME OF THE LAW!

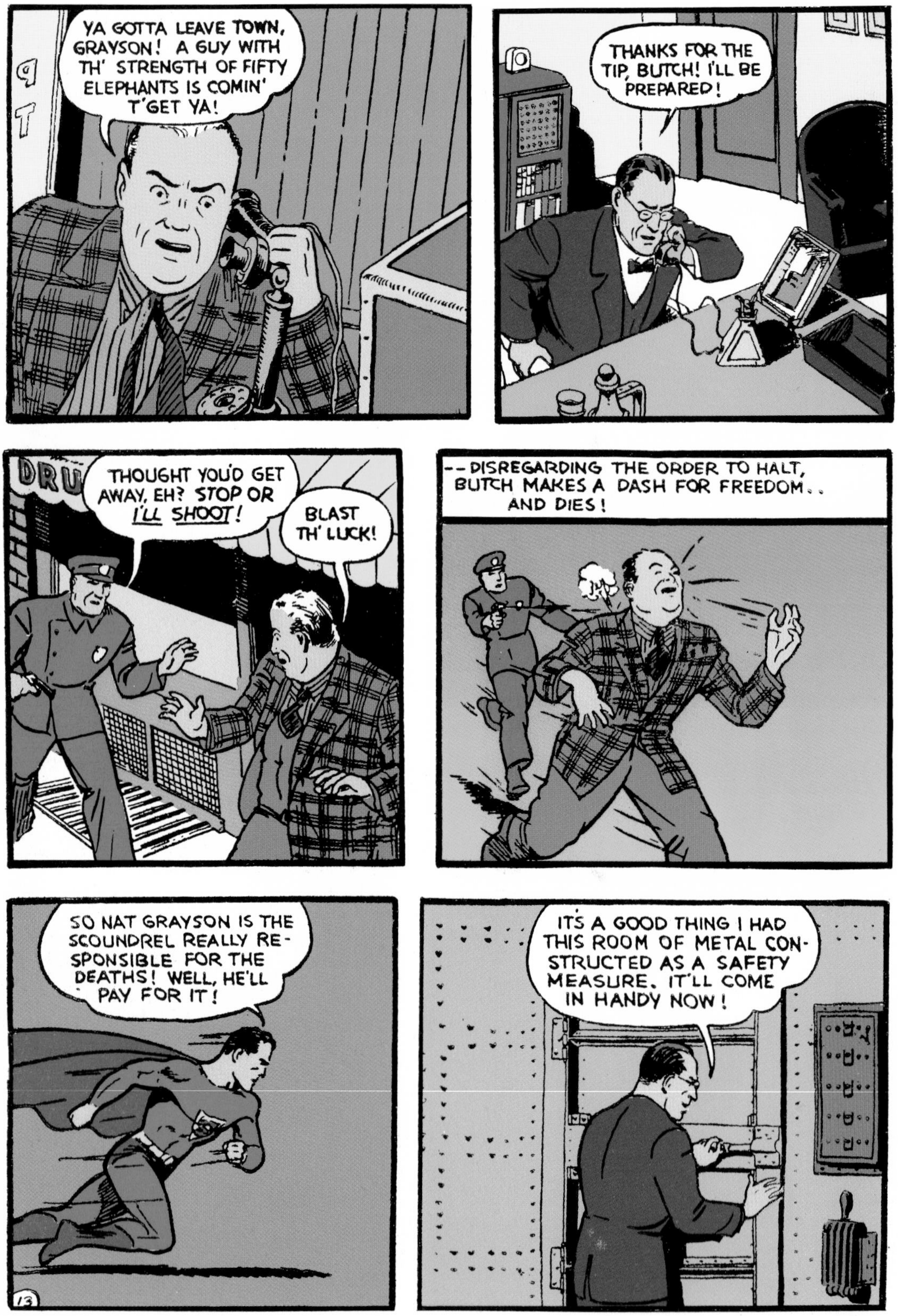
YA GOTTA LEAVE TOWN, GRAYSON! A GUY WITH TH' STRENGTH OF FIFTY ELEPHANTS IS COMIN' T'GET YA!
THANKS FOR THE TIP, BUTCH! I'LL BE PREPARED!
THOUGHT YOU'D GET AWAY, EH? STOP OR I'LL SHOOT!
BLAST TH' LUCK!
--DISREGARDING THE ORDER TO HALT, BUTCH MAKES A DASH FOR FREEDOM.. AND DIES!
SO NAT GRAYSON IS THE SCOUNDREL REALLY RE-SPONSIBLE FOR THE DEATHS! WELL, HE'LL PAY FOR IT!
13
IT'S A GOOD THING I HAD THIS ROOM OF METAL CON-STRUCTED AS A SAFETY MEASURE. IT'LL COME IN HANDY NOW!

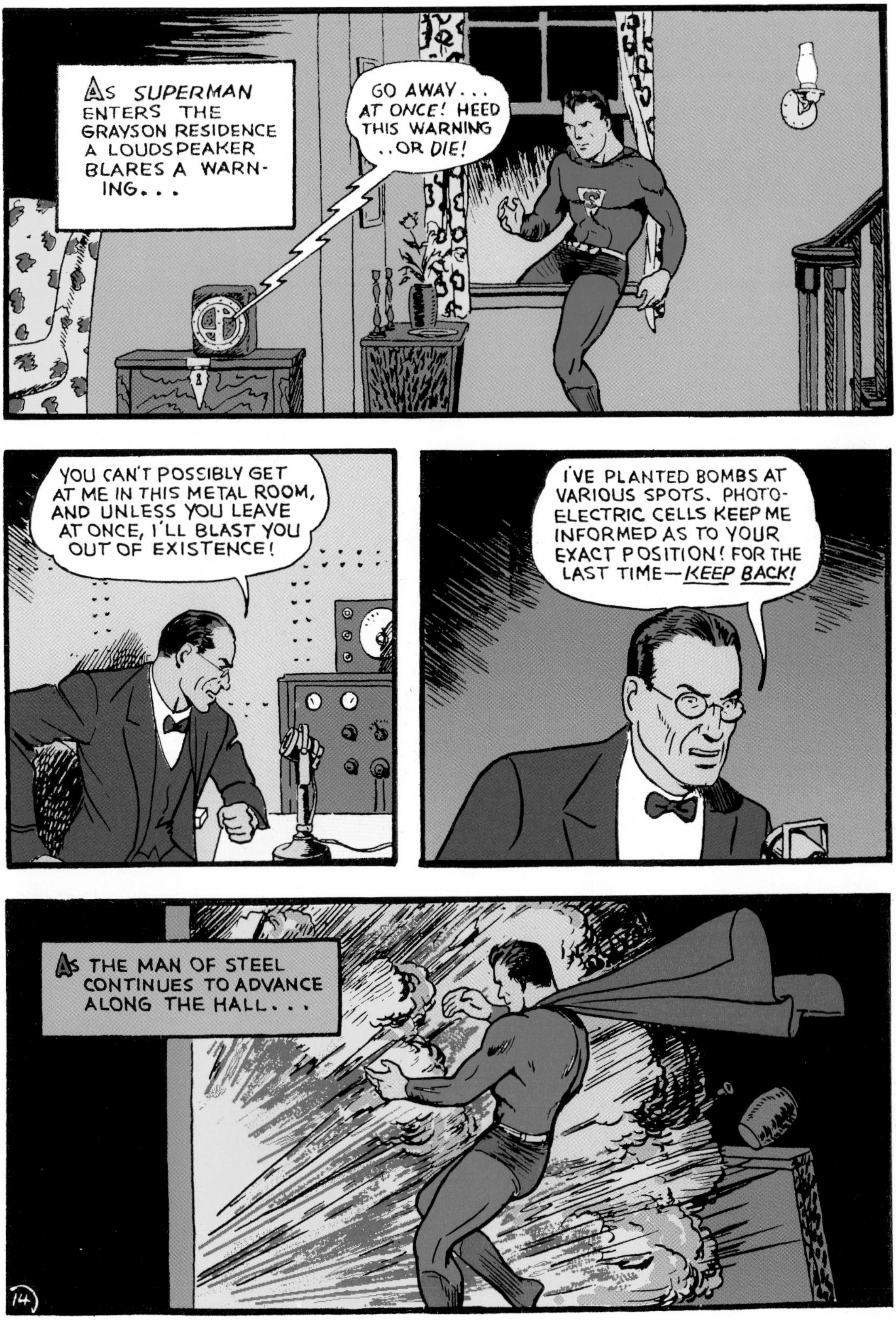
AS SUPERMAN ENTERS THE GRAYSON RESIDENCE A LOUDSPEAKER BLARES A WARNING...
GO AWAY... AT ONCE! HEED THIS WARNING ..OR DIE!
YOU CAN'T POSSIBLY GET AT ME IN THIS METAL ROOM, AND UNLESS YOU LEAVE AT ONCE, I'LL BLAST YOU OUT OF EXISTENCE!
I'VE PLANTED BOMBS AT VARIOUS SPOTS. PHOTO-ELECTRIC CELLS KEEP ME INFORMED AS TO YOUR EXACT POSITION! FOR THE LAST TIME—KEEP BACK!
AS THE MAN OF STEEL CONTINUES TO ADVANCE ALONG THE HALL...
14

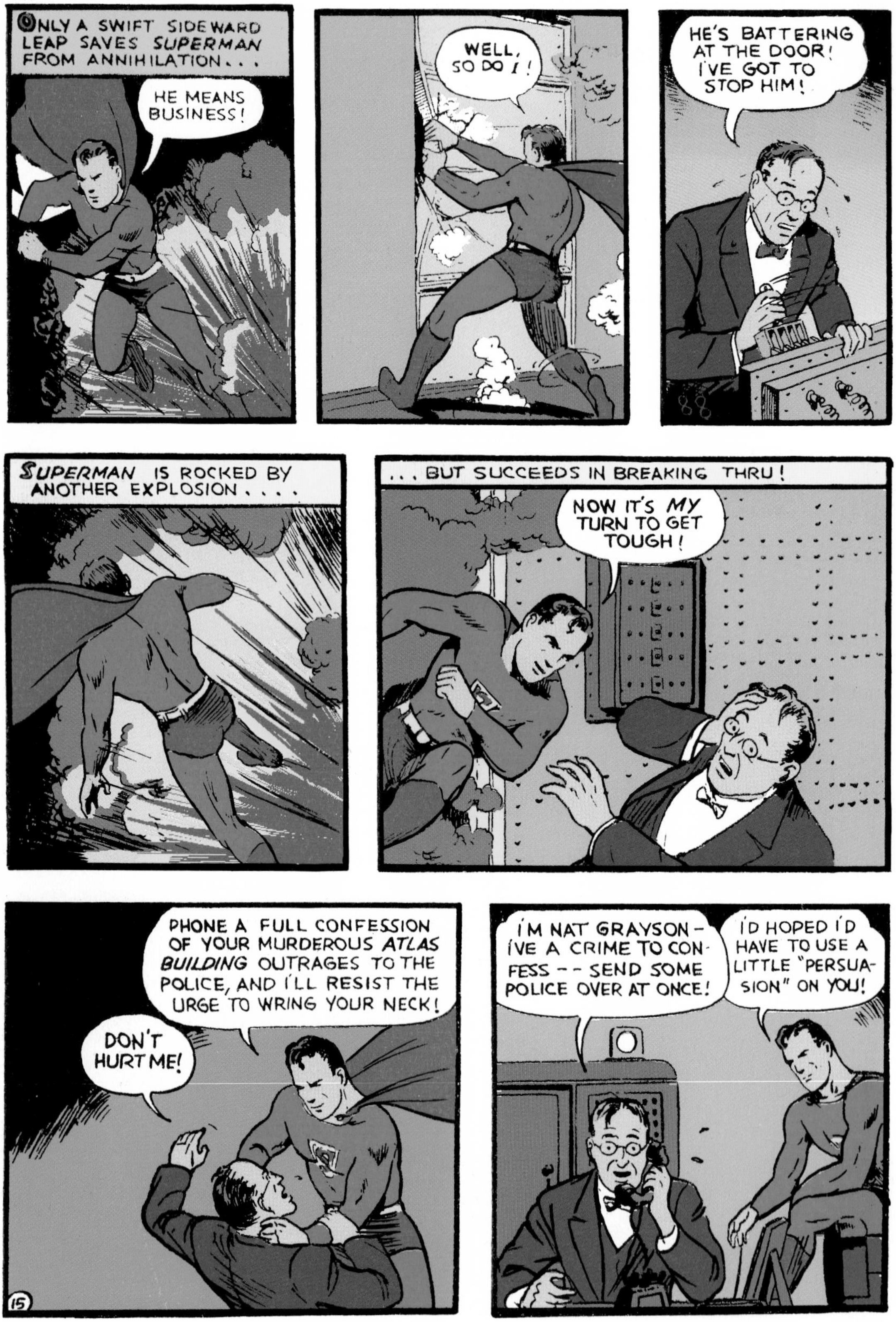
ONLY A SWIFT SIDEWARD LEAP SAVES SUPERMAN FROM ANNIHILATION . . .
HE MEANS BUSINESS!
WELL, SO DO I!
HE'S BATTERING AT THE DOOR! I'VE GOT TO STOP HIM!
SUPERMAN IS ROCKED BY ANOTHER EXPLOSION . . . .
. . . BUT SUCCEEDS IN BREAKING THRU!
NOW IT'S MY TURN TO GET TOUGH!
PHONE A FULL CONFESSION OF YOUR MURDEROUS ATLAS BUILDING OUTRAGES TO THE POLICE, AND I'LL RESIST THE URGE TO WRING YOUR NECK!
DON'T HURT ME!
15
I'M NAT GRAYSON - I'VE A CRIME TO CONFESS - - SEND SOME POLICE OVER AT ONCE!
I'D HOPED I'D HAVE TO USE A LITTLE "PERSUASION" ON YOU!

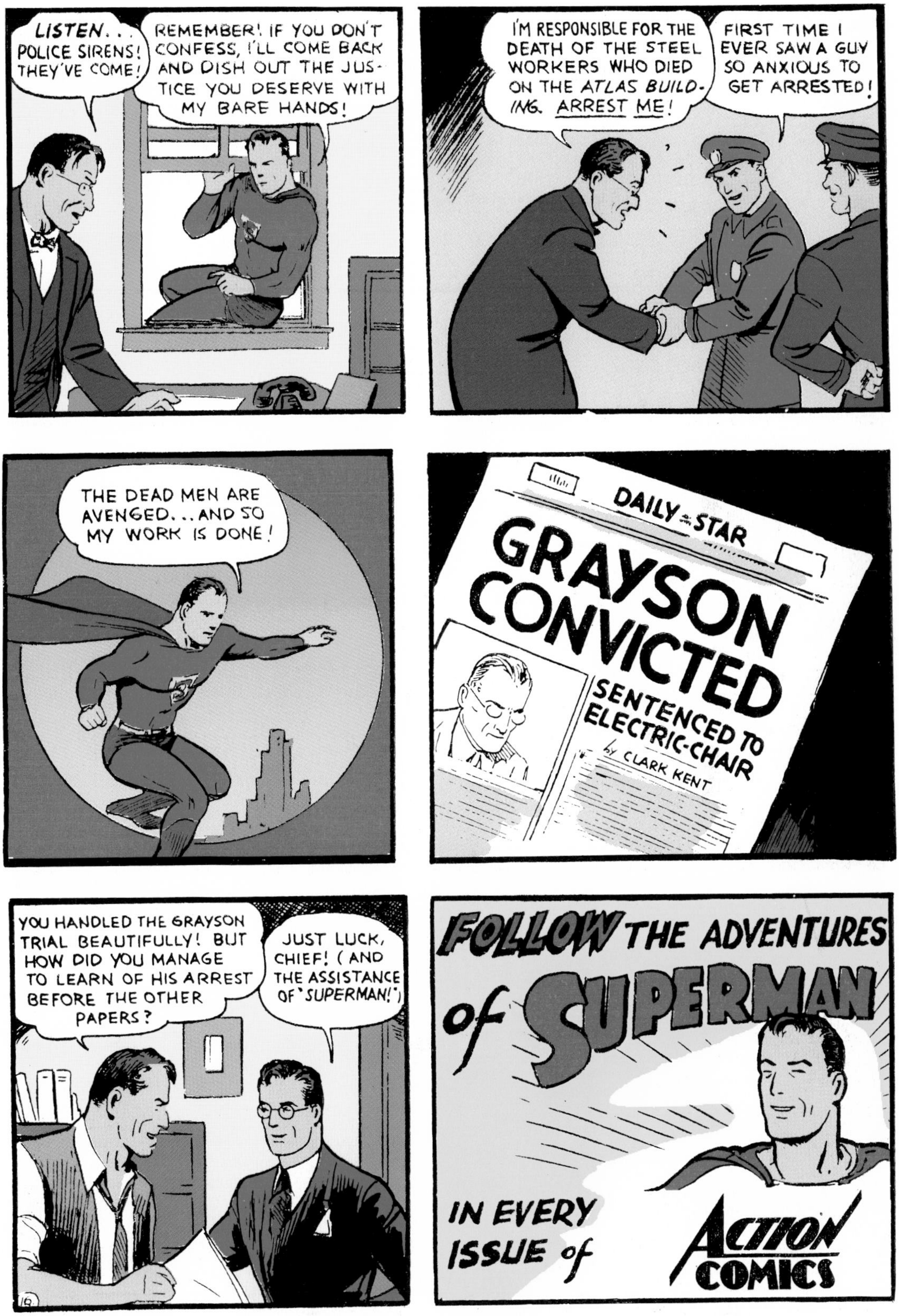
LISTEN... POLICE SIRENS! THEY'VE COME!
REMEMBER! IF YOU DON'T CONFESS, I'LL COME BACK AND DISH OUT THE JUSTICE YOU DESERVE WITH MY BARE HANDS!
I'M RESPONSIBLE FOR THE DEATH OF THE STEEL WORKERS WHO DIED ON THE ATLAS BUILDING. ARREST ME!
FIRST TIME I EVER SAW A GUY SO ANXIOUS TO GET ARRESTED!
THE DEAD MEN ARE AVENGED... AND SO MY WORK IS DONE!
DAILY STAR
GRAYSON CONVICTED
SENTENCED TO ELECTRIC-CHAIR
by CLARK KENT
YOU HANDLED THE GRAYSON TRIAL BEAUTIFULLY! BUT HOW DID YOU MANAGE TO LEARN OF HIS ARREST BEFORE THE OTHER PAPERS?
JUST LUCK, CHIEF! (AND THE ASSISTANCE OF "SUPERMAN!")
16
FOLLOW THE ADVENTURES of SUPERMAN
IN EVERY ISSUE of
ACTION COMICS

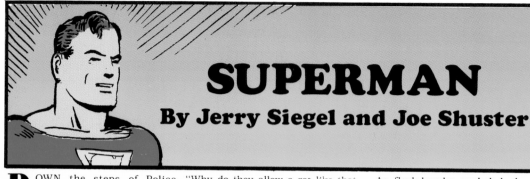

SUPERMAN
By Jerry Siegel and Joe Shuster

DOWN the steps of Police Headquarters hurried "Big Mike" Caputo, roughly shouldering aside any unfortunate figure that happened to bar his path. Huge, hulking in size, was the ruthless racketeer, and in his roughshod lumbering gait was revealed something of the brutality of the man.

A small mob of reporters hurried toward "Big Mike" as he hove into sight. "Hold it, Mike," one of them called. And then another piped up, "Let's have it. Just what went on in there between the Chief of Police and yourself?"

"Big Mike" paused in his stride, scowled, then assuming a false face of geniality, said, "Just a little friendly talk, that's all!"

Clark Kent, ace scribe on the *Daily Star*, commented: "Friendly, eh? Since when does the Police Chief of *Metropolis* get pally with a murderous hoodlum who has been kicked out of a dozen states?"

Mike's huge paw of a fist darted out, seized the luckless reporter by the shirt front. He cried: "Why, you little squirt, I'll—!"

His face ashen, the *Daily Star* reporter attempted to stutter an apology, but before he could get more than a few words out, Mike's fist smashed directly into his face. Kent went down like a sack. Caputo turned grimly toward the other waiting reporters. "Any more cracks?"

As no reply came, Mike continued on his way to the steps' bottom, crammed his great bulk into a taxi, and disappeared from view as it was driven off.

Eager hands assisted Clark Kent erect. "What hit me?" groaned Clark. "A sledge hammer?"

"No," replied one of the other reporters. "Caputo's fist! That was a pretty foolhardy thing to do: insult him to his face!"

Clark tenderly felt his jaw.

"Why do they allow a rat like that to roam the streets?"

"I can answer that," came a nearby voice.

The reporters' eyes swung to the doorway, and there stood the Chief of Police himself! "Caputo, since he was forced to leave several other cities, has been looking *Metropolis* over, and apparently thinks it's ripe for the plucking."

"And you're going to stand by and let him commit a crime," cried Clark.

"I warned him," said the Chief sternly. "I called him into my office and told him straight to his face...one false move, and it's into a cell he goes!"

"Nice goin', Chief!" applauded one of the reporters.

"Think so?" asked the Chief, smiling. "Then how about writing it up in your papers. And if you'd like some pictures of me to appear with the articles, well, far be it that I should argue with the Gentlemen of the Press."

As flash-bombs exploded about the Chief of Police, Clark Kent unobtrusively slipped away from the others. Amazingly enough, once he had succeeded in eluding the others, he no longer appeared like a man who had been on the receiving end of a terrific haymaker. No patting of a tender aching jaw, now...instead, that jaw was set firmly in an attitude of grim determination.

Shortly after, within a dark alley, Clark Kent glanced swiftly about, made certain he was unobserved, then swiftly stripped off his outer garments, revealing himself clad in the fantastic costume that was talked about from one end of the nation to the other: the uniform of SUPERMAN, Savior of the Helpless and Oppressed!

A huge leap carried the Man of Steel high into the air. One of his outflung arms seized the roof of a building and drew him safely up atop the edifice. There he poised, his great scarlet cloak whipping out behind him, glancing swiftly about in various directions. His eyes blazed with a fierce penetrating flame, as well they might, for he was surveying the surrounding vicinity with his amazing telescopic, X-ray eyesight. And in a few moments he had located the object of his search: Caputo leaving his taxi, and entering a dejected looking boarding house.

A GREAT spring carried the Man of Tomorrow out over the city, soaring high above the traffic below, and landed him near the boarding house. Several more cautious springs from building to building, and SUPERMAN found himself on a ledge outside the boarding house, staring into a window...and seeing within, Caputo seated at a table in conference with two hirelings.

Within the room, Caputo spoke

harshly, confidently, "It's a cinch. This town is just rolling in gravy, waiting to be plucked...and we're the men to do it! Listen, Sneer, and you too, Fink! Give me a month, and I'll have every business man paying tribute to me, 'Big Mike' Caputo—or else!"

The two remaining men in the room glanced hastily at each other, muttered under their breath, then dropped their eyes. Caputo instantly glared. "What's the matter with you guys?" he bellowed. "It's a great plan, isn't it? Then why the glum looks?"

One of the men spoke hesitantly. "It's not that we haven't got confidence in you, 'Big Mike'. It's that we happen to have been in this town longer than you, and we know..."

"The blazes with what you know..." rasped Caputo. "I say I can take over this town, and if you two weasels are getting chicken-livered...!"

"But—" interposed the other hireling, "—you're not counting on ...SUPERMAN!"

"SUPERMAN?" questioned Caputo. "And who in blazes is he?"

"That's just it!" whispered Sneer. "Nobody knows. He's a will-of-the-wisp...a phantom of the night. He preys on evil-doers who operate in Metropolis...and once that bozo's on your trail, brother, you're sunk!"

Caputo smashed his fist against the table, arose. "Yeah? Well, just let him watch out if he tackles me. I'm pretty tough myself!"

"You don't get it," interposed Fink. "The guy ain't human. He's got super-strength. He could take you, Caputo, and twist you into a pretzel, honest he could!"

Caputo roared, reached across the table, clutched at the helpless Fink. "He could what...?" he bellowed.

Fink tried to reply...but no words would come. Caputo smirked with satisfaction. They were afraid of him, these riff-raff were. Why with one smash of his fist he could ...Suddenly he paused, noting that though Fink was trembling, his eyes were fastened upon something behind Caputo's back. Abruptly dropping Fink, "Big Mike" whirled...then gasped.

For stepping thru the window, and regarding him coolly, was the strangest-attired man Caputo had ever seen. A man clad entirely in a skin-tight costume with the letter "S" emblazoned strikingly upon his chest—and upon his back, a flaring cloak.

"What th'—? exploded Caputo. "What is this? Wh- who are you?"

"It's him!" cried Sneer hoarsely. "It's—it's—SUPERMAN!"

For a moment, Caputo stood stunned, then he cried, "You fools! He's no more supernatural than you or me! Come on, let's rush him!"

Sneer and Fink rushed, all right —but directly from the room.

SUPERMAN smiled amusedly, then spoke, "It looks like your 'friends' have run out on you. It's between you and me, now—'Big Mike'...are you ready to make a bargain with me?"

"A bargain...?" asked Mike, suspicious.

"Yes," said SUPERMAN. "You seem to believe that you are physically my master. Well, what say, we find out? We'll fight it out, you and I. And the winner, it's pledged, leaves town in a jiffy! A battle between us, 'Big Mike', to decide whether good or evil rules this city!—Agreed?"

"Agreed!" shouted "Big Mike", and leapt directly at the costumed figure.

With a crash the two struck! Mike swung at his adversary, groaned with pain as his fist collided with granite-like skin. "Hey!" he cried.

Next instant, Mike was whirling up thru the air! Up he flew, then with a WHAM! crashed against the ceiling amidst a deluge of raining plaster. Down he hurtled, and into a relentless, steel grip. Around and around, he circled about SUPERMAN'S head.

"Just like on the Merry-Go-Round," grinned SUPERMAN, "Want a repeat-ride?"

"Big Mike" bellowed his protest. But in the middle of his cry, SUPERMAN loosened his grip, and Caputo went flying across the room...on...on thru the air... and OUT THE WINDOW!

Down thru space dropped Caputo, amidst a soul-tearing shriek. Down he hurtled...but a few moments later, steely arms encircled him from behind, as SUPERMAN, flashing down after him, gripped his figure. Down—smashing into earth, with SUPERMAN absorbing the fall! Then, he was dangling in the air, his collar gripped firmly in SUPERMAN's hand.

"Fergoshsakes!" wept Caputo. "Have a heart! Lemme go!"

"Done!" said SUPERMAN. "But I've your solemn word that you'll clear out of Metropolis pronto. We want none of your kind, here!"

"I'll do it!" cried "Big Mike", "I'll beat it outa here—gladly!"

"And just remember," SUPERMAN called after the fleeing racketeer. "If you decide to come back, I'll give you an encore of this that'll make our first match appear mild!"

* * *

That evening, the Daily Star carried the following headline on an inner page:

POLICE CHIEF MAKES
RACKETEER LEAVE TOWN
By Clark Kent

The End.

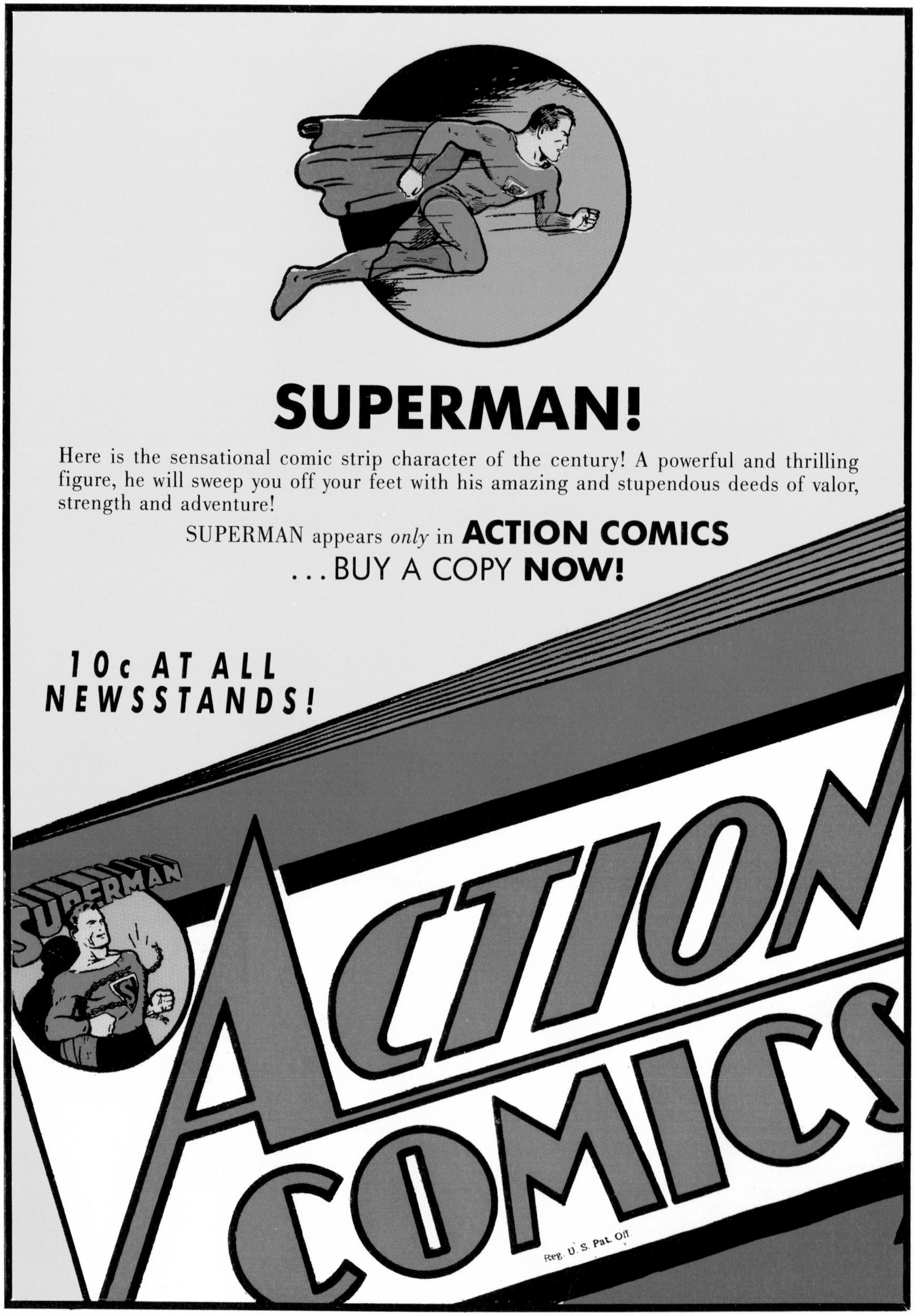
SUPERMAN!
Here is the sensational comic strip character of the century! A powerful and thrilling figure, he will sweep you off your feet with his amazing and stupendous deeds of valor, strength and adventure!
SUPERMAN appears *only* in **ACTION COMICS**
...BUY A COPY **NOW!**
10c AT ALL NEWSSTANDS!
SUPERMAN
ACTION COMICS
Reg. U.S. Pat. Off.

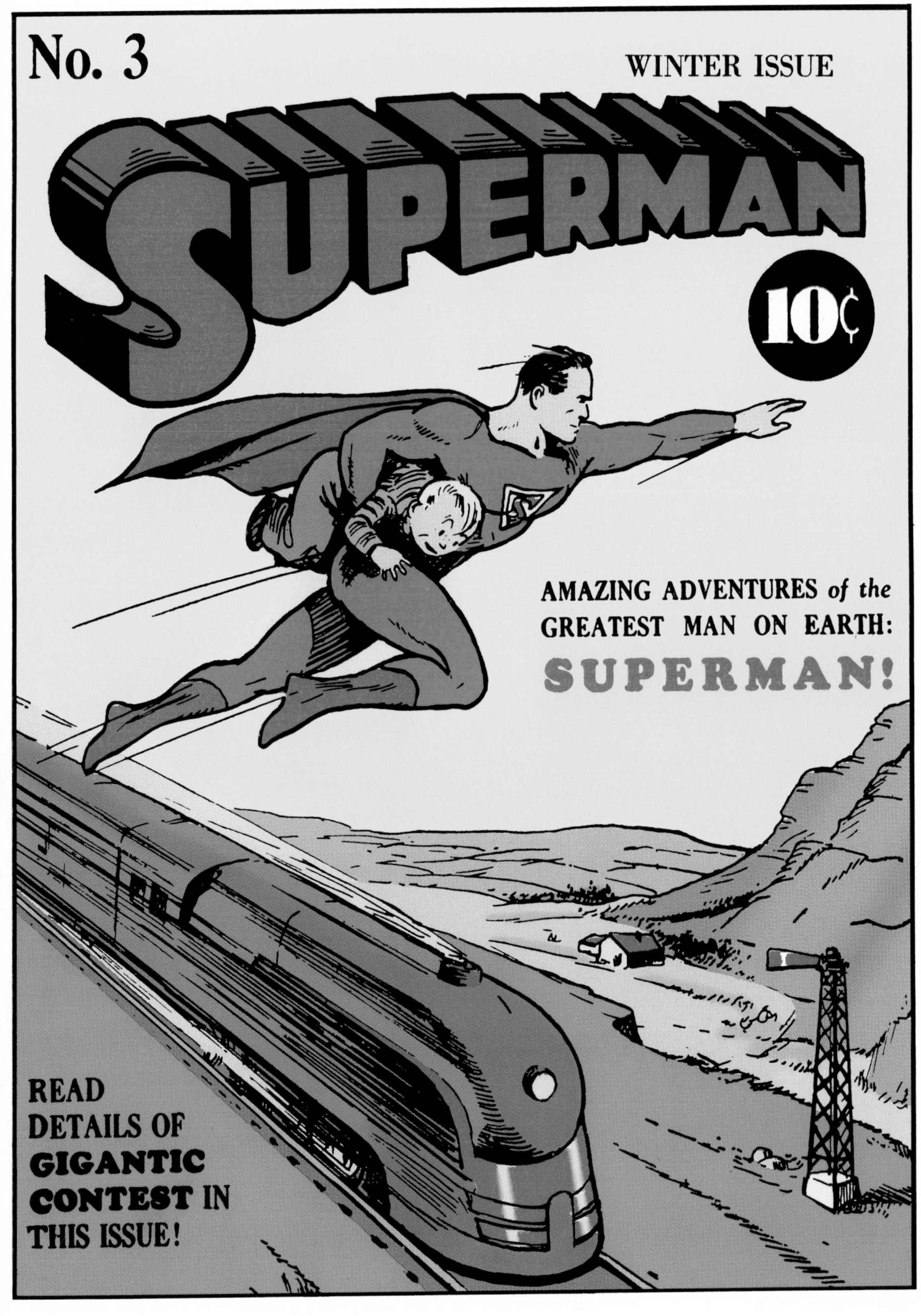
No. 3
WINTER ISSUE
SUPERMAN
10¢
AMAZING ADVENTURES of the GREATEST MAN ON EARTH:
SUPERMAN!
READ DETAILS OF GIGANTIC CONTEST IN THIS ISSUE!

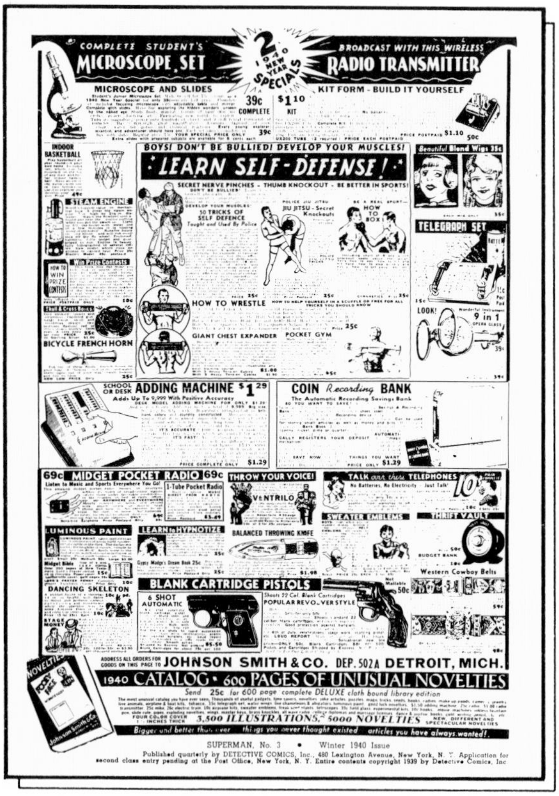
COMPLETE STUDENT'S MICROSCOPE SET
2 1940 NEW YEAR SPECIALS
BROADCAST WITH THIS WIRELESS RADIO TRANSMITTER
MICROSCOPE AND SLIDES
39c COMPLETE
$1.10 KIT
KIT FORM - BUILD IT YOURSELF
INDOOR BASKETBALL
BOYS! DON'T BE BULLIED! DEVELOP YOUR MUSCLES!
LEARN SELF-DEFENSE!
Beautiful Blond Wigs 25c
STEAM ENGINE
TELEGRAPH SET
HOW TO WRESTLE
GIANT CHEST EXPANDER
POCKET GYM
BICYCLE FRENCH HORN
SCHOOL OR DESK ADDING MACHINE $1.29
COIN Recording BANK
69c MIDGET POCKET RADIO 69c
THROW YOUR VOICE!
TALK over these TELEPHONES
LUMINOUS PAINT
LEARN to HYPNOTIZE
SWEATER EMBLEMS
THRIFT VAULT
BALANCED THROWING KNIFE
BLANK CARTRIDGE PISTOLS
6 SHOT AUTOMATIC
POPULAR REVOLVER STYLE
DANCING SKELETON
Western Cowboy Belts
NOVELTIES
ADDRESS ALL ORDERS FOR GOODS ON THIS PAGE TO JOHNSON SMITH & CO. DEP. 502A DETROIT, MICH.
1940 CATALOG · 600 PAGES OF UNUSUAL NOVELTIES
Send 25c for 600 page complete DELUXE cloth bound library edition
Bigger and better than ever things you never thought existed articles you have always wanted!
SUPERMAN, No. 3 • Winter 1940 Issue
Published quarterly by DETECTIVE COMICS, Inc., 480 Lexington Avenue, New York, N. Y. Application for second class entry pending at the Post Office, New York, N. Y. Entire contents copyright 1939 by Detective Comics, Inc.

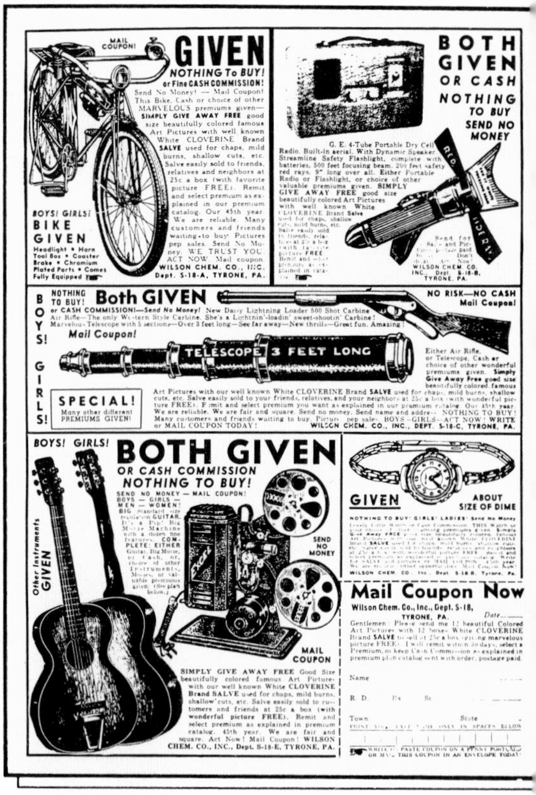
MAIL COUPON!
GIVEN
NOTHING To BUY!
or Fine CASH COMMISSION!
BOYS! GIRLS! BIKE GIVEN
WILSON CHEM. CO., INC. Dept. S-18-A, TYRONE, PA.
BOTH GIVEN OR CASH
NOTHING TO BUY
SEND NO MONEY
G. E. 4-Tube Portable Dry Cell Radio.
BOYS! GIRLS!
NOTHING TO BUY!
Both GIVEN
NO RISK—NO CASH
Mail Coupon!
TELESCOPE 3 FEET LONG
SPECIAL!
Many other different PREMIUMS GIVEN!
BOYS! GIRLS!
BOTH GIVEN
OR CASH COMMISSION
NOTHING TO BUY!
Other Instruments GIVEN
SEND NO MONEY
MAIL COUPON
GIVEN
ABOUT SIZE OF DIME
Mail Coupon Now
Wilson Chem. Co., Inc., Dept. S-18, TYRONE, PA.
CHEM. CO., INC., Dept. S-18-E, TYRONE, PA.

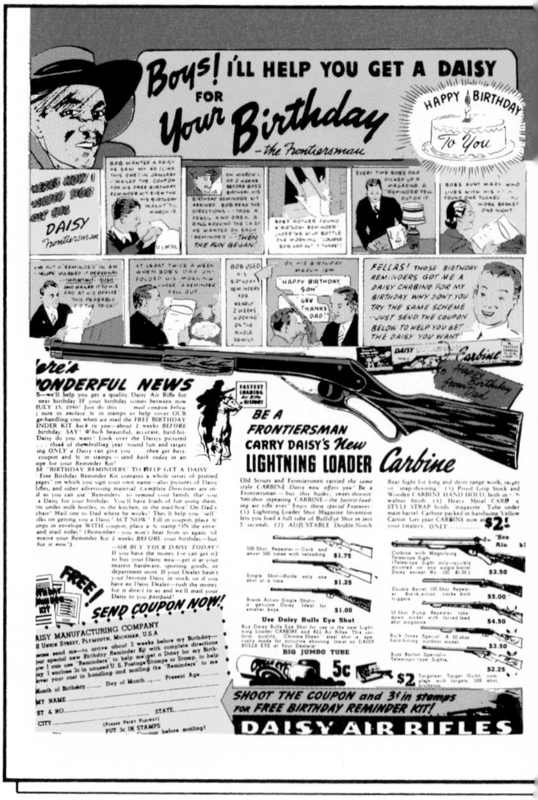
Boys! I'LL HELP YOU GET A DAISY FOR Your Birthday
- the Frontiersman
HAPPY BIRTHDAY To You
HERE'S HOW I HELPED BOB GET HIS DAISY
Frontiersman
THE FUN BEGAN!
HAPPY BIRTHDAY, SON
GEE THANKS DAD!
FELLAS! THOSE BIRTHDAY REMINDERS GOT ME A DAISY CARBINE FOR MY BIRTHDAY. WHY DON'T YOU TRY THE SAME SCHEME — JUST SEND THE COUPON BELOW TO HELP YOU GET THE DAISY YOU WANT!
Here's WONDERFUL NEWS
BE A FRONTIERSMAN
CARRY DAISY'S New LIGHTNING LOADER Carbine
FREE!
SEND COUPON NOW!
DAISY MANUFACTURING COMPANY
BIG JUMBO TUBE
5c
$2
SHOOT THE COUPON and 3¢ in stamps FOR FREE BIRTHDAY REMINDER KIT!
DAISY AIR RIFLES

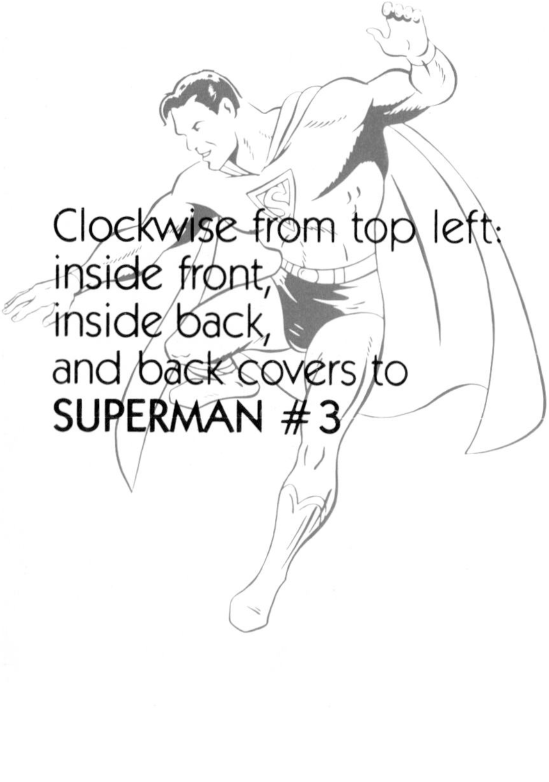

Clockwise from top left:
inside front,
inside back,
and back covers to
SUPERMAN #3

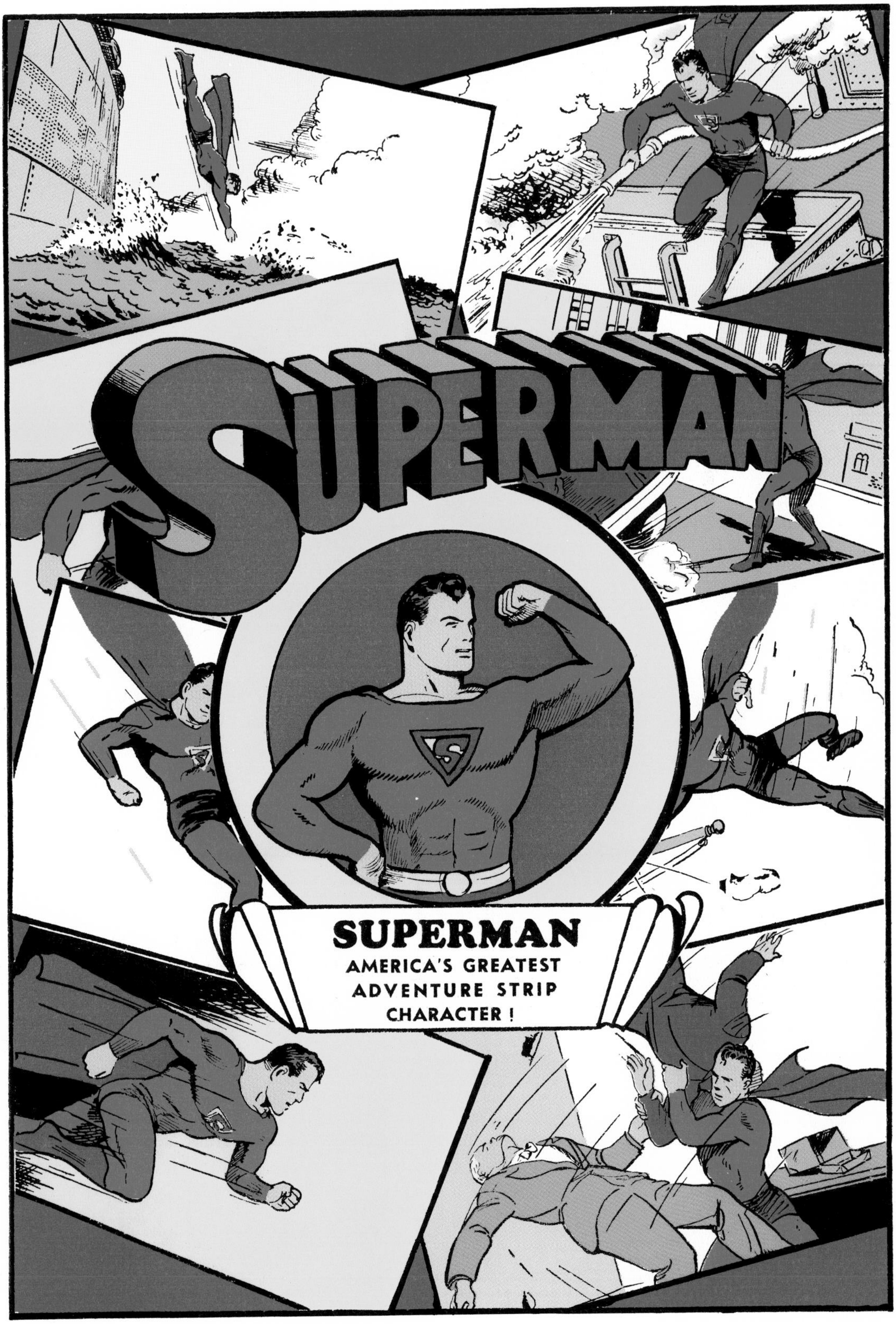
SUPERMAN
SUPERMAN
AMERICA'S GREATEST
ADVENTURE STRIP
CHARACTER !

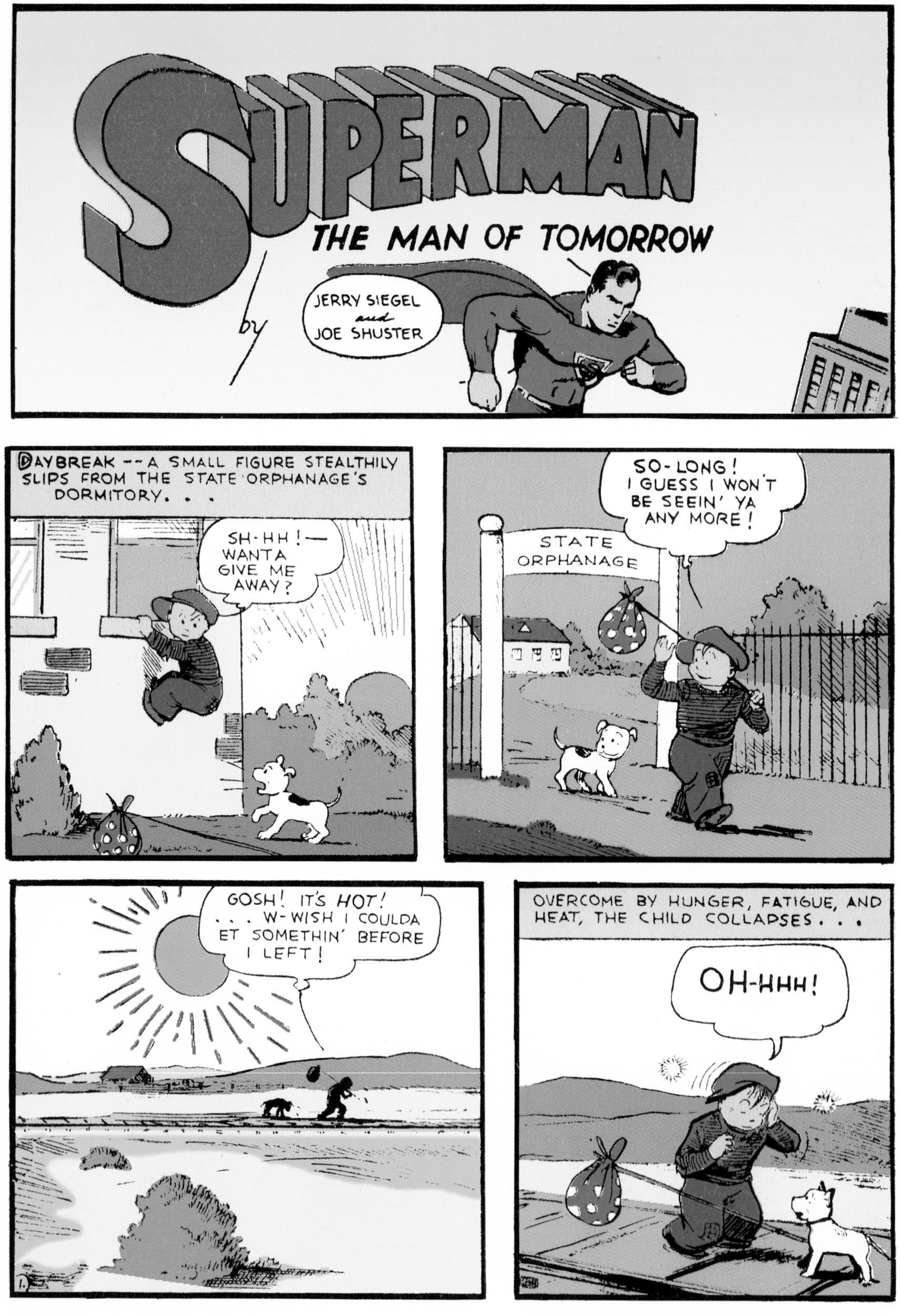
SUPERMAN
THE MAN OF TOMORROW
by
JERRY SIEGEL and JOE SHUSTER
DAYBREAK -- A SMALL FIGURE STEALTHILY SLIPS FROM THE STATE ORPHANAGE'S DORMITORY. . .
SH-HH!— WANTA GIVE ME AWAY?
SO-LONG! I GUESS I WON'T BE SEEIN' YA ANY MORE!
STATE ORPHANAGE
GOSH! IT'S HOT! . . . W-WISH I COULDA ET SOMETHIN' BEFORE I LEFT!
OVERCOME BY HUNGER, FATIGUE, AND HEAT, THE CHILD COLLAPSES. . .
OH-HHH!

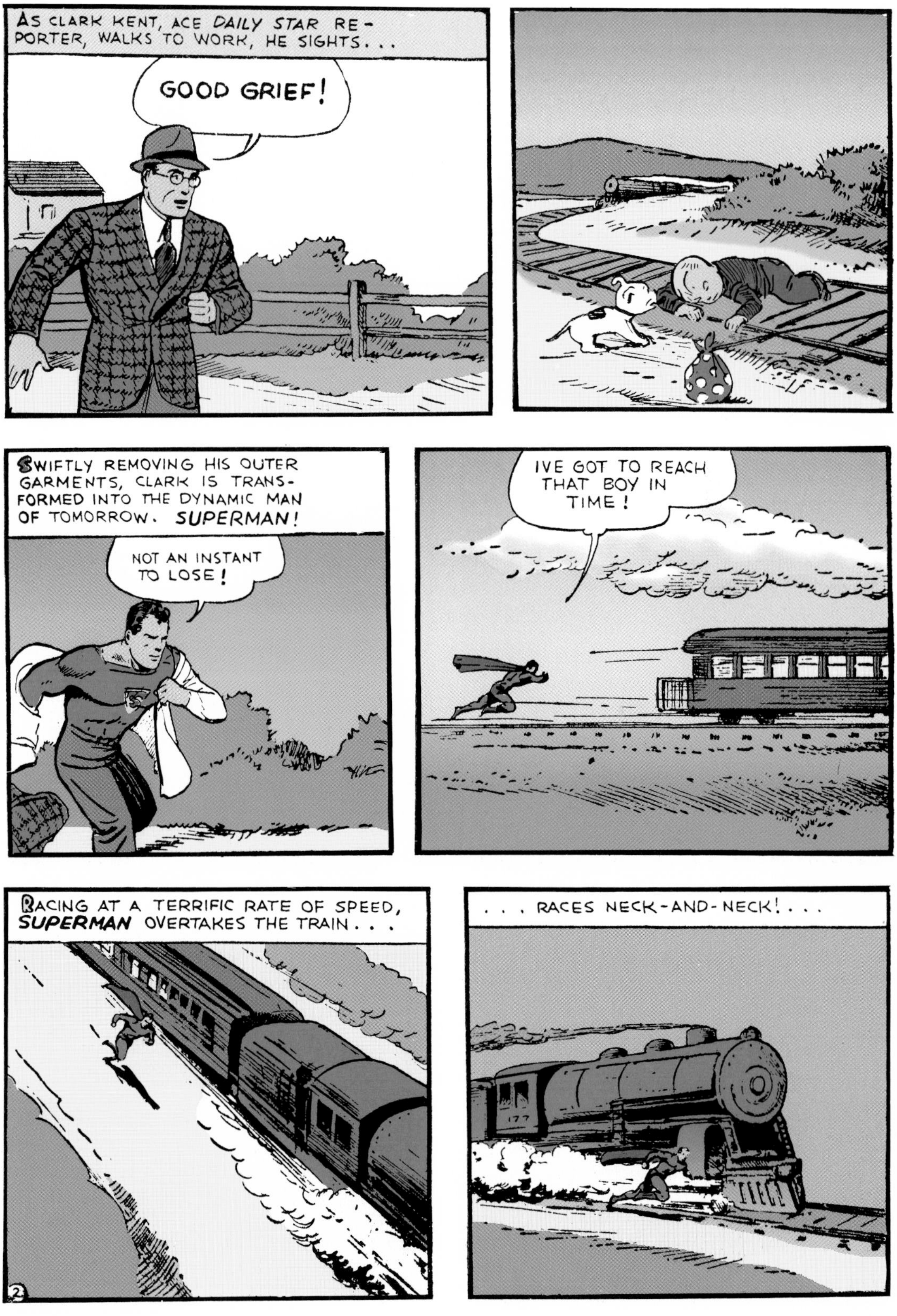
AS CLARK KENT, ACE DAILY STAR RE-PORTER, WALKS TO WORK, HE SIGHTS . . .
GOOD GRIEF!
SWIFTLY REMOVING HIS OUTER GARMENTS, CLARK IS TRANS-FORMED INTO THE DYNAMIC MAN OF TOMORROW. SUPERMAN!
NOT AN INSTANT TO LOSE!
IVE GOT TO REACH THAT BOY IN TIME!
RACING AT A TERRIFIC RATE OF SPEED, SUPERMAN OVERTAKES THE TRAIN . . .
2
. . . RACES NECK-AND-NECK! . . .
177

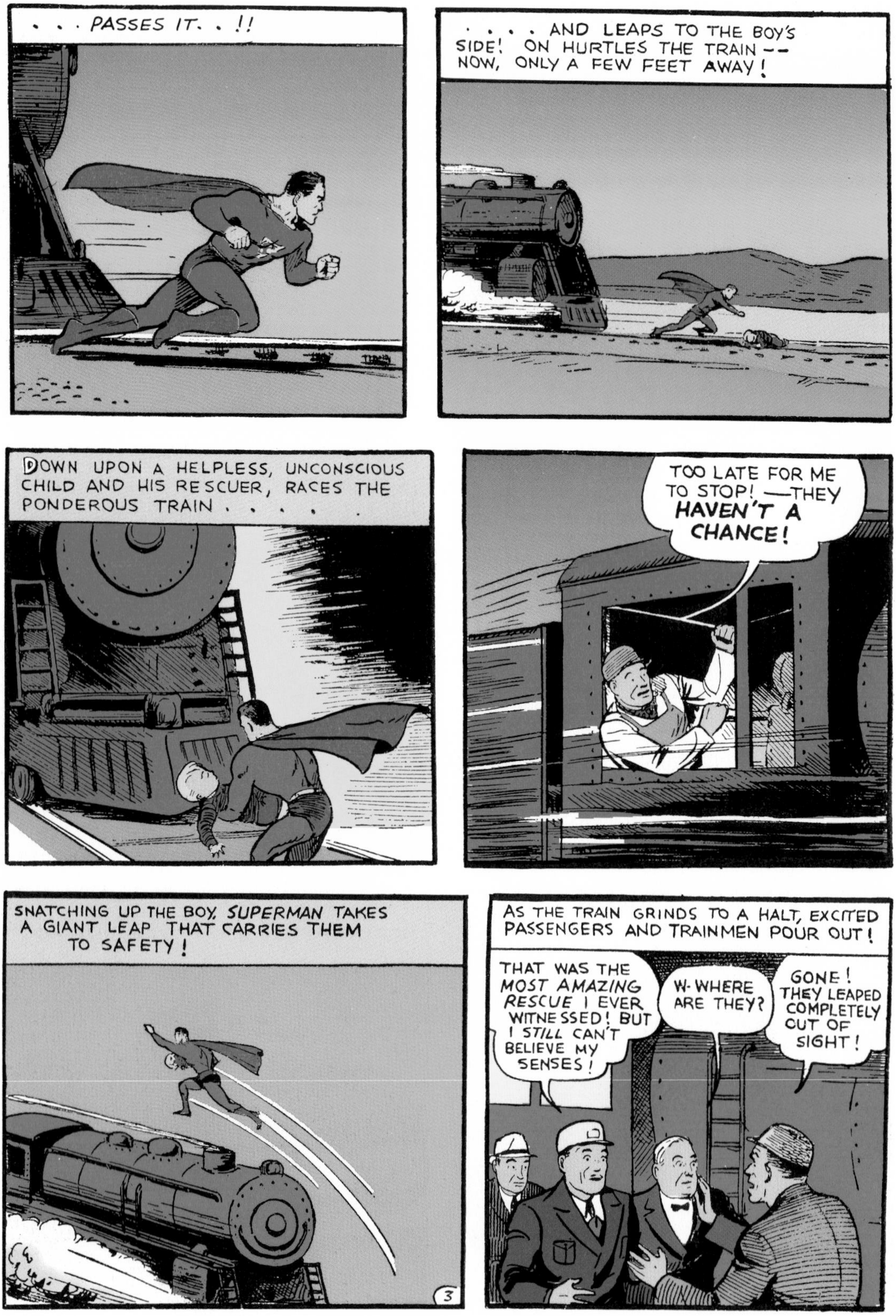
. . . PASSES IT. . !!
. . . . AND LEAPS TO THE BOY'S SIDE! ON HURTLES THE TRAIN -- NOW, ONLY A FEW FEET AWAY!
DOWN UPON A HELPLESS, UNCONSCIOUS CHILD AND HIS RESCUER, RACES THE PONDEROUS TRAIN . . . . .
TOO LATE FOR ME TO STOP! —THEY HAVEN'T A CHANCE!
SNATCHING UP THE BOY, SUPERMAN TAKES A GIANT LEAP THAT CARRIES THEM TO SAFETY!
3
AS THE TRAIN GRINDS TO A HALT, EXCITED PASSENGERS AND TRAINMEN POUR OUT!
THAT WAS THE MOST AMAZING RESCUE I EVER WITNESSED! BUT I STILL CAN'T BELIEVE MY SENSES!
W-WHERE ARE THEY?
GONE! THEY LEAPED COMPLETELY OUT OF SIGHT!

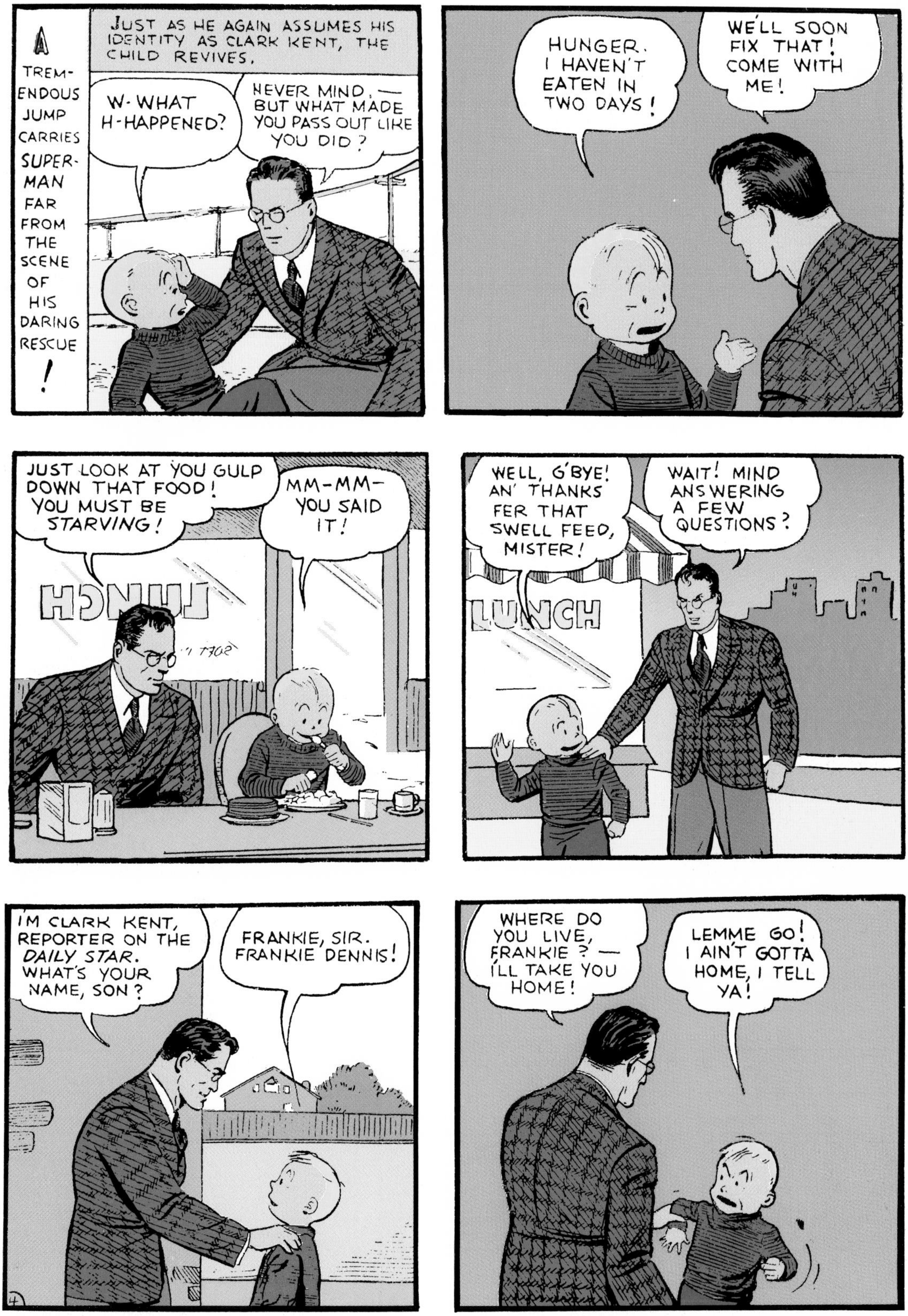
A TREMENDOUS JUMP CARRIES SUPERMAN FAR FROM THE SCENE OF HIS DARING RESCUE!
JUST AS HE AGAIN ASSUMES HIS IDENTITY AS CLARK KENT, THE CHILD REVIVES.
W-WHAT H-HAPPENED?
NEVER MIND, — BUT WHAT MADE YOU PASS OUT LIKE YOU DID?
HUNGER. I HAVEN'T EATEN IN TWO DAYS!
WE'LL SOON FIX THAT! COME WITH ME!
JUST LOOK AT YOU GULP DOWN THAT FOOD! YOU MUST BE STARVING!
MM-MM- YOU SAID IT!
LUNCH
WELL, G'BYE! AN' THANKS FER THAT SWELL FEED, MISTER!
WAIT! MIND ANSWERING A FEW QUESTIONS?
LUNCH
I'M CLARK KENT, REPORTER ON THE DAILY STAR. WHAT'S YOUR NAME, SON?
FRANKIE, SIR. FRANKIE DENNIS!
WHERE DO YOU LIVE, FRANKIE? — I'LL TAKE YOU HOME!
LEMME GO! I AIN'T GOTTA HOME, I TELL YA!

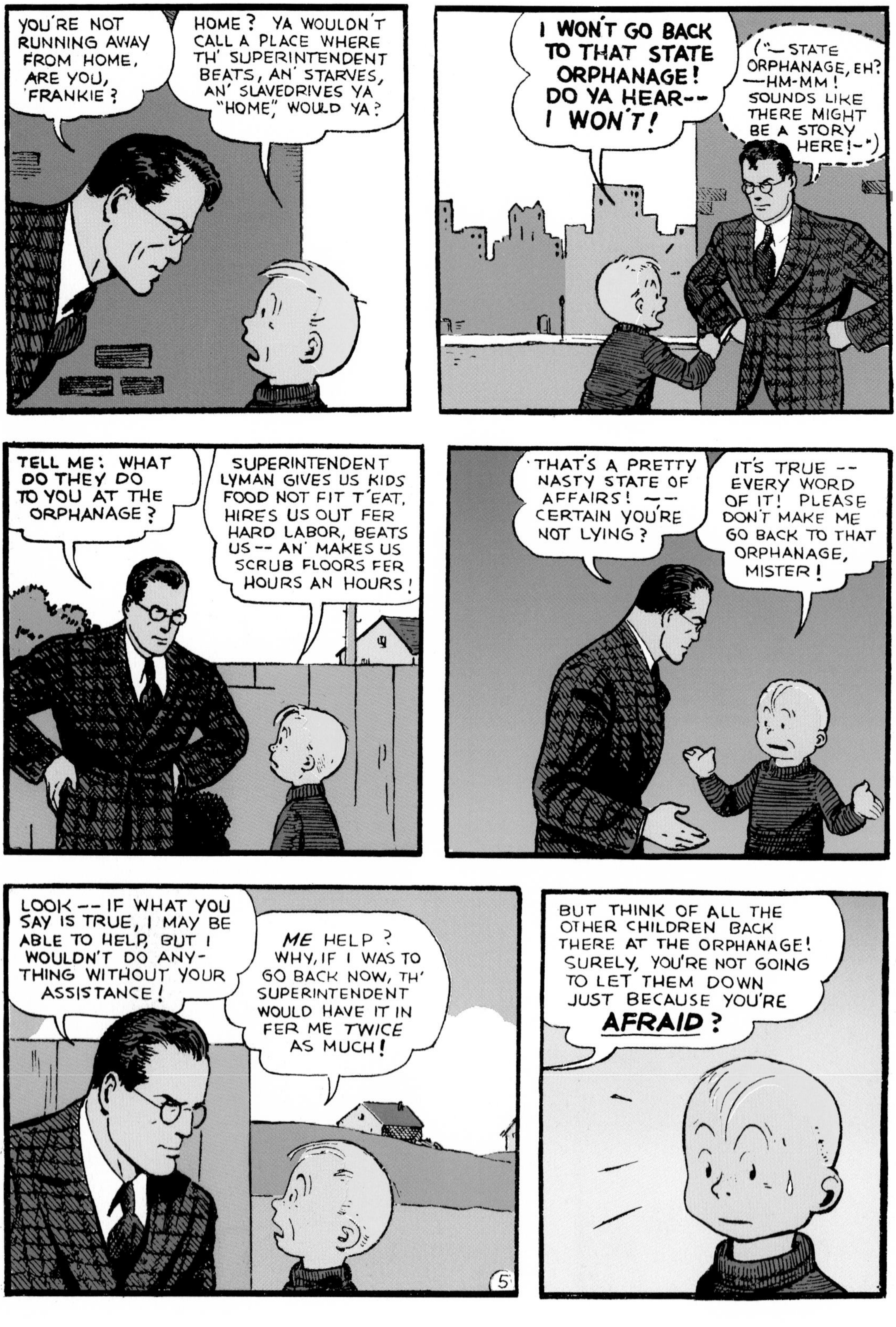
YOU'RE NOT RUNNING AWAY FROM HOME, ARE YOU, FRANKIE?
HOME? YA WOULDN'T CALL A PLACE WHERE TH' SUPERINTENDENT BEATS, AN' STARVES, AN' SLAVEDRIVES YA "HOME," WOULD YA?
I WON'T GO BACK TO THAT STATE ORPHANAGE! DO YA HEAR-- I WON'T!
("--STATE ORPHANAGE, EH? --HM-MM! SOUNDS LIKE THERE MIGHT BE A STORY HERE!--")
TELL ME: WHAT DO THEY DO TO YOU AT THE ORPHANAGE?
SUPERINTENDENT LYMAN GIVES US KIDS FOOD NOT FIT T'EAT, HIRES US OUT FER HARD LABOR, BEATS US-- AN' MAKES US SCRUB FLOORS FER HOURS AN HOURS!
THAT'S A PRETTY NASTY STATE OF AFFAIRS! -- CERTAIN YOU'RE NOT LYING?
IT'S TRUE -- EVERY WORD OF IT! PLEASE DON'T MAKE ME GO BACK TO THAT ORPHANAGE, MISTER!
LOOK -- IF WHAT YOU SAY IS TRUE, I MAY BE ABLE TO HELP, BUT I WOULDN'T DO ANYTHING WITHOUT YOUR ASSISTANCE!
ME HELP? WHY, IF I WAS TO GO BACK NOW, TH' SUPERINTENDENT WOULD HAVE IT IN FER ME TWICE AS MUCH!
5
BUT THINK OF ALL THE OTHER CHILDREN BACK THERE AT THE ORPHANAGE! SURELY, YOU'RE NOT GOING TO LET THEM DOWN JUST BECAUSE YOU'RE AFRAID?

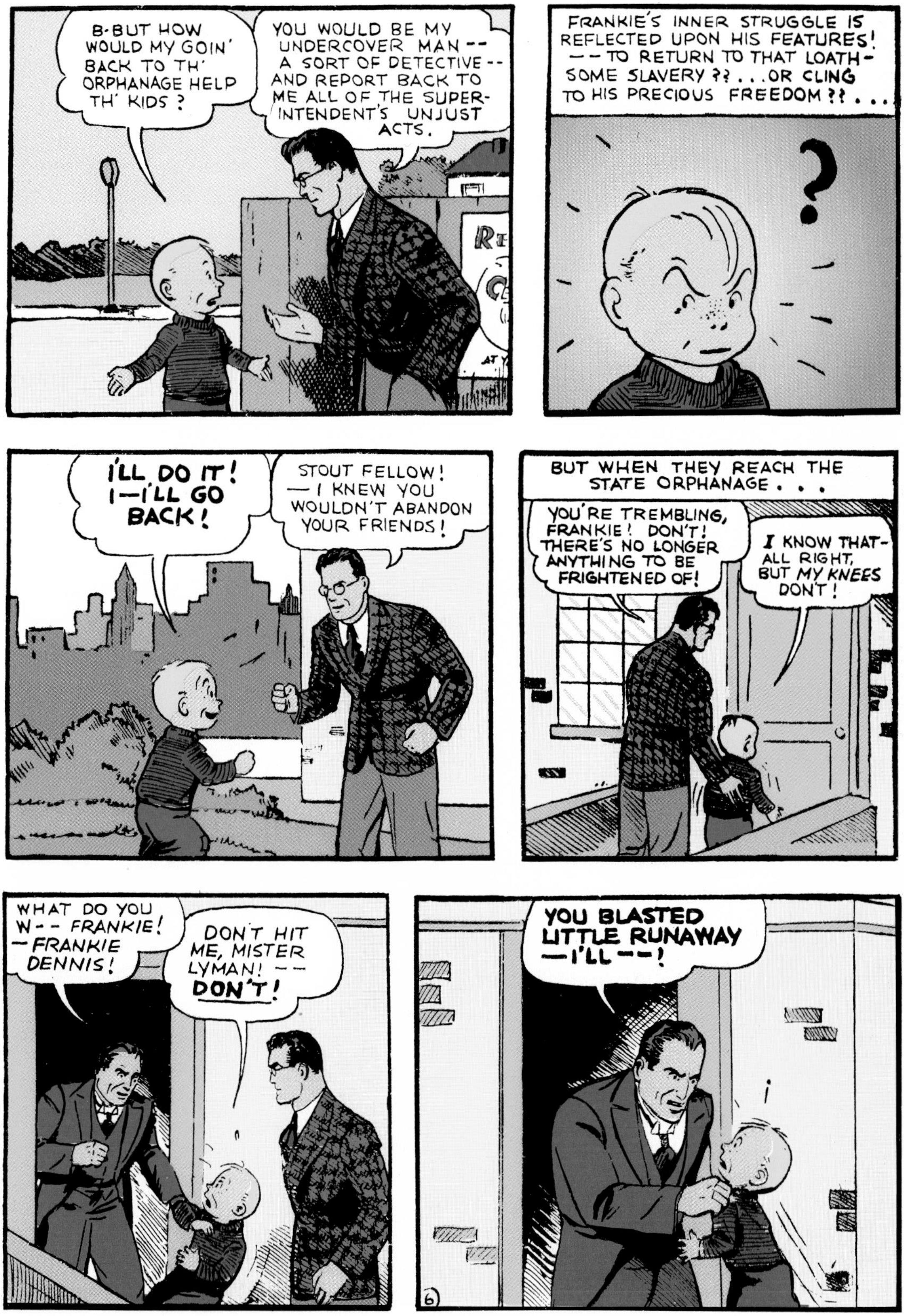
B-BUT HOW WOULD MY GOIN' BACK TO TH' ORPHANAGE HELP TH' KIDS ?
YOU WOULD BE MY UNDERCOVER MAN -- A SORT OF DETECTIVE -- AND REPORT BACK TO ME ALL OF THE SUPER-INTENDENT'S UNJUST ACTS.
FRANKIE'S INNER STRUGGLE IS REFLECTED UPON HIS FEATURES! -- TO RETURN TO THAT LOATH-SOME SLAVERY ?? . . . OR CLING TO HIS PRECIOUS FREEDOM ?? . . .
?
I'LL DO IT! I--I'LL GO BACK!
STOUT FELLOW! --I KNEW YOU WOULDN'T ABANDON YOUR FRIENDS!
BUT WHEN THEY REACH THE STATE ORPHANAGE . . .
YOU'RE TREMBLING, FRANKIE! DON'T! THERE'S NO LONGER ANYTHING TO BE FRIGHTENED OF!
I KNOW THAT-ALL RIGHT, BUT MY KNEES DON'T!
WHAT DO YOU W-- FRANKIE! --FRANKIE DENNIS!
DON'T HIT ME, MISTER LYMAN! -- DON'T!
YOU BLASTED LITTLE RUNAWAY --I'LL --!
6

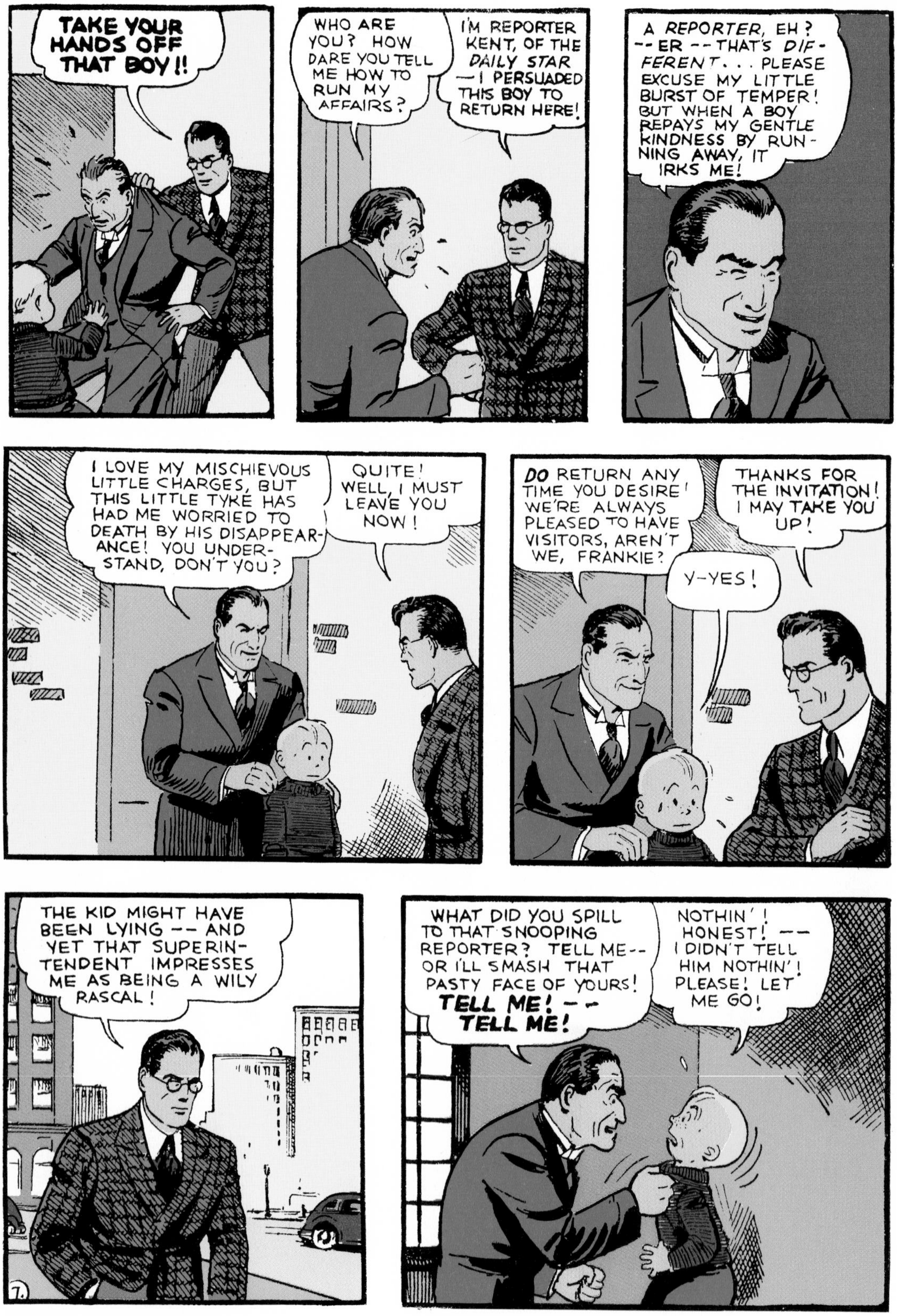
TAKE YOUR HANDS OFF THAT BOY!!
WHO ARE YOU? HOW DARE YOU TELL ME HOW TO RUN MY AFFAIRS?
I'M REPORTER KENT, OF THE *DAILY STAR* — I PERSUADED THIS BOY TO RETURN HERE!
A *REPORTER*, EH? -- ER -- THAT'S *DIF-FERENT*... PLEASE EXCUSE MY LITTLE BURST OF TEMPER! BUT WHEN A BOY REPAYS MY GENTLE KINDNESS BY RUN-NING AWAY, IT IRKS ME!
I LOVE MY MISCHIEVOUS LITTLE CHARGES, BUT THIS LITTLE TYKE HAS HAD ME WORRIED TO DEATH BY HIS DISAPPEAR-ANCE! YOU UNDER-STAND, DON'T YOU?
QUITE! WELL, I MUST LEAVE YOU NOW!
DO RETURN ANY TIME YOU DESIRE! WE'RE ALWAYS PLEASED TO HAVE VISITORS, AREN'T WE, FRANKIE?
Y-YES!
THANKS FOR THE INVITATION! I MAY TAKE YOU UP!
THE KID MIGHT HAVE BEEN LYING -- AND YET THAT SUPERIN-TENDENT IMPRESSES ME AS BEING A WILY RASCAL!
WHAT DID YOU SPILL TO THAT SNOOPING REPORTER? TELL ME -- OR I'LL SMASH THAT PASTY FACE OF YOURS! **TELL ME! -- TELL ME!**
NOTHIN'! HONEST! -- I DIDN'T TELL HIM NOTHIN'! PLEASE! LET ME GO!

WHEN CLARK REACHES THE *DAILY STAR* . . .

HOW ABOUT HAVING LUNCH WITH ME TODAY, LOIS?

SORRY—NOT INTERESTED!

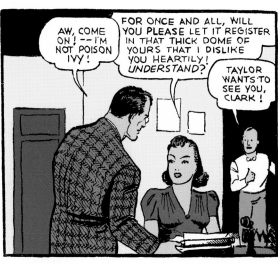

AW, COME ON!—I'M NOT POISON IVY!

FOR ONCE AND ALL, WILL YOU PLEASE LET IT REGISTER IN THAT THICK DOME OF YOURS THAT I DISLIKE YOU HEARTILY! *UNDERSTAND?*

TAYLOR WANTS TO SEE YOU, CLARK!

YOU KNOW THAT SPECTACULAR RESCUE BY AN UNKNOWN MAN OF THE RUNAWAY FROM THE STATE ORPHANAGE—— SEE WHAT YOU CAN DIG UP ON IT!

FINE, CHIEF!——I'D LIKE TO COVER IT!—— I'VE GOT A HUNCH ABOUT CONDITIONS IN THAT INSTITUTION!— WHY NOT HAVE LOIS HELP ME COVER THAT ANGLE?

SOUNDS SWELL!

('—WHAT A BREAK!— HO! HO! SHE'LL HAVE TO BEAR MY COMPANY NOW, WHETHER SHE WANTS TO OR NOT!—')

LOIS, CLARK HAS REASON TO BELIEVE THERE'S DIRTY WORK GOING ON AT THE STATE ORPHANAGE. THIS MAY TURN OUT TO BE A BIG STORY. GIVE HIM YOUR COMPLETE COOPERATION.

I'M SURE SHE'LL BE ONLY TOO DELIGHTED!

DELIGHTED!— WHY . . . !

I'M GOING WITH YOU ONLY BECAUSE I'M FORCED TO—AND DON'T YOU FORGET IT!

WHAT DIFFERENCE DOES THAT MAKE AS LONG AS WE'RE—ALONE?

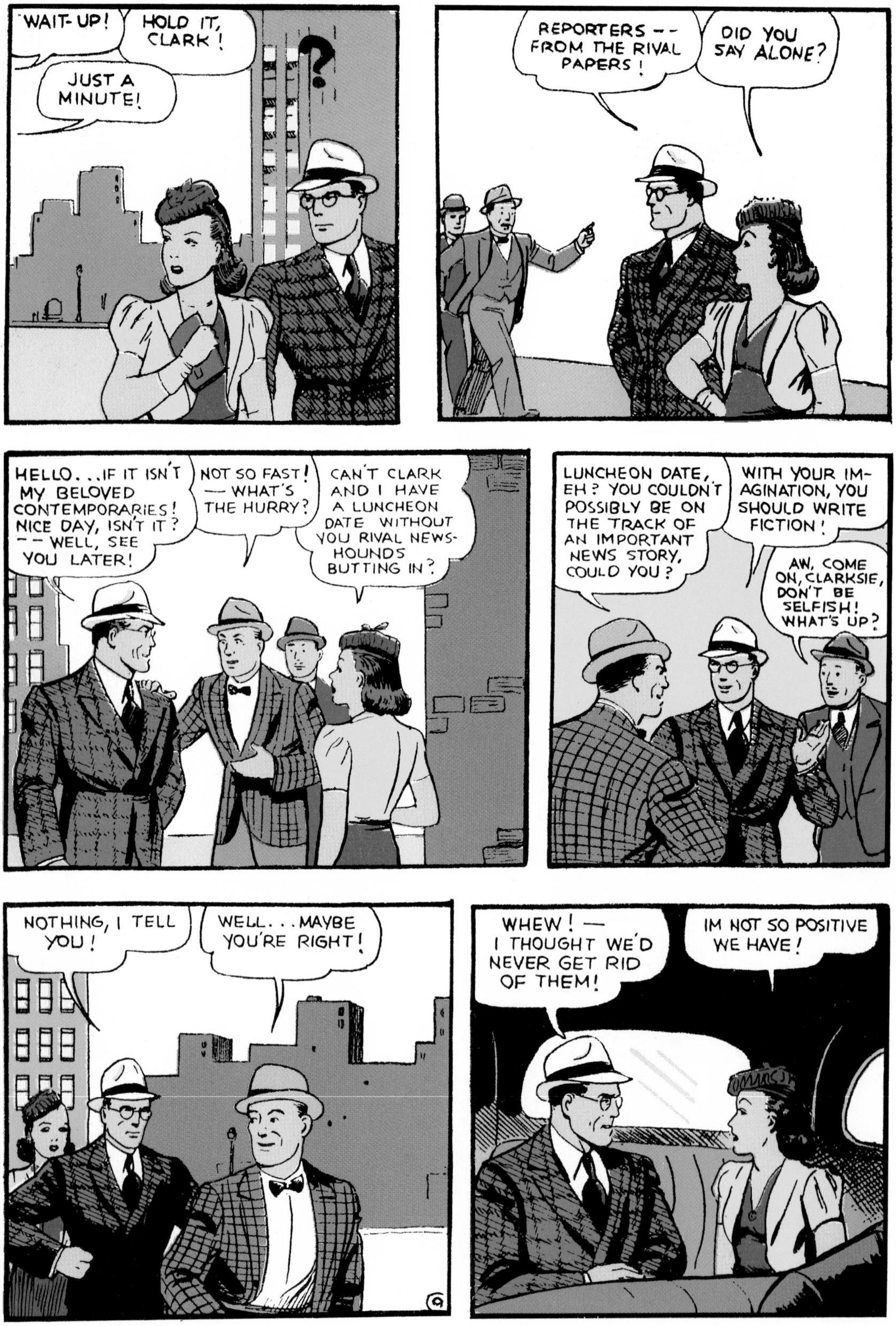
WAIT- UP!
HOLD IT, CLARK!
JUST A MINUTE!
REPORTERS -- FROM THE RIVAL PAPERS!
DID YOU SAY ALONE?
HELLO...IF IT ISN'T MY BELOVED CONTEMPORARIES! NICE DAY, ISN'T IT? -- WELL, SEE YOU LATER!
NOT SO FAST! — WHAT'S THE HURRY?
CAN'T CLARK AND I HAVE A LUNCHEON DATE WITHOUT YOU RIVAL NEWS-HOUNDS BUTTING IN?
LUNCHEON DATE, EH? YOU COULDN'T POSSIBLY BE ON THE TRACK OF AN IMPORTANT NEWS STORY, COULD YOU?
WITH YOUR IM-AGINATION, YOU SHOULD WRITE FICTION!
AW, COME ON, CLARKSIE, DON'T BE SELFISH! WHAT'S UP?
NOTHING, I TELL YOU!
WELL...MAYBE YOU'RE RIGHT!
9
WHEW! — I THOUGHT WE'D NEVER GET RID OF THEM!
IM NOT SO POSITIVE WE HAVE!

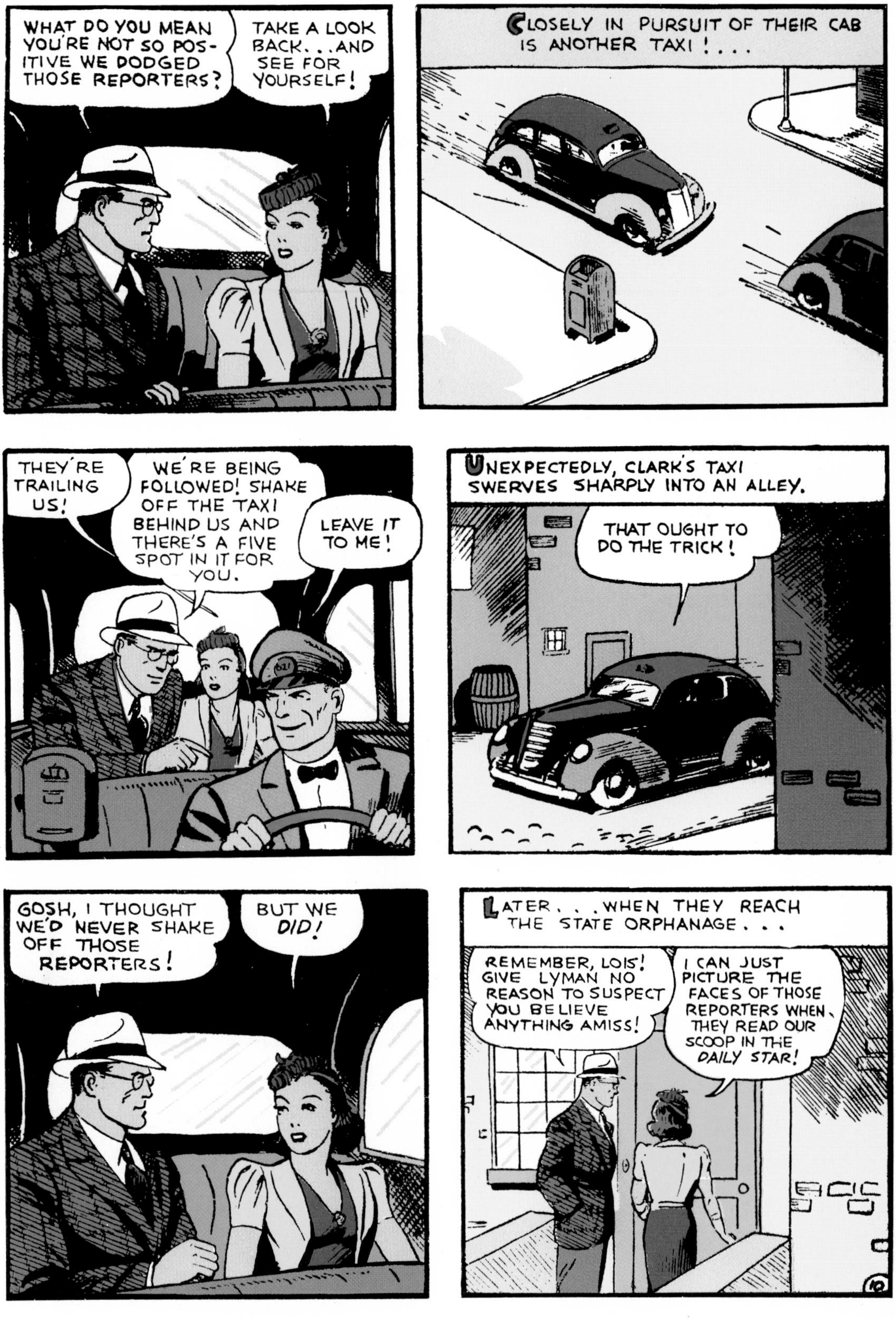
WHAT DO YOU MEAN YOU'RE NOT SO POSITIVE WE DODGED THOSE REPORTERS?
TAKE A LOOK BACK. . .AND SEE FOR YOURSELF!
CLOSELY IN PURSUIT OF THEIR CAB IS ANOTHER TAXI! . . .
THEY'RE TRAILING US!
WE'RE BEING FOLLOWED! SHAKE OFF THE TAXI BEHIND US AND THERE'S A FIVE SPOT IN IT FOR YOU.
LEAVE IT TO ME!
UNEXPECTEDLY, CLARK'S TAXI SWERVES SHARPLY INTO AN ALLEY.
THAT OUGHT TO DO THE TRICK!
GOSH, I THOUGHT WE'D NEVER SHAKE OFF THOSE REPORTERS!
BUT WE DID!
LATER. . .WHEN THEY REACH THE STATE ORPHANAGE . . .
REMEMBER, LOIS! GIVE LYMAN NO REASON TO SUSPECT YOU BELIEVE ANYTHING AMISS!
I CAN JUST PICTURE THE FACES OF THOSE REPORTERS WHEN THEY READ OUR SCOOP IN THE DAILY STAR!
10

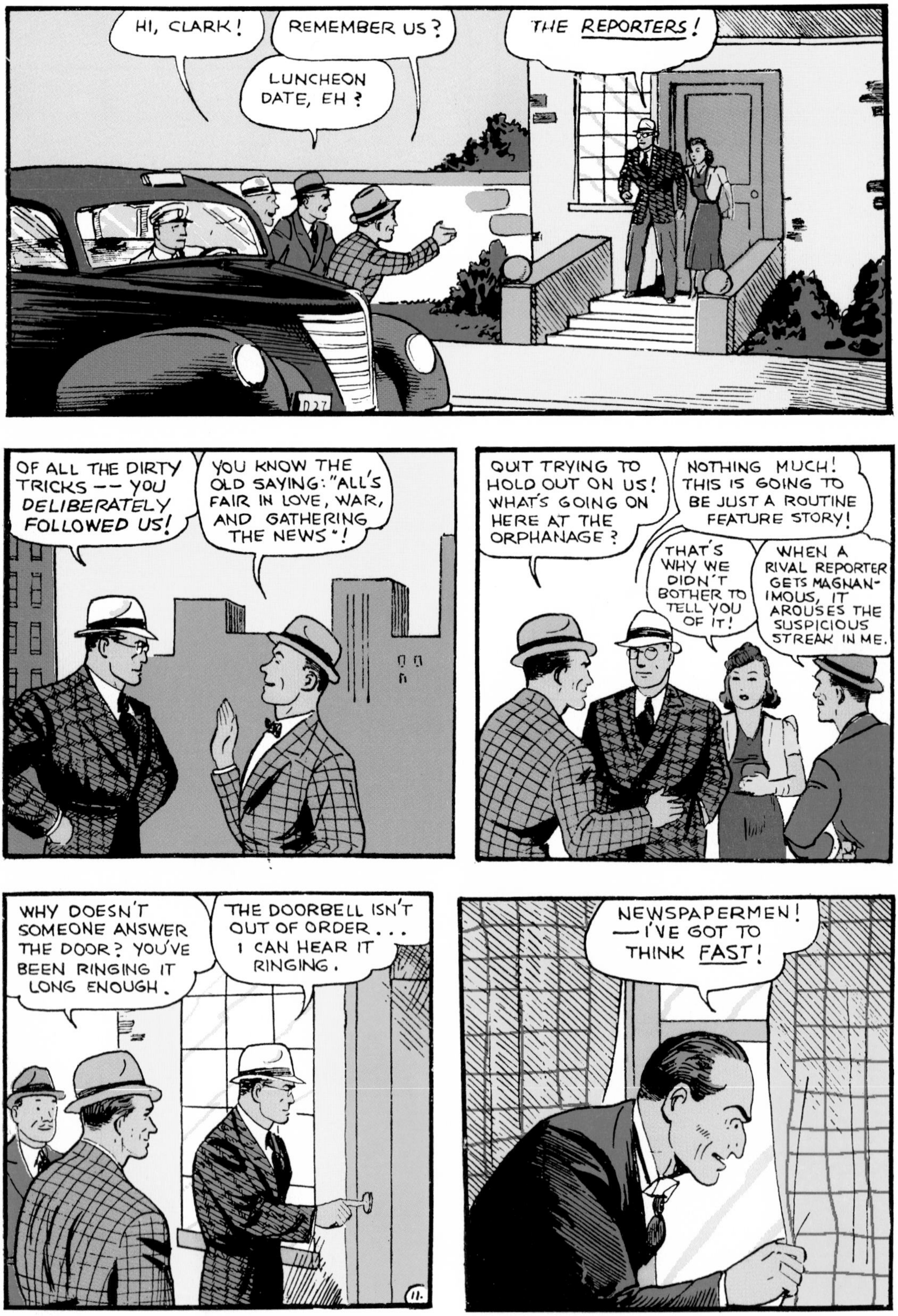
HI, CLARK!
REMEMBER US?
LUNCHEON DATE, EH?
THE REPORTERS!
OF ALL THE DIRTY TRICKS -- YOU DELIBERATELY FOLLOWED US!
YOU KNOW THE OLD SAYING: "ALL'S FAIR IN LOVE, WAR, AND GATHERING THE NEWS"!
QUIT TRYING TO HOLD OUT ON US! WHAT'S GOING ON HERE AT THE ORPHANAGE?
NOTHING MUCH! THIS IS GOING TO BE JUST A ROUTINE FEATURE STORY!
THAT'S WHY WE DIDN'T BOTHER TO TELL YOU OF IT!
WHEN A RIVAL REPORTER GETS MAGNAN-IMOUS, IT AROUSES THE SUSPICIOUS STREAK IN ME.
WHY DOESN'T SOMEONE ANSWER THE DOOR? YOU'VE BEEN RINGING IT LONG ENOUGH.
THE DOORBELL ISN'T OUT OF ORDER... I CAN HEAR IT RINGING.
11.
NEWSPAPERMEN! —I'VE GOT TO THINK FAST!

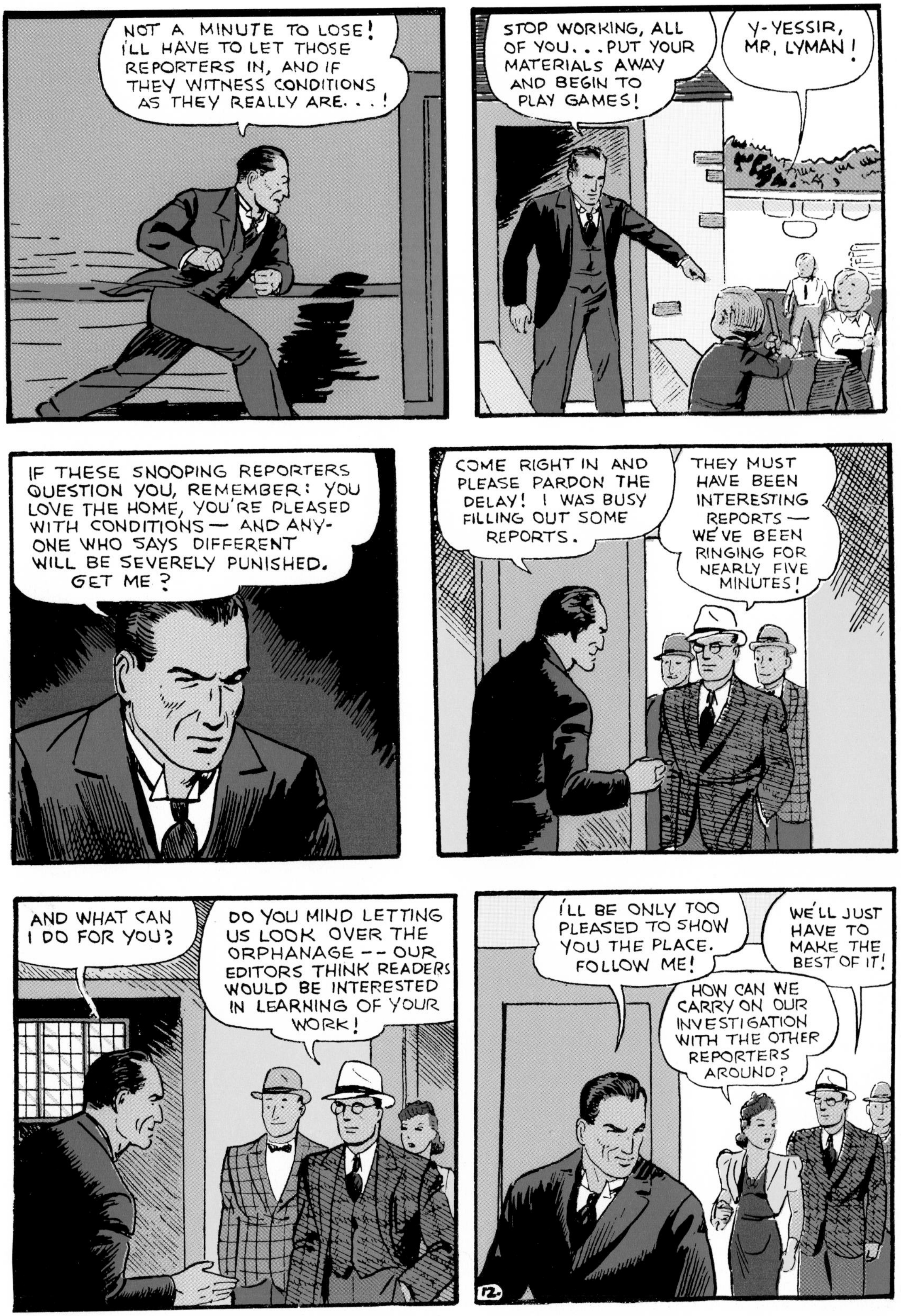
NOT A MINUTE TO LOSE! I'LL HAVE TO LET THOSE REPORTERS IN, AND IF THEY WITNESS CONDITIONS AS THEY REALLY ARE...!
STOP WORKING, ALL OF YOU...PUT YOUR MATERIALS AWAY AND BEGIN TO PLAY GAMES!
Y-YESSIR, MR. LYMAN!
IF THESE SNOOPING REPORTERS QUESTION YOU, REMEMBER: YOU LOVE THE HOME, YOU'RE PLEASED WITH CONDITIONS— AND ANYONE WHO SAYS DIFFERENT WILL BE SEVERELY PUNISHED. GET ME?
COME RIGHT IN AND PLEASE PARDON THE DELAY! I WAS BUSY FILLING OUT SOME REPORTS.
THEY MUST HAVE BEEN INTERESTING REPORTS— WE'VE BEEN RINGING FOR NEARLY FIVE MINUTES!
AND WHAT CAN I DO FOR YOU?
DO YOU MIND LETTING US LOOK OVER THE ORPHANAGE -- OUR EDITORS THINK READERS WOULD BE INTERESTED IN LEARNING OF YOUR WORK!
I'LL BE ONLY TOO PLEASED TO SHOW YOU THE PLACE. FOLLOW ME!
HOW CAN WE CARRY ON OUR INVESTIGATION WITH THE OTHER REPORTERS AROUND?
WE'LL JUST HAVE TO MAKE THE BEST OF IT!
12.

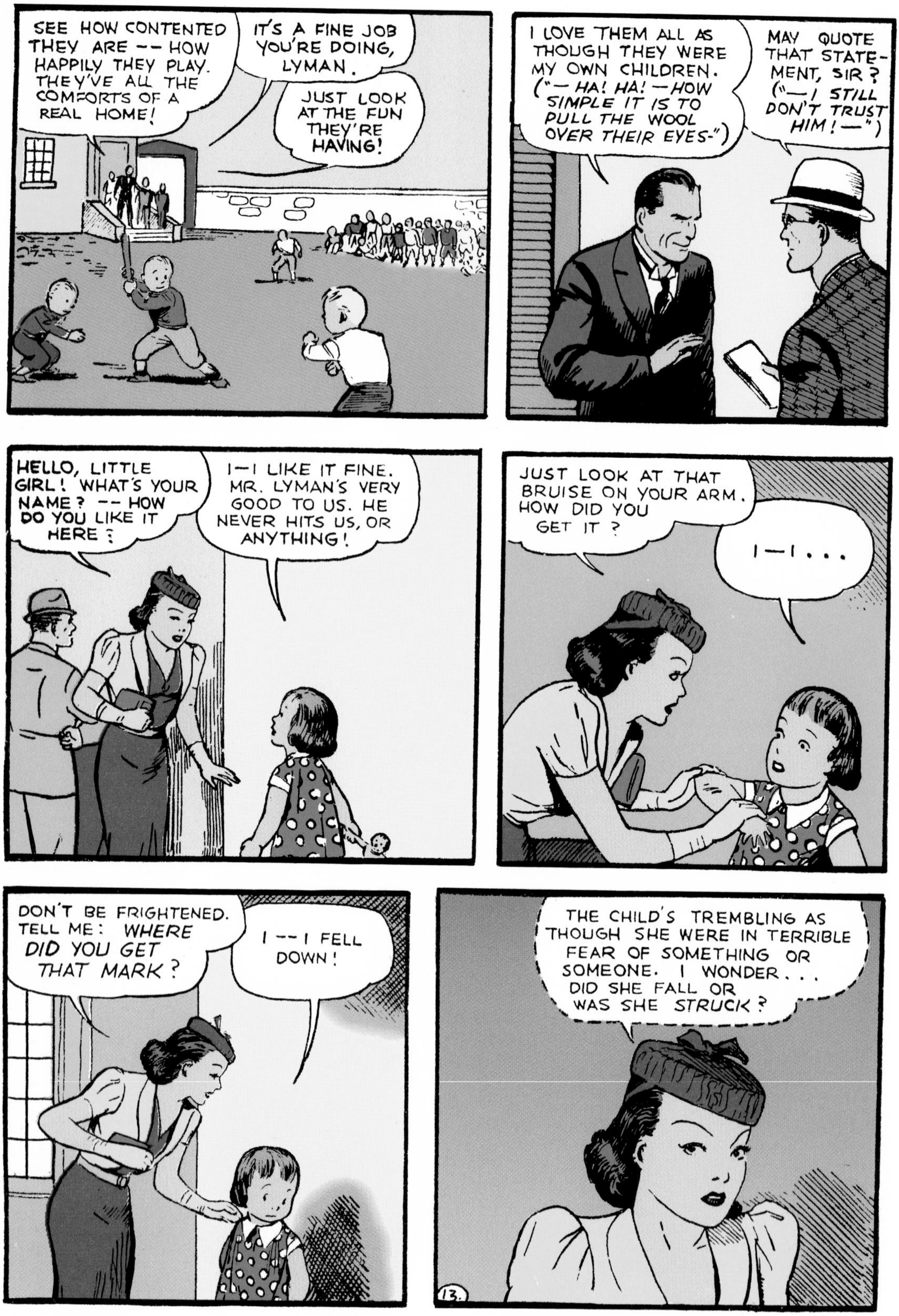
SEE HOW CONTENTED THEY ARE -- HOW HAPPILY THEY PLAY. THEY'VE ALL THE COMFORTS OF A REAL HOME!
IT'S A FINE JOB YOU'RE DOING, LYMAN.
JUST LOOK AT THE FUN THEY'RE HAVING!
I LOVE THEM ALL AS THOUGH THEY WERE MY OWN CHILDREN. ("— HA! HA! —HOW SIMPLE IT IS TO PULL THE WOOL OVER THEIR EYES-")
MAY QUOTE THAT STATEMENT, SIR? ("— I STILL DON'T TRUST HIM! —")
HELLO, LITTLE GIRL! WHAT'S YOUR NAME? -- HOW DO YOU LIKE IT HERE?
I—I LIKE IT FINE. MR. LYMAN'S VERY GOOD TO US. HE NEVER HITS US, OR ANYTHING!
JUST LOOK AT THAT BRUISE ON YOUR ARM. HOW DID YOU GET IT?
I—I . . .
DON'T BE FRIGHTENED. TELL ME: WHERE DID YOU GET THAT MARK?
I -- I FELL DOWN!
THE CHILD'S TREMBLING AS THOUGH SHE WERE IN TERRIBLE FEAR OF SOMETHING OR SOMEONE. I WONDER . . . DID SHE FALL OR WAS SHE STRUCK?
13.

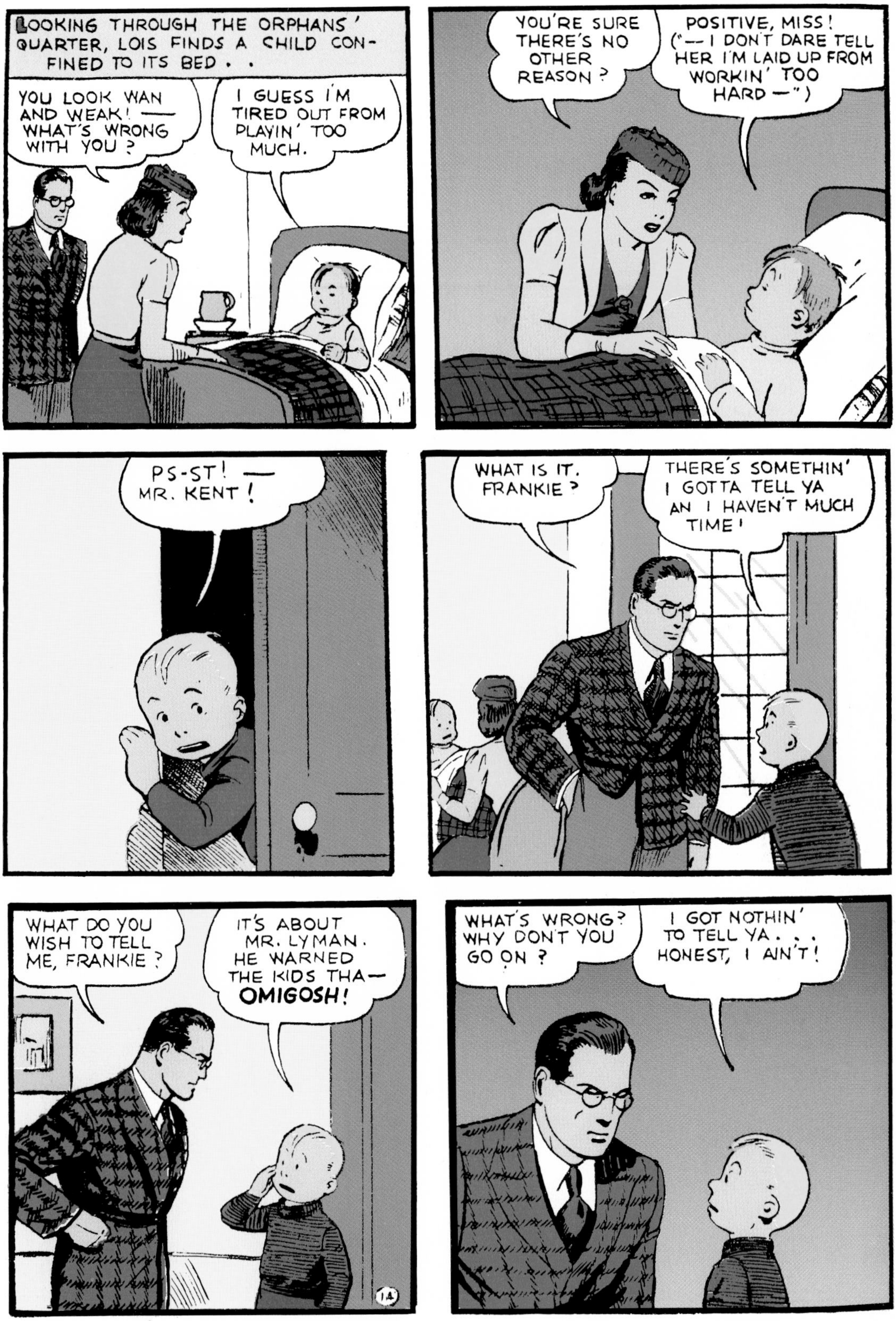
LOOKING THROUGH THE ORPHANS' QUARTER, LOIS FINDS A CHILD CONFINED TO ITS BED . .
YOU LOOK WAN AND WEAK! — WHAT'S WRONG WITH YOU?
I GUESS I'M TIRED OUT FROM PLAYIN' TOO MUCH.
YOU'RE SURE THERE'S NO OTHER REASON?
POSITIVE, MISS! ("— I DON'T DARE TELL HER I'M LAID UP FROM WORKIN' TOO HARD —")
PS-ST! — MR. KENT!
WHAT IS IT, FRANKIE?
THERE'S SOMETHIN' I GOTTA TELL YA AN I HAVEN'T MUCH TIME!
WHAT DO YOU WISH TO TELL ME, FRANKIE?
IT'S ABOUT MR. LYMAN. HE WARNED THE KIDS THA— OMIGOSH!
14
WHAT'S WRONG? WHY DON'T YOU GO ON?
I GOT NOTHIN' TO TELL YA . . . HONEST, I AIN'T!

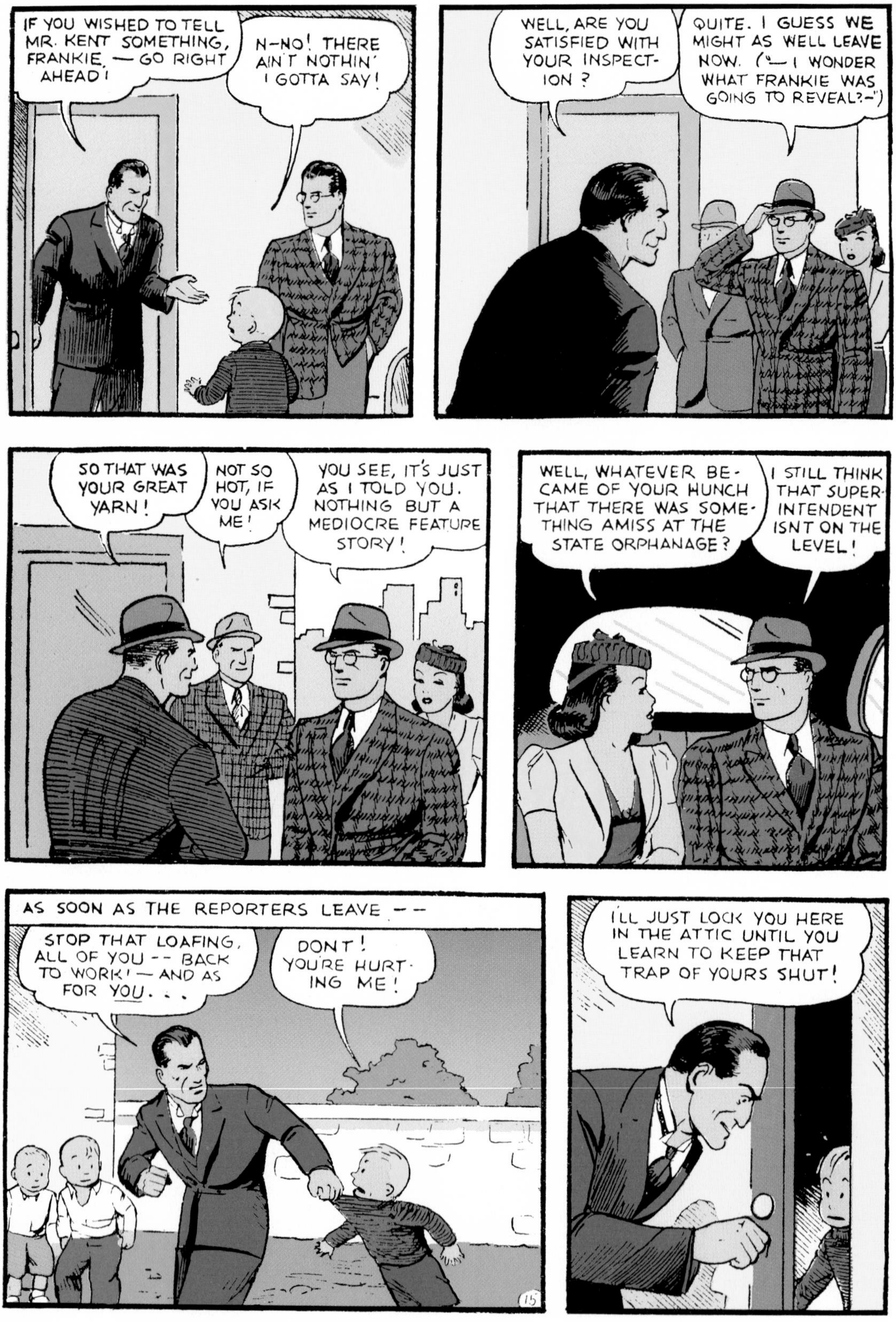
IF YOU WISHED TO TELL MR. KENT SOMETHING, FRANKIE, — GO RIGHT AHEAD!
N-NO! THERE AIN'T NOTHIN' I GOTTA SAY!
WELL, ARE YOU SATISFIED WITH YOUR INSPECTION?
QUITE. I GUESS WE MIGHT AS WELL LEAVE NOW. ("— I WONDER WHAT FRANKIE WAS GOING TO REVEAL?—")
SO THAT WAS YOUR GREAT YARN!
NOT SO HOT, IF YOU ASK ME!
YOU SEE, IT'S JUST AS I TOLD YOU. NOTHING BUT A MEDIOCRE FEATURE STORY!
WELL, WHATEVER BECAME OF YOUR HUNCH THAT THERE WAS SOMETHING AMISS AT THE STATE ORPHANAGE?
I STILL THINK THAT SUPERINTENDENT ISN'T ON THE LEVEL!
AS SOON AS THE REPORTERS LEAVE --
STOP THAT LOAFING, ALL OF YOU -- BACK TO WORK! — AND AS FOR YOU. . .
DON'T! YOU'RE HURTING ME!
15
I'LL JUST LOCK YOU HERE IN THE ATTIC UNTIL YOU LEARN TO KEEP THAT TRAP OF YOURS SHUT!

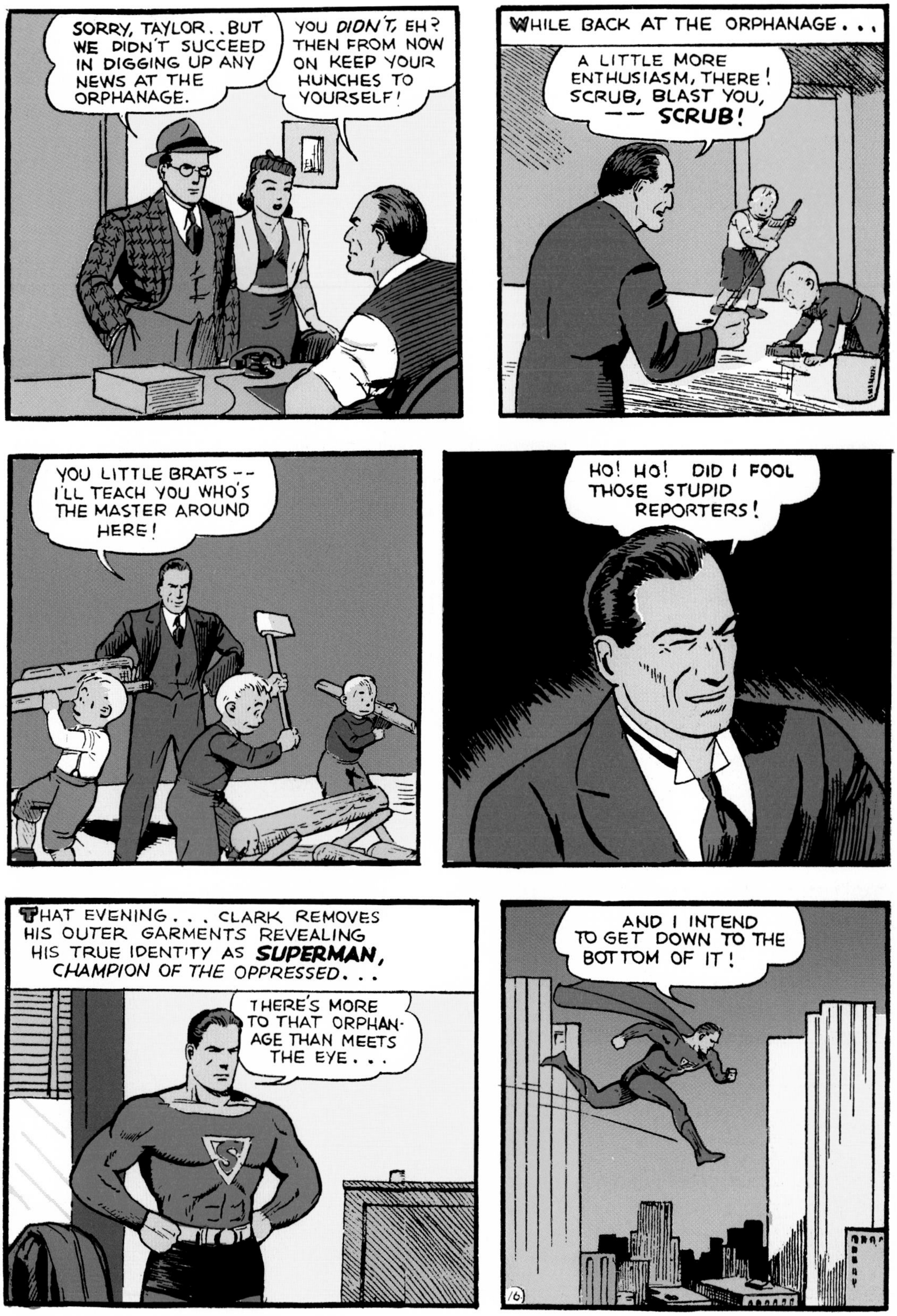
SORRY, TAYLOR..BUT WE DIDN'T SUCCEED IN DIGGING UP ANY NEWS AT THE ORPHANAGE.
YOU DIDN'T, EH? THEN FROM NOW ON KEEP YOUR HUNCHES TO YOURSELF!
WHILE BACK AT THE ORPHANAGE...
A LITTLE MORE ENTHUSIASM, THERE! SCRUB, BLAST YOU, -- SCRUB!
YOU LITTLE BRATS -- I'LL TEACH YOU WHO'S THE MASTER AROUND HERE!
HO! HO! DID I FOOL THOSE STUPID REPORTERS!
THAT EVENING... CLARK REMOVES HIS OUTER GARMENTS REVEALING HIS TRUE IDENTITY AS SUPERMAN, CHAMPION OF THE OPPRESSED...
THERE'S MORE TO THAT ORPHANAGE THAN MEETS THE EYE...
AND I INTEND TO GET DOWN TO THE BOTTOM OF IT!
16

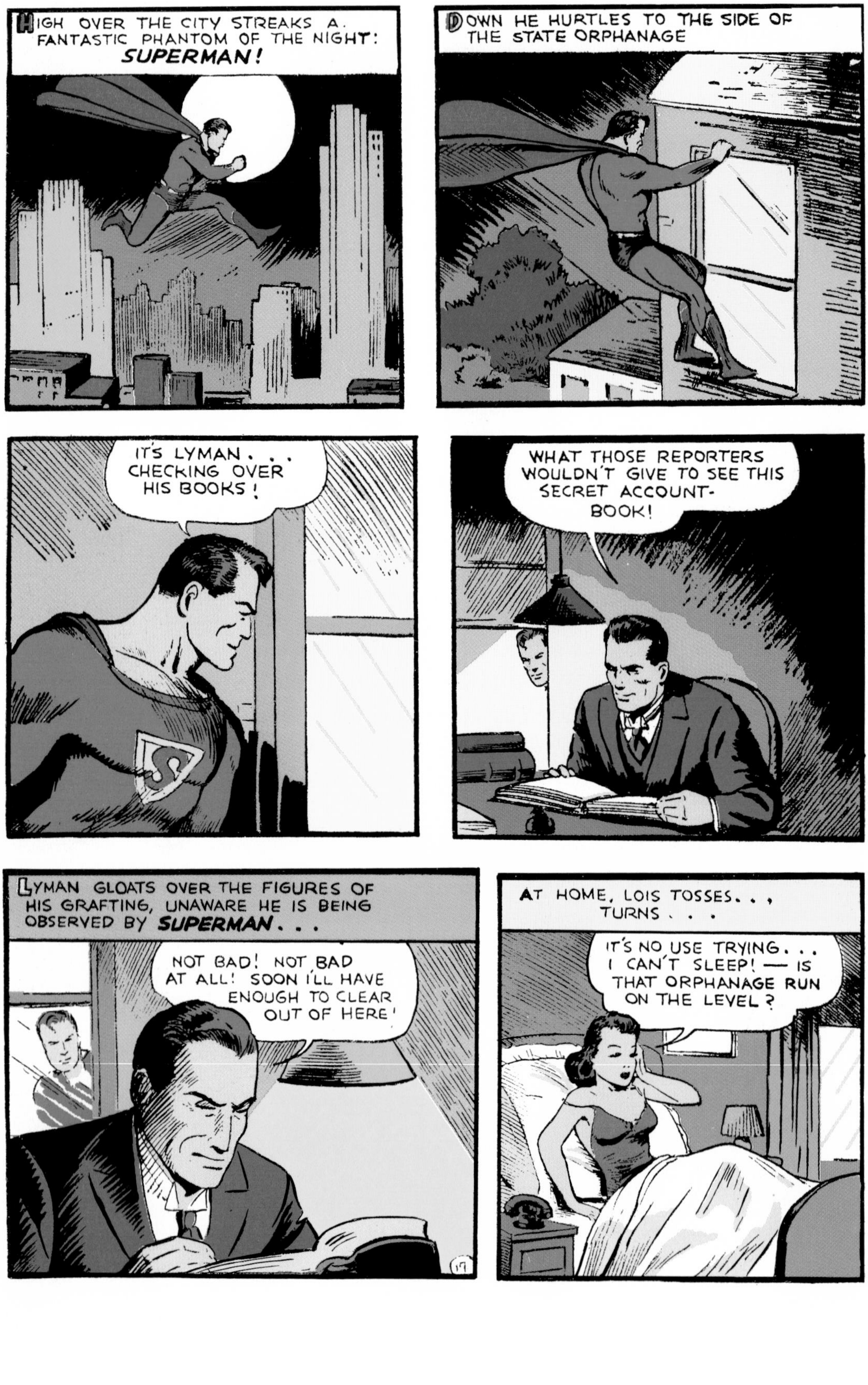
HIGH OVER THE CITY STREAKS A FANTASTIC PHANTOM OF THE NIGHT: SUPERMAN!
DOWN HE HURTLES TO THE SIDE OF THE STATE ORPHANAGE
IT'S LYMAN. . . CHECKING OVER HIS BOOKS!
WHAT THOSE REPORTERS WOULDN'T GIVE TO SEE THIS SECRET ACCOUNT-BOOK!
LYMAN GLOATS OVER THE FIGURES OF HIS GRAFTING, UNAWARE HE IS BEING OBSERVED BY SUPERMAN. . .
NOT BAD! NOT BAD AT ALL! SOON I'LL HAVE ENOUGH TO CLEAR OUT OF HERE!
AT HOME, LOIS TOSSES. . , TURNS . . .
IT'S NO USE TRYING. . . I CAN'T SLEEP! — IS THAT ORPHANAGE RUN ON THE LEVEL?

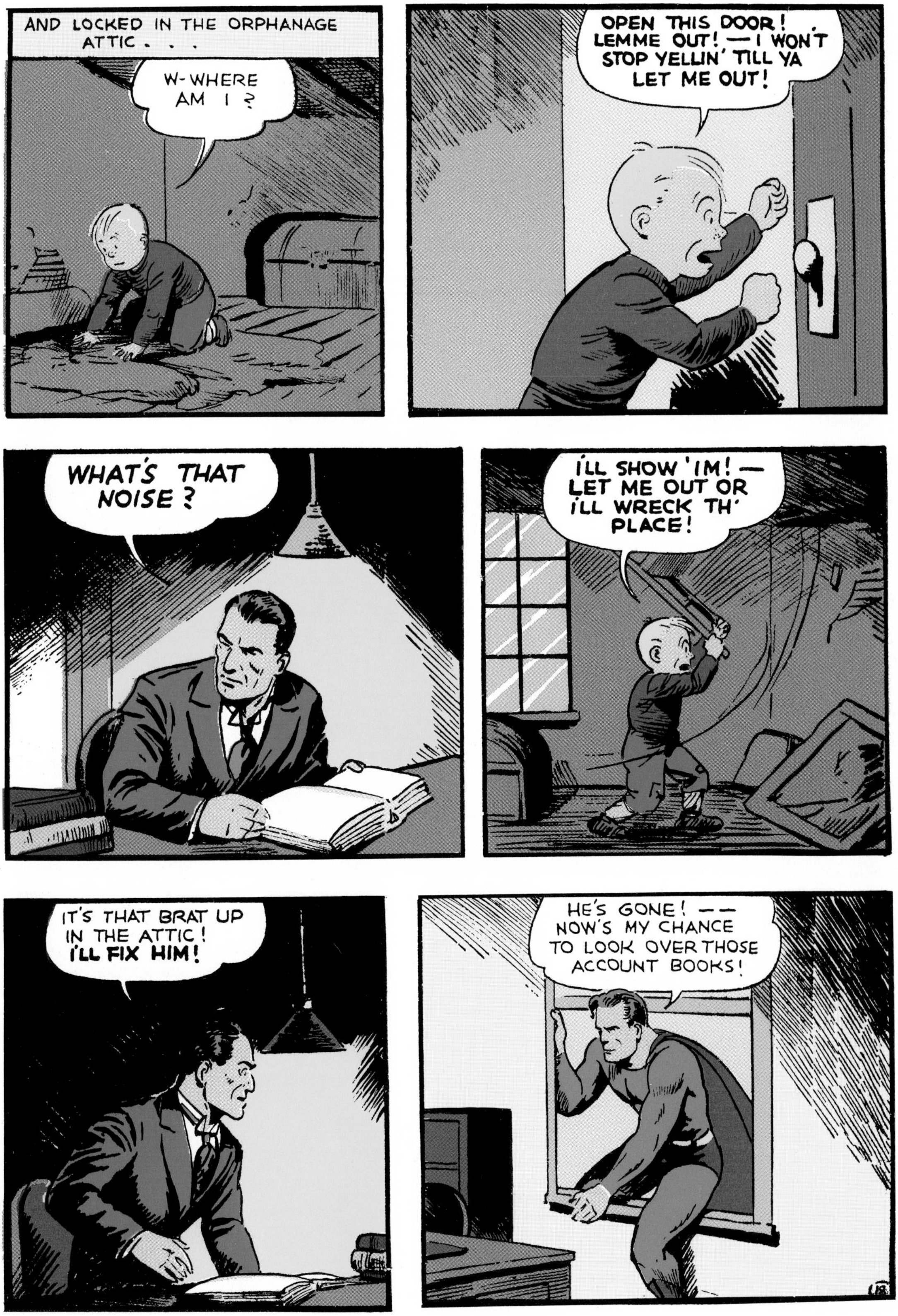
AND LOCKED IN THE ORPHANAGE ATTIC . . .
W-WHERE AM I ?
OPEN THIS DOOR! LEMME OUT! — I WON'T STOP YELLIN' TILL YA LET ME OUT!
WHAT'S THAT NOISE ?
I'LL SHOW 'IM! — LET ME OUT OR I'LL WRECK TH' PLACE!
IT'S THAT BRAT UP IN THE ATTIC! I'LL FIX HIM!
HE'S GONE! — — NOW'S MY CHANCE TO LOOK OVER THOSE ACCOUNT BOOKS!

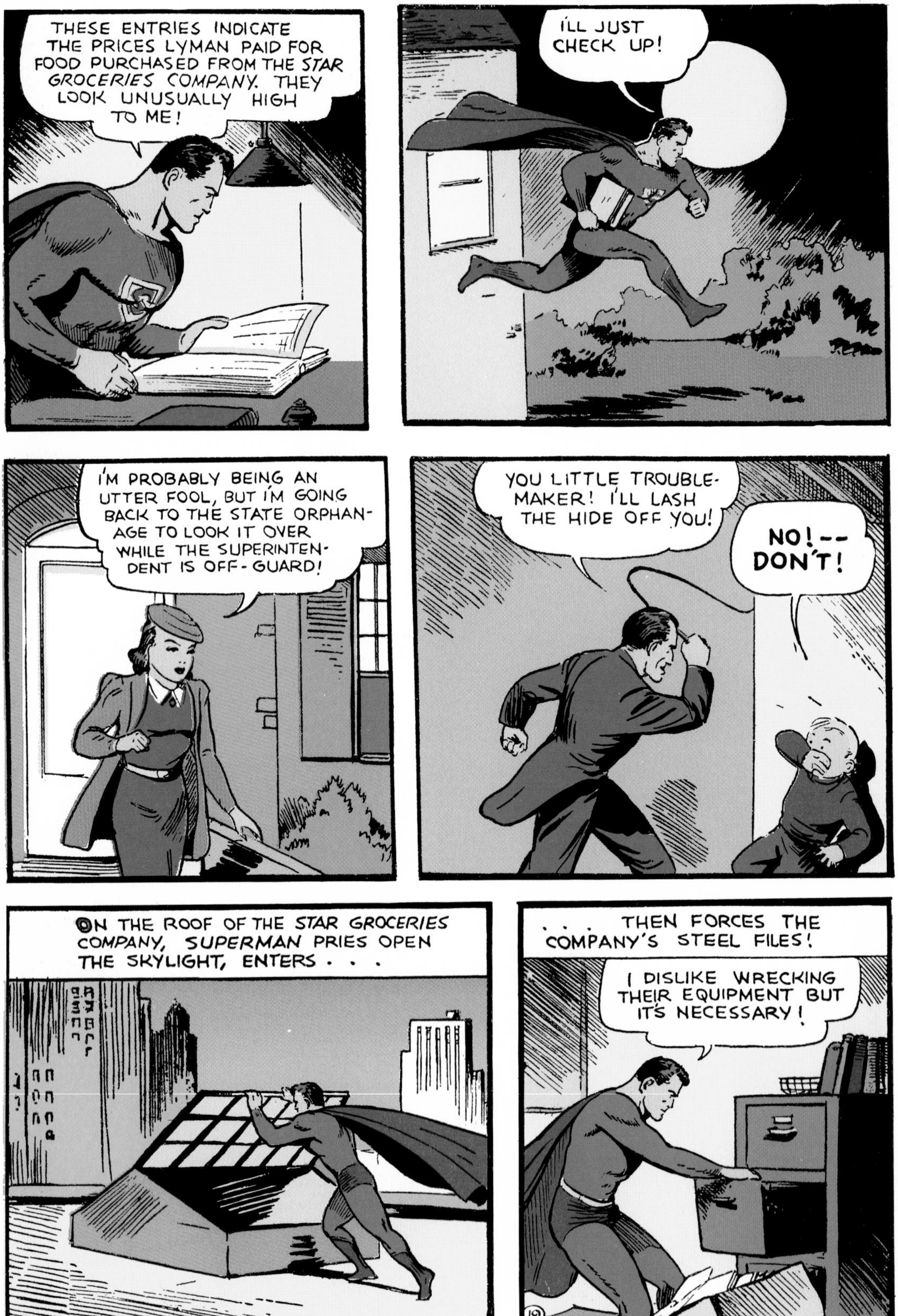
THESE ENTRIES INDICATE THE PRICES LYMAN PAID FOR FOOD PURCHASED FROM THE STAR GROCERIES COMPANY. THEY LOOK UNUSUALLY HIGH TO ME!
I'LL JUST CHECK UP!
I'M PROBABLY BEING AN UTTER FOOL, BUT I'M GOING BACK TO THE STATE ORPHANAGE TO LOOK IT OVER WHILE THE SUPERINTENDENT IS OFF-GUARD!
YOU LITTLE TROUBLE-MAKER! I'LL LASH THE HIDE OFF YOU!
NO!-- DON'T!
ON THE ROOF OF THE STAR GROCERIES COMPANY, SUPERMAN PRIES OPEN THE SKYLIGHT, ENTERS . . .
. . . THEN FORCES THE COMPANY'S STEEL FILES!
I DISLIKE WRECKING THEIR EQUIPMENT BUT IT'S NECESSARY!
19

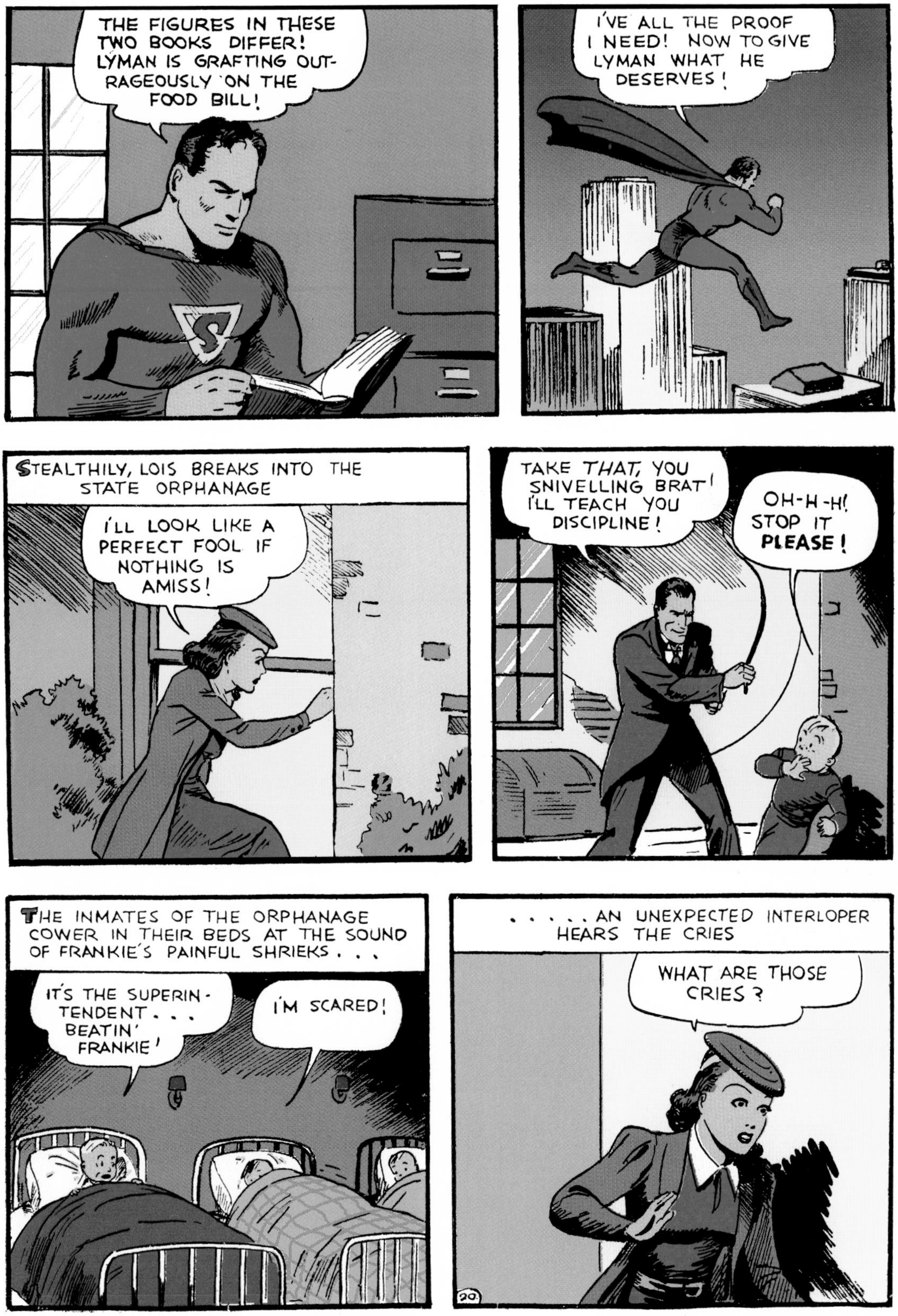
THE FIGURES IN THESE TWO BOOKS DIFFER! LYMAN IS GRAFTING OUT-RAGEOUSLY ON THE FOOD BILL!
I'VE ALL THE PROOF I NEED! NOW TO GIVE LYMAN WHAT HE DESERVES!
STEALTHILY, LOIS BREAKS INTO THE STATE ORPHANAGE
I'LL LOOK LIKE A PERFECT FOOL IF NOTHING IS AMISS!
TAKE *THAT,* YOU SNIVELLING BRAT! I'LL TEACH YOU DISCIPLINE!
OH-H-H! STOP IT **PLEASE!**
THE INMATES OF THE ORPHANAGE COWER IN THEIR BEDS AT THE SOUND OF FRANKIE'S PAINFUL SHRIEKS . . .
IT'S THE SUPERIN-TENDENT . . . BEATIN' FRANKIE!
I'M SCARED!
. . . . . AN UNEXPECTED INTERLOPER HEARS THE CRIES
WHAT ARE THOSE CRIES?
20

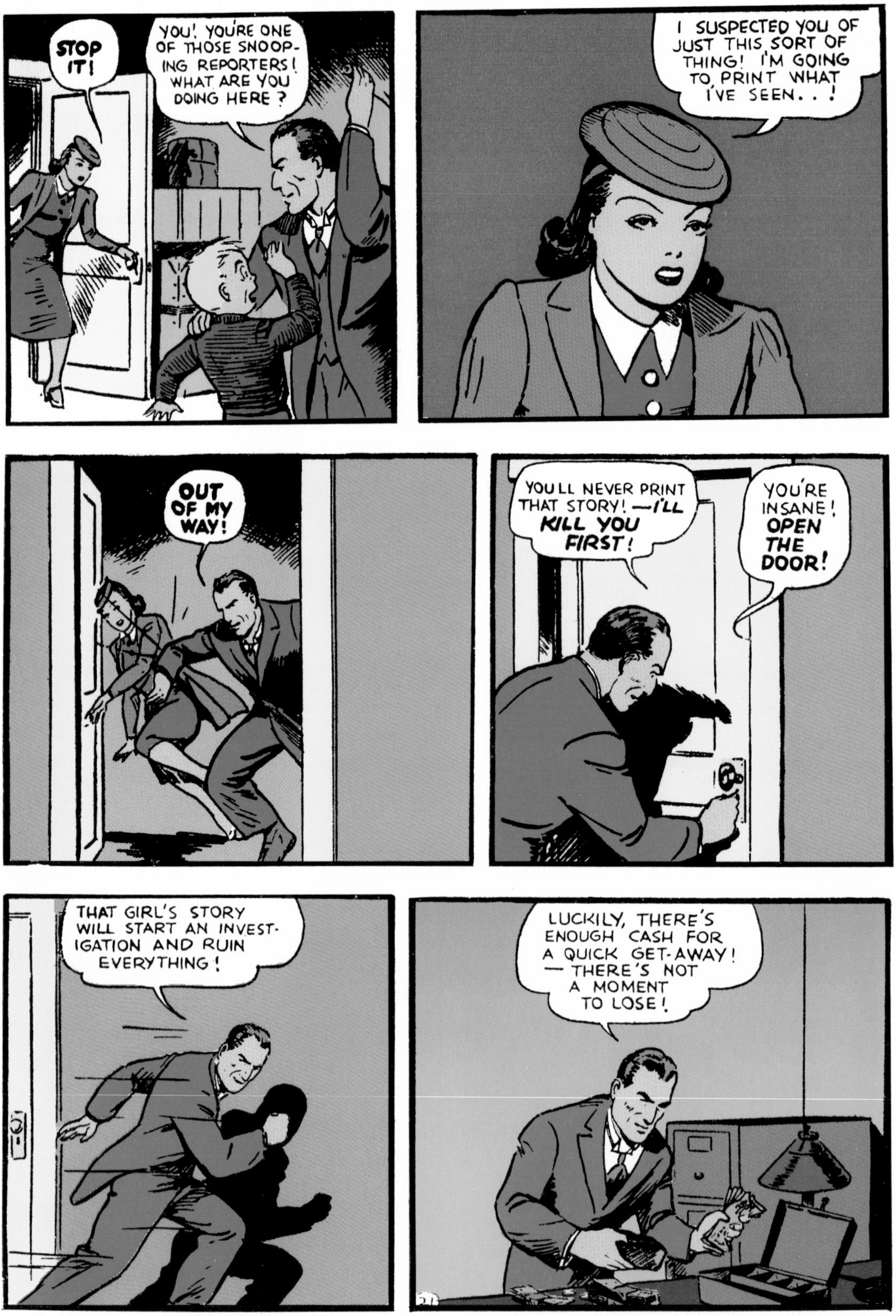
STOP IT!
YOU! YOU'RE ONE OF THOSE SNOOPING REPORTERS! WHAT ARE YOU DOING HERE?
I SUSPECTED YOU OF JUST THIS SORT OF THING! I'M GOING TO PRINT WHAT I'VE SEEN..!
OUT OF MY WAY!
YOU'LL NEVER PRINT THAT STORY! —I'LL KILL YOU FIRST!
YOU'RE INSANE! OPEN THE DOOR!
THAT GIRL'S STORY WILL START AN INVESTIGATION AND RUIN EVERYTHING!
LUCKILY, THERE'S ENOUGH CASH FOR A QUICK GET-AWAY! — THERE'S NOT A MOMENT TO LOSE!

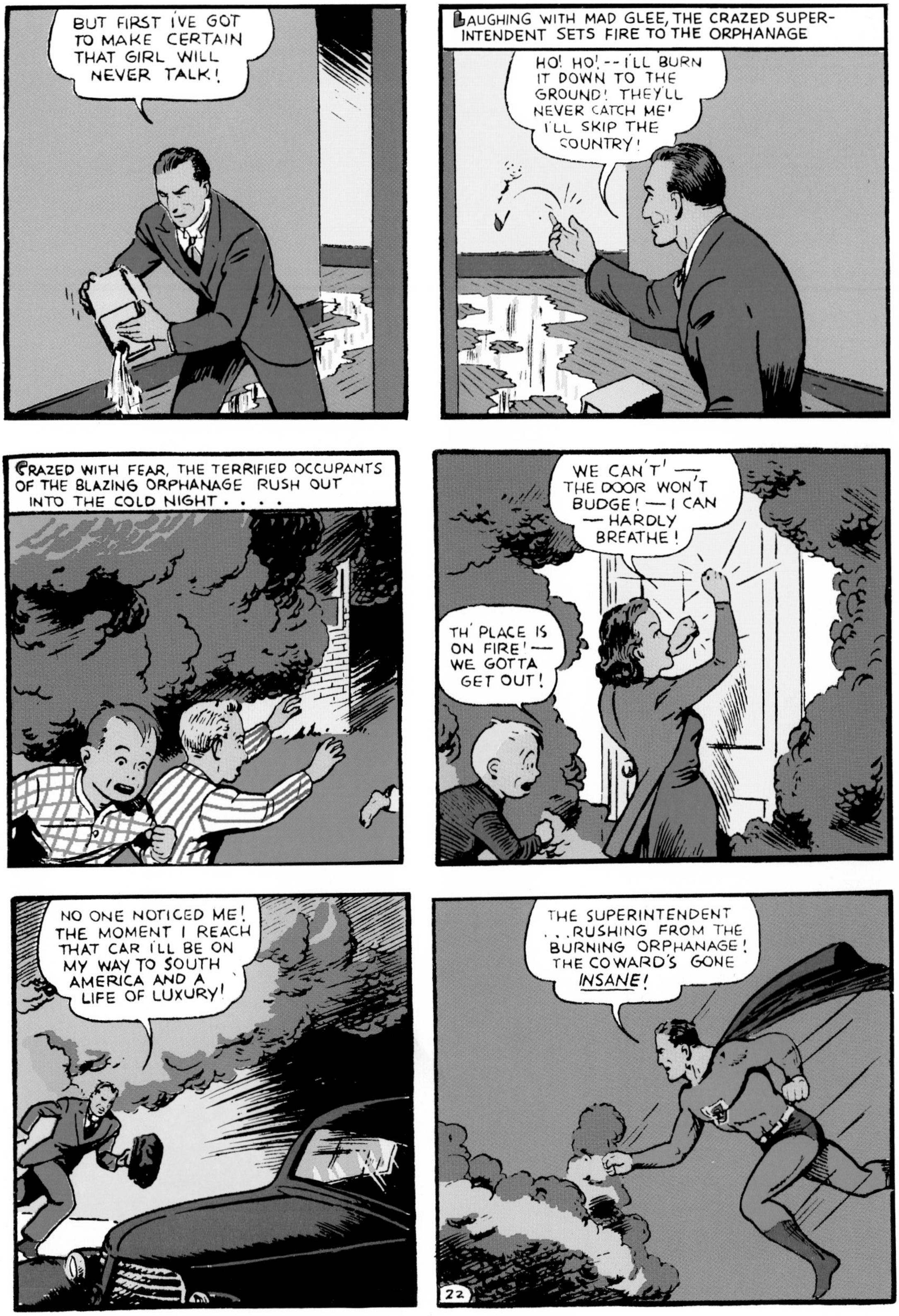
BUT FIRST I'VE GOT TO MAKE CERTAIN THAT GIRL WILL NEVER TALK!
LAUGHING WITH MAD GLEE, THE CRAZED SUPER-INTENDENT SETS FIRE TO THE ORPHANAGE
HO! HO! -- I'LL BURN IT DOWN TO THE GROUND! THEY'LL NEVER CATCH ME! I'LL SKIP THE COUNTRY!
CRAZED WITH FEAR, THE TERRIFIED OCCUPANTS OF THE BLAZING ORPHANAGE RUSH OUT INTO THE COLD NIGHT . . . .
WE CAN'T! — THE DOOR WON'T BUDGE! — I CAN — HARDLY BREATHE!
TH' PLACE IS ON FIRE! — WE GOTTA GET OUT!
NO ONE NOTICED ME! THE MOMENT I REACH THAT CAR I'LL BE ON MY WAY TO SOUTH AMERICA AND A LIFE OF LUXURY!
THE SUPERINTENDENT . . .RUSHING FROM THE BURNING ORPHANAGE! THE COWARD'S GONE INSANE!
22

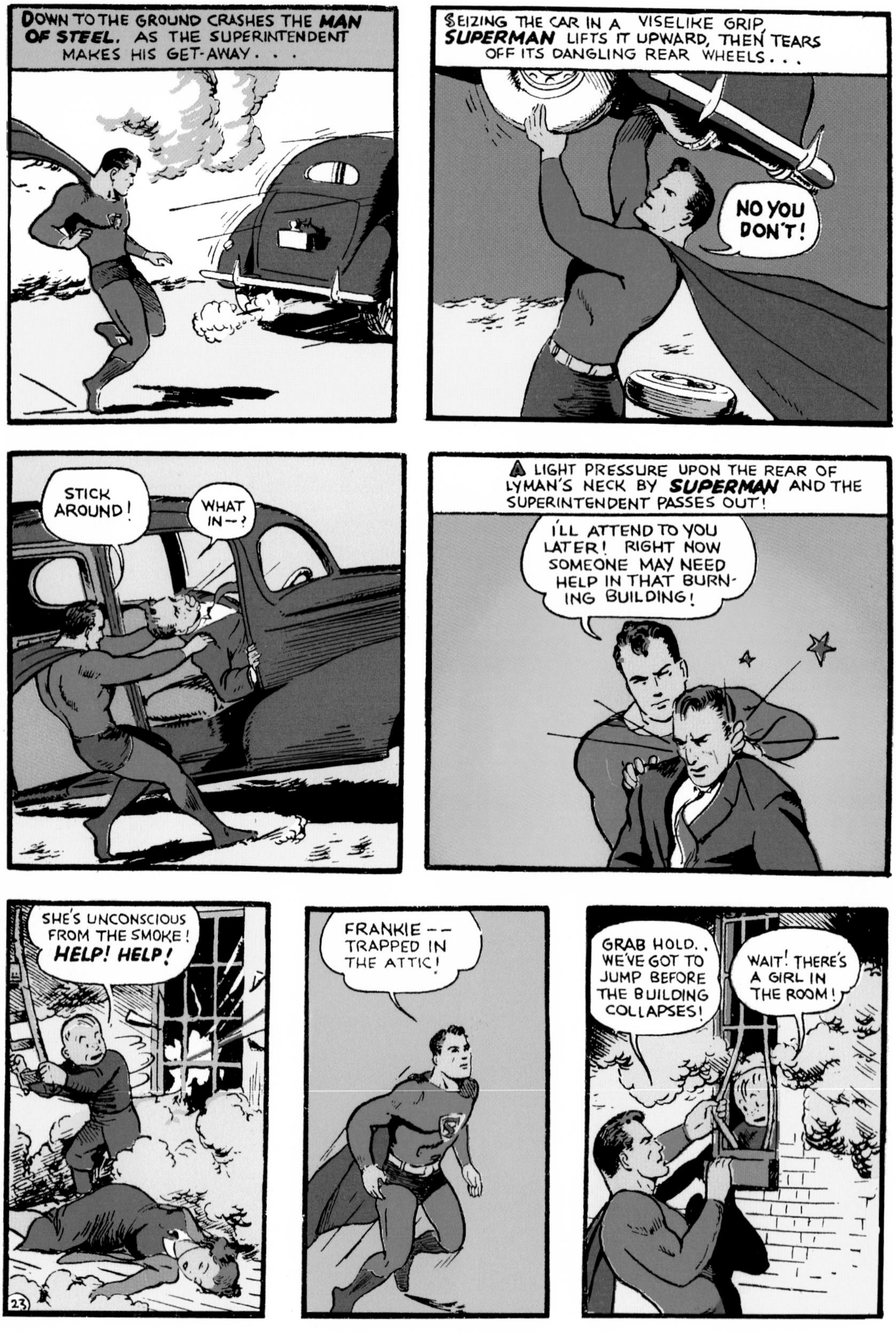
DOWN TO THE GROUND CRASHES THE MAN OF STEEL. AS THE SUPERINTENDENT MAKES HIS GET-AWAY . . .
SEIZING THE CAR IN A VISELIKE GRIP, SUPERMAN LIFTS IT UPWARD, THEN TEARS OFF ITS DANGLING REAR WHEELS . . .
NO YOU DON'T!
STICK AROUND!
WHAT IN--?
A LIGHT PRESSURE UPON THE REAR OF LYMAN'S NECK BY SUPERMAN AND THE SUPERINTENDENT PASSES OUT!
I'LL ATTEND TO YOU LATER! RIGHT NOW SOMEONE MAY NEED HELP IN THAT BURNING BUILDING!
SHE'S UNCONSCIOUS FROM THE SMOKE! HELP! HELP!
23
FRANKIE -- TRAPPED IN THE ATTIC!
GRAB HOLD.. WE'VE GOT TO JUMP BEFORE THE BUILDING COLLAPSES!
WAIT! THERE'S A GIRL IN THE ROOM!

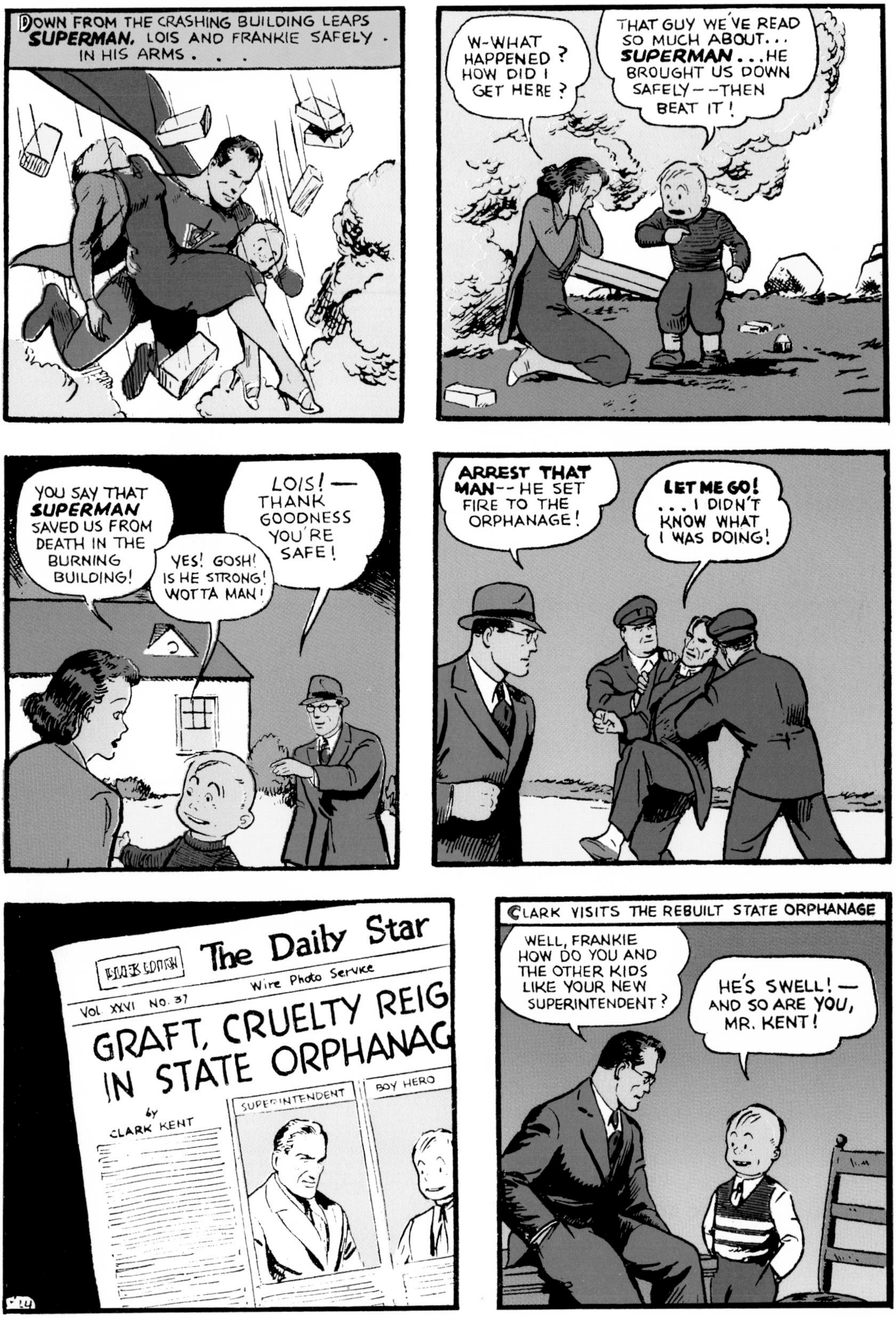
DOWN FROM THE CRASHING BUILDING LEAPS SUPERMAN, LOIS AND FRANKIE SAFELY IN HIS ARMS . . .
W-WHAT HAPPENED? HOW DID I GET HERE?
THAT GUY WE'VE READ SO MUCH ABOUT... SUPERMAN...HE BROUGHT US DOWN SAFELY--THEN BEAT IT!
YOU SAY THAT SUPERMAN SAVED US FROM DEATH IN THE BURNING BUILDING!
YES! GOSH! IS HE STRONG! WOTTA MAN!
LOIS!— THANK GOODNESS YOU'RE SAFE!
ARREST THAT MAN--HE SET FIRE TO THE ORPHANAGE!
LET ME GO! ...I DIDN'T KNOW WHAT I WAS DOING!
The Daily Star
Wire Photo Service
VOL. XXVI NO. 37
GRAFT, CRUELTY REIG
IN STATE ORPHANAG
by CLARK KENT
SUPERINTENDENT
BOY HERO
CLARK VISITS THE REBUILT STATE ORPHANAGE
WELL, FRANKIE HOW DO YOU AND THE OTHER KIDS LIKE YOUR NEW SUPERINTENDENT?
HE'S SWELL!— AND SO ARE YOU, MR. KENT!

THE GREATEST CONTEST IN COMIC MAGAZINE HISTORY!

THOUSANDS OF FREE PRIZES!

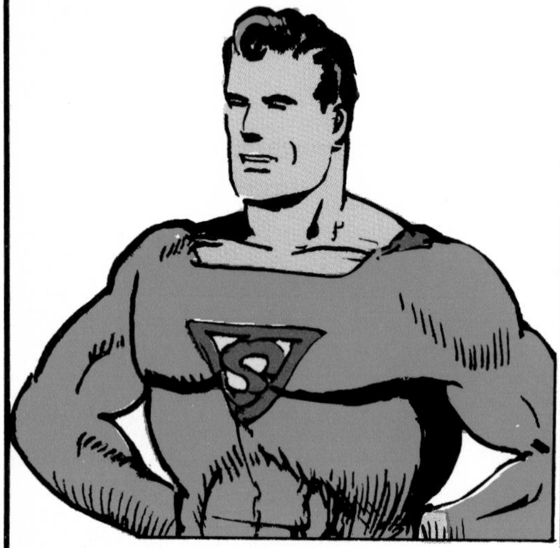

REMEMBER!

TO ENTER THIS CONTEST, YOU MUST BE A MEMBER OF THE SUPERMEN of AMERICA!

JOIN NOW!

FILL IN THE APPLICATION BLANK BELOW AND MAIL IT IN IMMEDIATELY!

Just think of it, Boys and Girls! Over 2,000 FREE Prizes will be given away in this immense contest! On the opposite page are pictured just a few of these beautiful prizes: Radios, flashlights, typewriters, Superman rings, roller skates, bicycles, footballs, hunting knives, boxing gloves . . . and numerous others that are not seen here!

However, you must meet one important requirement to take part in this contest . . . only those who are Members of the SUPERMEN OF AMERICA are eligible to enter! SO JOIN NOW!

SUPERMAN, S/3
c/o ACTION COMICS,
480 LEXINGTON AVENUE, N. Y. C.

Dear Superman:

Please enroll me as a Member of the SUPERMEN of AMERICA. I enclose 10c to cover cost of mailing. It is understood that I am to receive my Membership Certificate, Button and Superman Code.

NAME...AGE............

STREET ADDRESS...

CITY AND STATE...

Be sure to read the January issue of ACTION COMICS for complete details for this GIGANTIC SUPERMAN CONTEST!

It will be on sale everywhere about December 1st!

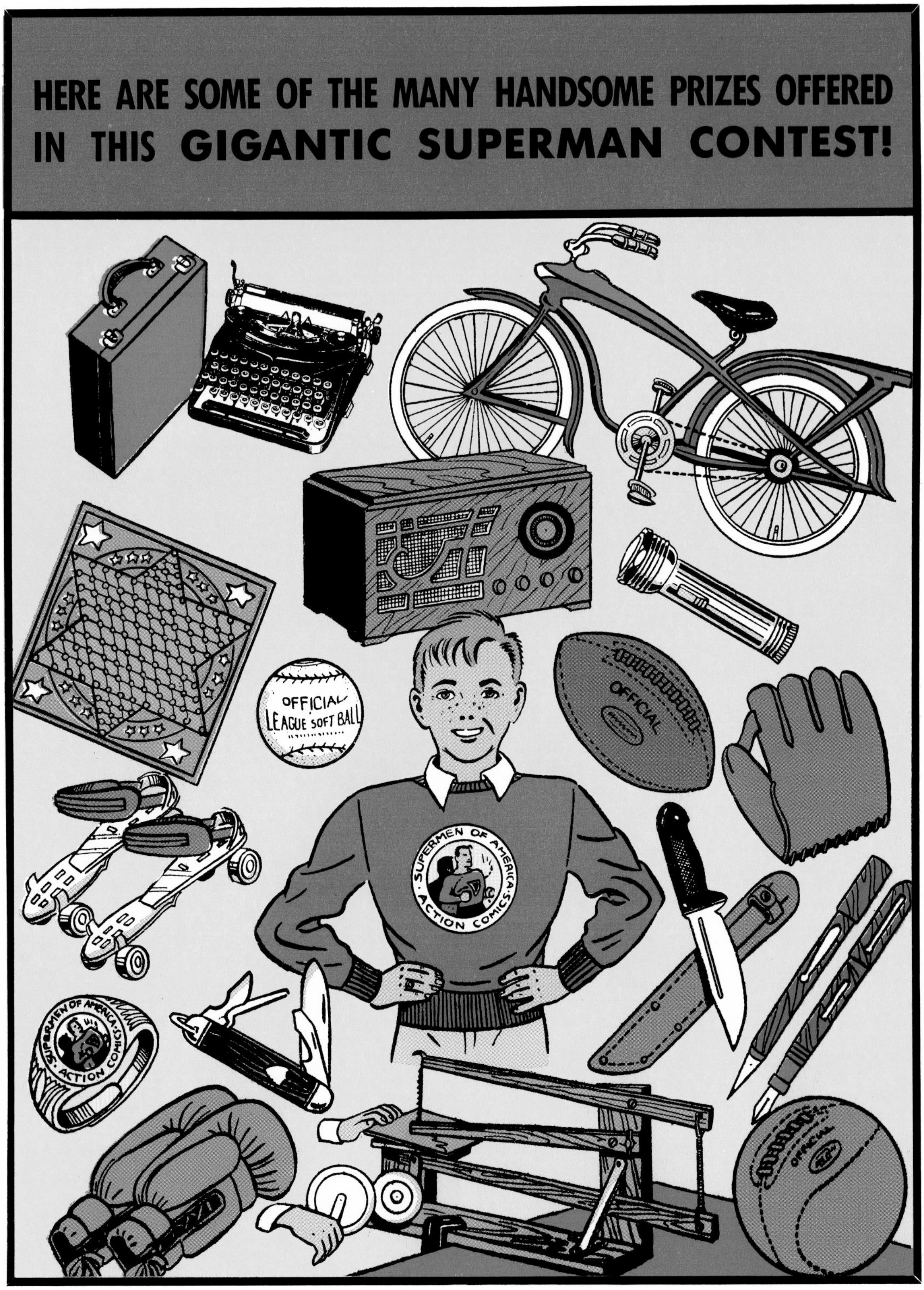
HERE ARE SOME OF THE MANY HANDSOME PRIZES OFFERED IN THIS GIGANTIC SUPERMAN CONTEST!
OFFICIAL LEAGUE SOFT BALL
OFFICIAL
SUPERMEN OF AMERICA ACTION COMICS
SUPERMEN OF AMERICA ACTION COMICS
OFFICIAL

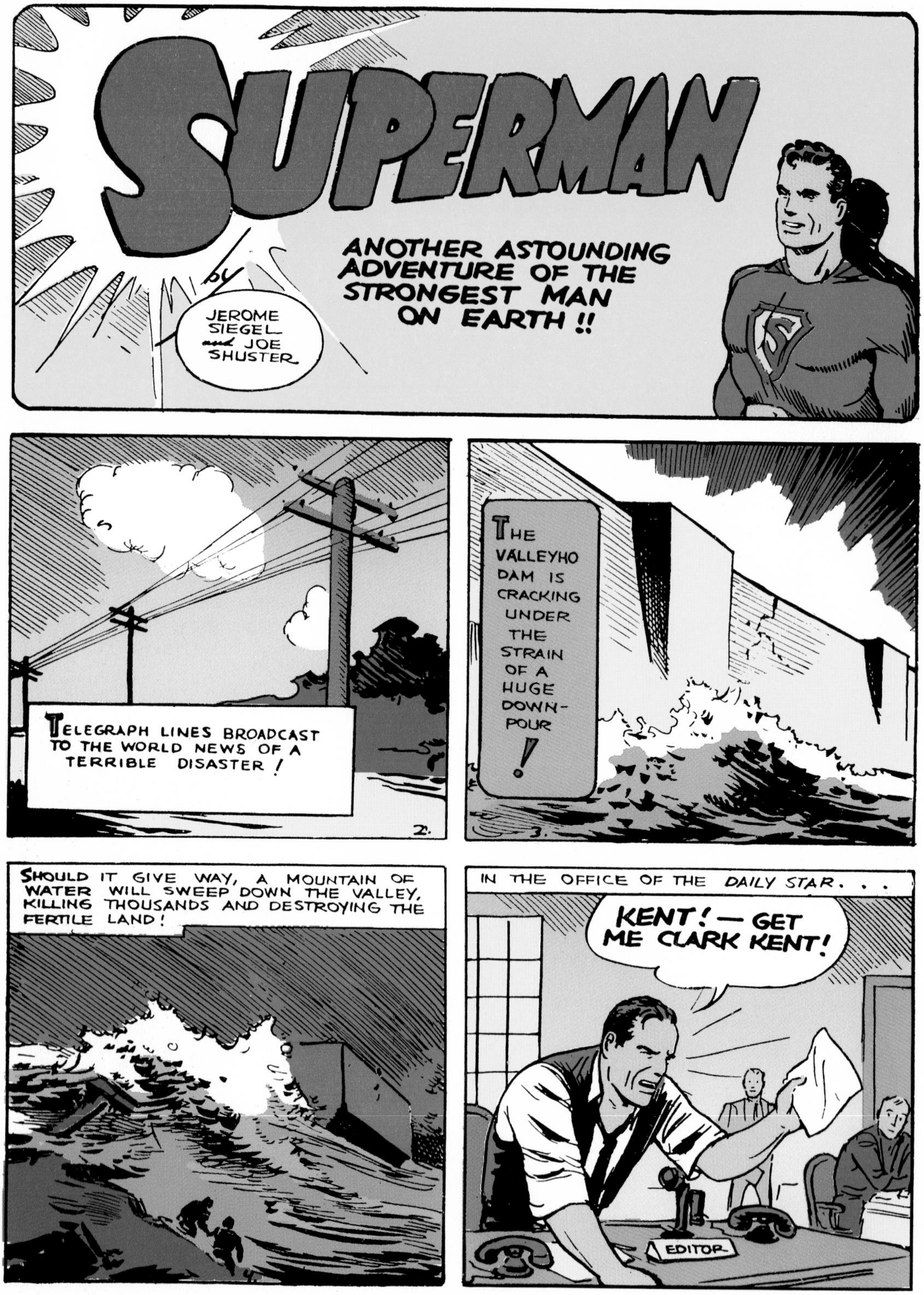
SUPERMAN
by
JEROME SIEGEL and JOE SHUSTER
ANOTHER ASTOUNDING ADVENTURE OF THE STRONGEST MAN ON EARTH!!
TELEGRAPH LINES BROADCAST TO THE WORLD NEWS OF A TERRIBLE DISASTER!
THE VALLEYHO DAM IS CRACKING UNDER THE STRAIN OF A HUGE DOWN-POUR!
SHOULD IT GIVE WAY, A MOUNTAIN OF WATER WILL SWEEP DOWN THE VALLEY, KILLING THOUSANDS AND DESTROYING THE FERTILE LAND!
IN THE OFFICE OF THE DAILY STAR . . .
KENT! — GET ME CLARK KENT!
EDITOR

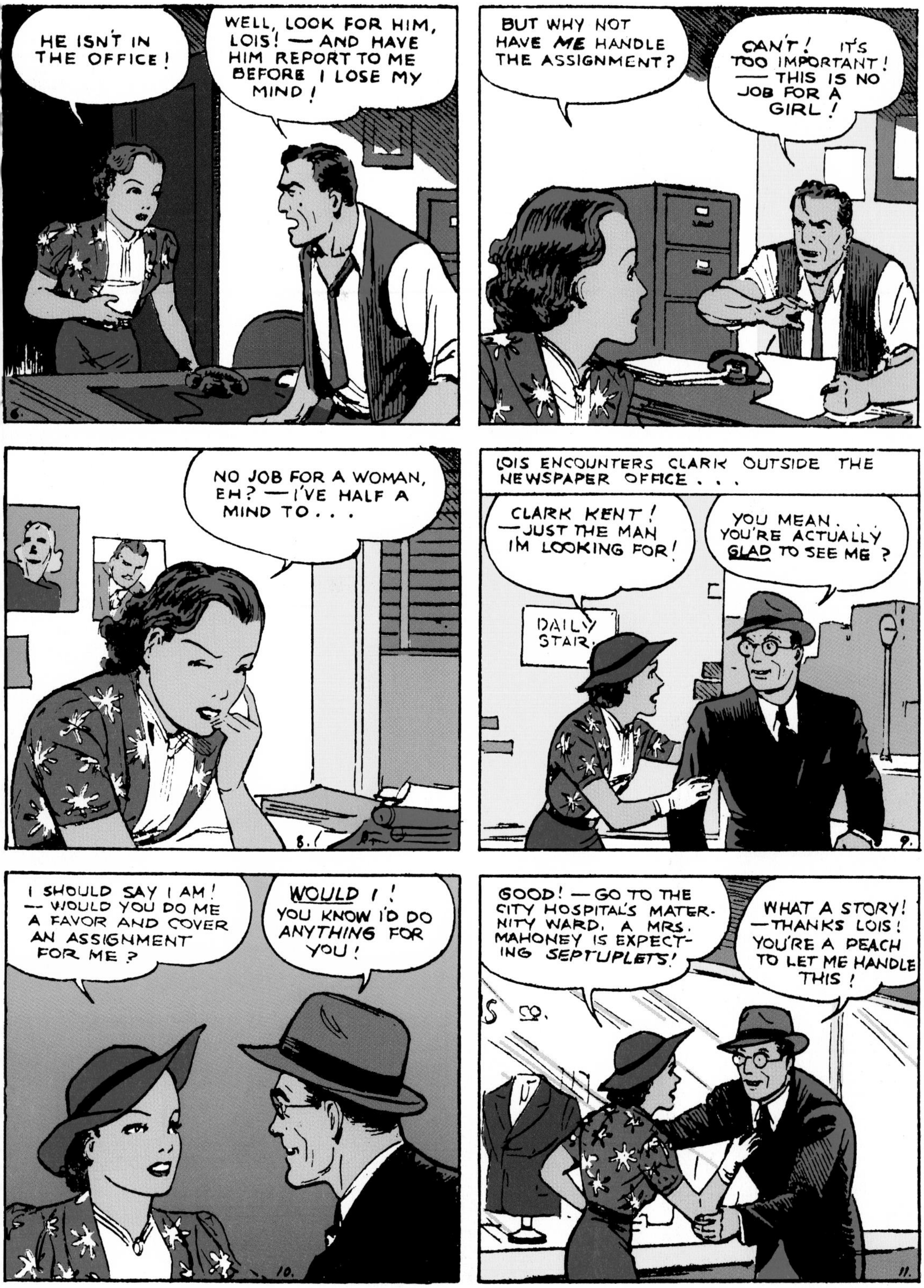
HE ISN'T IN THE OFFICE!
WELL, LOOK FOR HIM, LOIS! — AND HAVE HIM REPORT TO ME BEFORE I LOSE MY MIND!
BUT WHY NOT HAVE ME HANDLE THE ASSIGNMENT?
CAN'T! IT'S TOO IMPORTANT! — THIS IS NO JOB FOR A GIRL!
NO JOB FOR A WOMAN, EH? — I'VE HALF A MIND TO . . .
LOIS ENCOUNTERS CLARK OUTSIDE THE NEWSPAPER OFFICE . . .
CLARK KENT! — JUST THE MAN I'M LOOKING FOR!
YOU MEAN. . . YOU'RE ACTUALLY GLAD TO SEE ME?
DAILY STAR
I SHOULD SAY I AM! -- WOULD YOU DO ME A FAVOR AND COVER AN ASSIGNMENT FOR ME?
WOULD I! YOU KNOW I'D DO ANYTHING FOR YOU!
GOOD! — GO TO THE CITY HOSPITAL'S MATERNITY WARD. A MRS. MAHONEY IS EXPECTING SEPTUPLETS!
WHAT A STORY! — THANKS LOIS! YOU'RE A PEACH TO LET ME HANDLE THIS!

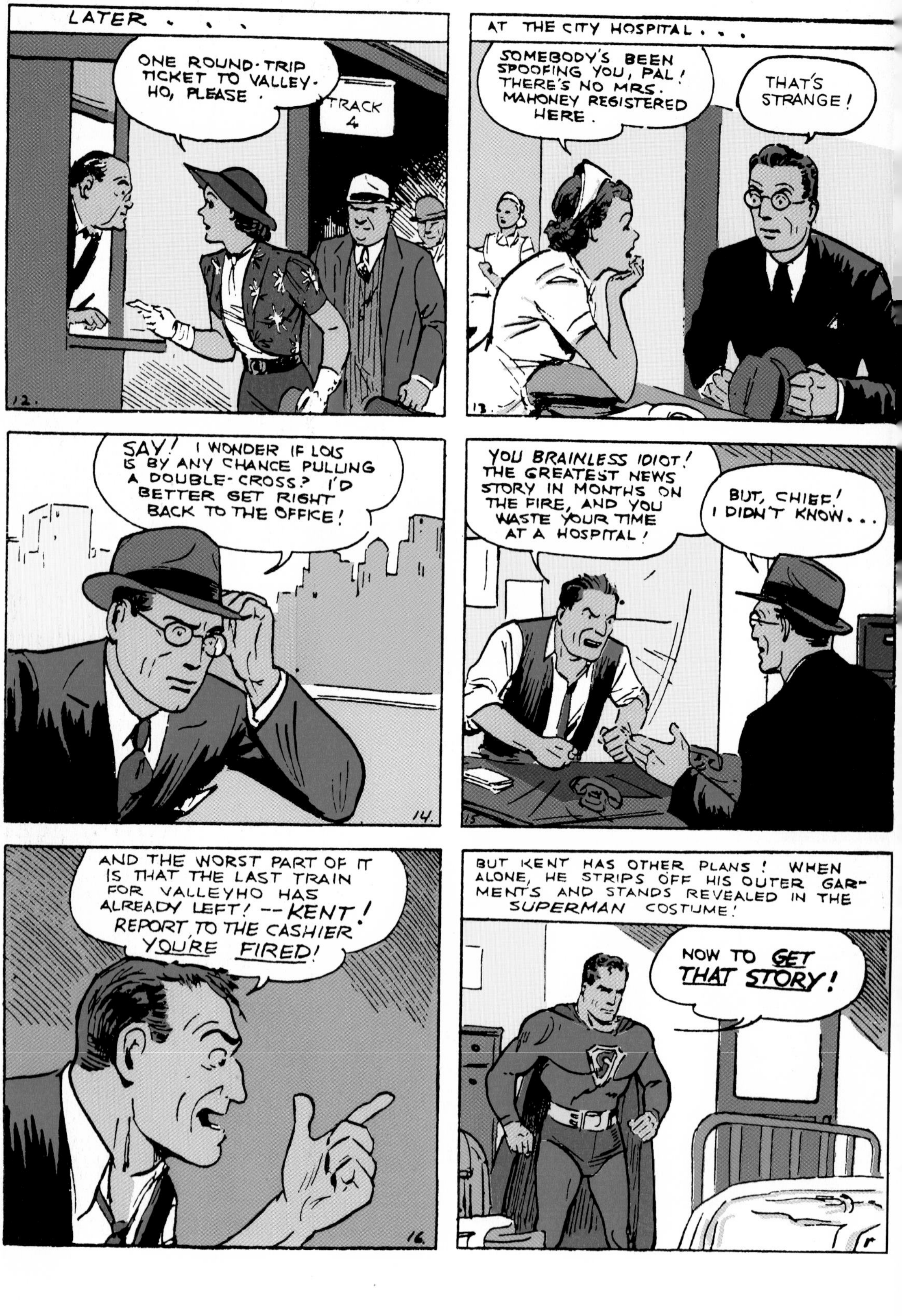
LATER . . .
ONE ROUND-TRIP TICKET TO VALLEY-HO, PLEASE.
TRACK 4
12.
AT THE CITY HOSPITAL . . .
SOMEBODY'S BEEN SPOOFING YOU, PAL! THERE'S NO MRS. MAHONEY REGISTERED HERE.
THAT'S STRANGE!
13.
SAY! I WONDER IF LOIS IS BY ANY CHANCE PULLING A DOUBLE-CROSS? I'D BETTER GET RIGHT BACK TO THE OFFICE!
14.
YOU BRAINLESS IDIOT! THE GREATEST NEWS STORY IN MONTHS ON THE FIRE, AND YOU WASTE YOUR TIME AT A HOSPITAL!
BUT, CHIEF! I DIDN'T KNOW...
15
AND THE WORST PART OF IT IS THAT THE LAST TRAIN FOR VALLEYHO HAS ALREADY LEFT! --KENT! REPORT TO THE CASHIER YOU'RE FIRED!
16.
BUT KENT HAS OTHER PLANS! WHEN ALONE, HE STRIPS OFF HIS OUTER GARMENTS AND STANDS REVEALED IN THE SUPERMAN COSTUME!
NOW TO GET THAT STORY!

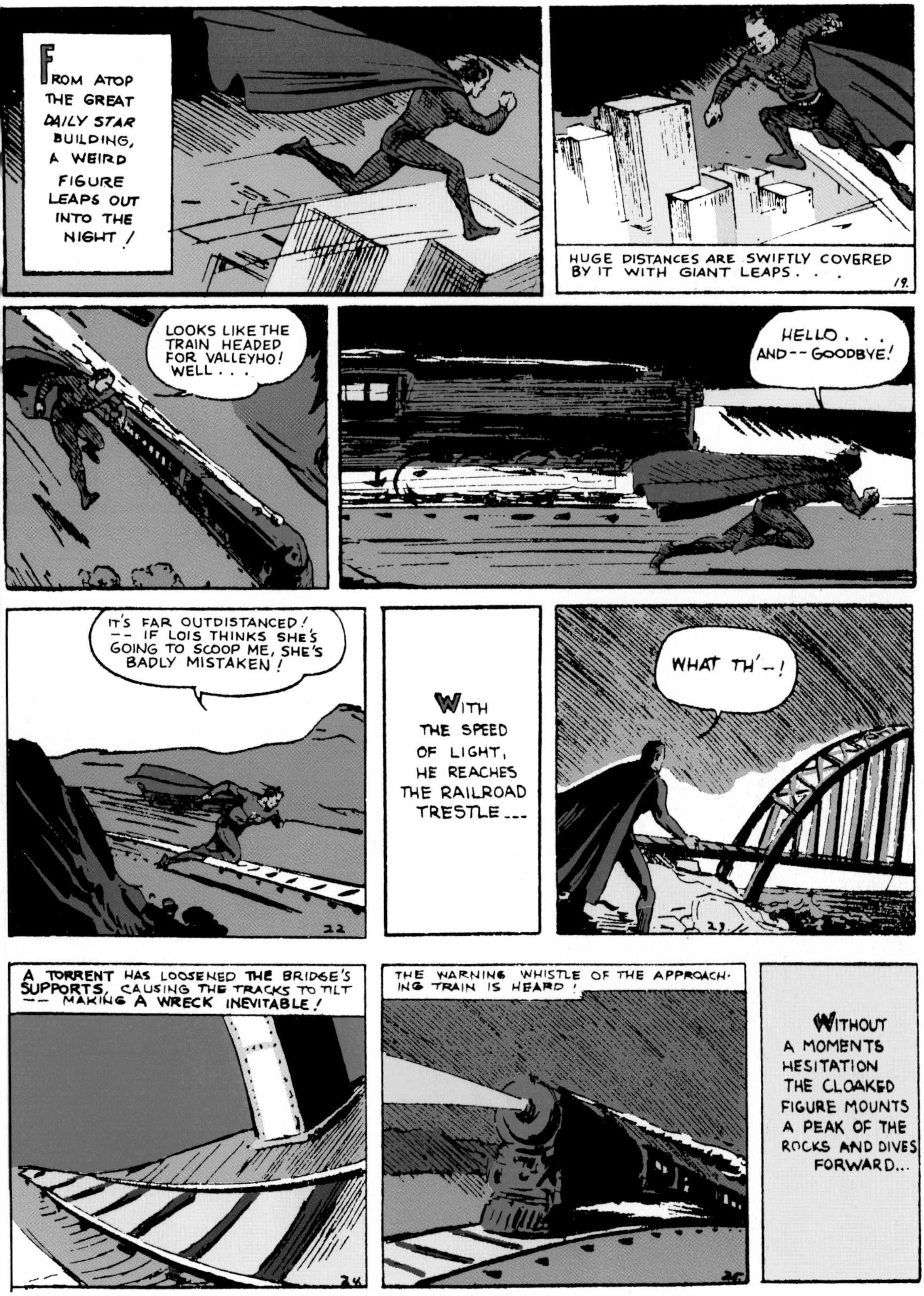
FROM ATOP THE GREAT DAILY STAR BUILDING, A WEIRD FIGURE LEAPS OUT INTO THE NIGHT!
HUGE DISTANCES ARE SWIFTLY COVERED BY IT WITH GIANT LEAPS. . .
LOOKS LIKE THE TRAIN HEADED FOR VALLEYHO! WELL . . .
HELLO. . . AND--GOODBYE!
IT'S FAR OUTDISTANCED! -- IF LOIS THINKS SHE'S GOING TO SCOOP ME, SHE'S BADLY MISTAKEN!
WITH THE SPEED OF LIGHT, HE REACHES THE RAILROAD TRESTLE...
WHAT TH'--!
A TORRENT HAS LOOSENED THE BRIDGE'S SUPPORTS, CAUSING THE TRACKS TO TILT -- MAKING A WRECK INEVITABLE!
THE WARNING WHISTLE OF THE APPROACHING TRAIN IS HEARD!
WITHOUT A MOMENTS HESITATION THE CLOAKED FIGURE MOUNTS A PEAK OF THE ROCKS AND DIVES FORWARD...

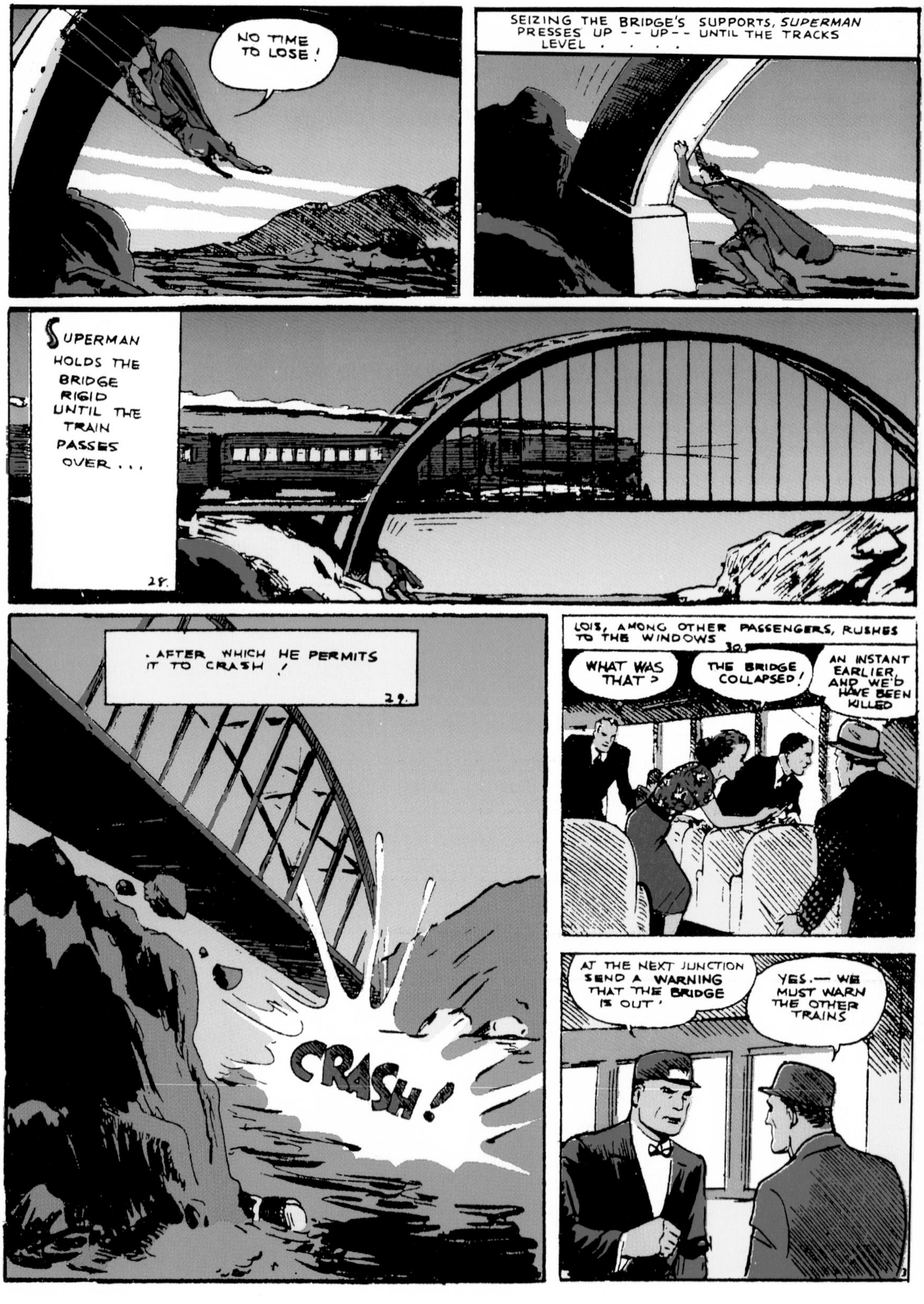
NO TIME TO LOSE!
SEIZING THE BRIDGE'S SUPPORTS, SUPERMAN PRESSES UP -- UP -- UNTIL THE TRACKS LEVEL . . . .
SUPERMAN HOLDS THE BRIDGE RIGID UNTIL THE TRAIN PASSES OVER . . .
28.
. AFTER WHICH HE PERMITS IT TO CRASH!
29.
CRASH!
LOIS, AMONG OTHER PASSENGERS, RUSHES TO THE WINDOWS
30.
WHAT WAS THAT?
THE BRIDGE COLLAPSED!
AN INSTANT EARLIER, AND WE'D HAVE BEEN KILLED
AT THE NEXT JUNCTION SEND A WARNING THAT THE BRIDGE IS OUT!
YES.— WE MUST WARN THE OTHER TRAINS

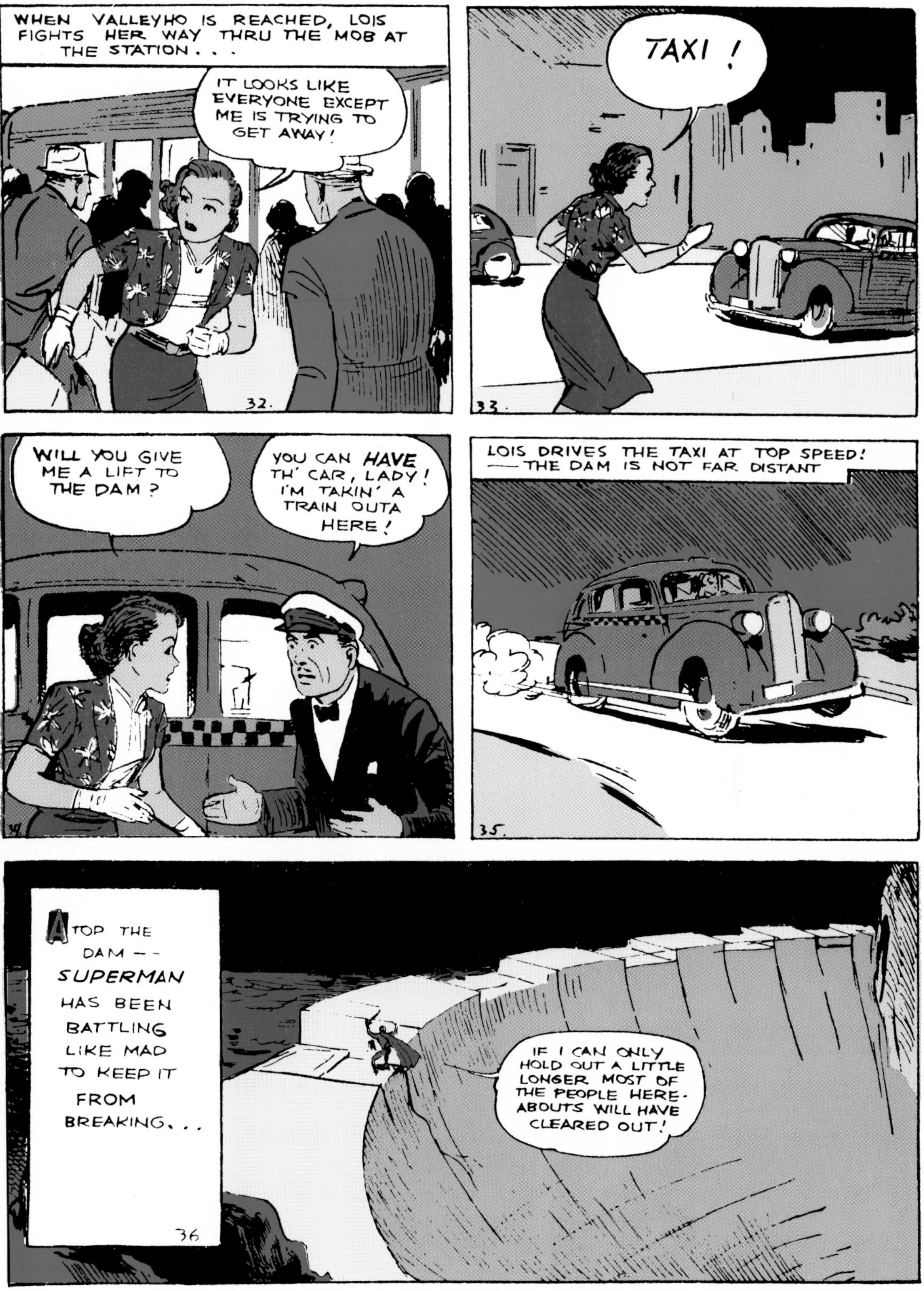
WHEN VALLEYHO IS REACHED, LOIS FIGHTS HER WAY THRU THE MOB AT THE STATION . . .
IT LOOKS LIKE EVERYONE EXCEPT ME IS TRYING TO GET AWAY!
32.
TAXI !
33.
WILL YOU GIVE ME A LIFT TO THE DAM ?
YOU CAN HAVE TH' CAR, LADY! I'M TAKIN' A TRAIN OUTA HERE!
34.
LOIS DRIVES THE TAXI AT TOP SPEED! —THE DAM IS NOT FAR DISTANT
35.
ATOP THE DAM -- SUPERMAN HAS BEEN BATTLING LIKE MAD TO KEEP IT FROM BREAKING. . .
IF I CAN ONLY HOLD OUT A LITTLE LONGER MOST OF THE PEOPLE HERE-ABOUTS WILL HAVE CLEARED OUT!
36

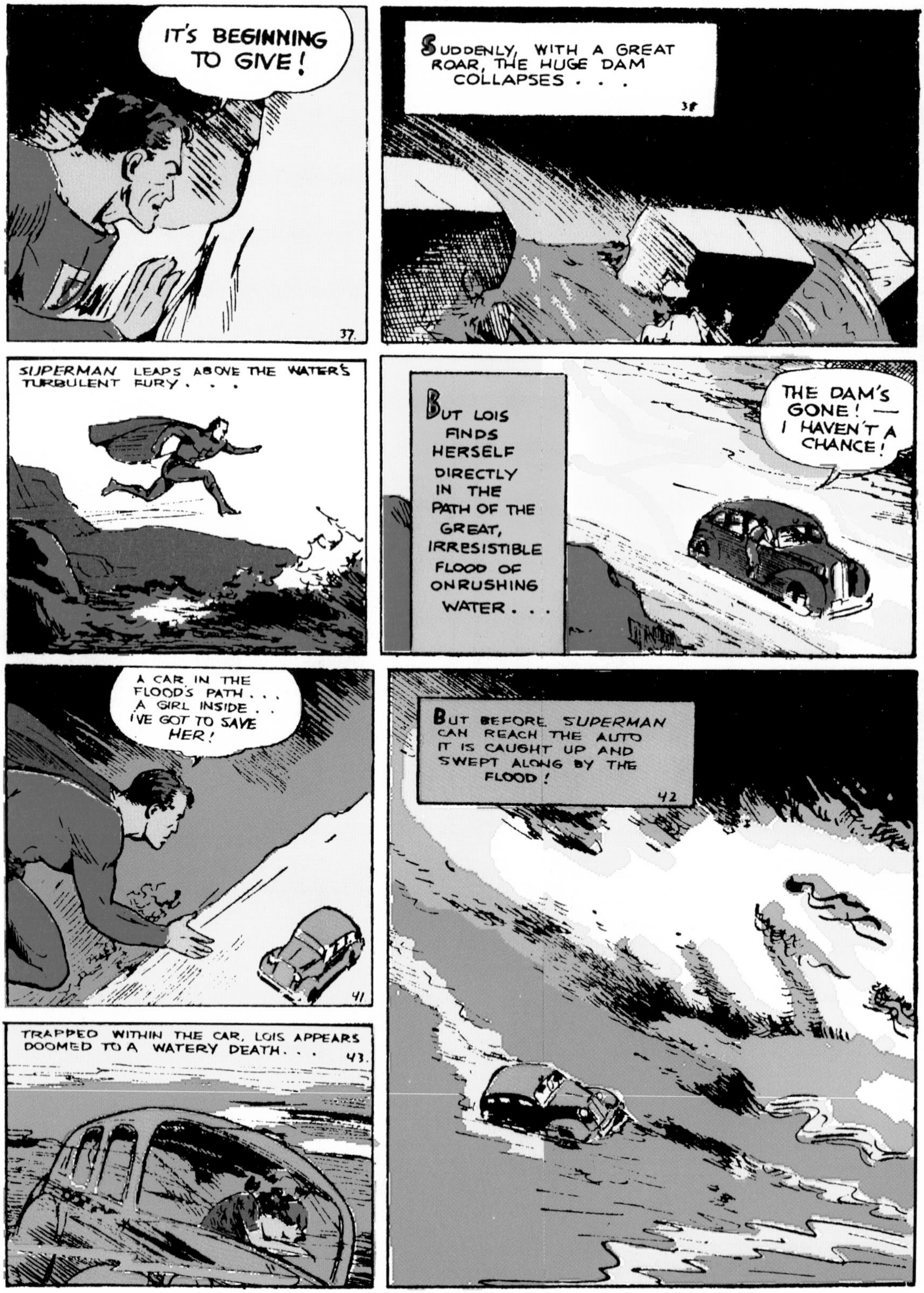
IT'S BEGINNING TO GIVE!
37.
SUDDENLY, WITH A GREAT ROAR, THE HUGE DAM COLLAPSES . . .
38
SUPERMAN LEAPS ABOVE THE WATER'S TURBULENT FURY . . .
BUT LOIS FINDS HERSELF DIRECTLY IN THE PATH OF THE GREAT, IRRESISTIBLE FLOOD OF ONRUSHING WATER . . .
THE DAM'S GONE! — I HAVEN'T A CHANCE!
A CAR IN THE FLOOD'S PATH . . . A GIRL INSIDE . . I'VE GOT TO SAVE HER!
41
TRAPPED WITHIN THE CAR, LOIS APPEARS DOOMED TO A WATERY DEATH . . .
43.
BUT BEFORE SUPERMAN CAN REACH THE AUTO IT IS CAUGHT UP AND SWEPT ALONG BY THE FLOOD!
42

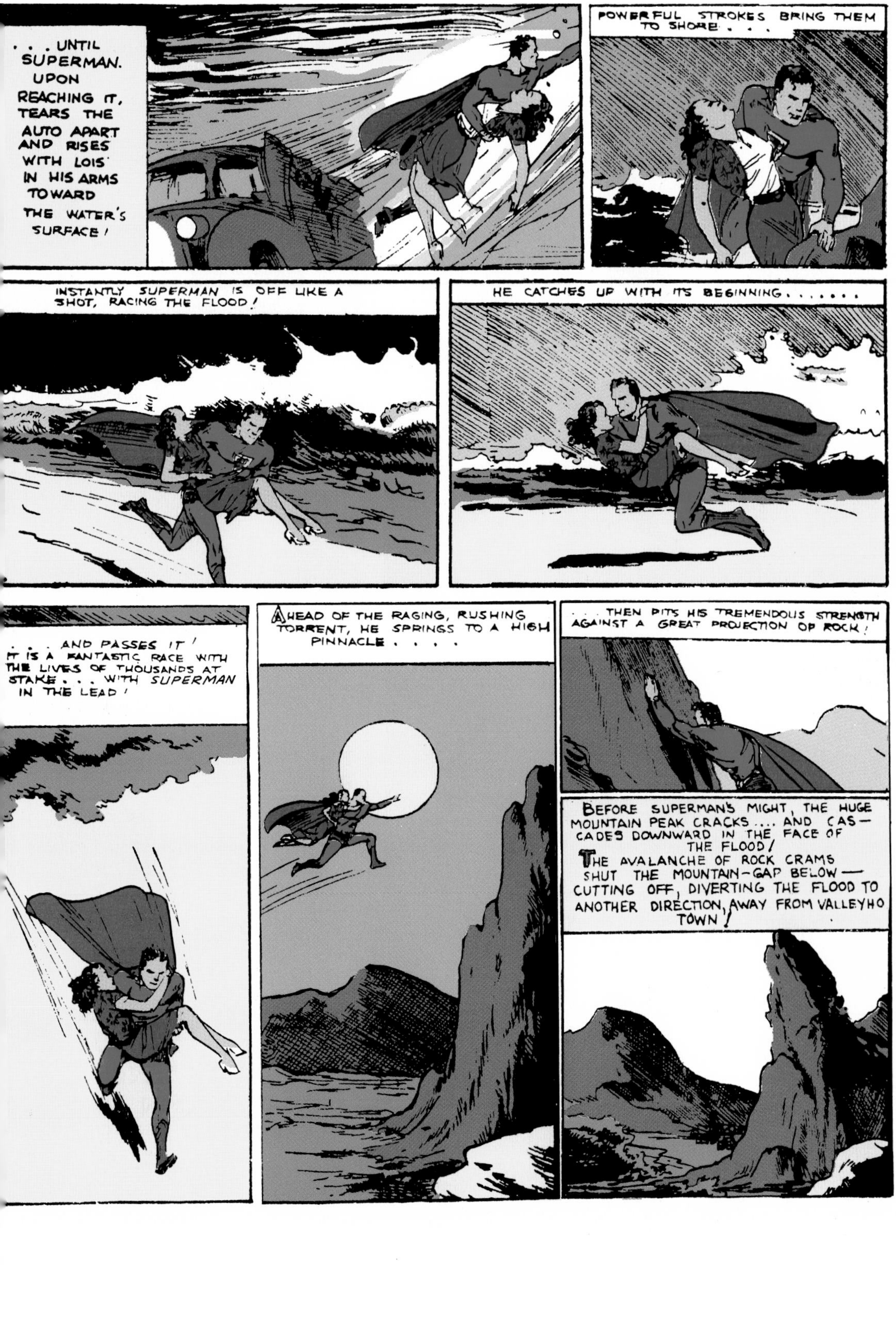
. . . UNTIL SUPERMAN. UPON REACHING IT, TEARS THE AUTO APART AND RISES WITH LOIS IN HIS ARMS TOWARD THE WATER'S SURFACE!
POWERFUL STROKES BRING THEM TO SHORE . . .
INSTANTLY SUPERMAN IS OFF LIKE A SHOT, RACING THE FLOOD!
HE CATCHES UP WITH ITS BEGINNING . . . .
. . . AND PASSES IT! IT IS A FANTASTIC RACE WITH THE LIVES OF THOUSANDS AT STAKE . . . WITH SUPERMAN IN THE LEAD!
AHEAD OF THE RAGING, RUSHING TORRENT, HE SPRINGS TO A HIGH PINNACLE . . . .
. . . THEN PITS HIS TREMENDOUS STRENGTH AGAINST A GREAT PROJECTION OF ROCK!
BEFORE SUPERMAN'S MIGHT, THE HUGE MOUNTAIN PEAK CRACKS .... AND CASCADES DOWNWARD IN THE FACE OF THE FLOOD!
THE AVALANCHE OF ROCK CRAMS SHUT THE MOUNTAIN-GAP BELOW — CUTTING OFF, DIVERTING THE FLOOD TO ANOTHER DIRECTION, AWAY FROM VALLEYHO TOWN!

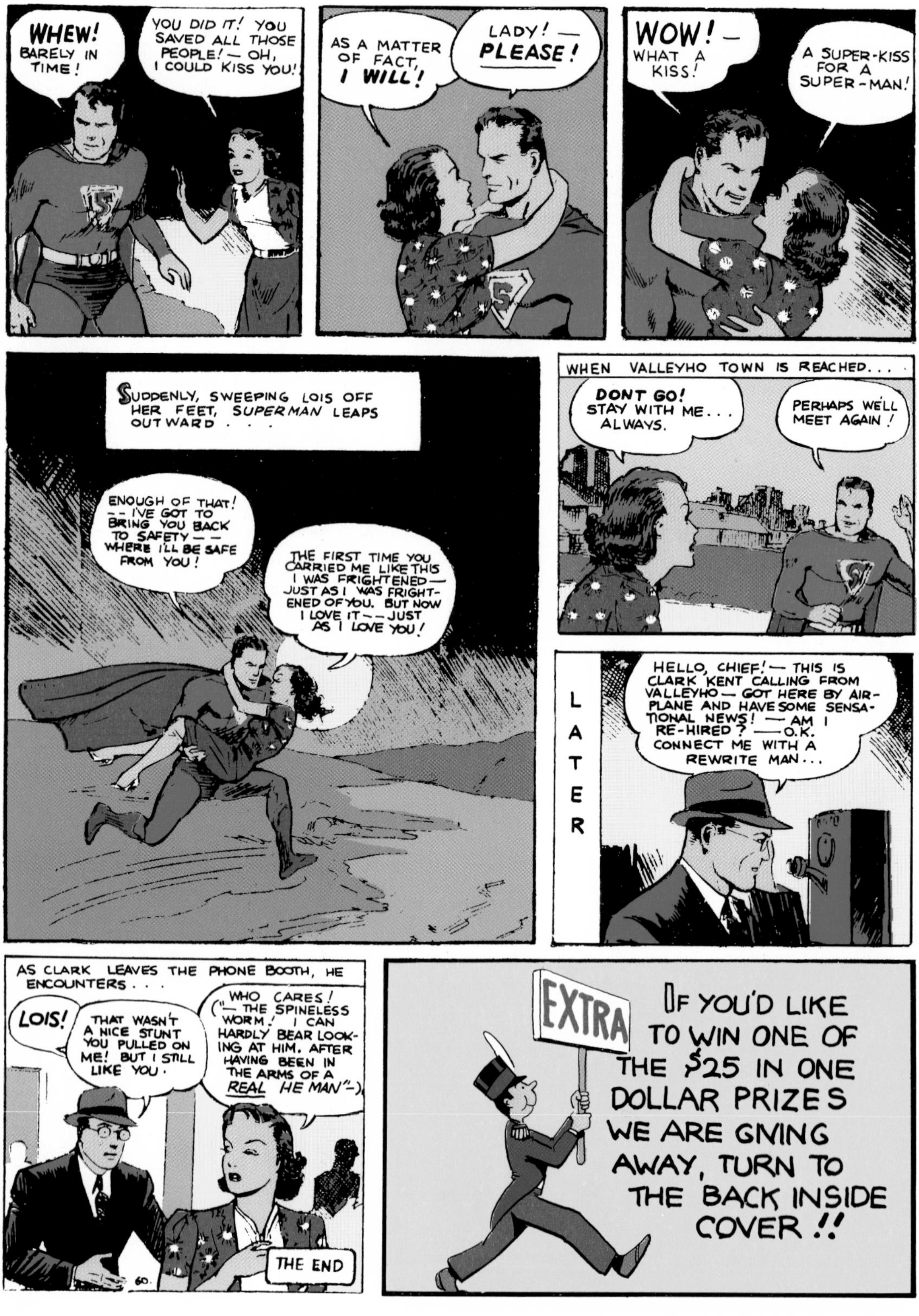
WHEW! BARELY IN TIME!
YOU DID IT! YOU SAVED ALL THOSE PEOPLE! — OH, I COULD KISS YOU!
AS A MATTER OF FACT, I WILL!
LADY! — PLEASE!
WOW! — WHAT A KISS!
A SUPER-KISS FOR A SUPER-MAN!
SUDDENLY, SWEEPING LOIS OFF HER FEET, SUPERMAN LEAPS OUTWARD . . .
ENOUGH OF THAT! -- I'VE GOT TO BRING YOU BACK TO SAFETY — — WHERE I'LL BE SAFE FROM YOU!
THE FIRST TIME YOU CARRIED ME LIKE THIS I WAS FRIGHTENED — JUST AS I WAS FRIGHTENED OF YOU. BUT NOW I LOVE IT -- JUST AS I LOVE YOU!
WHEN VALLEYHO TOWN IS REACHED . . .
DONT GO! STAY WITH ME . . . ALWAYS.
PERHAPS WE'LL MEET AGAIN!
LATER
HELLO, CHIEF! — THIS IS CLARK KENT CALLING FROM VALLEYHO — GOT HERE BY AIR-PLANE AND HAVE SOME SENSA-TIONAL NEWS! — AM I RE-HIRED? — O.K. CONNECT ME WITH A REWRITE MAN . . .
AS CLARK LEAVES THE PHONE BOOTH, HE ENCOUNTERS . . .
LOIS!
THAT WASN'T A NICE STUNT YOU PULLED ON ME! BUT I STILL LIKE YOU.
WHO CARES! ("— THE SPINELESS WORM! I CAN HARDLY BEAR LOOK-ING AT HIM. AFTER HAVING BEEN IN THE ARMS OF A REAL HE MAN" —)
THE END
EXTRA
IF YOU'D LIKE TO WIN ONE OF THE $25 IN ONE DOLLAR PRIZES WE ARE GIVING AWAY, TURN TO THE BACK INSIDE COVER !!

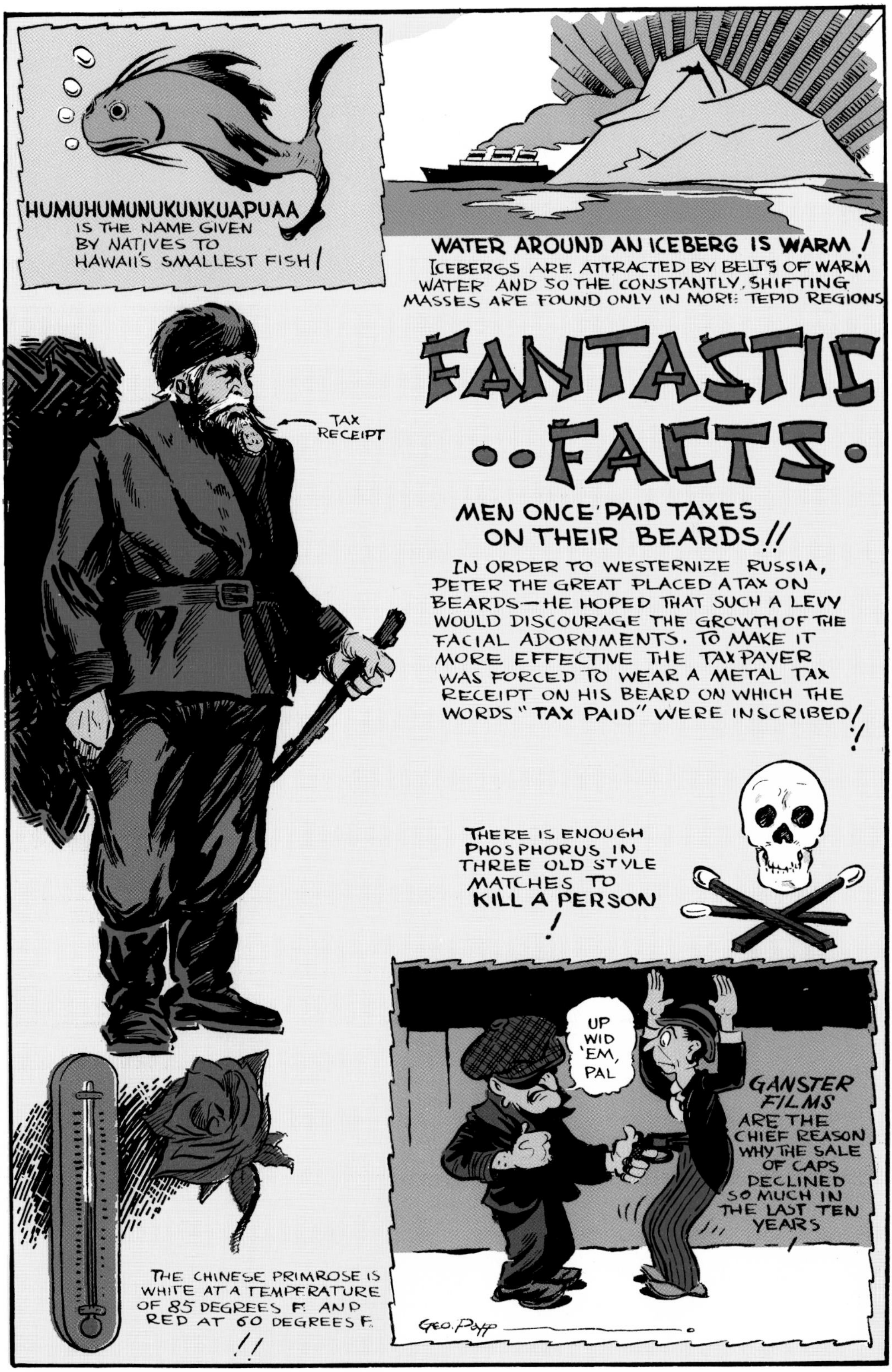
HUMUHUMUNUKUNKUAPUAA
IS THE NAME GIVEN BY NATIVES TO HAWAII'S SMALLEST FISH!
WATER AROUND AN ICEBERG IS WARM!
ICEBERGS ARE ATTRACTED BY BELTS OF WARM WATER AND SO THE CONSTANTLY SHIFTING MASSES ARE FOUND ONLY IN MORE TEPID REGIONS
FANTASTIC FACTS
TAX RECEIPT
MEN ONCE PAID TAXES ON THEIR BEARDS!!
IN ORDER TO WESTERNIZE RUSSIA, PETER THE GREAT PLACED A TAX ON BEARDS—HE HOPED THAT SUCH A LEVY WOULD DISCOURAGE THE GROWTH OF THE FACIAL ADORNMENTS. TO MAKE IT MORE EFFECTIVE THE TAXPAYER WAS FORCED TO WEAR A METAL TAX RECEIPT ON HIS BEARD ON WHICH THE WORDS "TAX PAID" WERE INSCRIBED!!!
THERE IS ENOUGH PHOSPHORUS IN THREE OLD STYLE MATCHES TO KILL A PERSON!
THE CHINESE PRIMROSE IS WHITE AT A TEMPERATURE OF 85 DEGREES F. AND RED AT 60 DEGREES F. !!
UP WID 'EM, PAL
GANSTER FILMS ARE THE CHIEF REASON WHY THE SALE OF CAPS DECLINED SO MUCH IN THE LAST TEN YEARS!
GEO. PAPP

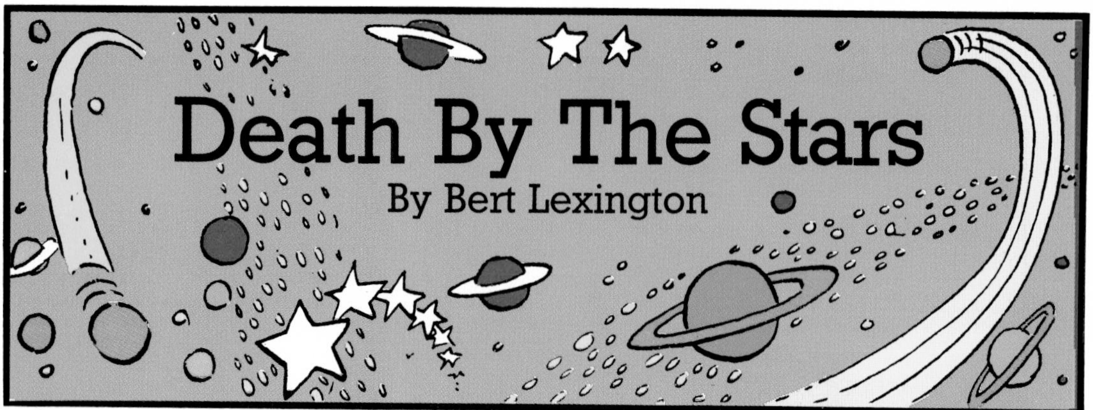

Death By The Stars

By Bert Lexington

"ONE minute to live!"

The voice was Emil Brandwan's—the tone, sardonic. A wry smile crossed the famous astrologist's features as he spoke. For a man pronouncing his own death sentence, Brandwan seemed to be enjoying himself immensely.

It had all begun with a little row in Marty's, a well-known Broadway eating-place. Brandwan had been extolling the virtues of Astrology when a caustic voice behind had stated simply: "Bunk!"

Whirling, Brandwan's angry expression changed to a mocking smile he saw that the person who had so rudely interrupted was none other than an amusing acquaintance, Detective Sergeant Steve Hanley. "Are you really dead-set against Astrology?" he had asked.

"Dead-set is putting it mildly," the Detective Sergeant had returned. "I'm convinced your favorite pseudo-science is an out-and-out fake!"

"Astrology is one of the most ancient of the sciences," dryly reminded Brandwan. "If it were only, as you say, just a delusion, then how has it managed to survive down through the centuries?"

"Don't forget that a lot of other silly superstitions are also still going the rounds. You can put Astrology's continued success down to the amazing credulity and ignorance of an over-dumb public."

That had really nettled Emil. "Sure of yourself, aren't you? But suppose I were to give a practical demonstration of Astrology's authenticity. Would that satisfy a hardened skeptic like you?"

"Possibly," admitted Hanley. "But it would have to be mighty convincing hocus-pokus to make me fall for it. But I'll warn you right now. I'm no sucker for mere coincidences."

That had been exactly a week ago. Tonight six men were gathered within the astrologer's exotic studio: Emil Brandwan himself, now clad in a star-studded robe... Detective Sergeant Hanley, a grin of disbelief upon his features... Professor Louis Morton, another eminent astrologer... Stephen Gregory, prominent scientist and consistent opponent of Astrology Jack Lowell, a personal friend of Hanley's... and Robert Shelton, Brandwan's close-mouthed assistant.

As Shelton inconspicuously closed the studio's doors, the seated men, grouped about a large table, had sufficient time to glance inquisitively about the room and note its queer decorations. Maps of the heavens... yellowed tomes on the sciences of Astrology... incense ... were everywhere, and everything about the room gave an uncanny suggestion of the mysteries of time and space.

Brandwan, studying the faces of guests with unconcealed amusement, began with: "Astrology, as you doubtless know, is the science of foretelling the future by interpreting the positions of the stars in relation to the date of your birth. Many, many thousands implicitly believe that their future existence can be forecast and guided by the heavenly bodies. But there are, unfortunately, unbelievers, among which you, my friends, number."

Professor Morton hastily interrupted. "With the exception of Robert Shelton and myself."

"With the exception of Shelton and yourself," agreed Brandwan, nodding his head slightly. "—I've gathered all of you here to give you proof of your colossal ignorance, a demonstration supreme of astrology's absolute integrity."

"Can the fine talk and let's have proof," interrupted Hanley.

"Very well. In investigating my own future in the stars, I made a disconcerting discovery. Gentlemen, I've learned that I'm doomed to die this very night!"

A chorus of startled exclamations went up at that. Emil Brandwan relaxed in his chair and smiled as he observed the sensation his words had provoked.

"But, Mr. Brandwan, surely..."

"Are you joking?"

"Do you really...?"

The Detective Sergeant's commanding voice drowned out the others', "Come now," he laughed, "You don't expect us to swallow that?"

"No," replied Brandwan. "I don't expect you to. But I base my reputation as an astrologer upon the statement that tonight, at exactly seven o'clock, I shall die! And that, gentlemen, I see by yonder clock, leaves me just... *one minute to live!*"

"If this is a jest," said Jack Lowell in the stunned pause that followed, "It certainly is in bad taste!"

Brandwan smiled broadly. "Is that the way to talk to a man who has merely forty-five more seconds to live in this world?"

Detective Sergeant Hanley arose from his chair, withdrew a revolver from his shoulder-holster. "If you're to die in half a minute that means there's going to be an attempt on your life. Have you received any threatening notes?"

"My dear Sergeant," said Brandwan, "you pain me. I am holding nothing back from you. No one told me I was going to die—no one but the stars!"

"Fifteen seconds left!" someone exclaimed.

"For heaven's sake," exploded Robert Shelton, "can't something be done? Must we just sit idly by and see a man die?" Then, to Brandwan. "I've worked beside you for years, believing in the science we both love, but now, for the first time in my career, I pray that Astrology has no basis in truth—I pray this, so that you'll live!"

Brandwan's face softened. "You're a true friend," he began, "but...uh-hhh!"

Abruptly he gave a choking gasp and toppled face forward on the table! Swiftly, Hanley sprang to his side, examined him as the others started to their feet with hoarse shouts.

Hanley grimly faced the others.

"What is it?" demanded Gregory. "Is he bluffing, or...?"

"He's DEAD!"

H ALF an hour later, the coroner completed his examination of Brandwan and stated to the Detective Sergeant, "There's no evidence to indicate he died of physical violence. It must have been a heart-attack."

After the coroner departed, the men stood around mutely, deeply impressed by the wonder they had witnessed.

"Can it be possible," whispered Gregory, half to himself, half to the others, "that I've been wrong all along—that Astrology *is* an actuality?"

Hanley shook his head in puzzled bewilderment. "So it appears!" Then, violently, "This has got me buffaloed! I'd have sworn that Astrology was the baloney, but now —*I'm beginning to wonder!*"

"You've got to believe him! He died, proving it to you! What greater proof could you demand?" It was Shelton, shouting in a rage. Then he quieted. Sorrowfully he knelt beside his dead employer, carefully brushed some disturbed strands of the dead man's hair back into place, with a handkerchief. "He was a good man," he said, "a good man!"

Something of his cockiness left Hanley. Gravely, he said, "We might as well leave now." But then, struck by a sudden thought, he knelt once more beside Brandwan, studied his features closely. The Detective Sergeant's jaw suddenly tensed.

Swiftly standing erect, he said to Shelton, "Quick. Hand me your handkerchief. I think I've discovered something!"

Shelton looked frantically through his pockets. "I—I seem to have misplaced it."

"Oh, here it is," said Shelton as he brought it to light. Hanley appropriated it, then stepped toward Shelton. "You're sweating," he said. "Mind if I wipe your brow?"

Shelton shrank back. "No! No!" he cried. "Don't touch me!"

Puzzled, Jack Lowell asked, "What does this mean, Steve?"

In answer, Hanley unfolded the handkerchief he held in his hand. "Look!" he said, simply.

The others swiftly crowded around, and exclamations of excitement arose as they noted, concealed within the handkerchief, a small needle.

"No wonder you don't want me to brush this against you," the Detective Sergeant said sternly to Shelton. "Robert Shelton! I arrest you for the murder of your employer, Emil Brandwan!"

"But, Steve!" Lowell cried "How could he have killed Brandwan? We saw the astrologer toppled

dead before our very eyes, when no one was within reach of him!"

"A few moments ago, Robert Shelton, under the pretense of brushing Brandwan's hair back in place with a handkerchief, pricked him with this poisoned needle, and killed him!"

"But," reminded Gregory, "that was *after* the medical examiner had officially pronounced Brandwan dead. How could Shelton have murdered a man who was no longer living?"

"That was the incredibly clever part about this crime. To murder a man *after* the law had declared him dead from heart attack would remove any possibility of anyone suspecting murder had been done. —How was it possible to murder a man already 'dead'? My belief is that Brandwan was really living all the time. He had put himself into a state of suspended animation. Tho in reality alive, he did not breathe, nor did his pulse or heart beat. When fish are packed in ice, to all appearances they are dead, but at times, when they are freed from the ice, they resume the characteristics of the living. So it was with Brandwan—he was only 'temporarily dead,' and fully intended to return to life later, and have the laugh on us. But his practical joke turned into grim tragedy when Shelton, who was in on the affair, double-crossed him!"

Shelton's complexion was turning paler with each second.

"But WHY," demanded Lowell, "should Shelton have killed his employer?"

"Because no doubt he's mentioned favorably in Brandwan's will. He must have needed money badly, and couldn't resist this opportunity to perform what he believed to be a 'perfect crime'!"

Abruptly, Shelton made a frantic dash for the room's door. But with one swift leap, Hanley was upon him. A powerful right to Shelton's jaw eclipsed the escape attempt.

As he handed the murderer's limp figure over to Lowell, the Detective Sergeant said, "I guess he's seeing enough stars right now to make a dozen horoscopes.—But I don't have to be an astrologer to know that his future lies in the electric-chair!"

Without further ado, Hanley telephoned for the wagon!

THE END

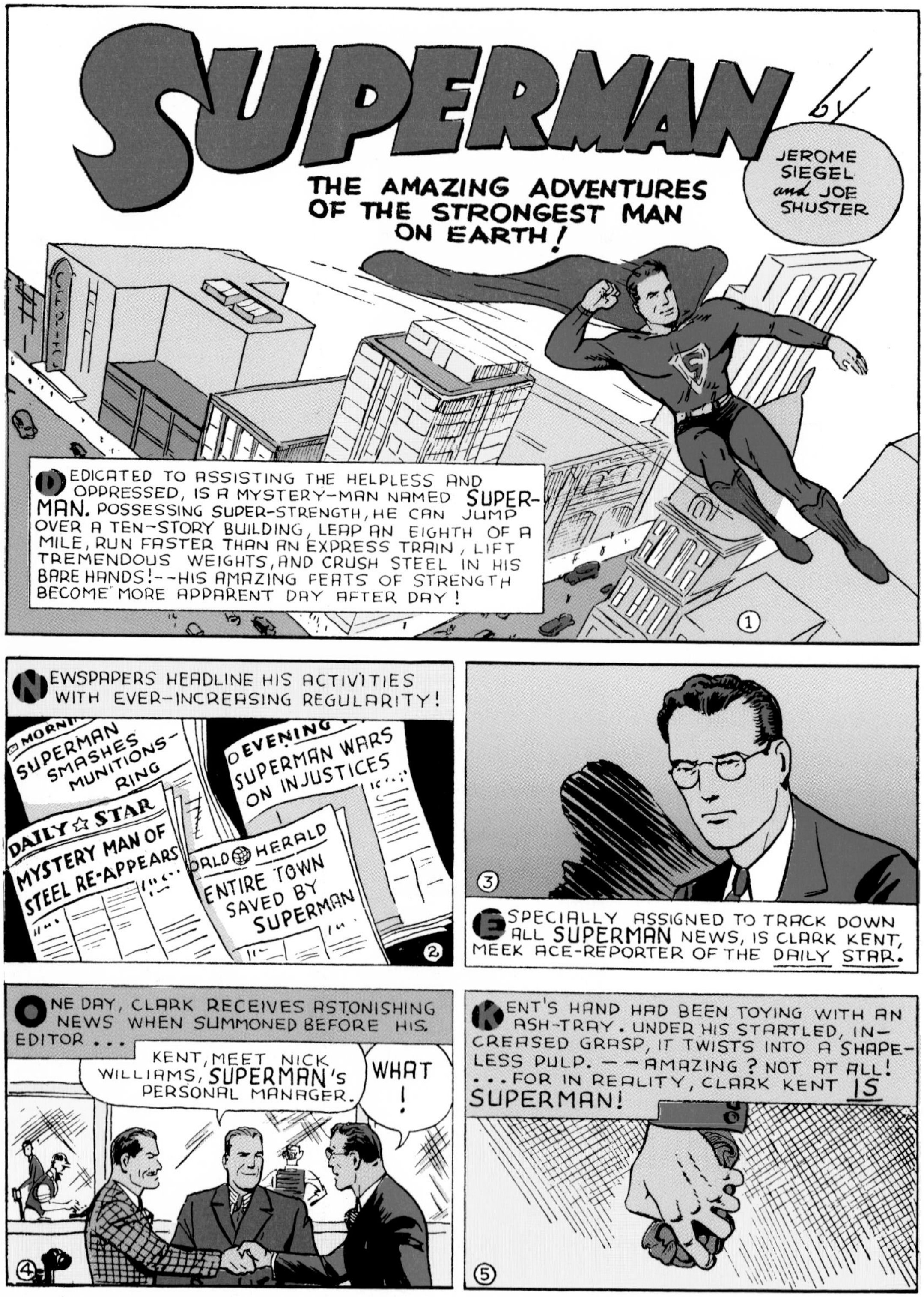
SUPERMAN
BY JEROME SIEGEL and JOE SHUSTER
THE AMAZING ADVENTURES OF THE STRONGEST MAN ON EARTH!
DEDICATED TO ASSISTING THE HELPLESS AND OPPRESSED, IS A MYSTERY-MAN NAMED SUPERMAN. POSSESSING SUPER-STRENGTH, HE CAN JUMP OVER A TEN-STORY BUILDING, LEAP AN EIGHTH OF A MILE, RUN FASTER THAN AN EXPRESS TRAIN, LIFT TREMENDOUS WEIGHTS, AND CRUSH STEEL IN HIS BARE HANDS!--HIS AMAZING FEATS OF STRENGTH BECOME MORE APPARENT DAY AFTER DAY!
1
NEWSPAPERS HEADLINE HIS ACTIVITIES WITH EVER-INCREASING REGULARITY!
MORNING
SUPERMAN SMASHES MUNITIONS-RING
EVENING
SUPERMAN WARS ON INJUSTICES
DAILY ☆ STAR
MYSTERY MAN OF STEEL RE-APPEARS
HERALD
ENTIRE TOWN SAVED BY SUPERMAN
2
3
ESPECIALLY ASSIGNED TO TRACK DOWN ALL SUPERMAN NEWS, IS CLARK KENT, MEEK ACE-REPORTER OF THE DAILY STAR.
ONE DAY, CLARK RECEIVES ASTONISHING NEWS WHEN SUMMONED BEFORE HIS EDITOR...
KENT, MEET NICK WILLIAMS, SUPERMAN'S PERSONAL MANAGER.
WHAT!
4
KENT'S HAND HAD BEEN TOYING WITH AN ASH-TRAY. UNDER HIS STARTLED, INCREASED GRASP, IT TWISTS INTO A SHAPELESS PULP. --AMAZING? NOT AT ALL! ...FOR IN REALITY, CLARK KENT IS SUPERMAN!
5

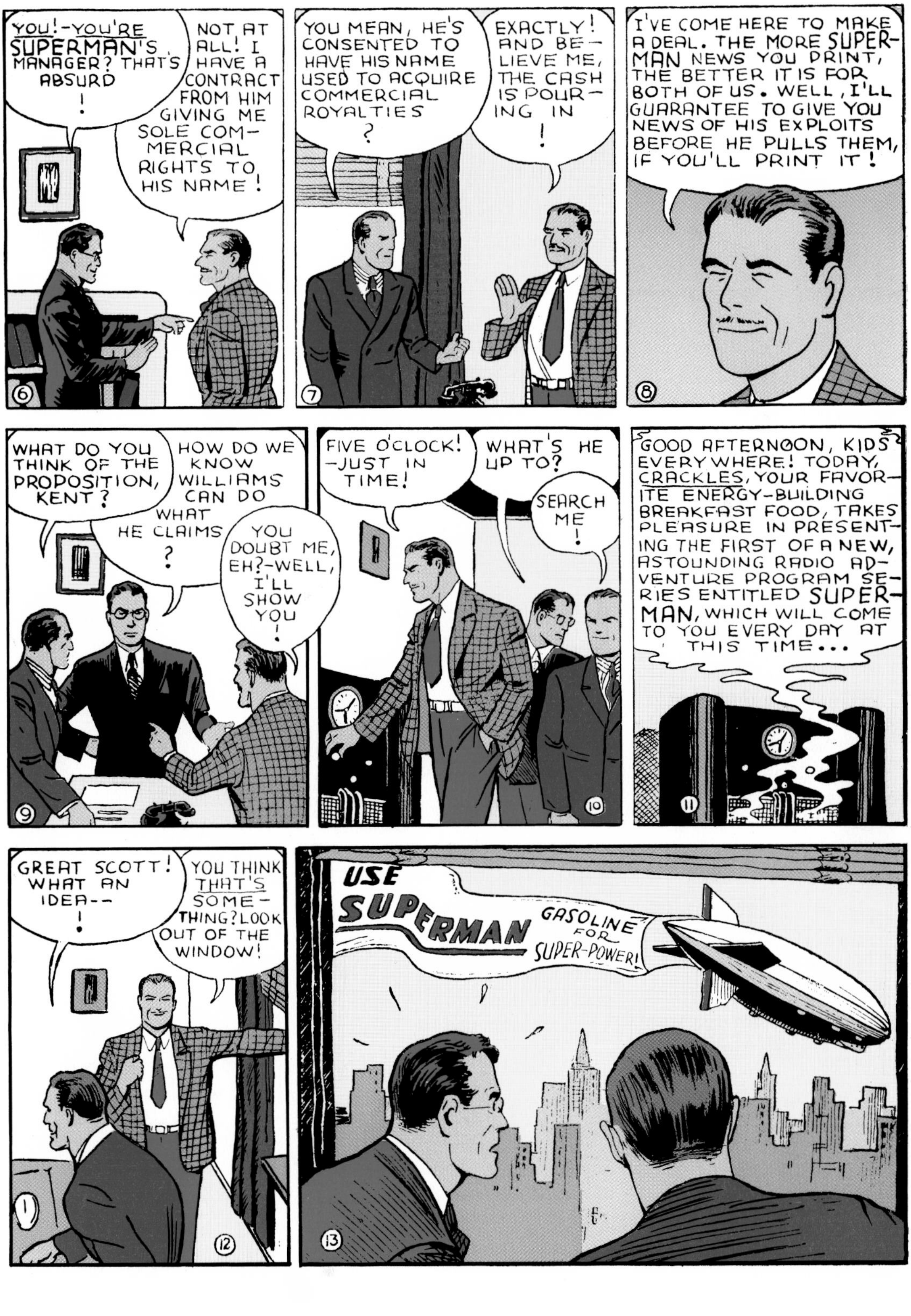
YOU!-YOU'RE SUPERMAN'S MANAGER? THAT'S ABSURD!
NOT AT ALL! I HAVE A CONTRACT FROM HIM GIVING ME SOLE COMMERCIAL RIGHTS TO HIS NAME!
6
YOU MEAN, HE'S CONSENTED TO HAVE HIS NAME USED TO ACQUIRE COMMERCIAL ROYALTIES?
EXACTLY! AND BELIEVE ME, THE CASH IS POURING IN!
7
I'VE COME HERE TO MAKE A DEAL. THE MORE SUPERMAN NEWS YOU PRINT, THE BETTER IT IS FOR BOTH OF US. WELL, I'LL GUARANTEE TO GIVE YOU NEWS OF HIS EXPLOITS BEFORE HE PULLS THEM, IF YOU'LL PRINT IT!
8
WHAT DO YOU THINK OF THE PROPOSITION, KENT?
HOW DO WE KNOW WILLIAMS CAN DO WHAT HE CLAIMS?
YOU DOUBT ME, EH?-WELL, I'LL SHOW YOU!
9
FIVE O'CLOCK! -JUST IN TIME!
WHAT'S HE UP TO?
SEARCH ME!
10
GOOD AFTERNOON, KIDS EVERYWHERE! TODAY, CRACKLES, YOUR FAVORITE ENERGY-BUILDING BREAKFAST FOOD, TAKES PLEASURE IN PRESENTING THE FIRST OF A NEW, ASTOUNDING RADIO ADVENTURE PROGRAM SERIES ENTITLED SUPERMAN, WHICH WILL COME TO YOU EVERY DAY AT THIS TIME...
11
GREAT SCOTT! WHAT AN IDEA--!
YOU THINK THAT'S SOMETHING? LOOK OUT OF THE WINDOW!
12
USE SUPERMAN GASOLINE FOR SUPER-POWER!
13

GOOD LORD! —WHAT NEXT?

TAKE A GANDER AT THAT BILL-BOARD OVER YONDER!

The SUPERMAN Streamline Special

AMERICA'S FAVORITE AUTOMOBILE

I'VE ALSO LICENSED SUPERMAN BATHING-SUITS, COSTUMES, PHYSICAL DEVELOPMENT EXERCISERS, AND MOVIE RIGHTS, TO NAME A FEW.--WHY, I'VE EVEN MADE PROVISIONS FOR HIM TO APPEAR IN THE COMICS!

ALL VERY INTERESTING! BUT HOW DID SUPERMAN CONTACT YOU?

HE DROPPED IN ON ME AND SPRUNG THE PROPOSITION. I LIKED THE IDEA, AND WE EVOLVED A PARTNERSHIP.

VERY INTERESTING --IF TRUE!

YOU DOUBT ME? VERY WELL THEN! WOULD A PERSONAL INTERVIEW WITH SUPERMAN INTEREST YOU?

I SHOULD SAY IT WOULD! —IN FACT, I'D LIKE TO MEET HIM VERY MUCH!

FINE! COME TO MY OFFICE TONIGHT, AND I'LL ARRANGE YOUR FIRST INTERVIEW WITH THE STRONGEST MAN ON EARTH!

GOSH!

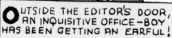

OUTSIDE THE EDITOR'S DOOR, AN INQUISITIVE OFFICE-BOY HAS BEEN GETTING AN EARFUL!

CAN Y'IMAGINE THAT, LOIS? CLARK KENT IS GOING TO SEE SUPERMAN TONIGHT, IN PERSON!

HE IS! --THEN SO WILL I!

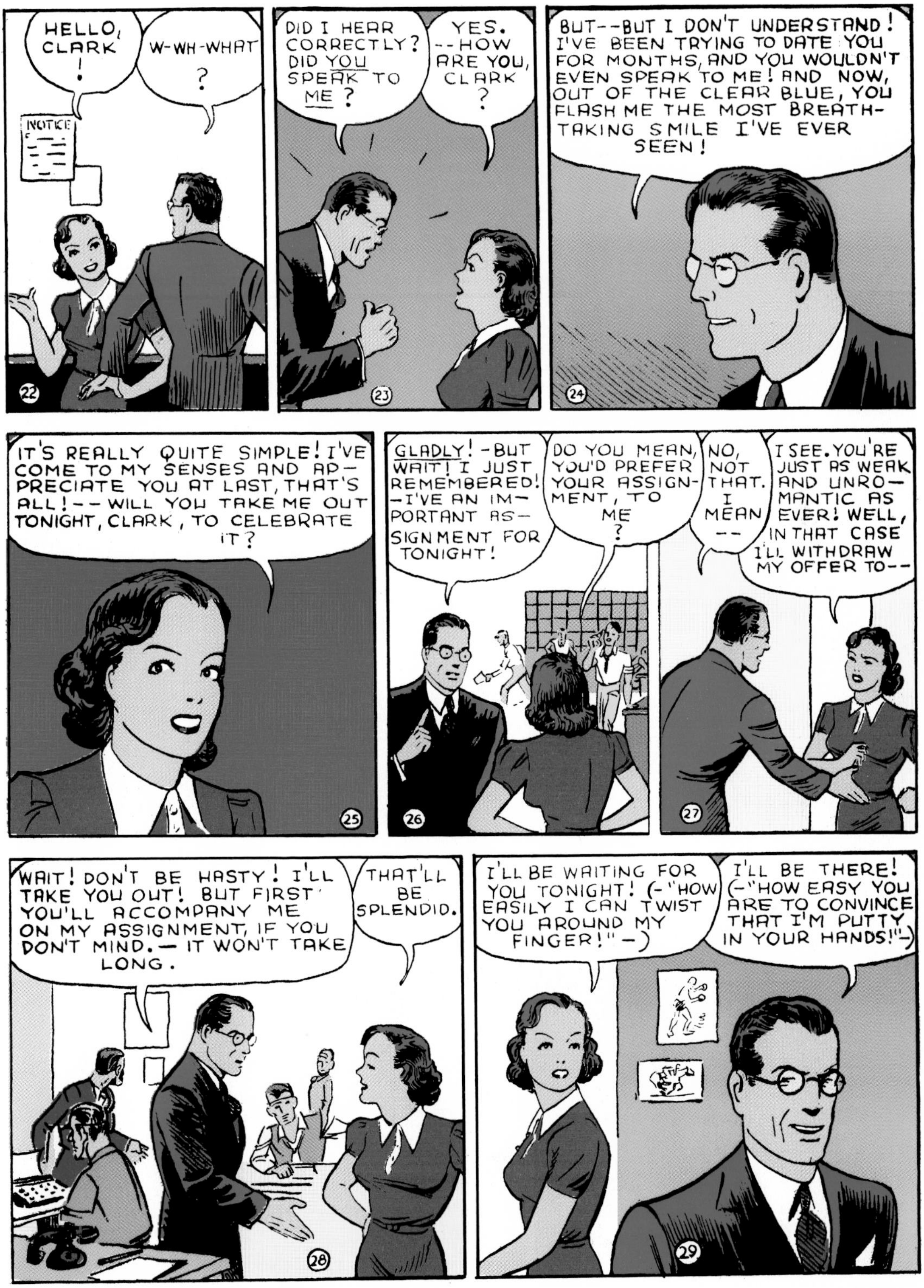
HELLO, CLARK !
W-WH-WHAT ?
NOTICE
DID I HEAR CORRECTLY? DID YOU SPEAK TO ME ?
YES. --HOW ARE YOU, CLARK ?
BUT--BUT I DON'T UNDERSTAND! I'VE BEEN TRYING TO DATE YOU FOR MONTHS, AND YOU WOULDN'T EVEN SPEAK TO ME! AND NOW, OUT OF THE CLEAR BLUE, YOU FLASH ME THE MOST BREATH-TAKING SMILE I'VE EVER SEEN!
IT'S REALLY QUITE SIMPLE! I'VE COME TO MY SENSES AND AP-PRECIATE YOU AT LAST, THAT'S ALL!--WILL YOU TAKE ME OUT TONIGHT, CLARK, TO CELEBRATE IT?
GLADLY! -BUT WAIT! I JUST REMEMBERED! -I'VE AN IM-PORTANT AS-SIGNMENT FOR TONIGHT!
DO YOU MEAN, YOU'D PREFER YOUR ASSIGN-MENT, TO ME ?
NO, NOT THAT. I MEAN --
I SEE. YOU'RE JUST AS WEAK AND UNRO-MANTIC AS EVER! WELL, IN THAT CASE I'LL WITHDRAW MY OFFER TO--
WAIT! DON'T BE HASTY! I'LL TAKE YOU OUT! BUT FIRST YOU'LL ACCOMPANY ME ON MY ASSIGNMENT, IF YOU DON'T MIND.— IT WON'T TAKE LONG.
THAT'LL BE SPLENDID.
I'LL BE WAITING FOR YOU TONIGHT! (-"HOW EASILY I CAN TWIST YOU AROUND MY FINGER!"-)
I'LL BE THERE! (-"HOW EASY YOU ARE TO CONVINCE THAT I'M PUTTY IN YOUR HANDS!"-)

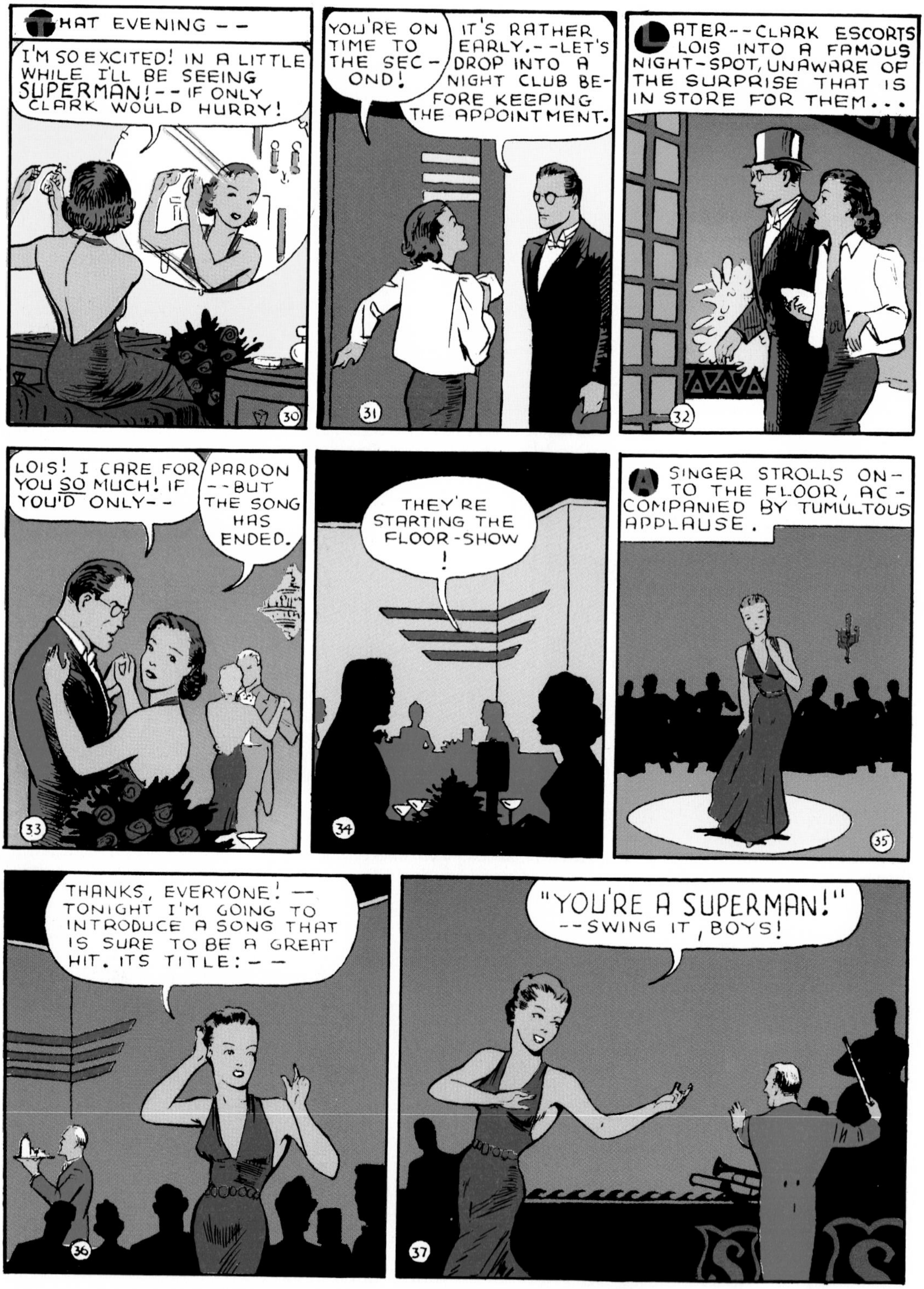
THAT EVENING --
I'M SO EXCITED! IN A LITTLE WHILE I'LL BE SEEING SUPERMAN!-- IF ONLY CLARK WOULD HURRY!
30
YOU'RE ON TIME TO THE SEC-OND!
IT'S RATHER EARLY.--LET'S DROP INTO A NIGHT CLUB BE-FORE KEEPING THE APPOINTMENT.
31
LATER--CLARK ESCORTS LOIS INTO A FAMOUS NIGHT-SPOT, UNAWARE OF THE SURPRISE THAT IS IN STORE FOR THEM...
32
LOIS! I CARE FOR YOU SO MUCH! IF YOU'D ONLY--
PARDON --BUT THE SONG HAS ENDED.
33
THEY'RE STARTING THE FLOOR-SHOW!
34
A SINGER STROLLS ON-TO THE FLOOR, AC-COMPANIED BY TUMULTOUS APPLAUSE.
35
THANKS, EVERYONE! — TONIGHT I'M GOING TO INTRODUCE A SONG THAT IS SURE TO BE A GREAT HIT. ITS TITLE:--
36
"YOU'RE A SUPERMAN!" --SWING IT, BOYS!
37

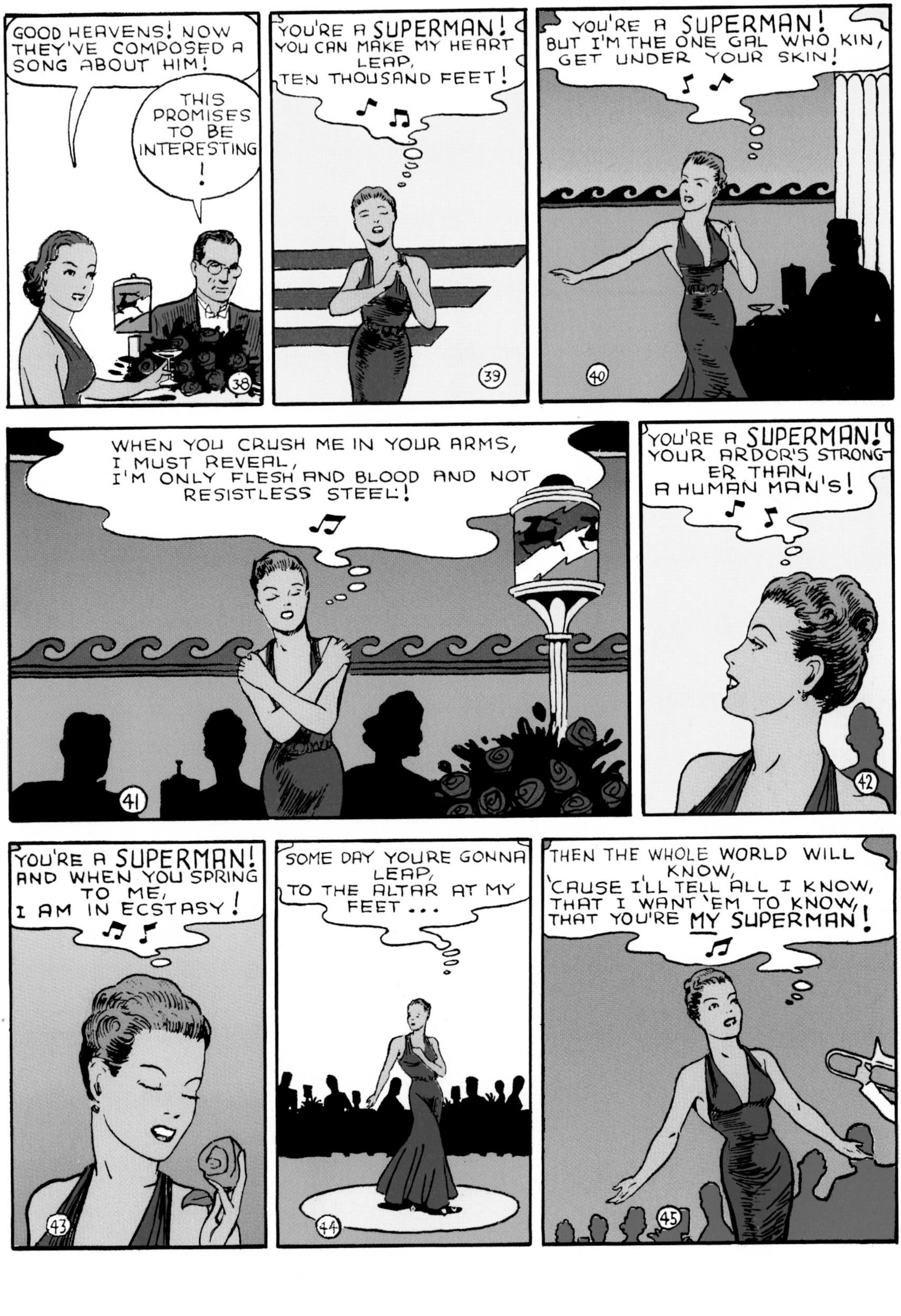
GOOD HEAVENS! NOW THEY'VE COMPOSED A SONG ABOUT HIM!
THIS PROMISES TO BE INTERESTING!
38
YOU'RE A SUPERMAN! YOU CAN MAKE MY HEART LEAP, TEN THOUSAND FEET!
39
YOU'RE A SUPERMAN! BUT I'M THE ONE GAL WHO KIN, GET UNDER YOUR SKIN!
40
WHEN YOU CRUSH ME IN YOUR ARMS, I MUST REVEAL, I'M ONLY FLESH AND BLOOD AND NOT RESISTLESS STEEL!
41
YOU'RE A SUPERMAN! YOUR ARDOR'S STRONG-ER THAN, A HUMAN MAN'S!
42
YOU'RE A SUPERMAN! AND WHEN YOU SPRING TO ME, I AM IN ECSTASY!
43
SOME DAY YOU'RE GONNA LEAP, TO THE ALTAR AT MY FEET...
44
THEN THE WHOLE WORLD WILL KNOW, 'CAUSE I'LL TELL ALL I KNOW, THAT I WANT 'EM TO KNOW, THAT YOU'RE MY SUPERMAN!
45

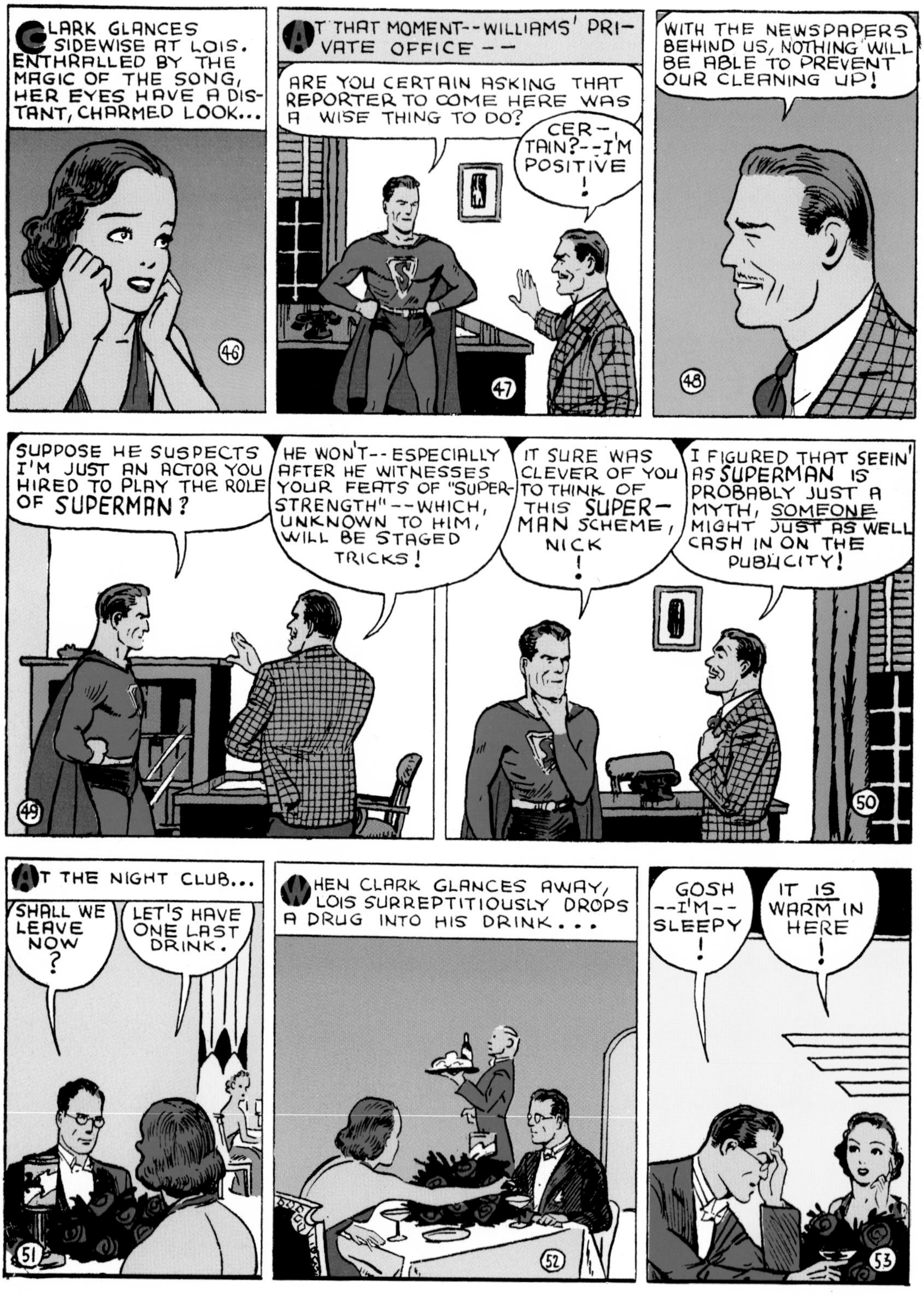
CLARK GLANCES SIDEWISE AT LOIS. ENTHRALLED BY THE MAGIC OF THE SONG, HER EYES HAVE A DISTANT, CHARMED LOOK...
46
AT THAT MOMENT--WILLIAMS' PRIVATE OFFICE --
ARE YOU CERTAIN ASKING THAT REPORTER TO COME HERE WAS A WISE THING TO DO?
CER-, TAIN?--I'M POSITIVE !
47
WITH THE NEWSPAPERS BEHIND US, NOTHING WILL BE ABLE TO PREVENT OUR CLEANING UP!
48
SUPPOSE HE SUSPECTS I'M JUST AN ACTOR YOU HIRED TO PLAY THE ROLE OF SUPERMAN?
HE WON'T--ESPECIALLY AFTER HE WITNESSES YOUR FEATS OF "SUPER-STRENGTH"--WHICH, UNKNOWN TO HIM, WILL BE STAGED TRICKS!
49
IT SURE WAS CLEVER OF YOU TO THINK OF THIS SUPER-MAN SCHEME, NICK !
I FIGURED THAT SEEIN' AS SUPERMAN IS PROBABLY JUST A MYTH, SOMEONE MIGHT JUST AS WELL CASH IN ON THE PUBLICITY!
50
AT THE NIGHT CLUB...
SHALL WE LEAVE NOW ?
LET'S HAVE ONE LAST DRINK.
51
WHEN CLARK GLANCES AWAY, LOIS SURREPTITIOUSLY DROPS A DRUG INTO HIS DRINK...
52
GOSH --I'M-- SLEEPY !
IT IS WARM IN HERE !
53

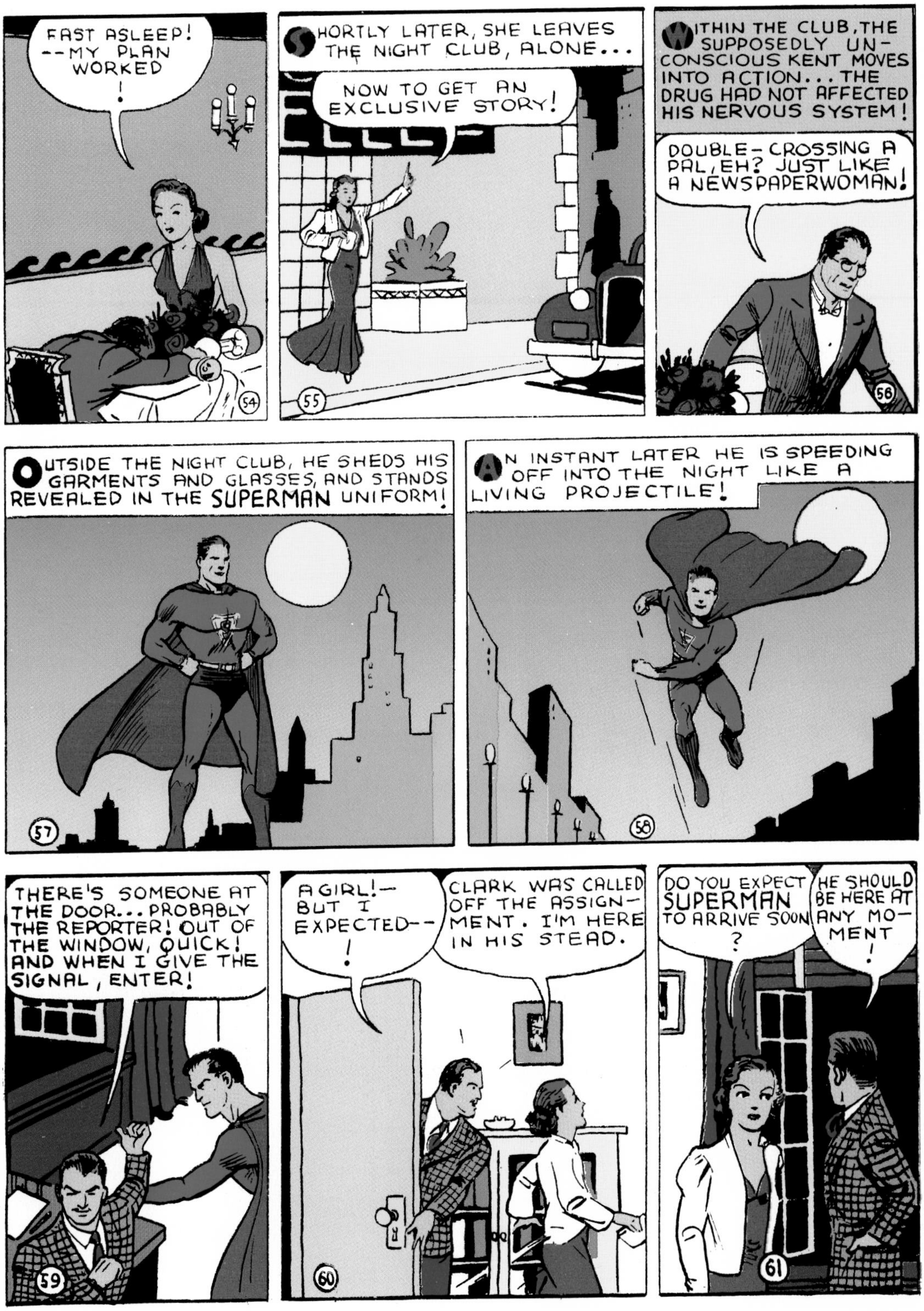
FAST ASLEEP! --MY PLAN WORKED!
SHORTLY LATER, SHE LEAVES THE NIGHT CLUB, ALONE...
NOW TO GET AN EXCLUSIVE STORY!
WITHIN THE CLUB, THE SUPPOSEDLY UNCONSCIOUS KENT MOVES INTO ACTION... THE DRUG HAD NOT AFFECTED HIS NERVOUS SYSTEM!
DOUBLE-CROSSING A PAL, EH? JUST LIKE A NEWSPAPERWOMAN!
OUTSIDE THE NIGHT CLUB, HE SHEDS HIS GARMENTS AND GLASSES, AND STANDS REVEALED IN THE SUPERMAN UNIFORM!
AN INSTANT LATER HE IS SPEEDING OFF INTO THE NIGHT LIKE A LIVING PROJECTILE!
THERE'S SOMEONE AT THE DOOR... PROBABLY THE REPORTER! OUT OF THE WINDOW, QUICK! AND WHEN I GIVE THE SIGNAL, ENTER!
A GIRL!— BUT I EXPECTED— —!
CLARK WAS CALLED OFF THE ASSIGNMENT. I'M HERE IN HIS STEAD.
DO YOU EXPECT SUPERMAN TO ARRIVE SOON?
HE SHOULD BE HERE AT ANY MOMENT!

PLACING HIS HAND BE-HIND HIM, WILLIAMS SNAPS HIS FINGERS...

SNAP!

THE SIGNAL!—NOW TO GO INTO MY ACT!

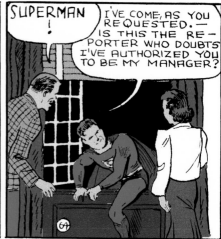

SUPERMAN !

I'VE COME, AS YOU REQUESTED.—IS THIS THE RE-PORTER WHO DOUBTS I'VE AUTHORIZED YOU TO BE MY MANAGER?

YES. BUT DEMONSTRATE SOME SUPER-STRENGTH! THAT SHOULD BANISH ANY DOUBTS THAT ARE IN HER MIND.

GLADLY !

BEHOLD! LIFTING A HEAVY DESK IS TO ME MERE CHILDSPLAY!

AND BENDING A STEEL BAR--WELL, I THINK NOTHING OF IT !

ARE YOU CONVINCED ?

NO !

AND I'M GOING TO PROVE THAT YOU'RE NOTHING BUT A PAIR OF FAKERS !

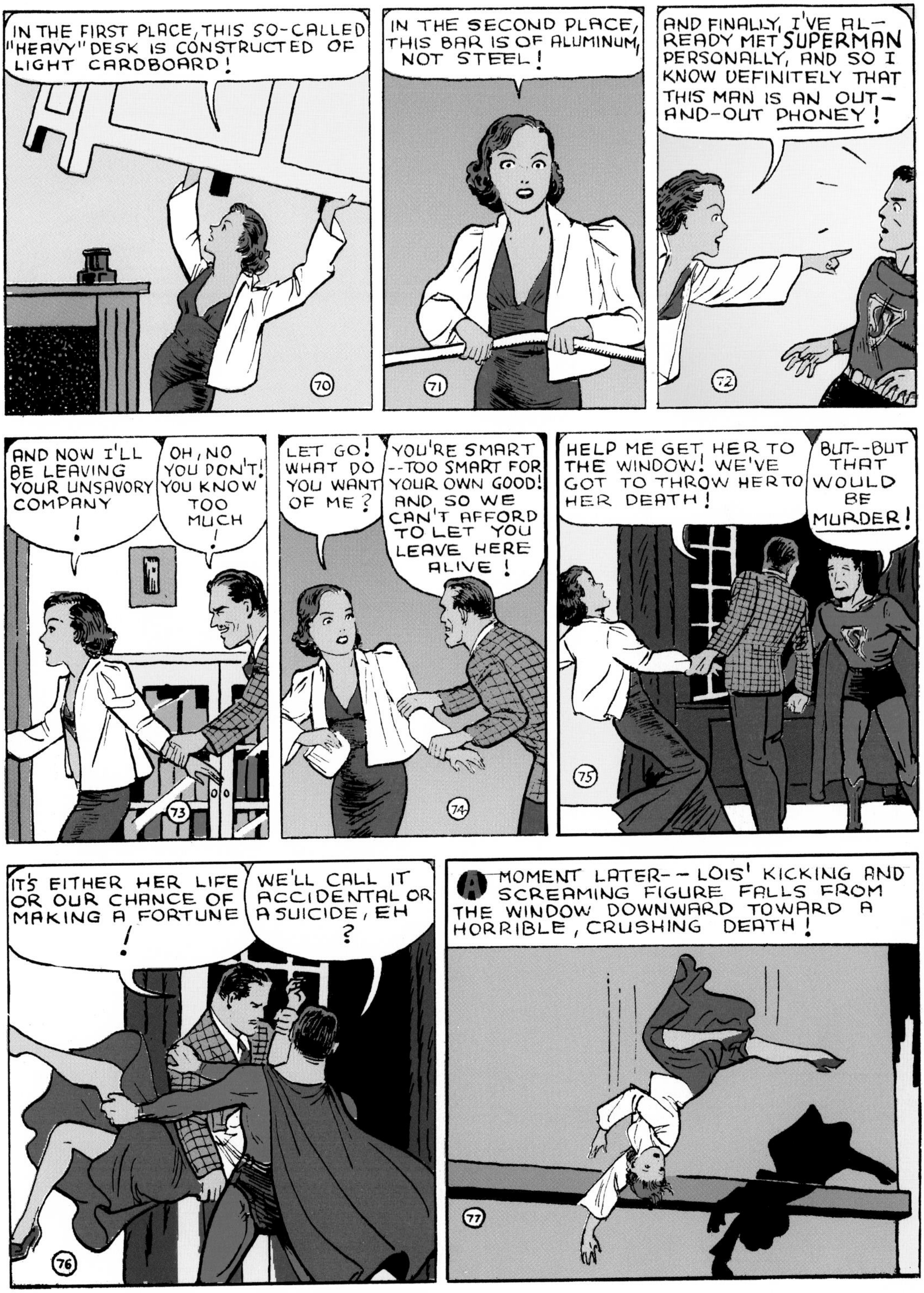
IN THE FIRST PLACE, THIS SO-CALLED "HEAVY" DESK IS CONSTRUCTED OF LIGHT CARDBOARD!
70
IN THE SECOND PLACE, THIS BAR IS OF ALUMINUM, NOT STEEL!
71
AND FINALLY, I'VE ALREADY MET SUPERMAN PERSONALLY, AND SO I KNOW DEFINITELY THAT THIS MAN IS AN OUT-AND-OUT PHONEY!
72
AND NOW I'LL BE LEAVING YOUR UNSAVORY COMPANY!
OH, NO YOU DON'T! YOU KNOW TOO MUCH!
73
LET GO! WHAT DO YOU WANT OF ME?
YOU'RE SMART --TOO SMART FOR YOUR OWN GOOD! AND SO WE CAN'T AFFORD TO LET YOU LEAVE HERE ALIVE!
74
HELP ME GET HER TO THE WINDOW! WE'VE GOT TO THROW HER TO HER DEATH!
BUT--BUT THAT WOULD BE MURDER!
75
IT'S EITHER HER LIFE OR OUR CHANCE OF MAKING A FORTUNE!
WE'LL CALL IT ACCIDENTAL OR A SUICIDE, EH?
76
A MOMENT LATER-- LOIS' KICKING AND SCREAMING FIGURE FALLS FROM THE WINDOW DOWNWARD TOWARD A HORRIBLE, CRUSHING DEATH!
77

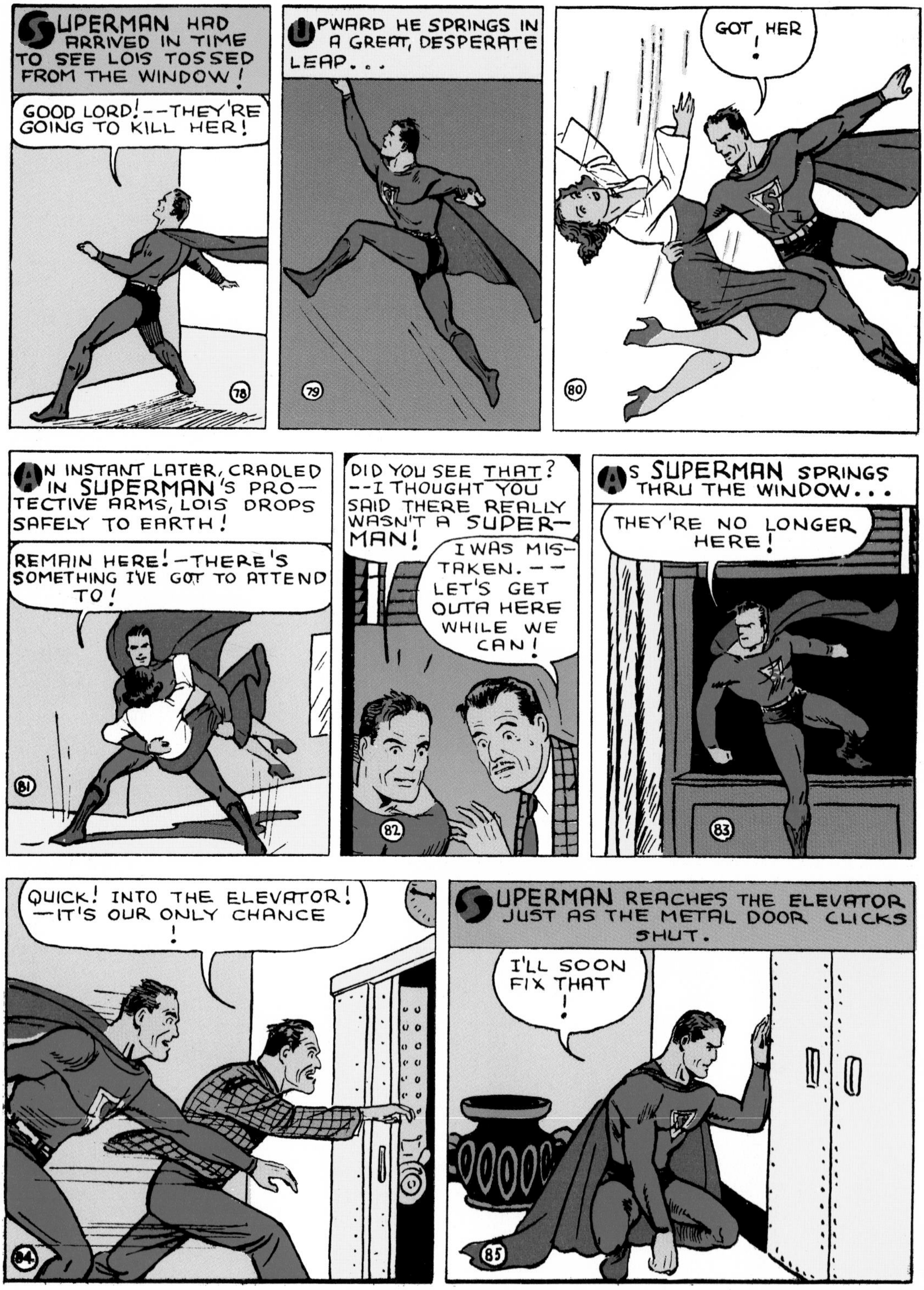
SUPERMAN HAD ARRIVED IN TIME TO SEE LOIS TOSSED FROM THE WINDOW!
GOOD LORD!--THEY'RE GOING TO KILL HER!
78
UPWARD HE SPRINGS IN A GREAT, DESPERATE LEAP...
79
GOT HER!
80
AN INSTANT LATER, CRADLED IN SUPERMAN'S PROTECTIVE ARMS, LOIS DROPS SAFELY TO EARTH!
REMAIN HERE!-THERE'S SOMETHING I'VE GOT TO ATTEND TO!
81
DID YOU SEE THAT? --I THOUGHT YOU SAID THERE REALLY WASN'T A SUPERMAN!
I WAS MISTAKEN.--LET'S GET OUTA HERE WHILE WE CAN!
82
AS SUPERMAN SPRINGS THRU THE WINDOW...
THEY'RE NO LONGER HERE!
83
QUICK! INTO THE ELEVATOR! -IT'S OUR ONLY CHANCE!
84
SUPERMAN REACHES THE ELEVATOR JUST AS THE METAL DOOR CLICKS SHUT.
I'LL SOON FIX THAT!
85

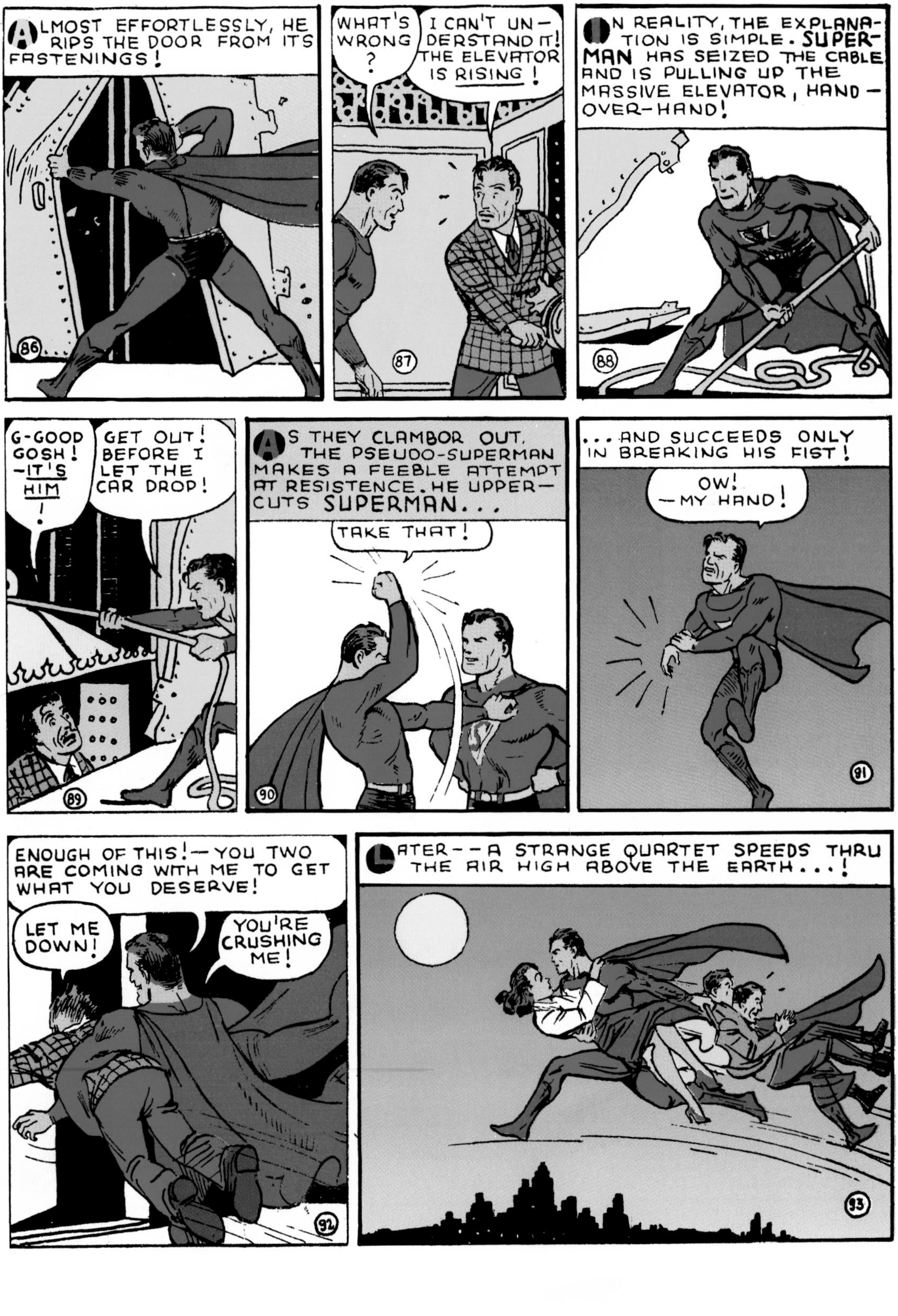
ALMOST EFFORTLESSLY, HE RIPS THE DOOR FROM ITS FASTENINGS!
86
WHAT'S WRONG ?
I CAN'T UNDERSTAND IT! THE ELEVATOR IS RISING!
87
IN REALITY, THE EXPLANATION IS SIMPLE. SUPERMAN HAS SEIZED THE CABLE AND IS PULLING UP THE MASSIVE ELEVATOR, HAND-OVER-HAND!
88
G-GOOD GOSH! -IT'S HIM!
GET OUT! BEFORE I LET THE CAR DROP!
89
AS THEY CLAMBOR OUT, THE PSEUDO-SUPERMAN MAKES A FEEBLE ATTEMPT AT RESISTENCE. HE UPPER-CUTS SUPERMAN...
TAKE THAT!
90
...AND SUCCEEDS ONLY IN BREAKING HIS FIST!
OW! —MY HAND!
91
ENOUGH OF THIS!—YOU TWO ARE COMING WITH ME TO GET WHAT YOU DESERVE!
LET ME DOWN!
YOU'RE CRUSHING ME!
92
LATER--A STRANGE QUARTET SPEEDS THRU THE AIR HIGH ABOVE THE EARTH...!
93

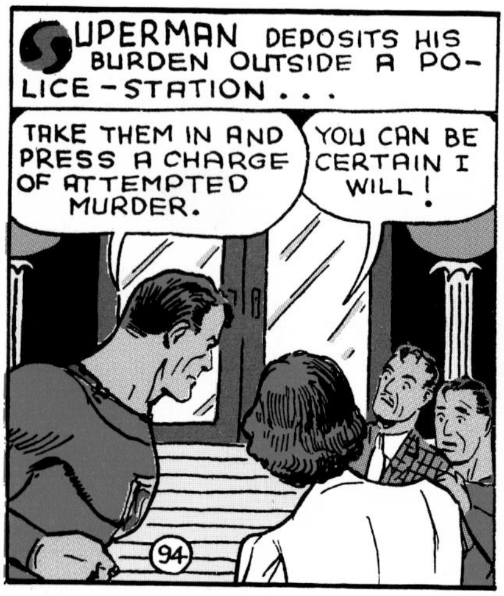
SUPERMAN DEPOSITS HIS BURDEN OUTSIDE A POLICE-STATION . . .
TAKE THEM IN AND PRESS A CHARGE OF ATTEMPTED MURDER.
YOU CAN BE CERTAIN I WILL!
94

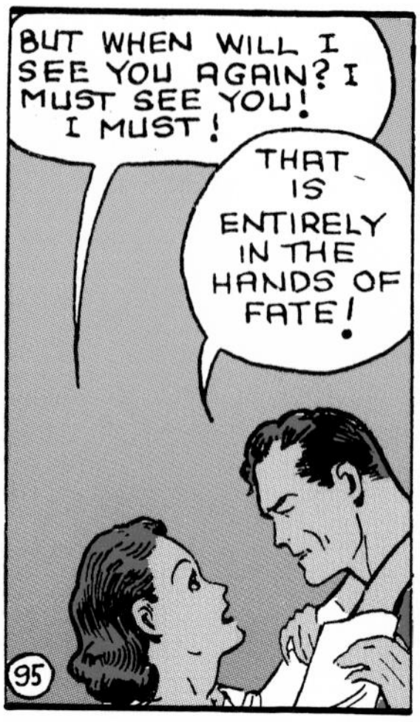
BUT WHEN WILL I SEE YOU AGAIN? I MUST SEE YOU! I MUST!
THAT IS ENTIRELY IN THE HANDS OF FATE!
95

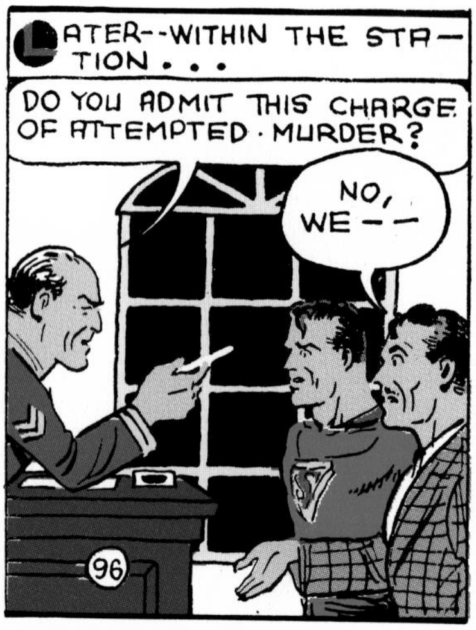
LATER--WITHIN THE STATION . . .
DO YOU ADMIT THIS CHARGE OF ATTEMPTED MURDER?
NO, WE--
96

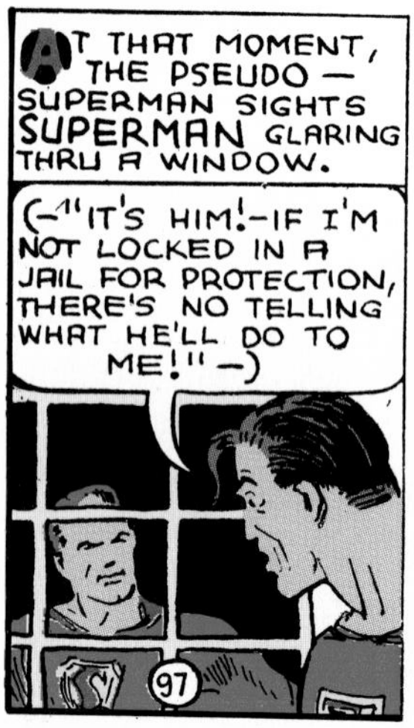
AT THAT MOMENT, THE PSEUDO—SUPERMAN SIGHTS SUPERMAN GLARING THRU A WINDOW.
(—"IT'S HIM!—IF I'M NOT LOCKED IN A JAIL FOR PROTECTION, THERE'S NO TELLING WHAT HE'LL DO TO ME!"—)
97

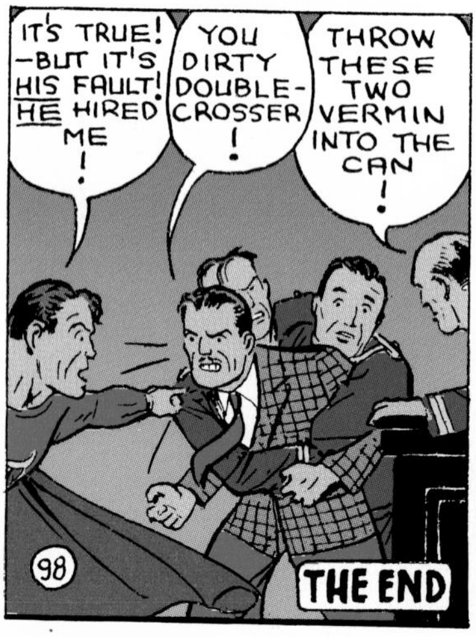
IT'S TRUE! —BUT IT'S HIS FAULT! HE HIRED ME!
YOU DIRTY DOUBLE-CROSSER!
THROW THESE TWO VERMIN INTO THE CAN!
98
THE END

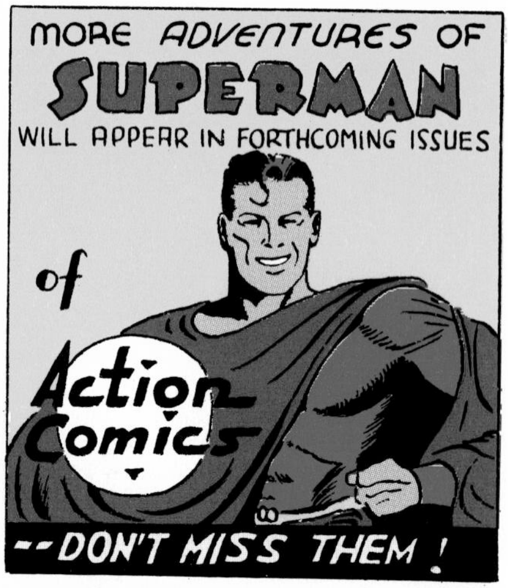
MORE ADVENTURES OF
SUPERMAN
WILL APPEAR IN FORTHCOMING ISSUES
of
Action Comics
--DON'T MISS THEM!

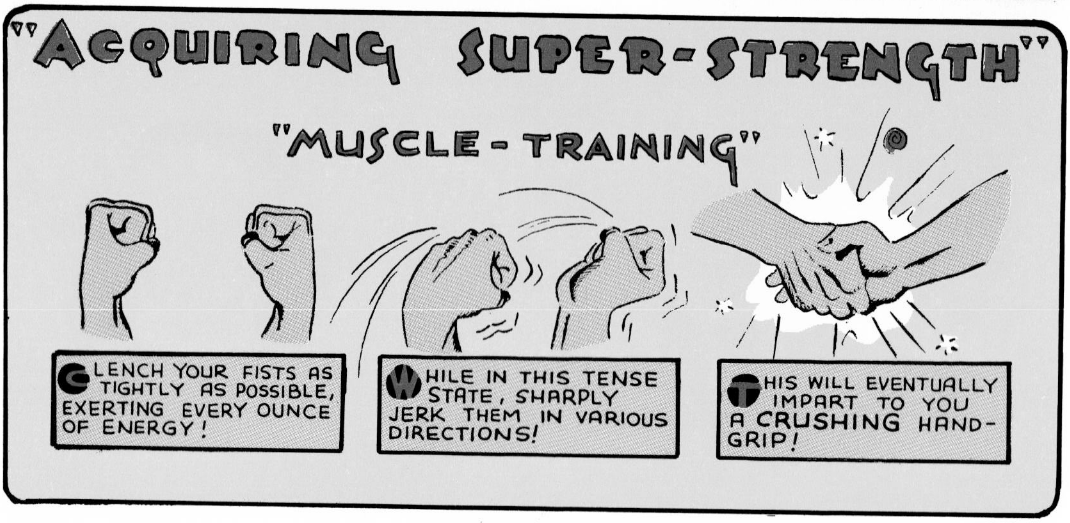
"ACQUIRING SUPER-STRENGTH"
"MUSCLE-TRAINING"
CLENCH YOUR FISTS AS TIGHTLY AS POSSIBLE, EXERTING EVERY OUNCE OF ENERGY!
WHILE IN THIS TENSE STATE, SHARPLY JERK THEM IN VARIOUS DIRECTIONS!
THIS WILL EVENTUALLY IMPART TO YOU A CRUSHING HAND-GRIP!

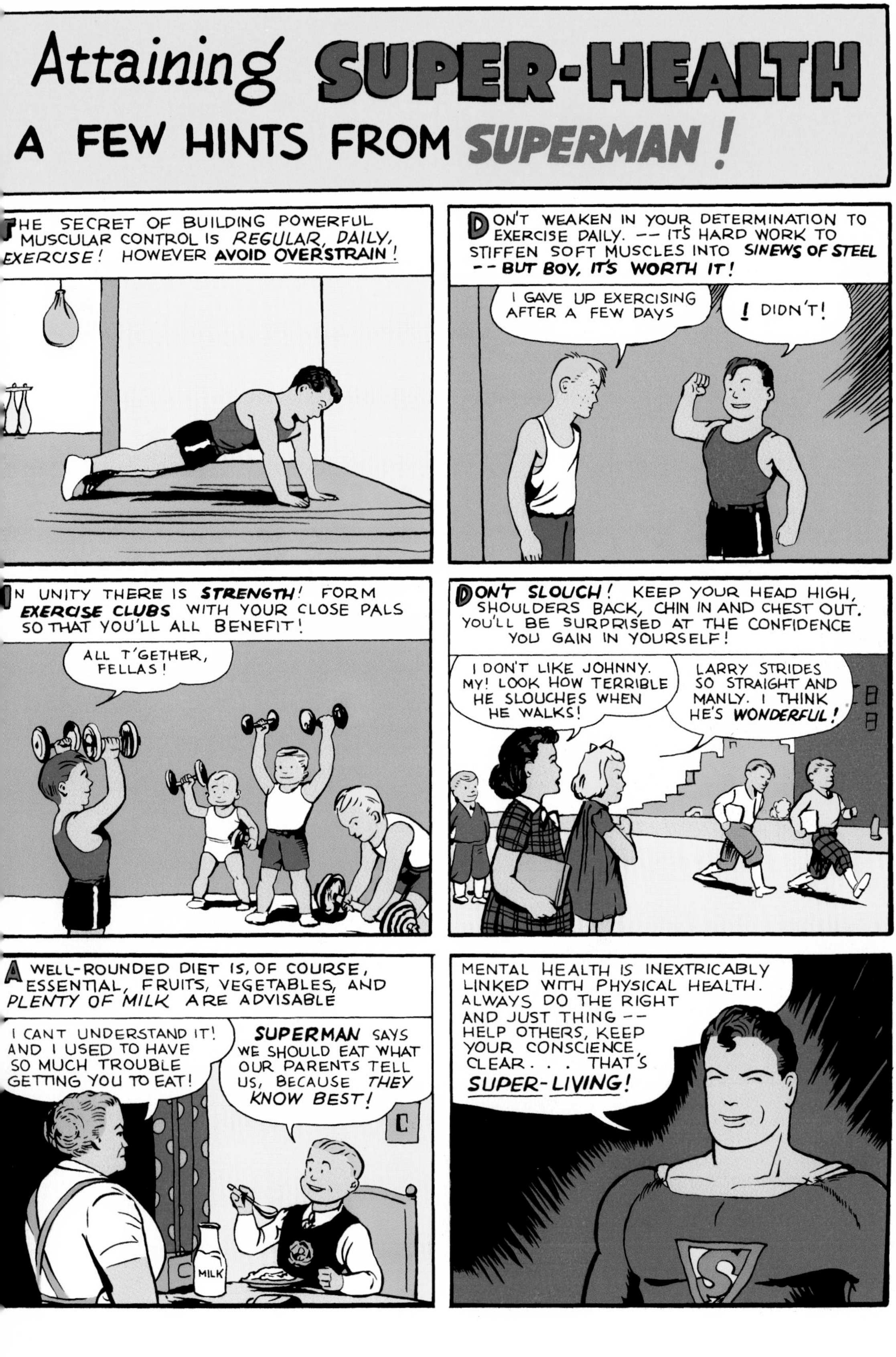
Attaining SUPER-HEALTH
A FEW HINTS FROM SUPERMAN!
THE SECRET OF BUILDING POWERFUL MUSCULAR CONTROL IS REGULAR, DAILY, EXERCISE! HOWEVER AVOID OVERSTRAIN!
DON'T WEAKEN IN YOUR DETERMINATION TO EXERCISE DAILY. -- IT'S HARD WORK TO STIFFEN SOFT MUSCLES INTO SINEWS OF STEEL -- BUT BOY, IT'S WORTH IT!
I GAVE UP EXERCISING AFTER A FEW DAYS
I DIDN'T!
IN UNITY THERE IS STRENGTH! FORM EXERCISE CLUBS WITH YOUR CLOSE PALS SO THAT YOU'LL ALL BENEFIT!
ALL T'GETHER, FELLAS!
DON'T SLOUCH! KEEP YOUR HEAD HIGH, SHOULDERS BACK, CHIN IN AND CHEST OUT. YOU'LL BE SURPRISED AT THE CONFIDENCE YOU GAIN IN YOURSELF!
I DON'T LIKE JOHNNY. MY! LOOK HOW TERRIBLE HE SLOUCHES WHEN HE WALKS!
LARRY STRIDES SO STRAIGHT AND MANLY. I THINK HE'S WONDERFUL!
A WELL-ROUNDED DIET IS, OF COURSE, ESSENTIAL, FRUITS, VEGETABLES, AND PLENTY OF MILK ARE ADVISABLE
I CANT UNDERSTAND IT! AND I USED TO HAVE SO MUCH TROUBLE GETTING YOU TO EAT!
SUPERMAN SAYS WE SHOULD EAT WHAT OUR PARENTS TELL US, BECAUSE THEY KNOW BEST!
MILK
MENTAL HEALTH IS INEXTRICABLY LINKED WITH PHYSICAL HEALTH. ALWAYS DO THE RIGHT AND JUST THING -- HELP OTHERS, KEEP YOUR CONSCIENCE CLEAR. . . THAT'S SUPER-LIVING!

Good Luck Charm

By Hugh Langley

TONY CARRENZO'S slitted eyes darted furtively across the prison yard's barren expanse, gleefully noted the turned backs of unsuspecting guards. From the corner of his scarred mouth, he spat: "All set?"

"Lucky" Malone promptly replied: "Set!"

Two pairs of feverishly gleaming eyes simultaneously swung to the truck parked nearby. "ACME REPAIRS" was the legend that truck bore, but to these two hardened lifers, the words appeared to spell: *escape!*

Automatically, "Lucky's" hand strayed beneath his shirt and stroked a small metallic object then: "NOW!"

Swiftly the two stepped to the truck's side, threw themselves down flat, and crawled beneath it. Reaching up, they seized the lower parts of the auto, and drew themselves up out of view.

"Lucky" slipped a small locket from under his shirt with one free hand and chuckled softly to himself.

"You crazy fool," Tony whispered harshly to him. "Stop that laughing! Wanta give us away?"

"Can't help it," "Lucky" chuckled. "This good luck charm has done th' trick again!"

Odd about that lucky piece. Years ago when Malone was just another strong arm muscle-man, he read in a newspaper that the wealthy hindu, Rhani Kor, was bringing a fortune in jewels with him to America. Later that same evening Malone, looking through a window in a mansion, saw the Hindu gloating over his precious jewels. A few moments later, Rhani Kor was sprawled on the floor with a bashed skull, and Malone was stuffing the jewels into his pocket. He was about to depart, when noting a locket about his victim's throat, he appropriated it, believing it might be valuable. But later, when he turned the jewels over to a fence, he held onto the locket, thinking it had brought him good fortune. There was some foreign script upon the face of the locket, but after puzzling over it briefly, Malone gave up.

It was then that people began calling him "Lucky" Malone. Good luck seemed to come his way with miraculous regularity. And "Lucky" always ascribed his successes to the good luck charm. One day "Lucky" murdered a double-crossing henchman and the law succeeded in pinning the crime on him. But again his good luck held sway, and he was given a life sentence instead of the chair.

The two cons held their breath as they glimpsed several pair of feet approach: guards! But then they heaved relieved sighs as the truck's gears clashed and the car leapt ahead. The strip through the prison yard seemed to last an infinity, but finally they were passing through the gates...and then, were out in the open world at last!

"Lucky" could not hide his jubilation. "You can't tell me now

that the locket doesn't bring... HEY!" His words were cut short by a series of gasps as the truck went over a bump in the road and he lost his grip.

Horrified at seeing "Lucky" dragging on the pavement, Tony shrieked: "Stop the car! Stop the car!"

The car swiftly slid to a halt. A terrible sight met the driver's eyes, as he glanced under the truck. When "Lucky" lost his grip, the locket had caught in the auto's mechanism, and he had been strangled by his good luck charm!

Shortly after, when "Lucky's" body had been freed, Tony questioned his dark-skinned captor, as the driver gravely read the inscription upon the locket. "Can you read that? What does it say?"

"It is written in Arabic," said the driver, a Hindu. "Translated, it reads: 'Wear me in Honor—or Perish!'"

THE END

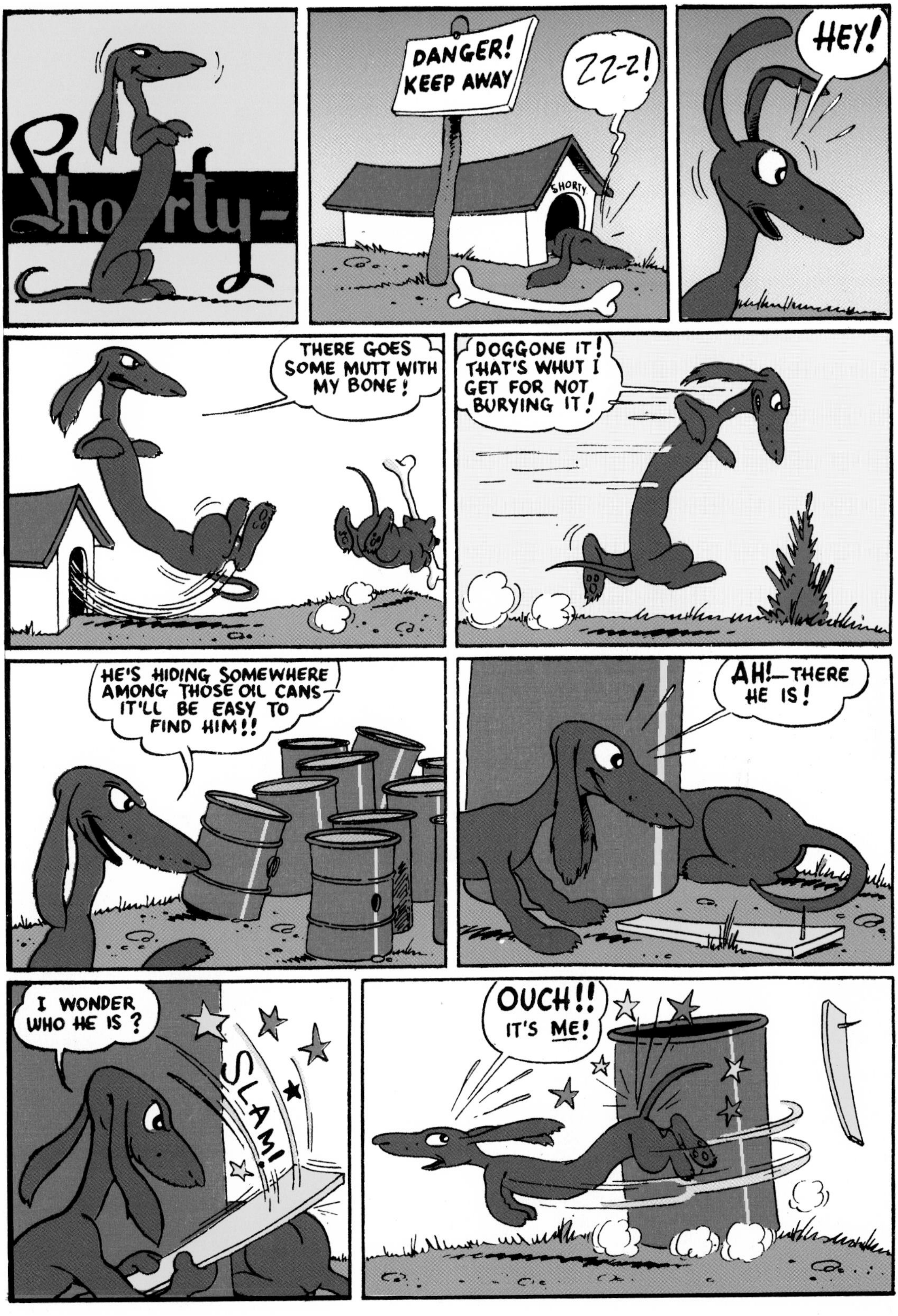
Shorty
DANGER! KEEP AWAY
ZZ-z!
SHORTY
HEY!
THERE GOES SOME MUTT WITH MY BONE!
DOGGONE IT! THAT'S WHUT I GET FOR NOT BURYING IT!
HE'S HIDING SOMEWHERE AMONG THOSE OIL CANS—IT'LL BE EASY TO FIND HIM!!
AH!—THERE HE IS!
I WONDER WHO HE IS?
SLAM!
OUCH!! IT'S ME!

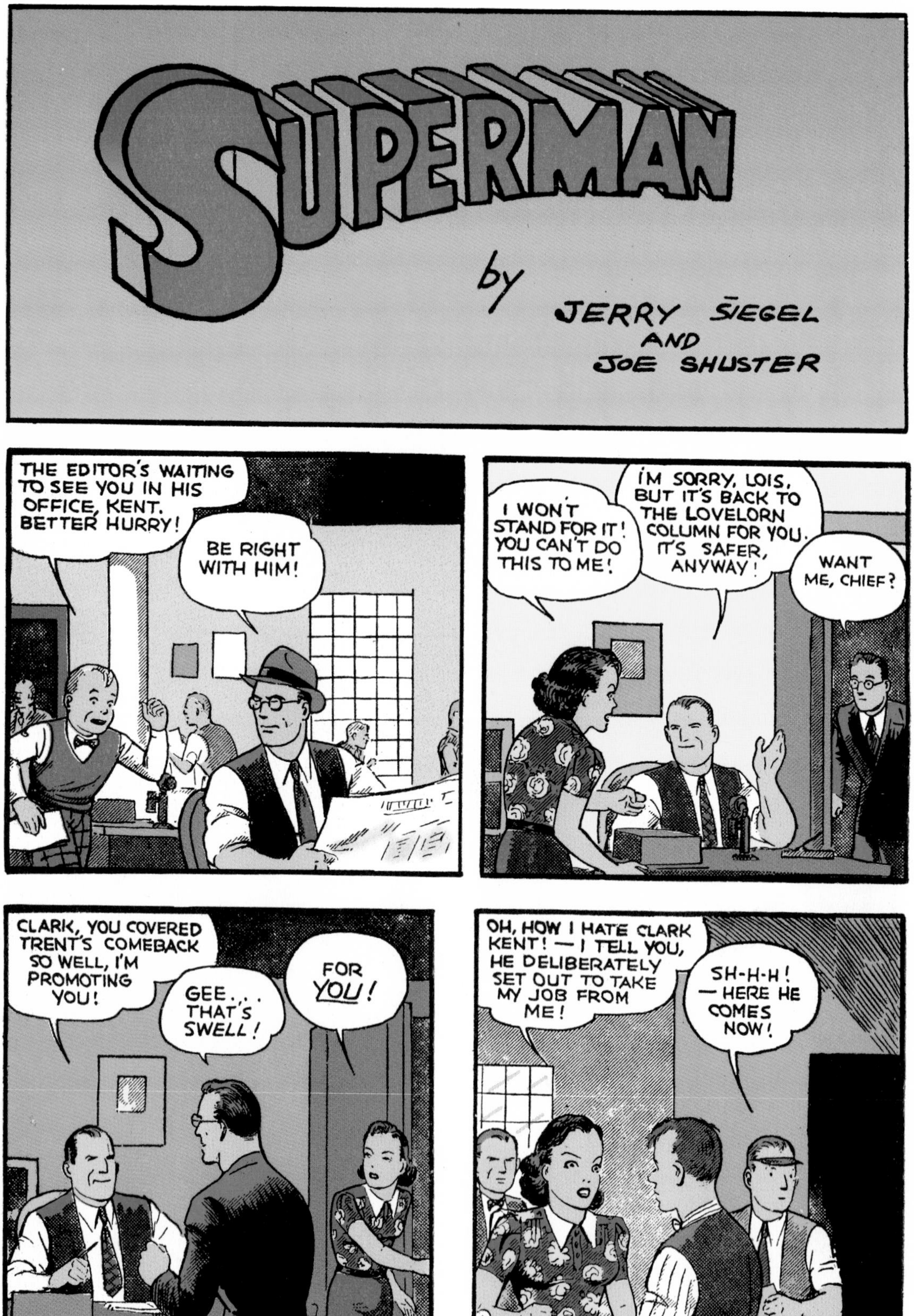
SUPERMAN
by
JERRY SIEGEL
AND
JOE SHUSTER
THE EDITOR'S WAITING TO SEE YOU IN HIS OFFICE, KENT. BETTER HURRY!
BE RIGHT WITH HIM!
I WON'T STAND FOR IT! YOU CAN'T DO THIS TO ME!
I'M SORRY, LOIS, BUT IT'S BACK TO THE LOVELORN COLUMN FOR YOU. IT'S SAFER, ANYWAY!
WANT ME, CHIEF?
CLARK, YOU COVERED TRENT'S COMEBACK SO WELL, I'M PROMOTING YOU!
GEE... THAT'S SWELL!
FOR YOU!
OH, HOW I HATE CLARK KENT! — I TELL YOU, HE DELIBERATELY SET OUT TO TAKE MY JOB FROM ME!
SH-H-H! — HERE HE COMES NOW!

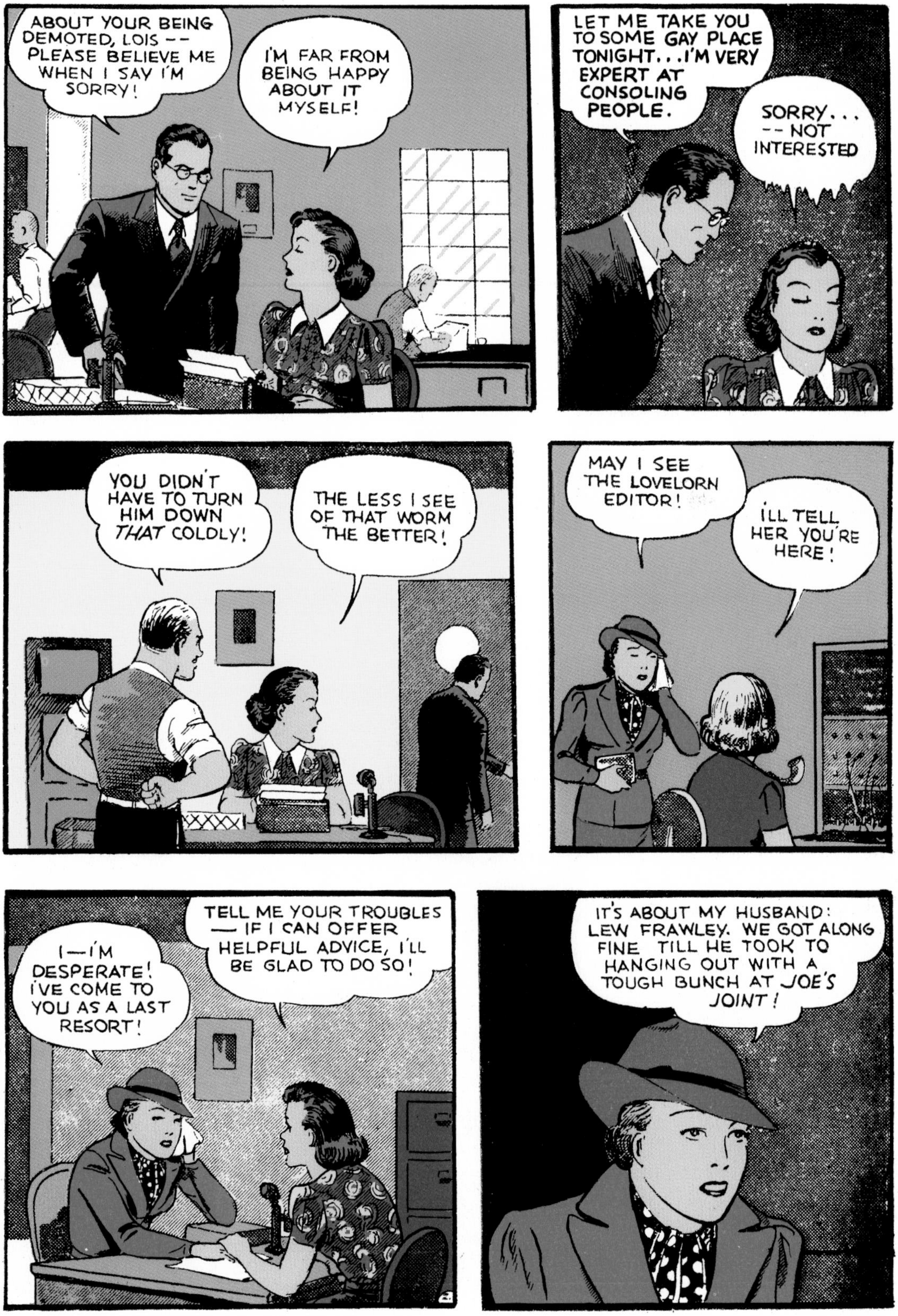
ABOUT YOUR BEING DEMOTED, LOIS -- PLEASE BELIEVE ME WHEN I SAY I'M SORRY!
I'M FAR FROM BEING HAPPY ABOUT IT MYSELF!
LET ME TAKE YOU TO SOME GAY PLACE TONIGHT. . .I'M VERY EXPERT AT CONSOLING PEOPLE.
SORRY. . . -- NOT INTERESTED
YOU DIDN'T HAVE TO TURN HIM DOWN *THAT* COLDLY!
THE LESS I SEE OF THAT WORM THE BETTER!
MAY I SEE THE LOVELORN EDITOR!
I'LL TELL HER YOU'RE HERE!
I—I'M DESPERATE! I'VE COME TO YOU AS A LAST RESORT!
TELL ME YOUR TROUBLES — IF I CAN OFFER HELPFUL ADVICE, I'LL BE GLAD TO DO SO!
IT'S ABOUT MY HUSBAND: LEW FRAWLEY. WE GOT ALONG FINE TILL HE TOOK TO HANGING OUT WITH A TOUGH BUNCH AT *JOE'S JOINT!*

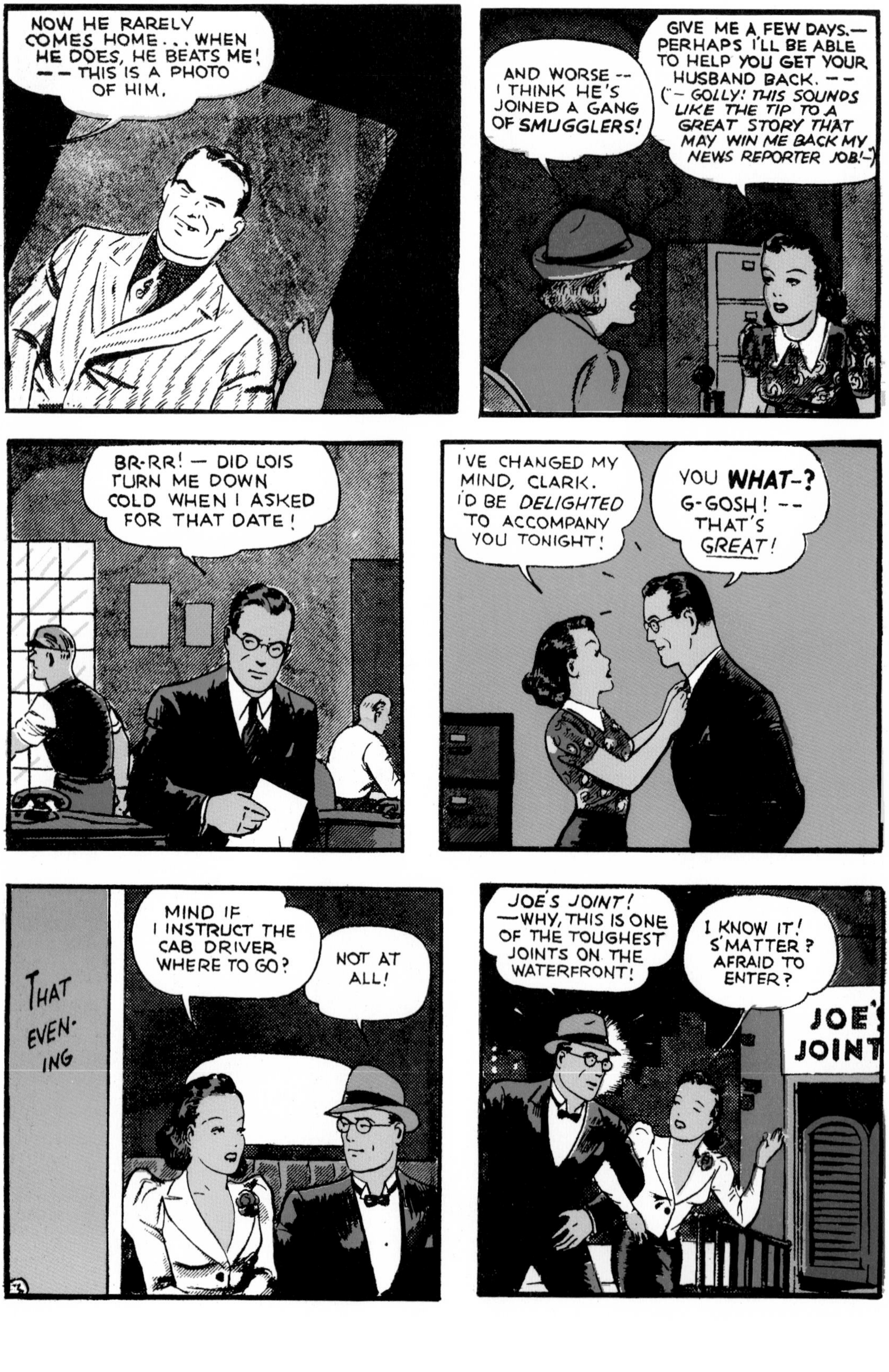
NOW HE RARELY COMES HOME . . . WHEN HE DOES, HE BEATS ME! -- THIS IS A PHOTO OF HIM.
AND WORSE -- I THINK HE'S JOINED A GANG OF SMUGGLERS!
GIVE ME A FEW DAYS.— PERHAPS I'LL BE ABLE TO HELP YOU GET YOUR HUSBAND BACK. -- ("— GOLLY! THIS SOUNDS LIKE THE TIP TO A GREAT STORY THAT MAY WIN ME BACK MY NEWS REPORTER JOB!—")
BR-RR! — DID LOIS TURN ME DOWN COLD WHEN I ASKED FOR THAT DATE!
I'VE CHANGED MY MIND, CLARK. I'D BE DELIGHTED TO ACCOMPANY YOU TONIGHT!
YOU WHAT—? G-GOSH! -- THAT'S GREAT!
THAT EVEN-ING
MIND IF I INSTRUCT THE CAB DRIVER WHERE TO GO?
NOT AT ALL!
JOE'S JOINT! —WHY, THIS IS ONE OF THE TOUGHEST JOINTS ON THE WATERFRONT!
I KNOW IT! S'MATTER? AFRAID TO ENTER?
JOE'S JOINT

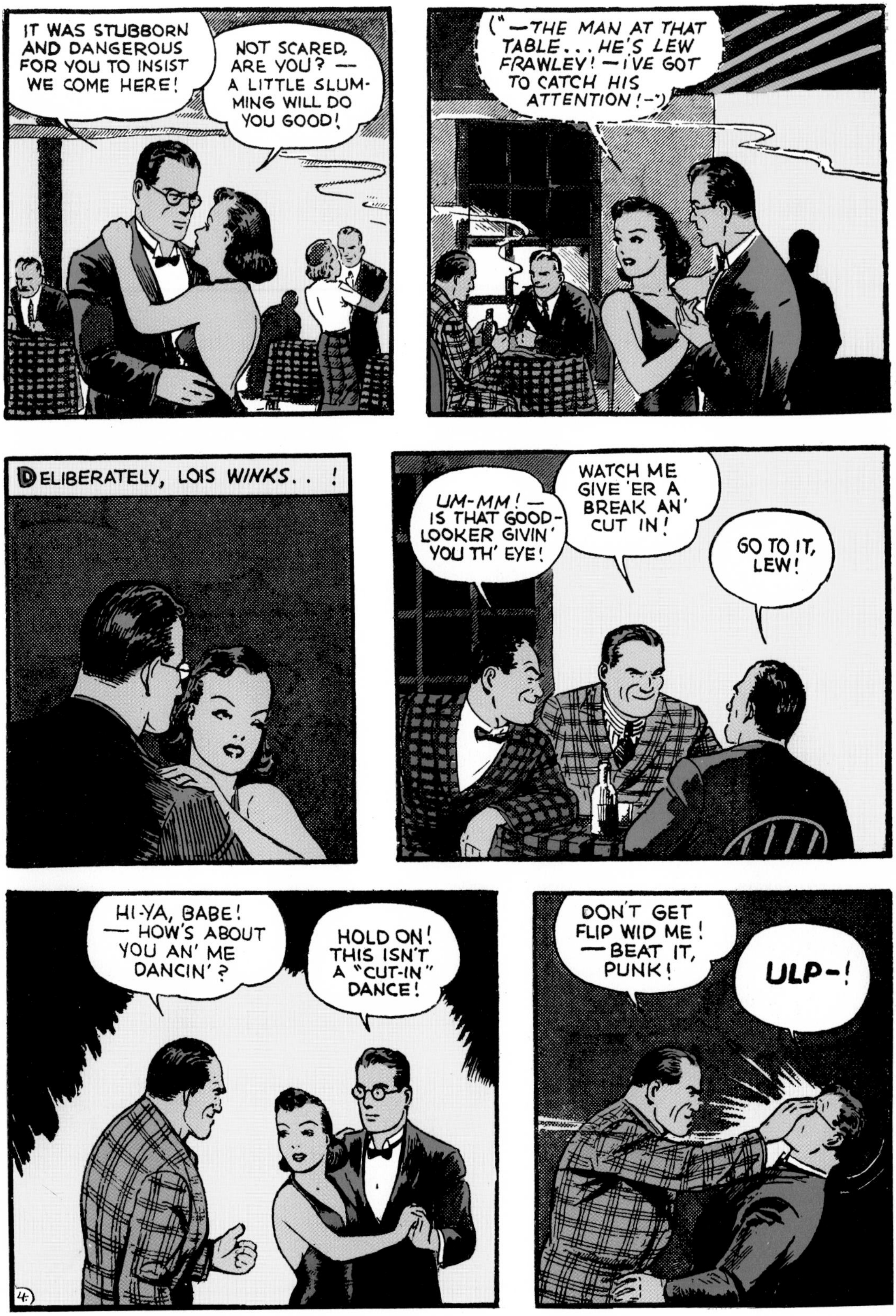
IT WAS STUBBORN AND DANGEROUS FOR YOU TO INSIST WE COME HERE!
NOT SCARED, ARE YOU? — A LITTLE SLUMMING WILL DO YOU GOOD!
("—THE MAN AT THAT TABLE... HE'S LEW FRAWLEY! —I'VE GOT TO CATCH HIS ATTENTION!—")
DELIBERATELY, LOIS WINKS.. !
UM-MM! — IS THAT GOOD-LOOKER GIVIN' YOU TH' EYE!
WATCH ME GIVE 'ER A BREAK AN' CUT IN!
GO TO IT, LEW!
HI-YA, BABE! — HOW'S ABOUT YOU AN' ME DANCIN'?
HOLD ON! THIS ISN'T A "CUT-IN" DANCE!
DON'T GET FLIP WID ME! —BEAT IT, PUNK!
ULP-!

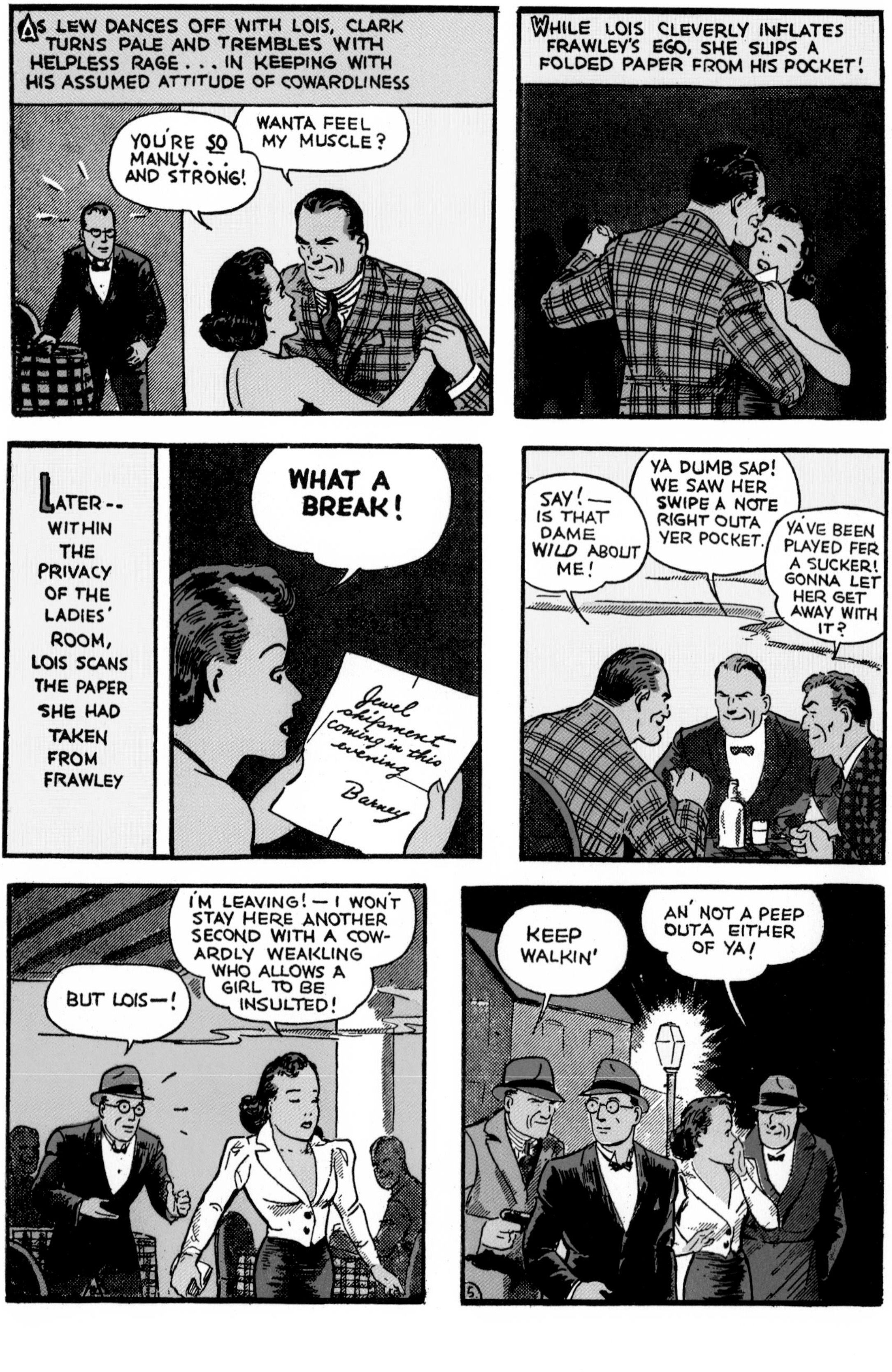
AS LEW DANCES OFF WITH LOIS, CLARK TURNS PALE AND TREMBLES WITH HELPLESS RAGE . . . IN KEEPING WITH HIS ASSUMED ATTITUDE OF COWARDLINESS
YOU'RE SO MANLY. . . AND STRONG!
WANTA FEEL MY MUSCLE?
WHILE LOIS CLEVERLY INFLATES FRAWLEY'S EGO, SHE SLIPS A FOLDED PAPER FROM HIS POCKET!
LATER -- WITHIN THE PRIVACY OF THE LADIES' ROOM, LOIS SCANS THE PAPER SHE HAD TAKEN FROM FRAWLEY
WHAT A BREAK!
Jewel shipment coming in this evening Barney
SAY! — IS THAT DAME WILD ABOUT ME!
YA DUMB SAP! WE SAW HER SWIPE A NOTE RIGHT OUTA YER POCKET.
YA'VE BEEN PLAYED FER A SUCKER! GONNA LET HER GET AWAY WITH IT?
BUT LOIS—!
I'M LEAVING! — I WON'T STAY HERE ANOTHER SECOND WITH A COWARDLY WEAKLING WHO ALLOWS A GIRL TO BE INSULTED!
KEEP WALKIN'
AN' NOT A PEEP OUTA EITHER OF YA!

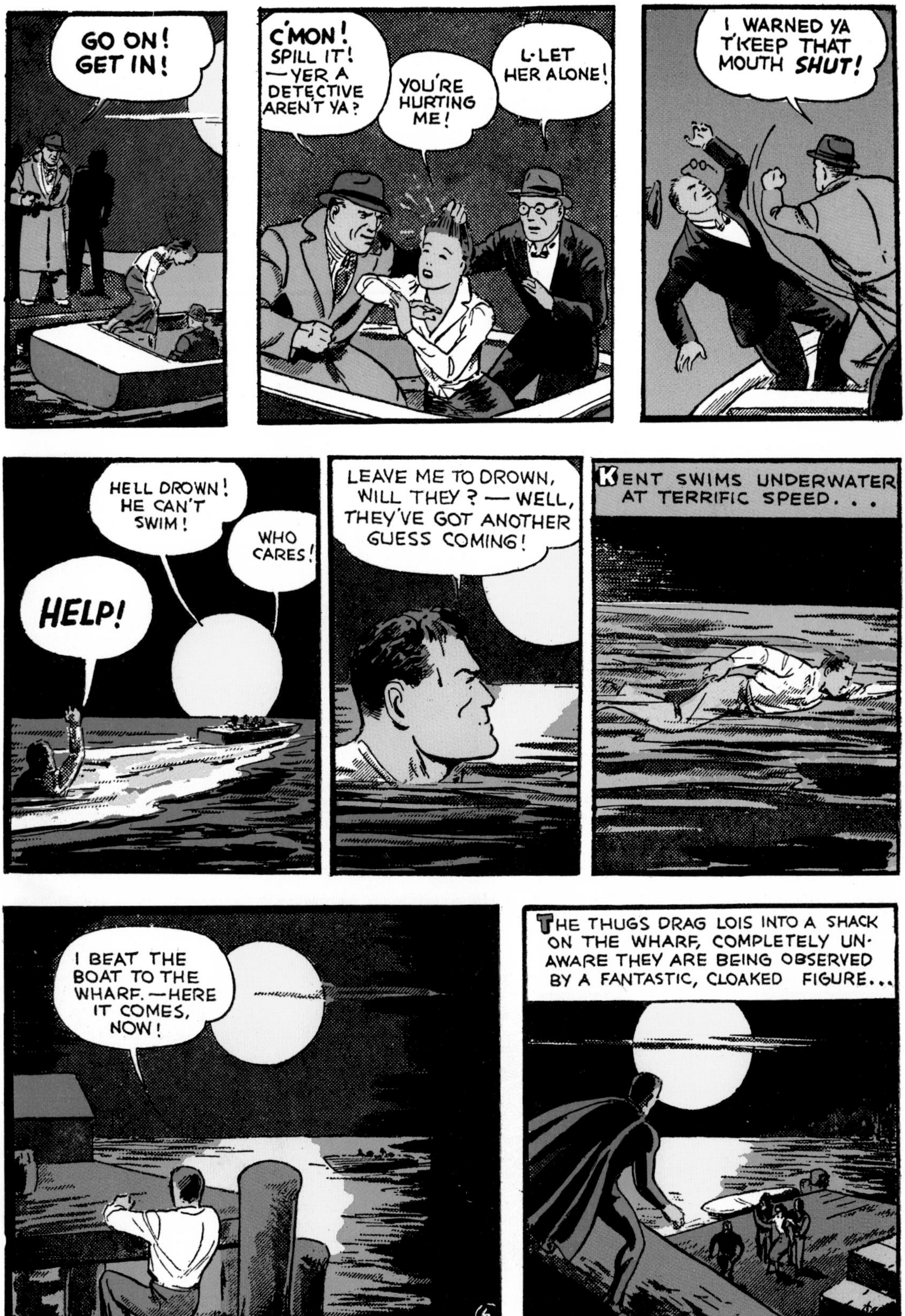
GO ON! GET IN!
C'MON! SPILL IT! —YER A DETECTIVE AREN'T YA?
YOU'RE HURTING ME!
L-LET HER ALONE!
I WARNED YA T'KEEP THAT MOUTH SHUT!
HE'LL DROWN! HE CAN'T SWIM!
WHO CARES!
HELP!
LEAVE ME TO DROWN, WILL THEY? — WELL, THEY'VE GOT ANOTHER GUESS COMING!
KENT SWIMS UNDERWATER AT TERRIFIC SPEED. . .
I BEAT THE BOAT TO THE WHARF. —HERE IT COMES, NOW!
6.
THE THUGS DRAG LOIS INTO A SHACK ON THE WHARF, COMPLETELY UN-AWARE THEY ARE BEING OBSERVED BY A FANTASTIC, CLOAKED FIGURE...

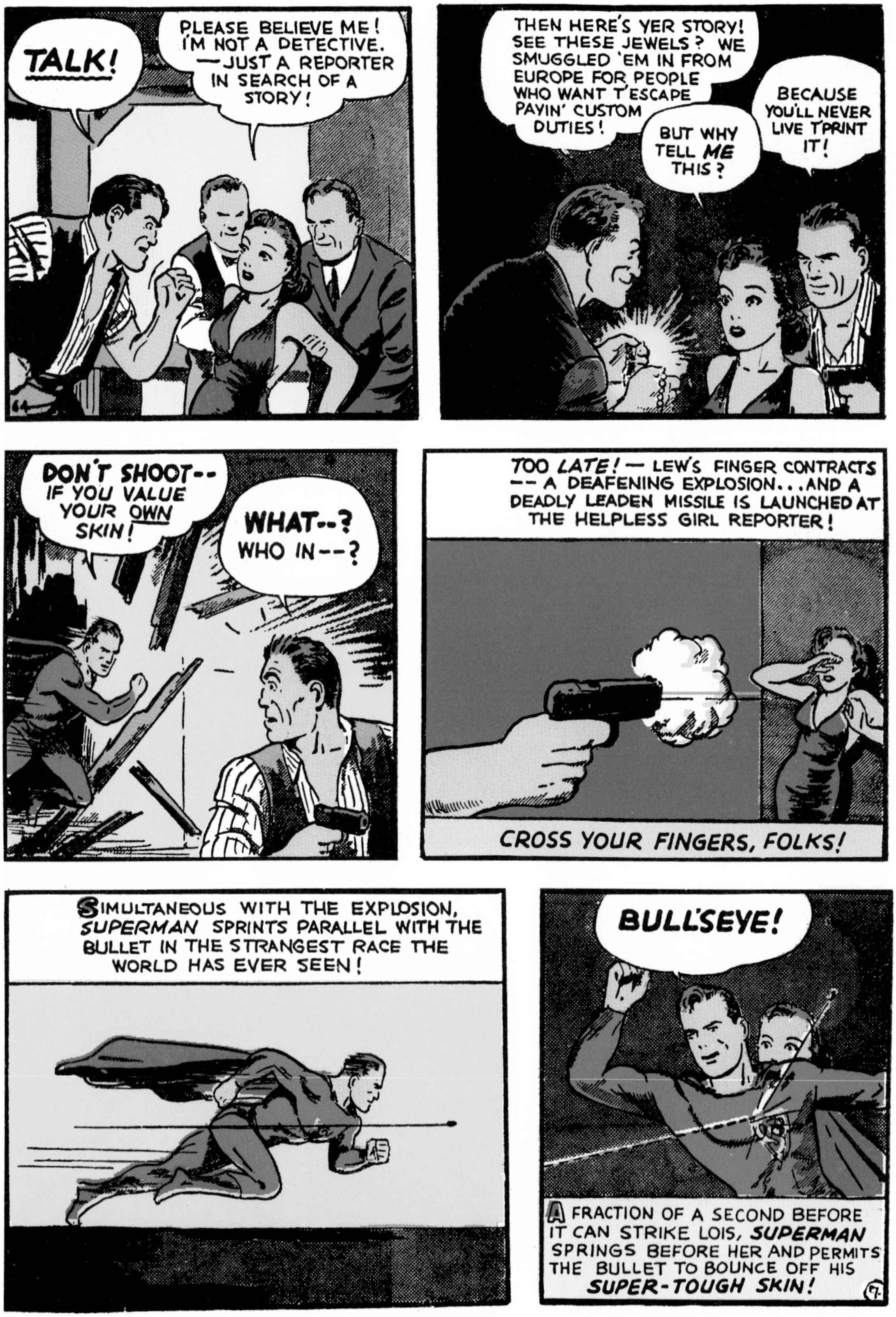
TALK!
PLEASE BELIEVE ME! I'M NOT A DETECTIVE. —JUST A REPORTER IN SEARCH OF A STORY!
THEN HERE'S YER STORY! SEE THESE JEWELS? WE SMUGGLED 'EM IN FROM EUROPE FOR PEOPLE WHO WANT T'ESCAPE PAYIN' CUSTOM DUTIES!
BUT WHY TELL ME THIS?
BECAUSE YOU'LL NEVER LIVE T'PRINT IT!
DON'T SHOOT-- IF YOU VALUE YOUR OWN SKIN!
WHAT--? WHO IN--?
TOO LATE! — LEW'S FINGER CONTRACTS -- A DEAFENING EXPLOSION...AND A DEADLY LEADEN MISSILE IS LAUNCHED AT THE HELPLESS GIRL REPORTER!
CROSS YOUR FINGERS, FOLKS!
SIMULTANEOUS WITH THE EXPLOSION, SUPERMAN SPRINTS PARALLEL WITH THE BULLET IN THE STRANGEST RACE THE WORLD HAS EVER SEEN!
BULL'SEYE!
A FRACTION OF A SECOND BEFORE IT CAN STRIKE LOIS, SUPERMAN SPRINGS BEFORE HER AND PERMITS THE BULLET TO BOUNCE OFF HIS SUPER-TOUGH SKIN!
7.

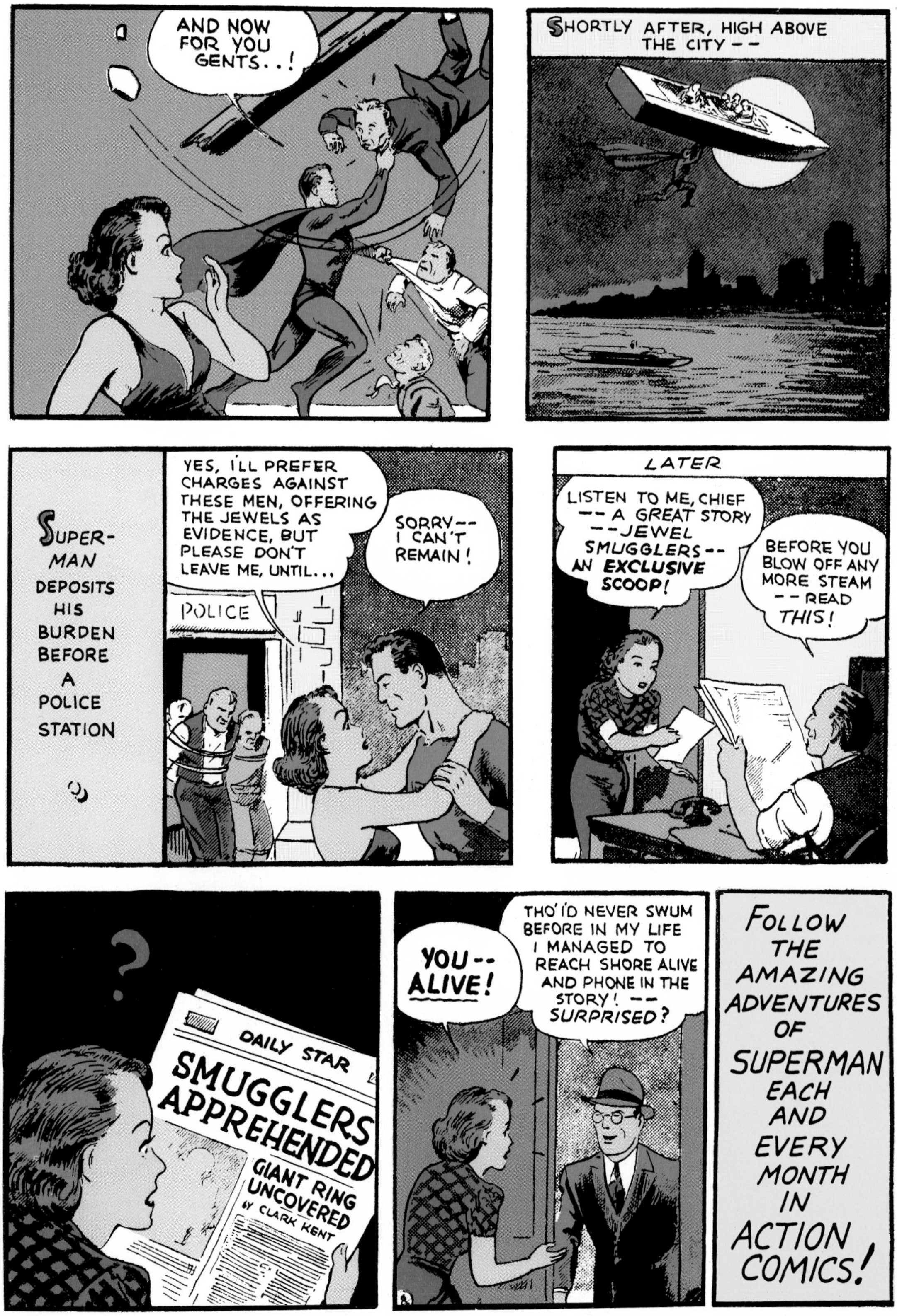
AND NOW FOR YOU GENTS..!
SHORTLY AFTER, HIGH ABOVE THE CITY --
SUPER-MAN DEPOSITS HIS BURDEN BEFORE A POLICE STATION
YES, I'LL PREFER CHARGES AGAINST THESE MEN, OFFERING THE JEWELS AS EVIDENCE, BUT PLEASE DON'T LEAVE ME, UNTIL...
SORRY-- I CAN'T REMAIN!
POLICE
LATER
LISTEN TO ME, CHIEF -- A GREAT STORY --JEWEL SMUGGLERS -- AN EXCLUSIVE SCOOP!
BEFORE YOU BLOW OFF ANY MORE STEAM -- READ THIS!
?
DAILY STAR
SMUGGLERS APPREHENDED
GIANT RING UNCOVERED
BY CLARK KENT
YOU-- ALIVE!
THO' I'D NEVER SWUM BEFORE IN MY LIFE I MANAGED TO REACH SHORE ALIVE AND PHONE IN THE STORY! -- SURPRISED?
FOLLOW THE AMAZING ADVENTURES OF SUPERMAN EACH AND EVERY MONTH IN ACTION COMICS!

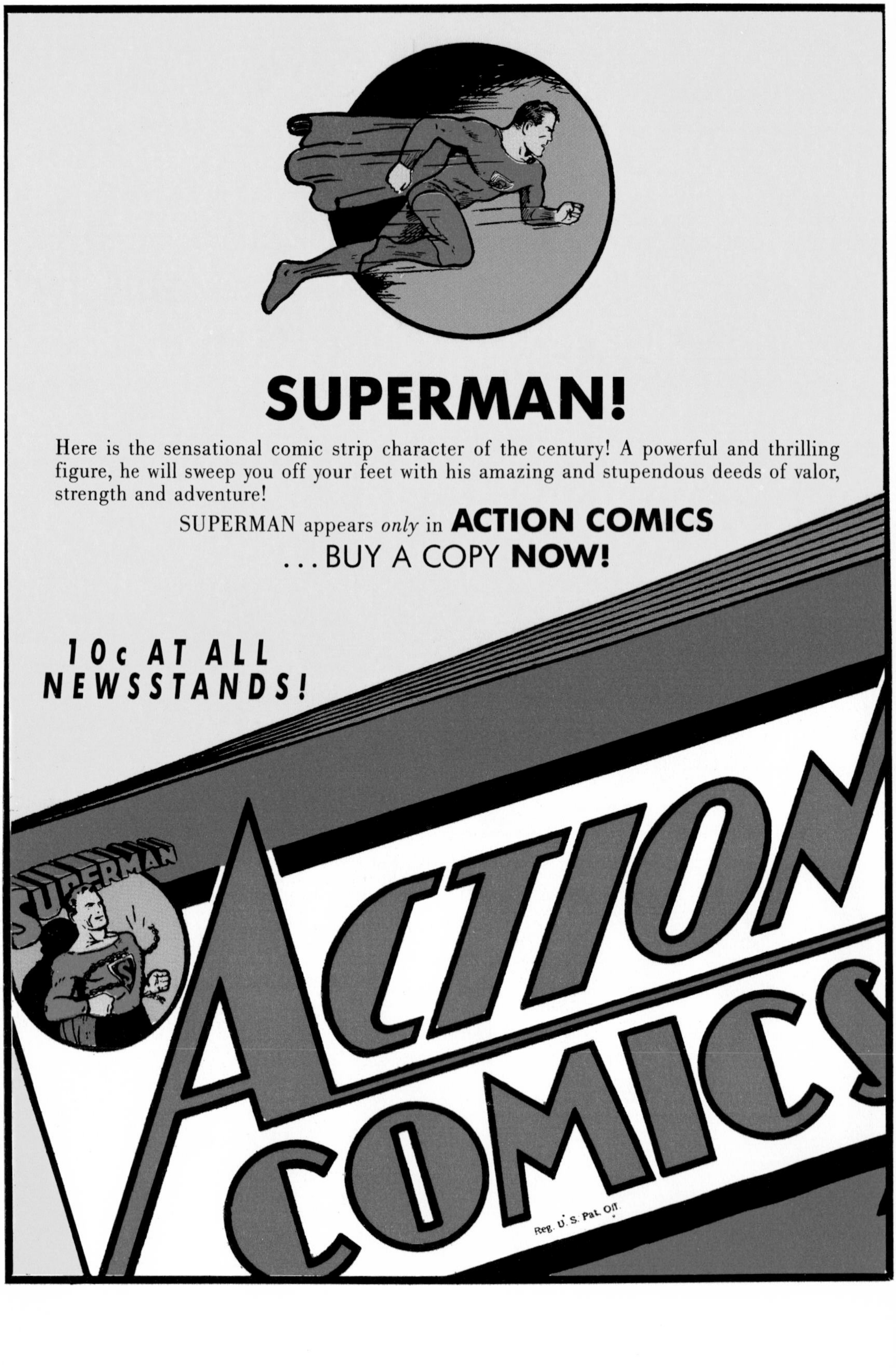
SUPERMAN!
Here is the sensational comic strip character of the century! A powerful and thrilling figure, he will sweep you off your feet with his amazing and stupendous deeds of valor, strength and adventure!
SUPERMAN appears *only* in ACTION COMICS
. . . BUY A COPY NOW!
10c AT ALL NEWSSTANDS!
SUPERMAN
ACTION COMICS
Reg. U. S. Pat. Off.

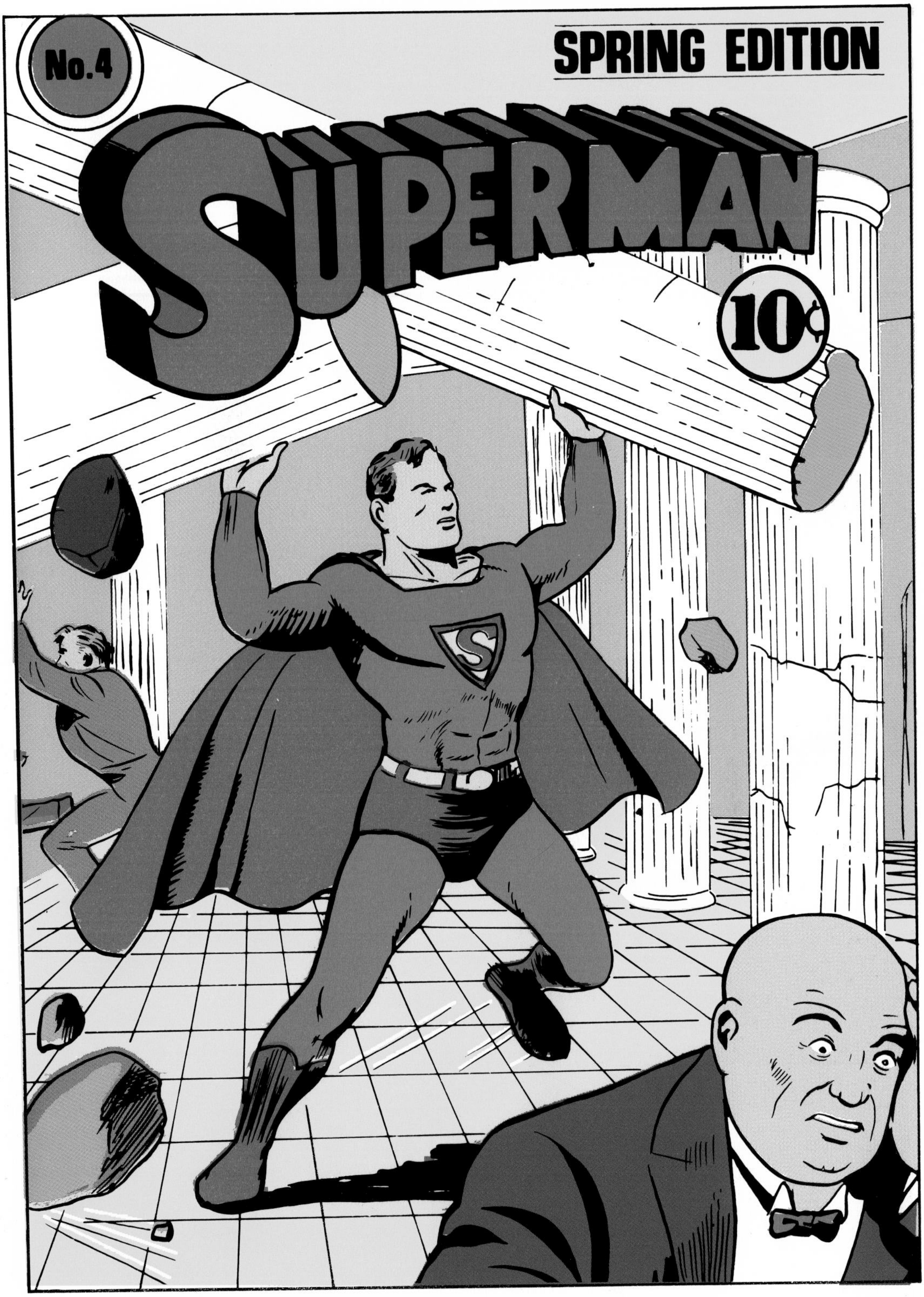
No.4
SPRING EDITION
SUPERMAN
10¢

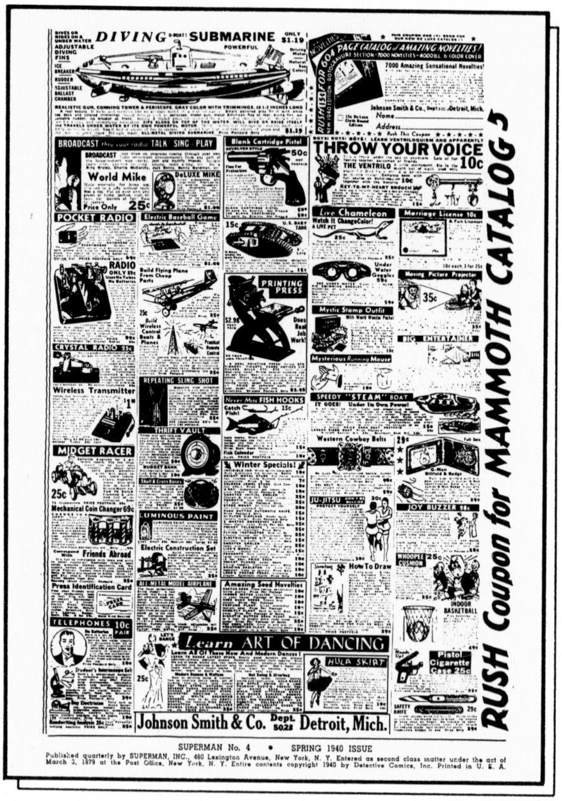
DIVING SUBMARINE
THROW YOUR VOICE
BROADCAST
World Mike
POCKET RADIO
PRINTING PRESS
MIDGET RACER
Learn ART OF DANCING
HULA SKIRT
Johnson Smith & Co. Dept. 502 Detroit, Mich.
RUSH Coupon for MAMMOTH CATALOG 5
SUPERMAN No. 4 • SPRING 1940 ISSUE
Published quarterly by SUPERMAN, INC., 480 Lexington Avenue, New York, N. Y. Entered as second class matter under the act of March 3, 1879 at the Post Office, New York, N. Y. Entire contents copyright 1940 by Detective Comics, Inc. Printed in U. S. A.

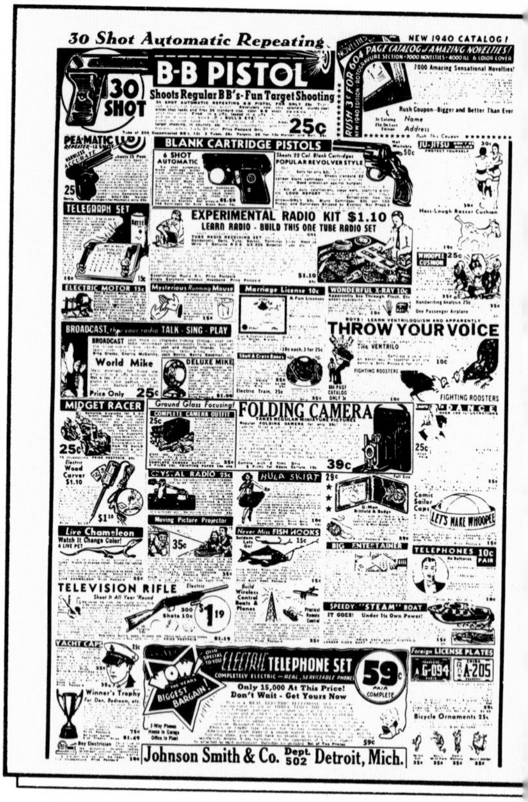
30 Shot Automatic Repeating
B-B PISTOL
Shoots Regular BB's-Fun Target Shooting
25c
BLANK CARTRIDGE PISTOLS
EXPERIMENTAL RADIO KIT $1.10
THROW YOUR VOICE
FOLDING CAMERA
TELEVISION RIFLE
ELECTRIC TELEPHONE SET
59c
BIGGEST BARGAIN
Johnson Smith & Co. Dept. 502 Detroit, Mich.

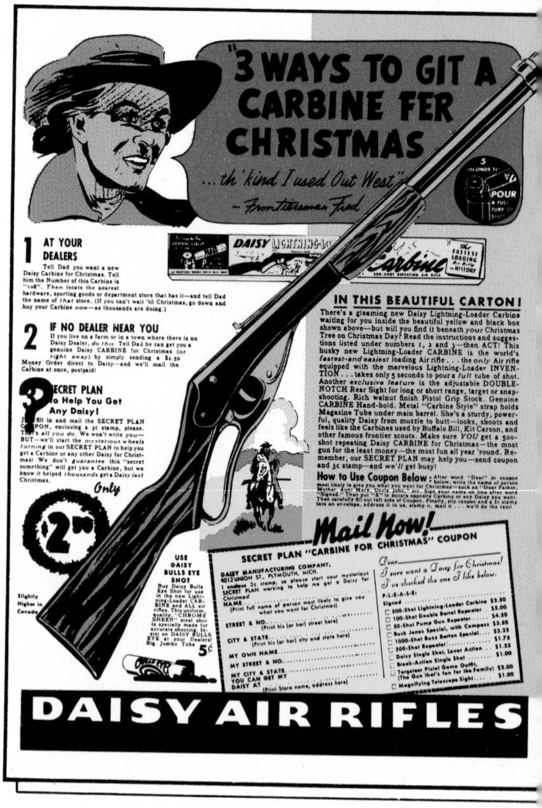
"3 WAYS TO GIT A CARBINE FER CHRISTMAS
...th' kind I used Out West"
—Frontiersman Fred
1 AT YOUR DEALERS
2 IF NO DEALER NEAR YOU
3 SECRET PLAN to Help You Get Any Daisy!
IN THIS BEAUTIFUL CARTON!
Only $2.00
Mail Now!
SECRET PLAN "CARBINE FOR CHRISTMAS" COUPON
DAISY AIR RIFLES

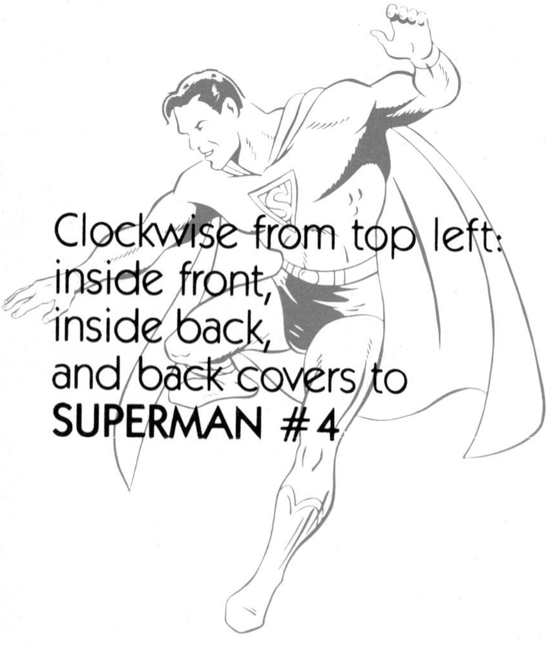

Clockwise from top left:
inside front,
inside back,
and back covers to
SUPERMAN #4

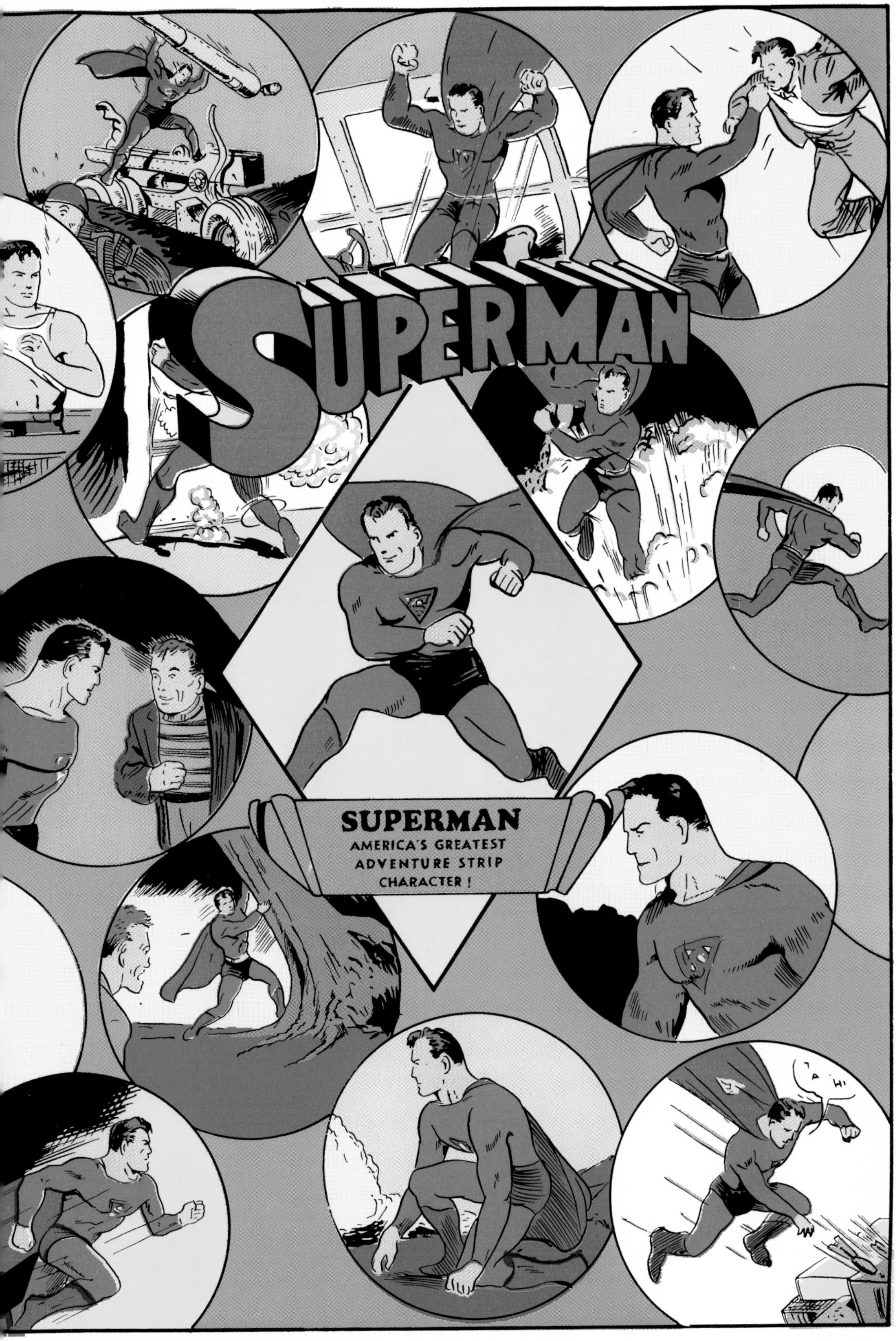
SUPERMAN
SUPERMAN
AMERICA'S GREATEST
ADVENTURE STRIP
CHARACTER !

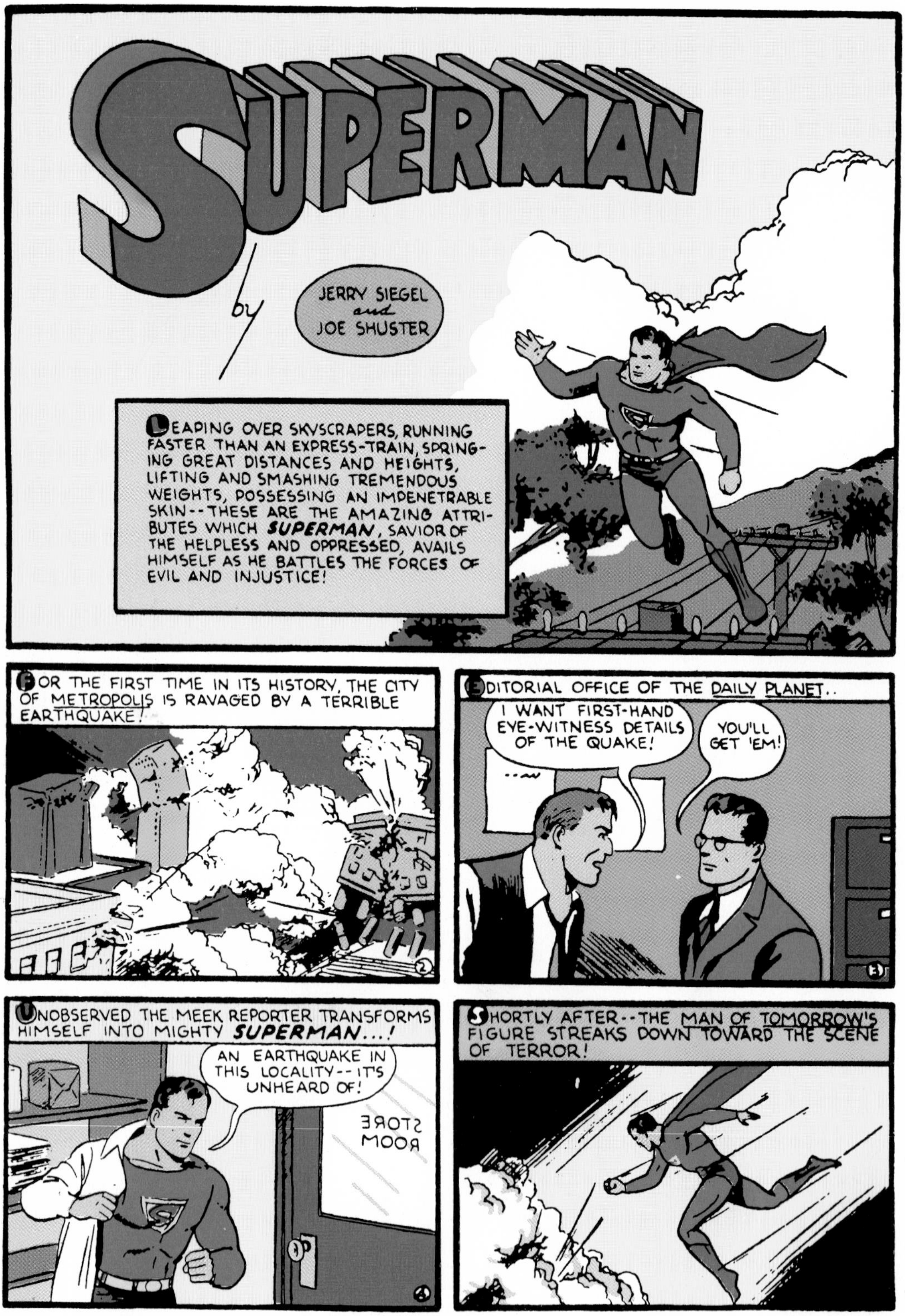
SUPERMAN
by
JERRY SIEGEL and JOE SHUSTER
LEAPING OVER SKYSCRAPERS, RUNNING FASTER THAN AN EXPRESS-TRAIN, SPRINGING GREAT DISTANCES AND HEIGHTS, LIFTING AND SMASHING TREMENDOUS WEIGHTS, POSSESSING AN IMPENETRABLE SKIN--THESE ARE THE AMAZING ATTRIBUTES WHICH SUPERMAN, SAVIOR OF THE HELPLESS AND OPPRESSED, AVAILS HIMSELF AS HE BATTLES THE FORCES OF EVIL AND INJUSTICE!
FOR THE FIRST TIME IN ITS HISTORY, THE CITY OF METROPOLIS IS RAVAGED BY A TERRIBLE EARTHQUAKE!
2
EDITORIAL OFFICE OF THE DAILY PLANET..
I WANT FIRST-HAND EYE-WITNESS DETAILS OF THE QUAKE!
YOU'LL GET 'EM!
3
UNOBSERVED THE MEEK REPORTER TRANSFORMS HIMSELF INTO MIGHTY SUPERMAN...!
AN EARTHQUAKE IN THIS LOCALITY--IT'S UNHEARD OF!
STORE ROOM
4
SHORTLY AFTER--THE MAN OF TOMORROW'S FIGURE STREAKS DOWN TOWARD THE SCENE OF TERROR!

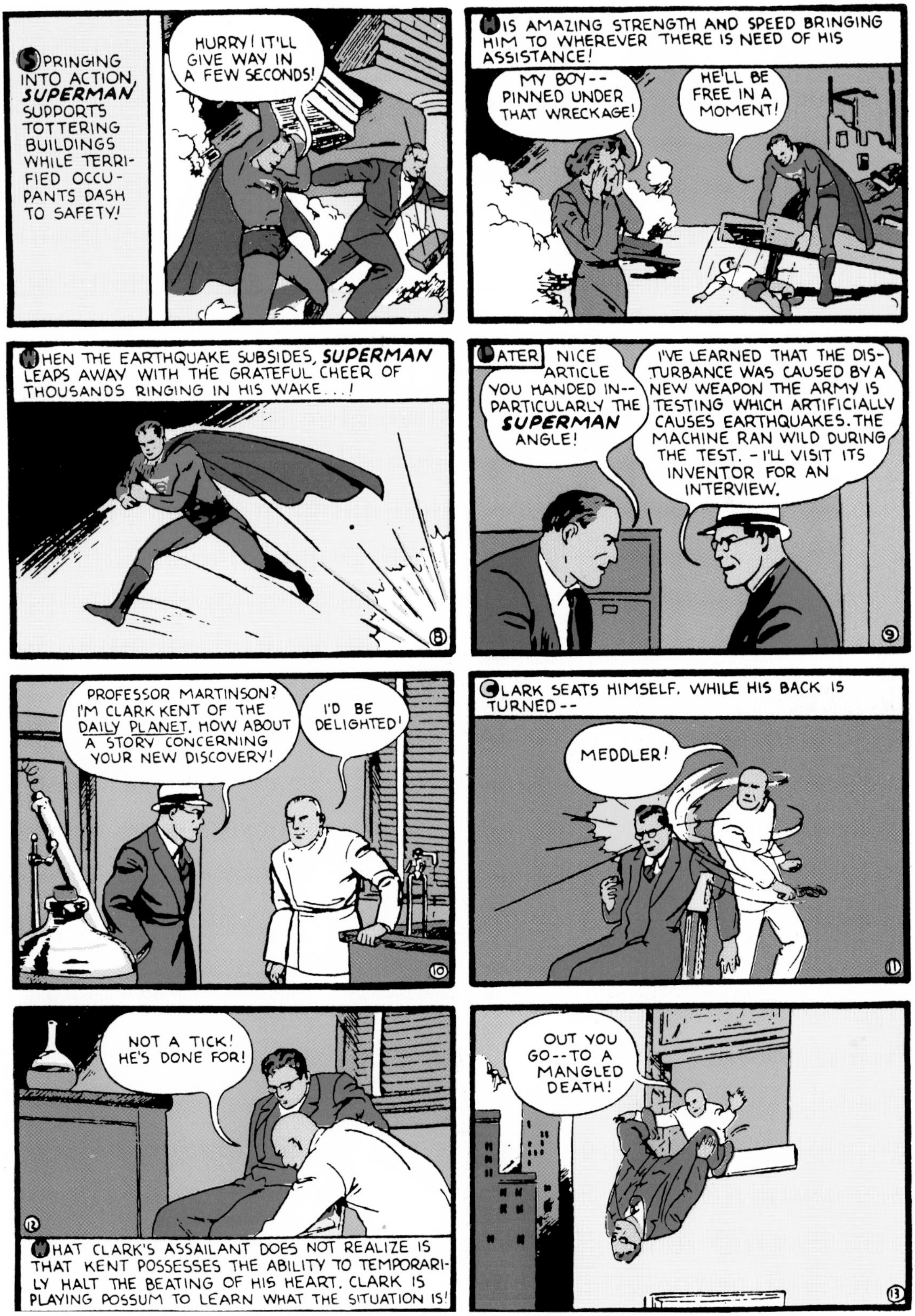
SPRINGING INTO ACTION, SUPERMAN SUPPORTS TOTTERING BUILDINGS WHILE TERRIFIED OCCUPANTS DASH TO SAFETY!
HURRY! IT'LL GIVE WAY IN A FEW SECONDS!
HIS AMAZING STRENGTH AND SPEED BRINGING HIM TO WHEREVER THERE IS NEED OF HIS ASSISTANCE!
MY BOY-- PINNED UNDER THAT WRECKAGE!
HE'LL BE FREE IN A MOMENT!
WHEN THE EARTHQUAKE SUBSIDES, SUPERMAN LEAPS AWAY WITH THE GRATEFUL CHEER OF THOUSANDS RINGING IN HIS WAKE...!
8
LATER
NICE ARTICLE YOU HANDED IN-- PARTICULARLY THE SUPERMAN ANGLE!
I'VE LEARNED THAT THE DISTURBANCE WAS CAUSED BY A NEW WEAPON THE ARMY IS TESTING WHICH ARTIFICIALLY CAUSES EARTHQUAKES. THE MACHINE RAN WILD DURING THE TEST. - I'LL VISIT ITS INVENTOR FOR AN INTERVIEW.
9
PROFESSOR MARTINSON? I'M CLARK KENT OF THE DAILY PLANET. HOW ABOUT A STORY CONCERNING YOUR NEW DISCOVERY!
I'D BE DELIGHTED!
10
CLARK SEATS HIMSELF. WHILE HIS BACK IS TURNED--
MEDDLER!
11
NOT A TICK! HE'S DONE FOR!
12
WHAT CLARK'S ASSAILANT DOES NOT REALIZE IS THAT KENT POSSESSES THE ABILITY TO TEMPORARILY HALT THE BEATING OF HIS HEART. CLARK IS PLAYING POSSUM TO LEARN WHAT THE SITUATION IS!
OUT YOU GO--TO A MANGLED DEATH!
13

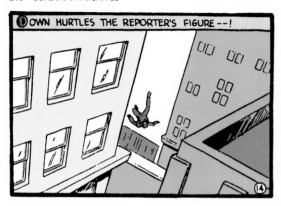

14. DOWN HURTLES THE REPORTER'S FIGURE--!

15. ABRUPTLY--OUT FLASHES ONE OF HIS HANDS, CLUTCHING THE SIDE OF THE SKYSCRAPER IN A STEELY GRIP, HALTING HIS PLUNGE!

TIME OUT!

16. IT TAKES BUT A FEW SECONDS TO REMOVE HIS OUTER GARMENTS....THEN HE COMMENCES TO CLIMB SWIFTLY BACK TOWARD THE LABORATORY ----AS *SUPERMAN!*

NOW IT'S *MY* TURN!

17. WITHIN THE LABORATORY---

A SNOOPING REPORTER INTERFERED WHILE I WAS GOING THRU THE PROFESSOR'S DESK. BUT I DISPOSED OF HIM!

SPLENDID! BUT IT'S UNFORTUNATE YOU COULDN'T FIND THE PLANS WE SEEK!

18. AT A DISTANT SPOT...

("--*SUPERMAN* EAVESDROPPING! I'LL ATTEND TO HIM!--")

19. SHORTLY AFTER--A WEIRD PLANE APPEARS IN THE SKY AND RELEASES A DEADLY BOMB DOWN TOWARD THE MAN OF STEEL'S FIGURE...

20. THIS HAS GOT TO STOP BEFORE BOMBS FALL ON INNOCENT PEOPLE IN THE STREET!

21. A FLIP OF *SUPERMAN'S* WRIST, AND THE BOMB HURTLES BACK TO ITS SOURCE, DESTROYING THE PLANE!

SWIFTLY *SUPERMAN* ENTERS THE LABORATORY--

NO SIGN OF THE MAN WHO PRETENDED TO BE MARTINSON!

SO! WE ENCOUNTER EACH OTHER ONCE MORE!

22

LUTHOR! THE MAD SCIENTIST WHO PLOTS TO DOMINATE THE EARTH!

PERMIT ME TO INTRODUCE PROFESSOR MARTINSON--A RETICENT INDIVIDUAL WHO REFUSES TO REVEAL TO ME THE DETAILS OF HIS DISCOVERY!

23

THEN YOU ADMIT FAILURE!

I DO NOT! IF MARTINSON PROVES UNCO-OPERATIVE, I MAY BE MORE FORTUNATE WITH THE ARMY ITSELF!

24

I WONDER WHAT LUTHOR HAS UP HIS SLEEVE? I'M SURE HE'S ABOUT TO SPRING SOMETHING!

25

THAT EVENING--WITHIN THE ARMY CAMP, *SUPERMAN* SEES ONE OF THE INVENTION'S GUARDS ATTACK THE OTHER.

THAT WAS SIMPLE!

26

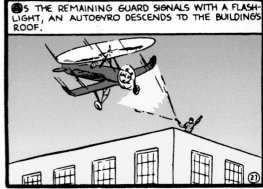

AS THE REMAINING GUARD SIGNALS WITH A FLASH-LIGHT, AN AUTOGYRO DESCENDS TO THE BUILDING'S ROOF.

27

BUT WHILE THE CONSPIRATORS ATTEMPT TO STEAL THE INVENTION, AN UNEXPECTED INTRUDER INTERFERES.

HEY!

OW-WW!

MUSN'T STEAL! IT'S NOT NICE!

28

GET BACK TO LUTHOR! AND WARN HIM TO ABANDON HIS ATTEMPTS TO GET THIS INVENTION!

WE'LL TELL HIM --ONLY DON'T HARM US!

29

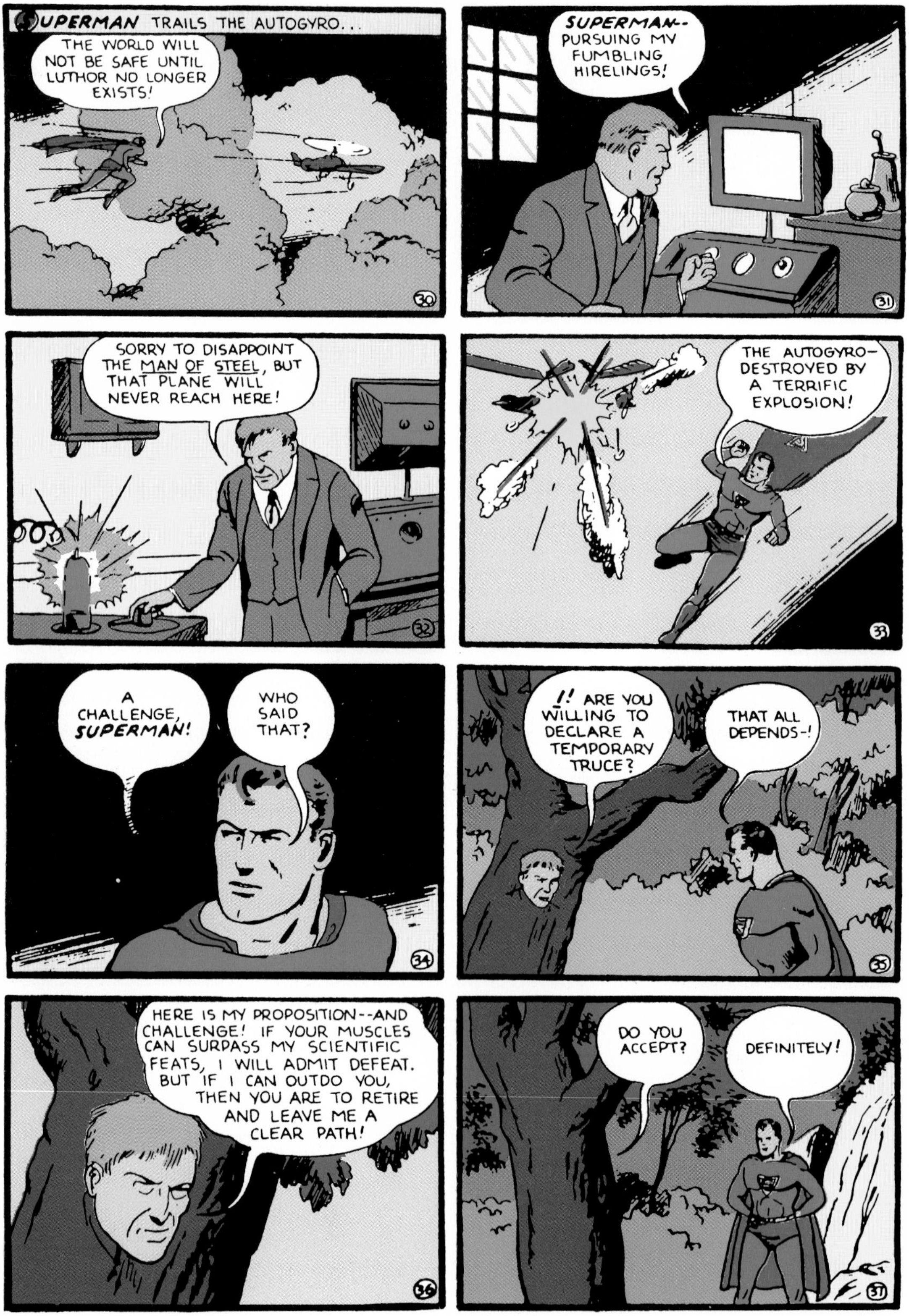
SUPERMAN TRAILS THE AUTOGYRO...
THE WORLD WILL NOT BE SAFE UNTIL LUTHOR NO LONGER EXISTS!
30
SUPERMAN-- PURSUING MY FUMBLING HIRELINGS!
31
SORRY TO DISAPPOINT THE MAN OF STEEL, BUT THAT PLANE WILL NEVER REACH HERE!
32
THE AUTOGYRO— DESTROYED BY A TERRIFIC EXPLOSION!
33
A CHALLENGE, SUPERMAN!
WHO SAID THAT?
34
!! ARE YOU WILLING TO DECLARE A TEMPORARY TRUCE?
THAT ALL DEPENDS-!
35
HERE IS MY PROPOSITION--AND CHALLENGE! IF YOUR MUSCLES CAN SURPASS MY SCIENTIFIC FEATS, I WILL ADMIT DEFEAT. BUT IF I CAN OUTDO YOU, THEN YOU ARE TO RETIRE AND LEAVE ME A CLEAR PATH!
36
DO YOU ACCEPT?
DEFINITELY!
37

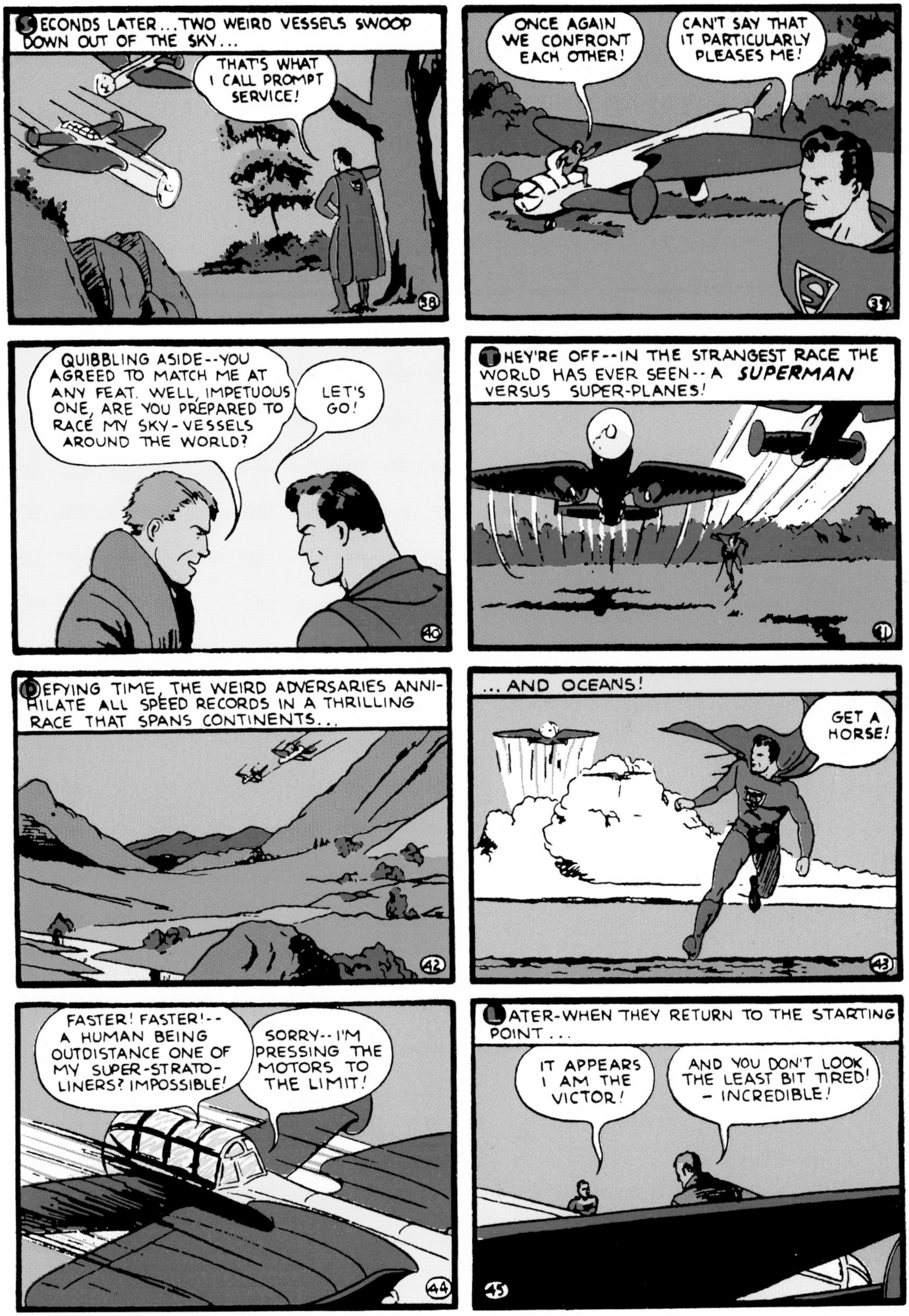
SECONDS LATER...TWO WEIRD VESSELS SWOOP DOWN OUT OF THE SKY...
THAT'S WHAT I CALL PROMPT SERVICE!
ONCE AGAIN WE CONFRONT EACH OTHER!
CAN'T SAY THAT IT PARTICULARLY PLEASES ME!
QUIBBLING ASIDE--YOU AGREED TO MATCH ME AT ANY FEAT. WELL, IMPETUOUS ONE, ARE YOU PREPARED TO RACE MY SKY-VESSELS AROUND THE WORLD?
LET'S GO!
THEY'RE OFF--IN THE STRANGEST RACE THE WORLD HAS EVER SEEN--A SUPERMAN VERSUS SUPER-PLANES!
DEFYING TIME, THE WEIRD ADVERSARIES ANNIHILATE ALL SPEED RECORDS IN A THRILLING RACE THAT SPANS CONTINENTS...
...AND OCEANS!
GET A HORSE!
FASTER! FASTER!--A HUMAN BEING OUTDISTANCE ONE OF MY SUPER-STRATO-LINERS? IMPOSSIBLE!
SORRY--I'M PRESSING THE MOTORS TO THE LIMIT!
LATER-WHEN THEY RETURN TO THE STARTING POINT...
IT APPEARS I AM THE VICTOR!
AND YOU DON'T LOOK THE LEAST BIT TIRED! - INCREDIBLE!

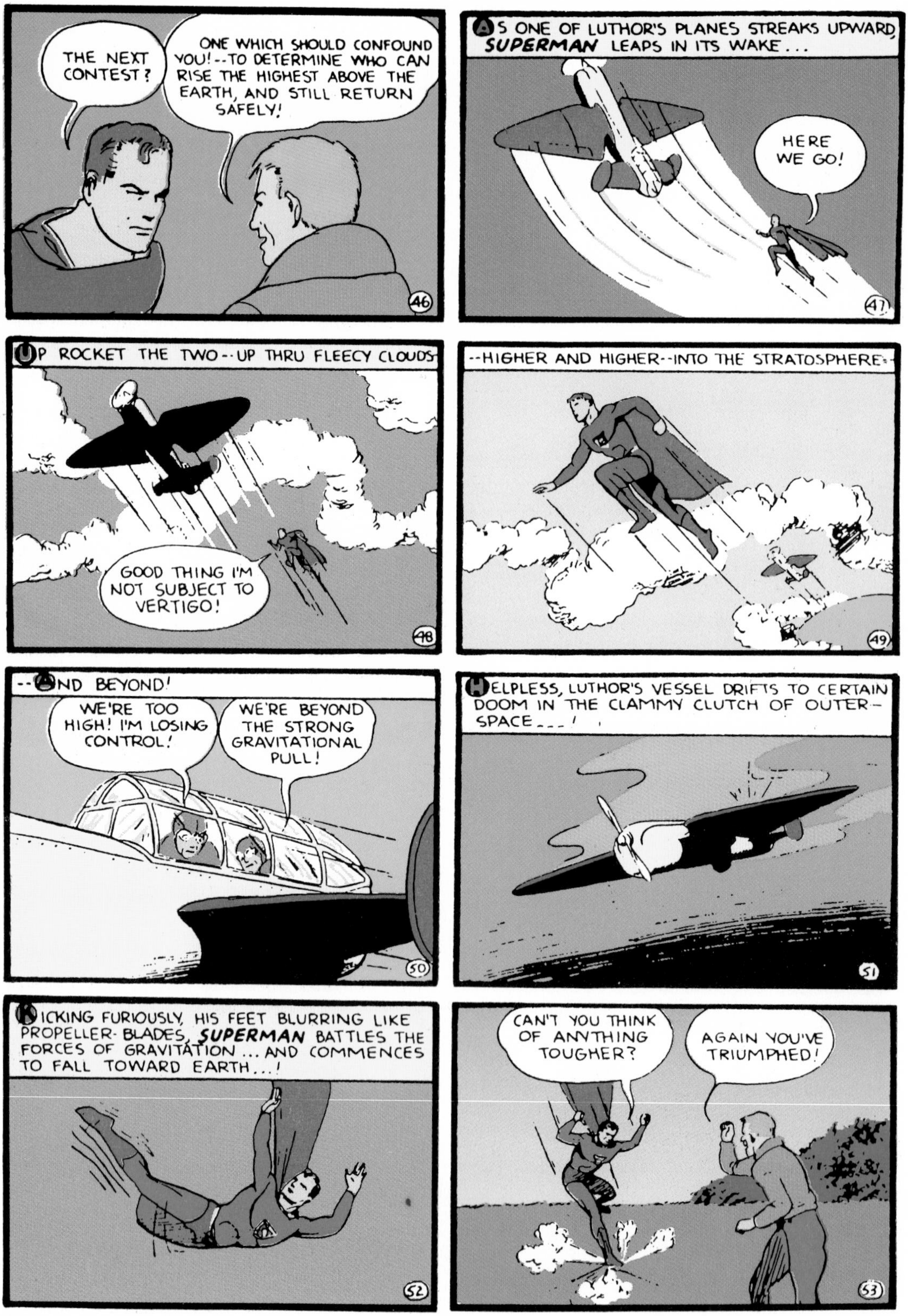
THE NEXT CONTEST?
ONE WHICH SHOULD CONFOUND YOU!--TO DETERMINE WHO CAN RISE THE HIGHEST ABOVE THE EARTH, AND STILL RETURN SAFELY!
46
AS ONE OF LUTHOR'S PLANES STREAKS UPWARD, SUPERMAN LEAPS IN ITS WAKE...
HERE WE GO!
47
UP ROCKET THE TWO--UP THRU FLEECY CLOUDS--
GOOD THING I'M NOT SUBJECT TO VERTIGO!
48
--HIGHER AND HIGHER--INTO THE STRATOSPHERE--
49
--AND BEYOND!
WE'RE TOO HIGH! I'M LOSING CONTROL!
WE'RE BEYOND THE STRONG GRAVITATIONAL PULL!
50
HELPLESS, LUTHOR'S VESSEL DRIFTS TO CERTAIN DOOM IN THE CLAMMY CLUTCH OF OUTER-SPACE...!
51
KICKING FURIOUSLY, HIS FEET BLURRING LIKE PROPELLER-BLADES, SUPERMAN BATTLES THE FORCES OF GRAVITATION ... AND COMMENCES TO FALL TOWARD EARTH...!
52
CAN'T YOU THINK OF ANYTHING TOUGHER?
AGAIN YOU'VE TRIUMPHED!
53

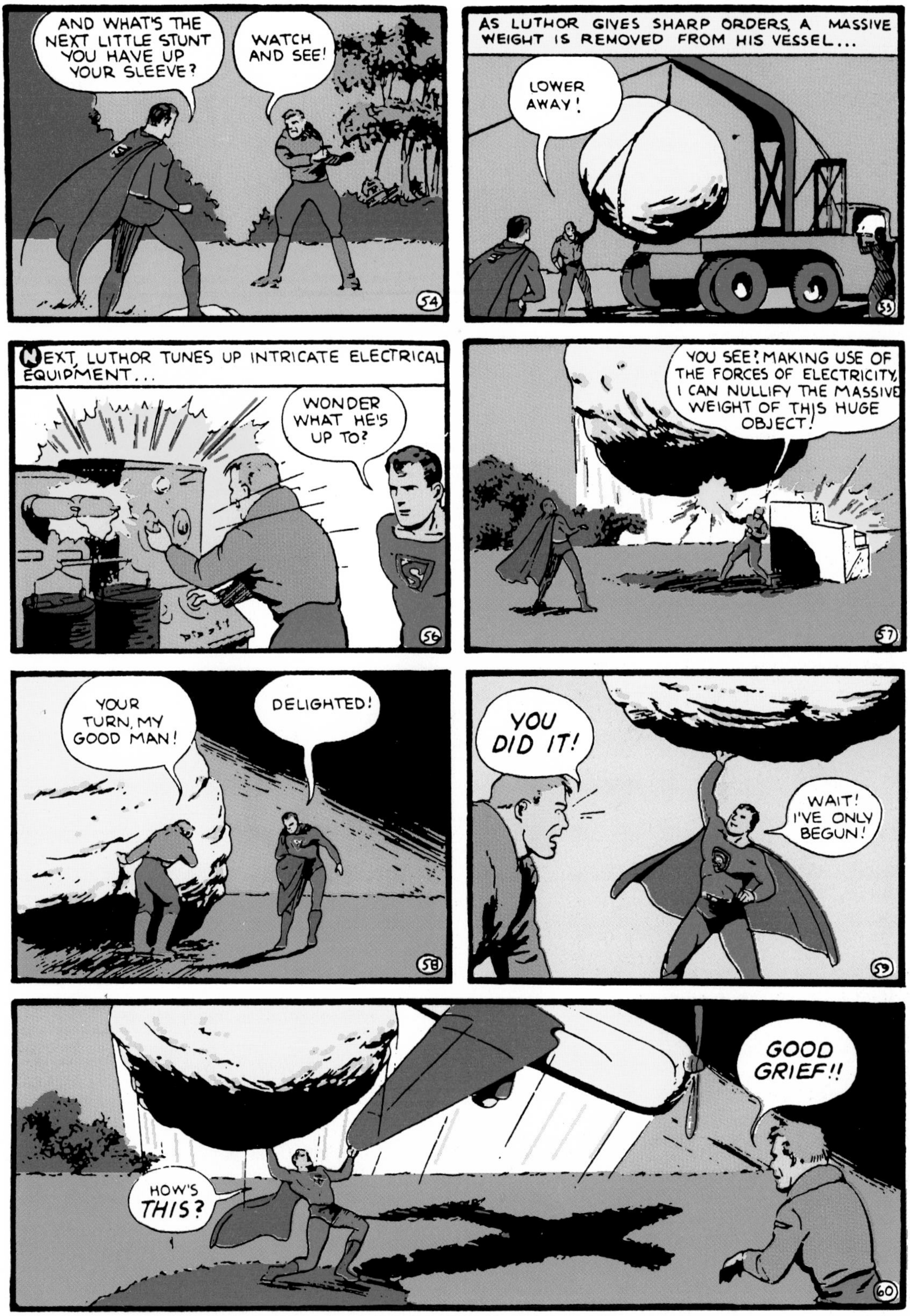
AND WHAT'S THE NEXT LITTLE STUNT YOU HAVE UP YOUR SLEEVE?
WATCH AND SEE!
54
AS LUTHOR GIVES SHARP ORDERS, A MASSIVE WEIGHT IS REMOVED FROM HIS VESSEL...
LOWER AWAY!
55
NEXT, LUTHOR TUNES UP INTRICATE ELECTRICAL EQUIPMENT...
WONDER WHAT HE'S UP TO?
56
YOU SEE? MAKING USE OF THE FORCES OF ELECTRICITY, I CAN NULLIFY THE MASSIVE WEIGHT OF THIS HUGE OBJECT!
57
YOUR TURN, MY GOOD MAN!
DELIGHTED!
58
YOU DID IT!
WAIT! I'VE ONLY BEGUN!
59
HOW'S THIS?
GOOD GRIEF!!
60

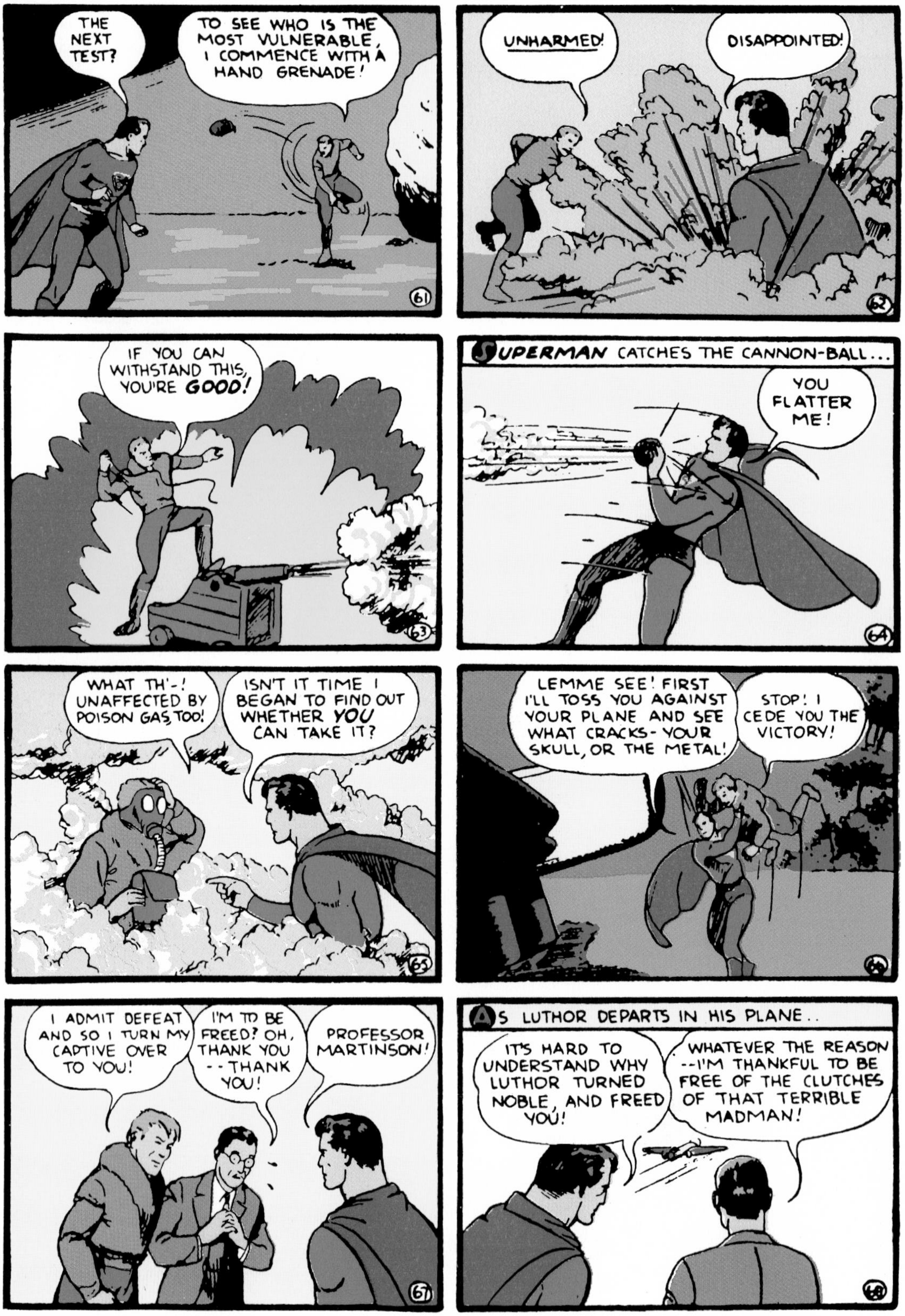
THE NEXT TEST?
TO SEE WHO IS THE MOST VULNERABLE, I COMMENCE WITH A HAND GRENADE!
61
UNHARMED!
DISAPPOINTED!
62
IF YOU CAN WITHSTAND THIS, YOU'RE GOOD!
63
SUPERMAN CATCHES THE CANNON-BALL...
YOU FLATTER ME!
64
WHAT TH'-! UNAFFECTED BY POISON GAS, TOO!
ISN'T IT TIME I BEGAN TO FIND OUT WHETHER YOU CAN TAKE IT?
65
LEMME SEE! FIRST I'LL TOSS YOU AGAINST YOUR PLANE AND SEE WHAT CRACKS - YOUR SKULL, OR THE METAL!
STOP! I CEDE YOU THE VICTORY!
I ADMIT DEFEAT AND SO I TURN MY CAPTIVE OVER TO YOU!
I'M TO BE FREED? OH, THANK YOU - - THANK YOU!
PROFESSOR MARTINSON!
67
AS LUTHOR DEPARTS IN HIS PLANE..
IT'S HARD TO UNDERSTAND WHY LUTHOR TURNED NOBLE, AND FREED YOU!
WHATEVER THE REASON --I'M THANKFUL TO BE FREE OF THE CLUTCHES OF THAT TERRIBLE MADMAN!
68

SEIZING MARTINSON, **SUPERMAN** LEAPS BACK TOWARD THE CITY...

I--I MUST BE DREAMING!

WITH YOUR EYES WIDE OPEN?

LATER--WITHIN MARTINSON'S LABORATORY...

SOMETIMES I'M SORRY I EVER INVENTED THE THING!

ATTENTION! **NEWS FLASH!**

QUIET-- LISTEN!

STARTLING NEWS HAS JUST COME OVER THE WIRE! THE ARMY'S MYSTERIOUS NEW WEAPON HAS BEEN STOLEN! EVERY EFFORT IS BEING MADE TO APPREHEND THE THIEVES!

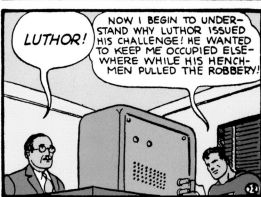

LUTHOR!

NOW I BEGIN TO UNDER- STAND WHY LUTHOR ISSUED HIS CHALLENGE! HE WANTED TO KEEP ME OCCUPIED ELSE- WHERE WHILE HIS HENCH- MEN PULLED THE ROBBERY!

IF THE INVENTION COULD ONLY BE DESTROYED! IT'S SO COMPLEX THAT NO ONE BUT MYSELF COULD BUILD ANOTHER!

FELLA-YOU'VE GIVEN ME AN IDEA!

TELL ME, QUICK! DO YOU HAVE ANY IDEA WHERE LUTHOR HELD YOU DURING YOUR CAPTIVITY?

I'M CERTAIN IT WAS IN **SATAN'S** CANYON!

ANOTHER NEWS FLASH! A PORTION OF THE CITY WAS JUST SHAKEN BY AN EARTHQUAKE. A MYSTER- IOUS CHARACTER NAMED **LUTHOR** DEMANDS THE CITY'S SURRENDER!

WAIT!

CAN'T! --NOT NOW!

I'VE GOT TO ATTEND TO LUTHOR--AND **FAST!**

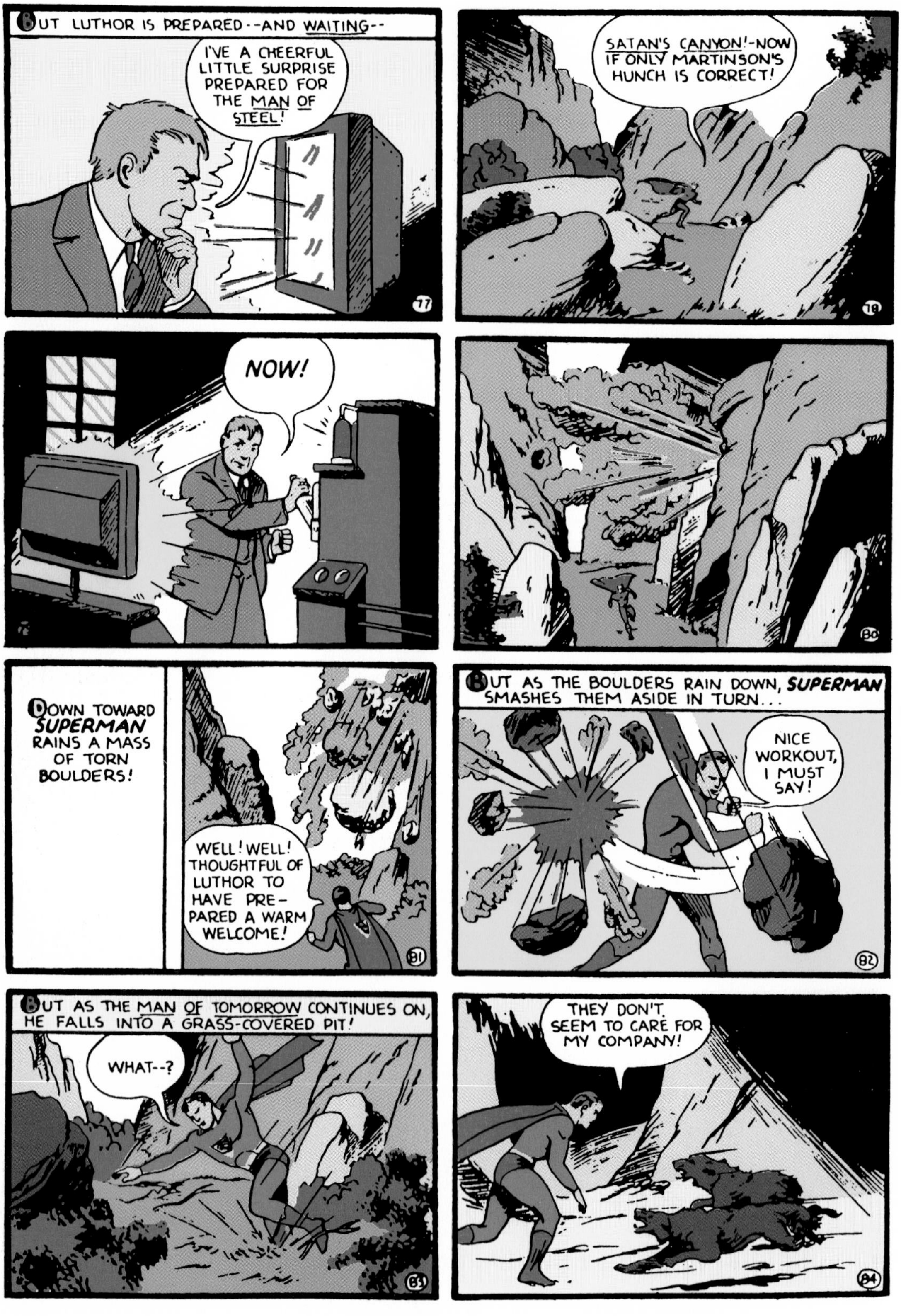
BUT LUTHOR IS PREPARED--AND WAITING--
I'VE A CHEERFUL LITTLE SURPRISE PREPARED FOR THE MAN OF STEEL!
77
SATAN'S CANYON!-NOW IF ONLY MARTINSON'S HUNCH IS CORRECT!
78
NOW!
80
DOWN TOWARD SUPERMAN RAINS A MASS OF TORN BOULDERS!
WELL! WELL! THOUGHTFUL OF LUTHOR TO HAVE PRE-PARED A WARM WELCOME!
81
BUT AS THE BOULDERS RAIN DOWN, SUPERMAN SMASHES THEM ASIDE IN TURN...
NICE WORKOUT, I MUST SAY!
82
BUT AS THE MAN OF TOMORROW CONTINUES ON, HE FALLS INTO A GRASS-COVERED PIT!
WHAT--?
83
THEY DON'T SEEM TO CARE FOR MY COMPANY!
84

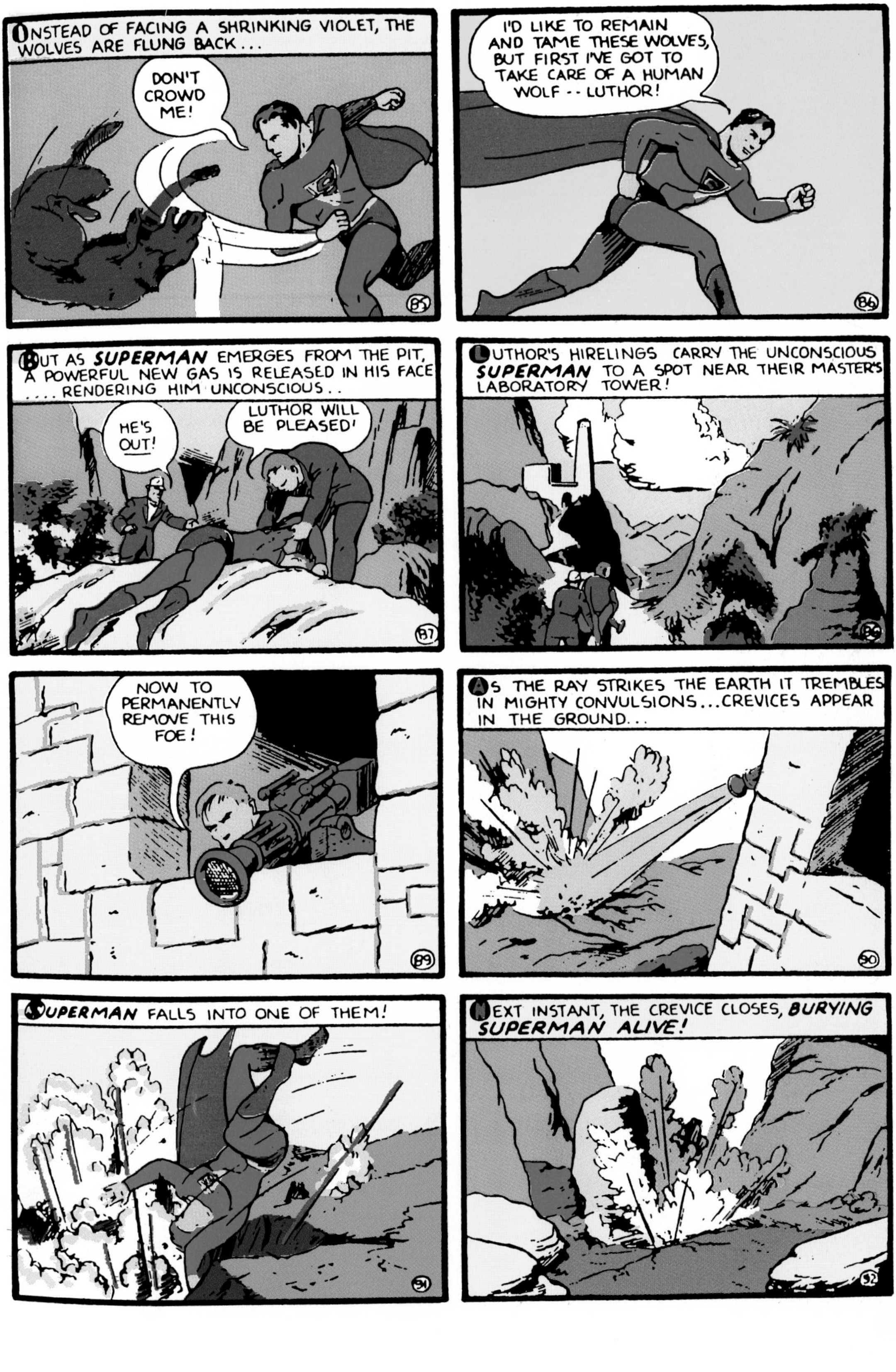
INSTEAD OF FACING A SHRINKING VIOLET, THE WOLVES ARE FLUNG BACK...
DON'T CROWD ME!
I'D LIKE TO REMAIN AND TAME THESE WOLVES, BUT FIRST I'VE GOT TO TAKE CARE OF A HUMAN WOLF -- LUTHOR!
BUT AS SUPERMAN EMERGES FROM THE PIT, A POWERFUL NEW GAS IS RELEASED IN HIS FACE .... RENDERING HIM UNCONSCIOUS..
HE'S OUT!
LUTHOR WILL BE PLEASED!
LUTHOR'S HIRELINGS CARRY THE UNCONSCIOUS SUPERMAN TO A SPOT NEAR THEIR MASTER'S LABORATORY TOWER!
NOW TO PERMANENTLY REMOVE THIS FOE!
AS THE RAY STRIKES THE EARTH IT TREMBLES IN MIGHTY CONVULSIONS...CREVICES APPEAR IN THE GROUND...
SUPERMAN FALLS INTO ONE OF THEM!
NEXT INSTANT, THE CREVICE CLOSES, BURYING SUPERMAN ALIVE!

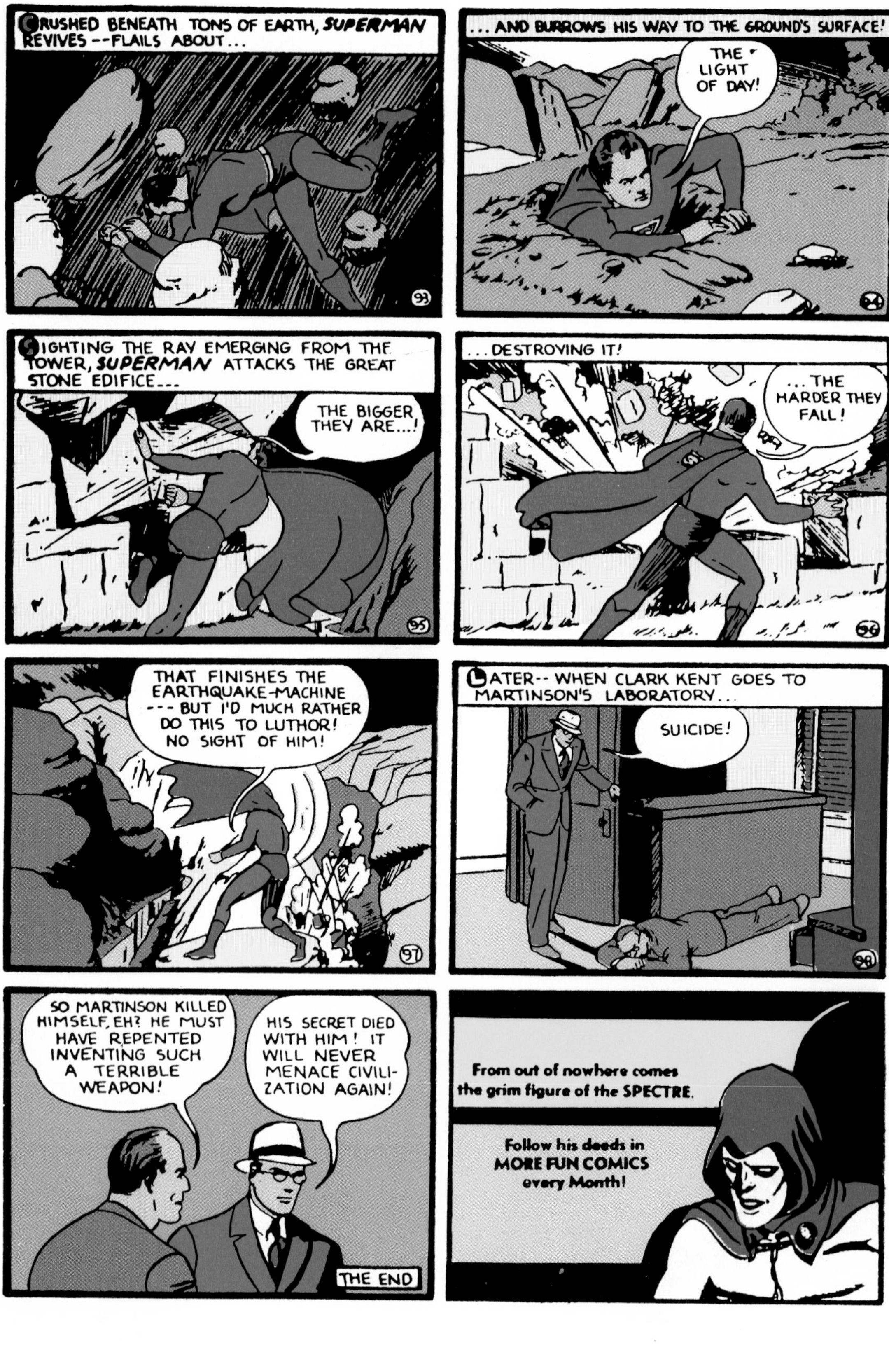
CRUSHED BENEATH TONS OF EARTH, SUPERMAN REVIVES --FLAILS ABOUT...
...AND BURROWS HIS WAY TO THE GROUND'S SURFACE!
THE LIGHT OF DAY!
SIGHTING THE RAY EMERGING FROM THE TOWER, SUPERMAN ATTACKS THE GREAT STONE EDIFICE...
THE BIGGER THEY ARE...!
...DESTROYING IT!
...THE HARDER THEY FALL!
THAT FINISHES THE EARTHQUAKE-MACHINE --- BUT I'D MUCH RATHER DO THIS TO LUTHOR! NO SIGHT OF HIM!
LATER-- WHEN CLARK KENT GOES TO MARTINSON'S LABORATORY...
SUICIDE!
SO MARTINSON KILLED HIMSELF, EH? HE MUST HAVE REPENTED INVENTING SUCH A TERRIBLE WEAPON!
HIS SECRET DIED WITH HIM! IT WILL NEVER MENACE CIVILIZATION AGAIN!
THE END
From out of nowhere comes the grim figure of the SPECTRE.
Follow his deeds in MORE FUN COMICS every Month!

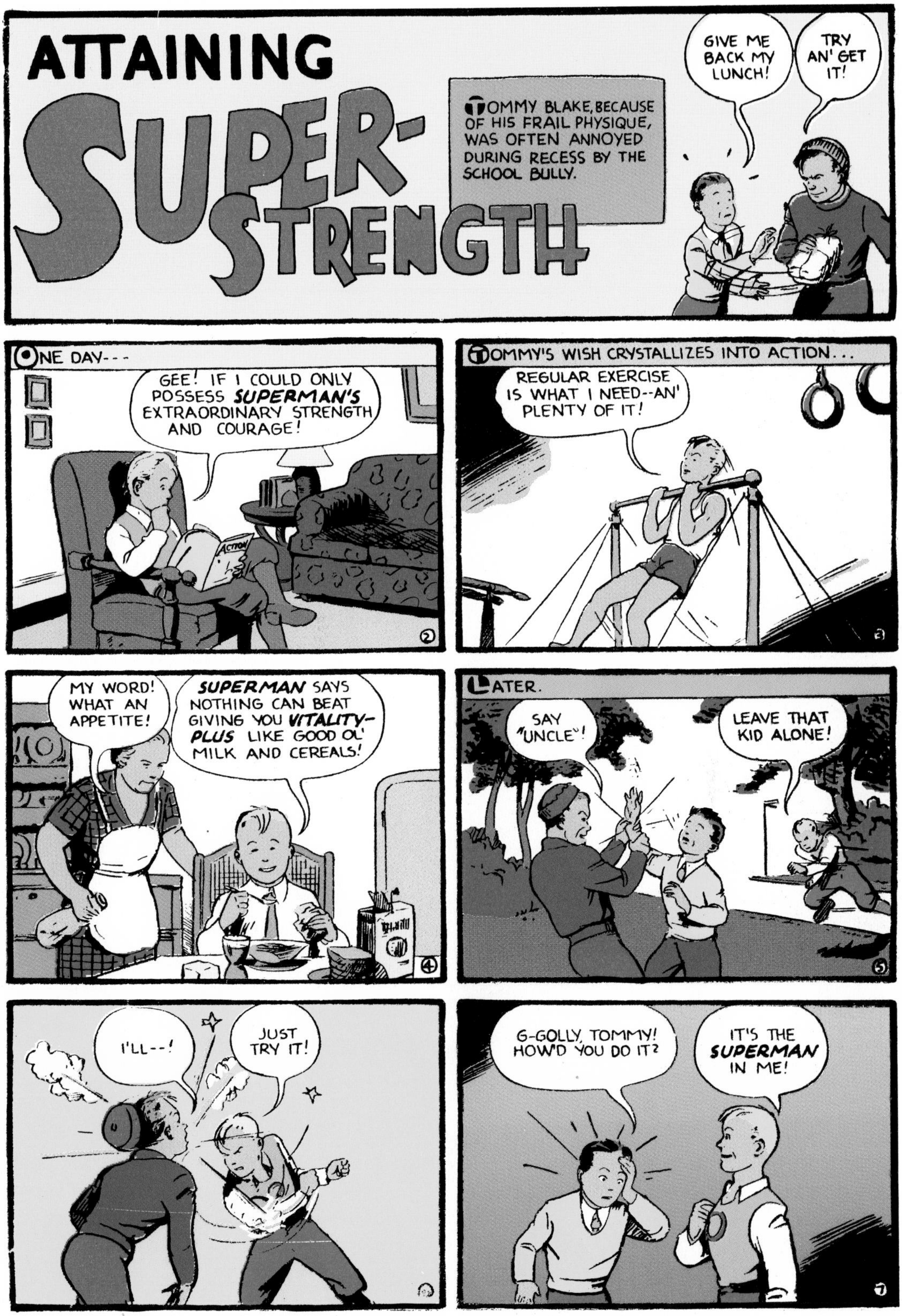
ATTAINING SUPER-STRENGTH
TOMMY BLAKE, BECAUSE OF HIS FRAIL PHYSIQUE, WAS OFTEN ANNOYED DURING RECESS BY THE SCHOOL BULLY.
GIVE ME BACK MY LUNCH!
TRY AN' GET IT!
ONE DAY---
GEE! IF I COULD ONLY POSSESS SUPERMAN'S EXTRAORDINARY STRENGTH AND COURAGE!
ACTION
TOMMY'S WISH CRYSTALLIZES INTO ACTION...
REGULAR EXERCISE IS WHAT I NEED--AN' PLENTY OF IT!
MY WORD! WHAT AN APPETITE!
SUPERMAN SAYS NOTHING CAN BEAT GIVING YOU VITALITY-PLUS LIKE GOOD OL' MILK AND CEREALS!
LATER.
SAY "UNCLE"!
LEAVE THAT KID ALONE!
I'LL--!
JUST TRY IT!
G-GOLLY, TOMMY! HOW'D YOU DO IT?
IT'S THE SUPERMAN IN ME!

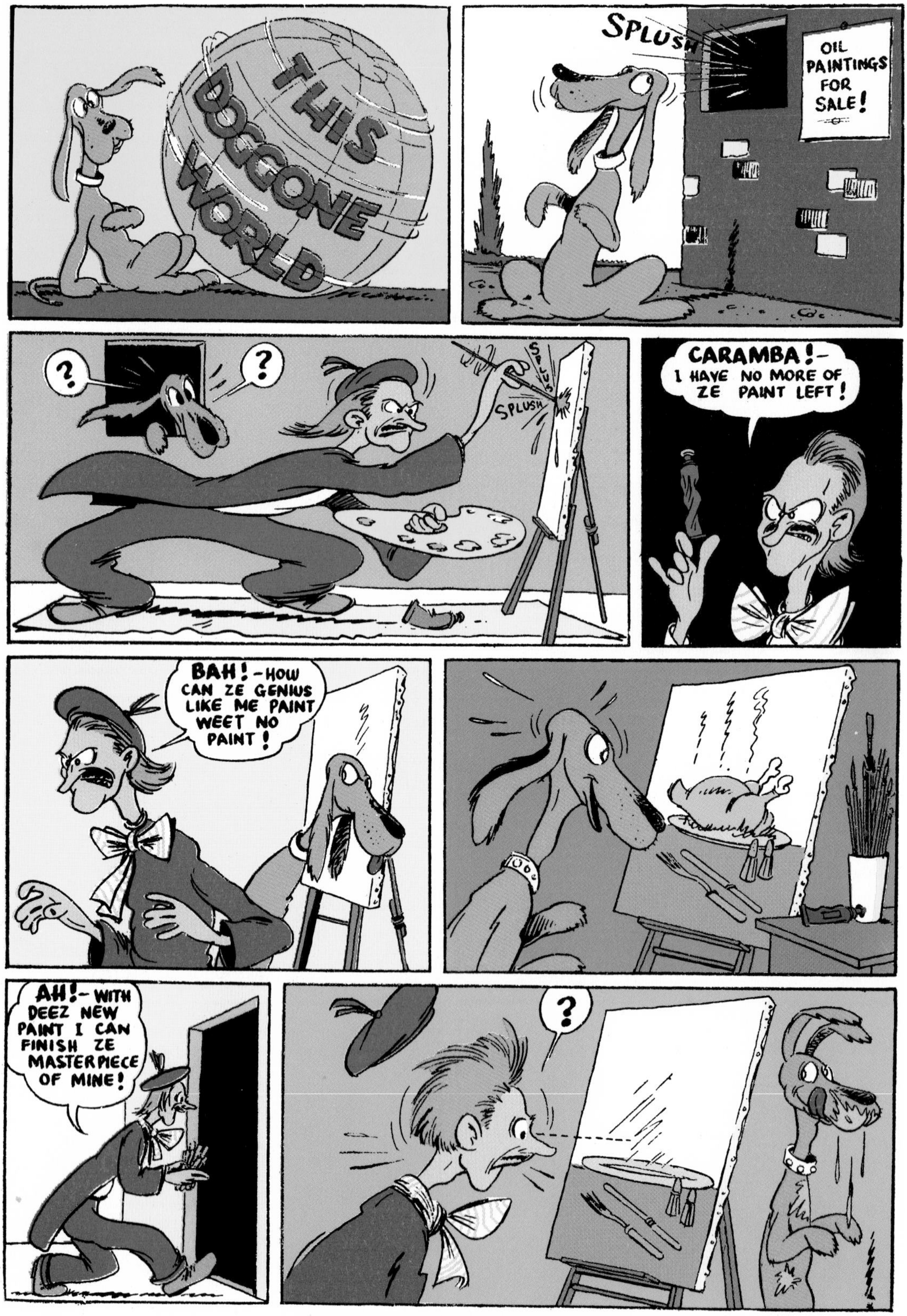
THIS DOGGONE WORLD
SPLUSH
OIL PAINTINGS FOR SALE!
?
?
SPLUSH
SPLUSH
CARAMBA!- I HAVE NO MORE OF ZE PAINT LEFT!
BAH!-HOW CAN ZE GENIUS LIKE ME PAINT WEET NO PAINT!
AH!- WITH DEEZ NEW PAINT I CAN FINISH ZE MASTERPIECE OF MINE!
?

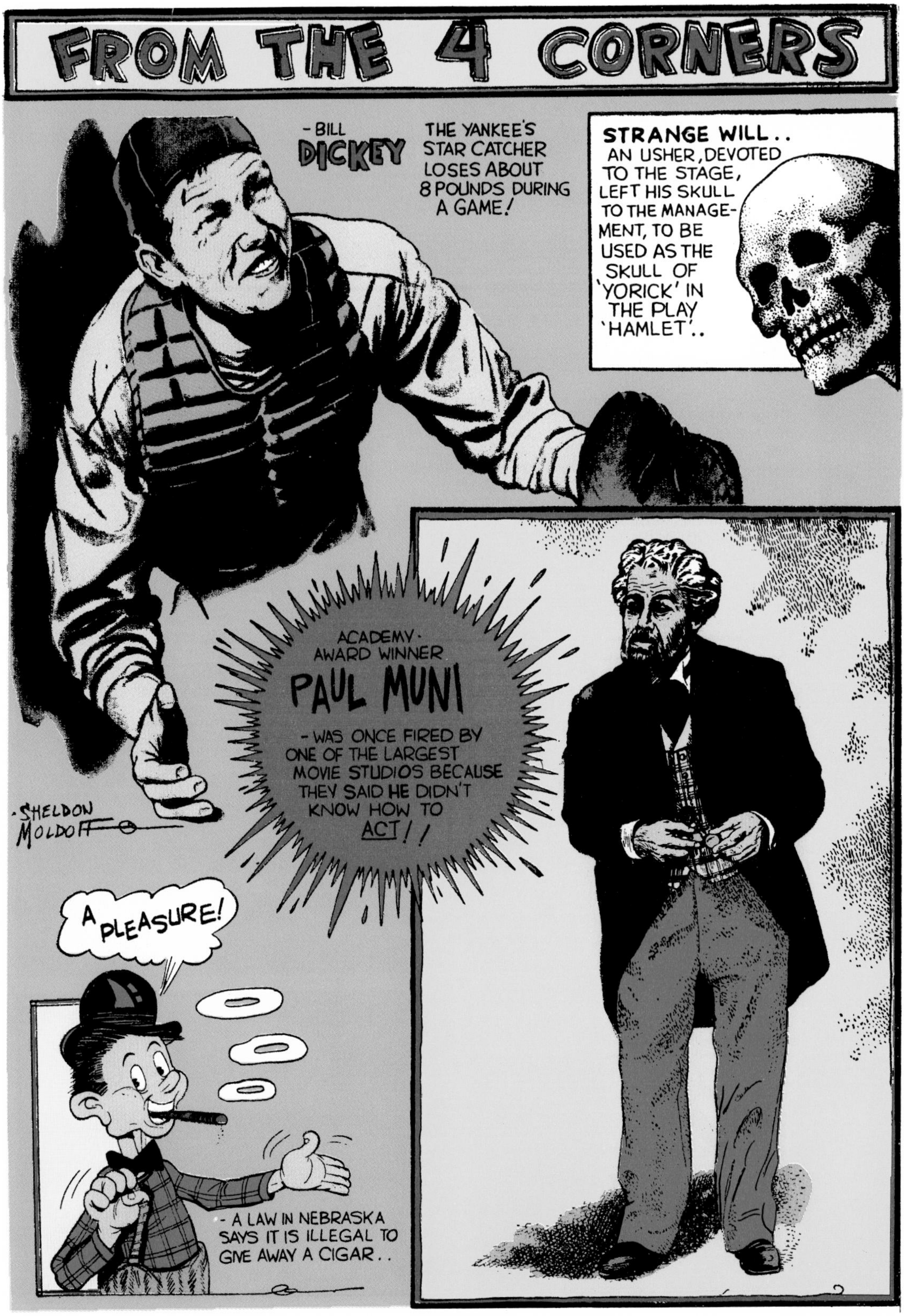
FROM THE 4 CORNERS
-BILL DICKEY
THE YANKEE'S STAR CATCHER LOSES ABOUT 8 POUNDS DURING A GAME!
STRANGE WILL..
AN USHER, DEVOTED TO THE STAGE, LEFT HIS SKULL TO THE MANAGEMENT, TO BE USED AS THE SKULL OF 'YORICK' IN THE PLAY 'HAMLET'..
ACADEMY AWARD WINNER
PAUL MUNI
-WAS ONCE FIRED BY ONE OF THE LARGEST MOVIE STUDIOS BECAUSE THEY SAID HE DIDN'T KNOW HOW TO ACT!!
-SHELDON MOLDOFF
A PLEASURE!
-A LAW IN NEBRASKA SAYS IT IS ILLEGAL TO GIVE AWAY A CIGAR..

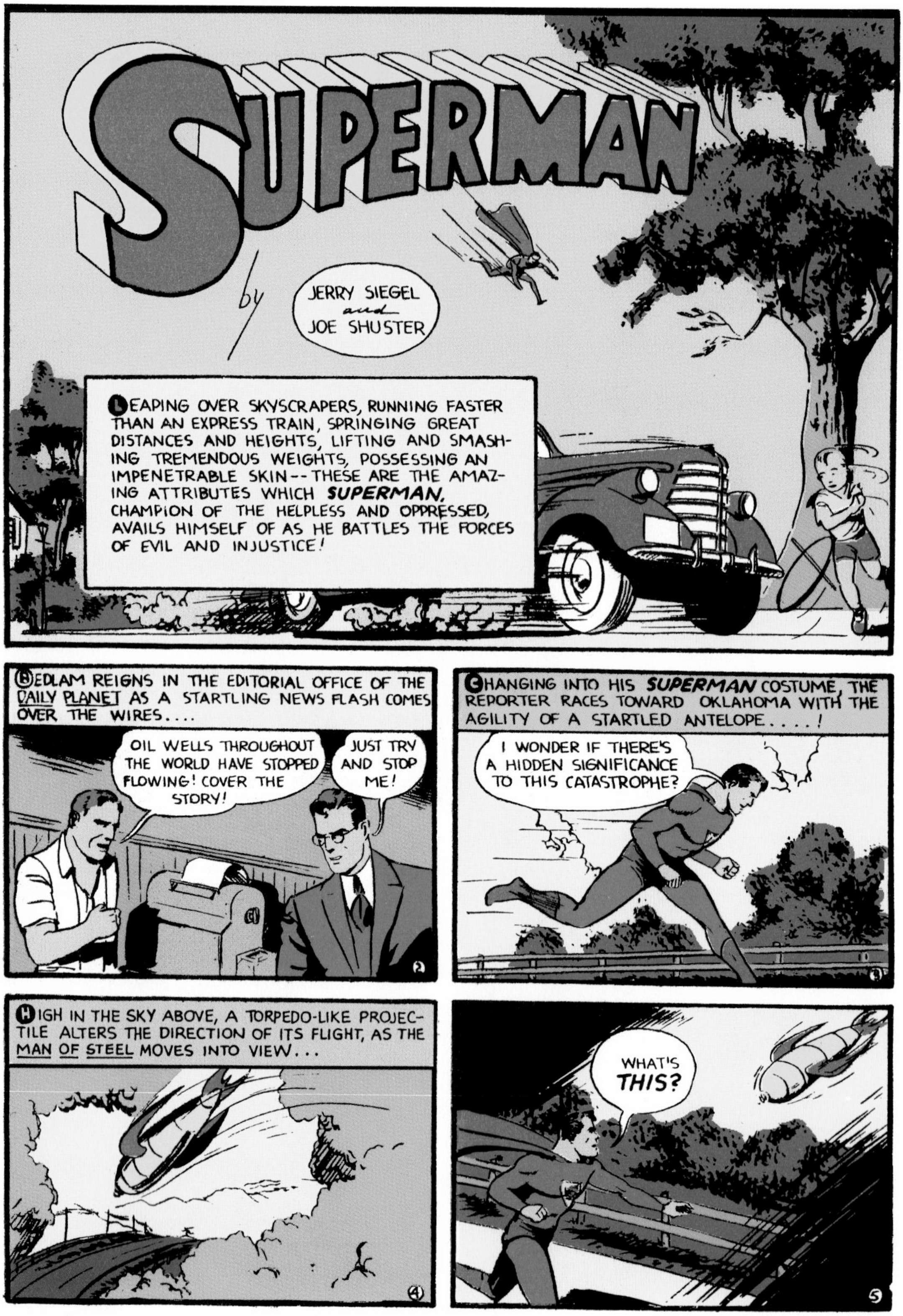
SUPERMAN
by
JERRY SIEGEL and JOE SHUSTER
LEAPING OVER SKYSCRAPERS, RUNNING FASTER THAN AN EXPRESS TRAIN, SPRINGING GREAT DISTANCES AND HEIGHTS, LIFTING AND SMASHING TREMENDOUS WEIGHTS, POSSESSING AN IMPENETRABLE SKIN--THESE ARE THE AMAZING ATTRIBUTES WHICH SUPERMAN, CHAMPION OF THE HELPLESS AND OPPRESSED, AVAILS HIMSELF OF AS HE BATTLES THE FORCES OF EVIL AND INJUSTICE!
BEDLAM REIGNS IN THE EDITORIAL OFFICE OF THE DAILY PLANET AS A STARTLING NEWS FLASH COMES OVER THE WIRES....
OIL WELLS THROUGHOUT THE WORLD HAVE STOPPED FLOWING! COVER THE STORY!
JUST TRY AND STOP ME!
CHANGING INTO HIS SUPERMAN COSTUME, THE REPORTER RACES TOWARD OKLAHOMA WITH THE AGILITY OF A STARTLED ANTELOPE....!
I WONDER IF THERE'S A HIDDEN SIGNIFICANCE TO THIS CATASTROPHE?
HIGH IN THE SKY ABOVE, A TORPEDO-LIKE PROJECTILE ALTERS THE DIRECTION OF ITS FLIGHT, AS THE MAN OF STEEL MOVES INTO VIEW...
WHAT'S THIS?

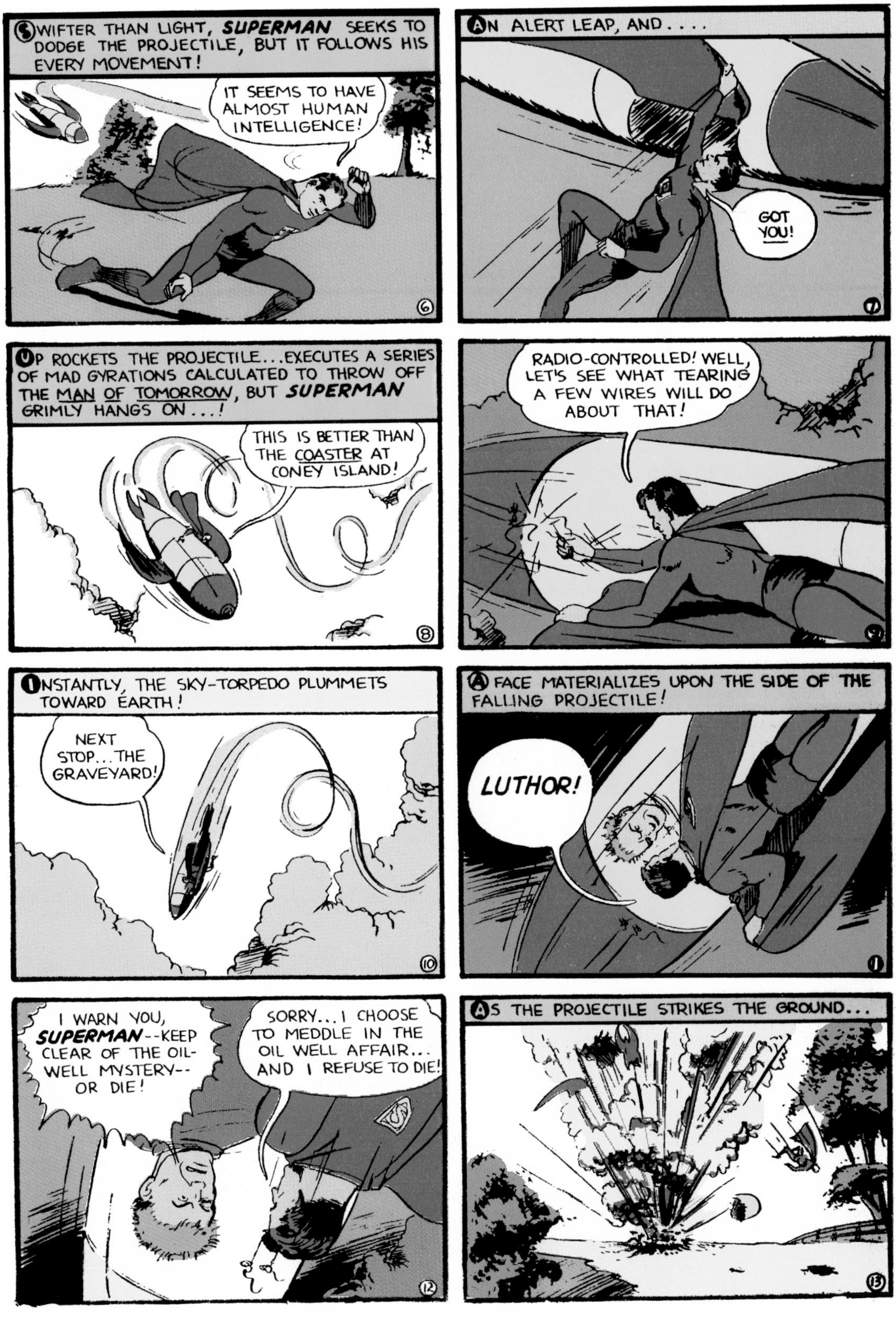
SWIFTER THAN LIGHT, SUPERMAN SEEKS TO DODGE THE PROJECTILE, BUT IT FOLLOWS HIS EVERY MOVEMENT!
IT SEEMS TO HAVE ALMOST HUMAN INTELLIGENCE!
AN ALERT LEAP, AND....
GOT YOU!
UP ROCKETS THE PROJECTILE...EXECUTES A SERIES OF MAD GYRATIONS CALCULATED TO THROW OFF THE MAN OF TOMORROW, BUT SUPERMAN GRIMLY HANGS ON...!
THIS IS BETTER THAN THE COASTER AT CONEY ISLAND!
RADIO-CONTROLLED! WELL, LET'S SEE WHAT TEARING A FEW WIRES WILL DO ABOUT THAT!
INSTANTLY, THE SKY-TORPEDO PLUMMETS TOWARD EARTH!
NEXT STOP...THE GRAVEYARD!
A FACE MATERIALIZES UPON THE SIDE OF THE FALLING PROJECTILE!
LUTHOR!
I WARN YOU, SUPERMAN--KEEP CLEAR OF THE OIL-WELL MYSTERY--OR DIE!
SORRY...I CHOOSE TO MEDDLE IN THE OIL WELL AFFAIR... AND I REFUSE TO DIE!
AS THE PROJECTILE STRIKES THE GROUND...

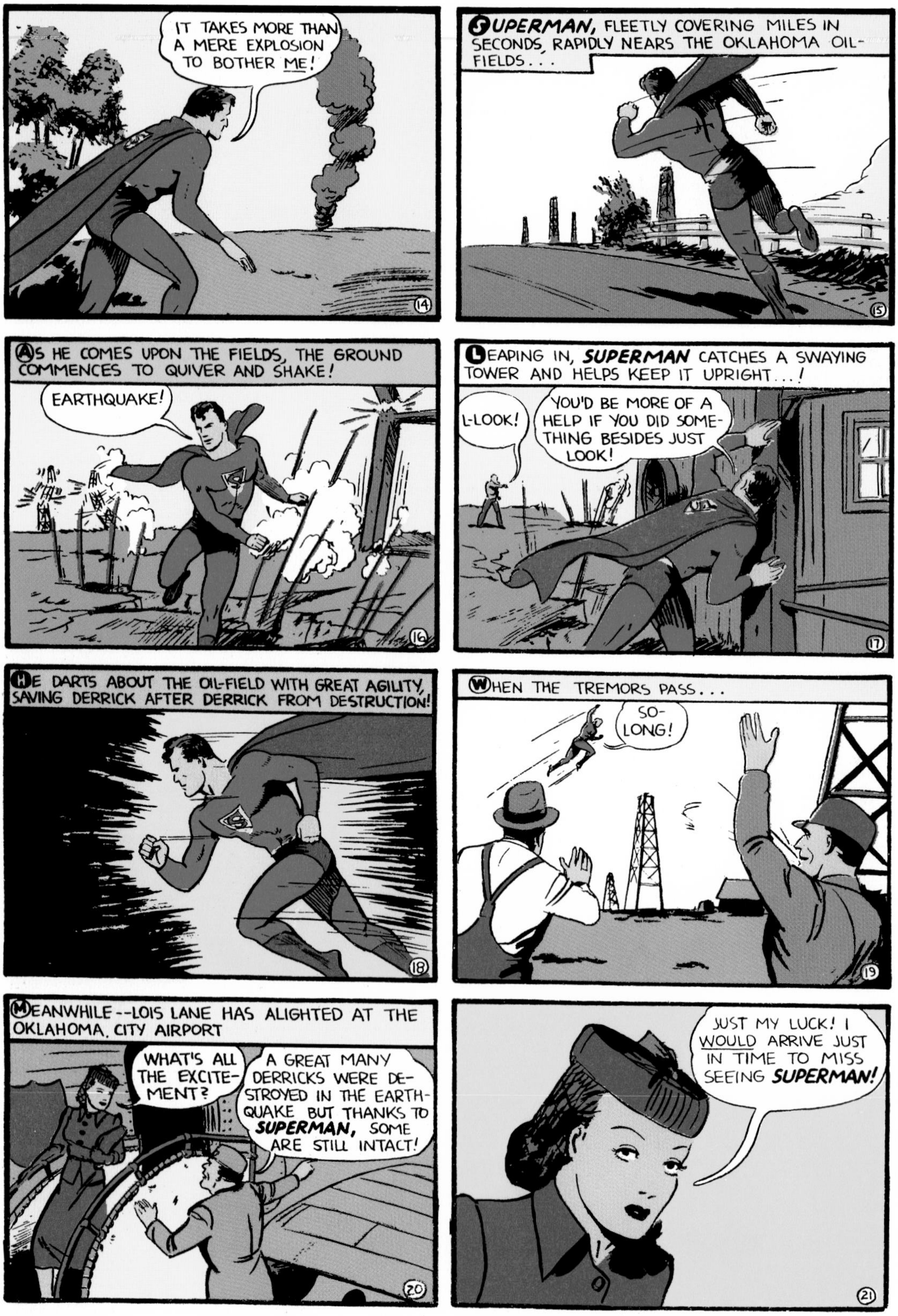
IT TAKES MORE THAN A MERE EXPLOSION TO BOTHER ME!
14
SUPERMAN, FLEETLY COVERING MILES IN SECONDS, RAPIDLY NEARS THE OKLAHOMA OIL-FIELDS . . .
15
AS HE COMES UPON THE FIELDS, THE GROUND COMMENCES TO QUIVER AND SHAKE!
EARTHQUAKE!
16
LEAPING IN, SUPERMAN CATCHES A SWAYING TOWER AND HELPS KEEP IT UPRIGHT . . . !
L-LOOK!
YOU'D BE MORE OF A HELP IF YOU DID SOME-THING BESIDES JUST LOOK!
17
HE DARTS ABOUT THE OIL-FIELD WITH GREAT AGILITY, SAVING DERRICK AFTER DERRICK FROM DESTRUCTION!
18
WHEN THE TREMORS PASS . . .
SO-LONG!
19
MEANWHILE--LOIS LANE HAS ALIGHTED AT THE OKLAHOMA CITY AIRPORT
WHAT'S ALL THE EXCITE-MENT?
A GREAT MANY DERRICKS WERE DE-STROYED IN THE EARTH-QUAKE BUT THANKS TO SUPERMAN, SOME ARE STILL INTACT!
20
JUST MY LUCK! I WOULD ARRIVE JUST IN TIME TO MISS SEEING SUPERMAN!
21

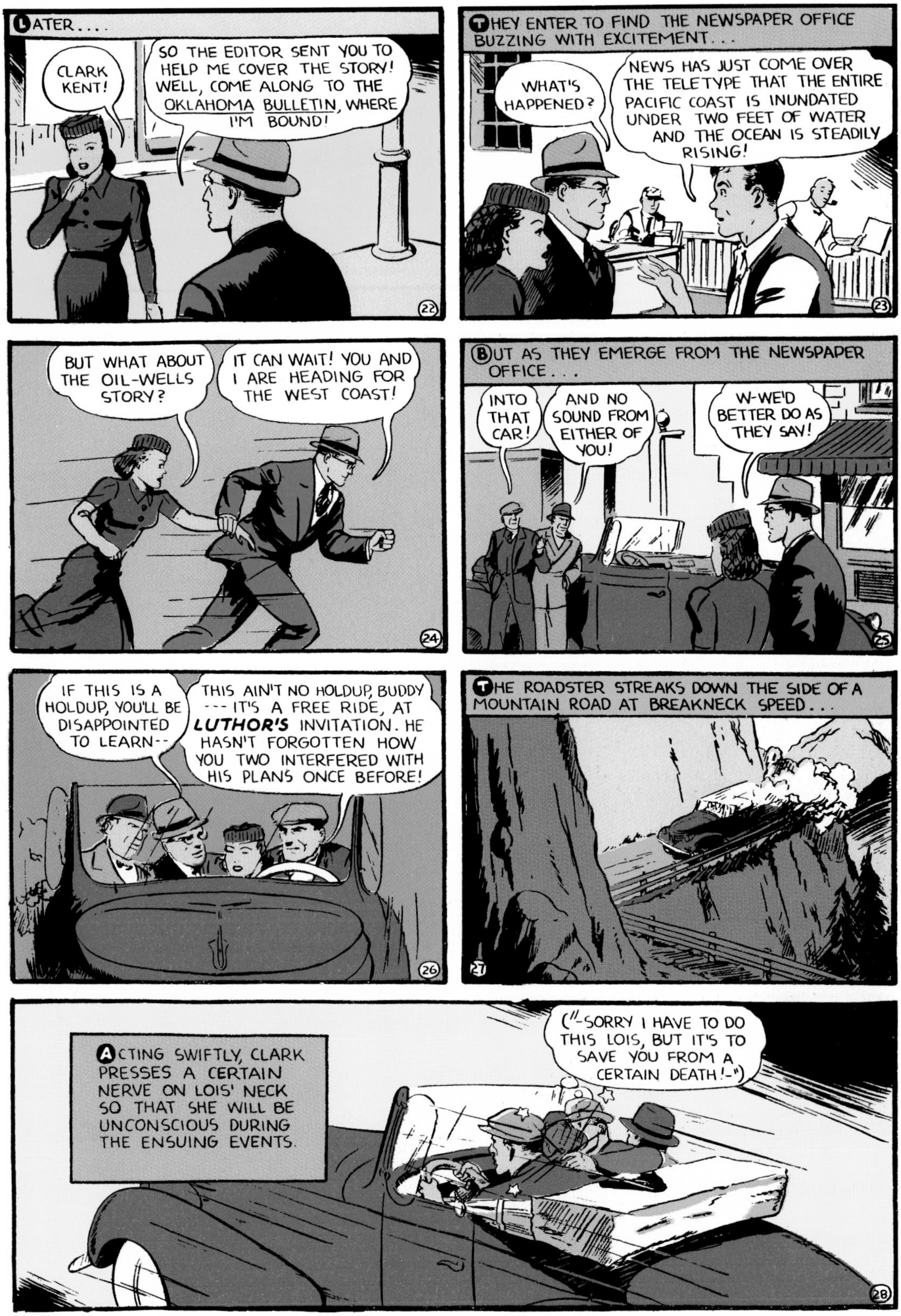
LATER....
CLARK KENT!
SO THE EDITOR SENT YOU TO HELP ME COVER THE STORY! WELL, COME ALONG TO THE OKLAHOMA BULLETIN, WHERE I'M BOUND!
22
THEY ENTER TO FIND THE NEWSPAPER OFFICE BUZZING WITH EXCITEMENT...
WHAT'S HAPPENED?
NEWS HAS JUST COME OVER THE TELETYPE THAT THE ENTIRE PACIFIC COAST IS INUNDATED UNDER TWO FEET OF WATER AND THE OCEAN IS STEADILY RISING!
23
BUT WHAT ABOUT THE OIL-WELLS STORY?
IT CAN WAIT! YOU AND I ARE HEADING FOR THE WEST COAST!
24
BUT AS THEY EMERGE FROM THE NEWSPAPER OFFICE...
INTO THAT CAR!
AND NO SOUND FROM EITHER OF YOU!
W-WE'D BETTER DO AS THEY SAY!
25
IF THIS IS A HOLDUP, YOU'LL BE DISAPPOINTED TO LEARN--
THIS AIN'T NO HOLDUP, BUDDY --- IT'S A FREE RIDE, AT LUTHOR'S INVITATION. HE HASN'T FORGOTTEN HOW YOU TWO INTERFERED WITH HIS PLANS ONCE BEFORE!
26
THE ROADSTER STREAKS DOWN THE SIDE OF A MOUNTAIN ROAD AT BREAKNECK SPEED...
27
ACTING SWIFTLY, CLARK PRESSES A CERTAIN NERVE ON LOIS' NECK SO THAT SHE WILL BE UNCONSCIOUS DURING THE ENSUING EVENTS.
("-SORRY I HAVE TO DO THIS LOIS, BUT IT'S TO SAVE YOU FROM A CERTAIN DEATH!-")
28

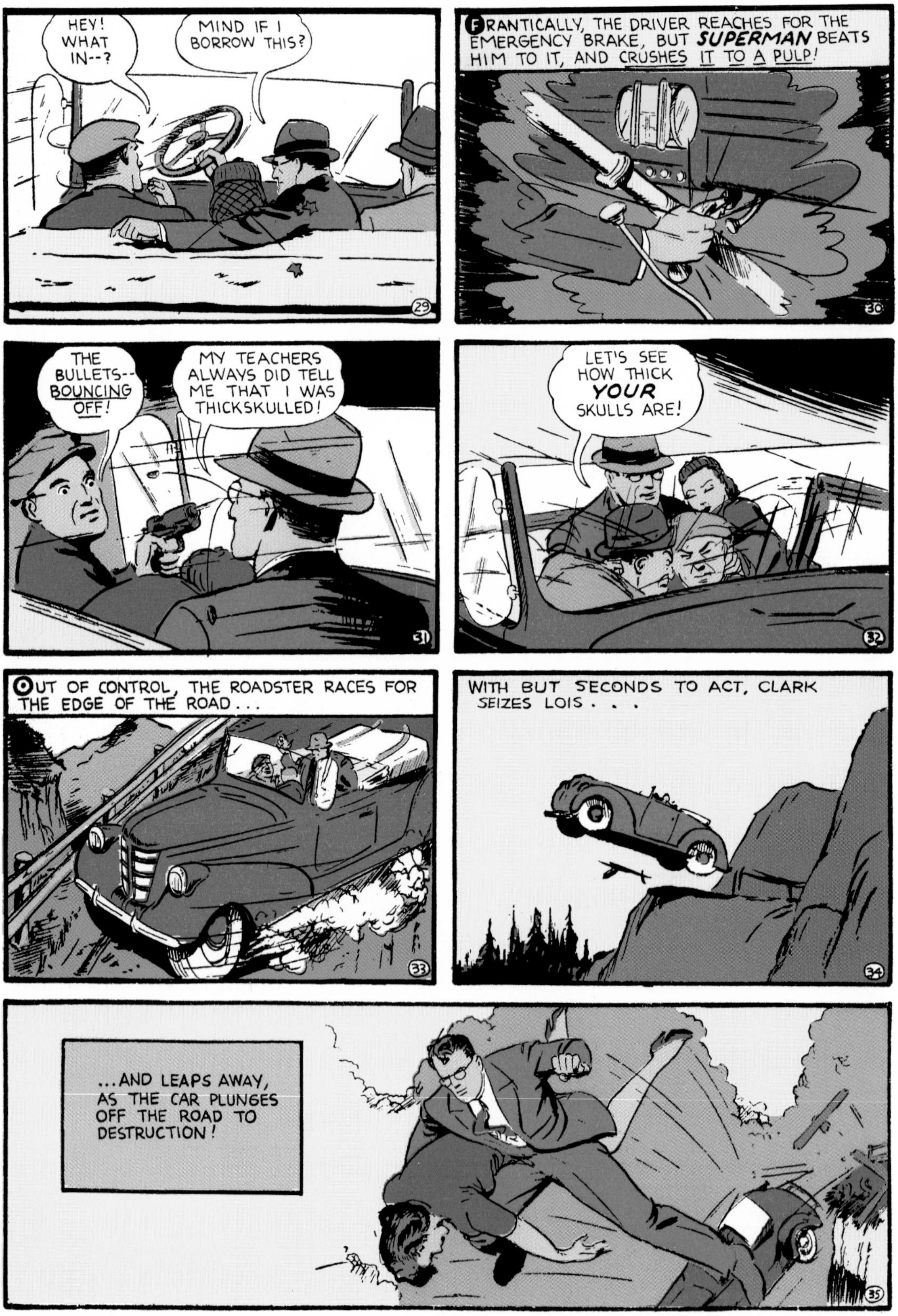
HEY! WHAT IN--?
MIND IF I BORROW THIS?
FRANTICALLY, THE DRIVER REACHES FOR THE EMERGENCY BRAKE, BUT SUPERMAN BEATS HIM TO IT, AND CRUSHES IT TO A PULP!
THE BULLETS-- BOUNCING OFF!
MY TEACHERS ALWAYS DID TELL ME THAT I WAS THICKSKULLED!
LET'S SEE HOW THICK YOUR SKULLS ARE!
OUT OF CONTROL, THE ROADSTER RACES FOR THE EDGE OF THE ROAD...
WITH BUT SECONDS TO ACT, CLARK SEIZES LOIS . . .
...AND LEAPS AWAY, AS THE CAR PLUNGES OFF THE ROAD TO DESTRUCTION!

AND NOW FOR THE FLYING-FIELD!

WHEN THEY REACH THEIR DESTINATION..

WH-WHAT HAPPENED?

THOSE THUGS RELEASED US WITH A WARNING TO ABANDON OUR INVESTIGATION!

WHAT SHALL WE DO?

PAY NO ATTENTION TO THEM, OF COURSE!

IT'S A DANGEROUS FLIGHT -- BUT I'LL FLY YOU THERE FOR $1,000!

IT'S A DEAL! LET'S GET STARTED!

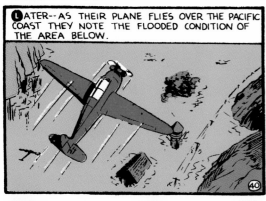

LATER -- AS THEIR PLANE FLIES OVER THE PACIFIC COAST THEY NOTE THE FLOODED CONDITION OF THE AREA BELOW.

CLARK'S SUPERVISION ENABLES HIM TO SEE...

("-A DISTURBANCE..FAR OUT ON THE WATER!-") PILOT, FLY OUT TO SEA!

LOOK- SOMETHING BULKY COMING UP THRU THE WATER!

I DON'T SEE ANYTHING!

A FEW MOMENTS LATER -- OUT OF THE WATER RISES A GLASS-ENCLOSED CITY OF ANCIENT, WEIRD DESIGN!

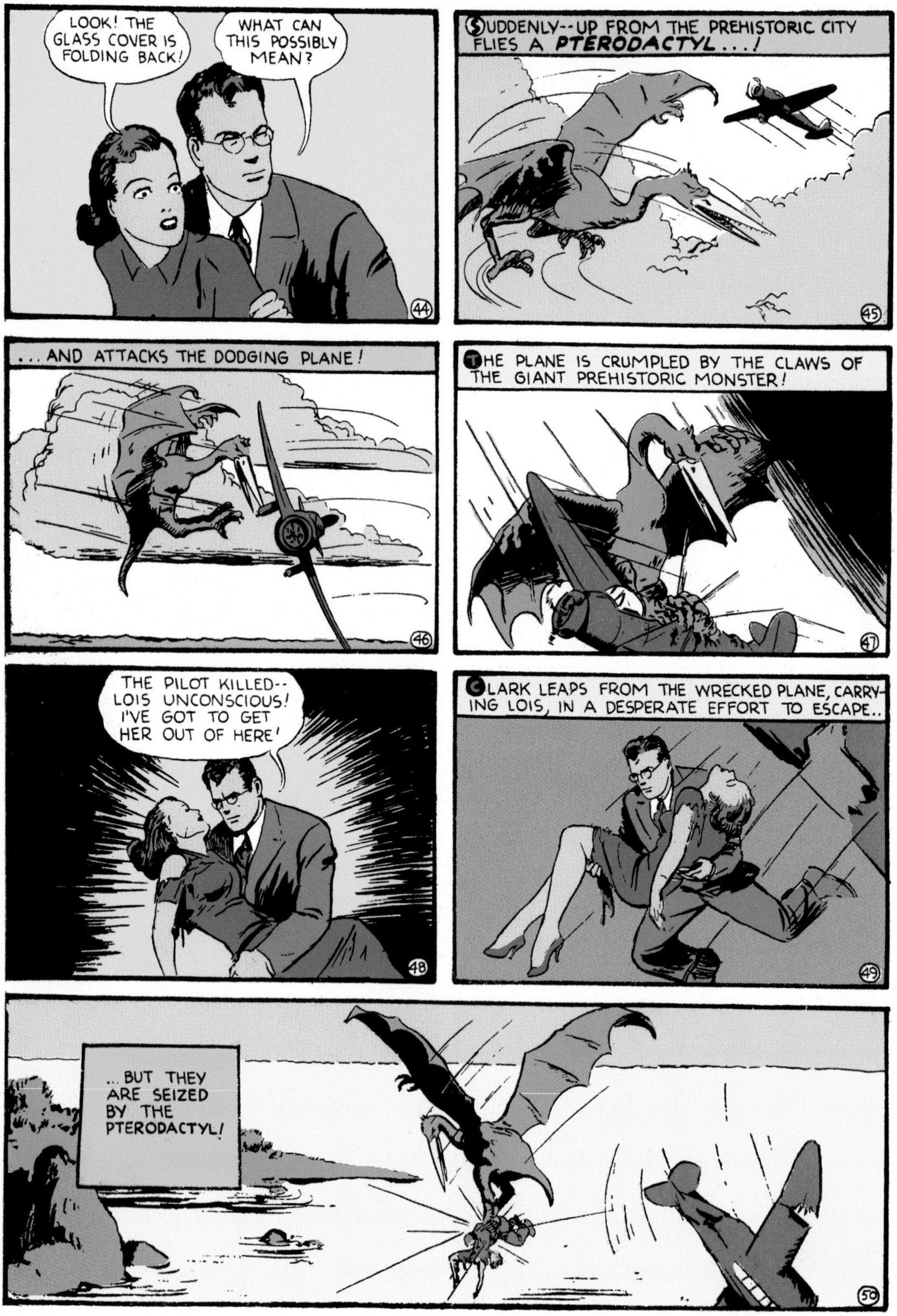
LOOK! THE GLASS COVER IS FOLDING BACK!
WHAT CAN THIS POSSIBLY MEAN?
44
SUDDENLY--UP FROM THE PREHISTORIC CITY FLIES A PTERODACTYL...!
45
...AND ATTACKS THE DODGING PLANE!
46
THE PLANE IS CRUMPLED BY THE CLAWS OF THE GIANT PREHISTORIC MONSTER!
47
THE PILOT KILLED--LOIS UNCONSCIOUS! I'VE GOT TO GET HER OUT OF HERE!
48
CLARK LEAPS FROM THE WRECKED PLANE, CARRYING LOIS, IN A DESPERATE EFFORT TO ESCAPE..
49
...BUT THEY ARE SEIZED BY THE PTERODACTYL!
50

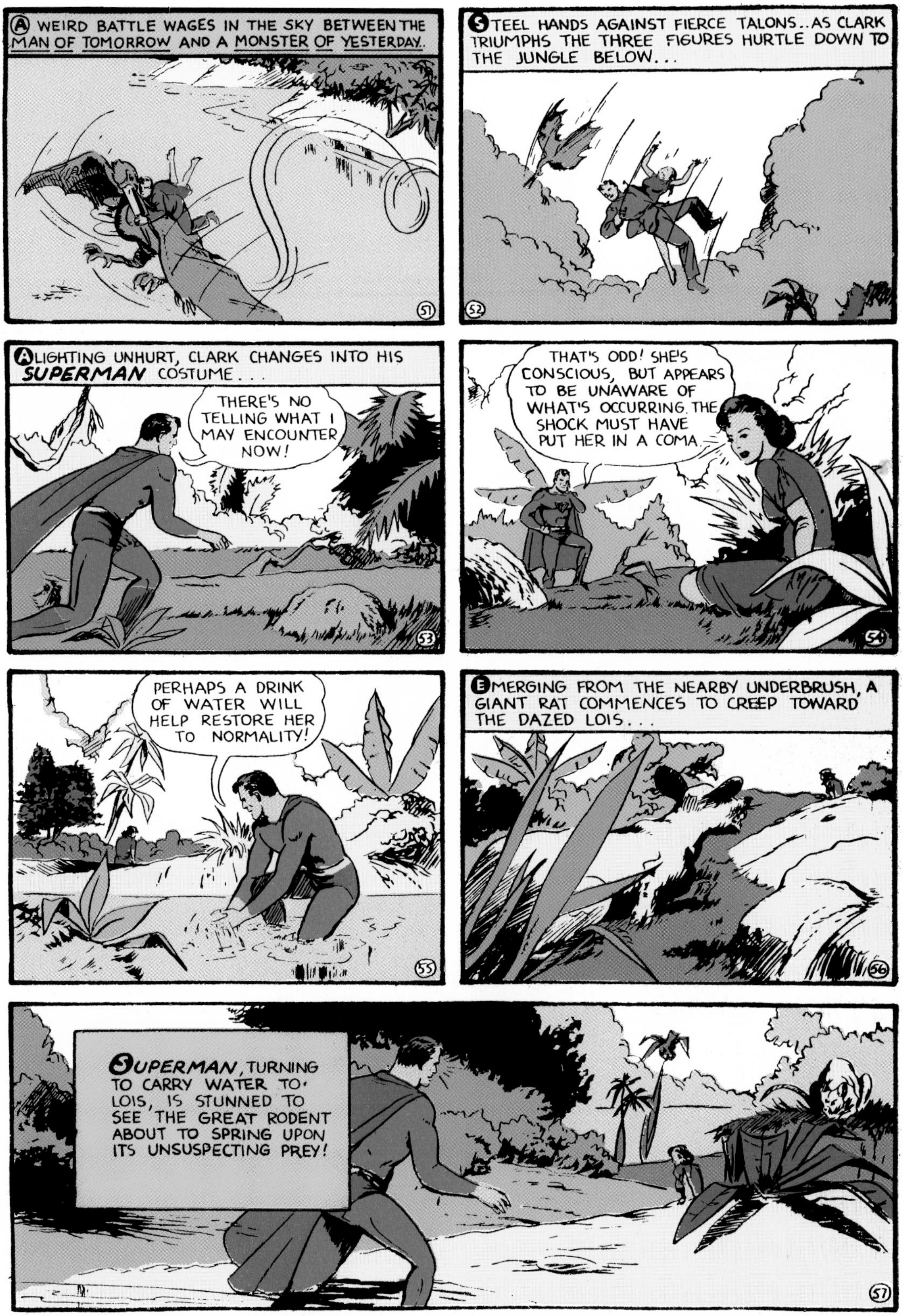
A WEIRD BATTLE WAGES IN THE SKY BETWEEN THE MAN OF TOMORROW AND A MONSTER OF YESTERDAY.
51
STEEL HANDS AGAINST FIERCE TALONS..AS CLARK TRIUMPHS THE THREE FIGURES HURTLE DOWN TO THE JUNGLE BELOW...
52
ALIGHTING UNHURT, CLARK CHANGES INTO HIS SUPERMAN COSTUME...
THERE'S NO TELLING WHAT I MAY ENCOUNTER NOW!
53
THAT'S ODD! SHE'S CONSCIOUS, BUT APPEARS TO BE UNAWARE OF WHAT'S OCCURRING. THE SHOCK MUST HAVE PUT HER IN A COMA.
54
PERHAPS A DRINK OF WATER WILL HELP RESTORE HER TO NORMALITY!
55
EMERGING FROM THE NEARBY UNDERBRUSH, A GIANT RAT COMMENCES TO CREEP TOWARD THE DAZED LOIS...
56
SUPERMAN, TURNING TO CARRY WATER TO LOIS, IS STUNNED TO SEE THE GREAT RODENT ABOUT TO SPRING UPON ITS UNSUSPECTING PREY!
57

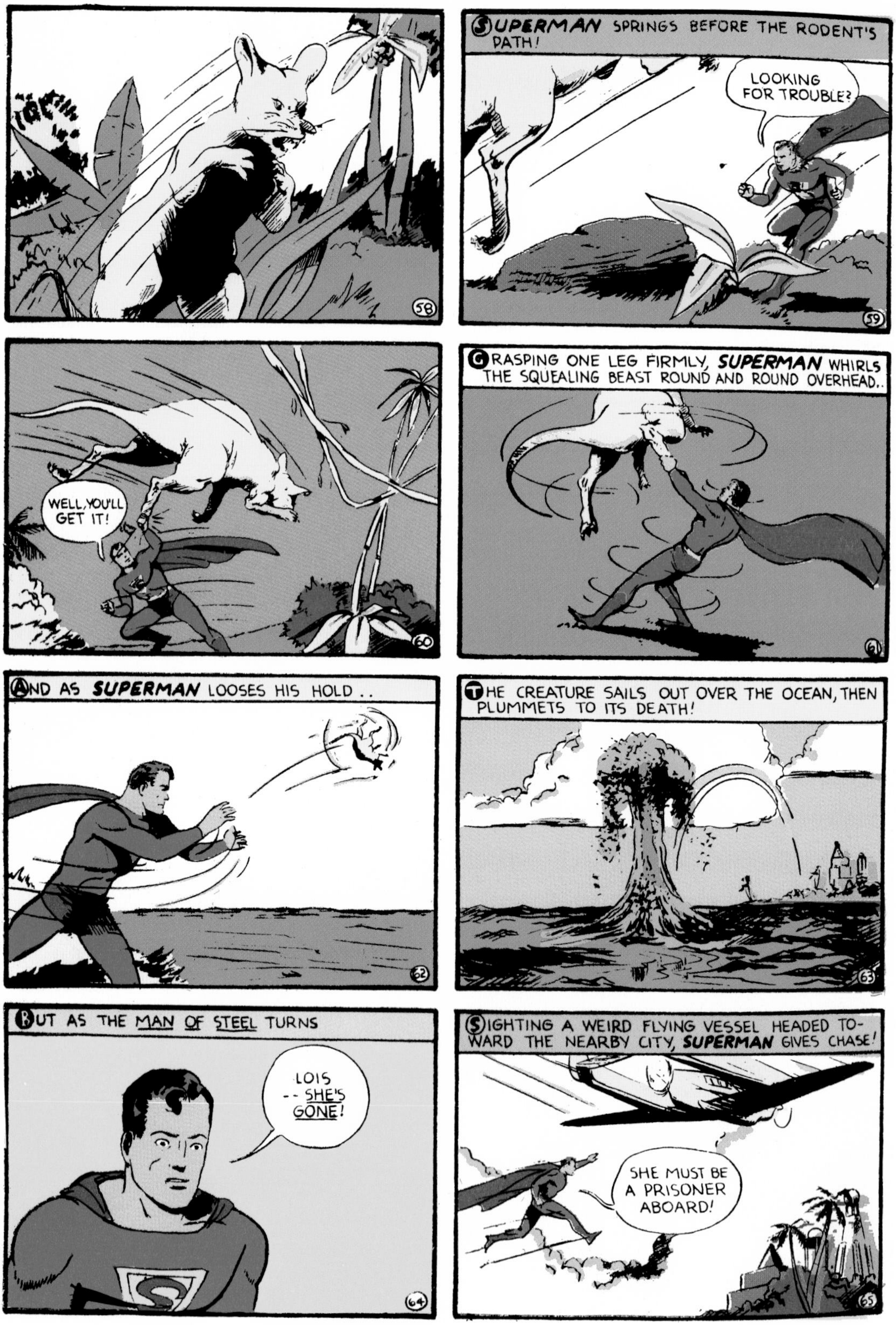
SUPERMAN SPRINGS BEFORE THE RODENT'S PATH!
LOOKING FOR TROUBLE?
WELL, YOU'LL GET IT!
GRASPING ONE LEG FIRMLY, SUPERMAN WHIRLS THE SQUEALING BEAST ROUND AND ROUND OVERHEAD..
AND AS SUPERMAN LOOSES HIS HOLD..
THE CREATURE SAILS OUT OVER THE OCEAN, THEN PLUMMETS TO ITS DEATH!
BUT AS THE MAN OF STEEL TURNS
LOIS -- SHE'S GONE!
SIGHTING A WEIRD FLYING VESSEL HEADED TOWARD THE NEARBY CITY, SUPERMAN GIVES CHASE!
SHE MUST BE A PRISONER ABOARD!

AS SUPERMAN NEARS THE CITY..
SUPERMAN! OFFER NO RESISTANCE--OR MISS LANE WILL BE DESTROYED!
LUTHOR'S VOICE!
FOR LOIS' SAKE, SUPERMAN STANDS PASSIVELY BY AS SHE LEAVES THE WEIRD VESSEL..
SO, MAN OF STEEL--WE MEET AGAIN!
SO-- IT'S YOU AGAIN, LUTHOR! AND AS EVIL AS USUAL!
I DON'T CARE WHAT HAPPENS TO ME-BUT IF YOU HARM THAT GIRL--
ON THE CONTRARY, I WILL HAVE HER TREATED SO THAT HER SENSES RETURN--TAKE HER TO THE GREEN LABORATORY, MEN!
SUPERMAN ACCOMPANIES LUTHOR IN A TOUR OF THE CITY...
HOW DID YOU CREATE THIS WEIRD CITY?
IT WAS CREATED YEARS AGO---I MERELY SALVAGED IT. WHAT YOU ARE WALKING UPON, IS A REMNANT OF THE SUNKEN CONTINENT, PACIFO!
YOU'LL ADMIT IT WAS A MIRACULOUS ACHIEVEMENT! WORKING UNDERWATER, I RAISED A GLASSOLITE-DOME OVER THE CITY, DRAINED OUT THE WATER, THEN RAISED THE CITY TO THE SURFACE OF THE OCEAN.
THEN IT WAS THIS TITANIC UNDERWATER UPHEAVAL THAT CAUSED THE OCEAN TO OVERFLOW! ...AND IT WAS YOU WHO TAPPED THE OIL-WELLS AND STOLE THE OIL FOR YOUR EVIL PURPOSES!
SHORTLY AFTER..
BEHOLD! IN THIS LABORATORY I HAVE RECREATED BIOLOGICAL MONSTROSITIES OF THE PAST. LOOSED UPON THE WORLD, THEY WILL BREAK ITS SPIRIT, ENABLING ME TO BRING IT UNDER MY DOMINATION!
BUT SURELY YOU WOULDN'T REALLY PERPETRATE SUCH AN INHUMAN CRIME---!
IF YOU GIVE ME YOUR ASSISTANCE, I WILL BE INCLINED TO BE MORE MERCIFUL WITH THE WORLD, OTHERWISE...! WELL, WHAT IS YOUR DECISION?
GIVE ME A FEW MOMENTS! I MUST THINK--THINK...!

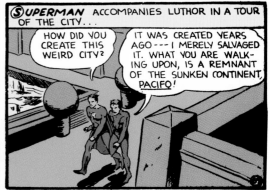

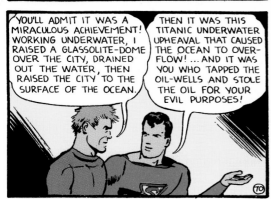

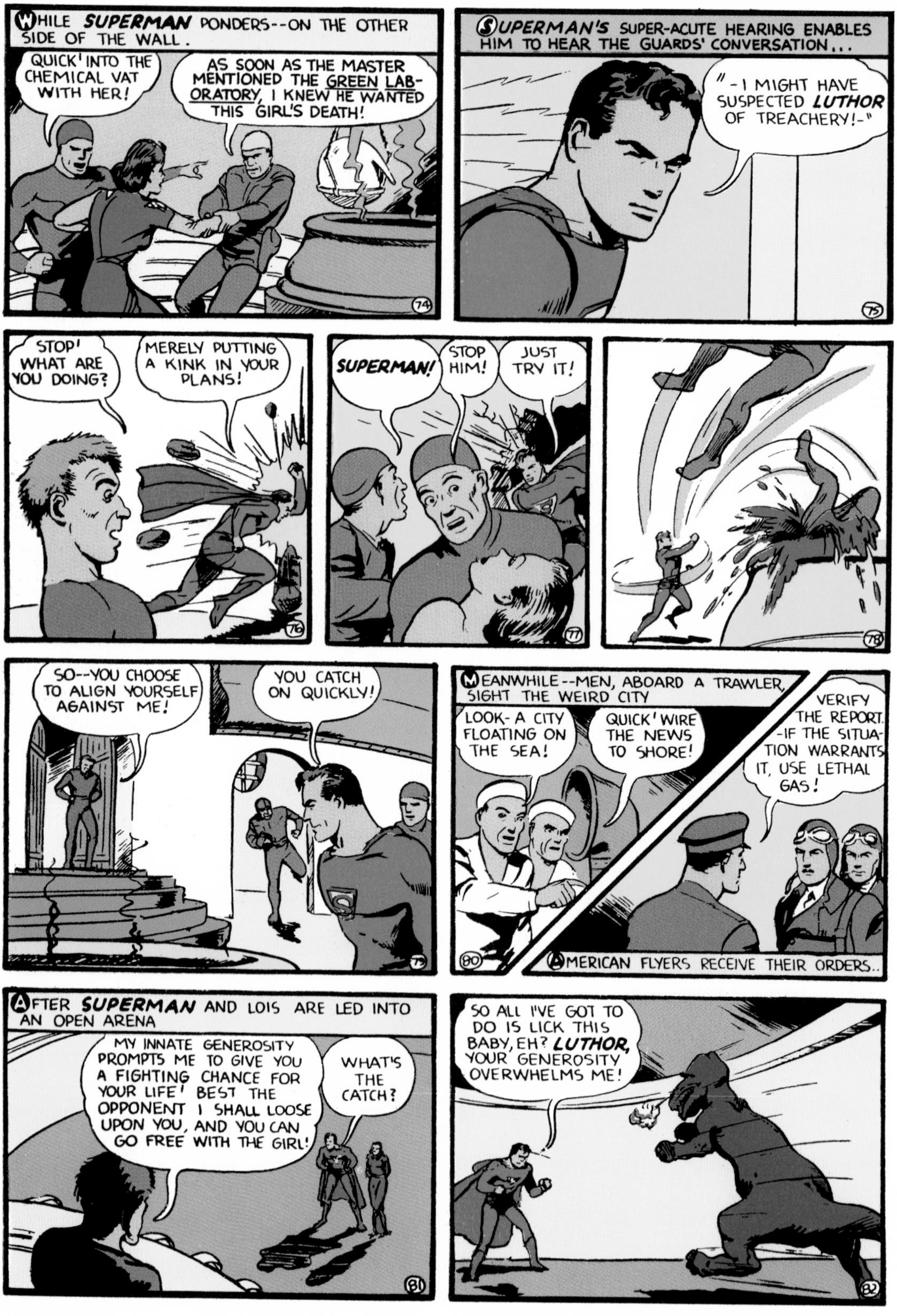
WHILE SUPERMAN PONDERS--ON THE OTHER SIDE OF THE WALL.
QUICK! INTO THE CHEMICAL VAT WITH HER!
AS SOON AS THE MASTER MENTIONED THE GREEN LABORATORY, I KNEW HE WANTED THIS GIRL'S DEATH!
74
SUPERMAN'S SUPER-ACUTE HEARING ENABLES HIM TO HEAR THE GUARDS' CONVERSATION...
"-I MIGHT HAVE SUSPECTED LUTHOR OF TREACHERY!-"
75
STOP! WHAT ARE YOU DOING?
MERELY PUTTING A KINK IN YOUR PLANS!
76
SUPERMAN!
STOP HIM!
JUST TRY IT!
77
78
SO--YOU CHOOSE TO ALIGN YOURSELF AGAINST ME!
YOU CATCH ON QUICKLY!
79
MEANWHILE--MEN, ABOARD A TRAWLER, SIGHT THE WEIRD CITY
LOOK-A CITY FLOATING ON THE SEA!
QUICK! WIRE THE NEWS TO SHORE!
80
VERIFY THE REPORT. -IF THE SITUATION WARRANTS IT, USE LETHAL GAS!
AMERICAN FLYERS RECEIVE THEIR ORDERS..
AFTER SUPERMAN AND LOIS ARE LED INTO AN OPEN ARENA
MY INNATE GENEROSITY PROMPTS ME TO GIVE YOU A FIGHTING CHANCE FOR YOUR LIFE! BEST THE OPPONENT I SHALL LOOSE UPON YOU, AND YOU CAN GO FREE WITH THE GIRL!
WHAT'S THE CATCH?
81
SO ALL I'VE GOT TO DO IS LICK THIS BABY, EH? LUTHOR, YOUR GENEROSITY OVERWHELMS ME!
82

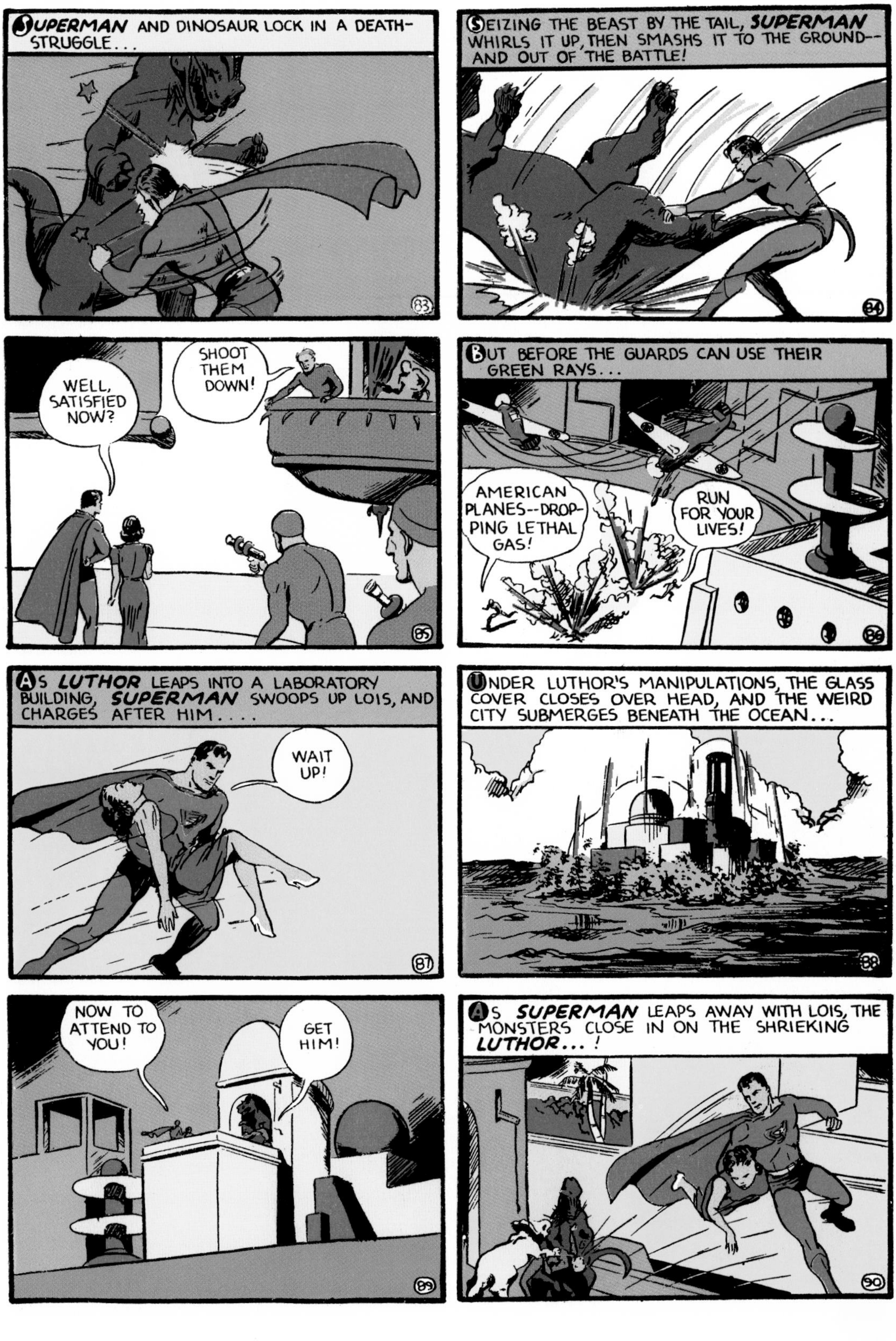
SUPERMAN AND DINOSAUR LOCK IN A DEATH-STRUGGLE...
83
SEIZING THE BEAST BY THE TAIL, SUPERMAN WHIRLS IT UP, THEN SMASHS IT TO THE GROUND-- AND OUT OF THE BATTLE!
84
WELL, SATISFIED NOW?
SHOOT THEM DOWN!
85
BUT BEFORE THE GUARDS CAN USE THEIR GREEN RAYS...
AMERICAN PLANES--DROPPING LETHAL GAS!
RUN FOR YOUR LIVES!
86
AS LUTHOR LEAPS INTO A LABORATORY BUILDING, SUPERMAN SWOOPS UP LOIS, AND CHARGES AFTER HIM....
WAIT UP!
87
UNDER LUTHOR'S MANIPULATIONS, THE GLASS COVER CLOSES OVER HEAD, AND THE WEIRD CITY SUBMERGES BENEATH THE OCEAN...
88
NOW TO ATTEND TO YOU!
GET HIM!
89
AS SUPERMAN LEAPS AWAY WITH LOIS, THE MONSTERS CLOSE IN ON THE SHRIEKING LUTHOR...!
90

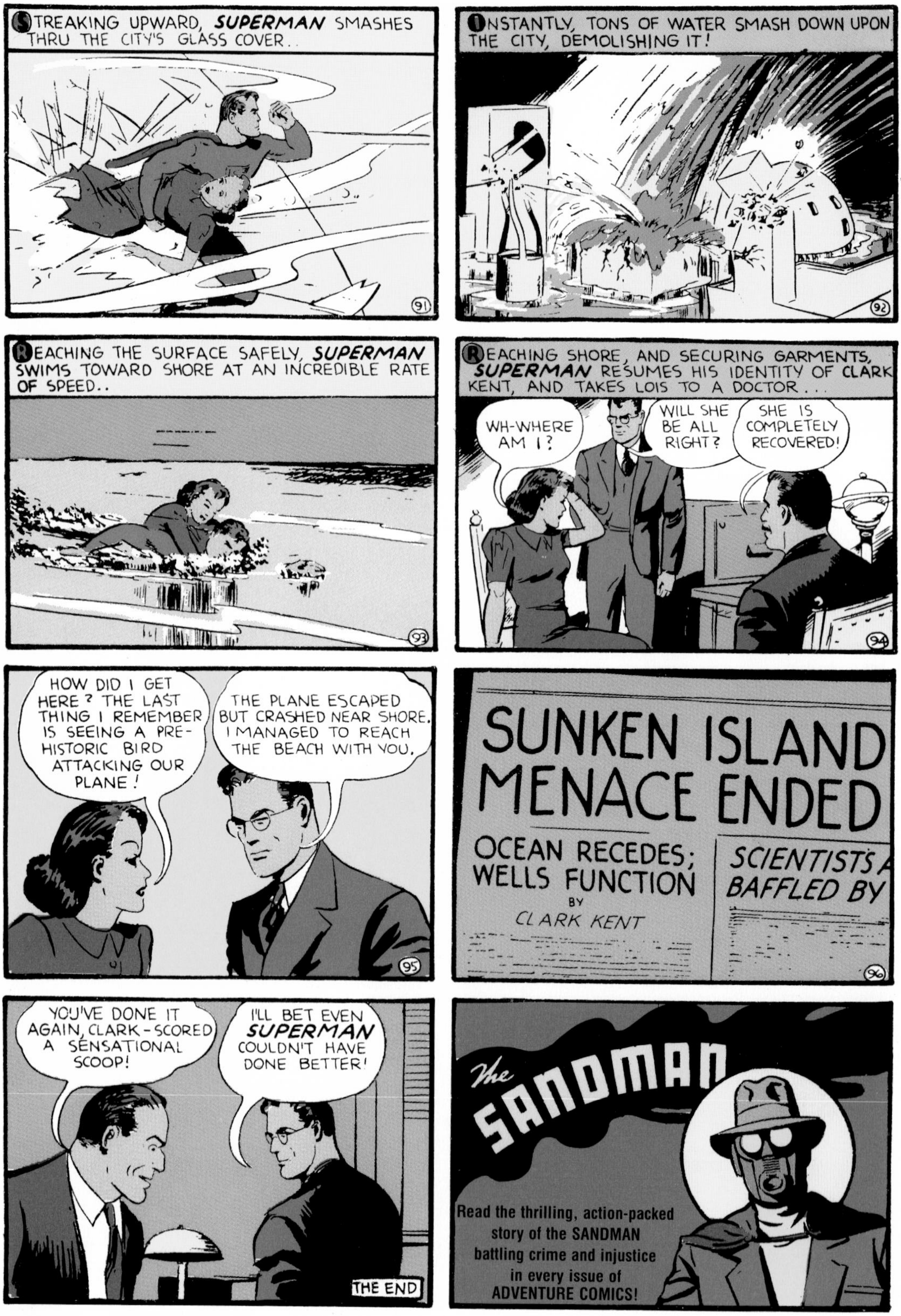
STREAKING UPWARD, SUPERMAN SMASHES THRU THE CITY'S GLASS COVER..
91
INSTANTLY, TONS OF WATER SMASH DOWN UPON THE CITY, DEMOLISHING IT!
92
REACHING THE SURFACE SAFELY, SUPERMAN SWIMS TOWARD SHORE AT AN INCREDIBLE RATE OF SPEED..
93
REACHING SHORE, AND SECURING GARMENTS, SUPERMAN RESUMES HIS IDENTITY OF CLARK KENT, AND TAKES LOIS TO A DOCTOR...
WH-WHERE AM I?
WILL SHE BE ALL RIGHT?
SHE IS COMPLETELY RECOVERED!
94
HOW DID I GET HERE? THE LAST THING I REMEMBER IS SEEING A PRE-HISTORIC BIRD ATTACKING OUR PLANE!
THE PLANE ESCAPED BUT CRASHED NEAR SHORE. I MANAGED TO REACH THE BEACH WITH YOU.
95
SUNKEN ISLAND MENACE ENDED
OCEAN RECEDES; WELLS FUNCTION
BY
CLARK KENT
SCIENTISTS A
BAFFLED BY
96
YOU'VE DONE IT AGAIN, CLARK-SCORED A SENSATIONAL SCOOP!
I'LL BET EVEN SUPERMAN COULDN'T HAVE DONE BETTER!
THE END
The SANDMAN
Read the thrilling, action-packed story of the SANDMAN battling crime and injustice in every issue of ADVENTURE COMICS!

SUPERMEN OF AMERICA

WELL, Members, the Big Prize Contest that ran in the January and February issues of ACTION COMICS has finally closed. And to say that I am happy about the number of entries would be sheer understatement; letters by the thousands poured into the office every hour from every State in the United States, from Canada and Alaska and even far-away Hawaiian and Philippine Islands. Right at this present time all these letters are being sorted and filed by a large staff of workers. When this task has been accomplished, the judges will then step in and start reading each letter to ascertain which entry is deserving of the highest credit. Of course, this will take a good deal of time when you consider the vast number of letters that have to be read and set aside into various groups according to their degrees of excellence. However, each and every member is as-

sured that his or her letter will receive the most careful consideration. Naturally some will be more outstanding than others and because of such they are entitled to the prizes that are to be awarded. Nevertheless, the names of the winners will be published soon in an early issue of ACTION COMICS so be sure to buy your copy each and every month. You may be one of the lucky prize winners!

Those readers of this magazine who are not Members of the SUPERMEN OF AMERICA can join by filling in the coupon on the bottom of the page. The list of Members has been increasing by leaps and bounds, so join now and send in your application immediately; march side by side with the thousands of other boys and girls, carrying aloft the inspirational banners of STRENGTH, COURAGE and JUSTICE!

The Names of the Winners of the Gigantic Superman Contest Will Be Announced in an Early Issue of Action Comics!

Every month in ACTION COMICS there appears a secret message from SUPERMAN, written in one of the nine codes which only the Members of the SUPERMEN OF AMERICA know. Those who are not Members may join by sending in the coupon on the right.

SUPERMAN,   MAR.
  c/o ACTION COMICS,
    480 LEXINGTON AVENUE, N. Y. C.

Dear Superman:

Please enroll me as a Charter Member of the SUPERMEN OF AMERICA. I enclose 10c to cover cost of mailing. It is understood that I am to receive my Membership Certificate, Button and Superman Code.

NAME..AGE...........

STREET ADDRESS..

CITY AND STATE..

CHANGER OF DESTINY

By Hugh Langley

GEORGE RANKIN could have doffed his laboratory-robe and walked out into the world, a billionaire. Things other than money, though, interested Rankin. A frown was upon the savant's features. Seated at a desk in his laboratory, he read:

"GANGSTERS SHOOT DOWN TWO-YEAR-OLD CHILD!"

His eyes shifted to another headline:

"WAR THREATENING!"

Tossing the newspaper aside, his hands reached out and caressed the objects which lay upon the bench: a hypodermic-syringe, and a bottle of yellow liquid. George Rankin filled the syringe then bared his arm. As he drove the plunger home, he permitted his eyes to rest upon the discarded newspaper. The glaring headlines caught his eyes, and again he frowned. His vision shifted to the open window. A lone sparrow was winging its way leisurely by.

Things began to happen to Rankin. His sight was growing misty. For an instant objects wavered, yawned grotesquely, as tho seen through an imperfect lens. A thunderous roaring was in his ears. He was attacked by a wave of nausea. Then the reaction set in. His vision cleared. Objects stood out sharply, more clear-cut than they had ever been before. He seemed gifted with the ability to peer into every remote corner of the room with a penetrating intensity that was almost painful in its thoroughness. Each detail stood out like a colossal landmark. The roaring in his ears subsided.

Rankin looked toward his window. He could not control the start or the nervous exclamation that sprang to his lips. For there, suspended motionless in the empty air, silent, unmoving as a graven statue, was the sparrow! It hung in space as though mounted in a solid object, yet there was no physical support!

Rankin's sensational discovery was a success! This was the discovery which could have netted him billions. But George Rankin had something

other than money in mind: a mission. He had no intention of revealing what he had discovered. It would not do to let the world know that George Rankin had succeeded in speeding up his time-rate! Rankin was living 31,536,-000 times faster than the rest of the planet. What to everyone else was a second, to Rankin was a complete year. The solution would be effective for one second of normal time. In other words, George had three hundred and sixty-five days in which to complete a task to which he had dedicated himself.

Still incredulous, though thunderstruck at the vision of the suspended bird, Rankin found himself moving toward his window. He stared out—and gasped!

It was noon. The sun shone high in the sky. The sidewalks were packed with pedestrians. The streets thronged with autos. But, within the range of his vision, there was not one single movement! George had expected to see this, but the weirdness of the sight was unnerving.

Walking swiftly, he descended to the street below. Directly before his laboratory two men stood rigid. They appeared to be the creations of a master sculptor. Their mouths were open and their arms were poised expressively in the air. One of the men was smoking a cigar. The other held a cigarette in an extended hand. George reached out, swiftly exchanged the cigar for the cigarette, then chuckled as he considered how great would be the amazement of the two men one year later—or rather, one second later—when they would become aware of the substitution.

But precious time was being wasted. George left the two figures and entered his automobile. Selecting a key, he slipped it into the proper slot, turned it. Then he stepped on the "starter."

Nothing happened!

Puzzled, Rankin again pressed the "starter," and once again there was no response! Abruptly he caught his breath as he guessed the answer. One year from now the motor would start! —it would take a full year for the electrical energy to travel the length of the car's mechanism! George pondered. A new problem had presented itself. What could he use for transportation? Certainly there was nothing on earth which could move at a speed which would even be apparent to his eyes. He shook his head slowly as he realized that he would have to depend upon his legs. That might

prove a serious setback to his plans, but there was nothing he could do about it.

* * *

Rankin was tired. It had taken three steady hours of walking to reach the other side of the city. He had passed through multitudes of motionless figures. A strange sensation, it had been: as though he alone were alive, while the rest of the world had been victimized by some fearful, ossifying malady. And at times it had appeared to Rankin that *he* were dead, and that the others lived an existence which his distored, dead vision interpreted as not normal.

Rankin was not only tired. He was also hungry and thirsty. Pausing beside a fruit stand, he helped himself to a banana and a pear. From his pocket he extracted a dime, placed it into the stiff, outstretched hand of the bronzed Italian merchant, saying, "Keep the change, Tony!"

A glance at a street sign informed him that he was nearing his destination. Refreshed, he walked a trifle more vigorously. But suddenly he stopped short in his tracks, before a bank.

Within, armed masked men had all the patrons and cashiers covered. The leader was striding forward toward the office of the bank's president. Rankin's attention swerved to another corner of the lobby. A man was withdrawing a pistol from a shoulder-holster beneath his jacket. George caught glimpse of a badge. Again Rankin's eyes swerved. He sighted a bandit, machine-gun raised, drawing aim upon the detective, his fingers already compressing the trigger.

George strode toward the detective, pausing at his side. He drew in his breath with an audible hiss at what he saw. Suspended in the air, separated from the breast of the detective by only an inch, was a bullet—the first to be launched by the bandit! Rankin reached forward, plucked the bullet out of the air, and tossed it into a nearby waste-paper container.

The next few minutes George was busy relieving the gansters of their weapons. Then he looked about until he located a cord, after which he went from one bandit to the other. When he was finished with his task, each was fastened to the other by a length of rope. George Rankin strode out of the

bank. He had had a small taste of the gigantic task which still lay before him.

Later, he strode up the steps of a brownstone mansion. Mechanically, he reached out to knock, then checked himself. Who wanted to wait an entire year for an answer to a knock? Grasping the handle of the door, he discovered that the door was unlocked. Passing through the doorway, he found himself within a long, lavishly furnished hall. There were several men in the hall; most of them had peculiar bulges in their hippockets. Disregarding them, George strode leisurely thru the different rooms of the house. Finally, he found his man.

The Great Man was seated alone in his library, resting in a luxuriously upholstered armchair, a book in his hands. Rankin noted the title. He said aloud: "I never knew, Spurnelli, that you were interested in poetry."

Drawing up a chair so that he faced Spurnelli, Rankin seated himself. "I've walked a long way to see you," he said. The motionless, reading figure said nothing. George reached forward, took the book gently away. Spurnelli's hands remained suspended in the air; he still stared straight ahead, as though scanning a printed page.

"Spurnelli," said Rankin, "you are the country's most dangerous thug. You have your finger in every cesspool of crime. The thousands of rackets which prey like myriads of bloodsucking parasites upon the people of this country, are your projects. You, the Big Shot, are the head of organized crime in this country. In order to remove crime, you, first, must be removed. That, I propose to do!"

Rankin arose. He leaned over the Crime King's motionless body, searching beneath a trim jacket; his hand emerged, clutching a short, ugly-looking automatic. George placed the weapon against the super-criminal's forehead. "For posterity!" he cried.

Then he pulled the trigger!

MONTHS of continuous walking had reduced George Rankin to a weary figure. But now, as he entered the country's capital, Washington, D. C., his tired body straightened. Above the ornate door of his destination was a huge sign. It proclaimed that this was the official office of a European ambassador to America. George entered and made his way to the office where he knew the ambassador would be found.

Opening an office door, George entered the holy of holies. Seated at a large sumptuous desk was the ambassador himself, a paunchy, swinish individual. Before him were seated several of his countrymen, their swarthy faces lighted with fervor. All had their eyes turned upon several documents spread before them on the desk. One of the ambassador's thick fingers was pressing heavily against the sheets, indicating a diagram.

Standing behind the ambassador, Rankin peered over his shoulder. A rapid intake of his breath indicated that what he saw startled him. Grimly, he gathered up all the papers, arranged them in a neat stack, then placed them in his pocket.

Twenty minutes later, George was mounting the steps of the White House. The President of the United States was sitting at his desk, frowning over matters of great importance as Rankin made his way forward and placed a number of sheets on the desk before him. "Now it's up to you!" said George Rankin.

As he departed from the White House, a tremendous weight eased off his mind. At last his task was completed! Suddenly, though, he felt immeasurably old and weary. He had been walking for days, months. In the act of crossing a thickly congested street, he paused and leaned against an immobile automobile for support. But instead of finding relief, his weariness seemed to increase. His entire body was aching and throbbing.

Abruptly, a thousand jagged frag-

ments of light burst and tore at his brain. A hoarse bedlam of sound numbed his ears. With a shock, George realized what was happening. The year was up. The drug was losing its effect! He was returning to his normal time-rate! No time to lose ...he must hurry...get out of the path of this moving auto...But his feet seemed weighted by remorseless lead. He could not move them. Valiantly, he fought, but despite himself, began to sway. He tottered back, his knees buckling—and suddenly crashed to the pavement. Slowly, it seemed to him, his fingers convulsively tore and scratched at the bricks. With all his energy, he strove to battle his way forward even an inch.

The thunderous roaring in his ears sounded like the laughter of a thousand demons. Distorted visions swam about his consciousness like blurred reflections on a troubled pond's surface. He raised his eyes to see the wheels of the car, towering above him, slowly move. Ponderously they turned at an infinitely slow speed—but with each fleeting second the velocity increased.

One superhuman effort Rankin made to escape the crushing doom that threatened, then all his strength oozed away, and he tumbled into pitch darkness. The last thing he heard was his own frantic scream...

* * *

The President of the United States stared open-mouthed at the documents spread on the desk before him. "What in——?" he exploded. "Documents proving that private moneyed interests are behind the threatening war! Good heavens! With these few scraps of paper I can outlaw the coming conflict!"

* * *

SPURNELLI SLAIN IN OWN STRONGHOLD

Amalgamated Press Release, March 8. Spurnelli, the nation's No. 1 Racketeer and Gangster, was mysteriously shot down early this afternoon by an unknown murderer. Spurnelli, it is known, was the head of organized crime in the United States. It is hinted that with Spurnelli out of the way, police will have a clear hand in cleaning up on the country's crime situation...etc....

* * *

TRAFFIC TOLL—147!!!

The body of an unidentified man was found lying on the street today where he had been left by a hit-and-run driver. This raises the traffic toll to 147. The Washington Ledger offers a reward of fifty dollars to anyone who can furnish a clue to the driver's identity. The victim will be buried in an unmarked grave in Potter's Field.

* * *

The End.

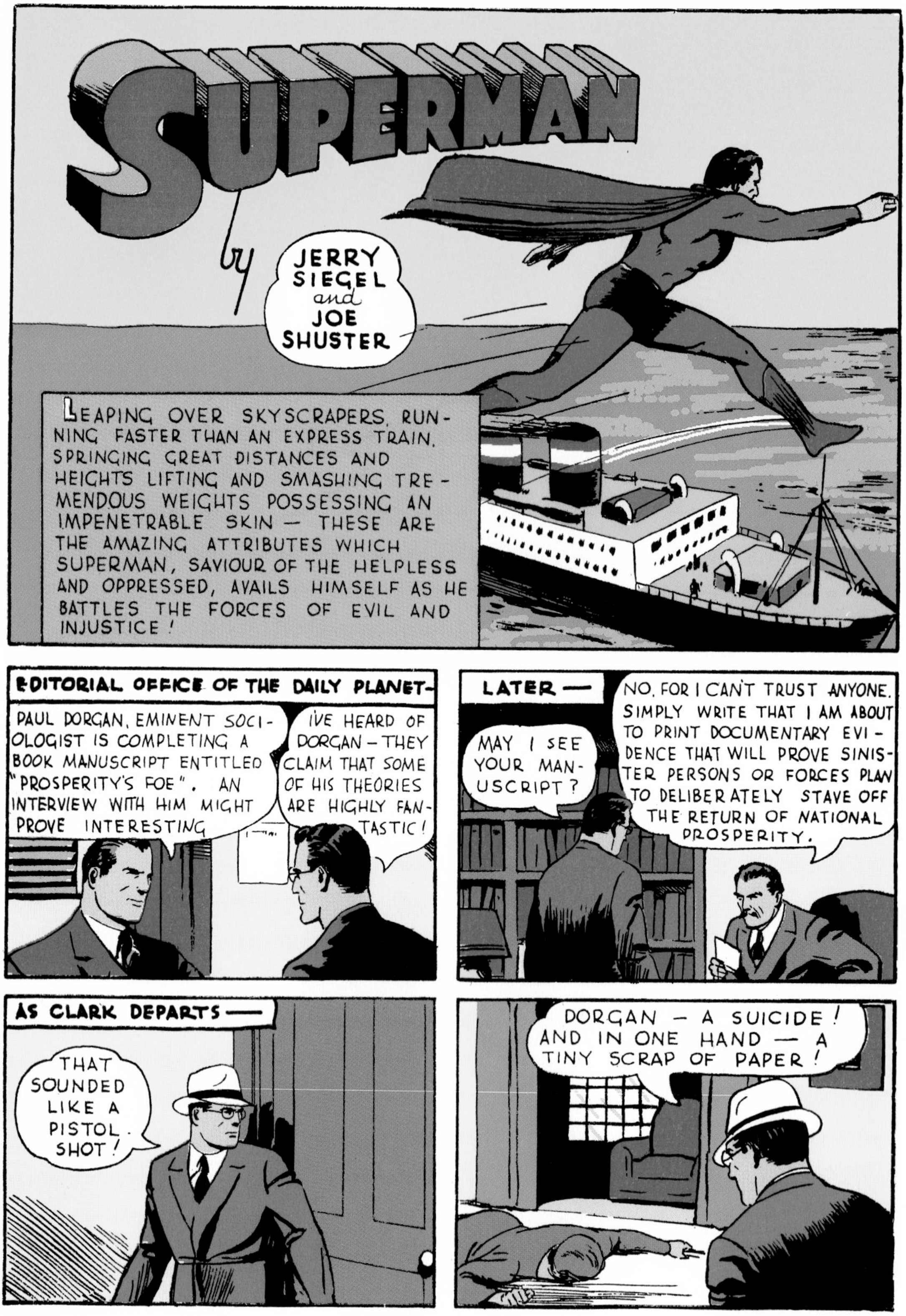
SUPERMAN
by
JERRY SIEGEL and JOE SHUSTER
LEAPING OVER SKYSCRAPERS, RUNNING FASTER THAN AN EXPRESS TRAIN, SPRINGING GREAT DISTANCES AND HEIGHTS LIFTING AND SMASHING TREMENDOUS WEIGHTS POSSESSING AN IMPENETRABLE SKIN — THESE ARE THE AMAZING ATTRIBUTES WHICH SUPERMAN, SAVIOUR OF THE HELPLESS AND OPPRESSED, AVAILS HIMSELF AS HE BATTLES THE FORCES OF EVIL AND INJUSTICE!
EDITORIAL OFFICE OF THE DAILY PLANET—
PAUL DORGAN, EMINENT SOCIOLOGIST IS COMPLETING A BOOK MANUSCRIPT ENTITLED "PROSPERITY'S FOE". AN INTERVIEW WITH HIM MIGHT PROVE INTERESTING
I'VE HEARD OF DORGAN — THEY CLAIM THAT SOME OF HIS THEORIES ARE HIGHLY FANTASTIC!
LATER —
MAY I SEE YOUR MANUSCRIPT?
NO, FOR I CAN'T TRUST ANYONE. SIMPLY WRITE THAT I AM ABOUT TO PRINT DOCUMENTARY EVIDENCE THAT WILL PROVE SINISTER PERSONS OR FORCES PLAN TO DELIBERATELY STAVE OFF THE RETURN OF NATIONAL PROSPERITY.
AS CLARK DEPARTS —
THAT SOUNDED LIKE A PISTOL SHOT!
DORGAN — A SUICIDE! AND IN ONE HAND — A TINY SCRAP OF PAPER!

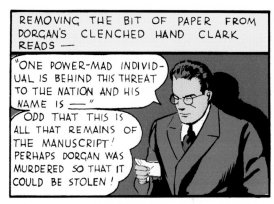

REMOVING THE BIT OF PAPER FROM DORGAN'S CLENCHED HAND CLARK READS —

"ONE POWER-MAD INDIVIDUAL IS BEHIND THIS THREAT TO THE NATION AND HIS NAME IS —"

ODD THAT THIS IS ALL THAT REMAINS OF THE MANUSCRIPT! PERHAPS DORGAN WAS MURDERED SO THAT IT COULD BE STOLEN!

CLARK SUMMONS THE POLICE AND IS RELEASED AFTER BRIEF QUESTIONING

WILL THAT BE ALL?

YES, YOU MAY RETURN TO YOUR NEWSPAPER!

WHAT'S ALL THE EXCITEMENT?

HAVEN'T YOU HEARD? THE NATION IS BEING PARALYZED BY A WAVE OF STRIKES IN ALL MAJOR INDUSTRIES!

THERE'S DISORDER EVERYWHERE!

SHIPS ARE SINKING AT SEA — AIRPLANES ARE MYSTERIOUSLY CRACKING UP! THE BUSINESS WORLD IS PANIC-STRICKEN!

WHEW! AND I HAD NO INKLING!

I WONDER IF AFTER ALL THERE ISN'T PERHAPS SOME BASIS OF TRUTH IN DORGAN'S CONTENTION THAT SINISTER FORCES SEEK TO RETARD THE NATION'S RETURN TO PROSPERITY? —

RETIRING TO A STOREROOM CLARK CHANGES INTO HIS **SUPERMAN** COSTUME

I THINK I'LL GIVE DORGAN'S HOME A THOROUGH GOING OVER. HE MAY HAVE LEFT SOME NOTES THAT WILL HELP ME!

MINUTE'S LATER — THE **MAN OF STEEL'S** INCREDIBLY POWERFUL FIGURE STREAKS DOWNWARD AND CATCHES HOLD OF A WINDOW —

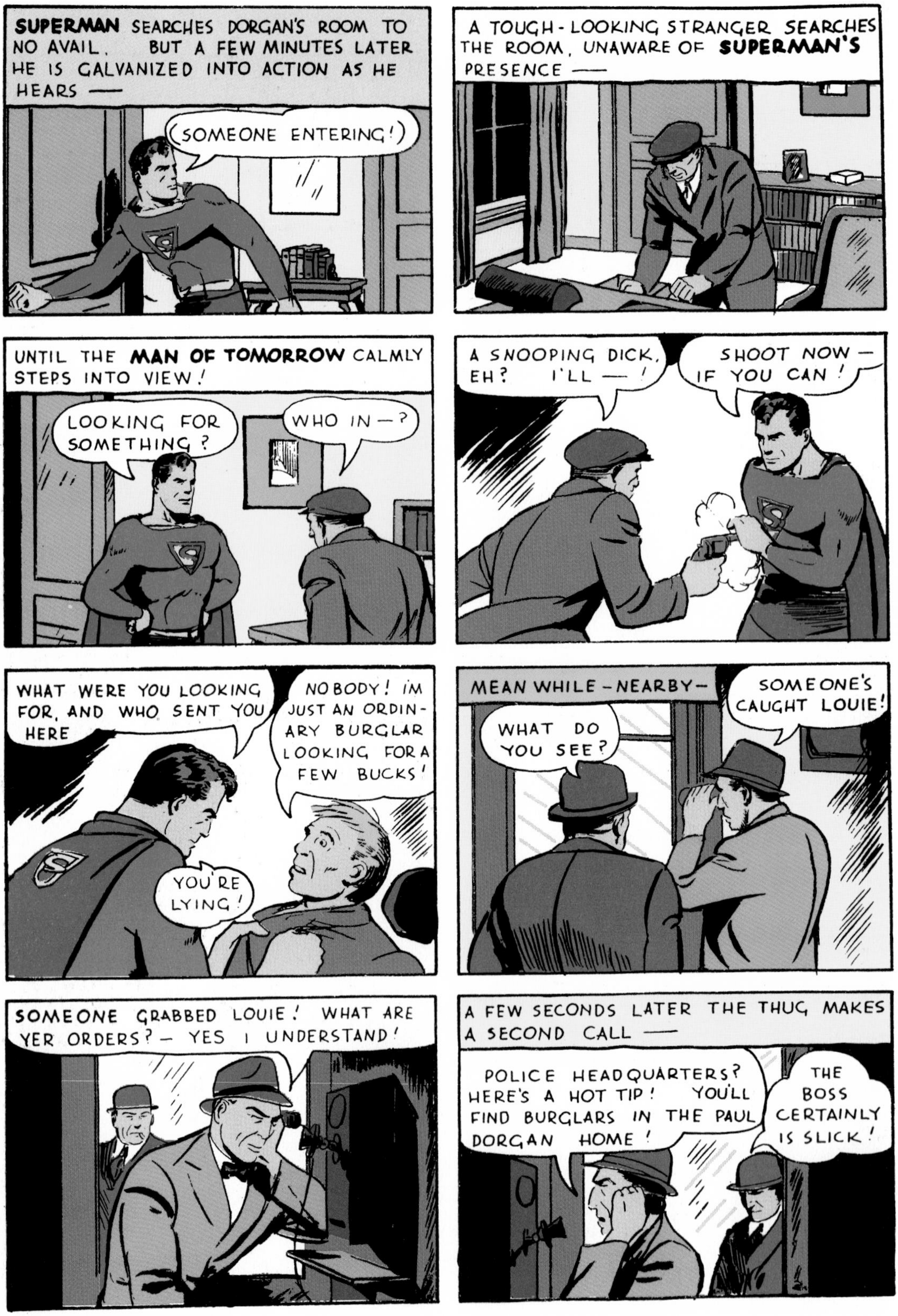
SUPERMAN SEARCHES DORGAN'S ROOM TO NO AVAIL. BUT A FEW MINUTES LATER HE IS GALVANIZED INTO ACTION AS HE HEARS —
(SOMEONE ENTERING!)
A TOUGH-LOOKING STRANGER SEARCHES THE ROOM, UNAWARE OF SUPERMAN'S PRESENCE —
UNTIL THE MAN OF TOMORROW CALMLY STEPS INTO VIEW!
LOOKING FOR SOMETHING?
WHO IN—?
A SNOOPING DICK, EH? I'LL —!
SHOOT NOW — IF YOU CAN!
WHAT WERE YOU LOOKING FOR, AND WHO SENT YOU HERE
NOBODY! I'M JUST AN ORDINARY BURGLAR LOOKING FOR A FEW BUCKS!
YOU'RE LYING!
MEAN WHILE — NEARBY —
SOMEONE'S CAUGHT LOUIE!
WHAT DO YOU SEE?
SOMEONE GRABBED LOUIE! WHAT ARE YER ORDERS? — YES I UNDERSTAND!
A FEW SECONDS LATER THE THUG MAKES A SECOND CALL —
POLICE HEADQUARTERS? HERE'S A HOT TIP! YOU'LL FIND BURGLARS IN THE PAUL DORGAN HOME!
THE BOSS CERTAINLY IS SLICK!

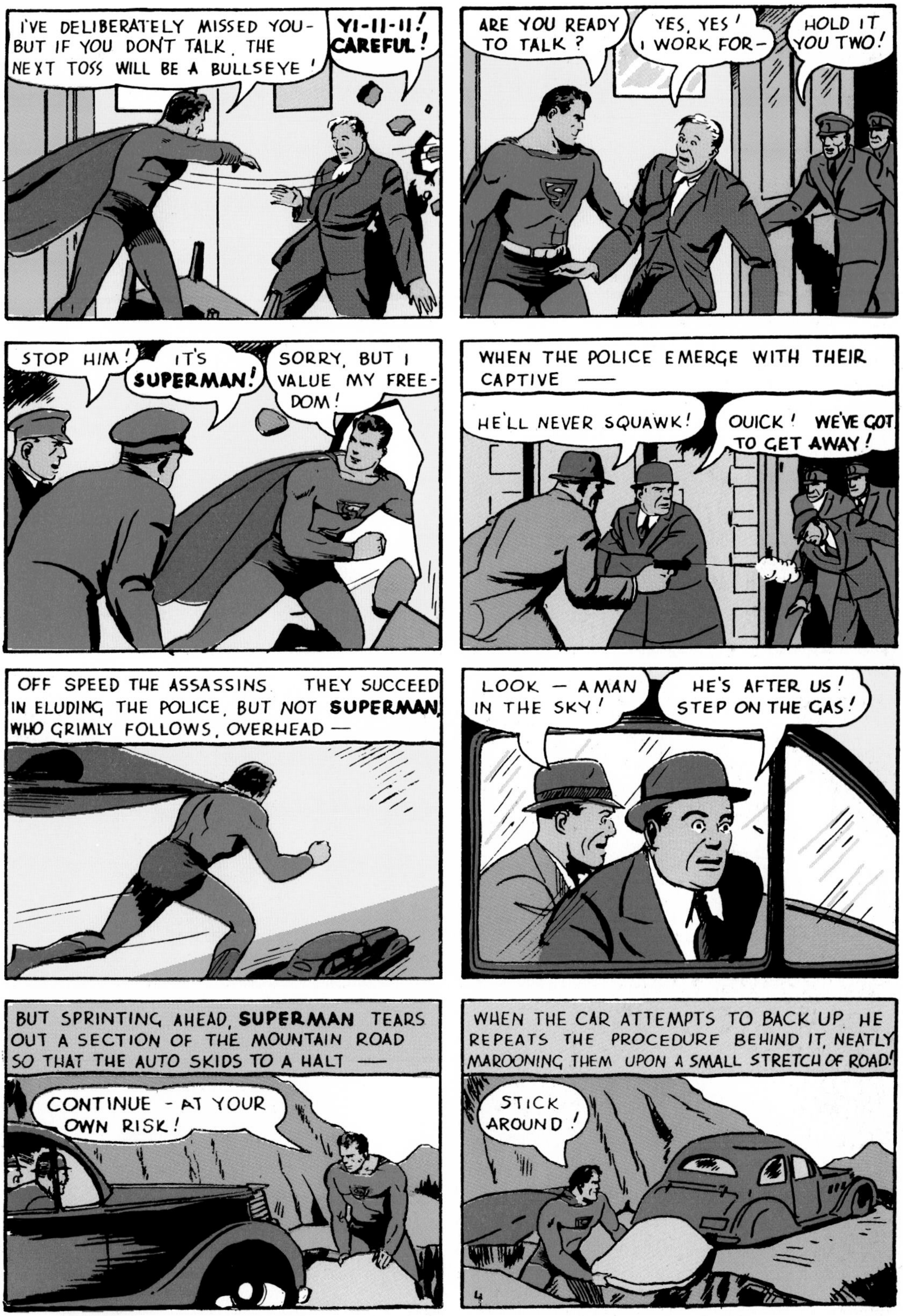
I'VE DELIBERATELY MISSED YOU- BUT IF YOU DON'T TALK, THE NEXT TOSS WILL BE A BULLSEYE!
YI-II-II! CAREFUL!
ARE YOU READY TO TALK?
YES, YES! I WORK FOR-
HOLD IT YOU TWO!
STOP HIM!
IT'S SUPERMAN!
SORRY, BUT I VALUE MY FREE-DOM!
WHEN THE POLICE EMERGE WITH THEIR CAPTIVE —
HE'LL NEVER SQUAWK!
QUICK! WE'VE GOT TO GET AWAY!
OFF SPEED THE ASSASSINS. THEY SUCCEED IN ELUDING THE POLICE, BUT NOT SUPERMAN, WHO GRIMLY FOLLOWS, OVERHEAD —
LOOK — A MAN IN THE SKY!
HE'S AFTER US! STEP ON THE GAS!
BUT SPRINTING AHEAD, SUPERMAN TEARS OUT A SECTION OF THE MOUNTAIN ROAD SO THAT THE AUTO SKIDS TO A HALT —
CONTINUE - AT YOUR OWN RISK!
WHEN THE CAR ATTEMPTS TO BACK UP, HE REPEATS THE PROCEDURE BEHIND IT, NEATLY MAROONING THEM UPON A SMALL STRETCH OF ROAD!
STICK AROUND!

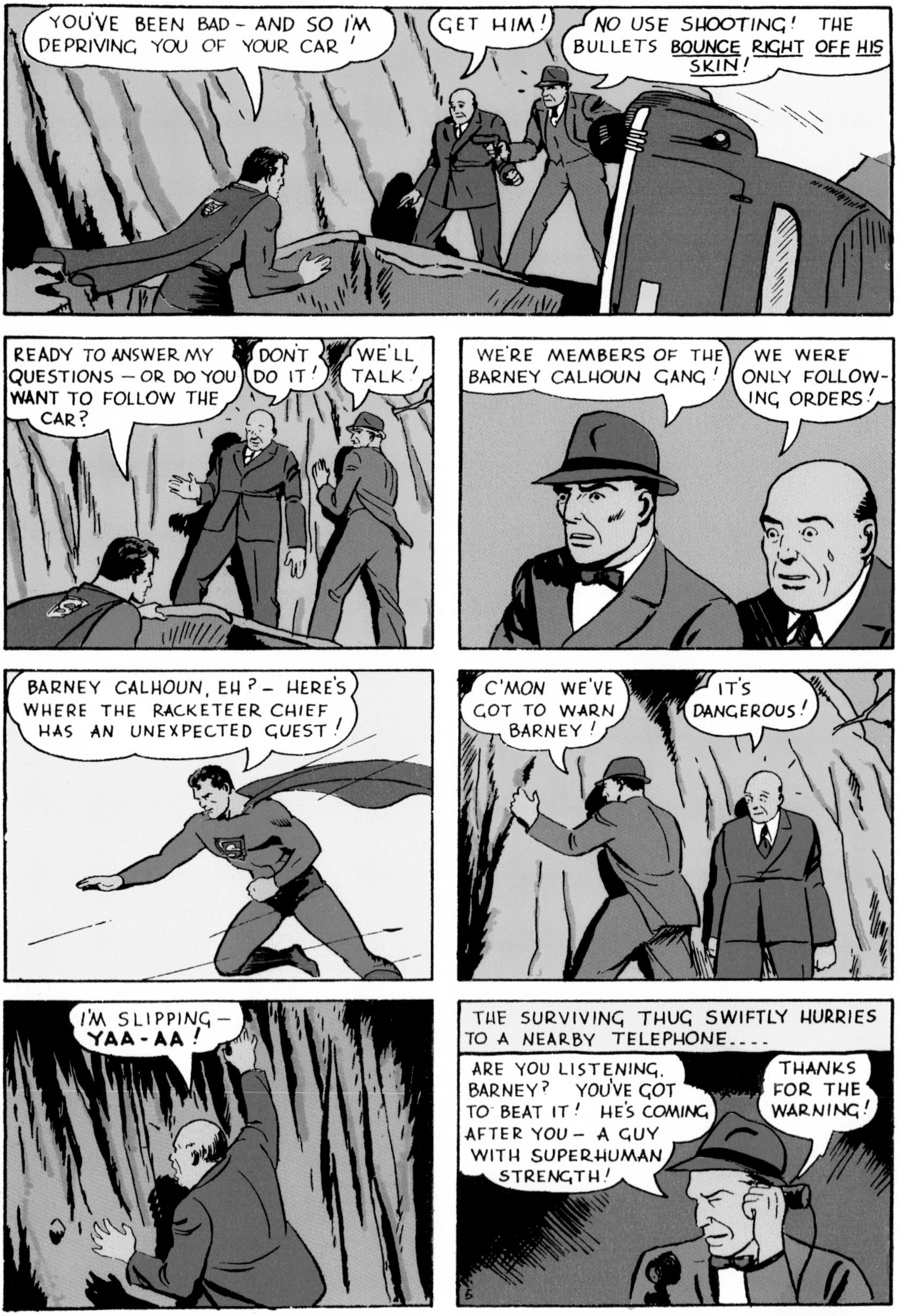
YOU'VE BEEN BAD – AND SO I'M DEPRIVING YOU OF YOUR CAR!
GET HIM!
NO USE SHOOTING! THE BULLETS BOUNCE RIGHT OFF HIS SKIN!
READY TO ANSWER MY QUESTIONS – OR DO YOU WANT TO FOLLOW THE CAR?
DON'T DO IT!
WE'LL TALK!
WE'RE MEMBERS OF THE BARNEY CALHOUN GANG!
WE WERE ONLY FOLLOWING ORDERS!
BARNEY CALHOUN, EH? – HERE'S WHERE THE RACKETEER CHIEF HAS AN UNEXPECTED GUEST!
C'MON WE'VE GOT TO WARN BARNEY!
IT'S DANGEROUS!
I'M SLIPPING – YAA-AA!
THE SURVIVING THUG SWIFTLY HURRIES TO A NEARBY TELEPHONE....
ARE YOU LISTENING, BARNEY? YOU'VE GOT TO BEAT IT! HE'S COMING AFTER YOU – A GUY WITH SUPERHUMAN STRENGTH!
THANKS FOR THE WARNING!

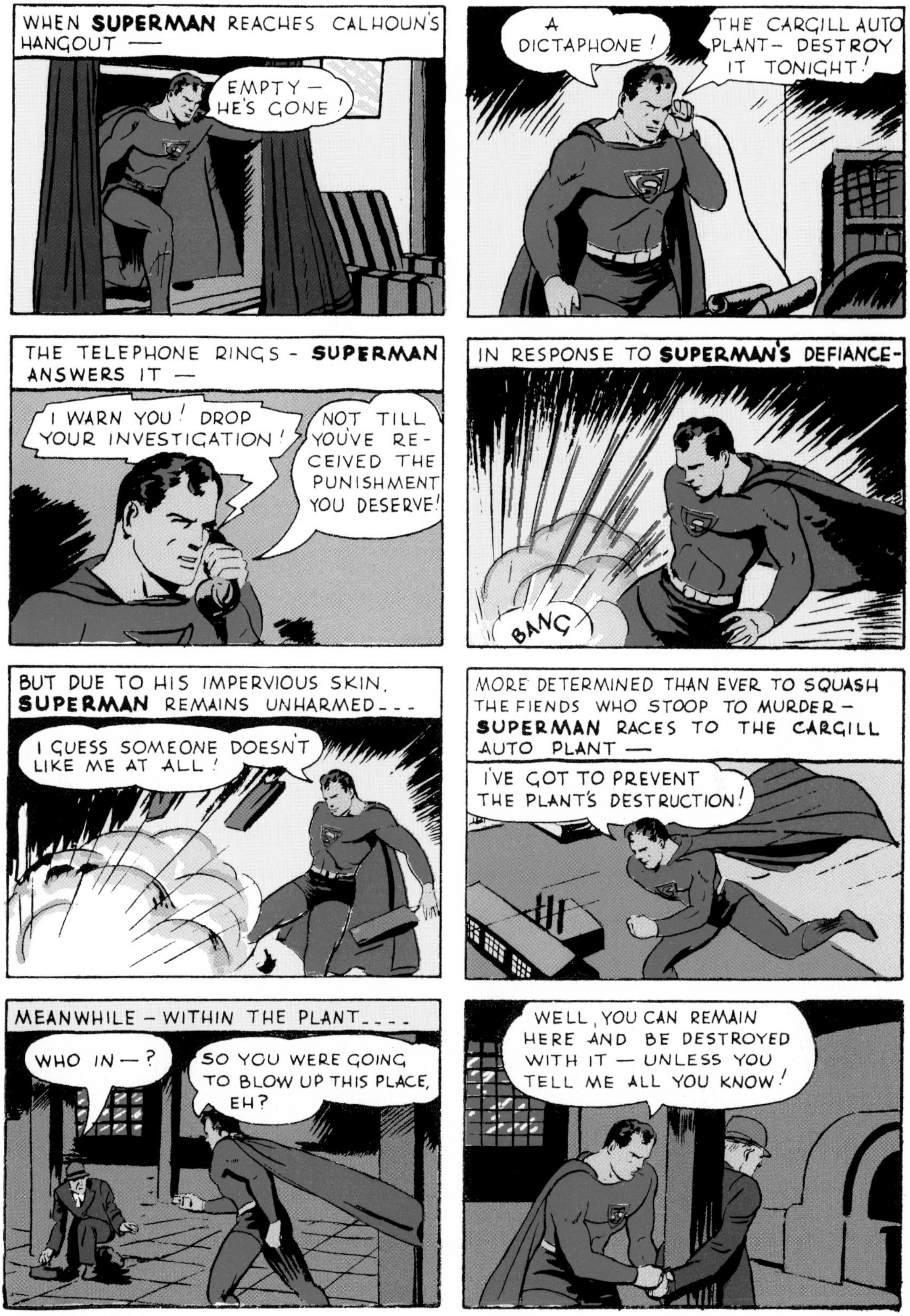
WHEN SUPERMAN REACHES CALHOUN'S HANGOUT —
EMPTY — HE'S GONE!
A DICTAPHONE!
THE CARGILL AUTO PLANT— DESTROY IT TONIGHT!
THE TELEPHONE RINGS - SUPERMAN ANSWERS IT —
I WARN YOU! DROP YOUR INVESTIGATION!
NOT TILL YOU'VE RE-CEIVED THE PUNISHMENT YOU DESERVE!
IN RESPONSE TO SUPERMAN'S DEFIANCE-
BANG
BUT DUE TO HIS IMPERVIOUS SKIN, SUPERMAN REMAINS UNHARMED---
I GUESS SOMEONE DOESN'T LIKE ME AT ALL!
MORE DETERMINED THAN EVER TO SQUASH THE FIENDS WHO STOOP TO MURDER— SUPERMAN RACES TO THE CARGILL AUTO PLANT —
I'VE GOT TO PREVENT THE PLANT'S DESTRUCTION!
MEANWHILE — WITHIN THE PLANT----
WHO IN —?
SO YOU WERE GOING TO BLOW UP THIS PLACE, EH?
WELL, YOU CAN REMAIN HERE AND BE DESTROYED WITH IT — UNLESS YOU TELL ME ALL YOU KNOW!

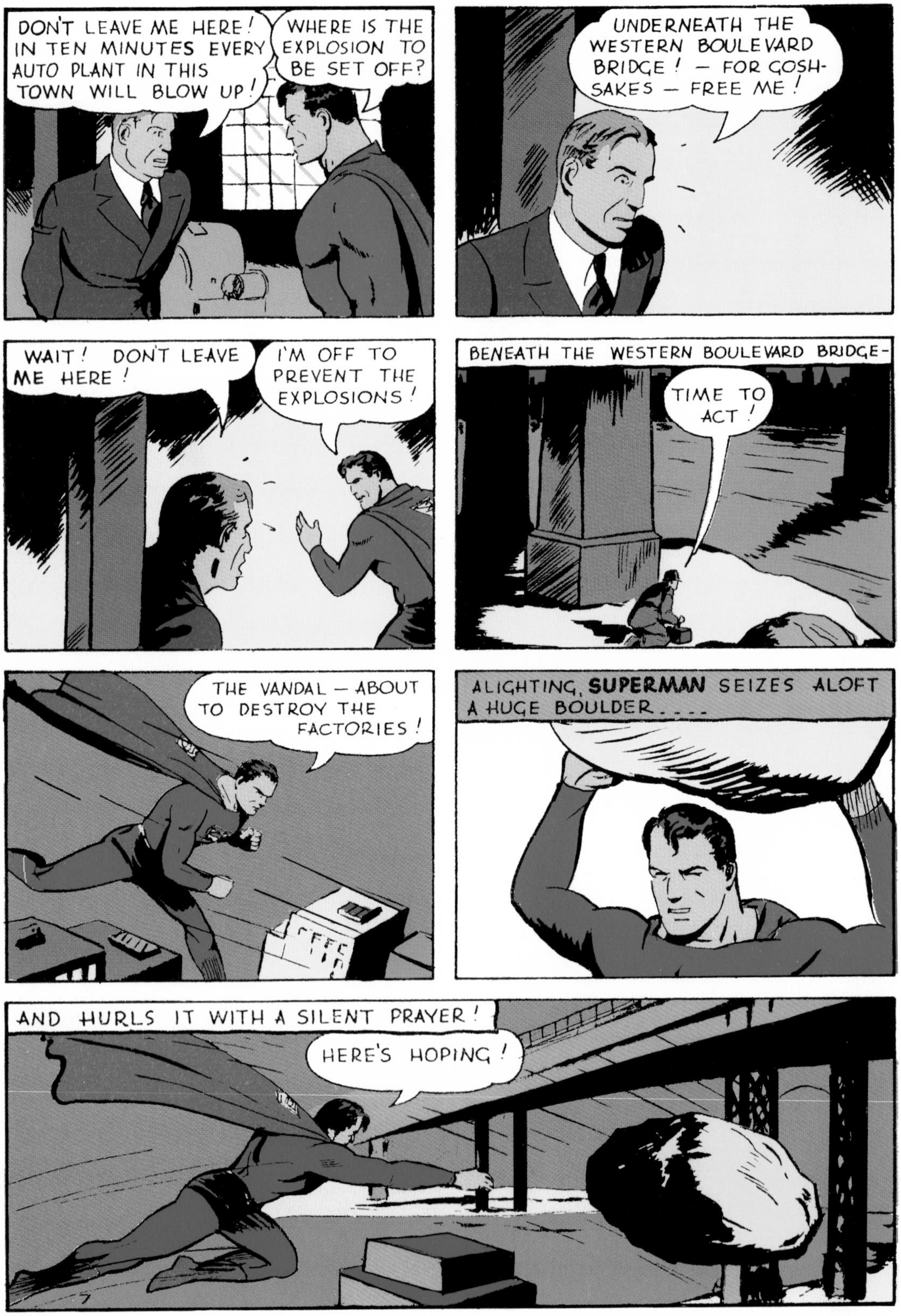
DON'T LEAVE ME HERE! IN TEN MINUTES EVERY AUTO PLANT IN THIS TOWN WILL BLOW UP!
WHERE IS THE EXPLOSION TO BE SET OFF?
UNDERNEATH THE WESTERN BOULEVARD BRIDGE! — FOR GOSH-SAKES — FREE ME!
WAIT! DON'T LEAVE ME HERE!
I'M OFF TO PREVENT THE EXPLOSIONS!
BENEATH THE WESTERN BOULEVARD BRIDGE-
TIME TO ACT!
THE VANDAL — ABOUT TO DESTROY THE FACTORIES!
ALIGHTING, SUPERMAN SEIZES ALOFT A HUGE BOULDER....
AND HURLS IT WITH A SILENT PRAYER!
HERE'S HOPING!

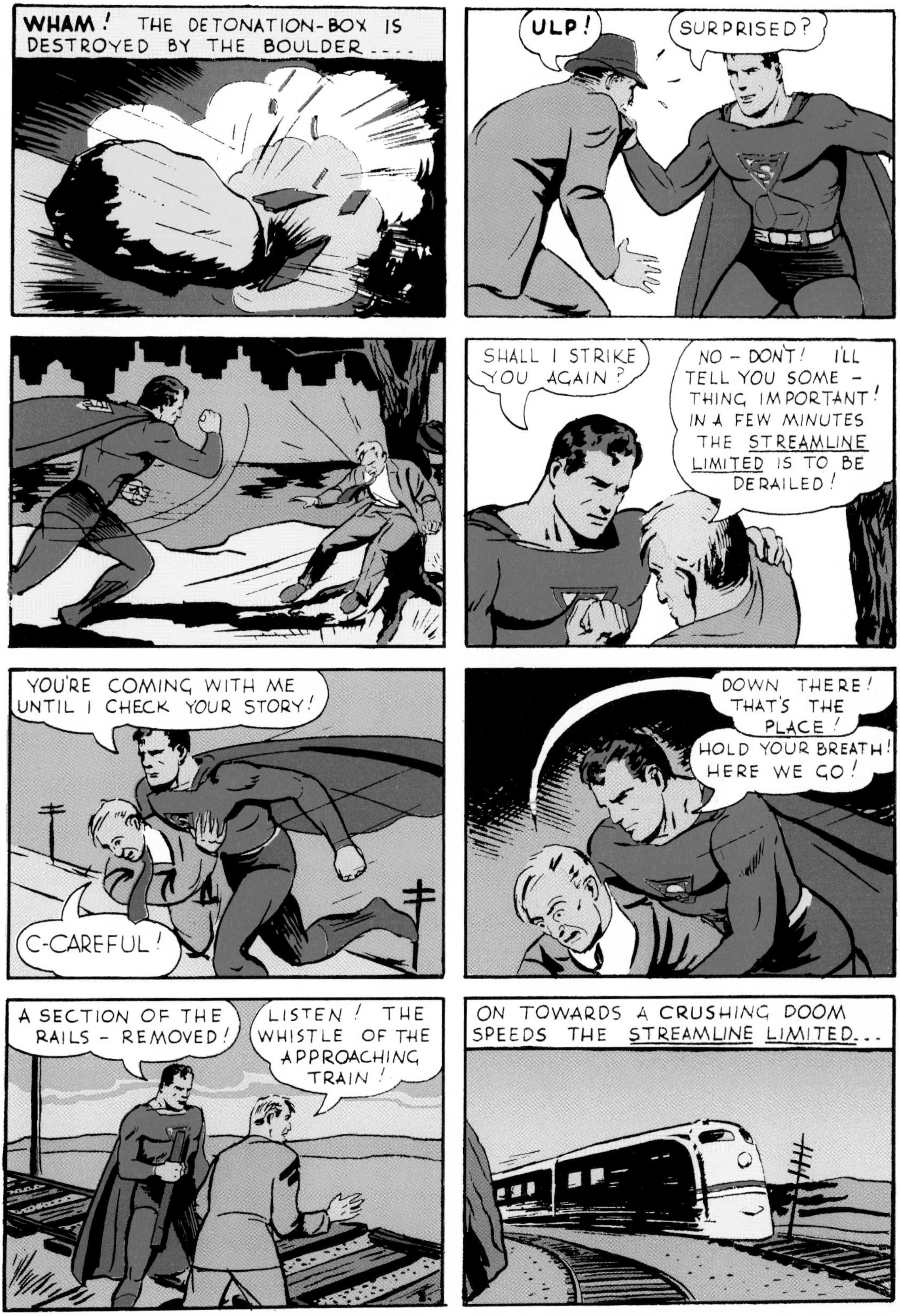
WHAM! THE DETONATION-BOX IS DESTROYED BY THE BOULDER....
ULP!
SURPRISED?
SHALL I STRIKE YOU AGAIN?
NO - DON'T! I'LL TELL YOU SOME-THING IMPORTANT! IN A FEW MINUTES THE STREAMLINE LIMITED IS TO BE DERAILED!
YOU'RE COMING WITH ME UNTIL I CHECK YOUR STORY!
C-CAREFUL!
DOWN THERE! THAT'S THE PLACE!
HOLD YOUR BREATH! HERE WE GO!
A SECTION OF THE RAILS - REMOVED!
LISTEN! THE WHISTLE OF THE APPROACHING TRAIN!
ON TOWARDS A CRUSHING DOOM SPEEDS THE STREAMLINE LIMITED...

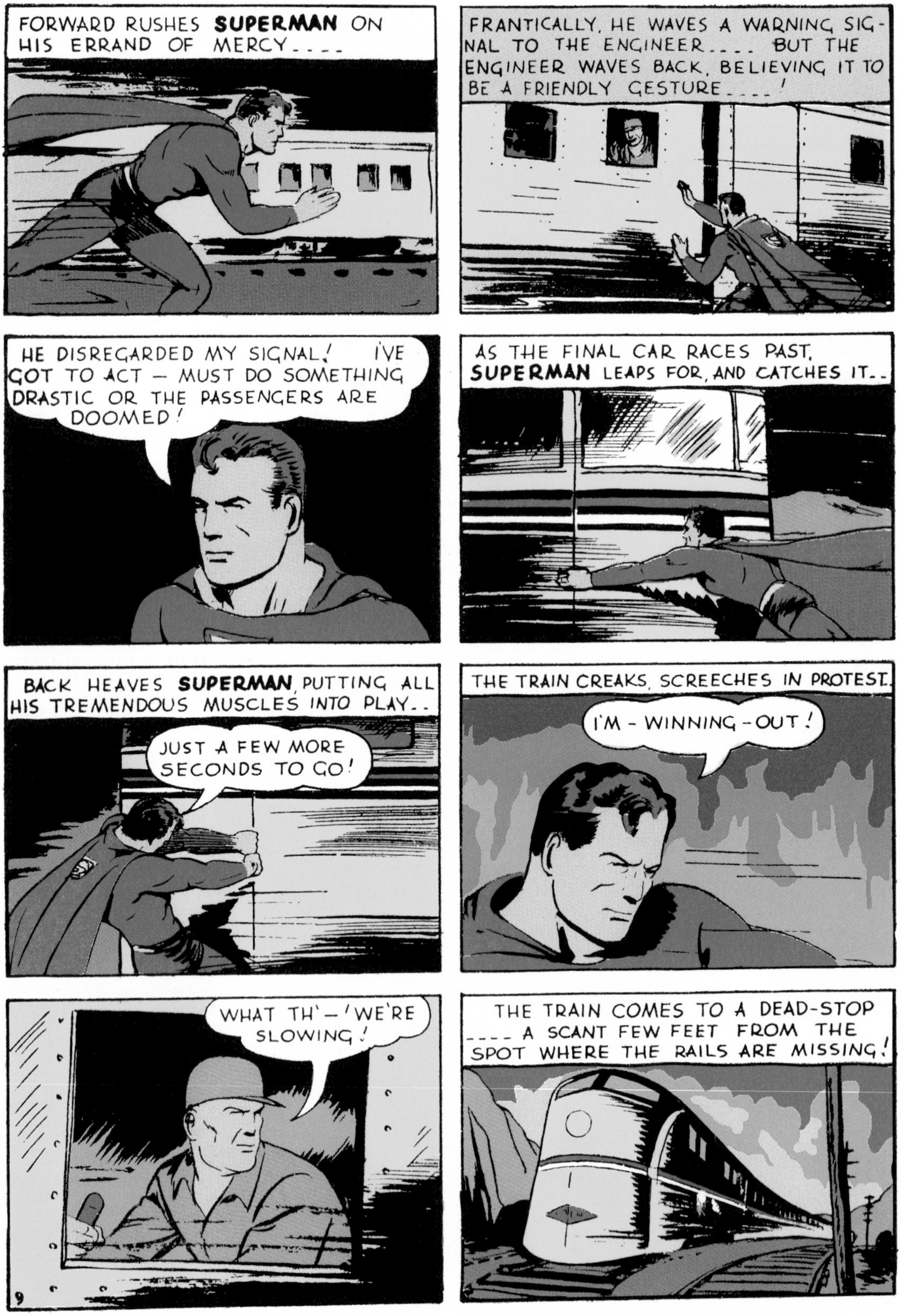
FORWARD RUSHES SUPERMAN ON HIS ERRAND OF MERCY----
FRANTICALLY, HE WAVES A WARNING SIGNAL TO THE ENGINEER---- BUT THE ENGINEER WAVES BACK, BELIEVING IT TO BE A FRIENDLY GESTURE---!
HE DISREGARDED MY SIGNAL! I'VE GOT TO ACT — MUST DO SOMETHING DRASTIC OR THE PASSENGERS ARE DOOMED!
AS THE FINAL CAR RACES PAST, SUPERMAN LEAPS FOR, AND CATCHES IT--
BACK HEAVES SUPERMAN, PUTTING ALL HIS TREMENDOUS MUSCLES INTO PLAY--
JUST A FEW MORE SECONDS TO GO!
THE TRAIN CREAKS, SCREECHES IN PROTEST.
I'M - WINNING - OUT!
WHAT TH'—'WE'RE SLOWING!
THE TRAIN COMES TO A DEAD-STOP ---- A SCANT FEW FEET FROM THE SPOT WHERE THE RAILS ARE MISSING!

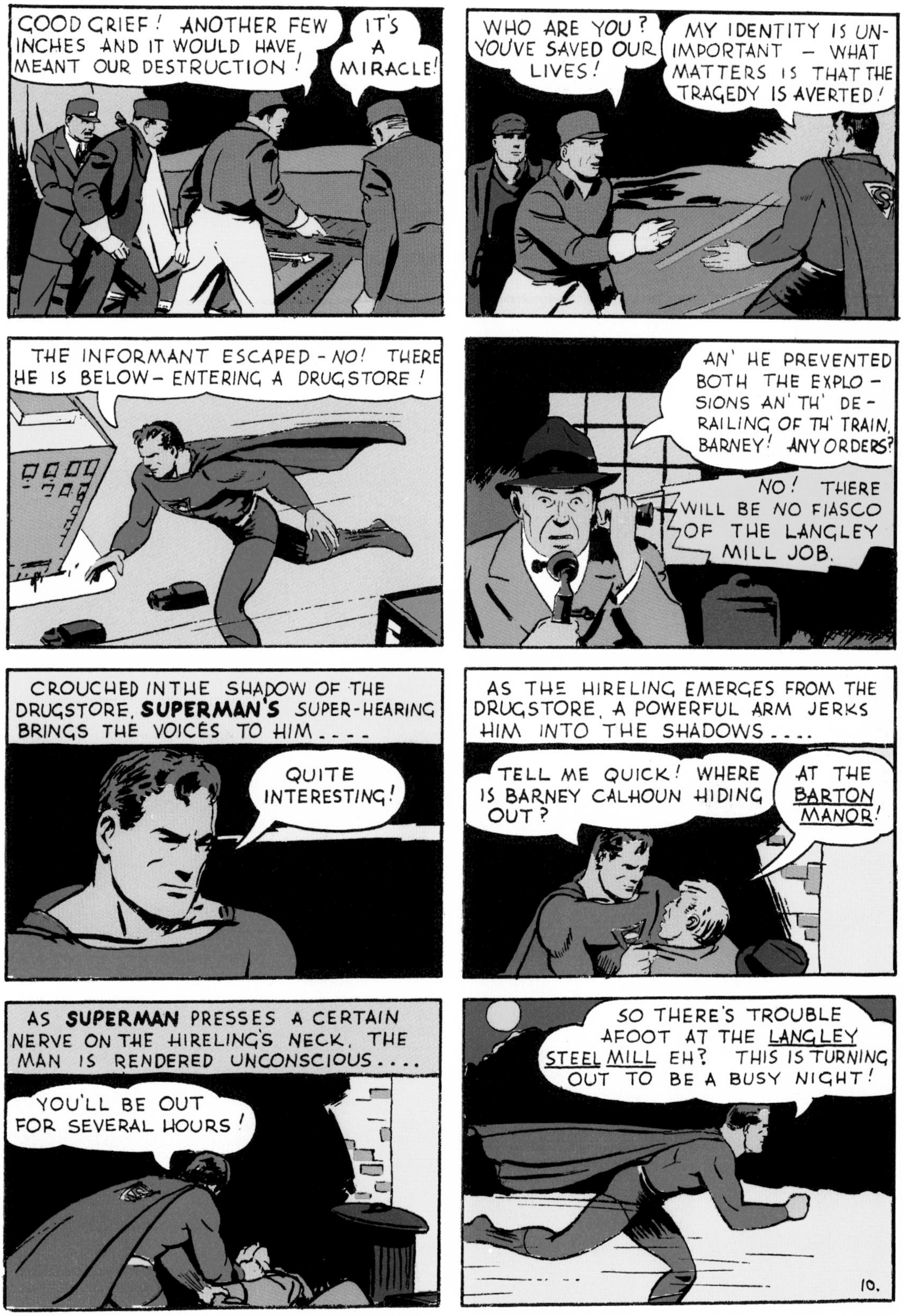
GOOD GRIEF! ANOTHER FEW INCHES AND IT WOULD HAVE MEANT OUR DESTRUCTION!
IT'S A MIRACLE!
WHO ARE YOU? YOU'VE SAVED OUR LIVES!
MY IDENTITY IS UNIMPORTANT — WHAT MATTERS IS THAT THE TRAGEDY IS AVERTED!
THE INFORMANT ESCAPED - NO! THERE HE IS BELOW - ENTERING A DRUGSTORE!
AN' HE PREVENTED BOTH THE EXPLOSIONS AN' TH' DERAILING OF TH' TRAIN, BARNEY! ANY ORDERS?
NO! THERE WILL BE NO FIASCO OF THE LANGLEY MILL JOB.
CROUCHED IN THE SHADOW OF THE DRUGSTORE, SUPERMAN'S SUPER-HEARING BRINGS THE VOICES TO HIM....
QUITE INTERESTING!
AS THE HIRELING EMERGES FROM THE DRUGSTORE, A POWERFUL ARM JERKS HIM INTO THE SHADOWS....
TELL ME QUICK! WHERE IS BARNEY CALHOUN HIDING OUT?
AT THE BARTON MANOR!
AS SUPERMAN PRESSES A CERTAIN NERVE ON THE HIRELING'S NECK, THE MAN IS RENDERED UNCONSCIOUS....
YOU'LL BE OUT FOR SEVERAL HOURS!
SO THERE'S TROUBLE AFOOT AT THE LANGLEY STEEL MILL EH? THIS IS TURNING OUT TO BE A BUSY NIGHT!
10.

WITHIN THE LANGLEY STEEL MILLS, THE THUG WHO HAD ESCAPED FROM THE MOUNTAIN ROAD GLOATS, FOR HE HAS TAMPERED WITH THE MILL'S MECHANISMS...

A COUPLE "ACCIDENTS", AND TH' MEN WILL REFUSE TO WORK HERE!

AS THE GREAT STEEL DIPPER TURNS, IT'S WEAKENED SUPPORTS BREAK, AND IT CRASHES DOWN TOWARD WORKERS BELOW, SPEWING MOLTEN METAL....!

LOOK OUT!

IT'S FALLING!

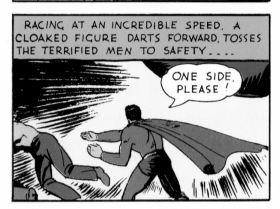

RACING AT AN INCREDIBLE SPEED, A CLOAKED FIGURE DARTS FORWARD, TOSSES THE TERRIFIED MEN TO SAFETY....

ONE SIDE, PLEASE!

....AND CATCHES THE GREAT, FALLING DIPPER!

B-BUT — IT'S — IMPOSSIBLE!

COME TO THINK OF IT, IT IS!

AS THE EYES OF SUPERMAN AND THE THUG MEET, THERE IS MUTUAL RECOGNITION....

YOU!

YOU WON'T GET ME!

THE THUG UNEXPECTEDLY TRIPS AND—

— HE TUMBLES INTO A HUGE BOWL OF MOLTEN ORE!

YI-I1-I1!

WITHIN HIS HIDEAWAY, CALHOUN CURSES AS BAD NEWS COMES OVER HIS 'PHONE...

THAT BLASTED SUPERMAN! IF I HAD HIM HERE, I'D-I'D....!

YOU'D WHAT?

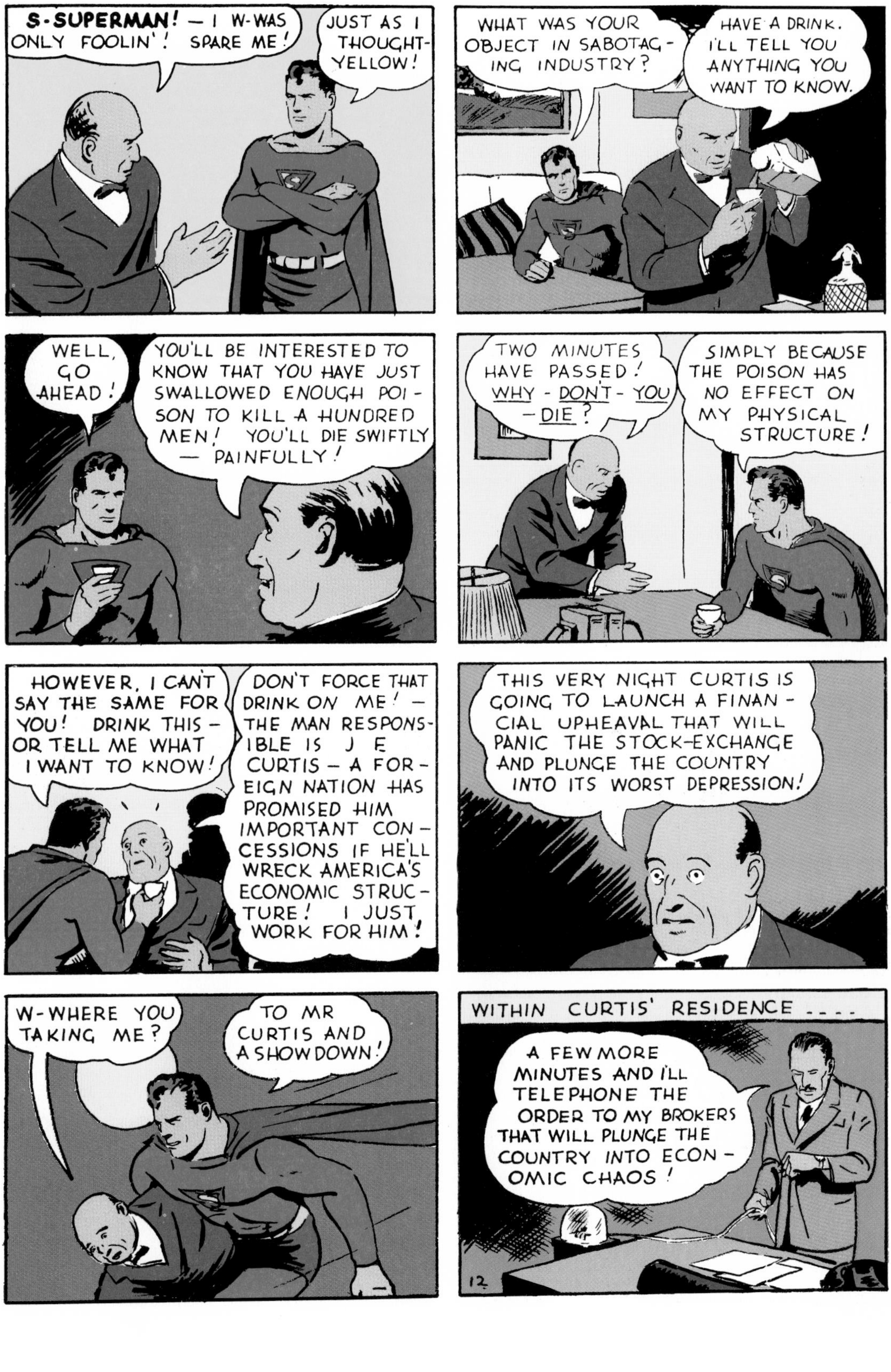
S-SUPERMAN! — I W-WAS ONLY FOOLIN'! SPARE ME!
JUST AS I THOUGHT- YELLOW!
WHAT WAS YOUR OBJECT IN SABOTAGING INDUSTRY?
HAVE A DRINK. I'LL TELL YOU ANYTHING YOU WANT TO KNOW.
WELL, GO AHEAD!
YOU'LL BE INTERESTED TO KNOW THAT YOU HAVE JUST SWALLOWED ENOUGH POISON TO KILL A HUNDRED MEN! YOU'LL DIE SWIFTLY — PAINFULLY!
TWO MINUTES HAVE PASSED! WHY - DON'T - YOU - DIE?
SIMPLY BECAUSE THE POISON HAS NO EFFECT ON MY PHYSICAL STRUCTURE!
HOWEVER, I CAN'T SAY THE SAME FOR YOU! DRINK THIS - OR TELL ME WHAT I WANT TO KNOW!
DON'T FORCE THAT DRINK ON ME! — THE MAN RESPONSIBLE IS J E CURTIS — A FOREIGN NATION HAS PROMISED HIM IMPORTANT CONCESSIONS IF HE'LL WRECK AMERICA'S ECONOMIC STRUCTURE! I JUST WORK FOR HIM!
THIS VERY NIGHT CURTIS IS GOING TO LAUNCH A FINANCIAL UPHEAVAL THAT WILL PANIC THE STOCK-EXCHANGE AND PLUNGE THE COUNTRY INTO ITS WORST DEPRESSION!
W-WHERE YOU TAKING ME?
TO MR CURTIS AND A SHOWDOWN!
WITHIN CURTIS' RESIDENCE ....
A FEW MORE MINUTES AND I'LL TELEPHONE THE ORDER TO MY BROKERS THAT WILL PLUNGE THE COUNTRY INTO ECONOMIC CHAOS!
12

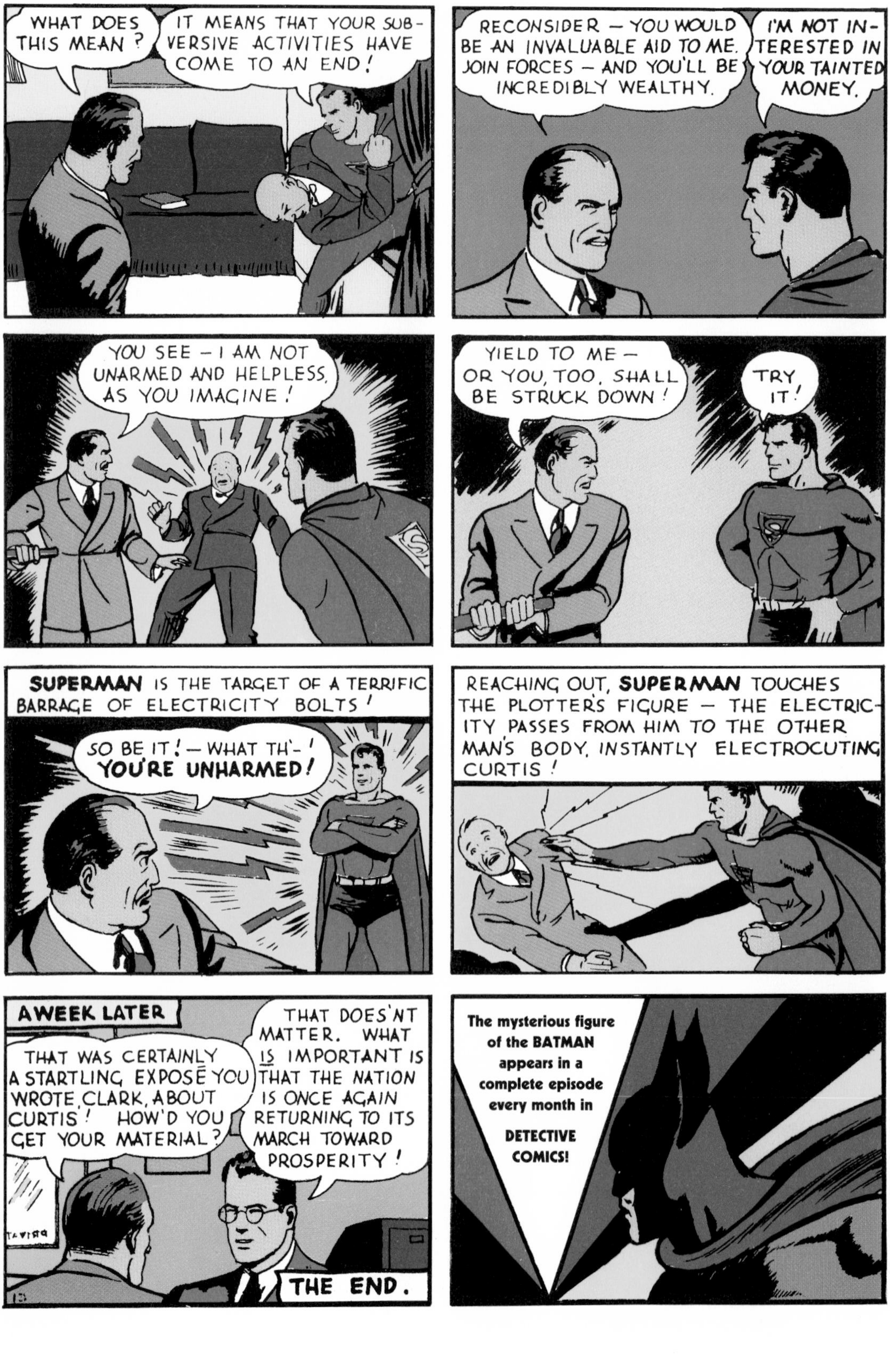
WHAT DOES THIS MEAN ?
IT MEANS THAT YOUR SUB-VERSIVE ACTIVITIES HAVE COME TO AN END !
RECONSIDER — YOU WOULD BE AN INVALUABLE AID TO ME. JOIN FORCES — AND YOU'LL BE INCREDIBLY WEALTHY.
I'M NOT IN-TERESTED IN YOUR TAINTED MONEY.
YOU SEE — I AM NOT UNARMED AND HELPLESS, AS YOU IMAGINE !
YIELD TO ME — OR YOU, TOO, SHALL BE STRUCK DOWN !
TRY IT !
SUPERMAN IS THE TARGET OF A TERRIFIC BARRAGE OF ELECTRICITY BOLTS !
SO BE IT ! — WHAT TH'- ! YOU'RE UNHARMED !
REACHING OUT, SUPERMAN TOUCHES THE PLOTTER'S FIGURE — THE ELECTRIC-ITY PASSES FROM HIM TO THE OTHER MAN'S BODY, INSTANTLY ELECTROCUTING CURTIS !
A WEEK LATER
THAT WAS CERTAINLY A STARTLING EXPOSÉ YOU WROTE, CLARK, ABOUT CURTIS ! HOW'D YOU GET YOUR MATERIAL ?
THAT DOES'NT MATTER. WHAT IS IMPORTANT IS THAT THE NATION IS ONCE AGAIN RETURNING TO ITS MARCH TOWARD PROSPERITY !
THE END.
The mysterious figure of the BATMAN appears in a complete episode every month in DETECTIVE COMICS!

SUPERMAN SAYS:

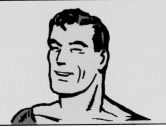

IN the many thousands of letters received in the big SUPERMAN CONTEST, it is evident that our readers, in telling us what they would do if they had the powers of SUPERMAN, realize the importance of an agile quick thinking mind as well as physical perfection.

It is only through this combination that the boys and girls of America can grow up into sturdy upstanding American citizens.

One of the important means of cultivating your mind so that you will have the keen mental powers so necessary, is to *read good books*. It is for that reason that the publishers of SUPERMAN, as well as ACTION, DETECTIVE, ADVENTURE, MORE FUN, FLASH and ALL-AMERICAN COMICS, have decided, beginning with the April issue, to review in each issue one good book—with a suggestion that if you like the review you go to your school library or the public library—get the book and thus get into the habit of reading at least one good book a month.

I am listing on this page a number of good standard accepted books for boys and girls. They are packed full of adventure, thrills, excitement and fun, and I know you will enjoy reading every one of them.

Lord Jim, *Joseph Conrad*
Swiss Family Robinson
Alice in Wonderland
Don Quixote
Captain Blood
Robin Hood
Anne of Green Gables
Moby Dick
The American Claimant, *Mark Twain*
A Connecticut Yankee, *Mark Twain*
A Tramp Abroad, *Mark Twain*
Hans Brinker and the Silver Skates, *Dodge*
Katrinka, *Haskell*
The Mysterious Island, *Verne*
War of the Worlds, *Wells*
Mutiny on the Bounty
Drums, *James Boyd*
Abraham Lincoln, *Carl Sandberg*
Everybody's Washington
Count of Monte Cristo
The Scarlet Pimpernel
The Black Tulip
The Prisoner of Zenda
The Man in the Iron Mask
Ivanhoe
Biography of Benjamin Franklin
Silver Chief, *Jack O'Brien*
Peter Pan
O'Henry's "Four Hundred"
The Alhambra, *Washington Irving*
The War in the Air, *H. G. Wells*
Tom Brown's Schooldays
20,000 Leagues Under the Sea, *Jules Verne*
Three Musketeers
Prince and the Pauper, *Mark Twain*
Two Little Confederates, *Page*
Huckleberry Finn
Captains Courageous, *Kipling*
Men of Iron, *Pyle*
King Arthur and His Knights, *Pyle*
Story of Roland, *James Baldwin*
Master Skylark, *John Bennett*
Puck of Pooks, *Kipling*
Kim, *Kipling*
The Wind in the Willows, *Kenneth Graham*
North Wind, *George McDonald*
Gulliver's Travels
Pinocchio
Pollyanna
Tom Sawyer
Seventeen, *Tarkington*
Penrod
Penrod and Sam
Oliver Twist, *Dickens*
The Old Curiosity Shop, *Dickens*
David Copperfield, *Dickens*
Great Expectations, *Dickens*
Tale of Two Cities, *Dickens*
Around the World in 80 Days, *Verne*
Little Men, *Alcott*
Black Beauty
The Spy, *Cooper*
Rip Van Winkle, *Irving*
The Headless Horseman, *Hawthorne*
THe Lighthouse at the End of the World, *Verne*
House of the 7 Gables, *Hawthorne*
Bambi, *Felix Salten*

The following six books will be reviewed in our April issues as follows:

In APRIL ACTION COMICS—Treasure Island.......*by Robert Louis Stevenson*
In APRIL DETECTIVE COMICS—Kidnapped.......*by Robert Louis Stevenson*
In APRIL FLASH COMICS—Robinson Crusoe.......*by Daniel Defoe*
In APRIL MORE FUN—Penrod.......*by Booth Tarkington*
In APRIL ADVENTURE COMICS—Call of the Wild.......*by Jack London*
In APRIL ALL-AMERICAN COMICS—Last of the Mohicans.......*by James Fenimore Cooper*

Be sure to get all these six leading monthly comic books for these book reviews, as well as for good, clean, exciting comic features!

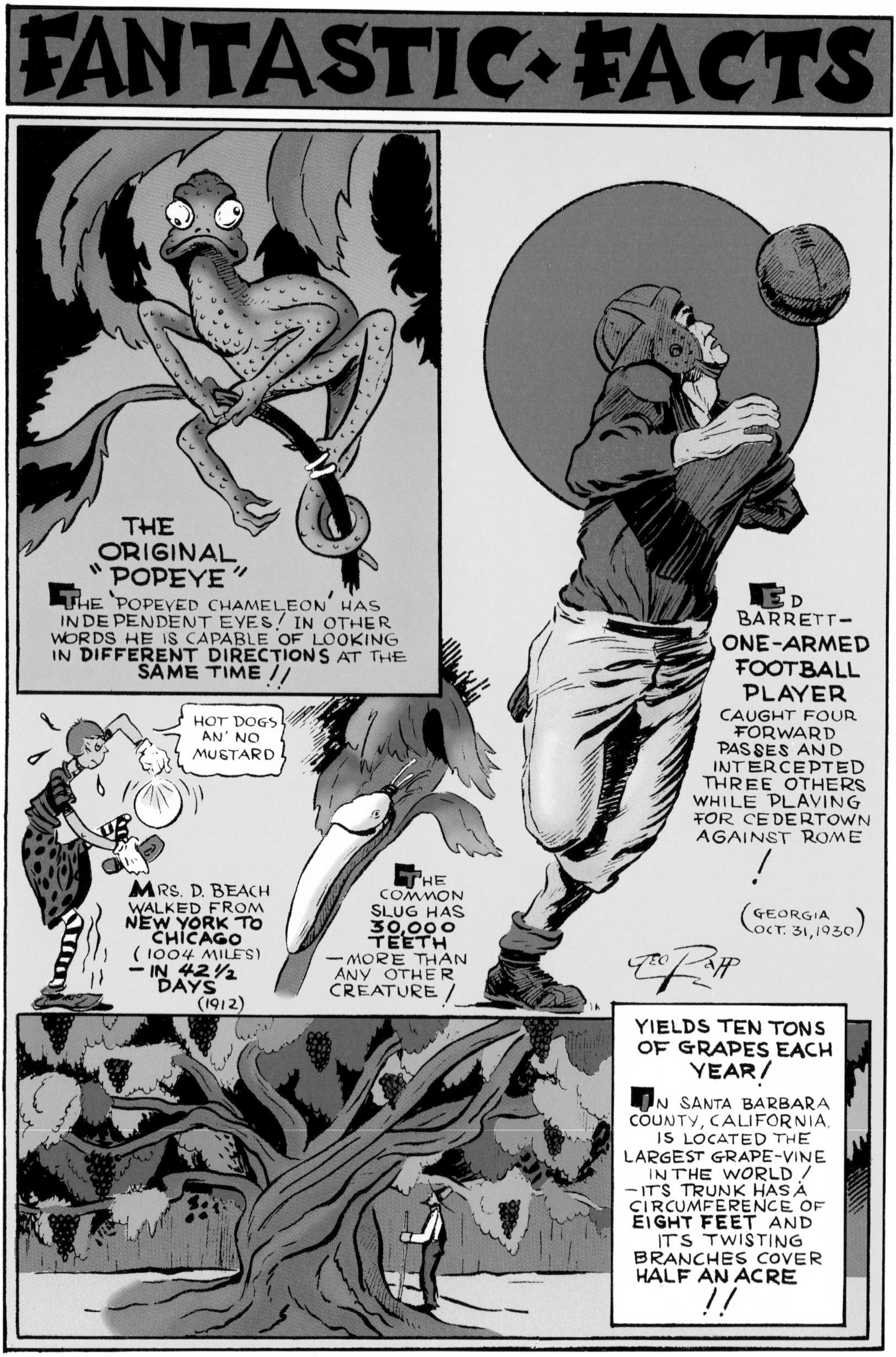
FANTASTIC FACTS
THE ORIGINAL "POPEYE"
THE 'POPEYED CHAMELEON' HAS INDEPENDENT EYES! IN OTHER WORDS HE IS CAPABLE OF LOOKING IN DIFFERENT DIRECTIONS AT THE SAME TIME!!
ED BARRETT— ONE-ARMED FOOTBALL PLAYER
CAUGHT FOUR FORWARD PASSES AND INTERCEPTED THREE OTHERS WHILE PLAYING FOR CEDERTOWN AGAINST ROME!
(GEORGIA OCT. 31, 1930)
HOT DOGS AN' NO MUSTARD
MRS. D. BEACH WALKED FROM NEW YORK TO CHICAGO (1004 MILES) —IN 42½ DAYS (1912)
THE COMMON SLUG HAS 30,000 TEETH —MORE THAN ANY OTHER CREATURE!
YIELDS TEN TONS OF GRAPES EACH YEAR!
IN SANTA BARBARA COUNTY, CALIFORNIA, IS LOCATED THE LARGEST GRAPE-VINE IN THE WORLD! —ITS TRUNK HAS A CIRCUMFERENCE OF EIGHT FEET AND ITS TWISTING BRANCHES COVER HALF AN ACRE!!

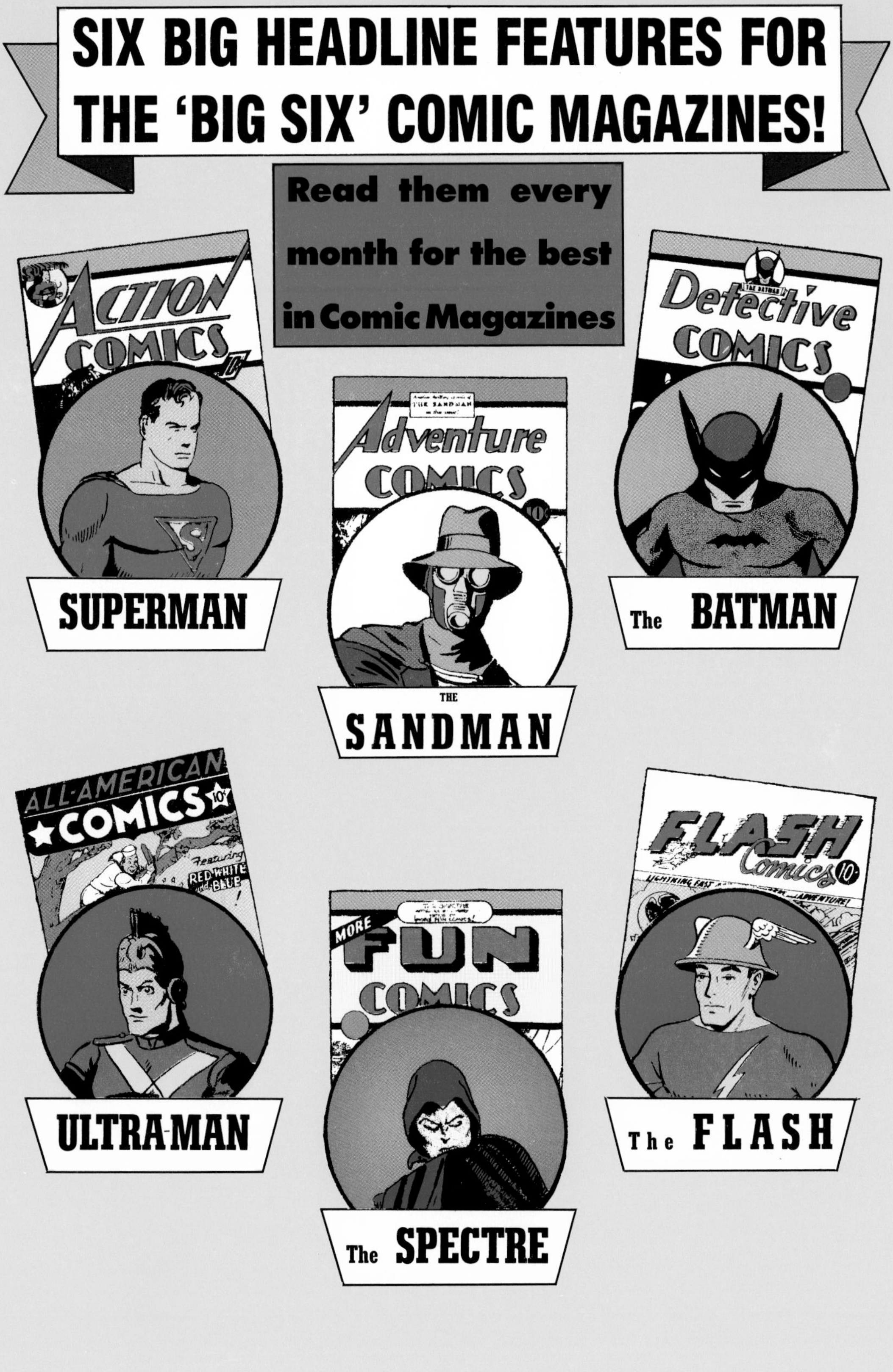
SIX BIG HEADLINE FEATURES FOR
THE 'BIG SIX' COMIC MAGAZINES!
Read them every month for the best in Comic Magazines
ACTION COMICS 10¢
SUPERMAN
Adventure COMICS 10¢
THE SANDMAN
Detective COMICS
The BATMAN
ALL-AMERICAN COMICS 10¢
Featuring RED WHITE and BLUE
ULTRA-MAN
MORE FUN COMICS
The SPECTRE
FLASH Comics 10¢
The FLASH

PIONEER INTO THE UNKNOWN

By Bert Lexington

A GREAT cheer arose from the assembled throngs as the sleek streamlined auto swept along the jammed streets to the foot of the great platform which rose a full hundred feet into the air. Atop the platform huddled a group of excited officials, more than one of which gazed up in awe at the huge crystalline globe above them. Out of the Mammoth Films Studio-Car jauntily stepped James Rolland. Swiftly, he raced up the winding runway in his customary virile style. As he reached the top of the platform, he laughingly bowed and waved to the shrieking, applauding multitudes.

Professor Graystoke, popeyed and breathless, dashed forward and enthusiastically wrung James Rolland's hand. "My boy, my boy," he fervently exclaimed. "This is the greatest day of my life! And this triumph—this brilliant culmination of all my experiments—I owe it all to you!"

"It's quite all right," replied Rolland with a frown, wishing the sweating little crackpot would let go of his hand and go away, or something.

Bixby came to the rescue with, "The audience is getting bored, Professor. How about slipping 'em a few words, before they listen to their protesting feet and take a walk?"

"Of course, of course," exclaimed the eccentric scientist, and stepping across the platform, stood on tiptoe and spoke into the microphone. "Long will we remember this day," he began. "Truly, it is the beginning of a new era. Without undue modesty, I admit that my space-folder is a scientific triumph of the greatest magnitude, but——!" He gasped for breath, then continued. "Engineers and idealists may plan and plot stirring things on paper, but it remains for pioneers of really tremendous stature to volunteer to put these very same plans into effect. You know to whom I refer in this instance, a man who has thrilled all of us on the silver screen—and who is now about to attempt an adventure greater than any he has performed in the movies—your idol and mine: JAMES ROLLAND!"

At the sound of Rolland's name the huge crowds went berserk. Men roared at the tops of their lungs. Women screamed and fainted. Mothers lifted their offspring so that they could get a better view.

Rolland stepped to the microphone, and looked out at the thousands stretching before him. He opened his mouth, and every ear strained anxiously. Apparently overcome with emotion, for the moment he could only mutter, and repeat, "My public!"

AGAIN cheering shook the vicinity. This time James Rolland permitted it to roar unleased for a good five minutes, then—"The time for speeches is over! Action is now imperative." And turning to Graystoke, "Sir! I am ready!"

As the tumultuous applause swept to even more ecstatic height, Rolland donned something quite akin to a diver's suit. Then, ponderously he made his way to the great translucent globe, and stepped into it, closing the entrance after him. But an instant later the entrance once again opened. He stepped out, bowed again and again, and re-entered the globe once more.

"He always did love his curtain-calls," acidly said Bixby.

Graystoke adanced toward the controls, seated himself, then extended a lean trembling hand toward the switch.

At that moment an overalls-clad man hastily poked his head thru the assembled officials and frantically attemped to signal Bixby. "Ps-st! Ps-st!"

Bixby sighted him. "Go 'way!" he ordered sharply. "Didn't I tell you not to——"

"But it's IMPORTANT," urged the laborer.

"Then make it snappy! What is it?"

"The trap-door! It doesn't work! *It's stuck!*"

Bixby swayed, gulped. "Wh-WHAT??"

"The trap-door," continued the laborer, "that you had me rig up. It was supposed to drop Rolland beneath the globe to safety. Later, you were to smuggle him away. Well, the trap-door doesn't work!"

"My gosh!" exclaimed Bixby. "I've got to do something!" He dashed toward Graystoke. "Hey! Stop!"

But he was too late! Down flashed the switch! Instantly, a terrific barrage of electricity engulfed the great crystalline globe—a thrilling sight, but one which sent clammy chills up Bixby's spine. "Oh-hh!" he moaned. "Oh-hh!"

The laborer clutched the press agent's arm. "It's *murder!*" he cried. "MURDER!"

Bixby wiped his sweating brow. "It's a nightmare, that's what it is! Or some hokum cooked up by the script department!—The invention's got to be a flop! It's *got to*—or I'll have to find me a new boss, and that's tough these days!"

The electrical display halted. As the Professor manipulated the lever, the entrance to the globe swung open revealing an empty interior. Graystoke turned to the microphone and hysterically screamed. "It's a success! A success!"

Bixby fainted!

* * *

As Rolland stepped within the globe, he could scarcely restrain the laughter which welled up within him. What a capital joke this was! All those yokels cheering madly out there when this was just a colossal hoax! The fools...to think that he would risk his neck, ten thousand dollars a week, and a home on Malibu Beach, just to satisfy their morbid curiosity. No siree! James Rolland wasn't that big a simpleton!

He advanced to the spot where he'd been instructed to stand, if things were to go as they had planned. He was to plummet into a concealed net below. A week later he was to come out of hiding, "magically reappearing from a trip to some distant spot in the universe!" As they stated it in Hollywood, the publicity would be terrific, stupendous, and clever old "J. P.," who had been hesitant about renewing his contract would sign on the dotted line, and at a substantial increase in salary. Uncle Sam would collect the increase in taxes, of course, but just think of the increased prestige!

James Rolland waited...and grew impatient. But before he could vent his rage, there came a gigantic explosion, and the world seemed to fly apart. It appeared to him that he was speeding thru dark, engulfing space. "What is this," he wondered. Then—"m-my gosh! The invention! It's *working*—on ME!"

The great movie star's next comments are unprintable, but they referred to the so-called capabilities of a certain "press-agent" named Bixby.

Suddenly, a brilliant light appeared ahead of him and swiftly waxed brighter. All else was forgotten in a sudden burst of panic. Next instant, his body was seared by unbearable heat, and simultaneously his vision was destroyed by the intensity of the blinding light.

Next instant, the tiny figure vanished in a brief *puff* as it dissolved into nothingness.

James Rolland had committed the unforgivable cosmic error of materializing within the heart of a giant sun!

* * *
* * *

Time: 1982, A.D.

Place: The Museum of Interstellar History.

Scene: A young child and his mother stand before a heroic bust.

Child: Who is that man, mother?

Mother: (reverently): That, my son, is James Rolland, the courageous pioneer who gave his life willingly so that interstellar travel might be advanced.

Child: Gosh! He must have been brave!

Mother: Yes, my son! When we reach home, I'll show you a personally autographed photograph my grandmother received from him when she sent twenty-five cents and a self-addressed stamped return envelope to the Mammoth Film Studio.

The End

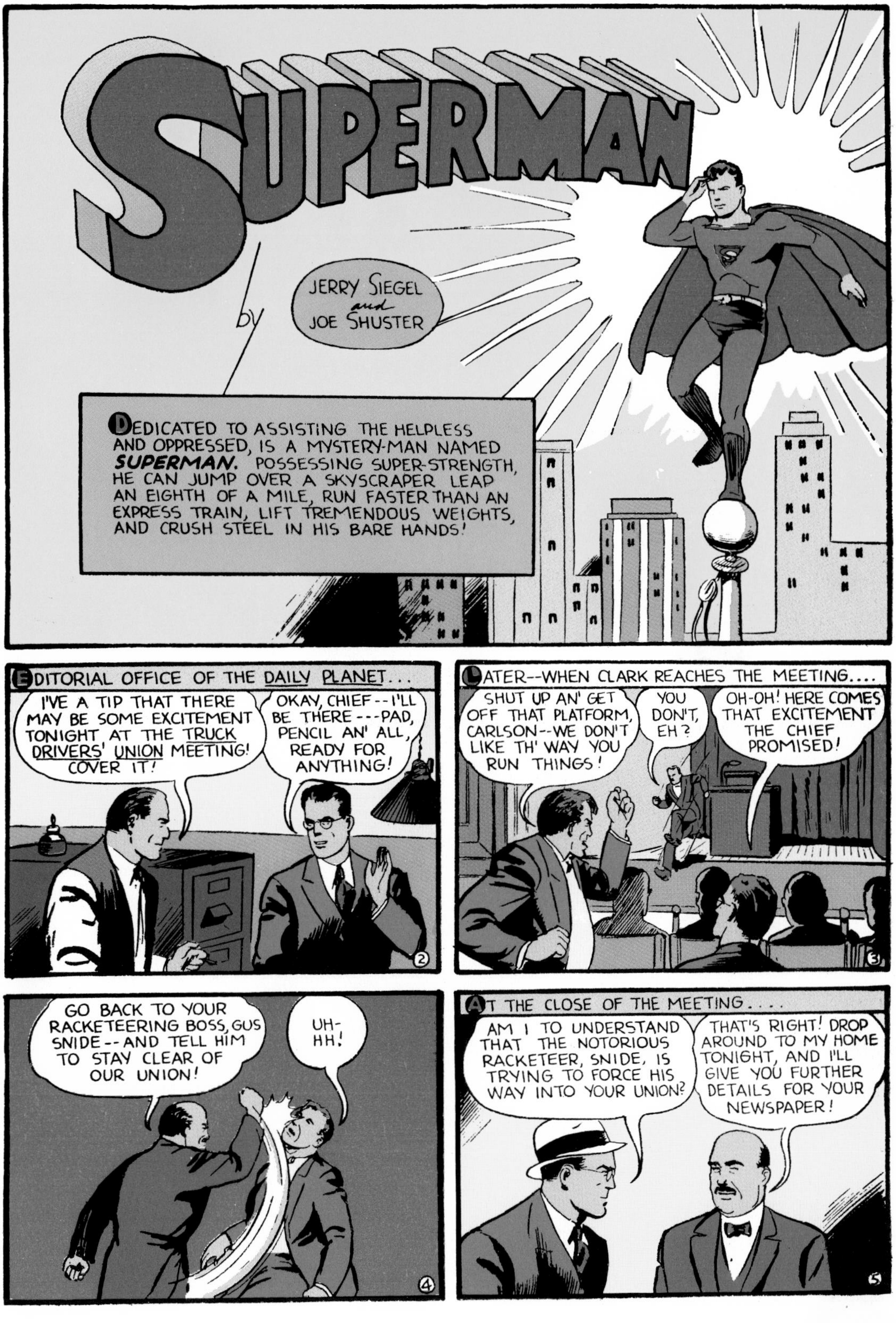
SUPERMAN
by
JERRY SIEGEL and JOE SHUSTER
DEDICATED TO ASSISTING THE HELPLESS AND OPPRESSED, IS A MYSTERY-MAN NAMED SUPERMAN. POSSESSING SUPER-STRENGTH, HE CAN JUMP OVER A SKYSCRAPER LEAP AN EIGHTH OF A MILE, RUN FASTER THAN AN EXPRESS TRAIN, LIFT TREMENDOUS WEIGHTS, AND CRUSH STEEL IN HIS BARE HANDS!
EDITORIAL OFFICE OF THE DAILY PLANET...
I'VE A TIP THAT THERE MAY BE SOME EXCITEMENT TONIGHT AT THE TRUCK DRIVERS' UNION MEETING! COVER IT!
OKAY, CHIEF--I'LL BE THERE---PAD, PENCIL AN' ALL, READY FOR ANYTHING!
2
LATER--WHEN CLARK REACHES THE MEETING....
SHUT UP AN' GET OFF THAT PLATFORM, CARLSON--WE DON'T LIKE TH' WAY YOU RUN THINGS!
YOU DON'T, EH?
OH-OH! HERE COMES THAT EXCITEMENT THE CHIEF PROMISED!
3
GO BACK TO YOUR RACKETEERING BOSS, GUS SNIDE--AND TELL HIM TO STAY CLEAR OF OUR UNION!
UH-HH!
4
AT THE CLOSE OF THE MEETING....
AM I TO UNDERSTAND THAT THE NOTORIOUS RACKETEER, SNIDE, IS TRYING TO FORCE HIS WAY INTO YOUR UNION?
THAT'S RIGHT! DROP AROUND TO MY HOME TONIGHT, AND I'LL GIVE YOU FURTHER DETAILS FOR YOUR NEWSPAPER!
5

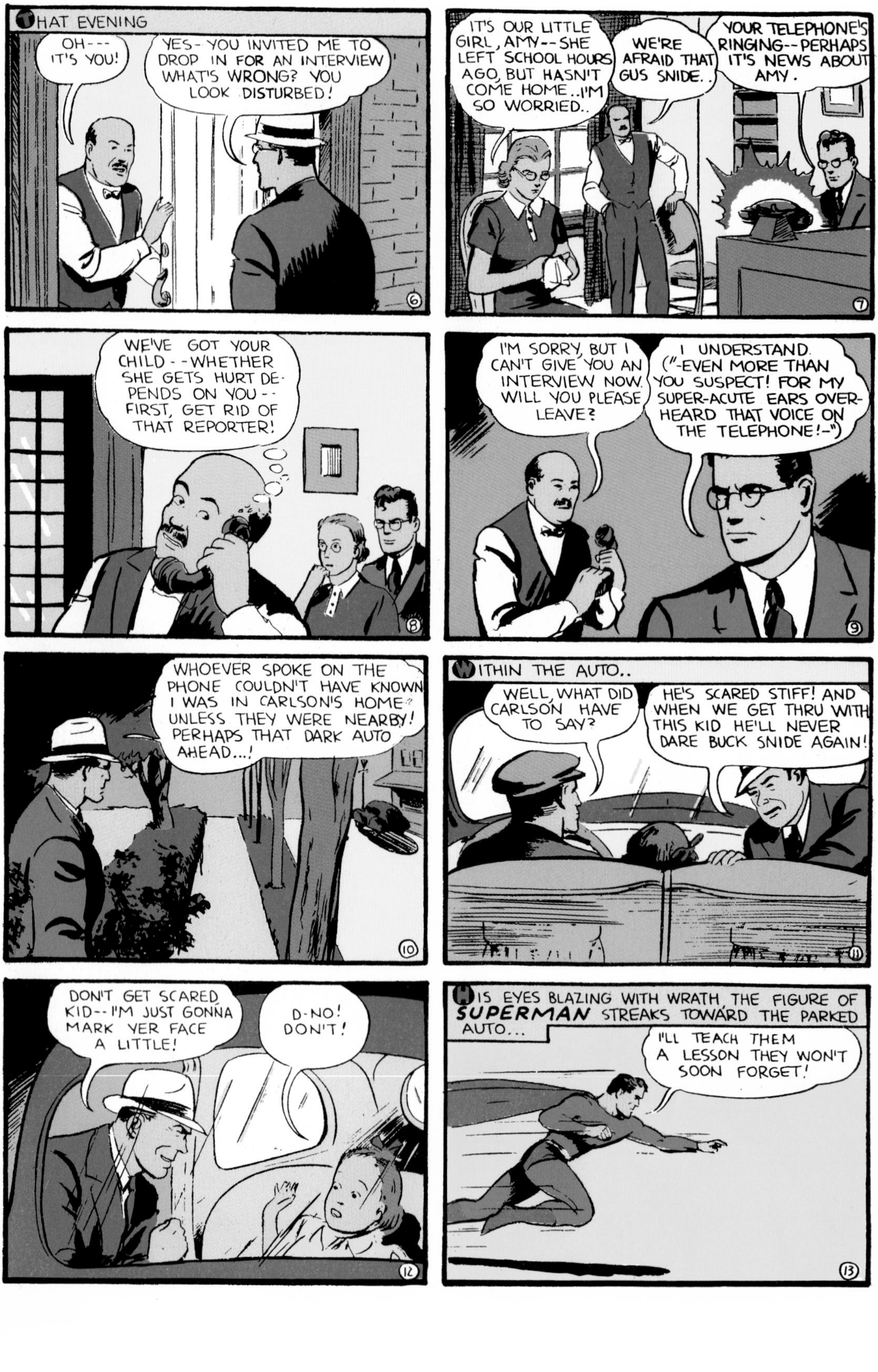
THAT EVENING
OH--- IT'S YOU!
YES- YOU INVITED ME TO DROP IN FOR AN INTERVIEW WHAT'S WRONG? YOU LOOK DISTURBED!
6
IT'S OUR LITTLE GIRL, AMY--SHE LEFT SCHOOL HOURS AGO, BUT HASN'T COME HOME..I'M SO WORRIED..
WE'RE AFRAID THAT GUS SNIDE..
YOUR TELEPHONE'S RINGING--PERHAPS IT'S NEWS ABOUT AMY.
7
WE'VE GOT YOUR CHILD--WHETHER SHE GETS HURT DE-PENDS ON YOU--FIRST, GET RID OF THAT REPORTER!
8
I'M SORRY, BUT I CAN'T GIVE YOU AN INTERVIEW NOW. WILL YOU PLEASE LEAVE?
I UNDERSTAND. ("-EVEN MORE THAN YOU SUSPECT! FOR MY SUPER-ACUTE EARS OVER-HEARD THAT VOICE ON THE TELEPHONE!-")
9
WHOEVER SPOKE ON THE PHONE COULDN'T HAVE KNOWN I WAS IN CARLSON'S HOME UNLESS THEY WERE NEARBY! PERHAPS THAT DARK AUTO AHEAD...!
10
WITHIN THE AUTO..
WELL, WHAT DID CARLSON HAVE TO SAY?
HE'S SCARED STIFF! AND WHEN WE GET THRU WITH THIS KID HE'LL NEVER DARE BUCK SNIDE AGAIN!
11
DON'T GET SCARED KID--I'M JUST GONNA MARK YER FACE A LITTLE!
D-NO! DON'T!
12
HIS EYES BLAZING WITH WRATH, THE FIGURE OF SUPERMAN STREAKS TOWARD THE PARKED AUTO...
I'LL TEACH THEM A LESSON THEY WON'T SOON FORGET!
13

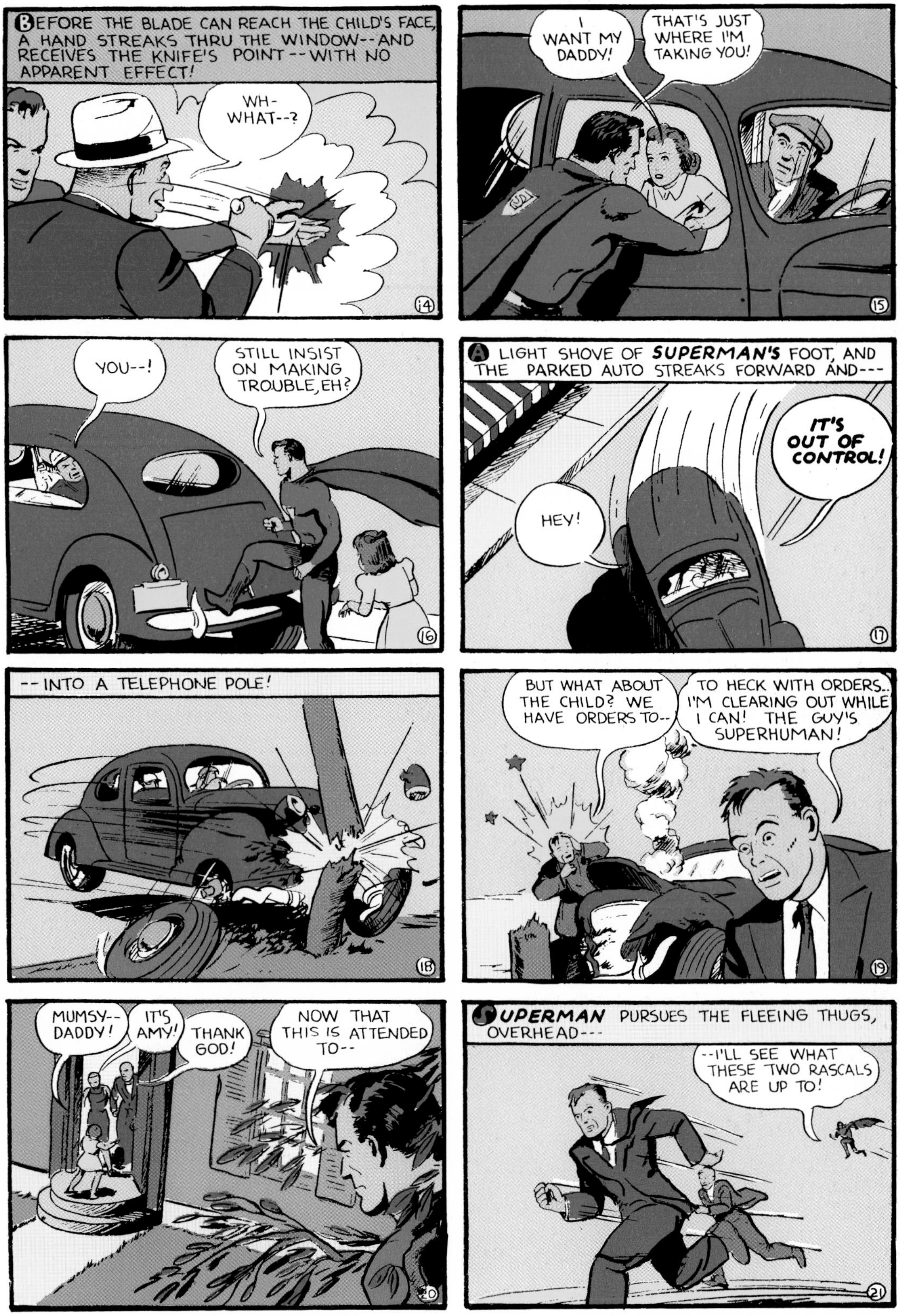
BEFORE THE BLADE CAN REACH THE CHILD'S FACE, A HAND STREAKS THRU THE WINDOW--AND RECEIVES THE KNIFE'S POINT--WITH NO APPARENT EFFECT!
WH- WHAT--?
14
I WANT MY DADDY!
THAT'S JUST WHERE I'M TAKING YOU!
15
YOU--!
STILL INSIST ON MAKING TROUBLE, EH?
16
A LIGHT SHOVE OF SUPERMAN'S FOOT, AND THE PARKED AUTO STREAKS FORWARD AND---
IT'S OUT OF CONTROL!
HEY!
17
--INTO A TELEPHONE POLE!
18
BUT WHAT ABOUT THE CHILD? WE HAVE ORDERS TO--
TO HECK WITH ORDERS.. I'M CLEARING OUT WHILE I CAN! THE GUY'S SUPERHUMAN!
19
MUMSY-- DADDY!
IT'S AMY!
THANK GOD!
NOW THAT THIS IS ATTENDED TO--
20
SUPERMAN PURSUES THE FLEEING THUGS, OVERHEAD---
--I'LL SEE WHAT THESE TWO RASCALS ARE UP TO!
21

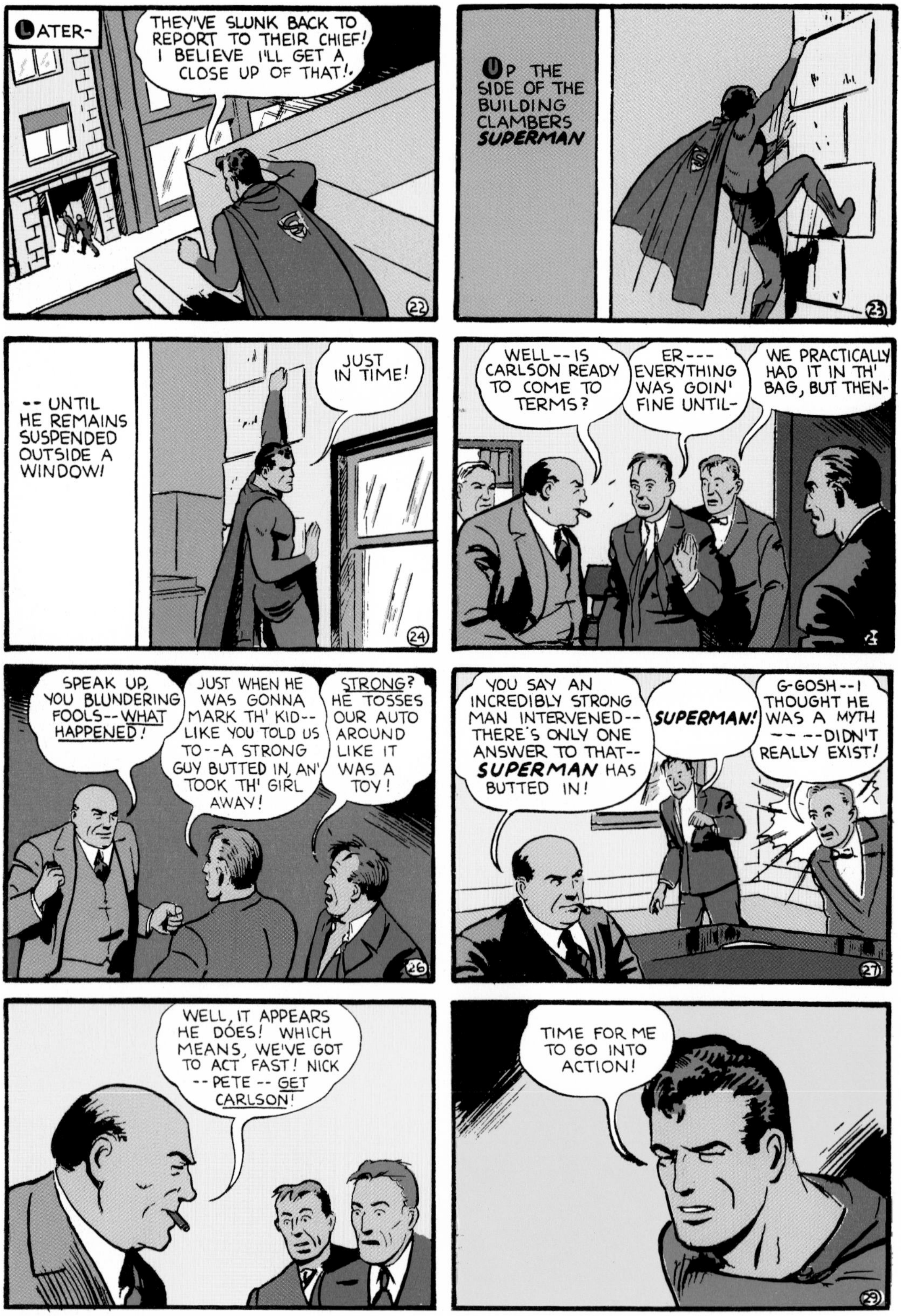
LATER-
THEY'VE SLUNK BACK TO REPORT TO THEIR CHIEF! I BELIEVE I'LL GET A CLOSE UP OF THAT!
22
UP THE SIDE OF THE BUILDING CLAMBERS SUPERMAN
23
-- UNTIL HE REMAINS SUSPENDED OUTSIDE A WINDOW!
JUST IN TIME!
24
WELL -- IS CARLSON READY TO COME TO TERMS?
ER--- EVERYTHING WAS GOIN' FINE UNTIL-
WE PRACTICALLY HAD IT IN TH' BAG, BUT THEN-
SPEAK UP, YOU BLUNDERING FOOLS--WHAT HAPPENED!
JUST WHEN HE WAS GONNA MARK TH' KID-- LIKE YOU TOLD US TO--A STRONG GUY BUTTED IN, AN' TOOK TH' GIRL AWAY!
STRONG? HE TOSSES OUR AUTO AROUND LIKE IT WAS A TOY!
26
YOU SAY AN INCREDIBLY STRONG MAN INTERVENED-- THERE'S ONLY ONE ANSWER TO THAT-- SUPERMAN HAS BUTTED IN!
SUPERMAN!
G-GOSH--I THOUGHT HE WAS A MYTH -- --DIDN'T REALLY EXIST!
27
WELL, IT APPEARS HE DOES! WHICH MEANS, WE'VE GOT TO ACT FAST! NICK -- PETE -- GET CARLSON!
TIME FOR ME TO GO INTO ACTION!
29

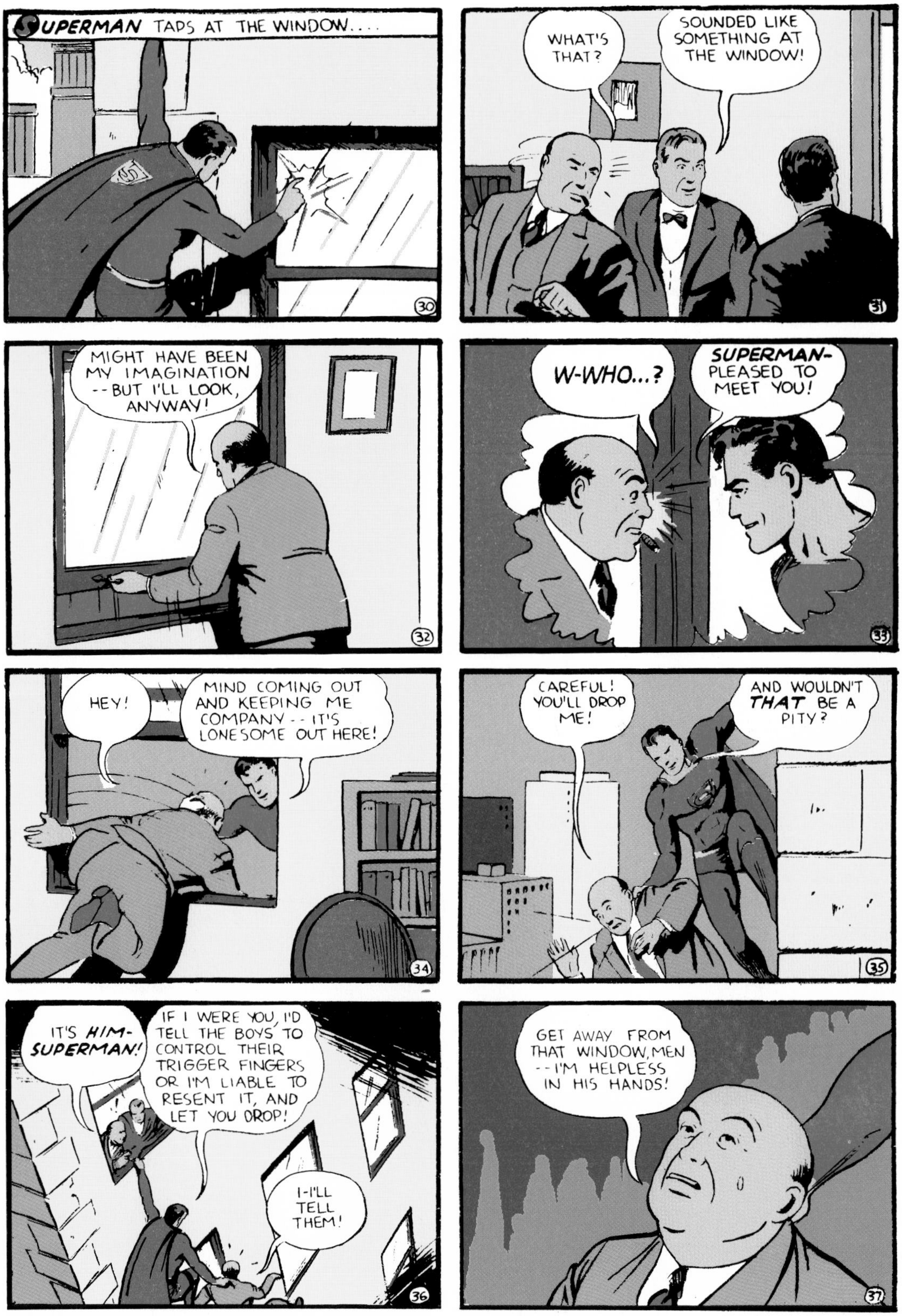
SUPERMAN TAPS AT THE WINDOW....
30
WHAT'S THAT?
SOUNDED LIKE SOMETHING AT THE WINDOW!
31
MIGHT HAVE BEEN MY IMAGINATION --BUT I'LL LOOK, ANYWAY!
32
W-WHO...?
SUPERMAN- PLEASED TO MEET YOU!
33
HEY!
MIND COMING OUT AND KEEPING ME COMPANY -- IT'S LONESOME OUT HERE!
34
CAREFUL! YOU'LL DROP ME!
AND WOULDN'T THAT BE A PITY?
35
IT'S HIM- SUPERMAN!
IF I WERE YOU, I'D TELL THE BOYS TO CONTROL THEIR TRIGGER FINGERS OR I'M LIABLE TO RESENT IT, AND LET YOU DROP!
I-I'LL TELL THEM!
36
GET AWAY FROM THAT WINDOW, MEN --I'M HELPLESS IN HIS HANDS!
37

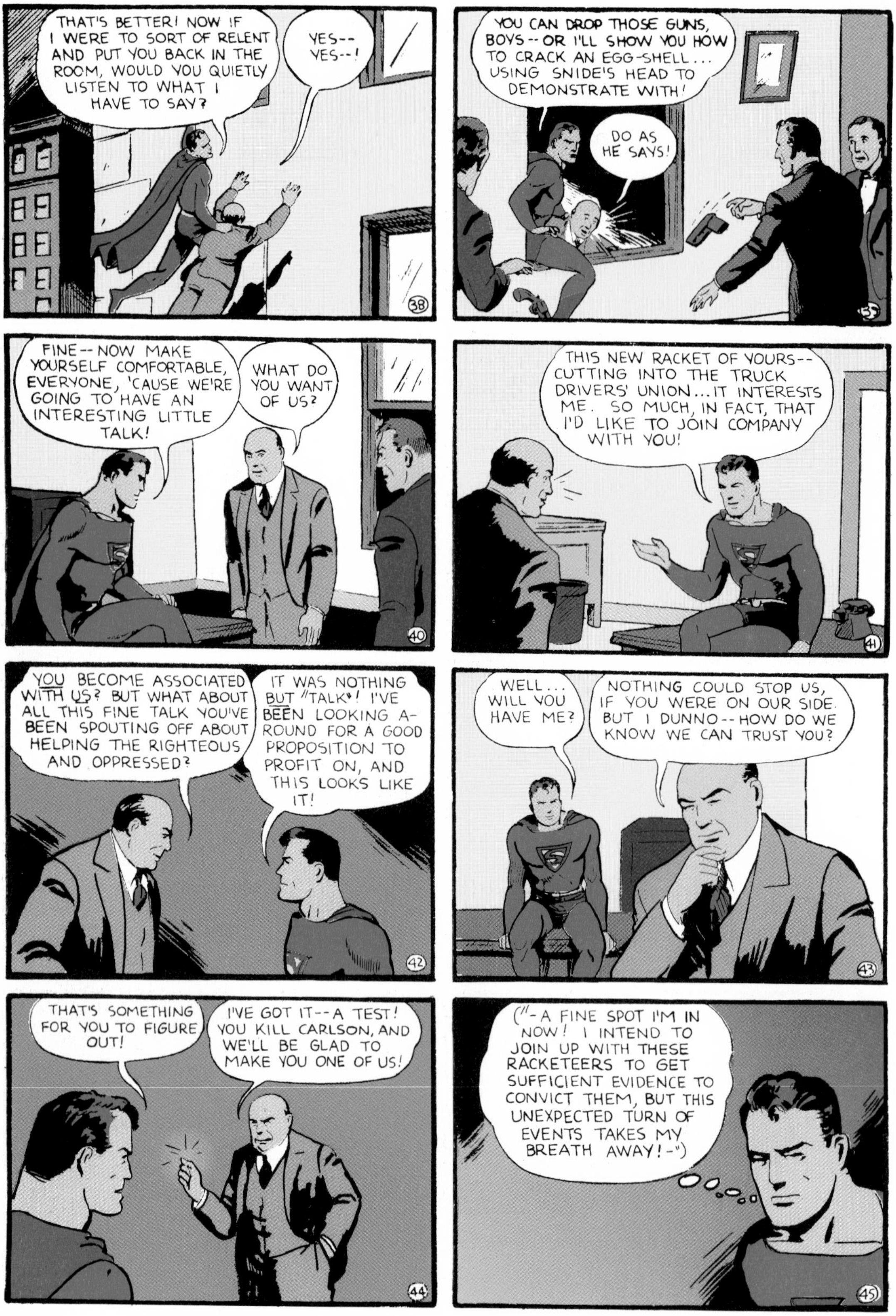
THAT'S BETTER! NOW IF I WERE TO SORT OF RELENT AND PUT YOU BACK IN THE ROOM, WOULD YOU QUIETLY LISTEN TO WHAT I HAVE TO SAY?
YES-- YES--!
38
YOU CAN DROP THOSE GUNS, BOYS--OR I'LL SHOW YOU HOW TO CRACK AN EGG-SHELL... USING SNIDE'S HEAD TO DEMONSTRATE WITH!
DO AS HE SAYS!
FINE--NOW MAKE YOURSELF COMFORTABLE, EVERYONE, 'CAUSE WE'RE GOING TO HAVE AN INTERESTING LITTLE TALK!
WHAT DO YOU WANT OF US?
40
THIS NEW RACKET OF YOURS-- CUTTING INTO THE TRUCK DRIVERS' UNION... IT INTERESTS ME. SO MUCH, IN FACT, THAT I'D LIKE TO JOIN COMPANY WITH YOU!
41
YOU BECOME ASSOCIATED WITH US? BUT WHAT ABOUT ALL THIS FINE TALK YOU'VE BEEN SPOUTING OFF ABOUT HELPING THE RIGHTEOUS AND OPPRESSED?
IT WAS NOTHING BUT "TALK"! I'VE BEEN LOOKING AROUND FOR A GOOD PROPOSITION TO PROFIT ON, AND THIS LOOKS LIKE IT!
42
WELL... WILL YOU HAVE ME?
NOTHING COULD STOP US, IF YOU WERE ON OUR SIDE. BUT I DUNNO--HOW DO WE KNOW WE CAN TRUST YOU?
43
THAT'S SOMETHING FOR YOU TO FIGURE OUT!
I'VE GOT IT--A TEST! YOU KILL CARLSON, AND WE'LL BE GLAD TO MAKE YOU ONE OF US!
44
("-A FINE SPOT I'M IN NOW! I INTEND TO JOIN UP WITH THESE RACKETEERS TO GET SUFFICIENT EVIDENCE TO CONVICT THEM, BUT THIS UNEXPECTED TURN OF EVENTS TAKES MY BREATH AWAY!-")
45

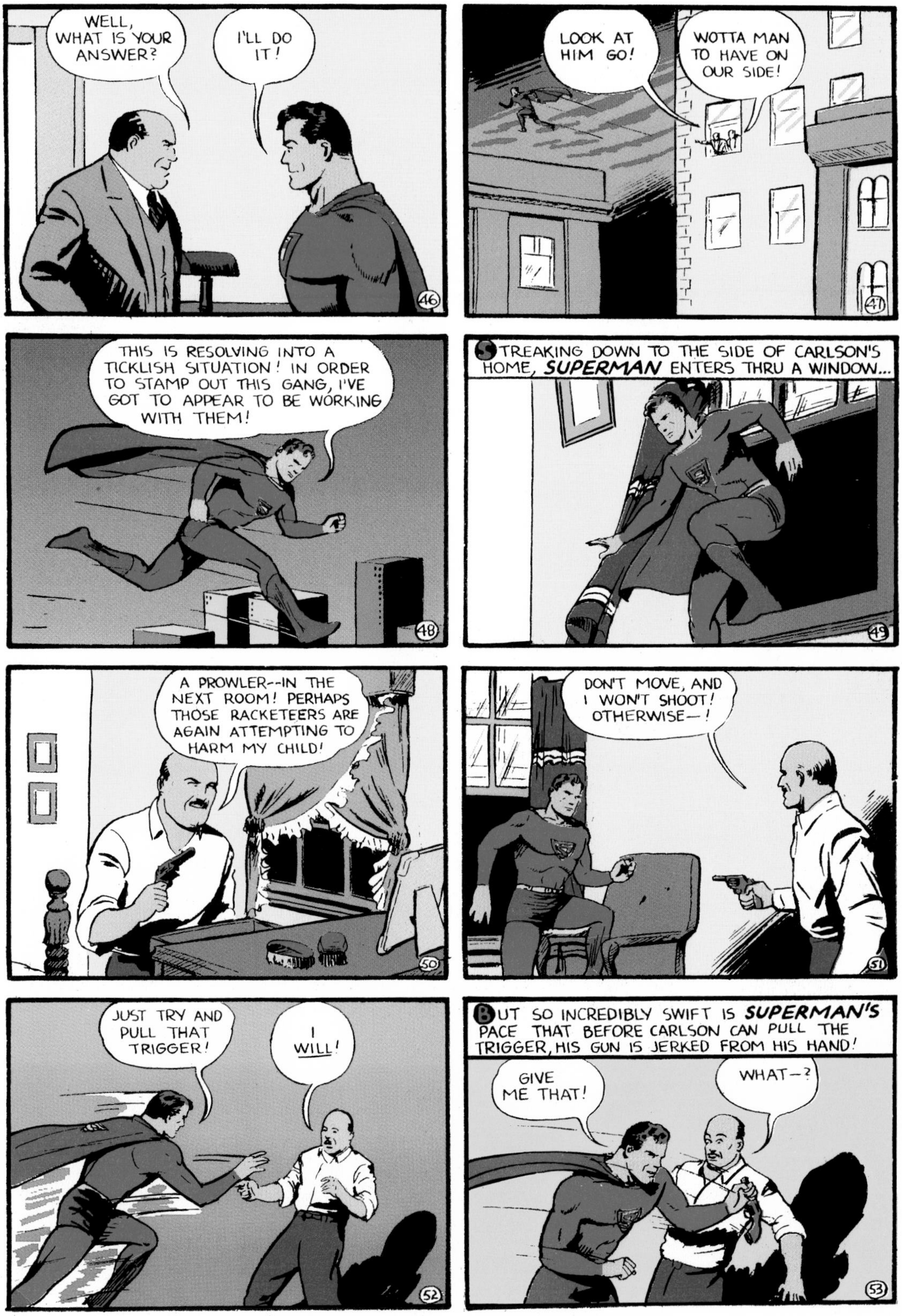
WELL, WHAT IS YOUR ANSWER?
I'LL DO IT!
46
LOOK AT HIM GO!
WOTTA MAN TO HAVE ON OUR SIDE!
47
THIS IS RESOLVING INTO A TICKLISH SITUATION! IN ORDER TO STAMP OUT THIS GANG, I'VE GOT TO APPEAR TO BE WORKING WITH THEM!
48
STREAKING DOWN TO THE SIDE OF CARLSON'S HOME, SUPERMAN ENTERS THRU A WINDOW...
49
A PROWLER--IN THE NEXT ROOM! PERHAPS THOSE RACKETEERS ARE AGAIN ATTEMPTING TO HARM MY CHILD!
50
DON'T MOVE, AND I WON'T SHOOT! OTHERWISE--!
51
JUST TRY AND PULL THAT TRIGGER!
I WILL!
52
BUT SO INCREDIBLY SWIFT IS SUPERMAN'S PACE THAT BEFORE CARLSON CAN PULL THE TRIGGER, HIS GUN IS JERKED FROM HIS HAND!
GIVE ME THAT!
WHAT--?
53

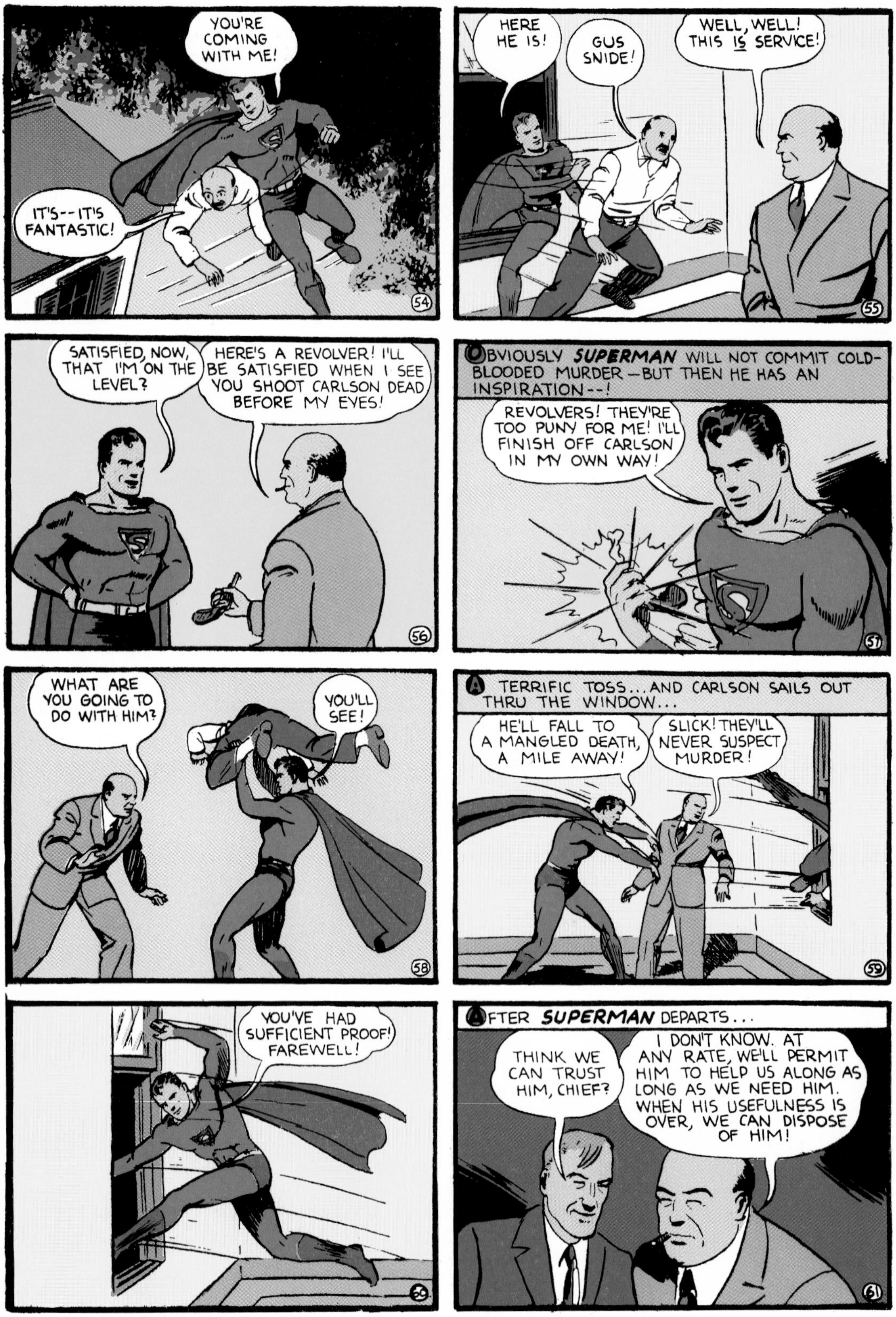
YOU'RE COMING WITH ME!
IT'S--IT'S FANTASTIC!
HERE HE IS!
GUS SNIDE!
WELL, WELL! THIS IS SERVICE!
SATISFIED, NOW, THAT I'M ON THE LEVEL?
HERE'S A REVOLVER! I'LL BE SATISFIED WHEN I SEE YOU SHOOT CARLSON DEAD BEFORE MY EYES!
OBVIOUSLY SUPERMAN WILL NOT COMMIT COLD-BLOODED MURDER—BUT THEN HE HAS AN INSPIRATION--!
REVOLVERS! THEY'RE TOO PUNY FOR ME! I'LL FINISH OFF CARLSON IN MY OWN WAY!
WHAT ARE YOU GOING TO DO WITH HIM?
YOU'LL SEE!
A TERRIFIC TOSS...AND CARLSON SAILS OUT THRU THE WINDOW...
HE'LL FALL TO A MANGLED DEATH, A MILE AWAY!
SLICK! THEY'LL NEVER SUSPECT MURDER!
YOU'VE HAD SUFFICIENT PROOF! FAREWELL!
AFTER SUPERMAN DEPARTS...
THINK WE CAN TRUST HIM, CHIEF?
I DON'T KNOW. AT ANY RATE, WE'LL PERMIT HIM TO HELP US ALONG AS LONG AS WE NEED HIM. WHEN HIS USEFULNESS IS OVER, WE CAN DISPOSE OF HIM!

AT THAT VERY INSTANT, *SUPERMAN* IS RACING FORWARD IN DESPERATE HASTE...

...FOR CARLSON IS COMMENCING TO DROP DOWN TOWARD EARTH, AND A CRUSHING DEATH!

WHEW!— ALMOST MISSED YOU!

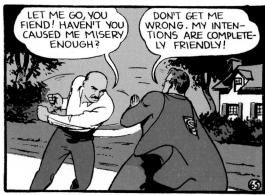

LET ME GO, YOU FIEND! HAVEN'T YOU CAUSED ME MISERY ENOUGH?

DON'T GET ME WRONG. MY INTENTIONS ARE COMPLETELY FRIENDLY!

CAN'T YOU SEE? I COULD HAVE EASILY DESTROYED YOU LONG AGO, IF I'D DESIRED TO. WHAT I WANT YOU TO DO IS HIDE OUT, UNTIL I AM READY TO EXPOSE THESE CRIMINALS!

IF THAT'S THE CASE, THEN I'LL CO-OPERATE COMPLETELY!

LATER— *SUPERMAN* RETURNS TO THE RACKETEERS' HEADQUARTERS...

NOW THAT CARLSON'S OUT OF THE WAY, I CAN EASILY ASSUME CONTROL OF THE TRUCK DRIVERS' UNION. MY PLAN IS TO MAKE ALL TRUCK DRIVERS STRIKE!

BUT WHY?

CAN'T YOU SEE? THE CITY'S FOOD DISTRIBUTION WILL BE PARALYZED! PEOPLE HAVE GOT TO EAT, AND THE EMPLOYERS WILL BE FORCED TO PAY ANY BLACKMAIL WE DEMAND!

GEE! WHAT A SWELL IDEA!

WE'LL CLEAN UP!

BUT LATER—

I'VE GOT TO DO SOMETHING TO UPSET SNIDE'S PLANS— AND I BELIEVE I KNOW JUST THE THING!

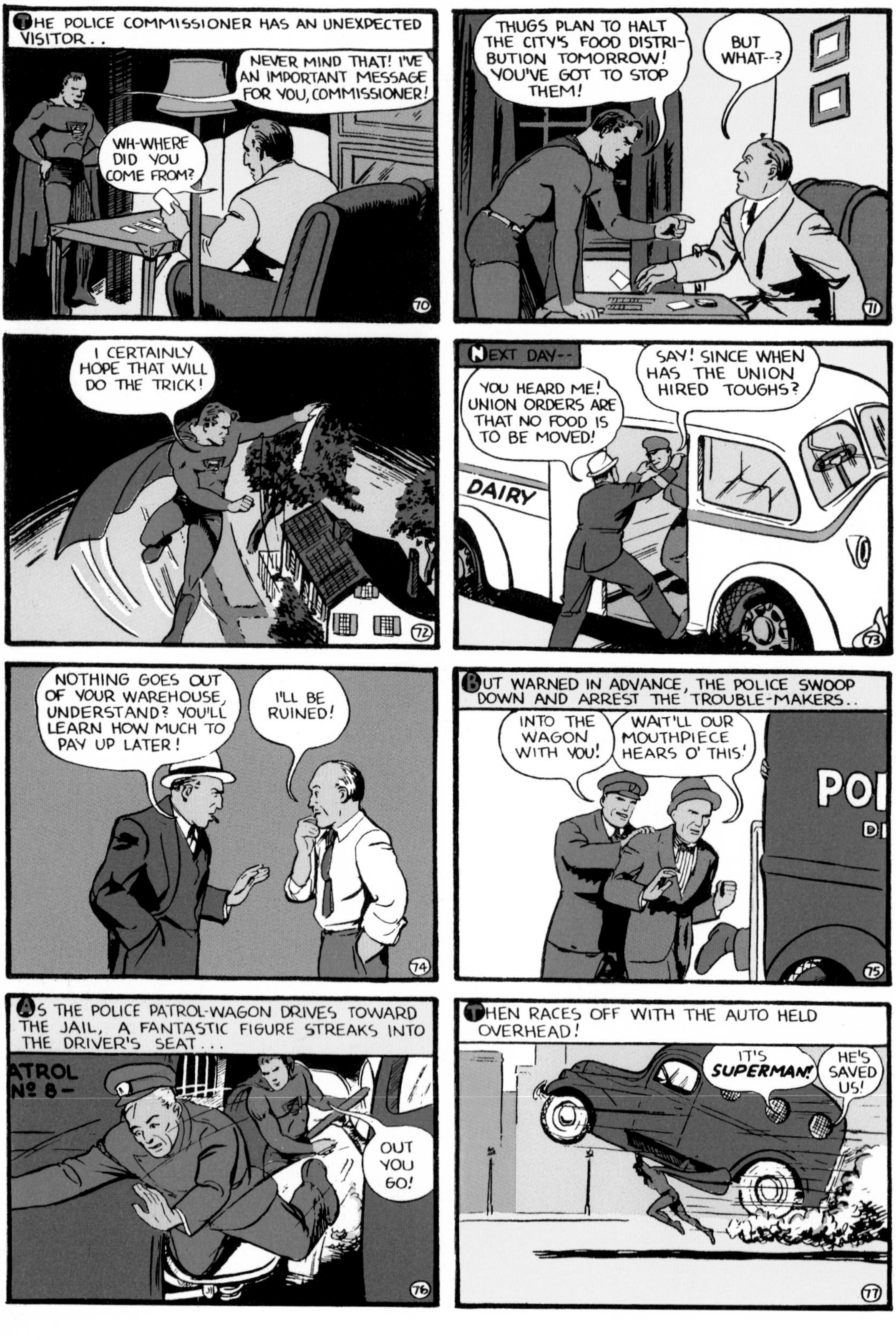
THE POLICE COMMISSIONER HAS AN UNEXPECTED VISITOR..
NEVER MIND THAT! I'VE AN IMPORTANT MESSAGE FOR YOU, COMMISSIONER!
WH-WHERE DID YOU COME FROM?
70
THUGS PLAN TO HALT THE CITY'S FOOD DISTRIBUTION TOMORROW! YOU'VE GOT TO STOP THEM!
BUT WHAT--?
71
I CERTAINLY HOPE THAT WILL DO THE TRICK!
72
NEXT DAY--
YOU HEARD ME! UNION ORDERS ARE THAT NO FOOD IS TO BE MOVED!
SAY! SINCE WHEN HAS THE UNION HIRED TOUGHS?
DAIRY
73
NOTHING GOES OUT OF YOUR WAREHOUSE, UNDERSTAND? YOU'LL LEARN HOW MUCH TO PAY UP LATER!
I'LL BE RUINED!
74
BUT WARNED IN ADVANCE, THE POLICE SWOOP DOWN AND ARREST THE TROUBLE-MAKERS..
INTO THE WAGON WITH YOU!
WAIT'LL OUR MOUTHPIECE HEARS O' THIS!
POL
DI
75
AS THE POLICE PATROL-WAGON DRIVES TOWARD THE JAIL, A FANTASTIC FIGURE STREAKS INTO THE DRIVER'S SEAT...
ATROL Nº 8-
OUT YOU GO!
76
THEN RACES OFF WITH THE AUTO HELD OVERHEAD!
IT'S SUPERMAN!
HE'S SAVED US!
77

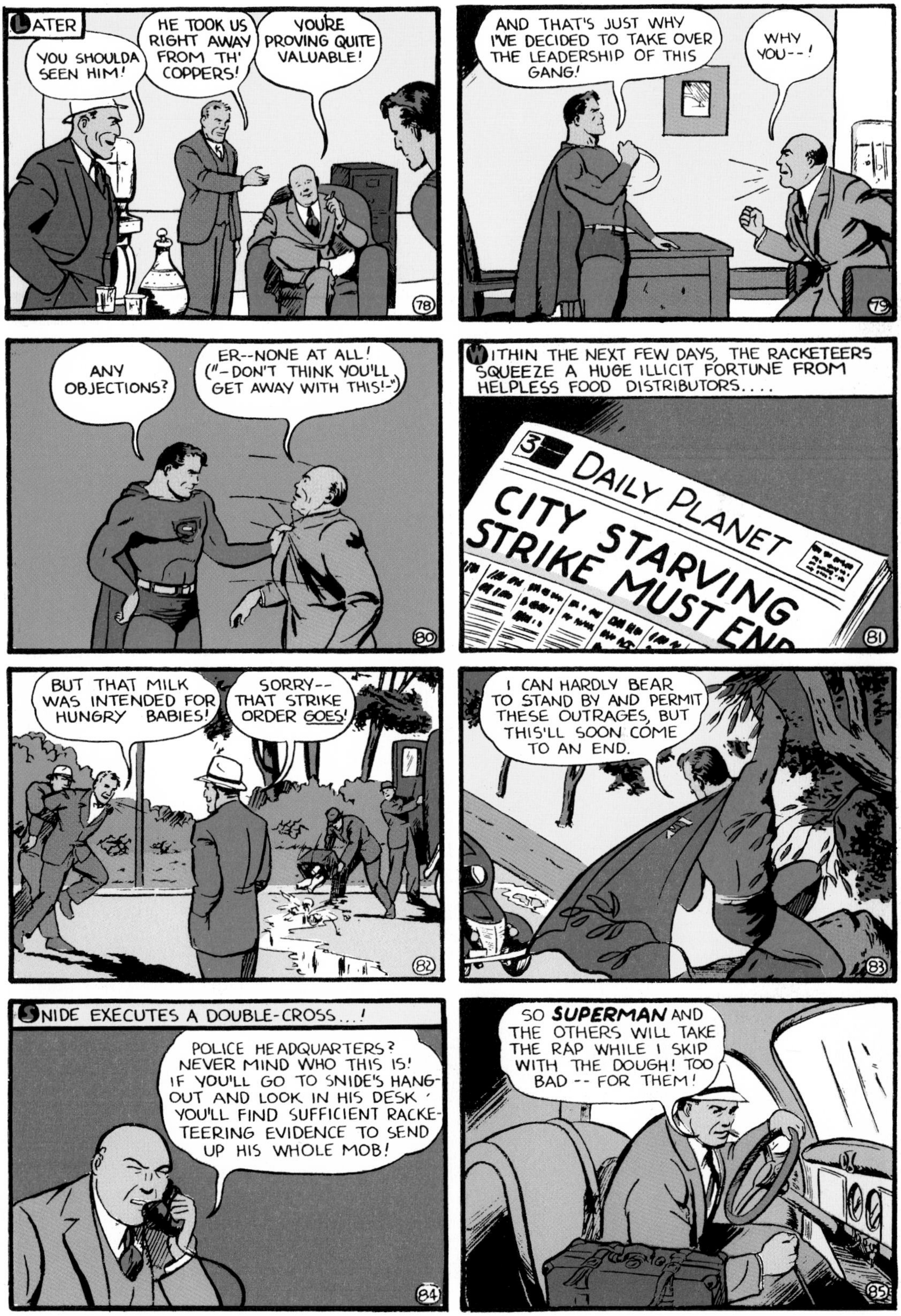
LATER
YOU SHOULDA SEEN HIM!
HE TOOK US RIGHT AWAY FROM TH' COPPERS!
YOU'RE PROVING QUITE VALUABLE!
AND THAT'S JUST WHY I'VE DECIDED TO TAKE OVER THE LEADERSHIP OF THIS GANG!
WHY YOU--!
ANY OBJECTIONS?
ER--NONE AT ALL! ("-DON'T THINK YOU'LL GET AWAY WITH THIS!-")
WITHIN THE NEXT FEW DAYS, THE RACKETEERS SQUEEZE A HUGE ILLICIT FORTUNE FROM HELPLESS FOOD DISTRIBUTORS....
DAILY PLANET
CITY STARVING
STRIKE MUST END
BUT THAT MILK WAS INTENDED FOR HUNGRY BABIES!
SORRY-- THAT STRIKE ORDER GOES!
I CAN HARDLY BEAR TO STAND BY AND PERMIT THESE OUTRAGES, BUT THIS'LL SOON COME TO AN END.
SNIDE EXECUTES A DOUBLE-CROSS...!
POLICE HEADQUARTERS? NEVER MIND WHO THIS IS! IF YOU'LL GO TO SNIDE'S HANG-OUT AND LOOK IN HIS DESK YOU'LL FIND SUFFICIENT RACKE-TEERING EVIDENCE TO SEND UP HIS WHOLE MOB!
SO SUPERMAN AND THE OTHERS WILL TAKE THE RAP WHILE I SKIP WITH THE DOUGH! TOO BAD -- FOR THEM!

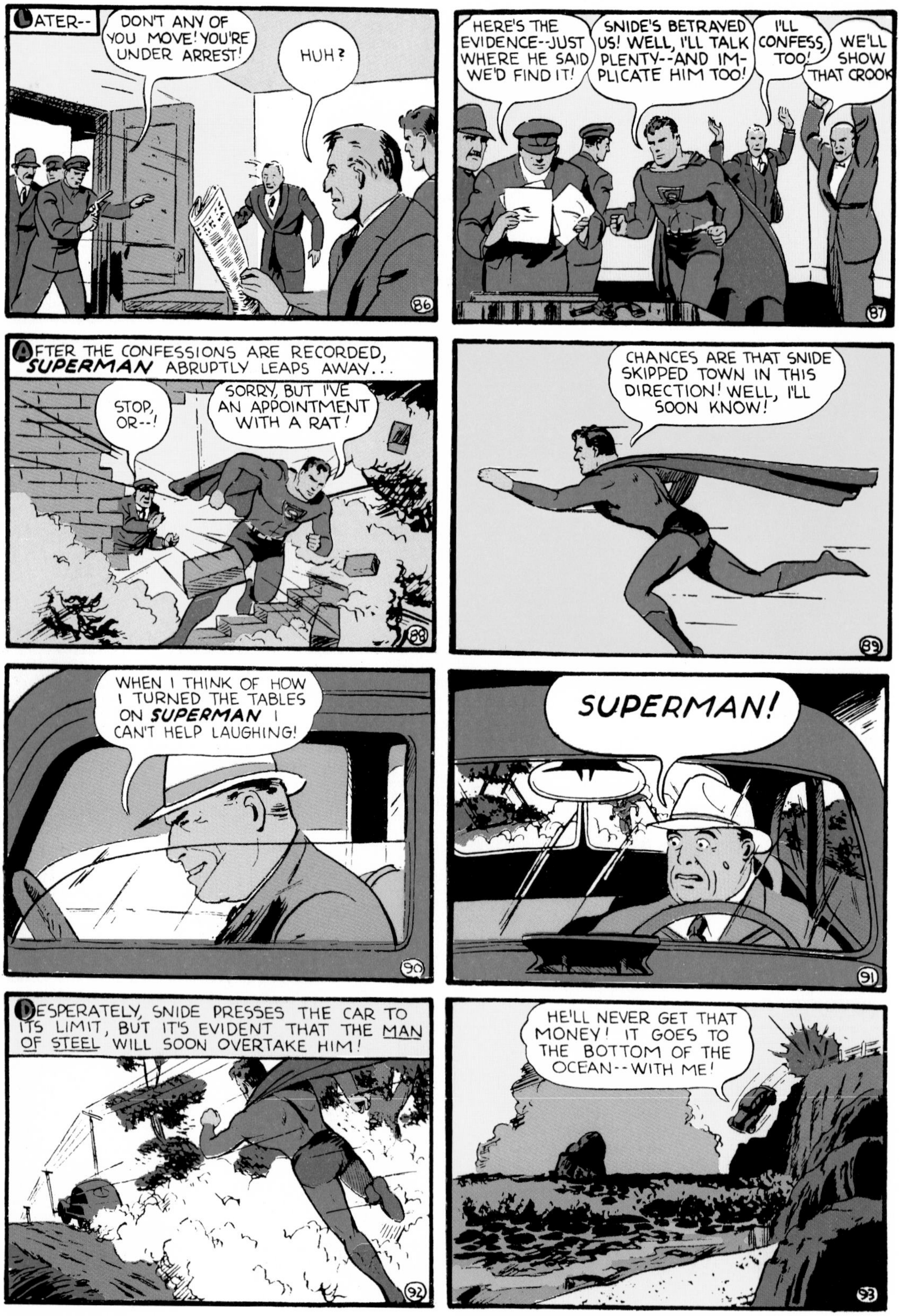
LATER--
DON'T ANY OF YOU MOVE! YOU'RE UNDER ARREST!
HUH?
86
HERE'S THE EVIDENCE--JUST WHERE HE SAID WE'D FIND IT!
SNIDE'S BETRAYED US! WELL, I'LL TALK PLENTY--AND IMPLICATE HIM TOO!
I'LL CONFESS, TOO!
WE'LL SHOW THAT CROOK
87
AFTER THE CONFESSIONS ARE RECORDED, SUPERMAN ABRUPTLY LEAPS AWAY...
STOP, OR--!
SORRY, BUT I'VE AN APPOINTMENT WITH A RAT!
88
CHANCES ARE THAT SNIDE SKIPPED TOWN IN THIS DIRECTION! WELL, I'LL SOON KNOW!
89
WHEN I THINK OF HOW I TURNED THE TABLES ON SUPERMAN I CAN'T HELP LAUGHING!
90
SUPERMAN!
91
DESPERATELY, SNIDE PRESSES THE CAR TO ITS LIMIT, BUT IT'S EVIDENT THAT THE MAN OF STEEL WILL SOON OVERTAKE HIM!
92
HE'LL NEVER GET THAT MONEY! IT GOES TO THE BOTTOM OF THE OCEAN--WITH ME!
93

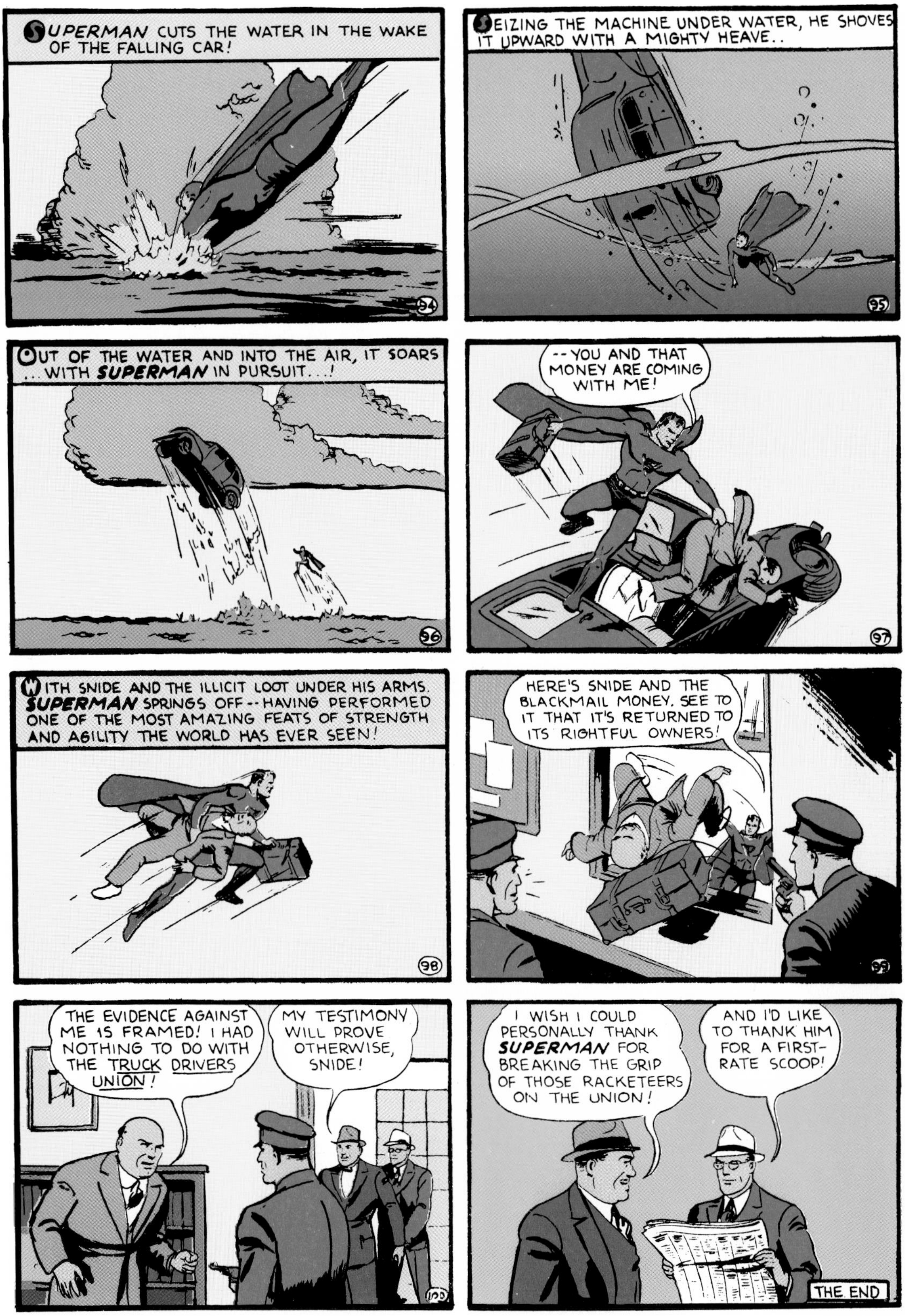
SUPERMAN CUTS THE WATER IN THE WAKE OF THE FALLING CAR!
SEIZING THE MACHINE UNDER WATER, HE SHOVES IT UPWARD WITH A MIGHTY HEAVE..
OUT OF THE WATER AND INTO THE AIR, IT SOARS ...WITH SUPERMAN IN PURSUIT...!
--YOU AND THAT MONEY ARE COMING WITH ME!
WITH SNIDE AND THE ILLICIT LOOT UNDER HIS ARMS. SUPERMAN SPRINGS OFF--HAVING PERFORMED ONE OF THE MOST AMAZING FEATS OF STRENGTH AND AGILITY THE WORLD HAS EVER SEEN!
HERE'S SNIDE AND THE BLACKMAIL MONEY. SEE TO IT THAT IT'S RETURNED TO ITS RIGHTFUL OWNERS!
THE EVIDENCE AGAINST ME IS FRAMED! I HAD NOTHING TO DO WITH THE TRUCK DRIVERS UNION!
MY TESTIMONY WILL PROVE OTHERWISE, SNIDE!
I WISH I COULD PERSONALLY THANK SUPERMAN FOR BREAKING THE GRIP OF THOSE RACKETEERS ON THE UNION!
AND I'D LIKE TO THANK HIM FOR A FIRST-RATE SCOOP!
THE END

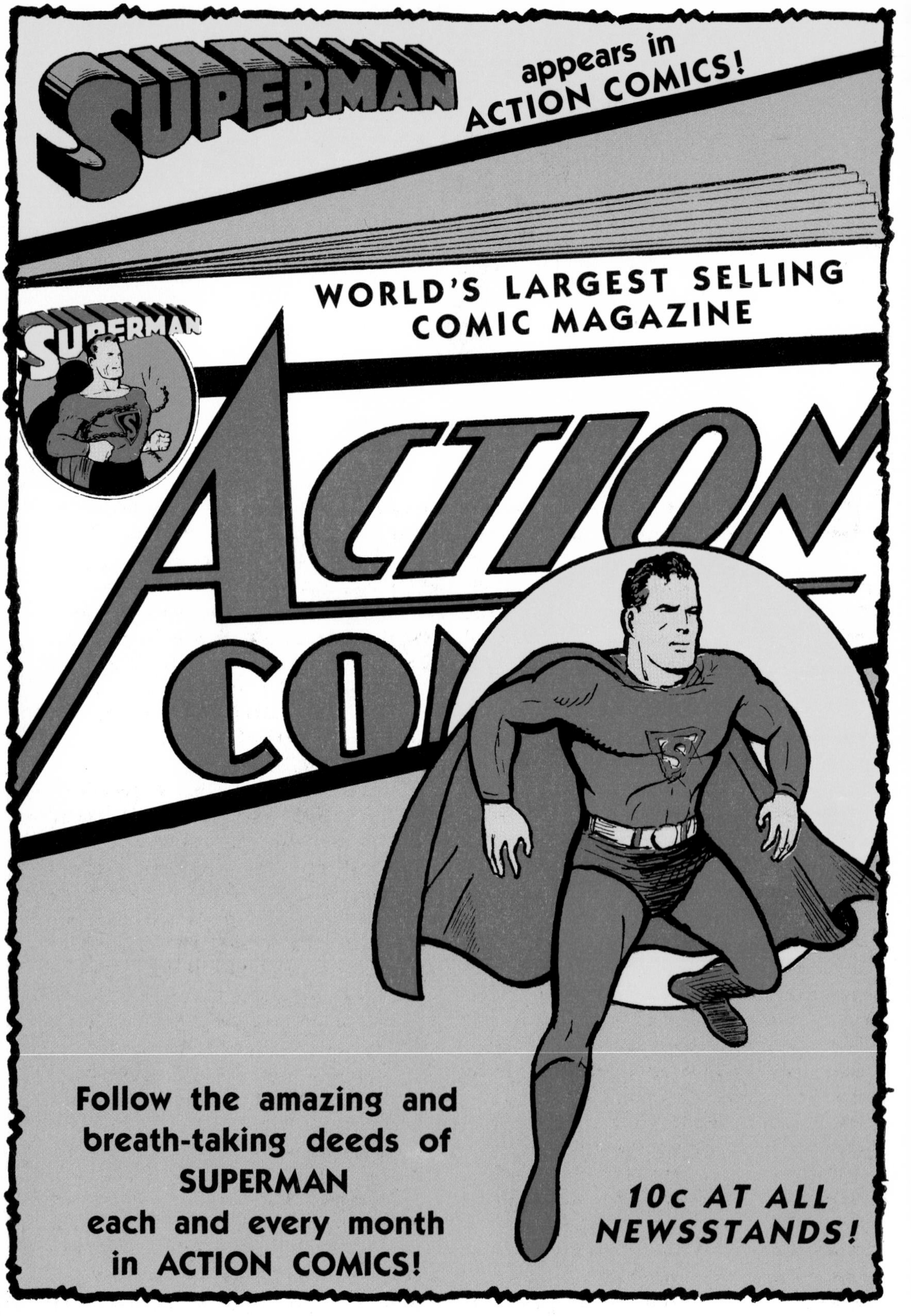
SUPERMAN
appears in ACTION COMICS!
SUPERMAN
WORLD'S LARGEST SELLING COMIC MAGAZINE
ACTION CO
Follow the amazing and breath-taking deeds of SUPERMAN each and every month in ACTION COMICS!
10c AT ALL NEWSSTANDS!

AFTERWORD

GARBED IN A BLAZE OF PRIMARY COLORS, Superman burst onto newsstands in **Action** 1 like a bombshell, setting imagination against reason as never before and forever changing the four-color medium. Just as his initial adventure redefined comics, it also laid the foundation for all Superman stories to come by firmly establishing the series' elements.

The first ground-breaking tale introduced the Kryptonian's dual identity (and answers speculation that he removes his pants before his shirt), his relationship with Lois Lane (including her utter disdain for Clark and his for her when he is Superman), and an appropriate series of super feats (such as hurling a soldier like a javelin into a grove of trees half a mile away).

The first adventure is noteworthy for a number of reasons, not the least of which is its length: 30 pages, including the two-page introduction. Although split over **Action** 1 and 2, the tale set a minor precedent in comics history. Most stories during the early period straddled the five-to-ten-page range, with few exceptions (Dell's Four-Color series, for example, featured 64 Sunday-newspaper pages in comics form for ten cents, but long original yarns were strictly experimental).

Pages 3-6 were obviously not part of the first story, but were redrawn by Shuster much later than the remainder of the pages, with no effort spent to match rendering styles (even the lettering is significantly different). Check out Superman's admission to being a newspaperman and the Jack Rubyesque

prisoner who confesses he is being held for the murder of Jack Kennedy but "didn't do it." Pages 7-17, inked with a heavy rendering technique, were obviously prepared for black-and-white newspaper reproduction. Two distinct sequences (the execution plot and the munitions plot) and the several short episodes they bookend constitute the 30-page adventure. Siegel and Shuster pay tribute to their roots in the initial tale by naming the munitions tycoon after top pulpsmiths Emile Tepperman and Norvell Page.

The next Adventure (from **Action** 3 and reprinted in **Superman** 1) is perhaps the most unusual in the early stories because it violates two basic tenets of super-hero comics. First, it relies more on dialogue than on action; with the exception of the mine cave-in splash, the yarn features only three super feats (actually the same one performed three times). Second, except in the third-panel throwaway scene, the Man of Steel never appears in costume. The story also has no real adversary with whom to develop conflict. As a 13-page morality play in the Elmer Rice social-reform tradition, it reverses Superman's violent approach of the first story ("That bar could just as easily be your neck!") to rely more on the justice of ironic circumstance.

Adventure 3 (from **Action** 4) embraces themes similar to those in the preceding tale. After an inappropriate two-page opening (a mini-morality tale), Superman uncharacteristically assumes a disguise (using makeup like the pulps' Secret Agent X), takes the malevolent coach to task (his accomplices escape unpunished), and plays Cupid for the clumsy athlete. Except for the perfunctory opening scene, he does not appear in costume—unthinkable behavior for a super-hero so early in the series (even today, the notion would be untenable).

Adventure 4 (originally the lead story in **Superman** 2) was another tale drawn for newspaper syndication (2/20/39 to 3/18/39). Like the first two pages of Adventure 1, the art is probably among the best of the early period. More accurate anatomy, specific light sources, a better spotting of blacks, tighter rendering, and improved lettering typify these easily recognized stories. While the plot echoes that of the previous yarn, it is richer in humor, action, and characterization—with a staggering four pages of Superman in costume!

Adventure 5, another newspaper conversion (5/1/39–6/10/39), finds Clark at **The Daily Star** again, working for editor George Taylor—now mysteriously transplanted in Metropolis, New York. The art reveals less Shuster input than any previous story: not only is the figure work different, but also panel composition and basic storytelling show another artistic sensibility at work (check the high collar of Superman in the sequence on page 6).

Adventure 8 (reprinted from **Action** 5 in **Superman** 3) forecast Superman's spectacular merchandising potential. (Harry Matetsky's 1988 megavolume **The Adventures of Superman Collecting** detailed the realization of 50 years of endorsements.) The song *You're Superman* says it all about the Man of Steel's popularity.

Adventure 10 is another episodic tale, distinguished by its use of Benday tones (a foul-smelling liquid applied to specially prepared paper develops the shaded areas) and by Clark's final assignment for **The Daily Star**.

Adventure 11 (the lead story in **Superman** 4) is a milestone for several reasons. Clark begins his tenure at **The Daily Planet** (it is possible that the **Star** was bought by a conglomerate which changed the newspaper's name), and Luthor (without the Lex, but with hair) is introduced. Because of the art's simplicity, the four-tier panel arrangement is quite pleasing. The tale fares less well, however,

with Superman clearly outwitted by his adversary and capable of responding only with brute strength ("I'll toss you against your plane and see what cracks—your skull or the metal!"). Foreshadowing a multitude of changes in his future brought about by advancing technology (especially when it is controlled by his enemies), the Man of Steel's powers are significantly increased. In addition to being able to suspend his heartbeat (but not capable of holding his breath long enough to survive poison gas), Superman leaps to the edge of outer space, violating his original "eighth of a mile" distance, establishing an escalating trend that limited the series' future dramatic possibilities. With this yarn, Superman conflict begins to move in a cosmic direction.

Adventure 12 takes another leap—into Flash Gordon territory. With movie-serial plotting and pacing, Superman is up to his insignia in danger as Luthor reappears with another world-domination scheme.

Adventure 13 returns the Man of Steel to familiar territory in an action-packed tale defining Superman's hearing powers. Those who label him a "goody two-shoes" hero are invited to count the bodies littering justice's wake, including that of the villain in the shocking climax.

Adventure 14 neatly links Metropolis's marvel with a labor-racketeering scheme to blackmail the city, amply showcasing Superman's mind and muscles (although one may wonder why he didn't simply check the desk for damning evidence), and ending with legal prosecution of the criminals, instead of super-vigilantism—a positive approach demonstrating that the strip's creators were finding an appropriate direction for the Man of Steel and his conscience.

Historically, the early Superman saga can be viewed as a series of experiments made by young pioneers struggling to determine the dimensions of an emerging art form called the comics. Typically, they stumble and fall; yet, in retrospect, their failures are often as interesting as their successes. In reading their efforts, we must remember they were establishing the guidelines of a vision, trailblazing in a new publishing medium where rules were tenuous, often nonexistent.   — STERANKO